Aphrodite's Cave

Books by N. Richard Nash

Novels
APHRODITE'S CAVE
THE LAST MAGIC
EAST WIND, RAIN
CRY MACHO

Poetry
ABSALOM

Plays
ECHOES
HANDFUL OF FIRE
GIRLS OF SUMMER
THE RAINMAKER
SEE THE JAGUAR
THE YOUNG AND FAIR
SECOND BEST BED

Nonfiction
THE WOUNDS OF SPARTA
THE ATHENIAN SPIRIT

Aphrodite's Cave

❖ ❖ ❖ ❖ ❖ ❖

A Novel by

N. Richard Nash

DOUBLEDAY & COMPANY, INC.
GARDEN CITY, NEW YORK
1980

Library of Congress Cataloging in Publication Data
Nash, N. Richard.
    Aphrodite's cave.
    1. Cyprus—History—Cyprus Crisis, 1974–
Fiction. I. Title.
PZ4.N254Ap   [PS3527.A6365]   813'.54
ISBN: 0-385-14294-3
Library of Congress Catalog Card Number 80–1069

Aphrodite

The Greeks on the beautiful island of Cyprus worship Aphrodite, the goddess of love. They pretend that they don't, that she is only a myth among the shards, a legend to beguile the tourists. But when they speak of her, their eyes have archaic shadows in them, and they recede a little, toward some private mischief. Even the sophisticated ones, while disclaiming her as a folk fantasy, smile secretly to one another, and their disclaimer is nullified.

In the fishing villages she is the goddess who, at dawn tomorrow, will rise dripping from the sea; in the tavernas she is the woman who will enter with the wine. Nor far from Paphos there is a monastery where a monk speaks nostalgically of her, as if recalling a love affair that ended ages ago, before he took his vows; in an abbey near Limassol an icon of Mary is the image of a statue of Aphrodite hewn long before the birth of Christ. Also in Limassol, there is a brothel called, simply, Her House.

There are those that say she is all love, and everywhere—in the warm seduction of the sea, in the passion of the wild red anemone of the field, in the voluptuous soar and yield of the mountain. She is in the people as well, for this little token of land in the soft Mediterranean waters is known as Aphrodite's Isle, she owns it, and her mortals here have been gentled by her amorousness; their welcome is an embrace and their currency is the smile, it is their legal tender. They say that love speaks with Aphrodite's voice, in all the winds and words of the island.

But there are others who believe quite differently. They charge that in Aphrodite's name much blood has been shed. If she is the patron goddess of the Cypriots, how can one explain the foreign hordes that have overrun their homes, the persecutions that have laid them waste, the tortures and mutilations in the brazen sun, the outcries in the night? And they are never-ending, to this day. So Aphrodite, for all her gentleness and amity, they say, has a lust for cruelty as well.

There is good cause. It will be remembered that Aphrodite's father was the almighty Zeus, who ruled Mount Olympus austerely, without suffering the misgivings of mercy; kindness was unknown to him; humanity had yet to be discovered. Her grandfather was the relentless Cronus, the so-called god of time, and down to the passing instant time has been intransigent.

Perhaps the forebear who touched her most—and from whom all of them descended—was the mad god Chaos, who raged in a void of nonexistence. Always, especially when dismayed, she turned to the demented deity, as if she had her genesis in him alone, as if love had sprung from Chaos. And must ultimately return to it, as home.

Zeus, Cronus, Chaos—it was not a lineage to bequeath felicity. And it is to be noted that none of her forebears was female. Who knows if she had a mother? And if she hadn't, what tenderness could come of a female born solely of males, all godly? Surely, to have been engendered, full-grown, on the spume of a wave or on a seashell, without the clemencies of a mother, was not conducive to the rearing of a goddess of pure love. Nor, as another version tells it, could being born through thunder in the cleft of a mountain have fostered a benign deity. Love could only be nurtured by love, according to mortal doctrine—and it was to mortals that she was relegated.

If love among humankind is nearly as often thought to be a malediction as it is a blessing, Aphrodite is not altogether blameless. It is said that on earth she was frequently a wanton, that she disported not only with gods but with mortals, that she made love to women as to men, that she dallied with children and woodland animals; and there is a legend of an aspen tree. Occasionally, when she could not have a creature she desired, she was vindictive. One of her most malicious tricks was to cause a spiteful coincidence— by confounding time and place, by exposing an evil or a grotesquerie, by unmasking a hideous face that was never meant to be revealed. An occurrence of this kind she could bring about with such cunning that it appeared to be a stroke of misfortune, a catastrophe of chance. Frequently, mortals would blame themselves for the ostensible accident, calling it the just retribution for a tragic blunder or for sin.

Although she was worshiped without reservation, she was not always propitiated. Sometimes she repaid devout petition with punishment. For example, there were the ugly virgins. Each of the misbegotten spinsters was forced to drudge menially in one of Aphrodite's temples until some male of great beauty would come along and ravish her. At times, there were many maidens in the same sanctuary, graying and wilting, unwanted. Some of them waited for years, some forever, longing for the love cruelty that would set them free. Many died while waiting, loathing the goddess and themselves.

But Aphrodite was finally punished. She had never known heartache until she came to live among the mortals. Age by age, they saddened her, until she knew what it meant to live on earth where the best that could be said for her gift of love was that it was a disorder. No matter how cruel and imperious love had been among the gods, it had been a categorical grandeur, not to be questioned or diminished, but simply to be breathed as the afflatus of the divine essence; it was the vast Olympian mystery. But among mortals the mystery dwindled to a mere complexity, to be quizzed and analyzed, to be rationalized and ratiocinated, to be poked and probed by the tines of doubt. On earth, love had no congruity, its pleasures were indistinguishable from its pains, its truths from its falsehoods. To Aphrodite, the contradictions were painful. She began to see that her beauty could be a betrayal, enticing the purblind and the superficial and the unnatural, and all the rapacious ones who demanded a bounty she had not promised. She found that she was inciting passions she could not consummate, sometimes passions that passed for love but were really rage. She even began to distrust the beauty of her body; her thighs, it seemed to her, were too opulent for the spareness of the rest of her, her breasts were too small and too firm; she wondered how men could be aroused by the rising of her nipples, she felt that the rosy hardening of them—which she had never noticed on Olympus— was a blemish, they were unsightly nodules on the smoothness of a divine configuration; and men's excitement over the phenomenal flaw was a disturbing perplexity to her. It suggested to the goddess that human lovemaking was a celebration of human fault.

Or was it a celebration of illusion, she asked herself, as she saw how men worshiped her delta, an eminence which had only an evanescent reality, disappearing when she spread her limbs; a deeper one, then, penetrating to the grotto of darkness where life and annihilation were confounded, and the last aching, desperate fantasy was hallucinated. What dream, what nightmare, what miracle, elixir, quintessence of life, did mortal man imagine was hidden in this darkness that he would go so recklessly in search of it? And, never finding it, what hopeless hope kept him forever going and going again?

Ultimately, Aphrodite came to believe that worldly love depended too meanly upon the concomitancies of the worldly apparatus, upon the size and form and texture of *things,* the beauty of the body, its shape and substance, its power and motion, the curve of the cheek and the infolding of the bosom, the crescent of back and buttock, the hardness and heft of the penis, the wetness of mouth and vagina, the hair and tears and multiform textures of the skin—lips, eyelids, tongue, the earlobes, the pink folds in hidden places—the dews and downs and musks, the slavers of eating and sucking; all these appurtenances seemed to her to be only the ponderous packings of love, the unbearable dunnage which kept it earthbound, far from the zenith of the Olympian mystery.

Yet . . . among the mortals, she began to take pleasure in the paradox, not comprehending how it was possible to derive so much gratification from an exercise of such painful confusion. The less she understood of it, the more desirable human love became to her, and the more insatiable she became. She loved and loved and could not love enough. She changed herself into many forms—man, woman, child, fawn, willow and linden tree, bull, rabid dog, flowing brook, music and stillness; into any form that would enchant or ravish or seduce, into any means that would bring her some charitable solace from her aching aloneness. But there was no remedy for her. Never having been broken to the agonies of love, as mortals are, the woman-goddess kept breaking and breaking. Her twilight came when the deity of love came to realize that she no longer had any hope of comprehending it. More terrible, she could not recall what she was seeking, or even if she would recognize it if she chanced upon it. Then one day she caught a glimpse of herself, her image in a pool of water, and saw that she was no longer beautiful. Nor was love eternal; she was no longer young. And it was no consolation to her that she had learned to weep.

It is not known what happened to the woman-goddess. Some say she wandered off into a wide meadow of summer grasses; some, that she walked into the sea. Some say she was revolted by the petty, transitory turmoils of humanity and, avid for a nobler furor, sickening for home, she fled to Chaos. Some say she started back to Olympus, but, as she caught sight of the snowclad crown, she could not bear to return to the frigid majesty and the capricious cruelty of the gods, so she entered a cleft in the mountain and tried to lose herself in the labyrinths of the dark cave. It is said that she still wanders there, smitten with madness and alone, asking the darkness whether she is human or divine, lamenting that she is no longer beautiful and no longer loved.

Aphrodite's Cave

1

At first, Ben thought it was a gamblers' fight. But if that had been the case, the other man at the *poka* table would have taken sides. Then he thought it was a squabble about a woman: the waitress walked as if she were wearing a body stocking, she had a bedroom eye, she served every drink with a fillip of tease; she was a likely issue. Both suppositions were wrong.

One of the disputants got up and made an abusive gesture, grinding his thumb into the palm of his hand, which vilified the other one as a traitor. Then he said the word "Turk" like an obscenity.

The two men were Greek, not Turkish, and for a moment it looked as though the three other card players at their table would succeed in making a farce of the whole unpleasantness. But the jokes fell dead, and the aggressive one kept saying traitor, informer, toad.

"You're a prostitute!" he shouted. "You have peddled yourself to the British, and now you peddle yourself to the Turks!"

The offended one replied, "Your mouth is a sewer! You would foul your own father and play big-man with your mother!"

The other one slapped him. A punch would have been more sufferable—face-slapping was for women. Another blow was struck, and another. The men grappled and a woman screamed.

There were eight card tables in the Platres Cazino, and one roulette wheel. And at least fifty people. But nobody did anything to stop the fracas, not even the owner. Because a knife had flashed.

Ben saw it come hacking down, slicing the empty air. He started to get up from the table.

"Stay out!" Yannis warned him. "Stay out!"

The old Greek, Yannis Petrides, was his friend and assistant.

He thought there were other things than bloodshed, and grabbed Ben's arm.

The American hesitated. "They'll kill each other."

"Stay out," Yannis repeated. "What you are—stupid?"

The men were clinched now. The knife quivered in the light.

"Stop them!" Ben shouted to everyone at large.

There was a twist, an impact, a hand broke free, the knife tore, again at nothing.

The men embraced, held, contorted one another, stumbled, fell to the floor, arose together.

The equilibrium won't last long, Ben thought, and when the balance is broken, someone will be dead.

The knife again, slashing.

Ben broke away from Yannis.

"Come back!" the old man called.

The American rushed to the fighters. He moved behind the man with the knife. As he reached him, the other one turned. Too late, however; Ben had his arm. He twisted it back, then snapped it upward, hard. The knife clattered on the tiles. Its owner dropped to his knees to retrieve it and Ben wrenched him away, threw the weight of his body onto him, forced him to the floor, then held him down with a knee in his belly and a hand at his throat.

But the knife was out of reach and the other man was after it.

"No!" Ben shouted. "Somebody—!"

"Ben!"

He saw Yannis leave the table.

As the other fighter almost had the knife, Ben's arm reached out, clutched at the man's jacket, had it and lost it. The Greek grabbed the knife. Ben again snatched at the jacket, caught it and yanked. He felt the lurch of the man's body, saw the dart of alarm, then didn't know what happened, only felt the stab of pain in his hand, and saw the blood. When the knife came down again, he struck the arm, then struck it again, gave all his strength to it. He heard the metal hit something, and saw it slide toward the roulette table.

Yannis was there then, rushing toward it. "Watch out!" he yelled.

The knife was behind the fighter and he whirled to it. It was between him and Yannis, both groveling, when the old man pitched forward and shoved the other one backward, just within Ben's reach. The American threw his arm around the man's neck and closed, headlock; he tightened. The hold was with his left hand; he saw his blood coursing down the other one's shirt.

Yannis had the knife.

The man on the floor, under Ben, was quite willing to have done with it. The other one, in the vise of Ben's arm, kept struggling a moment, then suddenly went limp, and Ben thought: My God, I've strangled him. He loosened his hold. The man broke free and shook himself like a wet dog out of the rain. He took a few unsteady steps, looked one direction, then another, saw Yannis with the knife, saw the doorway, staggered between the tables, and left the casino.

Slowly releasing the other one, Ben got to his feet. He felt a quaking in his body, and his hand hurt. There was blood on the floor and on the Greek. The man stood squarely to him now, shaking with rage.

"American scum!"

His arm shot out and he struck Ben a blow that staggered him.

Enraged, the American started to strike back, but stopped. It was over. He turned away.

Somebody somewhere laughed. It could have been derision, it could have been nerves; it didn't matter. Then he had a frightening thought: I wonder what it would have felt like to hit that man, to kill him?

The blood was coming faster. Yannis got rid of the knife and hastened to him. "Why you hold your hand down? Hold it up." The medical assistant giving orders to his boss, the medic.

"Come outside," Yannis directed.

The old man led him to the road ledge on the mountainside where the ambulance was parked It wasn't really an ambulance but a Land-Rover that Ben had converted to hospital specifications. Better equipped than the public vehicles, it had to be better, he had told himself, if he was going to be a private medic in the emergency business. First aid, his specialty, was needed tonight: the blood wasn't stopping.

Inside the ambulance, he sat on the cot while the old man started to tie a tourniquet around his forearm.

"Not so tight," Ben said.

Yannis was angry with him. "Shut your mouth, you stupid goat."

Ben grinned.

His assistant was annoyed. "Feel proud, yes?"

Laughing openly, "Bet your ass."

The Greek repeated that he was not an intelligent goat.

"What the hell was I going to do—let them kill each other?"

The old man pulled tighter on the tourniquet and Ben cursed at him. But he was doing it well, the medic observed; neat, quick, economical, just as confining as it needed to be. He's learned a hell of a lot in a couple of years, Ben thought.

The back door of the ambulance was open. There was a gentle mist in the mountain air, and a soft music of wind and birdsong; it was the summer of nightingales. He didn't know which he loved more, the mountains or the sea, but he knew he loved this island. . . . He felt good.

But he was still nettled by the fighters. "Those bastards," he said. "Do they want to make a war?"

"Do not move. I am finish, almost."

"They've got it better than they've ever had it. Christ, they're at peace!"

"Stay still." He was doing the bandage now.

"Why can't they let it alone?"

Yes, let it alone, this beautiful little paradise, let it draw an easy breath at last, now that the bitter war was over. It had been ten years since the big disturbances of '64, and with the republic of Greeks and Turks finally succeeding, why did a couple of fractious bastards roil the serene waters that bathed the island? They were leftover militants, obsolete, a vexation to everyone.

"Finished," Yannis said.

"Pretty good."

"Better than pretty good."

They genially traded indignities.

"How much you win tonight?" the Greek asked.

"Haven't counted. Over five hundred pounds, I think."

The old man rubbed his belly happily. "I won also."

"How much?"

"Two pounds." He giggled. "But is better than years ago. I was always losing. Now I win. We have to come more times, yes?"

"Yes," Ben promised, but guessed they wouldn't. They rarely had a free moment. One or another of the hospitals they served was always on the intercom, dispatching them.

"I'm hungry."

"Me also." Yannis nudged him. "You pay tonight."

Ben pretended to complain, but they both knew he would be glad to do it. Problem, however: it was getting late; all the restaurants might already be closed.

"The Wine Press will be open," the old man said. It was a taverna he had known a few years ago—if he could remember the way. "You can drive with that hand?"

"I've got another one," Ben replied. "Anyway, if I don't, who will?"

"Someday I will learn to drive."

"Bullshit."

The old man chuckled. "Yes—bullshit."

When they got into the cab, and Ben put both hands on the wheel, he could feel the blood oozing through the bandage.

Those sons of bitches, he thought. They both got away without a scratch, but he was bleeding.

Winning at the *poka* table tonight, Ben thought, was only symptomatic of how lucky he was. Even the fullness of moon and the bounty of stars, as he drove on the mountain road, told him how abundant his life had become. His Vietnam years over, he was fortunate to be living on this enchanted reef, far from the paroxysms of the world, doing the work he wanted to do, being successful at it, finding a crusty old man who had turned into a good friend, and coming finally into a serenity he had never known.

There was only one thing lacking this evening. He wanted to be with a woman. He had not spent the night with anyone for over a month, when he had been with the exchange clerk from Barclays Bank. She was an English girl from Coventry, with a low forehead but high breasts, and when she talked her moist mouth rounded in a suggestive way that was oddly attractive to him . . . whatever her name was, Gillian something. A dull woman with a metronomically monotonous voice, she spoke animatedly only about her hobby, sponge diving, and told the same underwater adventures over and over again in the same enervating detail; but she had a savory skin, sun- and sea-tanned, honey-colored, and she walked with a seductively disjointed gliding that made all her rounded protuberances seem separate, with a life of their own, individually alluring, trembling, inviting the hand to still the palpitation of her parts. It was a blandishment of his own mind, no doubt, a lie of self-teasing, but it stirred him to the radicle. In kissing, she had a busy tongue, in bed she hectically tossed her head from side to side, seeking pillows of comfort, her eyes closed until the gonging instance, then her lids came wide open and her pupils rolled back as if in trance, there was a quake of whiteness in them, then a surging of breast and a special flash of frenzy, operatic moan and moan until some extraordinary muscle came frantically to life inside her, a grabbing thing like thews or a sphincter, snatching and not releasing him, holding and holding, and as he agonized ecstatically, he was gone and she gone with him. Insanity, what a surprise she was! Who would have known that the dull-voiced diurnal bank clerk, dressed in deposit slips, would make such a nocturnal frenzy? He would have continued seeing her, glad of the steady custom, pleasuring in the rut—a word too apt—if not for one thing: she had an unrestrained panic for permanence. The private muscle within her that would not let go at night had its daytime counterpart, the unremitting clutch of desperation. How strange that he could not recall her full name; he regretted that he couldn't. He had a sad, immemorial erection. . . .

A mountain curve, more tortuous than usual, surprised him. He slammed the brakes on.

"One hand—you drive too fast," his companion said.

He realized it was not his one-handedness that was at fault. He had had a lot to drink, and he was not used to it. He slowed down, nearly to a crawl, and felt the pleasure of not having to race to an emergency. Yannis made a mistake in his directions, they got lost on a road that went downward instead of up, and when they found the village of Seismos—dark and silent and blue with moonlight—it was past eleven. There was little chance that the taverna would be open.

They rode through the town. High in the mountains, it was at the bottom of a shallow crater formed by an earthquake centuries ago, so the Seismans said. Even in these Troodos heights, always cool and windswept in the evenings, the heat of July crouched in the pit like a firedragon. It was a sultry heat, lying in wait, threatening to turn into something electrical and ominous. Since the crater was almost totally rimmed by hills, the springs of water did not flow into brooks or rivulets, but lay in the low places, making marshes which were barely visible, spectral, breathing gray witcheries of fog. The air was oppressive, but there was excitement in it, suggesting that the hazy vapors might soon start to swirl and become galvanized into a dazzling discharge of fireworks.

The restaurant itself was on an artificial lake that had been created by damming a ravine of tiny ponds. It was on the edge of this breastwork of landfill that the terrace of The Wine Press had been built.

As the road lifted a little, they saw the taverna. It seemed closed. Turning the corner of the building, however, they saw that the dining room was charily alight.

Inside, the place was empty. There weren't many tables, perhaps fifteen, and most of them were cleared; dinner was over. The room was smaller than it had seemed from the outside, and, viewed through the glass door, the terrace too appeared tiny, a table's width, no more.

And all of it dreary. It had a gloomily dutiful aspect, as if grudging effort had been exerted to keep it spotless and efficient, but the greeting of the place was niggardly, with no sign of affection. Ben couldn't tell why the taverna seemed moribund to him, clean as it was and orderly, but failure seemed to be its decorative style, dulling the paints and deadening the illumination. Yannis sensed it too; the restaurant was not as he remembered it. They both had the impulse to leave at once. But it was too late. The man appeared.

He was the owner of the restaurant and, at this time of night, its sole waiter. In his mid-forties, he had a haggardly unhappy face, with eyes that darted with suspicion. As he saw them in the room, he threw a napkin over his left wrist, and Ben saw that the forearm was withered.

"Kirios Menas," Yannis introduced, "this is my friend, Kirios Coram."

"How do you do—good evening," he said.

The words were well spoken but minimally polite. Dreading the dinner, and trying to bring to it what cordiality he could, the medic asked a friendly question, "Why is your place called The Wine Press?"

Menas drew no proprietary pleasure from the customer's interest; he merely pointed to the corner of the room. In the semi-darkness, Ben caught a glint of copper. The press was beautiful and extremely old. Not very different from a carpenter's vise, really, except that the jaws were large plates, the bottom one perforated by hundreds of holes, through which the grape extract could flow into the large copper vat. For all its incrustations of green sulfate and ancient lime, it seemed still workable. Ben touched it delicately, with admiring hands. "How old is it?"

The proprietor didn't know, probably a thousand years, it came with the restaurant when he bought it. He said it without profound engrossment in the subject. As Yannis turned the lever, the upper jaw came down a bit, and the owner was not pleased.

To fundamentals, then: "Is it too late for dinner?" Ben asked. "No."

The dining room was sweltering, and when Menas indicated a table, Ben looked through the window. "Could we sit outdoors?"

"It will not be cooler there. Besides, it is damp."

Seated—indoors—Ben ordered wine, a large carafe. After serving it, the man said unceremoniously, "What to eat?"

The usual courtesy while offering a menu—which Menas was doing now—was for the guest to be invited into the kitchen, to survey the display of provender. Not that the cuisine was widely various, you could generally count on the staples—moussaka, roast beef and chicken, occasionally a *kleftikon* of lamb, and all the customary vegetables and relishes, few surprises. While the purpose might be to whet the diner's appetite so that he would order more food than he had intended, Ben always felt that the origin of the impulse had been more generous, to welcome the stranger to the hearth. It was a friendly privilege. But it was not volunteered.

"Could we look in the kitchen?" he asked.

"There is hardly anything left—a little lamb and some moussaka." Then, tersely, "It is late."

It was an entirely reasonable answer. Yet, chilly for a Cypriot. Ben was puzzled. "Still—if you don't mind . . ."

The man's face tightened. "The chef does not want it."

Ben let it go.

The service was slow; setting the table took forever. Menas, with only one functioning hand, had to make many trips, and sometimes he dropped things. Once, when he was stooping to retrieve a saltcellar, he uttered a profanity; it was the first time they saw him smile, and it was in self-mockery. That instant, Ben felt sorry for him. The man was doing as well as he could, and bravely, wresting a crooked jest out of his infirmity, trying not to hear the plaintive wail of a child somewhere, hearing too well the annoyed clatter of the chef in the kitchen, ignoring the perspiration he could not wipe away because the hand that hung limp at the end of the shriveled arm was useless. Because he depressed them and because they were getting drunker, Ben and Yannis cracked the meretricious joke—Ben couldn't recall which of them told it—about the handicapped paperhanger, and they made book on whether he would drop the olive dish. He didn't. The droppages now were coming from the kitchen. And once, a muffled curse, unintelligible.

When the food arrived—lamb for both—it was not the best they had eaten, but it was gratifyingly good. The marrows were surprisingly not overdone, and the salad was crisp. The wine, local and inexpensive, was excellent, and they were on their second carafe. Yannis drank little and Ben, much. They ordered strawberries for dessert, coffee and brandy, and while they were being prepared, Ben went to the men's room.

As he was going toward it, he passed the kitchen, the door to which was closed; but on his return, it was open. He heard a clatter and looked in.

The chef was a woman. It would be difficult to tell what her age might be, but he would have guessed it somewhere near his own, say thirty-five, perhaps a bit older. By none of the customary standards could she be called beautiful, yet he imagined himself calling her that. There was a primitive vitality in her motion, and an animal, wildwood pride. She worked swiftly and impatiently, cleaning up the afterdinner mess. In the steamy, suffocating night, the kitchen must have been unbearable. Her dark hair was tightly tied back, but there were damp strands that had escaped the knot, her high cheekbones had a flaming heat flush, and she was the most hectically disturbing woman he had ever seen.

Ben realized why the chef wanted no visitors. She was practically naked. Moiling in the oven's heat, she had been cooking in nothing but her underwear. Not young, not thin, but with the lushness of a woman at the fullest time of life, she had ample Greek hips and a plenitude of breast not altogether imprisoned by her brassiere. It was this sense of imprisonment, not of breast alone but of everything about her, that seemed the erotic exponent of the woman—a vivid, sensual, high-bred animal in chains, hotly straining against entanglement, sweating in an oven of vexation, struggling against a bondage that seemed libidinous with heat, an obscene *ligotage* that might result in screams of orgasm or violence. She was an exquisite creature, bursting with rage and rut.

For all the allurements that her body had for Ben, it was the haunting expression in her face that held him. Her eyes, deep as they were, did not seem black enough or cavernous enough to hold all her despair . . . a devastation. He had never lost his sensitivity to affliction; sometimes he thought he was tropistically attracted to tragic people, as if their darkness were his light. And now, magnetically, he felt drawn to a havoc, calling it her essential beauty.

She did not know he was staring at her, and then she did. Discomposed, she looked away an instant, then turned to regard him fully. Her face was set in hot resentment and she stood there, motionless, as though she were arrogantly exposing herself, contemptuously exhibiting her semi-nakedness. Quickly, he stepped away from the doorway. As he went back to the table, he made the drunken declaration to himself: I have been slain.

At the table, he said to Yannis, "The chef is a woman."

"The chef is a big bullock name of Pugas and he weighs a good twenty stone."

"Not tonight. A beautiful woman."

"Oh—maybe Kalya."

"Kalya?" He had never heard the name before. He liked it. "What's her last name?"

Yannis pointed. "The same as his. Menas."

The meal turned sour in his stomach. "They're married?"

"No, they are not married, but they live together."

He looked at the man with the crippled hand and the failed face. "They live together?"

"For some years. They even have a child."

He felt moronic, parroting everything. "A child?"

"Two years—maybe more."

"If they . . . Why don't they get married?"

"He is a Greek, she is a Turk."

"She's Turkish?"

"Yes."

"You mean because she's Turkish, they have a child and don't get married?"

"You are more drunk than you should be."

More or less. In New York, or Boston where he came from, there would hardly be a raised eyebrow over two people having a child and living together, unmarried. But in Cyprus, the rupture of one convention revealed the rancor in another: Turks and Greeks don't intermarry. Even now, in these untroubled days, when the wounds had healed and there was accord again . . . Chagrined as he might be on other occasions to be benefiting by an old racial malice, he found himself rejoicing that the man was not her husband, and she might be available, she was free. He abused himself only a little for behaving so uncharacteristically like a crud, and he was happy. He extenuated the offense: he was drunk. But he did not want to be sober; he wanted to love this woman tonight, wanted to put a rose on one of her breasts and kiss the other, wanted to hold her, to enjoy all the benevolences of her body, wanted to make love to her, and love her.

"What else do you know?" he asked.

"About Kalya? Nothing."

"Come on—tell me more about her." He had a hunger. "Tell me."

The old man seemed to have a reluctance to talk about her, as if she were an evil legend. "Him—Savvas Menas—I can tell you something about him. He used to be a chicken farmer near Pendayia, the other side of the mountain. Even at this, he was a bad failure. People were always laughing at him, they would say his chickens were barren, they did not lay eggs, only shells. He sold his farm and opened a shop—very little—no more bigger than my pocket. Then he went away, nobody knows where. When he came back, he was with this woman. They had an infant child, only a few weeks old. They came here and found the old taverna. It was closed, no good. They took a lease and opened it once more. For a while it was successful, but now . . ."

"Where did he meet her—where did she come from?"

Yannis shrugged. "I do not know."

"What do you think? What do they say about her around here?"

The old man's face clouded. "They say . . . she is a room without a window."

He felt a chill. It was the same darkness he had seen in her: not looking out, not letting anyone look in, alone in there. Everything the old man had said about the woman intrigued him, but what he left unsaid was like a bewitchment. Each gauze of uncertainty that was draped over her suggested a more tantalizing nakedness underneath. He had a compulsion to peer through the webs of her mystery, he wanted to watch her awake and asleep, wanted to eavesdrop on her breathing.

Menas hovered at the entry counter, watching them, wanting them to go. They had eaten their dessert, had drunk their coffee and nearly all the brandy, there was nothing further to keep them here. Ben beckoned to the owner and the man came hurrying with the check.

The bill was less than four pounds, tax and service included. There was no need to leave any gratuity. Ben lay the four pounds on the yellow tab sheet, then put a twenty-pound note on top of it.

Menas looked at the extra money. Even ten shillings would have been more than enough . . . but twenty pounds?

The proprietor asked, "What is this for?"

"For the cook," the American said.

"It is generous," the man murmured.

"For the cook and the custom."

Menas knew the expression; they all did. Lost in the breach of old restaurant niceties, it was still the tradition if the observance was invoked. The cook, in all courtesy, would have to put in an appearance, come to the table to say thanks, and to be thanked in person.

Menas had no fat on his body, he was as lean as winter. He got leaner as he stood there. He didn't reach for the money.

"I do not think she will come," he said.

Ben pointed to the money. "Take it to her."

Menas took the four pounds first, and the yellow tab with it. He held them in his good hand. The twenty-pound note was still on the table. The Greek's body tensed. It seemed to cry emergency to all his energies. He mustered every muscle until, at last, his breath coming more shallowly, the withered arm stirred. It moved not more than a few inches. The hand, ostensibly dead, fluttered a trifle, and slowly the gray and wasted digits closed upon the note. Holding the money at an angle too askew, he walked away from the table and into the kitchen.

Ben and Yannis did not look at each other. The medic drank the tiny drop of brandy that was left in the glass. He waited.

The door opened and Kalya stood on the threshold. She held the twenty-pound note in her hand as if it were a lighted candle. The only concession she had made to her appearance was that she now wore a lightweight wrapper, but she had not combed her hair, had not even bothered to wipe the perspiration off her face. Yet, as she walked, it was as if the sleazy thing she wore trailed a train, and there were courtiers in her wake.

She didn't learn that walk in an impoverished village, he thought, or in a Turkish ghetto.

When she arrived at the table she paused and waited for

Menas to join them. Turkey out of Europe or Turkey out of Asia, Ben thought, and could not tell which; he wondered if it was the black and terra-cotta look of her that made her look so vivid, or whether it was the mystery. And which described her best, the pride or the distress? No woman is beautiful if she does not incite a question, but is she beautiful simply *because* she does?

Until Menas came to the table, she held her silence. When she spoke, her voice was deep and warmly modulated; her diction was as clean as pebbles. Nearly all the tradespeople on the island spoke English—Cyprus had been British—but it was what Londoners called Shopkeep, superficial. Hers, he suspected, had layers to it; he wondered how many, and how deep.

"You have left us quite a sizable tip," she said. And she put the money on the table.

Ben pointed to the currency. "Please keep it—with my thanks. The dinner was excellent."

She looked at him, dead on, holding his glance as if she would never release it. "It was not that good."

He smiled as amiably as he could. "Shouldn't you let me be the judge of it?"

"What is the money for?"

"My appreciation."

"Of something you have received?"

"Of course."

"Or of something you hope to receive?"

He stopped smiling. He became very still.

"What is the American buying?" she asked.

Menas took a step toward her. "Kalya . . ." He was on the verge of intervening, to soften the impulse or to make her more amenable. But she looked at him with such contempt that he turned away.

Back to Ben, she repeated the demand. "Well? What is the American buying?"

He hadn't meant to make an international incident of it. He felt befuddled—and ashamed—and angry—and wanted to think more clearly than the drink allowed. Mostly, he didn't want to talk about it anymore. "Please take the money," he said.

Then he did a spontaneous, foolish thing. He reached for the twenty-pound note, crumpled it, grabbed her hand, and shoved the money into it.

She opened her hand and looked at the lump of currency on

her palm. With utmost care, and without haste, she unwadded it, straightened it until it was smooth. When there was hardly a wrinkle in it, she meticulously curled the bill into a cone. Then, with the same slow precision, she reached down and picked up Ben's empty brandy glass. She put the cone of paper into the glass, and unhurriedly, with measured deliberation, gathered a mouthful of spittle. She let it drop into the money cornucopia. She set the brandy glass back on the table, exactly into the wet ring it had made on the tablecloth. She didn't return to the kitchen. The child was still crying mournfully in the distance, it might have been a feverish complaint, and she went outdoors to it, somewhere in the night.

Ben laughed more than the bathos warranted; Yannis, less. But the American wished he had not had a drink all evening, and wished he could call her back.

On a nearby hillside where there was no fog, the two men slept in the ambulance. Yannis had the built-in bed and Ben had the litter. When the Greek first went to work for the American, it was the other way around, Ben being tall and Yannis short, and the stationary bed being bigger and stronger. But every once in a while, when the old man's bones ached, the medic insisted on swapping with his assistant, and after a few months the Greek had the bed for keeps.

They had been lying down for nearly an hour when Ben heard him clear his throat. "What's up?" the younger one asked.

"Nothing—go to sleep."

"I am asleep."

"Goatshit. You think of that woman."

"Shut up."

"She will break your walnuts."

"I've got to see her again."

"She has already broke them." An instant. "What? You have become in love?"

"I didn't say I was in love." He did not believe in the power of love at first sight, certainly not at first drunken sight. And it occurred to him that *only* while drunk could he be subject to it. As soon as he was sober, the aberration would be gone. "I've got to see her, that's all," he repeated.

"After she spits on you?"

"She spits on him too. Did you see the look she gave him?"

"They live together."

"They're not married."

"They have a child. He has a right with her."

"What right—property? He doesn't own her, goddamn it."

"Ben . . . go to sleep."

"She's dying."

"What?"

"She's choking there. She hates that man and she despises her life."

"You know that in one evening?"

"I knew it in one minute."

The old man must have heard the intensity in his voice. He did not speak for a while. Then he said, with a little worry, "You have a crazy."

Yes . . . a crazy. The idiotic certainty, based on a single erratic evening, that he had come to an important moment—the end of his old life, and the beginning of a new one. Saying a thing like that, after a random and unsuccessful meeting with a woman— there was only hunch to go on, or lunacy.

Yet, he was a rational man who customarily behaved in a rational way. At the age of nearly thirty-five, he had already led a responsible life. Even if he did not consider himself a businessman, he managed his private ambulance in a practical way. He had satisfactory working relationships with the hospitals of four cities, he maintained radio connection with all of them and responded to every emergency, he paid his assistant generously and on time, he would go to any extremity to save a life or ease a pain. He was a bright man, competent and well trained. Reliable.

Not erratic, not a lunatic of love.

If he did confess to a bit of free verse in his soul, the body of him was commonsensical prose. If he had never ceased being an idealist, he did not dwell in dreamland. He was catholically well read for a man with a scientific specialty, but he didn't plumb deep distances inside himself in pursuit of an abstract idea, although he did—he had to admit it—in pursuit of a feeling. He was strong enough to be gentle—and he suspected that somewhere, ultimately accessible, there was a talent for loving. Not eccentric about love, however; not eccentric about anything. Sensible.

But he did have problems. One of them went back, many years. He was the only child of Boston parents, his father a doctor, a distinguished serologist who said that he was brought up to know, by instinct, the difference between good blood and bad. His mother was a public speaker, a brisk and cheery woman, formidable behind a podium, who spent her life fighting for hopeless causes, and winning. Both his parents were winners, by religion. And, loving him, they brought him up in the faith.

When Ben was just past twenty-five, he was not living at home but across the river in Cambridge, and was finishing his last year of medical school at Harvard. Three weeks before graduation, he packed his clothes, left school, never went back, and did not become a doctor.

His closest friend, the woman he was living with in Cambridge, was deeply upset by his decision. She was Drusilla Keating, also in medical school, a canny student, cool in her proficiencies, intent on being a surgeon. Strikingly attractive without being pretty, she was lean-faced and rawboned, with pert breasts and a hungry mouth, warm and willing in the night. Because she knew she was a keen-honed technical instrument, Drusilla made an exercise of appearing generous and cozy. She smiled inveterately, flashing teeth as perfect as dentures, a dazzle of them. But the smile was misleading—she had no time for cant, and had a satiric tongue; sugary ironies issued from her lips like maraschino cherries dipped in gall.

He was always deliciously surprised by how much sex she required. I like books and sailboats and fucking, she said, in variable order. Sometime, when we're sailing, I hope you'll screw me into the deck while I'm reading Proust. One Sunday afternoon they almost achieved the perfect simultaneity.

Drusilla was beautifully constructed, although she despaired of her attenuated, boyish figure, spare as a sapling. Particularly—and peculiarly, considering the criteria of current fashion—she despaired of her lean behind, and called herself Sparrowcheeks. Ben disagreed with her and said she had sweet round buns, warm from the oven; but it did not comfort her. Until she was naked. Then, suddenly, a transformation: she walked as if her backside were all pleasure to her, a festive bounty of soft rotundity, and she preened and tantalized with it, moving it lasciviously, shifting her world wantonly from hemisphere to hemisphere, teasing him with fleshly glissades of motion, enticing him, all pleasure and no hindrance. But always, after she had had her delectations from her nates, she berated them as if they were a pair of gluteal betrayers, wickedly colluding behind her back. This seldom love and sometime hate she had for her posterior struck Ben as being faithless to an apparatus that gave her pleasure, and he said that her derrière was, *au fond,* her worst hypocrisy.

But at the true fundament of things, Ben knew, Drusilla was no hypocrite. On the contrary, she rarely deviated from the honest position, as if afraid she might get lost and not find her way back to herself. The daughter of a rich public opinion pollster, she was resolutely opinionated and scrupulously frank. Dru had researched life definitively, and, in conversation, while pretending to listen open-mindedly, she never kept the ball in the air, but smashed every lob. She tried to smash Ben's idea of quitting medical school with the incontestable argument that it lacked prudential wisdom.

Prudence was Drusilla's fetish. On account of it, Ben had met her—in the bay off Marblehead. His tiny skiff—rashly too far from land, and engineless—was becalmed in a motionless sea of satin. In the darkening twilight, he heard her engine first, then saw her slender, natty sloop. She yelled across the water, offered a lift, hove to, and towed him home. Small as her craft was, it had two engines, an extra one in case. In case of what? he had asked. I don't want to be at the mercy of anything, she had answered, not wind, wave, or weather. Caution was the keystone in her arch of self-preservation.

Dru's morality was pragmatism. Justice was a public expedient; decency was a social lubricant; honesty, the best policy. Ben asked: No honesty for its own sake?

"Whose sake is that?" she replied.

Going to war, according to Dru, was for nobody's sake. Extremely impractical. Against the canon of common sense. It was a breach of a tenet she thought they understood about each other; she was shocked—and felt betrayed—that he would smash it. It was never mended. When he was overseas, she didn't answer his first letter, nor his second. He started his third letter, "Dear Dru . . ." and that was as far as he got.

His mother was away on a speaking tour when he decided to enlist, so he phoned her. She too was shocked that he was quitting the university. Although she couldn't for the moment recall what year he was in, her voice was achingly troubled and she tried not to cry. She sent him a compassionate letter saying she understood his need for a respite from the grueling exigencies of medical school. As a matter of fact, she thought the American Medical Association had much to answer for with respect to its arbitrary rigors and laxities, and she was preparing a lecture and promotional brochure on the subject. Enclosed, she said, please find check for five hundred dollars.

His father was in a rage. "What the hell do you mean, you won't be a doctor?" he said. "Define yourself."

His father had never had any difficulty defining *him*self. He was select. Born in a select house on Beacon Hill, he had a select Harvard education, and spoke as if he had personally selected his parents, using the Social Register as a catalogue. He was a parfit, gentil knight by blood, by morals, and by the exclusive heraldry of his profession. All the Corams had been doctors; they were so declared at birth. When he demanded that Ben define himself, he meant quite simply that there are doctors, and there are all those others of vague definition. Once, in his oaken linenfold-paneled office, a college friend of Ben's had observed the father-physician's Hippocratic pride and asked which gave him more self-esteem, being a doctor or a Boston Brahmin. To which the Bostonian had replied, with an engaging lack of affectation, that all doctors were Brahmins.

To be or not to be one? His father felt that the answer was obvious. "Get your degree and keep going. The doubts will pass. It's only a temporary indisposition, Ben—a low-grade infection."

"From what?"

"The Sixties."

The doctor always blamed everything on the Sixties, the wicked *Zeitgeist*. Perhaps this time he was right. Ben may not have caught all the fevers of the decade, but he had lived in the heat. As an undergraduate, even as a medical student, he had listened to most of the rhetoric and spoken some of it, had engaged in the forced marches for ethnics and civil rights and against the war, had hurled a brick or two, had run from sirens, police clubs, and, once, from tear gas. Unlike his father, he would not carry a conservative sword in a liberal sheath, yet he sensed that many of the valorous voices were loudest in empty rooms, and that frequently, when his companions refused to flee from their posts, it was not courage but a muscular listlessness brought on by the aftereffects of speed or blotter acid. He had driven to an outdoor prayer breakfast, not honking for Jesus; had become a Charismatic for a moment, without revelation; had Meditated deeply, but not for long. The tantras and mantras and mandalas did not usher him into the luminescence of the Great Mystery but into a dark cellar of mystification. He shouted the new cries in an old world and never stopped meaning many of them; he spat in the dirty bath water of success, yet he swam smoothly in Harvard's disinfected swimming pool, and saw the incongruity and was ashamed of it. He lived in plethora and void, and both were painful to him. Even the easy sexual freedom did not come easily to him; he disliked the busy thoroughfare of sexual traffic, with its few lights and casual signals, the effortless convenience of it, the quick emissions and the dry departures, sadder because there was no sadness in them, and the loud, loud loneliness. And at the sorry heart of everything, the new certainty —hitherto unreckonable to the mind of man—that the world was terminally ill, that the once beautiful and green earth had been betrayed once too often, and was inconsequentially coming to its sickly end. And like most of the accusers, even while shouting his outrage, he felt namelessly and helplessly guilty for all of it.

It would have been a relieving extenuation to agree with his father: his defection from medical school was not his fault, but the taint of the times. And that it was only a temporary aberration in him, it would pass.

But he knew it was an evasion. The cause of his dereliction was not in the Sixties alone, but in himself. Some deep lack or failing, some spot not visible to the X-ray of reason, a weakness, an ailment . . . a need.

If only he knew what it was. It plagued him that he didn't. And how strange that it had never become an unbearable question until he was almost ready to graduate. Why was he loath to become a doctor? For "loath" did he read "loathe"? Did he really hate the idea of becoming an MD? Was he afraid?

The one word that projected from the others, swelling into his consciousness like a tumor, was of course the word "afraid." It was always the word that harassed him. It was the goad that prodded him to pick fights when in high school, and play chicken in cars. Those pursuits never proved anything to him, neither his cowardice nor his bravery; only that he was a fool. And the question of courage still remained. Afraid.

It was the crux of another problem as well. He was a man of peace in a world that had been ceaselessly at war. Everywhere he went—and before arriving in Cyprus he had traveled a good deal —he saw bloodshed, the fact of it, or the memory or the preparation or the threat. He had at one time considered war a pathological state, a diseased condition of the social organism, but now, watching the world's habituation to it, he saw it becoming an acceptable normality. Not to him. His preoccupation with it was a sympathetic illness, and it tormented him that the heart of his malady was the venom, fear. I hate war not because of any highminded, incorruptible love of my fellowman, but because I don't want to get killed. As if that were a terrible reason.

It *was* terrible to him. Especially at that time, when he had so convulsively torn himself out of medical school, and forced himself into spasm after spasm of self-blame. Unhappiness about unhappiness, and fear about fear, and suddenly he realized that he was seeing war in ways he had never imagined. It might not only be a test of a man's courage and his ability to survive, but even a test of his *will* to survive. Whatever the test might reveal about the *world's* will to survive, it was an enlightenment he personally had never dreamed he would need. That he did need it scared him. So he enlisted.

There was a fitness about it, an almost too perfect patness. The recreant doctor becomes a paramedic; the fugitive gives himself up; the life-questioner studies the alternative. War would have been the perfect laboratory, if it hadn't been agony.

Stateside, he had always regarded the human body as a whole number, not a miscellany of fractions. As a student observer in the operating room, while viewing the most radical surgery, he took for granted that incisions and sectionings and carvings were performed on an integer, the body was an indivisible unit. Entity and sanctity, the saying went. But this was back home, before he saw what a mortar shell could do. The purpose of warfare, it seemed, was to fragmentize the body into as many segments as possible; and his job as a medic was to reassemble the bloody lumps and chunks, the faceless heads and limbless feet, the unassigned guts and gizzards, the leftover hearts that often continued to beat, tardily, after disjunction. Sometimes the reassemblages would not come out even, like jigsaw puzzles with pieces missing, or extra ones, unnecessary. Occasionally it would be a superfluous spleen or finger, an arm that was gratuitous; the medics called them spares. Often, especially when turning the odds and ends over to a burial detail, a short leg would be coupled with a long one, or ears of discrepant sizes; once in a while there were inconsistencies of skin color. But it was all the same in death, no prejudice. The stench, particularly, was democratic—the carcasses stank uniformly, the one, single, identifiable, unchangeable, belly-sickening stink-rot of the dead.

After four years as a medic, just as he thought he had become toughened to it—nothing, he believed, could appall or nauseate him anymore—he found himself lying face upward, eyes rigid, staring at the white ceiling of a field hospital.

There was nothing wrong with him; it was merely that he couldn't walk. He had no wounds to account for it, his limbs were all there, intact, there was no physical impairment or illness of any kind, and nothing hurt, except that "hurt" was his total condition, an absolute. He had no specific agonizing memory, no forlorn regrets, no acute pain to weep over at night; when the tears came, they were for nothing. He simply cried, softly and secretly, not disturbing the nurses, no bother to anyone.

However . . . occasionally—not too often—he screamed. It would not have been notably agitating in the ward, outcries being commonplace among the patients, if the word he shrieked had not been so terrifying:

Fire!

The first and second time it happened, it nearly caused a panic. Nurses, doctors, corpsmen, orderlies came running, all directions. Although it was not a psycho hospital but a medical one, some of the patients became hysterical at being disabled in a burning building, some shouted for help, some beat with spoons on bed frames or bedpans; the ambulatory ones scrambled toward the exits, tripping over crutches.

But the third time he screamed, a week after the first, there was little disturbance. A few of the men laughed, there was a spattering of curses; the rest of the ward was vaguely annoyed, another nuisance.

There was no way of preventing his outcry, or foretelling when it would happen. It could occur at nighttime or in broad daylight. He might go a whole week without uttering it, then suddenly it would tear out of him, ripping his throat, racking his body, fire! Since it had no predictable pattern, sedation did not serve to prevent it. Nor, most terrible of all, could Ben understand what the scream meant or where it came from. It was as if someone else, trapped inside him, were shrilling from the hollow depths of his being. He would be convulsed by it, shrieking the word again and again, in agony, trying to flee not so much from the imagined flames as from his own outcry, trying to lift his body off the bed, to bestir his immovable legs, scarcely able to budge, screaming and screaming, *fire!*

His psychomed was a first lieutenant named Nedley. He had dry palms and a clean nose, and he always steered the middle course, using all the clichés of compromise. He talked about give-and-take, striking a balance, the level head, and the happy medium. Even his hair was a middling color, between brown and blond, and he pursued a fifty-fifty morality, splitting the difference. He lived a lukewarm life. But he was not a stupid man, nor indeed insensitive. And since his promotion in the service might ultimately be accelerated by making use of what he heard, he had an ear acutely cocked for listening. In a psychiatrist, this was not a bad thing to have.

"You had another one last night," he said.

"Yes."

"Was it the same?"

"I suppose so."

"Did you actually see any flames?"

"I don't know—I don't think so."

"Feel any heat? Burning? Anything like that?"

"I can't remember."

"Did you try to walk? Run?"

"I think so. My covers were off."

"Couldn't make it, huh?"

"No."

"Why?"

"Up your ass."

Nedley's face equivocated between smile and frown. "You still can't remember an actual fire?"

"No."

"Have you tried?"

"Come on, come on."

"Did anybody ever order you to fire—a gun, I mean?"

"We've had this."

"We've had it and we haven't," he said in his halfway manner. "Did *you* ever order anybody to fire?"

"We've had this too. No."

"Ever get fired from a job?"

It was a new question. New ones were more worrisome than the others; the trails were overgrown, or booby-trapped. "I can't . . . no, I don't think so."

"Can't remember anything else today? How about the ambulance?"

"No."

"You sure? Where it was, where you left it, whether the VCs got it?"

"Nothing."

"Can't remember how you got to the field station?"

Not a memory, only a conjecture: "I may have . . . walked."

"Mm . . . Let's get back to the other thing. What *is* fire, anyway?"

Ben closed his eyes. He felt deathly tired. Quietly: "Let me alone."

"No, really. What is it?"

"Please."

"Come on—try. What's fire for?"

"Good for cooking."

"And?"

"Hotfoots."

"And?"

"Some say the world will end in it."

"Some say ice."

Things lifted a little; he wondered if the man meant Frost or frost. "From what I've tasted of desire . . ."

"What's desire got to do with it?"

Not Frost; too bad. "Nothing to do with it. Fire-desire—they rhyme."

"Rhyme or reason?"

"You mean was it reasonable for me to scream fire last night and scare the ass off the head nurse? No, it wasn't. Now, for Chrissake, let me alone, will you?"

"You want to get well, don't you?"

"Yes, but I don't want to talk about it, I want to do it!"

"By yourself?"

"By myself."

"We're thinking of transferring you to another hospital."

"I won't be put in psycho!"

"Don't call it that."

"I won't, goddamn it! I'll do it by myself! Now fuck off and let me alone! By myself, by myself!"

Point was, he couldn't be sure he did want to get well, if getting well meant: sane. There might be better states than sanity, a variety of them, some dementias suited to some people, others to others. Total forgetfulness, as an instance, might be just his kind, he might like that. And perhaps he was gratifyingly en route to it. Clearly, he had forgotten a good deal already—the origin of the fire terror, for example. He would also like to lose the memory of the boy running headless, and the Viet child with its belly . . .

Christ.

Not only memory, but reason—he would like to lose that, too. Trying to make a dialectic out of the illogical perversities, the stupid barbarities, the pig-eyed ignorances of war—the very attempt betrayed a loss of reason. And judgment—how easily he could give *that* up, knowing how it had betrayed him with illusions that the body, brain, and blood were magical, the romantic biological mysteries; and how quickly in a war he had learned what pulpy commonplaces they were—oh murder, the banality of blood! . . . Insanity might be quite the best of everything. And maybe, with a bit of luck, he was on his way.

But there was the one slender thread to sanity that would not let itself be severed: caring. God, what he would give to surrender caring! Or to know what it was he still cared about, how it was linked to tears, to the limbs that wouldn't move, to the outcry in the night of his mind.

Fire!

No, it was not necessary to his sanity to know why he awakened with it, or why he wept. Sanity was not a state in which all questions were answered, or any. Nor was locomotion a function of lucidity. Physical balance wasn't entirely dependent on mental balance: there were the walking lunatics. And, sane or demented, he needed to walk.

So, still yearning to know why the fire-word had come to him, he stopped crying it, and one day forced his left leg out from under the covers, then his right, and, a week later, walked.

He was not the first to go to Vietnam nor the last to leave, although it seemed that way to him. When he departed from Saigon in 1970, having handled every part of the human body attached or unattached to the corpus, having seen every mutilation known to butchery, he decided: I will never enter an ambulance again, I will never again look at a severed arm, a split skull or an open gut. I will pretend not to know the use of a hypodermic, a compress or a Band-Aid. I will look away from a nosebleed.

So he took his military earnings and traveled. Not wanting to feel too aimless about it, he told himself he was on a quest, but he couldn't tell for what. He saw bits and pieces of everywhere, of cities and villages and countrysides, of veldt and steppe and pampa. He was cold in the hot climates and feverish in the frozen ones, and lost in all of them. He wandered involuntarily one way and another, looked for love and would have settled for light—not the frightening firelight, of course, but some steady and bearable beam that would illuminate wherever the hell he was going, and where to go next. He was deeply and terribly lonely.

He wound up at last in the soft and mellow countries, those that had seashores on the Mediterranean or the Aegean. And at length he realized what it was he had been searching for: an island.

Thus, he discovered Cyprus. He came to it late in 1970 when the Cypriots were just beginning to forget that they had been at war, and to give credence to their peace. There were still a few ructions here and there, like the one in the Platres Cazino, but for the most part the peace was real, and it could be trusted. The British had been driven out a decade ago, and there had been no pitched battles between the native Turks and Greeks for a half-dozen years. The streets were free of British soldiery, people began to leave their doors unlocked again, you could make a Greco-Turkish jest in mixed company without outrage or mayhem. The new republic had a native Greek for its president and a native Turk for its vice-president, and the two races were starting to make a little *kouskousouria* together, a neighborly word that suggested back-yard gossiping. Hatred was out of style. Even among the effete wits of Nicosia, the hostile joke had lost its cachet. It was as though Cyprus were inviting its inhabitants to join a friendly, interracial club.

Ben joined. He fell in love with all of them, with the Greeks at first, because they were easier to know. He was warmed by their instant hospitality, the outstretched hand that held the goblet of wine, the readiness to laugh at his lamest quips as if he were Aristophanes, their unwillingness to wait for his reticent Anglo-Saxon show of affection—they would show theirs first.

Much more slowly, glance by glance, he came to love the Turks. The Turkish smile was always reluctant at the start; full of wanting, it was wary of injury. He noticed, early, that Turkish men were readier with the question than with the statement, and

Turkish women were hesitant about everything. He wondered about the stereotype: fierce. He met no fierce ones. An English journalist who had worked for *The Times* of London told Ben that the way you could tell a man was a Turk and not a Greek was that he was more stolid, more solid. Ben didn't record it with indelible ink. All he added, without expecting a prize for originality, was that he loved them both, but differently.

At the start of his first spring on the island, he felt he could live here, in its gentleness. Cyprus had made him whole again. One morning he awoke and said he did not want to be idle anymore, he wanted muscle-stressing work. He took a job as a *fortotis*, a stevedore, loading crates of produce onto cargo vessels docked in Limassol. When the season was over, he worked in a small metals-assaying laboratory, then did some enzyme research for one of the citrus institutes. Hermetically, he sealed himself off from anything that had to do with the healing arts. He had no remedies for anybody. It was a mistake to go in quest of a cure for the human condition; the need for it might in itself be a malady. Now that he himself was hale once more, he wanted nothing further to do with wounds and illness and dismemberments.

On an evening in June, a little boy was run down by a truck. Ben picked him up off the street, got into the cab next to the driver, and accompanied the child to the hospital. There was apparently no bodily injury, no concussion, nothing serious; but the boy's arm was fractured. The time was unfortunate—between shifts for medical residents—there was a surgeon around but he was in the operating room, and the only attending intern was raw and clumsily unskilled. The boy was in pain, he had to be sedated and put in traction. But there was no regular traction splint available, and if there had been, the callow intern would not have known what to do with it. So Ben fashioned a makeshift splint from the slat of a wooden bench, and miles of bandage.

When the surgeon came out of the operating room, he looked at the narcotized boy, asleep now, studied the improvised splint and said it need not be considered temporary, it was done as well as it need be done. Then, in a gush of generosity, he sounded a fanfare over Ben. You are very gifted, he kept saying over and over, very gifted. What a hurrah over a simple splint, Ben thought as he was walking away from the hospital, and his mind went to Phan Khe and Binh Lu, and amputations.

Thinking of the patient, Ben wondered how the boy would

feel when he came out of sedation. He hoped his parents had been found and, if he awakened in the night, someone would be near him. Perhaps, tomorrow, he would drop by, look in on the kid, see how he was getting along. Then he decided, no . . . But the following day, he did appear at the hospital, and the boy was doing well.

For hours thereafter, he tried to put the patient out of his mind. He couldn't. Through the rest of the day, the rest of the evening, he thought about the experience, and he hurt. For the first time in over a year he remembered the army hospital where he could not walk, the fire he still could not identify. And yet . . .

He knew he would have to go back to medicine. He put it off for weeks. Then he wrote a letter to the medical school. On the day he received the invitation to return and finish his work toward the degree, he broke into an illness of chills and fever. He couldn't go back.

Burrowing into a tunnel of depression, he was unable to work. He knew he needed help, but he reminded himself that he had gone it alone in tougher times than this, and he wouldn't surrender. He wanted desperately to believe that it was not apprehension, it was self-respect that kept him away from all such assistance; it was pride in his newfound psychic health—and he was entirely capable, on his own, of pulling himself together. But the small voice of his uncompromising honesty told him it was the naked dread of ripping the uncertain seams that bound him together; if he were to allow anyone to open a single stitch . . .

A new panic beset him. He was idle, he couldn't bring himself to look for a job, and he was running out of money. Actually, he was not by any means impoverished, he still had nearly a thousand dollars left, he had no dependents, and he could have managed quite a decent time, if at the end of that time he could see himself functioning again. But he couldn't. When the money ran out, he told himself, so would his life. He thought of squandering all of it in a single night.

Then, miraculously, something saved him. It was the chapter in his life that he called Sending for the Ambulance.

It started as the most minor of incidents. There was an advertisement in the Cyprus *Mail*. A Land-Rover was for sale—estate wagon on the cheap, the copy said—old, but in top-notch condition. Ben was living in a tiny rented shack on the beach at the time, and the Rover was over the mountain in Kyrenia. He took two buses to get there. The owner of the station wagon was an Englishman who had lived in Cyprus nearly all his life. He was a nervous, fidgety old man, and he did not share Ben's faith that the war years were over for the Greeks and Turks, he thought hostilities were inevitable. The mainland Turks'll come sabering in any day now, you-mind-your-arse-they-will.

Viewing the Land-Rover, Ben had gone green. It recalled the medic bus he had driven from Saigon to Tuy An, and then for an eternity thereafter. The meat wagon, they had called it, and this one was the same color of dun, the hue of mortality.

The Briton, seeing the hesitation, pointed out the merits of the vehicle, the rebuilt engine, extra fog lights, and the specially constructed partition which made an enclosure of the driver's cab area, for the more efficient use of heater and air conditioner. Then, commenting that Yanks enjoyed a bit of a haggle, he lowered his price. Ben bought it.

For a week it sat outside his shack at the water's edge and he couldn't bring himself to touch it. High tide, the waves washed up to the hubcaps. The sand and salt would wreck the thing, he knew, sooner or later. It was a four-wheeled incubus, it became an enormity to him.

At last he made himself drive it. One day he threw out the rear seats and bought a bed for it. For economy's sake, he gave up the shack and took to sleeping in the station wagon. Mile by mile, he made friends with it. Purchasing a couple of secondhand cabinets, one small, one large, he built some drawers. At a junk shop in Nicosia he paid a pound for a used cot, the legs of which he made collapsible; it would make a good litter. He rode down to Akrotiri one Saturday, to the British infirmary that was shutting down, and bought a mechanical heart-lung resuscitator for use during transport; it was hoarily out of date but was in good condition. There were other things he got there—a gas mask and anti-shock trousers and any number of hand instruments, much of it useless but most of it free. Within a month of his acquisition of the Land-Rover, it had become a working ambulance.

Without an appointment, one morning, he went to see the resident superintendent of the General Hospital in Nicosia. I'm a paramedic with my own paraphernalia, he said, and I want to offer the services of an auxiliary ambulance. It was not an offer that conformed to hospital custom, and the man said no, they had their own ambulances. So did the district health officer in Limassol. Even the private clinics turned him down.

Then Ben had an idea. None of the public ambulances had intercoms—and the districts were large. Sometimes a vehicle had to travel a hundred miles from a hospital; frequently, an hour away from a telephone. So he installed the two-way radio equipment in the cab of his Rover. And he selected a major city that had the fewest ambulances and the largest area to cover—Larnaca, with a fifty-bed hospital and only a single ambulance to serve a huge district.

He went. In the district health office, he put a carton on the doctor's desk. The box contained the partner set of intercom apparatus that could establish contact between the hospital and the ambulance. He showed the official how easy it was to operate, and he offered the equipment gratis.

The physician was a practical man, a good executive, and the staff ambulance was badly overworked. Most important, the man had a long memory of the old civil disturbances when one ambulance had been calamitously inadequate. Not that those times would ever come again, he said, but still . . . The only problem was tradition. The whole thing seemed so unprecedented, and so awkward—how would they pay him, for example?

Ben didn't much care how he got paid so long as he could earn his livelihood, but he knew that the pragmatic official would consider his offer unorganized unless he sounded like a hard-headed businessman. So he laid it out: the hospital's Emergency/Receiving desk would be in touch with him on the two-way radio. They would dispatch him to cases the hospital's ambulance could not handle. Ben would go wherever he was sent, tend the patient on the spot, and if it was first aid he could administer right then and there, he would do so—without billing the hospital, no charge. But if, at his own discretion, he felt it necessary to bring the patient in, he would then be paid—per patient.

"How much?"

"Prorate it according to what your own costs would be—one intern and one vehicle," Ben said. "I'll accept your figures."

The man smiled admiringly. "You are an American businessman," he said.

"No, I'm a medic who wants to stay in Cyprus."

They shook hands.

Within six months, Ben had made the same arrangement with the hospitals of three other major cities—Limassol, Paphos and Nicosia.

He was back in the freemasonry of healers again!

They had been three wonderful years for him. He hardly concerned himself with whether he was blessing anybody's life but his own; he was simply doing a job he wanted to do. Then, one day, an anonymous present arrived. With it was a card crudely written in Greek which said: "You are a man with goodness." The gift was a cigarette lighter and, although he didn't smoke, he carried it around for months. Another time a Turkish woman had kissed him and said he had a pure soul because he had pulled her ten-year-old daughter out of the sea. Then there was the hot afternoon when he was sent to a vineyard at grape-harvest time. A young woman was in labor. He delivered her on the flatbed of a farm wagon, and weeks later got a picture of the infant and was told that the child's middle name was Doctor, as if it were Ben's proper name. He realized that many others thought it was his proper name, and that people knew him in many places, Greek and Turkish, and that they liked him.

Three years, and he was healthy again. He had had an emergency, had sent for his own ambulance, and it had come. And he had done it himself, without head doctors; that was what pleased him most—all himself. Except for the aid of his providence:

Cyprus.

He felt, in some deeply touched way, that the island had worked a cure upon him. Serenely it told him that wounds could be mended, that outcries could be stilled. The island had soothed him out of his malady. Even—ridiculous phenomenon—the odor of him had changed. One evening, an autumn ago, looking at the sea, he discerned that he was giving off a different essence. There had been a time when all he ever smelled of himself, near or at a distance from a battlefield, was gangrene. But now he breathed a new and deeply agreeable scent. For days he told himself it was an illusion; what he was inhaling was the natural fragrance of the island, the smell of the shore, the clear penetrating pine of the hills, the hot pungency of nightshade in the open fields. But each time he crushed a leaf or broke a pod, it was quite another essence he was seeking, still elusive.

He mentioned it to Yannis and the old man said there was a proverb: the young lover thinks it is his betrothed who smells so sweetly, but it is himself, the scent of his happiness. Smiling, he added in Greek, "It is an ancient spice."

Ancient, as if all palliations were in the past. Perhaps so. Perhaps that was what he loved most about Cyprus, a sense of brutal animosities that had gentled into history, bitter battlefields that had become benignly mythic meadows. War was a myth.

This, all, was what Cyprus had done for him. And now the crowning benefaction of the island: it was fulfilling its promise as the Isle of Aphrodite, and casting a love spell upon him. The island had always made the prophecy that it would happen. Sooner or later, it had said, there would be some Kalya or other. There had been an amatory whisper in the wind. The sea, without oceanological reason, was always erotically warm. Once, on a mountaintop, at a long remove from Greece, he thought he heard the Delphic voice he had never heard in Delphi, and it had spoken auguries of love.

He had reveries of Kalya. The first one was her mouth close to his ear, whispering a secret to him, her breath making a stir on his earlobe and into the labyrinth, a soft susurration like the rustle of leaves, teasing, unbearably tantalizing, daring him to come. In another revery he saw her naked, hovering over him, moving slowly downward, inch by inch, so that her breasts were getting closer and closer to his mouth, and then just as he could smell a delicate, a delicious scent on her nipples, just as his lips touched one of them and parted to receive it, the revery faded, and he heard the taunting whisper again, telling him to come, to come.

Tomorrow evening he would go and see her again. No, too late. In the morning—while Yannis was having his coffee somewhere—he would go to her.

"I came to apologize," he said.

"It was not necessary."

She was setting tables on the terrace, spreading them with azure tablecloths that matched the color of the lake. The fog was gone, the water was a sheet of sky. He could hear Menas stirring in the dining room; he had the feeling the man was watching them, sidelong, in a furtive way.

Driving there, Ben had thought: I was drunk last night: what if all the beauty I saw in her was in the wine? And here she was, in the morning light, totally different from the way he remembered her, but just as beautiful. He wondered why she seemed so changed, and realized that last night she had been lighted by small candle lamps on the table; they had made her loom as large as drama—and now, in the total glare of sunlight, she was lifesize. So also was the pain in her eyes—lifesize and manageable. Or, perhaps not there at all; had he imagined it?

"I was quite drunk," he said.

"Wouldn't you have offered twenty pounds if you had been sober?"

He wanted to say that he would, that he would offer it right now, that the dinner was more beautiful in retrospect than it might have been in reality, that the food had been ambrosial and the wine had been mulled in magic.

"But I was telling the truth—it was a wonderful dinner."

A mistake. Not knowing his thought, the words she heard would strike her as rankly insincere, as distasteful as his flattery had been last night.

He was right. "Thank you," she said with cool detachment. "Now, would you excuse me—I'm very busy."

"Now, listen—I'm not drunk today. I came here to say I was sorry, but you've got a little to be sorry for as well. That twenty pounds had a taint in it—I admit that. But it wasn't offered without generosity. And it was the only way I could tell you—drunk as I was—that I was attracted to you."

"That's another bribe, isn't it?"

"What is?"

"Yesterday, money. Today—attraction."

The thought nettled him. "You think I'm trying to make a deal?"

"Of some sort."

In a jumble, he wondered where her defenses came from, where she got her pride, what her mouth would feel like, how she had learned to walk so well, what language he could use to get to her.

"I don't know what to say."

They were the first effective words he had spoken. She apparently saw how willing he was to make himself vulnerable, and something happened to her. The austerity, like splitting stone, began to fracture. "Don't let it bother you—it's not your fault."

It was not an abject apology, only acknowledgment of a lapse. But if that was all, her manner was more troubled than it should have been. Then he saw it again—as inescapably as he had seen it last night—the despair. It clouded her eyes like a cataract. Quickly, knowing herself exposed, she turned to go indoors, to be rid of him.

"Wait," he said.

She faltered only a moment.

He had this single instant, he told himself, and she would be gone. He would have to think of something to intrigue her, something bright to lure her out of the shadows, make her laugh. Instead—impulsive and unguarded—he blurted the truth of what he felt.

"You're in pain!"

"Please." She started to leave again.

There was no stopping now, no reversal. He walked after her, a step or two. "You're calling for help!"

"Don't."

"You are, you know that! You're in pain!"

Arrested for a moment, she turned to him. "Is that your ambulance out there?"

"Yes."

"Are you a doctor?"

"A paramedic."

"But pain is your business, isn't it?"

He was stung. There it was again: what is the American bargaining for? "I'm not trying to buy anything."

"Just offering help."

"Yes—offering help."

She took the time to believe him. When she did, her voice was kinder than it had been. "I'm sorry. I think you *are* generous. That is American. Except . . ."

"What?"

Clearly, she wanted to make amends, but didn't want him to think she was susceptible. "That's also a kind of purchase, isn't it?"

Such damn arrogance—and pride! They were near the doorway now, and once she crossed the threshold, it would be over, and he couldn't bear it.

"I'm glad I came a second time."

Something happened then, or he imagined it. She lowered her head, and he thought that she declined her eyes in order not to see his own; or it was the downward look of a somber moment when the mood is so heavy that it will not sustain the slightest glance of animation. She was looking at nothing and seeing nothing. But then—with a start—it occurred to him that she was staring at something, at him, at a level below their looks and glances, studying him to see if he showed, if there was an evidence or eminence, how susceptible he was. Instantly, flushed, he distrusted his observation, it was ludicrous—and unnecessary—he had come here openly to expose himself, he might as well be pulling the tab on his zipper. Disturbed by the notion, he realized it was not what she was looking at but what he wanted her to look at. He sensed the tightening cloth of his trousers and, realizing that in her gaze he was going to be erect at any moment, he felt like a randily embarrassed adolescent, and was on the point of a quick departure. But, holding his ground, he repeated, "I'm glad I returned."

She raised her head. Nothing in her face suggested that she had invaded his privacy. Only a look of gratitude. He had a need to be closer to her, to touch her, to experience the texture of her skin. On impulse, he reached out his hand to say goodby. He was surprised by her handclasp. Not because it was firm and strong— he had expected it to be—but something else. She held it longer than necessary, he thought, and just as he was about to withdraw, he felt a strange excitement of skin, palm to palm, a sudden warmth, a moisture, like lips held together. Then, at the final instant, just as he was withdrawing, she impulsively clasped his hand once more, as if she dreaded to relinquish a last chance. About to make something of it, he restrained himself: don't jostle her, he said. But he vowed silently that it was not her last chance by any means: he would see her again. And he felt that she had encouraged him to do so.

Yet, as he was driving away, he was disquieted. Perhaps the extra pressure of the hand meant nothing; he could be wrong in reading too much into it. He had certainly read too much into the other thing—the mere dropping of her glance into the disrobing of his cock—what an idiot! What a fool, to magnify the slightest blink or press of fingers into some yearning she might have for him. The pressure of her hand had meant nothing more than a last thank-you, a finality. And it could be that he had misinterpreted other signs as well—her cry for help, for example. He had jumped to that conclusion like an oversolicitous man, a fretful father. Worse, like a bad doctor. He had made his diagnosis without gathering all the symptoms. A mere look into her tragic eyes with his emotional ophthalmoscope and he had pronounced her a woman needing succor, and in pain. Ridiculous. What ailment? What was the history of the case, where did she come from, why was she putting her education to such odd use up here, how did a Turkish woman get mixed up with a Greek man, why was she living with him if she wasn't happy?

He determined to find out. He didn't know where he would start, or how he would make time for it, since he allowed himself only one free weekend a month, and this was Monday morning, the weekend over. But with a woman, there's a way, the Cypriot song said, and it excited him. What excited him most was his American self-certainty—let her ridicule it—that if he did his work well, if he put muscle and imagination to it, he would bring it to a successful conclusion. And as he gave this wonderful gift of confidence to himself, he tried not to notice that he was too stridently happy, that not all of his person was responding in the same way, some reserved part of him was holding back, tensing, balking . . . and his legs were getting numb.

"Fire!"

He thought he told his foot to press down sharply on the brake, but it didn't do it. The vehicle was picking up speed, plunging down the steep mountain road, and wouldn't stop. He reached for the hand brake, emergency.

"Fire!"

He pulled the brake. The ambulance came to a halt. His legs were nerveless; no feeling in them, none. He told them to move and they were rigid. Slapping the right one, he waited a moment, then punched it. He felt nothing. His left leg, harder, he smashed down on it with his fist, punished it as cruelly as he could, but received no hurt at all. He started to shake and couldn't stop himself.

"Fire!"

He saw the face of Mee Lanh. Out of somewhere—nowhere —the past, a past that might not even have happened—she returned to him, a glimmer on the windshield. Clearer, then, until she was as real as Kalya, as total a presence as if he had not left her on the ridge road, toward Dak Binh; she was here. And as soon as the Vietnamese girl's image became altogether luminous to him, he lost the image of the Turkish woman; the eyes of the older one became the eyes of the younger, and they both together—and the fire too—became his fault.

No, not the fire, nor the rigid limbs, not everything his fault. Only Mee Lanh was his failure, his singular offense; the other woman was as yet a stranger. But the virus of fault infected everything, and he was back again in the wartime butcher wagon with too many wounded, and some who would die before he could get them anywhere, and others, if he so much as touched them, and his medical degree never earned, and his father's dream in particles, and the war never ending, with too many arms in a pit and not enough bodies to go around, and not enough air to die in, and absurdities no longer laughable, and all his fault, his fear, his fault . . . and he didn't know why.

His legs still would not stir, no matter how he begged them. He was in a sweat, his shirt wet with perspiration, his hands not steady. He felt the tears coming and commanded them back. He had not wept in four years, and wouldn't now. Stop it, he said, nothing's hurting, nothing's hurting nearly enough, you'll have no feeling in your legs unless you make them hurt, start moving, give them pain and *walk*.

But nothing answered his command, no motion. Don't fall apart, he said, don't get the shakes, stay calm, take it slowly, easily. You're in Cyprus, he reminded himself, not Vietnam. Those days are gone, they'll never come back again. You're not on the ridge road with Mee Lanh, and you're not in a field hospital; you're here, on a lovely tranquil mountainside in Cyprus, not far from the sea. *In Cyprus* . . . and now—you've got no choice— you've got to walk.

He opened the car door, opened it as wide as it would go. He sat there a moment, gathering breath and courage. Then: the right leg—he tried to edge it outward. Move only a few inches, he begged it, only an inch or two. It remained inert. As if pain anywhere would be some help, he bit his lip until he tasted blood, then tried the leg again. The same. The hell with you, he said to it, I'll make myself fall out of the vehicle and drag you after me. He braced himself. With an angry, violent lurch, he shoved his shoulder sideways, heaved his body with it and fell outward on the road, the hot summer dust in his face, something twisting, aching—and the stab was in his leg! Move, you bastard!

And it did, a little. Now shove, he said, push at the goddamn ground, push earth away from you, push now, push!

He was standing, but on one leg only, hurting like dog's teeth in his flesh, and abruptly the other leg was hurting too, then a moment of imbalance—he might fall—and—moving—slowly at first, and going somewhere. Move faster, you bastards, you can do it, move faster, he said, move!

He was walking now, almost steadily, walking on the mountain road, five feet, ten, twenty, fifty . . . and all at once, without a tic of warning, the pain was gone, and his legs were good again.

Slowly he turned. Measuring every step, studying every footfall, he made his way back to the ambulance. His eyes were on his legs and he knew he mustn't do that, mustn't pamper them with excessive attention. Take them for granted, he said, take walking as your right, don't question it. But he couldn't help being grateful. He had a need to thank Someone or Something, thank everything, thank Cyprus that he was here, not elsewhere, that he could walk, that calling fire was only a reminder of what he was, and he need never be that man again.

He wondered, now that he was upright and in unimpeded motion, why he had thought of all three of them together—Kalya and Mee Lanh and fire—and if he would ever know. He would give a lot to comprehend it, might even be willing to suffer more pain in order to discover what it meant, why the images had come to him out of his past, and if they would ever totally disappear in his future. And most poignantly, he wondered why fire and Mee Lanh had never been associated before today, and why Kalya had brought them together, in a single place at such a distant time.

As he got into the ambulance, he was still perspiring and still a little shaky. But he felt fundamentally at peace with himself, felt as if he had conquered something, some fire demon that had tried to entomb him in his own body by setting the world aflame.

Abruptly he had a need to visualize himself more securely as part of Cyprus again, not only to be here but to belong here. Which meant an instant urgency to get down to the sea. The sea was everywhere in him, and he felt safe if he was near it. He put the car in gear and quickly made the rest of the descent.

There it was, the surf. The waves were high, unusually rough; the wind, while hot, was brisk. If only he knew where the fire cry came from. Mee Lanh's face had totally faded now, and he could see Kalya's eyes again, her mouth open, about to speak. With the woman's image returning, clearer and clearer, his hopes lifted. He watched the waves for a few minutes. It gave him a pleasure, a deep pleasure to know that for all their wild ferocity he was at peace with them. He took all of it, all he could get. He felt better. . . . In Cyprus, yes.

He had another pleasure that day. He was decorated.

As he arrived at the *kafenion* in the village where he was to pick up Yannis, the old man came running toward him, waving a week-old newspaper. "Your picture is in the paper, your picture is in the paper!"

He shoved the crumpled newspaper at him. It was *Hafta,* a modest four-page tabloid—Turkish—and on the third page, there they were, Ben and Yannis. It was head and shoulders, both of them grinning like simpletons, Yannis with a banana in his hand.

"Me too," the old man cried ecstatically. "Is me too!"

"Where did they get this picture?"

"Pharas, you fool, Pharas!"

He was cheered by the memory. It was a Turkish village, very poor, that they had tended months ago. There had been a typhoid epidemic, and after the Limassol doctors had departed, the two of them had remained, in charge. They had inoculated everybody and ministered to them for two weeks, and not a single mortality had occurred. On their last day, when the villagers had heard that Ben was not receiving any remuneration for his work, they had given them a *kutlama* under the trees, with food and music; that's when the picture was taken.

Ben pointed to the article. "What does it say?"

"It says you are the great—and I am the great also." His grin was as wide as his face.

"Read it."

The old man was a Turkophile—a Greek policemen had once accused him of liking Muslims better than his own people—and, having grown up with Turks, he was proud that he could make sense of their language. However much he could actually read and however much he was making up, Ben got the gist of it; they were both friends of humanity and of the Turkish people, and worthy of decoration.

"But they make a mistake here," Yannis said. "First they call you an American, then they call you a Swiss."

"Swiss?"

"Yes. Or maybe is a German word—*Schweitzer.*"

"Yes—*Schweizer*—it is a German word."

In his mind, he was spelling it as he heard it. Then: "Let me look at it." As the Greek pointed to the word, he saw the letter "t." He didn't speak for a moment. "It's the name of a great doctor, a great man—Albert Schweitzer."

"They call you that?"

Bemused, Ben didn't answer. He pointed to the ambulance. "Come on—let's go."

"You like it?"

Of course he did. But it had an ache in it. "Yes."

As they were driving away: "You do not like it that they say this about you?" the old man asked.

"I said I liked it."

"Then why you are not happy, the way I am happy?"

"I am."

"No, you are not. You look like they insult you."

"Quit it."

"No—I want to know why. If this was a Greek paper you would be happy, yes? But because it is Turkish, it means nothing."

"That's not true!"

"A Turkish honor is nothing!"

"I didn't say that!"

For a long while the old man didn't talk. He was ashamed. He had said something he had not meant, something he knew was untrue, and he didn't know how to apologize. "Sometimes I am foolish," he said.

"It's all right."

He understood the old man very well. He was touchy on the subject of Turks, and had frequently gotten into trouble for saying good words about them. Even in times of peace, he was sensitive and edgy. Their first meeting, in fact, when Ben was starting to be successful, had been marked by it.

There was, at that time, a large importation of cheaply made Turkish trousers, meant to undersell the market. The materials were good enough but the workmanship was sloppy and the trousers were skimpily cut. The Greeks would not buy them, but the Turks did, as a matter of pride and for economy's sake. They were called Ankara pants.

One day, while Ben was at lunch at a taverna on the road to Paphos, he heard an emergency call from the outdoor *pissoir*. The old man stood not far from the urinal. He was wearing dark blue

Ankara pants, and cursing painfully at his dingus, which had gotten caught in the broken zipper. Yelling lustily, he screamed for help but didn't want any.

"Go away—go away," he howled, as Ben and the restaurant proprietor hurried toward him.

When Ben, offering medical assistance, extended his hand in the appropriate direction, the old man let out a roar. "No— nobody will touch my *vila!*"

"He's a doctor," the proprietor said.

The old man twitched a few times, and jiggled; then, because every slight movement was painful, he allowed the medic to approach. Ben leaned over and studied how the loose skin under the glans had been caught between the teeth and the slide of the zipper.

He seemed to be taking more time than the patient was prepared to give. "Hurry," he said. "You know to take the zipper from the *vila*, yes—not the *vila* from the zipper?"

"Either way." Ben was teasing.

"Not either way, not either way!" Yelping: "You will circumcise an old man!"

The medic turned to go to the ambulance. "Where do you go?" the Greek called.

"To get some cutters."

The wounded man saw the specter of botched surgery. "Oh, the saints!"

In a moment, Ben returned with a pair of sharp-nosed wire cutters, scissors and an orthopedic pack. With the snips, he cut the zipper tapes, first above, then below the captured skin. Gently he applied the chilling anesthetic to the trapped area.

"You freeze my cock off!"

"Be quiet."

The Greek wasn't quiet, but he did stop complaining. Pretending to be brave, he maundered of other times. "In our village, when I was a boy, we all are having buttons on our flies. I am the first one in the whole town who has a zipper. Every day I am showing how I can open my pants very quick—for any good reason—and how quick I can close up again. Everybody is very jealous of me—and I am very proud. How do I know that with this new little machine, I help to destroy the world?"

Ben was finishing. Carefully, both hands at once, he was rotating the two sides of the zipper apart from each other. Now, lifting ever so gently, he loosened the grip. The skin was free.

"You did it?" the old man asked. He looked down and could not believe the operation had been completed so rapidly and painlessly. In a haste of embarrassment, he started stuffing his member back into his trousers.

"Wait," Ben said, and turned to the proprietor, who had not left the surgical scene. "Do you have any ice?"

"Why you want ice?" Yannis asked.

"To keep it from swelling."

"No ice!" the Cypriot said. "If it will swell, I will shout *oorah!*"

Laughing boisterously not only from relief but to cover his discomposure, he put his hand on the fly that could no longer be zippered shut, and hastened away. He had not commented on Ben's speed or skill, nor had he uttered a word of gratitude.

A few minutes later, however, as Ben was reentering the taverna, he saw the Greek again. Sitting on a bench under a medlar tree, the old man raised his hand and made a vague motion in the air, meaning for the younger man to approach.

"It does not feel cold anymore, but even warm it does not hurt."

He was paying tribute to the medic's expertise, and obliquely saying thanks. Then, the laggard word: *"Efharisto."*

Ben appraised him. The work was getting heavy these days, with four hospitals to cover. More and more, recently, he had been relying on the help of the chance passerby; it was not only time consuming, it was hazardous. He needed an assistant. The old man looked healthy—a little dirty, but Ben could scrub him up. He was obviously intelligent, he had a bright personality, and his movements were quick. He liked him.

"You want to go to work with me?"

Silence. The old man looked away as if not trusting what he had heard. "To do what?"

Ben pointed to the ambulance.

"For a doctor?" He couldn't hide his eagerness.

"I'm a paramedic."

Despite the Greek prefix, the man did not understand. When Ben explained that he had been nearly through medical school but had not become a doctor, the man looked suspicious. For someone to be within one stride of Olympus and not take the final footstep suggested deception of some sort.

The medic smiled. "Yes, I didn't believe it either."

"You say you offer a job. This much is true?"

"Yes, true."

He could see that the Greek yearned for it but didn't trust the reality. "I am too old for this."

"Why? You're not sick, are you? Aren't you strong?"

Forgetting the unclosable fly, the old fellow jumped up. A short man but feisty, he pranced away from the bench. Raising his arms, he flexed them, flapped them like wings, strutted like a bantam, and started to cackle and crow.

Ben sensed that there would be more praise in sobriety than in laughter. "You're okay," he said.

To make his offer tangible, Ben suggested what salary he could afford—not magnanimous but respectable. When the Greek did not respond: "Isn't the money enough?"

"Money is not of importance."

Something was bothering Yannis. No matter how much the man wanted the position, he had some hidden reservation, and he apparently could not bring himself to speak of it. Then Ben saw the glance. A quick one, hardly perceptible, the slightest reference to his trousers again, and he sensed what was disturbing the old Cypriot. He was still embarrassed about the accident; he had been seen looking ridiculous, an oaf. It was the wrong way to start a kinship.

Gently: "Forget about that," Ben said.

"How can I?" The old man reddened with chagrin. "How can I work with you? You will think I am a man without *axia*."

Literally it meant worth. Ben measured his words. "Whether or not you have *axia*—I will have to find out. And you will have to find out the same about me."

It had never occurred to the old Greek that the dignity of a young man, an American, a medic who owned an ambulance, might also be in question. It was a revelation, a cheering one that made him smile; he was happy.

The arrangement concluded, Ben saw the man holding his fly together with his hand. Opening his wallet, he offered Yannis a few pounds. "You'll need a new pair of pants."

"No. Many thanks."

"Go on—you can pay me back if you want."

"I do not want a new pants."

"You can't fix that zipper."

"I will use pins."

"Those pants have had it." Ben extended the money again. "Go on—take it. The pants are no good."

Inexplicably, the man lost his temper. "Why? Because they are Turkish? They are as good as yours! If you do not like Turks —the hell with you!"

It was not reasonable but Ben responded as if it were. Quietly he said that he did like Turks. It placated Yannis, but he did not take the money.

For two days the old man did as he said he would—he used safety pins. On the third day, when he at last agreed to borrow the money, he told Ben why the subject of Turks was such a sore one.

In the disturbances of 1964, he was a widower with two sons. Both of them were killed by Turks. The farm he owned was no longer manageable by him. He had nothing, he had nobody. For two years afterward, he lived in a demented rage against the enemy. Even the friendly Turks, his neighbors, people he had known all his life—he could not stand the sight of them. Then one day he realized he couldn't stand the sight of himself either, and knew he would die of hatred. After a while, by painful degrees, he became well again, and went back to the Yannis he could live with. All people, at last, became his friends again; only war was his enemy.

Occasionally, to this day, because it was a subject close to the quick, he was too defensive. As he had just been with Ben. And he didn't know how to make things right.

It was such a small thing to get angry about—not the tribute in the Turkish paper, which was consequential to both of them— but the petty misunderstanding. He wanted to reassure Yannis, to comfort him, and didn't know what to say. The old man was pretending it was over. He was doing what he always did when things were less than perfect, talking about his childhood in Paphos, about oranges at festival time, and cakes made of buckwheat and sesame and currants; as if there were no wars when he was young, as if nobody had ever hurt him, nobody had ever lied to him, and even *things* were truer then.

"Read me the article again," Ben said.

The old man looked at him doubtfully a moment, not trusting the happy turn, then saw that his face was serious. He started to translate it, and his voice got husky; he stopped and went on again. When he got to the name Schweitzer he could not continue.

They drove along in silence. No messages came in on the intercom. There were no emergencies, nobody was in an accident, nobody was hurt, nobody was in pain. The day was beautiful and serene. They were very close.

At last the old man spoke again. "It is in a Turkish paper, it is about an American and a Greek."

It was about peace.

Everything was possible in peacetime. The world did not fly into fragments. It had singleness and continuity. The days related to the nights, and the seasons to the years. There were futures. Love had something to do with tomorrow, not with yesterday— and he could think hopefully of Kalya, in a time of peace. And it occurred to him that peace was not a placid, inert thing; it was like the steady throb in the bloodstream, the surge of living.

That day—Monday, July 15, 1974—the war began.

2

In Ben Coram's opinion, Nikos Giorgiades Sampson, who became the president of the republic of Cyprus, was a roach. The medic had heard him speak once, two years ago in a crowded police station in Famagusta, and had even then strongly suspected the man was a roach. And most Cypriots, the Greeks as well as the Turks, now had the same, clearly focused picture of him: *katsarida,* roach. And they charged him with starting the war.

He denied everything. He said the war did not start in 1974 but twenty years previously, and had never ceased. It began, he claimed, when a tiny boatload of arms, most of them secondhand, costing approximately six hundred pounds, was landed on a lonely stretch of beach in western Cyprus. With this meager arsenal, General George Grivas, the hero of the revolution, led the guerrilla campaign to drive the British into the sea. He was a man of mulish obstinacy and titanic courage, with a dream that needed both: to cleanse the island of its English corruption, as they called it, and to achieve an enosis, a union of Cyprus and her mother country, Greece. The hope for the blood-league of island Greeks with mainland Greeks—the lamb returned to the fold, the pamphlets said—was an old family yearning, and enosis was a cry from the heart. The word appeared everywhere, on walls, on pavements, on menus, on blackboards; sometimes, it was scrawled on the lorries of the English military, and Tommies found it on chits of paper in their water canteens. There was no other graffito anywhere.

Grivas's guerrilla band was called the EOKA. They hid themselves in the Troodos Mountains, in abandoned archaeological digs, in caves, on fishing boats, under the floorboards of kitchens, in the sacristies of churches. Their raids were daredevil, their audacity was maniacal. English barracks vanished between dusk and darkness, English tanks disintegrated, communication centers went dead in the middle of sentences. Grivas said that British cannon were not as deadly as Cypriot spittle.

If he was the muscle of the revolution, Archbishop Makarios was its heart and soul. In the city streets, in the village schools, from the bemas of churches, he chanted the one watchword: enosis. He was a practical man and a canny politician, and—most potently—a priest; when he spoke of union with Greece it was similar to union with the Holy Spirit. Enosis was his prayer and his promise.

But the Turks had no such prayer or promise. Not enough that they were a minority, they were also in the middle, caught between their Greek neighbors and the British authority. The revolution against England frightened them. With the first forays of Grivas's guerrillas, they remained warily in the background, vigilant, apprehensive. They could not believe that the Greek insurrection would succeed, but there was always the dread possibility. Not that the Turks loved the English, but being under the protection of the Union Jack was safer than being under the hegemony of mainland Greece, their historic enemy. Irrespective of who had been at fault, there were afflictions and atrocities to remember, and Greece would not forget. Enosis was a terror to the Turks; it would leave them unprotected in Cyprus, at the mercy of their ancient foe, and Muslim blood would spill.

Their hope that the Greek rebellion would fail soon looked futile. As more and more British soldiers were killed, as ammunition dumps were detonating, the Turks began to help the British. Secretly at first, they turned against their Greek acquaintances, informing on them, sabotaging them in subtle ways. Then, with crisis following crisis, their collaboration became open, and they took to wearing uniforms.

The war was now an unreserved barbarity. Nighttime massacres, pitiless mutilations, the bombing of schoolhouses, the torture of prisoners.

After nearly six years of war, a truce was declared. The peace treaty, like all postwar covenants, was not universally popular. The British were to leave, but there was to be no enosis with Greece. Cyprus would be a republic, governed by its native populations, Greeks and Turks together, both races represented proportionately, according to their numbers, with a hope for equity.

Grivas thought the treaty was an abomination. Peace without enosis was, to him, no peace at all; his hope of union with the motherland had been shattered. By Makarios. To Grivas, the Archbishop was no better than a traitor, for he had compromised the dream. If the priest's treaty with the English had come as a result of his desperate prayer for an end to bloodshed, he had prayed to the wrong god.

Many Cypriots felt as the General did, but most of them were war-weary and at the end of anguish, and they called the Archbishop their peacemaker; they blessed him as he had blessed them.

Among those who never forgave him, Nikos Sampson was perhaps the most rabid. Rabidity was Sampson's signal energy. The publisher of a frenetic newspaper, *Mahi,* he was one of Grivas's guerrillas, always in a state of advanced hysteria. He was a thug and a convicted thief. The British called him a cutthroat and a sadist. Many who knew him in Famagusta, his native city, remembered him as a fool. Those who tried to find a good word to speak in his behalf soon abandoned the search.

From the moment the republic began, he did his best to undermine it. But he didn't effect very much. There was a saying in Nicosia that Sampson was the bellwether of black sheep. As the republic began to succeed, people laughed at him, covertly at first, and then to his face. And it was a joke of the fates for him to have become president.

The fates of Greece. A coup happened in Athens. The democratic government was routed and a military junta seized the country. The press was stifled, dissidents were jailed, there were executions in alleys; and artists, actors, writers fled. For all its pockmarked walls, the fascist Junta was powerless, and failed. As it realized it was failing, it scurried for causes, seeking any shibboleth, any banner under which the defecting populace would unite. To kindle patriotic fervor, it needed a war. And Cyprus would be an easy one. So Athens decided to "free" the island.

Free us of what? the Cypriots asked. Greek and Turk, they asked: Of what?

Of Makarios, the Junta answered. Of the priest who had been a Judas. Of the archbishop-president who had promised the Greeks enosis and had sold them a bill of republic.

The plan was simple: The Junta would engineer a coup. Makarios would be assassinated. A new president—a dupe of the

Athenian military—would be installed in Nicosia. Cyprus would be joined to Greece: enosis.

They cast about to find the new president. It was an honor no Cypriot hastened to accept. They offered the prize to seven well-known men of Cyprus, and all of them spurned it. Farce: they could not find a dummy. Finally, they found their straw man, Nikos Sampson.

The coup took place on Monday, the fifteenth of July. The presidential palace, inside which Makarios was playing host to a party of visiting schoolgirls, was bombed, mortared, and strafed with machine guns. It would have been easy to capture the Archbishop, or to kill him. But Sampson, adding shrewd generalship to his inventory of talents, had neglected to order his soldiery to watch the back door. So the Archbishop bid farewell to the schoolgirls and took his leave. He went to Paphos and Malta, then to England and America.

Sampson was made president of the dummy republic, and stayed in office for four days.

On Saturday, July 20, Turkey bombed the island. Ankara stated its purposes: to safeguard the Greco-Turkish republic of Cyprus in the absence of Makarios, and to protect the Cypriot Turks from the Athenian Junta, which had taken over the island. The Turkish Government called it a police action and a peace operation; the Cypriot Greeks called it an invasion.

One term or another, it was a war. Bombs were dropping. Nicosia was on fire. Kyrenia was falling. Turks were killing Greeks, and Cypriots were killing one another.

In Ben's ambulance, the intercom wouldn't cease. He was dispatched in all directions at once, as if the wounded were everywhere. Finally the signals stopped being so discordant. One place kept calling more necessitously than all the others—Nicosia. Please come to Nicosia. Hurry.

It was a war that did not know its business. The bombers came over and hit a mental hospital, and missed the National Guard barracks, which were within walking distance. Fighter planes zoomed down and strafed a school, and left the armory untouched. A squad of Greek soldiers walked down the middle of a street in Nicosia, fully armed and an easy target; grenades lobbed across from the Turkish line; the soldiers went unscathed but an old lottery-ticket seller fell down dead.

In the Nicosia General Hospital, they moved sick patients into private clinics to make way for the wounded. The wards filled, then the hallways. At first they put cots all over, but when the cots ran out, they lay the patients on the floors. In some corridors, doctors and nurses could not get through to the patients; there was no room to walk.

Operations went on everywhere—in the reception rooms, in the pediatric ward, on the fire escape, in moving elevators. And everybody was a surgeon. Middle-aged psychiatrists and pathologists who had not held a knife in twenty years were slicing into bellies as if they were melons.

The instant it became known that Ben knew the difference between the handle of a scalpel and its blade, he became a specialist. There was no time for consultations or blood tests or X-rays or urinalyses. The word was: cut. Even Yannis became a surgeon of sorts. He stood alongside Ben and stitched up sutures, and called himself a tailor.

For days and days they did not see the ambulance. It was being run by two *gymnasion* students—sisters—who loaded and unloaded it as if it were the school bus. The older one never went home, never slept or ate or complained; the younger one cried a lot, but it did not slow her down.

For nearly two weeks Ben and Yannis could not leave the hospital. Ben started to grow a beard without realizing he was doing it; Yannis began to stink.

The pandemic ailment was shock. Everybody had it. There was the purely physical insult that was happening to patients—the damaged skull, the shaken cerebrum, the concussion after wound or collision, the chill after surgery, the profound depression of the vital processes. Then there was the physical shock that everyone was suffering—the sound of bombardment and the earthquaking tremor that caused a frantic electricity in the body and a convulsion of the spirit.

But the most untreatable shock was psychic. It had followed a hemorrhage in the sanity of the world. Everything had been going so well in Cyprus; how could this have happened? Had it been a peaceful time, or were they just imagining that it was? Or were they imagining *this?* It was something for the psychiatrists, but they were doing surgery.

Meanwhile the Turks were bombing Nicosia and their destroyers were in Morphou Bay. It was a certainty that they had taken the lovely city of Kyrenia. Somebody, between patients, said that the International Airport had fallen; somebody else said not yet. There were paratroopers landing in the north of the capital; if you looked out the hospital windows, you could see them floating down like soap bubbles. Water and air were disordered; shortages of one, and the other too dust-laden to breathe, full of gray smoke and clouds of sand and the reek of gelignite. Alarms kept sounding and sounding, until they lost their power to quicken. No matter how swiftly one hurried, there did not seem any right place to be.

Then the news came, incontrovertible, that the sixteen-mile road between Kyrenia and Nicosia was totally in the hands of the Turks, and the capital city would have to fall. For a day or so, the streets had been deserted, but now the evacuation started, and the thoroughfares became busy with fleeing people. A greasy smudge filled the air and rockets grazed the hospital.

The napalm cases started coming in. The first time he had seen a napalm victim, in Vietnam, it had reminded him of a coal-scorched baked potato on which oil had been rubbed. There were no features to identify; only a smoking charcoal, black and moist. And the fire of the flesh kept burning, from the outside inward, unquenchable by water or medicine or any means at all. Even if wrapped in blankets, the patient continued to roast. When a body was left in the woods, the animals would go to the charred remains; a succulence.

He felt that he could stand anything except the sight of napalm again, and as the first case arrived, he opened his mouth wide, made no sound, but could not close it for a while. Yannis saw Ben do it; looking at him, the old man began to cry.

Suddenly—unbelievably—hardly before the war was begun, it was over. Well, not over exactly, but a cease-fire had been declared, a temporary truce so that a peace could be negotiated.

It was too good, Ben thought, such a short war, too civilized to be true! He wanted to cheer, to stand on the roof of the Ledra Palace Hotel and shout how happy he was, he wanted to run through the streets and rejoice with the others.

Later, when he did run through the streets, nobody was there. The shops were shuttered tight. The pavements were strewn with broken glass, spent bullet casings, sandbags whole and ruptured, barbed wire going nowhere. There were bloodstains on walls and windows. But no people. Only cats. The city had been taken by the cats. As he turned to go inside again, he saw one of them lapping at a red puddle. Remembering the whilom gaiety of the place, its gossipy busyness and happy prosperity, and seeing it now, so desolate and deserted, hiding in a shadow, cringing like a small, beaten creature, he felt alien from life, and sorrow-stricken. He had lived through, worked through, suffered through the recent days and nights of bloodshed with hardly a tremor of the hand, with no faltering of courage, and now he began to dread that his strengths were deserting him. He was overcome with a deep sadness, deeper even than in the days of his fire illness, deeper than he felt he could endure. Oh God, he said, don't let me be sick again!

It was dusk, going quickly to darkness, and out of the lowering twilight he heard a plaintive sound. It was the crying of a child, he thought, a small child, an infant perhaps. He walked slowly down the length of the street, the crepuscular light becoming more and more opaque, the visibility lessening. While the sound of the lament continued, eerily as if in an echo chamber, he saw no sign of the infant, or of anyone. Where the narrow thoroughfare intersected a still narrower alleyway, he turned into the passage, onto a cobblestoned footpath even dimmer, it seemed, and more forbidding in the silence that carried the softly weeping utterance like a feather in the air. The baby lamented and was still, then lamented again, and as he stopped to listen, it occurred to him that it was a whimpering that he knew, or understood in some deeply hidden recess of his memory. Then, as he recalled it, he realized it was not an actual presence but was indeed a recollection, a wailing in the past. Kalya's child—the crying he had heard in the restaurant the first time he had been there, on that drunken night when he had met her and offered the misbegotten gratuity. It was her baby's lament to which Kalya had gone, outdoors, to some undefined place, in darkness.

Out of that undefined obscurity she returned to him now, in remembrance, as he had first seen her. Again he stood on the threshold of the kitchen, looking into the hot and steamy half light at the nearly naked woman as she prepared a dinner that was meant for him to eat. Tonight, however, with the luxurious privilege that memory conferred, he did not hurry away from the open door but stood gazing at her, slowly filling his recollection as if it hungered for a longer vision of her, closer, for a deeper knowing of what the vision signified. How beautiful she looked tonight, he thought, just as beautiful as she had looked when she had caught him in his first espial of her. This time, not drunkenly immobilized or routed by the dazzle of her semi-nakedness—ah, this time he hauntedly crossed the threshold of his memory and walked into the soft smoke and mist of a charcoal brazier burning low, of fumy cooking pans and savors of redolence. He couldn't take his eyes off her. She moved slowly and abstractedly, the bare-shouldered woman, almost in a trancelike music, convoking the edibles of the meal with a slow ceremoniousness, as if she were preparing a charm for sorcery. He knew she was performing an ordinary, fundamental ritual too commonplace to be romanticized, yet in his memory there was enchantment in the half-hidden room, in the vaporous haze, in the scents of thyme and coriander and pungent sage, in the dense muskiness of roasting meat; and it seemed to him that the enchantress was pouring pungent philters of aromatic wine and valerian vinegar and the juice of the erotic cardamom into viands that would tempt and excite him, seducing his eyes, his nostrils, his lips, his palate, and make an exquisite liquid fire on his tongue. As he took a few steps deeper into the room, her back was turned to him and she did not know that he was behind her. When she shifted a little, sideways, the light flickered fitfully on her high cheekbone, and he saw that her pale amber skin was flushed with scarlet heat, and thought she must be burning with it. He observed her silently, filled his hungry gaze with her, the soft undulation of her shoulders, the ripeness of flesh as it mounded and fell away, like a crescendo and diminuendo of sound, how it came to roundness at her hips, her buttocks sliding softly away to the lovely slimness of her legs. His eyes moved as her body moved, to follow every sinuousness of her motion, to glisten in the silken promise of her skin. Oh, her skin, how he wanted to feel the satin of it, to monitor every stir and quiver with his fingertips, to touch its softness with his lips, to taste it with his tongue!

She bent, then, into a posture he had not anticipated, forward, so that her buttocks came to a new receptive fullness, and he couldn't stand how alluring they were, and felt himself rising to his need to be between them. As he took a step toward her, however, she was upright again, but he knew there was to be no halting now, he had to continue forward, toward her, had to extend his hand to touch her, his arms to hold her, had to move in upon her. Slowly, inch by inch, he shortened the distance between them. He could see the perspiration on her back, her shoulders; as she raised her arm, he watched a droplet course downward and vanish in the tuft of shading in her armpit, and other drops, like pearls, drifting down to her waist, losing themselves in the elastic band that held the sheer undergarment on her hips. Through the silky translucence of the moist cloth he saw her silkier flesh and the cleft of darkness down her buttocks, and could not bear how the fabric loosed and captured her, how the flesh stirred and stilled, stirred and stilled. He kept approaching with the slowest motion, tantalizing himself with his own deliberation, indulging it as if certain that the ecstasy must not be hurried, for it would never in his lifetime occur again. And now at last, he was close enough to touch her. Quiver by quiver, he raised one hand to her shoulder, let his fingertips gently rest on the warm moist skin; then the other hand on the in-curve of her body, under her arm. Slowly then, moving his right hand, he allowed it to slide down the valley of her back until it touched the rising mound below her waist. Both hands moved together now, both came to rest on the jointure of her brassiere, on the hint of metal, the cold hook that entered the cold eye of capture, and he slipped the top hook free. Then the bottom one. It was as if the surfeit of breast had burst the tabs asunder and the tails of cloth fell free, dangling loosely under her shoulder blades. Closer, he came closer until his body was pressed firm and warm against her warmth, and he put his arms around her, his hands on her belly first where the soft elastic just barely touched her navel, and with all memorial time to spare, with all eternity to touch her, he slowly let his hands glide upward to where the brassiere now loosely covered her breasts. He slid one hand under the cloth and cupped the breast in it, gently holding it as the fabric had held it, the other hand on the other breast, and his hands were not enough, the bounty of them was all he could hold and more, the discrepancy a joy and an ache of wanting, and he felt he couldn't stand it. Rounder than roundness, warmer than warmth, firm and soft as a fruit lost in Eden—he felt a yearning of mouth and stomach and mind and testes, a craving in every part of him that had a sensibility. He shoved his loins closer to her buttocks, gave muscle to his cock, driving, ramming it into the valley between fleshes, and as he impelled his hardness into her softness, he desperately became aware that there was a hindrance, a fantasy hymen, a cobweb condom, a filmy forbiddance between his prick's desire and the woman, and it didn't matter that the barrier was no denser than gossamer, no more substantial than the wing of a butterfly, no matter how seemingly impalpable it was, no matter how real or imaginary, it was *there,* and he had done nothing to remove it, might even fail to remove it if he tried. . . . And the reverie was over, and he had not been gratified.

The streets were totally dark and silent, and in the war-deserted stillness he returned to the hospital. He and Yannis stayed there for the rest of the week. But they were needed outside again, the superintendent said, so Ben reclaimed his ambulance. It was in surprisingly good shape, except that the supplies had been used up and it badly needed a cleaning. It was a pleasure to do it—it seemed like a return to normalcy. Suddenly, as Yannis was scrubbing the paintwork and Ben was cleaning out the drawers, he saw Kalya again, studying him as if she were there. He had seen her twice this week, a figment. When would he see her, real? Why was he waiting?

The intercom was going. Be careful, the Paphos Hospital said, reporting an emergency. Although the occurrence was not in the war zone, the casualty seemed suspiciously of military origin—an explosion, followed by a fire.

"Stop!"

Yannis again said stop, and cursed.

Ben didn't stop but he did jam on his brakes, too abruptly. He heard the clank in the rear, and hoped the oxygen tank wouldn't slip from the mounts, as it had done this morning. Everything needed an overhauling.

"Don't drive so crazy."

"I was driving fast, not crazy."

"You are thinking about her again—like she is in the focking road."

The Greek was right. She was always there, these days. She might have been a mirage on the sun-scorched highway, miles ahead and unapproachable.

"If you will not get her out of your mind—"

"—she will break my walnuts."

He had intended to go back and see her, but he had lost his nerve. The rejections had grown, in his memory, into an enormous ogre. When he thought of returning for what might be a third ignominy, he couldn't stand it. But still, he could not forget her. Mirages . . . Get off the road, he said to her, get off.

Switching the radio from the Paphos Hospital, he got the news. The peace negotiations were going on in Geneva, with delegates from England, Greece, and Turkey. The island was not represented—neither by Greeks nor Turks—the Cypriots would attend the later meetings. Meanwhile, said the Greek commentator, the Turks were breaking the truce—continuing to land troops in the north, shelling villages; and there was sporadic gunfire in Nicosia.

"He's a liar," Yannis said.

"How do you know he's a liar?"

"We were in Nicosia three times yesterday. Did we hear gunfire?"

"You think he's making it up?"

"He's a Greek."

"So are you."

"I am a Cypriot."

"Turkish?"

"Go to hell." He let it settle, his mind wandering. "When I was a child, there was a Turkish boy—and we used to fight. Then one winter we made a snow house together. Inside, we did not fight —we made faces at each other, and laughed."

"Snow melts."

"It lasts a long time if you do not piss on it." Then, half to himself; "For me it lasted sixty years."

Ben was sorry he had sounded a cynical note. Still, much though he loved the old man, there was some pap in his idealism. They both had to face the facts—the Turks *were* breaking the cease-fire; fugitives from the north had all told the same story.

What if the war broke out again?

He would have to think of leaving Cyprus. He had not come here for another bloodshed, but to escape the last one, and all others. He couldn't endure another protracted war, he couldn't live through it.

But what about Yannis? While Ben could escape simply by shipping out, what could the old man do? True, the old Greek had no family who would be harmed, no house of which he could be dispossessed as the northern Greeks were being dispossessed, and he was not important enough to be persecuted. He was an old olive tree, barren, and his insignificance would confer a certain physical safety upon him. But he would sicken. Seventy years old, he was still a humanist, still persuaded by goodness, and his soul would wither in another war.

There would not be any.

Ben had to believe it as faithfully as Yannis did; had to believe in the good faith of those men in Geneva, in their sweat and their devotion. More practically, in their common sense. The war was over.

The heat, now August, was unmerciful. And today, as if the hot rage of the afternoon were not enough, they were going to a fire. It's all right, he said, don't worry it. You're okay now. You came through the last few weeks in the hospital—dead, wounded, even napalm—and you did very well. You are yourself again.

They saw the smoke a good two miles away, a thin black curve of it, like a steer's horn. The fire was in a foothills village. A few of the houses were cubicles of whitewash, the others were made of wood and trellises, old vines that twined and tightened, and kept the shacks from falling. It was one of the wooden houses that was burning; already it was mostly ash and ember. Not far away, a gray sheep watched the smolder and bleated. It was the only sound; the people made none.

They stood around, perhaps two dozen of them, villagers, middle-aged and old, some of the women shawled even in the heat, a few men in the baggy trousers of bygone times, the youngest people at the furthest distance from the smoking cinders, restraining children. Nobody moved. There was nothing more to be done, the house was a ruin. When they talked, their words were not audible, they appeared only to be mouthing them. It was the silence, not the words, that spoke the tragedy. They stared at the graying loss.

Nobody looked at the man on the ground. He was too horrible to gaze at. He lay in the middle of the dirt road where he had been carried and set down for dead. He wasn't actually dead, but they knew what they knew.

Even when the ambulance arrived and the two medics hurried toward the victim, the neighbors scarcely looked at him. How different it was from napalm, Ben thought, because it was a comprehensible horror. He understood the burned hair and the blisterings on the forehead. He knew the pattern of the fire because the clothes on the left side of the body were intact, and the right was burned clean, the skin peeling, the flesh red, brown, yellow, varying degrees of incineration. He could make himself look at the thumb which was charred bone; the other fingers made a loose fist of pulp and plasma. The one hideousness he had to force himself to view was the extruded eyeball, running like the white of egg.

Yannis glanced once, then rushed to the ambulance, opened the rear doors, and started reaching for the litter.

"No!" Ben waved the stretcher back. "Salt solution."

There weren't many alternatives. The man's breath was scarcely anything, his pulse thready. His single functioning eye barely blinked at all, stared wide as if entranced. There was no moving him, not now. They would have to augment the circulating volume of his blood, pour fluids into him by vein.

"Hurry up!" Ben called.

But the old man continued pulling the stretcher out. "We take him to the hospital!"

"No! I said salt solution!"

He knew what was in Yannis's mind. Here or in the hospital, the man would die. Better to cart him there, then, while he was still alive, for otherwise Ben would not get paid. He was not an undertaker, he was a lifesaving attendant. His deal was that he had to bring them in alive, or no fee. No breath, no money. The old Cypriot, for all his humanism, was practical, and Ben was not.

The younger man was already in the ambulance, foraging for the infusion pump and the saline solution. As he rushed past Yannis and returned to the dying man, he could see the change. In the exposed flesh, everywhere, through the bloody areas and even through the exposed skin, the pale plasma was no longer transuding through the capillaries, it was flooding through, not colorless as usual, but yellow and dense, bubbling; it was as if the body, in hot anger, was expelling all its liquids.

And, anomalously, the man shivered with a chill. Through the burned mouth, a murmur, and a hissing as if against frost. Then, compounding contradictions, the face burst out in sweat.

Ben lifted the left arm. Rubbing at the skin, he looked for the vein, reached up as Yannis readied the needle.

"Hold still," Ben said. "You'll have to hold it steadier."

"Give fast." The old man raised the bottle so that the tube was straight.

Ben plunged the needle. He had sterilized nothing, not arm, not instrument. He pressed the tube, knowing that he had to hurry, and knowing that it didn't matter. Not relying on gravity, he pressed again, pressed harder. "Hold the bottle higher," he said.

He thought he saw a more rapid flutter of the man's eyelids, then the licking of the lips. Good, he said, as if any good would really come of it. A few more minutes of life, perhaps another hour, a day in the hospital with his skin debrided, grafts, transfusions, then what?

"Higher."

Another licking of the lips, a faster blinking, a hopeful breath and then another. Hopeful, hopeful.

It all stopped. The man was dead.

He looked at the body and thought: How strange. It didn't appear much different before, yet a moment ago it was a human being and now it was a carcass. Death had again become banal for him in those few weeks in the hospital, and here he was—less than a week away from it—and it had become a shock once more. His concept of essence must be fickle, he thought; his mind might be betraying him. Unsettled, he wondered as he always did: If I had been a doctor, a real doctor, might I have prolonged the man's life? And what would I be prolonging? . . . And why did I try so hard?

Yannis was cleaning up. A petty irony, watching him sterilize the needle now, after the fact, when they hadn't done it before. No rush anymore; plenty of time. The race against mortality, which he righteously told himself was the hideous part, was its sick ecstasy as well. The doctor game . . . Was that why I tried?

He saw the little girl. She was twelve, perhaps, not more. She had black hair, very long, almost to her waist, not gathered in any way, and her face was all eyes. She separated herself from the others and walked toward them, looked at the dead man, then quickly away, and up to Ben.

"*Nekros?*" she said.

He nodded.

She didn't cry, simply said *ochi*, meaning no, almost without inflection, as if merely disagreeing on a sum or a spelling.

"He's your father?" Ben asked in Greek.

She said he was, already adjusted to the past tense. It occurred to him: How long has she been adjusted to it? I wonder if she knew her father was going to die. But how could she know? Then he remembered that the Paphos Hospital said the fire had been reported as developing from an explosion, and that it might be suspicious.

She was gone. He hardly saw her disappear, saw only the in-

gathering of the villagers, readier to view the body now than when
it had been alive.

"Finish, Ben," Yannis said, and handed him the clipboard
with the accident sheets. There was no necessity to fill one out; the
police would do that, since the patient was dead. But he would fill
it out anyway, a courtesy to the hospital.

"What's the man's name?" he inquired. It was a general question, asked of anybody who would answer. But nobody did.

He asked it again. Still, nobody answered.

He felt Yannis touch him quickly, tug at his sleeve to come
away. He turned. The old man was trying to warn him in some
manner. But there didn't seem to be anything to warn him about.
He wondered if he should go looking for the girl.

"Doesn't anybody know who he is?"

"I will give you the details."

The medic turned to the voice. He saw a pleasant-looking
man of middle size and middle age. His face was sensitive, almost
delicate, and while he seemed somehow too special to belong here,
there was no real identifiability about him. Even his speech seemed
indeterminate; it had a Greek weight to it, but it could have been
English or American. A nondescript man. Except for the eyes.
They were arresting—brilliant blue in a dark Mediterranean face.
At first glance, they belonged to an intellectual, overworked and
overstrained, needing glasses perhaps, squinting too much. But
when they opened wide and gave permission for entry into the person of the man, there were humor and suffering and kindliness,
and—anomalously—not a little cruelty.

"If you have questions . . ." he said.

"Who was he?"

"His name was Doros Philbas. He was a plasterer."

"How did the fire start"

"Who knows? We think it was the Lux."

"What's the Lux?"

"It's a lamp—an old-fashioned petrol lamp." It was an educated voice. It spoke with quiet authority and exactitude. "They
are a nuisance, those lamps. You have to pump them. Perhaps he
was trying to light it."

"In the middle of the day?"

The man shrugged. "Or cleaning it—an explosion."

"You think that's what it was?"

"No, I am guessing—like everybody else."

"Is everybody guessing?"

He didn't know what he meant by it; neither, apparently, did the man. "You think we can do more than guess?"

It occurred to Ben that they could. Or this one could. It was a disturbing thought, and not his business. But he made one more try. He turned to the others and asked, "Who reported the fire?"

Again, nobody answered. The crowd started slowly to disperse.

He shoved the pencil back into the sleeve of the clipboard and walked toward the vehicle.

As they drove away, the thought of the crowd still bothered him. But the little girl bothered him more. Her face loitered in his vision. Her expressionless certainty, despite the *ochi* she had uttered, that her father was dead. She was too young to know death as a certitude; it was a word that should have retained its improbability. But Mee Lanh had been sure of it as well, and not much older than this one. But no other similarities; another country, another war. But was it the same fire, solely in his mind? No, this one was real—as the other must have been—as real as the unidentifiable man with the unidentifiable voice. And his unbelievable Lux lamp explanation.

He asked Yannis. "The man who talked to us—do you know him?"

"Only a little. I was living some miles from here."

"What's his name?"

"Mano."

"Mano? Is that a Greek name?"

"Yes. Manolis Falkos."

"Who is he?"

Yannis didn't answer immediately. "A schoolteacher."

Ben was puzzled by the reluctance. "Do you believe that—about the lamp?"

". . . No."

"What do you think?"

Yannis took so long that Ben thought he wouldn't answer the question. Then: *"Patriotis."*

It could mean, simply, that Falkos came from Yannis's part of the country, which apparently he did, or it could mean a patriot. Then it occurred to him: "Is he a guerrilla?"

". . . He was. With Grivas."

"Grivas is dead."

"Falkos is not."

The old man was uncomfortable talking about it, and Ben did not press him.

They made one more stop before dinner—a false heart attack that was really indigestion—then turned toward Xeno's Kapelion. It was a wineshop that had grown into a restaurant, on the beach, east of Limassol. It was not a good eating place. The meat—invariably lamb—was always shish-kebabbed to dry durability and had to be wetted down with gallons of lemon juice; the fish, monotonously mullet, was skeletal. But it was all outdoors, all home-made pavilions, bamboo poles spread with palm and grape leaves, with a shade-giving mulberry seemingly always in lush bloom. It was refreshing and cool at Xeno's, and sometimes, on summer evenings, the tide would wash up and one could take shoes and socks off, roll up trouser legs, and—while eating sugared raspberries and drinking ouzo—feel the warm lapping of the Mediterranean, fondling underfoot.

But tonight there were no such delectations. The tide was out, there was no sea breeze, the air was torpid, the sting-flies were a pestilence. And the man was there.

Manolis Falkos, waiting, as if he had known they would arrive sooner or later, and they had had an appointment to meet. Ben had never seen him here before, yet here he was tonight, sitting at the very table they usually occupied. He was drinking the sweet Commandaria wine and nibbling at lime rinds. He looked up and did not smile.

"*Kopiaste*," he said.

One didn't ignore the welcome without giving offense; sometimes hospitality became duress. The teacher was making it more forceful by pulling out one chair, then another. At least a moment or two, he pleaded, would they sit with him, would they have a drink?

"Would you care for brandy?"

"No, the Commandaria will be fine," Ben said. There were already glasses on the table, three of them, the larger wineglasses, not the small ones for brandy; wine was what the man had intended.

"I lied to you this afternoon," Falkos said.

Ben picked up a bit of lime rind and nibbled at it.

Falkos continued. "The fire was not an accident. We bound

Philbas to his kitchen stove, we turned the gas on, then threw a *hartoroketta* through the window."

Strictly, a firecracker, but guerrillas meant a bomb.

"Why?"

"He was a traitor."

"How?"

"Never mind." It was all he was going to say, but he realized it required more. "He disappeared from his home for a week and we learned why. He was in Kyrenia. He and two others—they limed a field near Karavas—for the pilots to see. We knew it for certain. He might just as well have come home with chalk on his hands."

"Why didn't you let the police take care of it, or the National Guard?"

His smile made Ben feel ingenuous. "These are not leisurely times, Mr. Coram."

He thought of a little girl with big eyes, asking *nekros?* "Did you have to burn the house? Why didn't you just shoot him, or stab him?" Murder, he thought, as merciful irony. "Where will his family live now?"

"There is no family—only Annetta. She will live with my cousin and his wife. I will see that she is taken care of. She was in my classroom, she is a good child. It was a choice—to leave her the house, and let it be known that her father was a traitor, or destroy the house—as if by accident—and force her to move to another village where she might never find out about him. . . . It was not a heartless decision."

Ben had a vision of him in the classroom, a good teacher, not unkind. Then the image became too neat: chalk on the teacher's hand and on the hand of the plasterer.

"We need a favor of you, *kirie*." He said the "sir" with a special deference, almost a plea.

The sun had almost set. The tide was coming in a little, not much, not enough to bathe one's feet. The Commandaria was too sweet; Ben wondered if, without offense, he could switch to brandy. Yannis was not looking at either of them; down into his glass, his face as dark as the pole shadow that crossed the tabletop, bisecting it.

"We are in a bad way up north," Falkos said. "And it will get worse."

"The cease-fire—"

"—does not exist. Not to the Turks, anyway. They haven't observed a single day of it. Merchant ships are landing munitions on the northern coast. Helicopters are dropping troops all over the mountains. They've taken the village of Myrton, and they're shelling Lapithos. And on Monday night they took the Monastery of St. Timotheos."

"The Monastery? Why?"

"It's on a height. The plateau surrounding it—where the vineyards used to be—is a good landing field for planes. It can command the island in three directions. They're landing aircraft secretly—a plane at a time—and even small tanks."

"Tanks—by air? Do you believe it?"

"Yes. Before they cut the telephone line, we heard from Father Demetrios." His glance contracted like an arrowhead coming to its point. "It was Father Demetrios who asked for the favor."

"He asked for me—particularly?"

"No, not for you particularly." Then, quickly: "Why? Do you know him?"

"Yes, I met him a number of years ago." There was more to it, but it was a treasured experience—and frail—and he kept it in a private place.

Falkos, sensing something, grasped at the unexpected advantage. "Good, good."

"But if it's a military favor—"

Hastily, "No—medical."

"How?"

"Father Demetrios is very ill. He needs a doctor, but the Turks are of course suspicious—they won't allow anyone to see him. If you were to go, however—if they were to inquire about you, they would know you're a neutral." He smiled with genuine admiration. "In fact, I'm told you've become quite a figure on the island—you're much appreciated. By everybody." As an afterthought: "You and Yannis."

Ben thanked him; Yannis didn't.

Falkos continued. "The Turks would let you through—no difficulty—and you could treat the old man."

"It's palsy—there's hardly anything . . ."

"It's worse than that. He has a kidney ailment. He's feverish, there's blood in his urine. His voice was so weak, he could hardly be understood. Someone has to take medicine to him—make him comfortable—perhaps one of those machines—"

"Dialysis."

"Yes. I understand you can get one at Nicosia."

"Yes."

"Will you go?"

Impulsively, he was on the verge of saying yes; then, the nudge of caution. "If they won't allow a Greek doctor, why not a Turkish one?"

Falkos looked puzzled. "I see you don't remember Demetrios."

He did remember him very well, the patriarch's almost clairvoyant vision, yet his blind side about Turks. God's anathema, he had called them; he would suffer damnation before allowing one near him. Ben had known the answer to his own question, but had asked it investigatively, feeling his way through a vague cloud of suspicion.

"Will you go?" Falkos asked.

"Yes, of course," he said. "At once."

"Well . . . not at once," the teacher said. "I can't work that fast."

The cloud was becoming more dense. "Fast enough for what?"

Falkos didn't address the question directly. He hesitated. Ben looked at Yannis, who didn't meet the glance. The old man was ahead of him, apparently, having suspected something from the start.

"You have a built-in bed in your ambulance," Falkos said. "It's a unit with drawers, isn't that so?"

"Yes." Narrowly.

"I would like those drawers removed."

"Why? They have medical equipment in them."

"I will take their place."

"You?"

"Yes. You will hide me there."

He could feel the heat, then the chill. "With what? A few grenades?"

"A small mortar, to be exact."

"To blow up a monastery?"

"It's not a monastery any longer, Mr. Coram. It was built in the fourteenth century as a fortress—and now it's an arsenal. It's very dangerous to us—and we need your help."

"Go to hell!"

He got up and Falkos arose with him. "Please, Mr. Coram—the whole point of the thing—"

"I know the point—don't tell me the point! You want to use the fact that people trust me—! You want to turn my ambulance into an armored tank!"

Enraged, he turned to get away. At the fringe of vision, he saw someone—another man, long-limbed, gaunt—bearing down on their table.

Greeks are not, as a telling characteristic, prodigious in stature. This one was lean and extraordinarily tall, with an aura of personage. His face was craggy and worn; it was ineffably kind. Weariness was in it, a profound weariness, to the soul. As he approached, Falkos seemed relieved to see him; the teacher's manner to the older man was deferential, this side of reverence.

Falkos introduced them. "Pavlos Chartas—I present Benjamin Coram."

Chartas extended his hand and for the moment Ben was reluctant to take it. When he did, the tall man looked grateful. He turned to Falkos. "He has said no, of course." When the schoolteacher nodded, Chartas said to Ben, "May I try again?"

"No."

"Please," he said, with an uneasy reticence. "I know your point of view can't possibly be ours. But you've lived with us for a number of years, and—as a friend—would you listen a while longer?" As Ben hesitated: "You are under no constraint, believe me—but please sit down."

Ben looked at Yannis, who was standing and had no intention to stay. But the old Greek was in a position where he did not have Chartas's eyes to deal with, and the supplication in them. And if the man had claimed he was using no constraint, he was wrong; it was the compulsion of his gravity.

The medic sat down again, and after a moment so did the others, Yannis included.

"I've just come from the north," Chartas said. "I cannot begin to calculate how many Greek casualties there have been. The wounded are not being tended—the Turks will not admit them to the hospitals. Nor are they burying our dead. Nearly all of our people have been driven from their homes—the houses will be occupied by Turks who will be imported from the mainland. The roads are glutted with refugees."

"You don't have to tell me the horrors of war, *kirie*," Ben said.

"The point I was getting to is that the war has not ended, it has just begun—and we are in a worse state than you can imagine. We have lost our airport, our northern harbor has been taken, Nicosia is helpless, there are forty thousand Turkish troops on the island. And now—with the taking of the Monastery—the enemy has made its intention clear."

"To do what?"

"To take the whole country."

"I don't believe that."

"You don't? Then look at the island." He moved the wine-glasses to one side and drew with his forefinger on the tabletop. "Here is St. Timotheos, at the top of the mountain. Here is its vineyard from which the planes can take off. Here are the three roads down which the tanks and troops can move. This road goes to Limassol and this one to Morphou. Limassol is our major port— Morphou is our food center. They've already taken the road to Nicosia. These roads are next. . . . There it is. It isn't as though we have an alternative—we must retrieve the Monastery."

"With an ambulance?"

"Don't smile, my friend—we are not naïve," he said quietly. "We could shell it, we could bomb it with a single pass of an airplane, we could mine the arch gate and blow it up. But besides being a fortress, it is also a religious institution, and we leave the bombing of churches to the Turks. Still, we do need to open it up, so that our armored vehicles can follow. And with one armored car—and a little surprise—we can do it."

"I'm sorry, *kirie*," Ben said quietly. "I can't be the armored car and the little surprise."

"Mr. Coram—"

"There's a cease-fire."

"Who recognizes it?"

"Your own army."

"We have no army! The National Guard gave in to Sampson without a whimper. Now that he has run, they're running too. *We* are the army."

"Then *you* have to recognize the cease-fire."

"The Turks took the Monastery *during* the cease-fire."

"Kirios Chartas, right now—right this minute—there's a peace conference going on in Geneva!"

Chartas's weariness seemed suddenly to have overcome him. He appeared unable to summon the strength to answer an argument the like of which he had probably addressed a thousand times in his now elderly life. He had been, no doubt, a Grivas man, and had seen action in the hills, summers of drought, freezing winters, hardships and risky raids and terrifying departures. He looked like a man who suffered from headaches that would last him forever, and was possibly having one now.

"Yes, there is a peace conference," he said, with a spent voice. "It is attended by England, Greece, and Turkey. We have not been invited."

"You will be—after the preliminaries are over."

"Yes, after everything has been decided. Meanwhile—every day—as the Turks get stronger here, they get stronger in Geneva. When finally we *are* invited to the meetings, what will we do there —cry? Do tears move conferences?"

"Justice . . ." He stopped, feeling foolish at the sound of the simplistic word.

"You believe there is such a thing, Mr. Coram?"

"Yes. And I suspect that you do too."

"Yes . . . somewhere." He said it longingly like a man who had not yet given up a flagging hope. "But not in Geneva. . . . We will get sold out, *kirie.*"

"The conferences have hardly begun."

"It's as if they have already ended." Then, insistently repeating the same expression, "We will get sold out. By England, by Greece—and by America."

"America isn't even *in* them."

"America is in all of them. And she will sell us out. Because we are a small, forgotten people on a little island somewhere. But Turkey is a buffer against Russia. Your country will send us a few tourists—and she will send Skyhawks to Turkey. And one of her friendliest tourists will have a little Land-Rover—and deny us a few days' use of it."

"It's not a Skyhawk," he said quietly. "And I'm not a soldier, I'm a medic. I spent four years in Vietnam saying that, and I'm not going to say anything different in Cyprus. I don't want you to think I'm unfeeling, *kirie*—I'm not. I'll tend the wounded—it's all I can do, it's all I'm good for. As to the rest—no matter what you say about Geneva—I have to believe in it. Not because it makes sense to believe in it, but because it's all we've got."

It was over and Chartas knew it. He said nothing. He only lowered his head a little. But as Ben was pushing his chair back, Falkos spoke: "If you can't view this through our motive, Mr. Coram—view it through your own. You say you're a medic—a healer, a man of good feeling—fine! There's a priest up there—his life is at stake."

"Then I'll go up there alone—without you."

"You'll never get there," Falkos said.

The threat was explicit.

As Ben departed, he heard Yannis padding softly after him.

The old man snored. He lay on the built-in bed while Ben lay on the truss-supported stretcher, and with a brassy nasal trumpeting Yannis made the ambulance tremble.

It was no use trying to sleep. Even if there weren't any snoring, Ben knew he would be awake. That plaguing, dotard patriarch on a distant mountaintop, that loving man, that rancorous man— that ineffable artist!—was up there, dying of a bad waste-disposal unit, pickling in his own urine. And he, Ben Coram, medic of mercy, was standing inert at a waterside, gazing at a black-blue-purple sea, counting planets and a star or two. Doing nothing. Not offering a single diuretic pill or a barbiturate or the palm of comfort, nothing.

Why didn't he just chance it, and drive up alone?

You'll never get there.

The threat was not idle. The roads would all be covered, with guerrillas everywhere. Suddenly out of the calm of cedar woodlands, a grenade would fly. An ambulance would require only one of them; it could be done economically.

Sorry, Demetrios.

He had met the old priest a little over three years ago, in the dismal time before he had bought the Land-Rover and converted it into an ambulance. Rootless, in early fall of that year, he had gone on a week's walking trip. The week had become a month, then two months, and he had trudged his way drearily into winter. It didn't matter where he went; his only itinerary was unhappiness. He had seen every cape and headland on the island, every vineyard and orchard, all the hills, valleys, meadowlands, and now for the second time he was traipsing the cedar forests of the Troodos Mountains.

One afternoon, walking through a wooded area that was really not very dense, he got lost. And it began to rain. It was not a good rain, it was cold and bleak, as mean as envy. The cedars were not thick enough to give good shelter, and a dripping poplar tree was worse than nothing. There was no cave to flee into, no shelf of rock under which he could take refuge. His clothes were soaked, his hair was sopping wet, and his boots became so full of water that they gurgled as he walked. Step by step, with no direction any more purposeful than any other, he was getting colder, more desperate, and the shivering began. The rain was turning to sleet, frozen pellets stabbing him, a punishment of needles.

When the snow started, it was a blessing for a while. The onslaught had whitened and gentled; it didn't tear his skin. For the first hour or so, it was endurable, even welcome. Then he got colder and colder and began to feel a tingling in his feet. It was the burn-and-itch that the soldiers used to call trench foot; but when the numbness started, he knew it could be the onset of ice gangrene, and he was frightened. He did not know which was more worrisome, being lost or being frozen, and he realized that his mind too must be turning gelid if he couldn't perceive that one was a function of the other.

He barely saw the wall, and wasn't sure what it was. The arched wooden part had a huge brass thing on it, which, through the swirl of snow, looked familiar in some way, something that was meant to be pulled. But he certainly couldn't manage it, his hands were useless. The fingers would not open anymore. They were long tentacles of ice now, and he was afraid to force them, for they were brittle, as shatterable as glass. All he could do was thump his body against the wood and augment the noise with throat sounds, guttural and not much louder than the fall of the snow. Then something that had held him up gave way inside him, and he sank into the whiteness.

He awoke to someone bathing his hands and feet with warm wet compresses. He was lying on a bed in what he later learned had once been the abbot's retreating room but was now an infirmary of sorts—and an old patriarch was bustling over him. The man had palsy and could not manage the compresses very adroitly, but his hands were the only part of him that seemed unsteady. He had a strong, intense face and a white beard that contrasted with the black fervency of his eyes. They were eyes that looked at nothing with indifference.

All of Ben's body was piled high with blankets, and under

them he felt the voluptuous warmth of hot-water bottles, but in his extremities he felt nothing. Some say the world will end in fire, he thought, some say in ice. He wondered why the words came back to him. The priest did not for one moment stop his attendances. For hours he went on, compress after compress, carefully wrapping each hand, each foot with heated cloths, pausing only to call for warmer water. When he did, a gnome of a man, Brother Modestos, came good-naturedly giggling into the room with another agate basin. For hours the procedure continued without pause or relaxation, until Brother Modestos could scarcely stand or giggle any longer, and when he started spilling the water, Father Demetrios dismissed him to bed and carried on the ministrations alone. All night, in dogged silence.

Toward morning, as Ben was feeling better but still had no sensation in his right foot, he begged the old man to quit and get some rest. Demetrios did stop, but only for a minute.

"If I do," he said in excellent Greek-accented English, "you will lose the use of your right foot. I do not intend for that to happen."

It wouldn't dare happen if Demetrios didn't intend it to. He was the strongest man Ben had ever met. And the priest had his way. In two days the patient had regained full sensitivity in all four limbs.

But he had pneumonia.

"Nonsense," Father Demetrios said. "You do not have pneumonia. You have only a slight cold."

Ben knew his own symptoms very well. There was no question about it: pneumonia. But the old man treated it like common laryngitis. He wheeled carts in with steaming teakettles on them, and he filled the air with the dampness of aromatic herbs and spices— boiling tarragon and hyssop that made Ben sneeze. Hyssop *should* make you sneeze, the priest assured him, the word *sounds* like sneezing, that's how they made it up.

It was Demetrios who made it up. He made up lots of things, he was the final authority on everything. Friar's balsam is just the same as tincture of benzoin, he claimed, but since it is of religious derivation, it clears the nostrils better—every good doctor knows that.

A week later, treated for mild laryngitis and the common cold, Ben was on his feet again. The old man scolded him: "I'm glad you gave up being a doctor. Any man who does not know that friar's balsam is better than tincture of benzoin . . ."

He was only half teasing. He had already invested something of himself in Ben, and it bothered him that the young man had given up his profession. Then he looked intently into Ben's eyes and asked, "Why do you think the difference between friar's balsam and benzoin is important?"

"Isn't it important to you?"

"Not at all. Why is it to you?"

Ben had started to think of Demetrios as a man of some thought, and this question seemed too naïve. "Well, if they aren't different . . . Father, isn't there a difference between, say, arsenic and aspirin?"

"Come now, Benjamin, don't reduce it to absurdity. You know what I'm talking about—all medicines have the same basic ingredient."

"Faith, you mean?"

"You don't believe that?" Then, as Ben didn't answer: "You wouldn't, of course, agree that a picture can cure the smallpox?"

"A picture?"

"A painting—a portrait. Can it cure the smallpox?"

"Well, I wouldn't call it the prescription of choice."

"Come with me," the old man said.

The patriarch led him out of the refectory, across the snow-covered cloister yard. The building they were going to was called the winery. The monks and lay brothers of the St. Timotheos Monastery had once been excellent vintners of an exotically aromatic wine. Where now there was a plateau meadow there used to be broad acres of vineyard, and the winery had been prosperous, until all of Cyprus had become a competing vineyard. The winery building was used for other things now, as Ben would see.

Demetrios preceded him up the wooden steps that led to what was once a loading platform. He opened a narrow door within a wider one, and ushered Ben into a broad and open space, lighted by clerestory windows.

Ben gasped. The vast room shimmered with color. It was an artist's studio and the walls were hung with the most vivid paintings he had ever seen. Some of them were ornately Byzantine— glowing gilts and viridian and ecstatic blues; some burned with the scarlets and madders of the Umbrian hills, some had a psychedelic scream to them, brashly modern.

They were all icons. Saints, real and imaginary; apostles, in bliss or in agony; and the rapturous faces of Christ. The pictures were radiantly beautiful.

"Where did they come from?" Ben asked.

"I painted them."

"You—all of them?"

"Demetrios of Timotheos—you don't know my name? I am famous."

He said it without egotism, only as a matter of reference. Ben had to confess that he had never heard of him.

"Well, let us say I *was* famous."

"Do you sell them?"

"I used to—except those I could not bear to part with." Then, amusedly, "Of course, not many people buy them these days. There was an American dealer here—he said they are no longer a 'hot item.'"

"And you're still painting them?"

"Hot or cold."

Reflexively, Ben looked at the palsied hand, and wished that he hadn't. Demetrios saw the glance, did not embarrass the young man by commenting on it, and smiled with some secret amusement.

But the priest had wandered from his point and now returned to it. "You know what an icon is? It is not only a portrait, my friend—it is a medicine, it is a cure. It's the face of a saint gazing on someone afflicted. It's the merciful eye of Christos, saying have faith and you will be whole again. Do you know that for many centuries the icon was the *only* cure? It gave sight to the blind, it mended the sores of the leprous—and if there was faith enough, it would cleanse a plague. These are miracles, you would say—and we are not always forgiven for believing in them. But they have happened. Icons have been known to weep with pity, did you know that? And one of them—I think it is somewhere in the Vosges—has been seen to bleed for the bleeding. Not centuries ago, Benjamin—recently!"

"Do yours have cures in them?"

"No—and that's my point. If I had more faith, they would."

Having uttered it so starkly, it unnerved him. While he was not recanting, he tried to soften the severity of what he had said about himself. He smiled and made a forlorn joke. "Perhaps it is not only my faith that is at fault, it may be my art as well. Perhaps, in modern times, the saints do not know how to bless in the old idiom. So I have tried to paint more modernly."

He pointed to his modern canvases—a saint, a grouping of them, a Maria, a Christos. They were executed with self-conscious primitiveness, as a child might paint them—the colors flat, hardly any chiaroscuro, no face with any depth or distance. They were by no measure the best in the room. But the artist, while he had never become comfortable with the technique, felt he had to justify it:

"Well, even if it is a naked kind of painting, a saint is not ashamed to be naked. Sainthood *should* be unadorned. Divinity needs no decoration."

Trying to convince himself, he was not succeeding. He stopped in the midst of it, as if he had lost his place in a book and didn't know where to resume reading.

Ben felt sorry for the old man. He had done beautiful work, but it had not satisfied him. All his paintings were merely works of art, not what he wanted them to be: curatives. To him they were paintings, not icons. They had no gift of healing.

Which Ben might have. So while he envied the young man, he also, in this brief fortnight, came to love him. How easy it was for Father Demetrios to love! It was, probably even more than his painting, his one great art.

Except where Turks were concerned. And that was the blind spot in the man. He had come as an orphan to the Monastery, had lived his whole life here, had probably met few Turkish people, yet he said he knew them to be cruel. He had no heart for cruelty, nor any time to discuss it—they were not a suitable subject for cloister conversation.

But Ben forced it a little. "How do you know they are cruel?"

"People have told me—people I trust."

"If you spoke to the Turks, you might trust *them*."

"Speak to a *Turk*? What is the advantage of living *here*, if I cannot escape what is hateful?"

Prejudice as escape. If he spoke to a Turk, he might get another truth—but how many verities did he need? If there were too many, the heart would be spread too thin. Give all you are to a small number of selected beliefs. As few as possible. One, if there is faith enough.

They disagreed violently, and agreed on nearly all else. How could the old man be so wise in other things? Ben spent practically every waking moment with Demetrios. He watched him paint, and marveled at how he managed. He would take the brush in his palsied hand and barely be able to maintain his grasp on it. The arm quaked, the stricken fingers did not seem capable of holding onto anything for more than a minute. Then, as the hand with the paintbrush slowly approached the easel, as the bristles touched the canvas, it was as if the saint he was about to paint was already healing *him!* If the old man only knew it, Ben thought, if he only knew he *was* painting a true icon, even without being a saint—!

A few days after the thought occurred to him, he tried to express it to the priest. When he did, the old man trembled beyond his infirmity, and did not seem able to accept the possibility that he had already been blessed. It was a joy too culminative, and he was not ready for it.

On the day of his departure, Ben asked him, "If there were one affliction you would want your icons to heal, which would it be?"

"Fear."

Walking down the mountainside, Ben wondered when it was that Demetrios came to that single-word response. Had he thought of it long ago, or did it occur to the old man for Ben's benefit? The American believed it was the latter. Don't be afraid of being a doctor, he was saying, don't be afraid to heal.

The following week Ben bought the Land-Rover. So the old man was a healer after all.

And now Ben, three years later, yearned to go up that mountainside and repay him. With perhaps only a day of comfort, an hour's respite from pain.

Goddamn those warring ones, he thought, who wanted to load his ambulance with bombs and turn it into an armored tank. Goddamn the Greeks and Turks alike.

He would have to leave this place, this beautiful island. They didn't deserve this beauty, none of them, this lovely sea, this ache-provoking sky, this soft wind out of an eastern mystery. But how could he ever leave it, this night enchantment, just as some voice was about to impart a love secret he had never dreamed would be revealed? Would the voice also tell him how to get the courage to return to her, and risk humiliation once more? Sometimes, sensible man though he was, he yearned to believe—as many Cypriots did, even the self-styled sophisticates—that Aphrodite would come to a lover's assistance. She would rise at daybreak out of the sea, drenched in an amniotic perfume, and show the way; she would lead him back to Kalya. Sometimes, while drunk, he almost believed in a goddess who . . .

What a romantic cretin he was turning out to be. A man in his mid-thirties, a number of women behind him, and a war or two. A doctor manqué who had disappointed a doctor father, a toughened man who had seen the human condition, blood, belly, and balls, and should be left with nightmares and no dreams, dreaming about a woman who was bound to be unattainable. Wasn't he old enough to know the real from the illusory—or, as the Cypriots put it, Pegasus from a jackass?

A terrible truth hit him. Thinking of Kalya and Demetrios, he was afraid that he hadn't the courage to ascend to the heights of either mountain, not to Seismos or St. Timotheos.

. . . He had been standing by the shore, and now he turned. He heard a strange sound. It wasn't sea or wind or anything to do with the night. Perhaps it had been his foot in sand, on sea pebbles. Motionless, he heard the sound again. It was coming from the ambulance. He felt a scurry of alarm.

He ran across the rocks, he stumbled, ran again. Heart pounding, he called to the open back door of the ambulance, "Yannis!"

There was no answer.

He jumped up onto the rear step, looked inside. Both beds were empty.

"Yannis!"

He heard the sound again.

It was an unusual noise on the intercom. He ran around to the cab of the vehicle. Yannis was inside, bent over, listening intently to the blurry chatter.

"What is it?" he asked.

"I don't know—sounds like airplanes."

They were still.

It wasn't airplanes, it was foghorns. Then the voice, in Greek. "Limassol—port. This is the new port. Limassol port, calling hospital."

They heard the voices, the hospital and the port speaking. There was no ambulance, Emergency was saying, they were both in the north, there was fighting somewhere.

"Can you break in?" Ben asked.

"I try—they cannot hear me."

"What's at the port?"

"Somebody sick—dying—"

Ben rushed to the other side of the ambulance, into the cab. Instantly, he had the motor running. "Break in if you can—tell them we're on the way."

"I cannot get in."

The old man talked softly, loudly, fidgeted with dials. "They cannot hear me," he said. Then, in Greek, irascibly, "Hospital, get off—we have it now—we are going."

It was useless. The only answer was speed—and, for Yannis, the siren. We don't need that bastard noise, Ben said, the road's deserted. But Yannis kept it going. It made him feel they were driving faster, or that the patient would hear it and be comforted.

"He has had three attacks," the harbor master said. "The *Thessaloniki* landed at two o'clock. As he came down the gangplank—right out there where the light is—he had the first one. We brought him into the office. About fifteen minutes after he recovered, he had another one, much worse. When he got over it, I told him to sit there for a while. He did, and everything was fine. Just as he got through customs, another big one. Now he seems all right."

He did seem all right. He lay on the concrete floor of the improvised waiting room—the new port had just opened recently—and he was fast asleep. A young man, a boy really, sixteen or seventeen, he was dark-complexioned—Turkish or Greek, it was hard to tell. His features were as fine as a Praxiteles, but he was quite pale, with a fleck of foam at his mouth. He stirred a little, made a soft murmuring with no intimation of pain, without the faintest hint of discomfort. He could be having a pleasant dream, Ben thought, a pleasant postepileptic reverie, some veiled glimmering of where these damn things come from. He couldn't be sure it was epilepsy, but the two big ones and a little one, what else could be so grand and petit, with the touch of sea froth on the lips? He wondered if the man dreaming so serenely heard water flowing, ebbing, tides.

"Where does he come from?" Ben asked.

"His passport is American," the official answered. "His name is Mark Achille. It could be French—he's been there." The middle-aged Greek paused, and said with studied casualness, "He has also been to Turkey."

The man was worried by it. Affably, to ease his concern, Ben said, "We see spies in everything, even in epileptics."

"He might not be an epileptic."

The medic teased him. "Faking, you mean—to attract attention? Classic spy procedure?"

The official heard the irony and flushed. Wanting nothing more to do with it, he twisted stiffly away and marched out of sight. Yannis was kneeling at the patient's side.

The boy's eyelids were fluttering. They opened a moment, closed, then fluttered again. I could give him something, Ben thought, but I don't know what he's been taking, and I better not mix things. Anyway, he seemed to be reviving quickly. Too quickly, the medic thought, with a kind of obsessive urgency, trying to speak, unable to manage words; starting to get up, unable to manage muscles.

Ben knelt on the other side of him. "Not too fast," he said.

The words themselves seemed to propel the young man upward, as if in flight from that object on the ground that had been himself. He was fully erect now, but unsteady.

"Hold it," Ben said. "Come and sit down."

He gestured to the wooden bench, not five feet away, put his hand on the sick one's arm, to help him there. The boy pushed his hand away, started under his own power toward the bench, turned to smile as though to say he had done it unassisted. Then suddenly his head twisted, his eyes rolled back, his body contorted, his throat emitted the sound of vomit. Foam, suds of foam, like a washing machine overflowing, issued from his mouth, and he seemed to choke on it.

Yannis started to encircle him with his arms. "Don't confine him," Ben said. He held the boy loosely, letting him down slowly, not on the bench but on the floor again, flat.

The mouth started to chew at the tongue. The medic reached for his handkerchief and shoved it between his teeth. The boy's head began to shake, to beat itself on the concrete floor. Ben put his hand under it. He felt the blows of the patient's head against his palm, like hammer strokes, smashing his knuckles against the floor.

Yannis again started to confine the boy, holding his head.

"Let go," Ben said.

"Your hand—!"

"It's okay."

His hand hurt, the large knuckle was injured. Hurry it up, he said silently to the boy, get rid of the damn thing. Again the hammer blow.

It was over.

The boy was sleeping once more. The peaceful invalid, oblivious of any bleeding hands, was back in his dreams again.

Then the awakening, slower this time, the urgency not so feverish. After a while, they helped him to get up and the boy sat between them on the bench. His eyes were far away and he was shivering a little but not spastically; his whole demeanor was calm and grave, in another world. He paid no attention to Ben's taking of his pulse, his blood pressure, his temperature; he suffered everything as if it were being done for someone else. Now that the foam was off his lips and his forehead bathed in cool water, he seemed more composed and certainly better groomed than either of them. He looked well kept, a boy of means perhaps, to whom detachment might be a function not only of illness but of superiority.

His first engagement with his surroundings came not with people but with time. He raised his eyes—barely his head at all—to look at the clock on the wall.

"Nearly dawn, isn't it?" he said.

"Yes," Ben answered.

"How many have I had?" As if he had to keep track of the number of seizures.

"A few," Ben said.

"How many?" Insistently.

"Three or four."

Surprisingly, the boy smiled. "I've been away for quite a spell, huh?"

The pun was intentional, and he had probably used it before, Ben thought. He had no vast experience with the ailment, but self-mockery had never been mentioned as one of its phenomena. Embarrassed, the boy was trying to sound aloof from it.

"You've had this diagnosed, I assume," Ben said.

"Oh yes—epilepsy." With studied nonchalance.

"Do you carry anything for it?"

"I don't anymore, no," he said. "I've taken everything. Dilantin, Peganone, Tridione—you prescribe it, I've taken it. It's all poison—I'd rather have the fits. . . . Were you here for all of them?"

"No, only for the last."

"It was a gorilla, wasn't it?"

"Large, yes."

The boy started to get up and was a little unsteady. "Take your time," Ben said. "Don't rush it. Sure you don't want something? I've got some phenobarb."

"Old standby. No, I don't think so," he said with elaborate boredom.

Then, unexpectedly, he became something altogether different. No longer the blasé worldling, indifferent to remedy, he was a little boy, sick in a foreign country, alone and vulnerable. "My name is Mark Achille," he said, as if he expected to be punished for it. "I'm really very grateful, Doctor."

"I'm not a doctor. Ben Coram. This is Yannis Petrides."

It was hardly a time for tourists; he wondered why the kid was coming to Cyprus at such an unsettled moment. He could see Mark realizing they were about to leave him, and the boy's sense of loss. "Could we drop you somewhere—are you going into Limassol?"

"No, Nicosia." Then, quickly, "Is it safe?"

"Not altogether—but there *is* a cease-fire."

"I understand there's a bus that goes to the hotels."

"To some of them. Which one?"

"The Delos." The boy apparently saw Ben's raised eyebrow. "Isn't it any good?"

"Well . . . it's kind of a joint."

"No, it is not," Yannis said. The old man went there for wine and to sit at the outdoor bar. He remembered it from the days when the streetwalkers didn't patronize it. "It is friendly."

It could be rough, too. "How did you happen to choose that one?" Ben asked.

"I haven't much money."

It was a factor. He had an uneasiness about the boy's going there, but then perhaps it would be only a day or so, and someone would join him. "Do you know anybody in Nicosia? If your Greek isn't good, I could call them for you."

"My Greek is excellent," he said with a grin. "And it would be hard to call her."

"Let's try. Where does she live—what's her name?"

"Aphrodite."

The boy was joking, of course. But how uncanny that he had chosen that particular jest, the name on Ben's mind less than an hour ago. Yet, it was not such a coincidence after all; the island was Aphrodite's realm, she was the house goddess, the institutional fantasy, the love lure to snare the myth-hungry tourist.

He threw the flippancy back to the boy. "Is she a relative?"

"Yes, I'm going to dig her up."

There was something sober about it. "In what way?"

"In the most specific way. I'm an archaeologist."

"You are?"

"You don't believe I am?"

Everybody was an archaeologist. He had noticed, when he first came to the Middle East, that every female tourist guide had called herself an archaeologist or a prospective one. Sometimes it was true, but sometimes it was only a catchall phrase for student or part-time shard collector; sometimes it was the subterfuge of a woman who had not yet found herself, or had found herself a whore. In Boston or Los Angeles or New York, an arraigned prostitute might pass herself off as a model or an actress, someone in the arts; here, where the preoccupying art was buried in the past, she was an archaeologist. Men too were archaeologists, hawking particles of illicit pottery, fake scarabs, a bit of copper that had been artificially greened; in their case, archaeology was a fictive word for thief. He wondered what it meant in Mark Achille's case.

"Have you ever dug before?"

"No," the boy said. "But I'm ready for it. I have my master's in archaeology."

It was clearly a lie. He could not have been more than sixteen or seventeen. "You're young for that."

"I'm nineteen."

"With a master's?"

"I'm a genius."

He said it uninflectedly, as a simple fact. The boy might not be lying after all; at least he himself seemed to believe what he was saying. He might damn well *be* a genius, too, announcing it so indifferently, with even a hint of convincing contempt for it. Nor was his genius necessarily inconsonant with his illness. Julius Caesar had epilepsy, so did Dostoevski; and Hercules, an epic model; one or two of them, if they took the snap courses, might satisfy the requirements for a master's degree.

But somehow everything about the young man was awry, shimmering in a shapeless way, like an image under water. "Are you serious about digging for the grave of Aphrodite?"

"Dead serious."

"As a scientist, you know she was a goddess, not human. A fable. A myth."

"So?"

The boy was patronizing him. Ben tried not to show his annoyance. "So you don't actually go digging in the earth for a myth, do you?"

He smiled engagingly. "You have to start somewhere."

"In the earth?"

"You search in any way you know."

He was not patronizing him at all, Ben decided, but taking him into his confidence. Under the engaging smile, there was an unruly thing moving, panic. It passed, however, and he recaptured his air of superiority. Almost. Still, somewhere, a lingering nervousness. Ben thought: He *is* lying, and any instant he'll tell me the truth.

But it was too late. The boy saw the bus arriving. "Is that it?" he asked.

It had to be; there was only one. Mark smiled and nodded once, a second time, unnecessarily. As he got up from the bench, he said that he was grateful. He was not unsteady anymore. He looked around for his suitcase and Yannis brought it to him. It was canvas, badly abraded and none to clean. He lifted it and turned to go.

"By the way," he said, "your hand is bleeding."

Ben looked down at his knuckle. It was skinned raw and wet with blood. "Yes, it is."

"How'd that happen?" the boy asked. "You should do something about it."

The myth . . . you search for it any way you know.

That boy, staying in his mind, a mild irritant at first, was now an infuriation. At his age, what the hell did he know of myth-searching, except in a textbook or two?

But what right had he to be so disdainful of the boy's innocence? He himself, a half generation older, was deluded by an image as hallucinatory as the ancient Aphrodite. He was beguiling himself with a love mirage, making a real woman into a myth. Goddamn it, he said, why am I doing it, why am I appeasing myself with a reverie, a mirage? Any moment, she'll appear again, as naked as my hunger for her, with her skin gleaming in half light, with her breasts in my hands and her tongue quivering, and her legs spread to receive me, and my cock as big as Gargantua, and I'll be dying with wanting her, and thrust, drive, ram, rip through the silken membrane, fuck her home to happiness, and it's only a *dream!* Only a dream, goddamn it, whack my cock and brain off, jack myself off on a myth! *Why don't I make her REAL?*

Why didn't he? Why couldn't he make her materialize again? She could be with him in the flesh, breathing and being breathed upon, with real breasts that could be touched if he dared reach for them, with a mouth that could bring love if he weren't afraid that the lips would once more open in contempt. She might be a tangible presence, someone he could rejoice in with all his senses, and even, if she were willing to talk to him, with some part of his mind, perhaps a part that had not recently been awake. But until he went back to Seismos, until he *dared* to go back, she was a myth.

But maybe, if he did return, she might still be a myth. Even if he got to know her intimately . . . Sometimes, in closest propinquity, a woman vanishes. A man as well. One's self, often. Thinking this way can make everyone disappear, he thought. It was as if the boy had said: You either go in search, you make her come alive, or you let her die, a fantasy.

A vision of Kalya's face appeared to him, Mee Lanh's as well —and again, completing the triad, the fire word trembling in his throat, not uttered. The two of them together—why do they enkindle this raging synergy? he thought. Like plutonium: hold two sticks of the element, one in each hand, at a distance from each other, and nothing happens. Put the sticks together and there is an explosive nuclear madness. How did the Turkish woman and the Vietnamese girl, strangers, a world apart, come to this rendezvous, in a flame? And which of them must he exorcise if he was to extinguish it?

"I'm taking the afternoon off."

Yannis was surprised. "Where do you go?"

He avoided the question. "I'll drive you to Paphos—Nicosia —anywhere you want."

"Where do you go?" the old man repeated.

"None of your business."

"Oh, there." He said nothing about walnuts.

So here he was now, alone and plying his foolhardiness, rushing to another rejection, perhaps, driving like fury westward toward the Temple of Apollo, then north through Pakhna, Omodhos, the heat broiling, en route for the mountains, and Seismos.

Seismos, earthquake village, built upon a fault. It was an absurdity, nobody believed it, but why was the weather always so unseasonable up here, fogged over when it was sunny everywhere else, snow blizzards in July? And why did Ben feel the temblor even before he was within sight of the place? Not temblor, you fool, only trembling, and nothing to do with a seismograph.

He felt exhilarated and a little loony. He was going to see her again! Faster in the old Land-Rover, faster, eighty, ninety, a hundred miles an hour on the beat-up road, head over honkers if he wasn't careful, *disjecta membra,* spray and splay through the windshield, bone bloody confusion, whose spleen is this, whose chitlings, a cat will run off with the medic's bellybone, he was going to see her again! . . . The road was getting rockier now, and the ascent steeper. Incredibly, with drought below, it was raining up here, a dull and misty rain, a warm and sticky wetness. In a little while he saw the faded sign pointing to Seismos. He realized he was still driving with incautious speed, recklessly up windy, twisting roads, and now, for the first time, he felt his foot lighten on the gas pedal as if, the end being in quick reach, he might change his mind and not go the entire distance.

But there it was: The Wine Press—*panta thia pantes*—everything for everybody.

And it was closed. Not closed for a few hours, for the afternoon, but irrevocably closed. A heavy chain was pulled across from the entrance sign to the one marked exit. And hanging from the chain, the rough board with the homemade lettering, *kenos.* What an incongruous word it was—not "closed" or "no admittance," but "empty." And he wondered if the doomed, unhappy place had ever been more than a void.

Gone, then, both of them gone, and his trip had been in vain. He had waited too long, a war intervening, and now, likely, he would never find her. Still, they might have left something on the building—a sign of some sort—giving a new address, a telephone number.

He got out of the cab of the ambulance, stepped over the chain, and started down the dirt and gravel path toward the restaurant. Already—it had been less than a month since he had been here—brambles and catchweeds were taking over. What his mother had called goosegrass, growing in the backyard of a country house they had once rented, now entwined itself around the olive trees and the rank, untended grapevine. He picked his way through it.

Arriving at the raised portico that led to the entrance, he went up the steps to the door. It was locked and there was no note on it, no forwarding message of any kind. The windows, right and left of the door, were shuttered; all he could see through the open slats was blackness. He turned to go.

As he stepped down onto the gravel again, he heard a sound. Stopping, he listened. It was a dullish noise, leaden, as if it came from animation almost given over, yet doggedly steady and rhythmic. Then it ceased.

Not certain what direction it had come from, or even if he had actually heard it, he waited. But it did not occur again.

Retracing his steps, toward the ambulance, he started to feel the dampness through his clothes. What a miserable place, he thought, and what a waste of time and hope.

He heard the sound again.

Turning once more, he cocked his head in one direction, then acutely in another, like a gun dog. In the relatively open space around the taverna, where the sound should have been louder than before, it was inexplicably fainter.

Ben walked faster. He crossed past the restaurant and halfway around it to a place that showed an older than month-long neglect, a thicket. He beat his way into it. No path at all here, not even an overgrown one, only the twisting vine tendrils, the scrub, the swamp-born wild willows and the indecent sword points of spiteful nettles. One of the thorn bristles caught him indecorously by the ear. Hold still, he said, stop struggling with it; he yanked it loose, the wrong direction, and it hurt like murder. Inanely, he laughed at his own complaint. When his sound was over, so was the other. Silence.

For a long while, he remained there, indecisive, annoyed, not knowing which way to go. Just as he was about to give it all up, he heard it again, a swishing noise, clearer, closer.

Ben turned right angle, going toward the lake, deeper into the swampland. He had stopped minding the boggy sump underfoot, didn't seem to notice it any further, just going, stalking the whisper.

But it was no longer a whisper. It was the noise he had originally been conscious of, the repeated thump, the leaden, rhythmic sound. He had not noticed until that instant that the rain had stopped. The mist, on a caprice, had lifted a little, not much, only enough to mitigate the thicket's darkness. And just that quickly, Ben was out of the heavy growth, with an open view of another clearing.

He saw Menas first. The man had his good arm akimbo; his withered one hung lower than Ben remembered it, as if it had become heavier. He was looking into a ditch.

Hearing Ben break through, the Greek turned long enough to fix him in his mind, then muttered something to the person in the trench. Whatever he said didn't seem to make any difference, for the noise continued with no break in rhythm, a shovel sound, spade after spade after spade. When he got to the ditch, Ben could see her.

What she was doing seemed meaningless, demented. There was a slow and steady flow of water into the trough, and she appeared to be fighting it, shoveling slush and earth out of the pit, trying to stay ahead of the flow of wetness. The muck kept wriggling away from her and still she shoveled at the Augean ditch.

She did not seem to notice Ben's arrival. She just kept frantically at it, mindless that she was up to her knees in mud, that her clothes were covered with it, that she was dabbing slime on her forehead when she stopped to brush her straggling hair away. She looked up for an instant and saw him; rather, she turned her sightless eyes on him, perceiving nothing.

"What are you doing?" he shouted at her. Then, when she didn't answer, he turned to the man. "What the hell are you making her do?"

There was a tiny springhouse nearby, a few paces away; it was run down and overgrown with vines. Menas moved toward it. He put his hand on the rubblestone wall and picked at the crumbling mortar as if it were a significant occupation.

Ben pursued him. "What is she doing?"

"She is insane," the man said.

Irrationally, Ben shouted at him. "Why are you letting her do that?"

"I have tried to make her stop."

"I'm going to get her out of there!"

The man's voice stopped him. "Wait. Let her finish."

"Finish what, for Christ sake?"

"A week ago, our child died," he said. "He is buried there."

"Oh, Jesus." But it still made no sense; less, in fact, than the death of a child. "What happened?"

The man was too locked in to answer anything. Then, abruptly, something seemed to give way in him, he was compelled to tell it, to get rid of it.

"We have been getting letters," he said. "Even before the war, we got them. Full of curses and threats. They were in different handwritings, but always Turkish. They called her the Greek's whore. Leave your Greek cripple and go hide yourself, they said, go tie yourself to the bumper of an automobile. Then, the night of the invasion they came and broke the windows, they smashed everything, the furniture, cooking stoves, the child's toys. They tore apart the baby's bed and ripped his clothes off—they left him lying naked on the floor. He was already sick—he has always been a sickly one—and a week ago he died. Last night there was an explosion—a grenade, a bomb, I don't know—and it struck the dam. The wall has not burst, but there is water—it is coming through the earth. . . ." His voice seemed as lame as his arm. "I don't know how this happens. . . . The child's grave will be flooded . . . it will be flooded."

He pointed. "She has dug another grave—you see it?" Ben had not noticed the second mound of dirt. It was on a dry place, higher and closer to the road.

Wretchedly, Menas was muttering to himself. "Such a useless thing . . . to do this for a dead child. What difference? . . . She has lost her wits."

He rubbed his cheek with a slow, rough motion. His gray beard stubble made him seem older than Ben remembered. "Lost her wits," he repeated.

Ben went back to the trench.

The coffin was exposed now, a small thing, bare wood. She started to pull at the handle of it. Mired, it wouldn't budge.

"Oh, Christ," he muttered. He jumped into the grave with her.

"No!" she said.

"I'll help you."

"I don't want any help!" Possessed, she screamed at him. "Get out!"

For an instant, he hesitated. She yanked at the handle, pulled with all her might, made animal sounds in her throat, tugged, struggled, then slipped in the muck. The bathos enraged him, and the sadness and the lunacy.

"Goddamn it!" he said.

He grabbed the other handle and with the strength of his anger he pulled the box a few inches out of the mud.

"Let it go!" she cried. "I don't need anybody—let it go!"

But he kept pulling at it, and in a moment had it halfway up the slope. When she saw he would not listen to her, she took hold of the handle again. With both of them lifting, the coffin was now clear of the wetness, but when she slipped once more, he kept pulling it without her, to the higher ground. Quickly, she clambered to the surface, and together they carried the coffin to the freshly dug grave.

Wildly, as if the race against the water hadn't stopped, she ran back for the shovel. Returning, she would not give it to him when he reached for it, but said no, no, and started to work feverishly with it again. To help her, he kicked at the dirt, cursing it, vehemently pushing piles of it with his feet; and soon Menas did the same.

It was not a deep grave, not nearly as deep as the other, and they filled it rapidly. When the earth was mounded over, she summarily seemed to emerge from her madness; she saw herself, her filthiness.

She said nothing. Leaving them, she made her way to the place where the dam was at its lowest, at the water's edge. There, she started to rid herself of her mucky clothes. Piece by unrecognizable piece, she stripped them off until she was dressed only in the pulpy remnants that still stuck to her. On the water, near the bank where the wild rushes grew, there was an edge of green duckweed. With a motion of her foot she kicked it apart and began to wash herself. She took notice of nobody; washed as if no one were there; bathed all of her in the most intimate detail, making her own privacy. Then, when she was as clean as the corrupt water could make her, she walked into the lake, away from the sludge. She fully submerged herself, rose and stood breast high in the water. Her face was turned away from the men, she looked to the far rim of the crater, to the mist that hung over it. She was as serene, as still as the velvet green duckweed on the water.

With utmost grace, she turned and walked out of the lake. She was clean, she was beautiful, and slimmer than Ben had thought she might be. Her breasts were further apart and the areolas were a faint flush, almost invisible. She walked past them. She did not see either of them, apparently, nor did she take notice of the graves she had dug. Leaving the open space, she entered the thicket.

Ben hurried after her. He could see her threading her way surefootedly through the undergrowth, and he could hear Menas following him. They emerged from the dense growth and came out upon the restaurant clearing just as she was opening one of the back doors of the building, presumably to their living quarters.

Menas was mumbling something to himself. "What?" Ben asked.

"I think she will be willing to leave Seismos now."

"And go where?"

"Who knows? I will go to work somewhere—on a farm, perhaps."

"You'll go without her?"

"Now that the child is dead, she will not want to stay with me."

"What will she do, then? Can she work? Can she cook for someone?"

The Greek smiled grimly. "Who will hire her in these times? A Turk who has been living with a Greek . . ."

"What will she do?" Ben repeated. "What can she do?"

He held his breath. It was going to happen to him. He had wanted it differently, had wanted *her* differently, but any way at all he would take her with him if she would agree to go.

"Will she go with me?" he said quietly.

The man did not seem at all taken aback by the question; on the contrary, he appeared to have expected it. "Ask her," he said.

She was coming outdoors, wearing the same wraparound as he had seen the first time they had met. It was as if the donning of the garment had brought her back to phenomena, to palpable and calculable substance. She saw real objects now, not fixations; she saw people, she saw *him*.

Menas said something to her in Turkish, barely a whisper. She did not answer at once. They looked at one another closely, she and the man she had lived with; the silence was heavy and afflictive. Then she murmured, *"Evet."*

He asked her something else. This time she looked at the American. It took her even longer to answer the Greek's second question. Also, it required more than a single word. When she had finished, she turned to Ben.

"He asked me if I wanted to leave him."

"What did you say?"

"I said yes."

An instant. Then she continued. "He also said you want me to go with you."

"That's right."

She wanted to make sure. "You do want me to go with you?"

"I said yes. . . . Will you?"

She did not respond immediately. Her thoughts seemed not to be on him at all, but only inward; her words, mostly for herself. "I do not care where I go," she said. She turned her gaze outward again, and fixed it upon him. "How much is it worth to you?"

Astonished: "Worth?"

"You buy things. How much am I worth?"

He had an impulse to hit her, but he was morbidly fascinated. "How much do you want?"

"I don't want anything," she said. "But he has been kind to me—I have a debt to him."

"How much of a debt?"

"I thought—five hundred pounds."

In the truck, hidden under the lining of a safety helmet, Ben had hidden more than five hundred pounds, more like a thousand, left over from his casino winnings. The money meant nothing to him, he would have given it all to her in an act of generosity. But not in a purchase.

He was infuriated. She was back to the old insult: the American as buyer. They were both in it, in fact, playing the Yankee for his money, making his wanting of her a matter of cheap commerce, the only thing an American could understand. And they were selling themselves as well, each of them, her especially, because they were both vendors, aliens to one another except as merchants; a money transaction was all they could have together. It was contemptuous and contemptible.

Besides, even as deals go, it was a cheat. The money would be delivered, and then how long would she stay with Ben—a week, a night?

Yet, even a single night . . .

The hell with the money; he hadn't earned it, merely won it; he wouldn't mind losing it. And the hell with pride as well; if he had to buy her, he had to buy her. A night of loving her, whether she loved him or not, would be worth—how much in terms of racing blood that would warm the chilled pride? God, a single night with her, as against never seeing her again—how much in terms of the forestalling of regret?

If only he didn't see the contempt in her eyes.

"No deal," he said.

Walking away, he realized he had gotten what he deserved. She was right. It wasn't Kalya who had started this business of buying and selling a woman. He himself had made an offer, twenty pounds. He didn't know what the hell he was being so self-righteous about. It was simply that the price wasn't right.

And there was something else to be said for her. She wanted the money for Menas—not for herself.

What *did* she want for herself? What would she ever ask for, or hope for? It couldn't be money, it couldn't be an ordinary thing. It would have to be something wonderful, or terrible.

3

The desk clerk in the Delos Hotel wore a glossy brown toupee, a wig really, not a natural hair showing, and what made it notable was that there was dandruff in it. Unpleasant as it was to look at, Mark couldn't take his eyes off the hairpiece as he puzzled the enigma.

The room clerk was measuring the guest as well, his rumpled clothes, his beat-up suitcase, and his youth. "You'll have to pay in advance," he said.

The man had kept Mark waiting, he was surly, and now he was disparaging his honesty. The boy started to see the anger stripes, the longitudinal flashes of light, and knew that if they merged and his mind went to gray, he would have another seizure. So he tried to pull away from it. He told himself how insignificant the clerk and the circumstance were, and he made his voice work evenly and rhythmically, like a slow-swinging pendulum, saying he had no objection to paying for his room in advance, would it be all right to pay in dollars? He needed a victory over the grays right now, needed it badly; the night had been tough with seizures, and he was worn out. The longitudinal lights were fading, the stripes were dimming, but blessedly the grays didn't rush in to take their place. Gone. He had conquered them, and he could have cried with relief.

An hour later he was lying on the bed, relaxed but wakeful. The room was dingy, but he didn't mind; he was still congratulating himself for warding off another mal. He could ward off many more of them, he told himself, if the warnings were consistent. Most epileptics who had advance notice had the same premonitory aura all the time; it was comforting, and you could learn to handle it—sit down, slow down, don't breathe too deeply, pull over to the side of the road. The aura would be like a visitor, and friendly. But his varied too much—the grays had been away for quite a long time; latterly, there was the rush of air, an aura he didn't like, always too quick, it never gave him time.

It was morning and he hadn't had any sleep, unless he counted his absence during the mals. But he could feel himself recovering from fatigue. The sun was coming through the narrow window, lighting up the flowers of the wallpaper. The colors were hideous but the design was interesting, and surprisingly unsimple in its mathematical progressions; a violet every fourth flower, but a daisy every sixth, and the little yellow and blue ones seemingly haphazard. But he knew it couldn't be so, there would have to be a machine-made formula. He could do an algebraic game with them, he thought, set them up in two equations, binomial, x-daisy by y-violet equals, and so forth; or he could do a nonsense game: divide them all by pi, lump them all together, multiply by zero, and come up with nothing. Irrational numbers. He wished he could go back and repeat that course in the calculus of variations; it had been wonderful, math had always been wonderful. How had he ever gotten off into archaeology, dumb fool?

He could see that he wouldn't sleep. He debated whether to unpack. The room was more dreadful now that he could see it so clearly in the light, and it was pervaded by a sickly mildew that seemed an impossible condition in hot summer. He hated the place and was glad he wouldn't stay. Nor had he intended to; he had work to do elsewhere.

Not that he knew where elsewhere was, or how to begin or who might give him his start, or even what questions to ask. But somehow he would dig around and discover something.

Not dig, not literally dig. He had told the medic and the old man a half lie. He was indeed an archaeologist by education, but not by intention—he was not in search of Aphrodite. It was simply an extension of the same lie he had told to win the two-thousand-dollar fellowship that had made the trip possible. *Aphrodite, the Classical Conceit,* he had written on the application form, followed by all the academic gibberish, the thesis gabble-babble that had made the project—pertinent, was their word. Pertinent to what? he wondered. But the paper was unimportant, he could write it anywhere, here or in Greece or in Yonkers. Actually, while his real purpose in coming here had nothing to do with metaphysical research on a love goddess, he would like nothing better than to go running in the fields of old folk tales, to descend into the dark caves of old religions, to look for potsherds of the past, and reassemble shadows. Aphrodite, born in the sea—what a game it would be to pretend he was going in search of her, going to submerge himself down the fathoms of the deep Mediterranean waters, then float upward with her, moist with the discovery of the deity of passion. I've come up, he would say as a digger might dream of saying, with a shard of seashell which proves conclusively that on this shore the goddess lived and loved. What a ridiculous thing, an adolescent's fancy, what a soft thing it was.

Anger was a hard thing. Anger was a fact: you could trust it. It was the metal armature which kept him erect, without which he would be a falling form. And the falling sickness was the worst of him.

He would have to get to the task, then, right away.

He didn't bother to unpack his clothes, only his toilet articles. He washed his face, combed his hair, brushed his teeth, and tried to gargle away the odor of last night. He looked at his image in the mirror and instructed himself: Be vain. He had a right to be. He had a strong face. He wished his features were not so delicately formed; they made him seem younger than his nineteen years, as young as he often felt himself to be. But his eyes made up for it— they were black and angrily black-browed, full of fury, like the Eumenides. He didn't actually like the way he looked—he wasn't vain, far from it—and when he was away from a looking glass he couldn't visualize any feature of his face. He hadn't any.

Because enclosures made him nervous, he didn't take the elevator downstairs. It was still early when he got outdoors, but already at the sidewalk cafe coffee was being served. He would not sit down at once, he decided, but walk a little. This was the inner town of Nicosia, the ancient place of narrow, twisting passageways, crooked and cobblestoned. Without seeking it, he came upon a wider thoroughfare, Regaena Street—the place of *pornia kai akatharsia,* of prostitution and putridity. It didn't look as whorish and filthy as the Athenian guidebook had described it, only drab and noisy. Already, this early in the morning, the bouzouki-gone-rock ruptured the eardrums. Two blind men competed, across the street from each other, hysterically hawking wares—one sold artificial flowers; the other, incense. A small boy peed in the drinking fountain. A sweet-faced old woman sold sesame rolls. Mark bought two of them, which she wrapped in a piece of brown paper, the ends of which she twisted.

It puzzled him that he saw no signs of the war. Perhaps the truce was not so uneasy as the medic had suggested.

Back at the outdoor cafe of the Delos Hotel, Mark untwisted the parcel of rolls, started to eat one, and ordered coffee, *metrio*. When it arrived, he drank the cool water that came with it, rubbed the lemon rind on his sesame roll as he saw someone else do, and drank the strong, deep coffee.

At the next table a middle-aged woman was recuperating from a night of trade. "I hear they're still fighting in the north," he said in Greek. "Is that true?"

The streetwalker stared at him blankly. She had cold sores around her mouth and perhaps opening her lips was painful; clearly, she didn't care to talk. She answered him in English, apparently not wanting to dignify his foreign-accented Greek. "The subject does not interest," she said.

He couldn't believe that the subject didn't interest her, and felt that in some way he hadn't made it clear how sympathetic he was to the Greeks. He told her that he was of Greek extraction himself, and he commiserated with the refugees from Kyrenia. "Are there many of them here?" he asked.

She told him to go masturbate.

He finished his coffee, walked the streets again, went to a bank and got pounds for his dollars, bought some dental floss. Toward ten o'clock, he stopped at a pushcart that sold nuts, raisins, and a variety of beans. Not knowing the nuts which were immediately edible from the beans which were inedible until cooked, he bit into one of the latter and nearly broke a tooth. The old vendor didn't laugh but gave him elaborate sympathy, apologized for not having warned a visitor, and offered reparations of nameless sorts.

"Is it possible to go to the Turkish quarter?" Mark asked.

The vendor was very still. He looked at the American with bewilderment. Mark couldn't tell what he saw in the man's face—disbelief or hostility, or plain fright.

"No, it is not possible," the Greek said.

As the morning wore on, the boy tried to ask subtler questions but he got no friendlier answers. There was something in every encounter that he could not understand. It perplexed him why people shuffled away from a discussion of the war as if it hadn't happened. Midmorning, he understood what nobody had told him, what the

English-language newspapers had not described in any detail. He hadn't realized that he was right in the midst of the destruction.

The battle border, the Green Line, was only a half mile from the hotel. The barricade was made of barbed wire and oil drums and sandbags, some of which were still bloodstained. On both sides of the makeshift impediment there were the signs of the Turkish bombing. Two buildings were a heap of rubble; a number of others had been shelled and strafed; nearly all were blind of windows. And last night a few mortars had come over; this morning, they were still digging for the dead.

On this side, three Greek soldiers paraded, passing one another intermittently.

On the other side, nobody was in sight.

Then, beyond the barricade, he saw a gray-green truck arrive. It stopped and a half-dozen soldiers got out. He was close enough to hear their Turkish voices. One of them deployed the others. They didn't seem to notice anybody on this side of the barricade; it was as if nobody were there.

If Mark had come to find Turks, he had found them. There they were.

He began to tremble.

But there was no aura, he was pleased to note; it was ordinary trembling, fear or rage. He could handle it.

He went back to the Delos outdoor cafe for lunch, and just as he had finished and was paying his check, he saw the old man enter. For an instant he was not sure it was Yannis, the medic's assistant; his perceptions had not been all that clear last night. But when he heard him ordering wine in the good-humored voice that was half chuckle and half cackle, he was certain it was the man.

Mark considered whether to approach him. He went to the men's room, tried to imagine how the old fellow might be of help, then walked slowly to Yannis's table. The Greek had a dish of olives and white radishes before him, and he was drinking retsina. Mark could smell the wine, the turpentiny tang of pine resin, even before he sat down.

"Have olives," the old man invited. "Also radishes, but not retsina. It is no good for you."

"I drink wine occasionally," the epileptic said.

"Is not wise. The devils will fight."

"I have no devils."

"The wine devils, I mean," the old man said quickly.

It wasn't what the old man meant, but Mark let it pass. "Yesterday—you and the ambulance man—I lied to you."

"You are not nineteen."

"Yes, I am."

"What, then?" He guessed again. "You are not an *archaeologos?*"

"I'm that too." The boy smiled sheepishly. "But I'm not here to dig up Aphrodite."

"Good—she will be happy to hear it. . . . What you are here to do?"

"Join the army."

The old man finished an olive, deposited the pit, and took a sip of wine. "Which army? There are many of them now. We have the National Guard and the National Police, the United Nations has send us Danes and Swedish and—"

"The Greeks, of course—the Cypriots."

"Ah—that is nice," he said, with studied blandness. "But perhaps the army will not take you—you are American."

"My mother was Greek—she was a Cypriot. I was adopted by Greeks. My name is not really Mark Achille—it's Markos Achillides. I like the original name better—I don't know why they changed it. People go to America, they do stupid things."

"Names . . ." the old man said, half to himself, as if he was bored with differences. "Why do you want to join the army?"

I must be careful how my voice sounds when I say this, Mark warned himself. Strike a balance between casualness and anger. "To kill Turks," he said.

The radish the old man was eating was crisp; it crunched in his mouth. He finished chewing. "You miss your chance. Where were you a few weeks ago?"

"The minute I heard about the war, I was on my way. But the Nicosia airport was closed, and so were the ports. Nothing could get in. I even tried to get here by way of Turkey—but no luck. And before I knew it, the war was over."

"If we know you are coming, we would wait."

Mark cautioned himself not to hear the sarcasm, and certainly not to take offense. "In a way, you did wait. I hear the war's not over."

"It is over."

"Not in the north."

"You cannot get to the north."

"I hear there are guerrillas. . . . Will you help me?"

"Me? Go home."

"I can't go home! I have to do it!"

The old Greek let the vibration of the boy's intensity die away. Quietly: "Why you want to kill Turks?"

"I told you—my mother was Greek."

"So? She sent you on a little errand, maybe? 'Go buy a loaf of bread and kill some Turks'?"

"She's dead."

Bitingly: "My mother is dead too. Christos!"

The old man was angry and Mark didn't know why. He would have thought an old Cypriot Greek would have applauded his sentiment and, in typical home-style fashion, taken him to his bosom. Instead, this mordant ridicule. He started to get up and go.

"Wait a minute, young man." Mark hesitated. "Sit down—I am sorry I show ugly teeth with you. I see you are a good boy—maybe with a good heart. Maybe you are angry, but we do not need angry people here—is a truce now—we are trying not to be angry. So go home. Your home is five thousand miles away. These Turks—any Turks—they cannot be a matter of life and death to you."

"Of sanity and insanity."

Damn it: he wished he hadn't said the melodramatic words. He had been doing it fairly well until now, speaking more lightly than he felt. And now the old man would mock him again, sneer at his schoolboy histrionics. Or, worse, he would think him a weirdo, a raving crackpot who should be tied up and packed away safely in absorbent cotton. But, surprisingly, the old man was looking at him soberly, as if surprised by the boy's maturity.

"Is this real talk or book talk?" Yannis said.

How could he prove to him how real it was? "I'm going to try to get up north—even if I have to do it by myself."

"You will kill yourself."

Quietly. "Not if you help me."

Ruefully, the old man looked away. "Everybody . . ." he said heavily. Then he repeated the word as if to bemoan a world gone lunatic.

"The army will not take you, boy," Yannis said. "But . . ."

Mark was totally still. Let the old man talk himself into it, he thought.

"I will tell you the name of a man," Yannis started. "He is a . . . patriot. You will have to take a bus to go there, then to walk a little something—two miles, maybe three. It is a small village—Lythia. The man's name is Manolis Falkos. You will tell him I sent you—old Yannis Petrides, from Paphos."

"Who is he?"

"He is a schoolteacher. An educated man—like you. He says what you say—sanity or insanity." Then, dispiritedly to himself: "He has found a good reason for killing people."

Mark thanked him. Then, tentatively: "Could I have a little wine?"

"Help yourself," the old man said.

Early the following morning, on the bus to Lythia, Mark wondered if he might at last be coming to his journey's end. A journey that had begun, in a figurative sense, when he was nine years old.

On his ninth birthday, he had tried to brain his older brother with a brick. He held the thing in his hand and he hit Renos not once, not twice, but until the blood came. When he saw it coursing down his brother's face, he got frightened and ran.

Hours later, he was on a grass incline alongside the Saw Mill River Parkway, watching the cars go by, dividing the numbers of one license plate by the numbers of another, and crying. He knew he could not go home. His father would beat him, he had no doubt of it. Even if his mother interceded, which she would do weakly, the punishment would happen. His father would start striking him first with an open hand, then, if Mark didn't cry, with a fist until he did.

Perhaps Renos had told him the truth, perhaps he *was* adopted. It would account for the fact that his father loved Renos and not him. Until now, Mark had been inclined to think that his father's hatred of him had been his own fault—he had been mean to the man. The boy was the brightest in the family—a prodigy, he was called—and his father, the most stupid. There was nothing Mark despised as he did stupidity; it made him feel unwashed. Almost from the moment he could read, he had fought the bullhead, mocking the slowness of his mind and the lumpish way he talked.

The hatred had gone both ways. And now, looking back, he realized there was an even deeper reason for his father's rage against him: the man could not even take genetic credit for the boy's intelligence; the only blood they had between them was bad.

Weighing it all, Mark would have wanted it otherwise. He'd settle for being not so smart, and better loved. Even by them.

They were not such awful people, his so-called parents. On the contrary, they were decent, well-meaning American Greeks—hard-working, both of them. They went to their jobs early and came home late. His father worked at a stamping machine in his uncle's imitation-leather factory, and his mother worked there too, as a bookkeeper. They lived in a comfortable little row house in Yonkers, and ate clean, filling food—moussaka too often, Mark thought; it was a food he didn't like—hot, warm, or cold, it had no suitable temperature. . . . But they were all right, his parents, not bad at all. If only . . .

He sat on the grassy incline and it was getting dark, and he was cold and miserable. Sooner or later there wouldn't be light enough to make out the numbers on the license plates, and there would be nothing left to count, not even that comfort, and he would have to start making numbers in his mind, but sometimes he lost track of what he was doing.

Adopted? Maybe Renos had lied. Maybe, when he got home, he could find out the truth from his mother, if he could talk to her alone. But generally his father was there, and from him Mark only got answers that gave him pain. "Face the fact," his father generally began every answer. It was a thick, pulpy cudgel with which he beat Mark on the head until it ached.

When he got home, his father did beat him, literally. You made Renos bleed, he said, and I won't stop until *you* do. Stop, his mother said, please stop.

Later that night, his Uncle Lexi came over, and they told him the truth.

"You'll have to face the fact, what Renos told you," his father said. "You're not our child."

"We would have had you if we could," his mother hastily added. "But when Renos was born the doctor said: no more. I couldn't have any more, I wasn't happy. Then your uncle came back from Cyprus. He said he found you there."

"I did—I found you there." Lexi nodded.

"You were only about a year old," she went on. "You were

very pretty—like a little girl. I wanted you right away." Then, with quick reassurance: "So did your father—honest—we both wanted you."

"That's true," Lexi said, but his father said nothing.

"We don't know exactly where you came from," the woman murmured.

His father seemed more certain. "Your mother was a Greek and your father was a Turk. Right, Lexi?"

"Yes—right." His uncle was drinking raisin brandy. He put the glass down. "What we're telling you is absolutely true."

"The rest of it might not be true," his foster father said.

"Then don't tell it, Frankos." She looked alarmed. "Don't tell it."

"We have to tell it," he insisted. "You don't tell him half and let him imagine the other half. He has to face the fact. Right, Lexi?"

Lexi said right, and went on with it. "It was the time of the disturbances. People were hurting each other. Who knows what stories were true, but the Turks—this part *is* true—the Turks were terrible."

"Don't tell it," she said.

"Terrible," Lexi continued. "Your real mother, being a Greek, should not have married your father. He was a brutal man, but he was a Turk—how could he help himself, what else could he be? They don't really know what happened—somebody said she was trying to run away from him—and he ran after her—and he—"

"Don't tell it," she pleaded.

"—cut her breasts off," his father said.

"Jesus, Frankos, did you have to say that?" Lexi asked.

"We said we'd tell him the truth."

"You could have said he killed her, just he killed her."

Mark's mother was trembling. "Greeks are brutal too—telling that to a nine-year-old."

"Nine years is not too young to hate the Turks," his father said.

His uncle smiled sadly. He didn't agree with his brother on everything, but agreed on that point.

A strange thing happened to Mark after they told him: he didn't feel a thing. They were looking at him very closely, watching, being especially gentle with the boy; even his father, gentle.

But in his mind Mark felt it wasn't necessary, this extra solicitude, he didn't need it.

He went right to bed. He lay in the dark, and the only aftermath of what they told him was a lightening sense of relief. He could hate his foster father if he wanted to. They were not related, the man had never been kind to him, he clearly despised the adopted boy because half of him was Turk, and none of him belonged to Frankos, who had never wanted him in the first place. But the thing that puzzled the boy was that he had no rancor against the man. He had been told to hate the Turks and, for some reason he could not understand, it was easier to do that than to hate the man who had been cruel to him. It was certainly easier to hate someone outside the house than someone in it; life with the foster father would have been insufferable without a real father to despise.

About a month later, in school one afternoon, he had his first attack of epilepsy. He thought, after the seizure was over, that he had simply gone away somewhere, on a trip, far from Yonkers, on a vacation.

He had a number of attacks in the next few months and each of them gave him the same feeling of having gone to a vague and distant hinterland, which he took to calling No Place. It was not an uncomfortable bourn to visit. It was, in fact, rather nice and easygoing. You didn't have to carry to it any unnecessary baggage of remembrance, there were no responsibilities in it, no school to attend, no homework, chores, relatives. It was only on the return that something was vaguely dreadful. He felt sleepy and sad, and wanted to weep and seemed helplessly to have forgotten how to do it. He had no way to describe the stillness, the silent awfulness of it, until much later, after many attacks, and then he accepted an imprecise description of it: it was incurable loneliness.

Sometimes he needed to ascribe this feeling, not to the seizures, but to the fact that he had no parents. Except that the illusion that he *had* parents had never made him feel less alone. He couldn't recall a single conversation with them in which anyone had ever tried to discover what someone else was saying.

They had a language problem. His foster parents spoke three languages: Yonkers English, Macedonian Greek, and Money. Their English, since they had immigrated when they were in their twenties, was still accented and unsure; their Greek they were rapidly forgetting. The language in which they were comfortable was

Money; its parts of speech were intelligible, its syntax was reliable. When all other forms of communication caused mayhems of family misunderstanding, Money was dependably unambiguous. And it could be spoken anywhere—the lingua franca of the world, better than Esperanto.

One day, a few months after Mark had been told that he had no parents, he pointed out that Money was rapidly becoming his father's only tongue, to which the man had retorted, "Do you have a better one?"

No, not better, Mark thought, but a secret one of my own. It was a language called Skipping. It got him into trouble.

The first time he discovered he had a talent for it, he was punished as if he had done something lewd. He was working away in the schoolroom, doing an arithmetic test, a problem in multiplication. Even considering that he was in the accelerated section, the problem was difficult—a five-figure number to be multiplied by a four-figure number. The process involved four steps in multiplication and one in addition. Mark resorted to Skipping—he eliminated all the steps and simply wrote down the sum total: 148,058,476.

The teacher, seeing no sign of any calculations, no penciled scribblings on the margins of the page, asked how he had arrived at the accurate result. He told her by Skipping. She was in no mood for impertinence; she pursued the question. Since he gave her a no more convincing answer, she was certain he had cribbed the number off the next boy's page, where all calculations were dutifully indicated. Mark insisted he had not cheated, had no need to cheat—it was more a blow to his vanity than to his honesty. When she called him a little liar, he referred to her lack of intelligence and her pimples. She lost her temper and thwacked him, in a cloud of powdered chalk, with a board eraser.

That night his father hit him again. "You cheated, yes?"

"No."

"Then how did you make the answer?"

"By using zero."

"Zero is nothing—how did you do it?"

"By zero."

"Zero is *kaka!*"

"It's not *kaka*—it's the most important number in the book!"

"It's nothing!"

"It's nothing and it's the end of nothing!" With a flare for rhapsody, "It's a poem!"

"A poem is a lie! How did you do it?"

Mark didn't know and couldn't tell, and just as his father raised an arm to strike him, the boy struck first. He punched the man, he kicked him, he scratched at his face with his nails. His foster parent started to strike back. Only one blow, however, which Mark did not feel; he fell to the floor in a writhing fit.

The following day his mother, not angry at Mark or her husband, but at the boy's teacher, went to see the principal. There ensued, then, a barrage of tests which revealed an I.Q. incalculably above 200, an exceptional facility with space and number, and even, surprisingly, with language.

At the age of ten Mark was in high school. The day he arrived, a boy in the geometry class asked how he had made it at such a young age. Mark replied: by Skipping.

In the next few years, he became a curiosity of the medical profession. Undoubtedly a child genius, the crucial question was: What relationship did his seizures have to his mental brilliance? Were his fits truly epileptic, an explosion of neurons in the brain, or were they a personality derangement, or a toxemia perhaps, or a disorder brought on by low blood sugar or some other metabolic imbalance? Or could his ailment be the neurosis of a boy traumatized by hearing how his mother had been brutalized?

He went to any number of doctors in any number of clinics. For all three months of a summer vacation, in a research center in Syracuse, he was assayed and groped and tested, he was punctured and spine-tapped and force-fed and peed, he was X-rayed and brain-scanned and encephalographed. In the fall, he was cycloplaned and made to sleep in unnatural positions; he was brain-shocked twice and Rorschached often. For four years he went to a psychotherapy clinic in the Bronx.

He ate a billion pills; nearly all, it seemed, ended with -arbital or -uximide; he hated the names of them. And there were any number of side effects—nausea, dizziness, drowsiness, fatigue, skin rash, blurred vision—and the total absence of libido.

The last, since he was now approaching sixteen, was a matter of some curiosity to the medicos. "Anything going on down there?" one of them asked.

Mark was getting bored with variations on the theme. He pretended not to understand. "You mean am I peeing?" he asked.

"No, I mean any trouble. Getting it up."

"No trouble. But not up."

The medic wrote it down.

The bustle and bother in Mark's life became too much and he started eliminating things. Though he kept going to his therapy sessions, he discontinued his visits to clinics and research laboratories. One day, just as he was about to take a pill called diamsuximidophenoprimarbital, he became violently offended by the medical blabber and threw the unpronounceable horror into the john. He flushed all his other pills after it, and emptied the medicine chest of all its side-effect tormentors. Three days later, at the age of sixteen, for the first time in his life, he had a first-class, full-fledged erection.

What a wonder it was, what a magnificence! He was tempted to run from his bedroom and wave the object at all and sundry, and cry out exaltedly: Look-a-*me,* look-a-*this,* look at The Great Agog!

It was indeed a marvel to behold. It suggested to him such an illimitable promise of pleasure that he didn't know what to do with it. Masturbation was out of the question, because too soon it would be gone. Yet, he could not make an *objet* of it, a museum piece, he couldn't put it under glass. So he talked to it quietly, as one might to a pal. Thereafter, it was with him nearly always, it was his alter ego. Although he never brought it to climax—why make an issue of it?—he consorted with it in a number of ways. Sometimes it was an affectionate creature that only wanted fondling; sometimes it was a talented listener to whom he rendered his observations about sums and substances, light and shade, and the way of the world; occasionally, it was a lonely thing that needed kindness and understanding, like a forlorn child or a puppy that had been abused. He tried not to think of it in connection with a female, although at times it was difficult to disassociate the two. One night when he couldn't avoid its rapport with the subject, it came and went. It was joy and pleasure and, most of all, an ecstatic mischief—and he thought, with delight in the aptness, that he had pulled a trick on the world. From that time onward, he pulled it often.

His whole life became happier. Until now he had been an isolated child—living alone, thinking alone, playing alone; now, playing with himself took on a felicitously double meaning. It was all pure delight; he had no shame about it, none whatever; on the contrary, he felt he had found an equitable compensation for his malady, as if boys who had no such ailment weren't similarly accommodated.

He had only one regret about his newfound pastime: that he hadn't come upon it sooner. It was all those damn drugs. And now that he was off them—and onto his penis—he realized that his seizures were becoming more moderate. They were lessening, in fact; in the last six months, approaching his seventeenth birthday, he had had only one grand mal. Blissfully, he looked forward to his complete recovery, and he laid the credit for his convalescence to his cock.

And to Amélie Françoisette.

A lusciously rounded black Haitian woman in her late twenties, she was a psychotherapist at a social welfare agency in the Bronx. Within five minutes of their first meeting, she told him she was a Wellesley graduate, but New England had done nothing to chill the warmth that radiated from her mouth, her breath, her skin. She was all curves, all continuously yielding festoons and loops and ellipses; her breasts were globular. He never missed a session with her. Almost as much as gazing at her bosom, Mark loved listening to her voice. Haitian-accented, it was mellifluous, like honey and ripe guava, and came melting off the tongue. He imagined her words licking him with sweetness, like liquefied caramels.

Although he never touched her, she was always touching him. She comforted him with pattings on the hand and caresses on the cheek. If a lock of his hair fell in his eyes, she smoothed it gently in place and touched the newly naked skin as if she had uncovered a baby sleeping. If he said something she disapproved of, she put her fingertips on his lips.

In his weekly ninety minutes with her, he had a perpetual erection. He didn't mind having it while he was sitting down; in fact, he always looked forward to its companionable arrival. But departure from the room was always a torment of embarrassment. How to get away without her catching sight of it?

He invented all sorts of ruses and dissimulations for distracting her. What's that, out the window? he would yelp—the Goodyear blimp? Do you smell smoke? Is that a cockroach? As she would look up or down or out or under, he would rearrange his doodle, shove it down his pant leg, and scramble for the door. At exit time his cock was such a real nuisance to him that he thought, occasionally, of tying or strapping it. Drastic measures, he realized, but temperate ones—get down!—had availed him nothing. Still, it was an exquisite anguish.

Almost as delightful as his fantasies. His sleeping images of Amélie Françoisette were, he believed, the ultimate *raison d'être* of all dreams. He would see her naked, often, but never totally so; always there would be one breast discreetly covered, or a buttock behind veils; and only once did he allow himself a glancing glimpse of pubic hair. Something told him, something out of some No Place in his mind, told him not to go too far, or he would rue it. So he tried to monitor his dreams, tried to avoid seeing her altogether in the nude; and when awake, masturbating with her image before his eyes, he rationed how much of her he saw, only a curve here, an arc of softness there; the rest of her was all hiatus.

One night he could not help himself. As his penis enlarged, as his hand tried to hold it back from emission too soon, the whole scene of the woman came to him, nothing veiled, everything available to all his senses, breast, buttock, hair, quivering flesh and glowing skin, all there, all his.

"What you got there, big mon?" she said in the fantasy. "Show me what the big mon got."

He showed her. She came nearer and studied his parts, close at hand. "Somebody cut him, yes?" she said.

"I've been circumcised."

"Ah."

With a pang, he realized that even in fantasy she didn't like circumcised men. It couldn't have been anti-Semitism, because she knew he wasn't Jewish; it was simply a slur on the reduced dimension. "I'm sorry," he said.

"It's not your fault. What can you do—put it back?"

"If I could . . ."

"No. Maybe hard will make up for little. Let me feel." She reached and held him. "Hard as a policeman," she said.

It was apparently her highest encomium and, haughty of cock, he was ready for anything. She stood there, in the middle of his trance, with her arms spread wide, her palms turned upward as if she carried the Eastern Hemisphere in her left hand and the Western in her right, and her breasts were as huge as the hemispheres. Before he knew what he was doing, he had dashed her onto the deep velvet carpet of his mind, and was onto one of her breasts with his hand and the other with his mouth. Her nipple was huge and purple, like a damson plum. He sucked and sucked at it, the fruit juice flowing into his mouth and out of it.

He felt her hand on him, somewhere, playing with some part of him he didn't know he had. "Don't waste yourself on titty, bebby," she said, "or you'll wet the world. Come in out of danger, bebby—come inside me, don't catch cold."

He did as he was told, felt how long the passage was, how short, kept measuring it with his penis, back and forth for size, for ecstasy, for pain, for all the joys and agonies he had ever dreamed of, for all the promises her body had made to him, on which it now made good.

Then she was gone. The fantasy having faded, he lay in his proud exhaustion and wondered if the real Amélie could ever be as fabulous as he had dreamed her. He wondered, too, if he could be.

In the next six months of fantasy with Amélie, he didn't have a single attack. Since his first convulsion at the age of nine, this was the longest period he had ever been totally free of them. I've become well, he started to tell himself, I've recovered from my illness. The seizures have all gone, all—the mals great and small, the terrifying auras, the grays, the cold clutchings, the icy drafts of wind—and the loneliness I thought incurable—all a horror of the past. I've routed my sickness! Love and lovemaking have made me well!

Then, things got even better. Instead of the fantasy woman, he found a real one. Until now he had met nobody with whom he could, in actuality, fall in love; or, to be more candid with himself, nobody who might fall in love with an epileptic. But now, as he saw himself coming out of his illness, he entered a blessedly new phase of his life. For the first time, he began to look at girls and actually see them. It was as if they had hitherto been hiding from him, wearing masks or yashmaks to conceal themselves, and they had now stripped away all their coverings and were exposed, baring their loveliness to him. And how beautiful they were! Then it occurred to him, like a bright and unexpected meaning one discovers in the dictionary, that they were uncovering themselves because, for the first time in his timid existence, so was he!

He became confident. He began to have trust not only in his brain but in his physical person. Formerly, his habitual gait had been a slinking from one place to another, as if to escape apprehension. Now he let himself be seen; in fact, he exhibited himself a little, cutting a slow swagger, with his pelvis slightly in advance of the rest of him. One day, as he was strutting along a college pathway, he met a girl who stopped to talk, or, rather, to accost. "You're cocksure of yourself, aren't you?" she asked. "You use words well," he answered, and went to bed with her.

He had just entered Columbia to do his master's work, and in a very short time after his first meeting with her—Lissa—he knew he was in love. The way he knew it was that she was not particularly beautiful. On the contrary, to get right down to it, she was commonplace-looking. All that was special about her derived from her fragility. She was as tall as a filament of glass and moved without bending, as if afraid to shatter. Outdoors, when they walked together, Lissa never raised her voice above the noise of the traffic, yet her softest utterance murmured its way through the hubbub, and he could hear every syllable she spoke. She was moderately talented, a competent pianist who was going to be a composer, until she wrote a sheaf of poems, two of which got printed; then she knew that forever afterward she would be trapped in words.

He loved her words, everything about her. She was just as enthralled as he was, and said that keeping up with his mind was a soaring from flash to flash, like flying a trapeze. Falling in love had been very quick, very simple; they turned a corner and they were there. They made a quivering resonance together—with music, with numbers, with the beauty of a world that was so tremulous that they dared to touch it only with their fingertips. Everything they did was delicate, their talk, their silences, their lovemaking, as if life was at its best in hesitation. They made an effort not to talk of mundane things; they behaved as if neither of them ever had to pare toenails; they tried not to catch each other eating.

Mark didn't tell her that he had been an epileptic. He started to do so once, but she seemed so beautiful to him, and it was so ugly. Maybe, he rationalized, there might never be a need to tell her; he had already come nearly a full year without an attack. But, facing the inevitable, he knew he couldn't keep it from her forever; sooner or later, he would have to reveal it. He would wait, he at last decided, until the full year of freedom from seizure had been achieved. Then, it would be like relating a childhood ailment, over and done with, and to be forgotten. Meanwhile . . . happiness.

One night they went to a piano recital at Carnegie Hall. While waiting for the music to start, she quoted a line from a poem she couldn't identify, he scoured about for John Donne's name and found it, she kissed his wet raincoat, he said her eyelids were moths, she said he smelled of quince. The recital, whether it was or not, was elegant. When it was over, they reached under their seats for their raincoats, found everything, handbag, programs, brief-case, umbrella, but couldn't find her hat. They were sitting in the first row of the fourth gallery, and she remembered putting her rain cap on the balcony rail. It must have dropped below, he said, onto a higher-priced head. They giggled and hurried down the stairs to retrieve it.

As they got halfway down, he felt a chilly draft.

They recovered her hat from an usher and started toward the exit door and Fifty-seventh Street. In the middle of the lobby, with the crowd pressing on every side of him, there was an empty space everywhere. He said, Oh God.

There were only a few steps that led down to the pavement; he was sure he could get down them. He saw the bus, the taxi, the flash of lights, the grays.

How much later it was he didn't know. The crowds were gone. He was sitting on one of the steps of Carnegie Hall. The rain had stopped but the wet streets rippled with lights. He had the thought: The ripples aren't mine, they're real. A policeman was looking down at him. An elderly man was sitting beside him.

Lissa was not there.

"Are you all right?" the policeman asked.

It was always the same question, always the same answer. "Yes."

They talked about names and people to phone, and did he knew where he lived? Yes, he knew. The elderly man, whether truthfully or not, declared that he was going Mark's way, and would drop him at the university dormitory. Which he did.

"Do you think you can manage?" he said as Mark fiddled with his key.

"Yes—fine. And I do thank you—very much."

The man nodded, successfully effected a smile, and departed.

Mark looked at his dormitory room and, small as it was, it was more space than he seemed capable of filling. As the minutes wore on, he felt himself becoming less and less. He was frightened. He was cold. The incurable loneliness had not been cured.

The phone rang. Are you all right? she said. Are you sure you're all right? Yes, okay, don't worry, he replied. She was crying. She was ashamed, she said, for running away, she wanted to die of shame. She had panicked, gone completely berserk, run, run, wanted to die of shame, die. Don't worry, he responded, please don't worry. She couldn't stop crying. Why didn't you tell me? she kept saying, why didn't you tell me? He wondered whether the question signified that if she had known she would not have become involved with him, or if she had known, she would not have abandoned him tonight. He didn't ask. Crying. Don't worry, he repeated.

After that night he saw her a number of times, but nothing was the same. Soon they started breaking dates with each other, always with legitimate excuses, exams, parents, overdue papers. One day, entering Butler Library, they met by accident and he realized he had not seen her in over three weeks; the next time, months later, he saw her at a five-and-ten-cent store, a few counters away, and they waved at each other. She seemed vaguely like someone he had known.

During that semester, things started to slip away from him. While still an undergraduate, he had given up working in mathematics. His talent in "quantitation," as he derogatively called it, was too easy, nothing more than a lucky knack he had been born with, it was sleight of mind. He looked upon it as an eccentricity, and God knows there was enough that was weird about him, he thought, so he got away from the embarrassment of it and went into more serious studies—philosophy first, then archaeology. Now, in graduate school, doing his master's in archaeology, he wondered if he hadn't made a mistake. He longed for the clean security of numbers, and the promises they kept, feeling he had strayed too far from home. So he started, as a hobby, to go back to them. And a terrible thing had happened: they no longer gave him the certainty he remembered, they were not as amenable to him as they used to be, they didn't come to him intuitively, he had to "work them up." Even his grasp of principles was not as secure as it had been; sometimes he lost the point of a simple axiom, and he thought wryly: All my numbers are irrational. There was a dread in this.

Then there was anger.

His seizures became worse. One month there were twenty of them, four grand mals on a single Sunday afternoon. He hardly slept. His appetite dwindled and he became very thin. In order not to be too afraid, he started—consciously—to make himself more and more angry, he wasn't sure at what. Mornings, he would go up into the library stacks and stay as long as he could. He would hide himself in his carrel and hope that if he had a seizure nobody would notice. And if he saw one coming, he would try not to cry out, not to make that bird sound. Occasionally, just as he was about to have an attack, he would imagine the outcries of the kids in grammar school—Oh look, Mark is having a fit!

Finally, when things became unbearable, he went back to the clinics. He heard the palaver all over again: A human being has over ten billion neurons in the central nervous system, and if only six or eight of them go haywire, a seizure can happen. Or: It's not behavioral, it's physiological—cerebral cortex—abnormal electrical discharges. Bloodstream, bloodlines . . .

Lies.

He knew, no matter how many tests they gave him, no matter how many blood samples they took, that he had never had a seizure until shortly after he had learned how his real mother had been killed.

One of the doctors said Mark should make a list. There are certain seizure triggers, the man reminded him, that set off attacks. They act like agitators and should be avoided. For example, some patients are set off by a sound of a certain galvanizing pitch, others turn dizzy at great heights; some fits are induced by offensive foods, and alcohol can be a dangerous incitement. He gave the patient a sheet of paper and told him to list anything that might be likely to provoke him into seizure. Mark wrote only one item:

Breasts.

That too was a lie, Mark knew. He had never been set off by the sight or thought of any kind of breast, beautiful or bleeding. Then why had he listed it?

I don't know what I'm thinking anymore, he said. I don't know who I am, I'm a rumor of myself, an unfounded rumor, totally disputable, all contradiction, a brain-damaged genius, a realist mathematician who used to get his results by fantasizing. I'm all abrasion, broken glass, all rage. But what can I rage at, except myself?

He got an important clue. He hadn't as yet selected the subject of his master's thesis. He came upon his topic—he would have sworn it happened this way, impossible as it seemed—in the midst of a petit mal. The following day he told a panel of three professors that, with their approval, he would like to do his thesis on the title: *Troy: Pre-Homeric Ilium and the Greco-Turkish Rages.*

The professors all expressed their doubts. One of them said: What will your sources be, your authorities, who's to bear witness? The second said: Who's to judge it? The third: Rages? A bit on the subjective side, isn't it?

But Mark was a favorite, and they allowed him to go ahead.

Small facts make large legends. Adduce a bit of history to an atrocity or two. The turks disemboweled the Greeks, and dined on human entrails. The Turks hung children upside down. The Turks . . .

. . . hacked off the breasts of women.

Come now, what authorities, who's to bear witness? Who's to judge?

Rages? A bit on the subjective side, isn't it?

He finished the thesis and it was approved.

On the last day of school, when he was taking a makeup examination which would discharge his final obligation to Columbia, he sat in a sunlit room, drawing geological earth strata, and his hand began to quiver. Then he lost it altogether. As he felt existence moving from him, as he felt a wetness of his mouth—

He raged, "No!"

He kept shouting the fury, kept shouting, didn't stop.

Out of a daytime nightmare, out of wrath, he saw the black-browed Turkish face, not unlike his own, the ferocity familiar, the mercilessness that had no fear of blood and no pity in shedding it. He knew that weapon, that it could sever anything.

"No!"

He reached, he struggled for it. He didn't know how he had made it happen, but it was his, the scimitar was in his hand. The blade flashed cold and dry at first, then hot red, and he was wielding it, he, Markos Achillides, Greek.

Turks . . . somewhere . . .

The seizure did not happen.

He sat in the examination room, his real arm slowly returning, his hand, the earth strata he had been drawing, the arrows designating now one era, now another. The last arrowhead: he drew it.

The seizure had not happened. He had enraged it out of existence.

Nonsense. For days he could not believe what he had imagined in that examination room. It was foolishness—abracadabra—it was the conjuring idiocy that desperate people beguile themselves with when they have no other nostrum.

But the image would not leave his mind. Rationally he tried to understand what it meant. He wondered why he so rejected it when he had not rejected all those alchemical pills and punctures and potions that had done him no good, and had not rejected all the incantatory gibberish he had spoken to doctors and therapists and psychologists and neurologists. What tortured him most—giving the scientific shamans their due—was whether he had missed saying the simplest open-sesame which might have unlocked the door of his imprisoning sickness—the simple magic of exorcising the bedevilment in himself, the Turkish evil, the bestiality that had killed his mother, had made him an orphan with a sick curse on him, alone in No Place.

Exorcise the Turkish in himself.

Rid his world of its cruelty. But do it as civil men do it, on the side of a cause, redressing imbalances, rectifying wrongs, rescuing the persecuted, crusading for the good and the kind and the just. It would be what his delving into the past had meant for him to discover, it would put his own misbegotten life into the reference of the Greco-Turkish rages. It would be his own *Iliad:* kill Turks.

And as if the fates were telling him that he was making the right decision—the great coincidence—war broke out in Cyprus.

Kill Turks.

"How did you know about me?" Manolis Falkos asked. "Who sent you?"

"Yannis Petrides," Mark replied.

The man appraised him silently. He didn't offer the boy the hospitality of the garden, the typical drink of welcome, not even one of the rattan chairs in front of the tamarisk hedge. He simply went on watering, out of a black iron teakettle, four young lime saplings, no higher than his waist. He treated them gently; they were as spindly as a single foal uncertain of its legs. The kettle was empty now, so he crossed the dooryard garden and went into the whitewashed cubicle of a house. Like the garden, it too was tiny, but what more did a middle-aged bachelor schoolteacher need, Mark had mused as he had gone through, than a plastic table, a few plastic chairs, and a wallful of books?

Falkos returned with the teakettle. "Who is Yannis Petrides?"

The question threw Mark off balance. Yannis had given him

the impression the two men knew each other. "He's an old man I met," he said vaguely.

"Where?"

He must not tell him that he had met the Greek professionally, as the American medic's assistant. The next question would have to be: Why? To which he would have to answer that he had been sick, an epileptic. There were too many rejections in the word. "I'm staying at the Delos Hotel," he said evenly. "Yannis goes there occasionally—the sidewalk tables. I had a drink with him."

"What does he do?"

Cautiously: "I'm not sure. I think he's a medical assistant somewhere."

"Oh, that one." His tone was airy. "He's a roughneck, that one. Very bloodthirsty."

It's a trap, Mark thought; he wants to know if I'm lying. He knows damn well that Yannis is not what he described, but peaceable. "I didn't find him that way." His voice was equable. "On the contrary, I felt he was too willing to see the Turkish side of it."

"And you?"

Stay good-humored, he told himself: grin. "I want to kill them all."

The watering kettle was again empty. The schoolteacher seemed undecided whether or not to go inside and fill it once more. He set the container down. There was something appealing about the man; he had a nice face with a bookish absentmindedness about it, as if it had been blurred with library dust. And extraordinary eyes, Aegean blue, with a kindliness he seemed at pains to hide.

"Why do you want to kill them all?" He sounded casual.

"Because I'm Greek." He was glad he had not said half-Greek.

"I'm Greek too. But I think after a little negotiation, I would allow some of them to live." Then, quickly, seeming to regret the ridicule, he said soberly, "Do you really hate them so much?"

"Yes. Don't you?"

"No." He didn't elaborate. "This hatred—an American—how do you come by it?"

Don't talk too personally, he cautioned himself, don't get on the subject of brutalities, or you may set yourself off; stick to the generalities. "I've read a lot. All the cruelties the Turks have perpetrated—the Greeks—the Armenians. I have a strong social feeling about that. Call it racial *Angst*—call it the Greek *agonia*—"

"Call it hogwash."

Blather wouldn't work.

"My mother was brutalized."

The man studied him and said nothing. He didn't give an inch of leeway, not a hint of curiosity, not a syllable of sympathy. The boy was getting more defensive. "I'm sure these tales of atrocity are old stuff to you. But if you experience them personally—" Coolly, the man was watching him, not helping, not filling the silence. Despite every resolution, Mark lost control. "Goddamn it, I came over here for this one purpose!"

It was more effective than the gibberish. "Specifically, what did you plan to do?"

"Join something. The army."

"There is no army."

"Join you, then."

"Have you ever been a . . . soldier?"

"No." He was angry. "And I understand that you used to be a teacher."

For the first time, Falkos allowed the boy a small smile. And it suddenly occurred to Mark: The man's not making fun of me, he likes me.

"Have you ever fired a rifle?" Falkos asked.

"No."

"Any kind of gun?"

"No."

"Have you ever thrown a grenade?"

"No. But what the hell's so tough about throwing a grenade? You just pull the pin and throw."

"Have you ever set a land mine?"

"You know damn well I haven't!"

"What *can* you do?"

"*I can learn!*"

Falkos took a while to gauge him more carefully. "Yes, you probably can . . . Are you as bright as you look?"

"I'm probably brighter than you are."

"You've just proved that you aren't." But this time his smile was generous.

Openly, in the most cordial manner, Falkos extended his hand. As the boy gratefully took it, thinking it was a gesture of acceptance, the teacher said, "I want to thank you for coming here. I do appreciate it—very deeply. And now I think you ought to take the first ship home."

Mark dropped the hand. "You've been making fun of me!"

"No, I haven't."

"Then why don't you give me a chance?"

"Listen, my friend. Even if you came here a fully trained fighter—even if you struck me as the perfect ally—do you suppose I would trust you after only a ten-minute meeting?"

"You mean after you get a line on me . . . ?"

Falkos gave him an enormous noncommittal shrug. He looked at his watch. "There will be a motorbus back to Nicosia in about twenty minutes."

He was being dismissed. He turned to leave the garden and, as he reached the threshold of the house, he heard Falkos's voice: "Just a moment."

Turning, he saw that the Greek was debating something. Starting to speak, he desisted, as if to discard a notion that was too unlikely. Then, apparently, he went back to it. But clearly he was addressing it with caution.

"What does your family think about this?"

Mark considered: whether to prevaricate a little. But the facts were on his side—he was disassociated—no family to make trouble if something happened to him. "I only have foster parents—and I don't get along with them. I haven't seen them in over a year."

"What do you live on?"

"Scholarships, fellowships. Scholastic handouts." He smiled wryly as if he were in on a racket. "I'm on a grant now—research on Aphrodite."

"Whom would we inform—if you got killed?"

He's giving me a rough shot, to see if I'll flinch, Mark thought, and I'm not even blinking. "Nobody," he said. Then, the casual afterthought: "Oh, you might inform Dr. Meyer Axelberg at Columbia University. He's a professor of classical history. I got my grant through him."

He had the distinct feeling that the man was impressed, more by his easy manner than by what he had told him. The Greek took a long time before asking the next question.

"Can you drive an automobile?"

Reflexively, he was on the verge of telling the truth—that he had lied about his epileptic seizures when applying for his New York driver's license, then he had had an accident after which he had lost his right to drive.

"Yes, I can."

"Have you ever driven an English car with steering on the right?"

"Yes—once—in college—it was a little MG."

"This would be larger—a Land-Rover wagon." Then, quickly, "What I'm getting at—you'd be driving on the left side of the road. If you were to get confused—"

Interrupting, "I wouldn't get confused."

"Well . . . let me think about it." He looked at him a little more pointedly now. "The Delos Hotel, did you say?"

"Yes."

"I may be in touch with you. Meanwhile, go back to Nicosia and—"

"Be quiet."

"On the contrary. Let everybody know who you are. An *American.*" He touched the boy lightly on the shoulder. "Come on, I'll walk out with you."

Falkos escorted him through the house and out onto the rubble-paved street. As the boy started away, the older man said with a quiet smile, "How many?"

"How many what?"

"Turks would you like to kill?"

Mark smarted. The man was mocking him once more.

"A thousand, would you say?" Falkos asked. "A dozen?"

"You're making fun of me again."

"How about only one? Would one be enough?"

There was something perverse about the mockery. And for a man who had struck him as being so kind, it seemed uncharacteristically cruel. Mark was vaguely disturbed. He had been in the midst of admiring the man, liking him, and suddenly he wasn't sure.

Disconcerted, he turned away and walked rapidly down the hill. A thousand—a dozen—how many? He had met very few Turks in his life—a few students, a teacher of zoology when he was in high school, a girl who practically lived in her carrel, studying linguistic roots in Indo-European languages. There was an old Turkish numismatist who had given him a few friendly bargains in coins when, as a child, he had started collecting them. He had hated none of them; the linguistics girl he had flirted with; the numismatist he had been fond of.

How about only one? Would one be enough?

He must not listen to such counsels of restraint. The man had obviously—some way or other—lost a lust for action, or for violence, or vengeance. He wondered what the Cypriot would have said if they had actually talked of atrocities—his Greek mother mutilated by his Turkish father—would he still sound as moderate, and as mocking?

Mark felt the rage again.

How about only one?

But wait—perhaps it was the telling question. One might be enough.

One.

Not all Turks, only one. This was why he had come to Cyprus. To find one Turk. His father. And to kill him.

4

The old man had a hangover. All morning he lay in the back of
the ambulance, moaning and groaning and berating himself for
having drunk so much retsina in the afternoon and so much ouzo
in the evening. Conscientiously, he did his best when there was a
patient, but luckily there was only one case—a woman who had
fallen down a flight of stairs, and when they lifted her onto the litter, he had carried his share of the stretcher's weight. Toward
midafternoon, however, he had to get out of the ambulance for
fear he would throw up, and he lay on a pebbly beach listening to
soft wind on soft sea. Ben knew that the vitamin B and the whiffs
of oxygen he dispensed could relieve only part of the old Greek's
misery. Something else was plaguing him.

"What happened to you yesterday?"

"I am no good," Yannis said.

"I know that, but what happened?"

"I know every whore on Ragaena Street—you realize this important fact?"

"I've made a note of it."

"Every focking one of them came to my table at the Delos,
every focking one. 'How are you, Yannis?—How are you, old
friend?—How is the silk around your corncob?' Last night, one of
them—Maria Lepos—she says to me, 'Come in to me, old man, it
will cost you nothing.' When a whore says this to you, she is making you an Apollon, and you cannot refuse it. But I think to myself: She smells of old olive oil, and maybe not since the day she
was baptized has her hair felt a sprinkle of water. So I say no to
her. But soon I know that I have not told to myself the true reason.
'Why are you lying to yourself, old manure? You know that even if
she smells of cloves, you are not able to fock her. You are become

nothing more than a damp night man, who dreams that he is young and brave—and to every woman he is a great something.' . . . So I go to sleep on the beach last night, and the moon is talking to me and the sea is talking to me, and they are saying, 'Make love to us!' And I am not able. I am a dry old man on a wet beach. . . . I am not worthy of my walnuts."

A Greek-deep depression. Ben got him into the truck and gave him another whiff of oxygen. "You are good to me," the old man said. The medic put his arm around his assistant, who looked up. "You are the only American who touches another man. Are you a *kolibrion?*"

The word, meaning hummingbird, was slang for homosexual. "Yes," Ben said, "you excite me."

The old man made a valiant effort to smile but couldn't do it, so Ben pummeled him a little and Yannis laughed helplessly, reached to his hungover head and begged for mercy. Then, gravely, "You went to see her?"

"Yes."

Yannis waited for him to go on. Ben was about to tell him everything—the ditch—the baby's grave—the five hundred pounds. But it depressed him, and he didn't.

Sensitive, the old man changed the subject. "That boy was a liar."

"What boy?"

"The one with *epilepsia.*"

"You saw him?"

"Yes, at the Delos. He did not come here for some goddamn Aphrodite. It was a cocking wool story."

He meant, of course, a cock-and-bull story. "What did he come for?"

"To kill Turks."

Ben turned to him. The old man was looking better now, and enjoying the gossip. "Did he tell you that?"

"Yes, and is not important—is like he is talking shish kebab. He wants to join something, he says. So I sent him to Falkos." Then, uncertainly, "I think he may be *trellos.*" He tapped his forehead.

"I don't think so, Yannis."

"I think he was lying about he is a genius. He is a fool."

Ben thought the boy might be both, but why not *trellos* as

well? Fool, genius, and lunatic, not a prepossessing parlay, he mused, especially when the concomitant was epilepsy.

The day was getting hotter, and they were thinking of shade trees and white wine when the intercom went off. It was the Emergency at Paphos, with a relief man who spoke no English. His Greek was none too clear, either, garbled by the machine, and Ben became impatient.

"You get it," he called to Yannis. The old man hurried into the cab, listened a minute, cursed under his breath, then shouted at the intern to speak more slowly. In a little while, he was nodding his head.

He clicked off. "He says to go to Seismos."

"Seismos?"

"The Wine Press. There was an incident."

Ben's breath caught; something had happened to her. "An incident? You mean an accident."

Yannis pointed to the intercom. "He says *peristatikon*—this means incident, no?"

The ambulance, siren screaming, was already on the roadway. "Incident to whom?" Ben asked.

"He did not say."

"Why didn't he?" Nerves. "Why the hell didn't you ask?"

"I did ask—you are deaf? Somebody calls him and tells him nothing. So this is what I tell you—nothing. Stop—not so fast!"

The ambulance skidded on the sand-coated asphalt. It careened, tried to right itself, then screeched to a stop. It was stuck in a soft shoulder of sand.

The old man started to open the door. Ben, all irritation: "Don't get out."

"I want to see."

"Stay there."

He turned the motor on again, slammed at the wheel angrily, right and left and back again, pumped up and down on the accelerator. With a lurch, they were free and hurtling onward in the craziness of the hot sun. Oh, please, he thought, no delays today, no refugee trucks on the road, let me get there fast.

He twisted off onto the mountain road. Climbing, he jammed from gear to gear, none of them powerful enough, all too sluggish, too laggard in goading wheel to wheel.

He saw the chain and stopped. The same rusted links of barrier, still stretched across from post to post, still forbidding entrance, still the same damn mist as yesterday.

"Hello," he cried. Then, nonsensically, "Where?"

Yannis beside him, he thrashed through thickets and brambles as he had done the day before. He went, illogically, to the back door, where the grave could be seen, as if certain this was where he would see her again. There was no one there.

"Hello," he called again, "hello."

Yannis was already moving toward the back door, and Ben followed him. Precipitously it occurred to the medic—what should have occurred sooner—an incident, as they had called it, could mean anything, danger.

"Wait!" he called. "Let me go first."

The old man was paying no attention. Ben ran to catch up. "Goddamn it, wait!" he shouted. He pulled the Greek away from the door and entered ahead of him. Through the dark hallway now, and past a bedroom, then another, then out into the kitchen, through its desolation, toward what had been the dining room.

It was a shambles of destruction and filth. The tables were smashed, the black iron lamps as well. There wasn't a chair that stood on four legs. It was wreckage, all of it, except for one large table, which, as he recalled, had been used to spread the display of coffee service and desserts.

Then he saw the wine press. The body lay between the jaws of it. The plates had been turned down tight on the naked torso of the man—Savvas Menas—his head and shoulders hung free on one side, his legs on the other. Even dead, his bloody juices were still running through the holes and into the vat below.

Dear God, he heard the old man say, as he walked closer to it. Holding his arms across his chest, Yannis rocked sideways, back and forth, as if he were lulling a child. *Ptochos, ptochos,* he said.

Yes, poor, poor—and loathsome, Ben thought, and cruel, those barbaric bastards.

Then the terrifying thought: What had they done with *her?*

Swiftly he looked around the room, searched everywhere, the cloak alcove, the space behind the cashier's counter, the closets where the linens were stored. He rushed back into the kitchen, opened every pantry door.

"Look in that other bedroom," he said, pointing to what must have been the child's room. He himself went into the nearer one.

There it was, the double bed where they had slept together,

and the clothes closet they had shared, and her table where she might have sat to put on whatever makeup she had worn. There was another closet in the passageway, not altogether empty, some of his clothes still there, some of hers as well, run-down work shoes, and a pair of black satin pumps that might never have been used. Leaning against the back wall of the closet, the collapsed playpen of a child, with a half-inflated blue balloon dangling from one of the wooden bars, hanging wrinkled nearly to the floor. And nothing else.

No sign of other bloodshed.

"Nothing," Yannis said, joining him.

Nobody in the bathroom. No track of her to follow; she had not left the slightest token to help him guess where she had gone.

Ben started to say he was going to search outdoors, when he stopped, midsentence. Apparently Yannis heard the sound too, a car approaching. They remained motionless, silent, to hear if it might be on the road, and passing. But it was closer than that, coming onto the long driveway of the property, crunching on the dirt and gravel pathway, stopping as they had stopped, at the chain.

He hurried to the window. It was useless—even if the window looked out in the right direction, which it did not, there would be no way he could see through the hedge and thickets.

Distantly, they heard the car door open and close. Men's voices. Not loud, but not particularly hushed. Then, total quiet.

The stillness lasted too long. They would have been able to walk here by now, he thought.

He heard them once more, closer now—footsteps on gravel, perhaps no more than thirty yards away.

He was unarmed. So was Yannis. If they were Turks, and instinctively he knew they were, perhaps they had come back to find the woman. They would search the place as thoroughly as he and Yannis had done. The Turks, however, would have more success in finding someone—two medics, one of them a Greek. I'm an American, Ben said, I must make some use of that. But Yannis— what could he do for his assistant? Yet, surely, they wouldn't hurt the harmless old man. Unless they were to question him. What did he know about Savvas Menas—or about Falkos, for that matter?

The footsteps were closer.

There were two voices, at least two.

If he and Yannis could slip out the back way, he thought, and skirt the lakeshore—but that would be no good because they would ultimately have to get back to the roadway, and be seen. If they made a run for it, there would be rifle shots, or whatever else the Turks might have in store for them.

The footsteps outdoors stopped.

There was silence now, then the softest whispering.

Ben looked at Yannis and marveled at his calm. He had an enigmatic smile on his face, like a mask, but it didn't cover everything; the eyes were frightened.

A screaking sound. It could have been a sticky hinge, a door opening. They were in the vestibule of the restaurant, he imagined. Another door. He heard them walking slowly in the dining room, heard the loose floorboards make a soft, complaining noise. It ceased. Stillness again.

Yannis didn't even pretend to smile anymore. He put his gnarled hands into his trouser pockets. Ben had the irrelevant thought: I bought him those pants quite a while ago; he paid me back; he needs another pair.

The stranger stood in the doorway.

And Ben heard Yannis laugh.

"It's Pig Hands," the old man said.

The stranger denounced him in Greek, and Yannis told him in the same language to do unmentionable things to his sister, if he had not already done them. Clearly they were continuing a discourse they had begun in brawnier days.

"When you arrive here, he is already dead, yes?" Pig Hands asked.

"Yes."

He inquired if they had seen any sign of Turks, and a few other questions, the answers to which were obvious. Neither of the Greeks wanted to talk about the dead man, so they pretended a raffish mirth that neither of them felt. Pig Hands, doughy and slow of speech, asked if there was any truth to the rumor that Yannis had died; the old man replied yes, while in bed with the other's wife. The oafish man laughed uncertainly, reached down, and scratched himself. Ben noted that the further east he traveled the more energetic the scratching. They belabored the crudities industriously; it was hard work forgetting the dead man.

A stir at the threshold, and Manolis Falkos stood there.

His face was stormy. "They did a good job," he said. Then the same question: "He was not alive when you got here?"

"No. I don't imagine he's been alive for quite a while."

"Yes, he was," Falkos replied. "He called me not more than an hour ago. He said he heard them coming."

"Was it you who called the hospital?"

"Yes."

"The woman," Ben said, "what about her?"

Falkos glanced at him quickly, seemed surprised to have been asked. He didn't answer for an instant. Something puzzled him. "Menas said she left him last evening." He seemed to be making choices. "You know Kalya?"

Some instinct told Ben not to be too direct. "Not really. I used to come to the restaurant."

Used to, he had said, without strict accuracy, meaning to sound as casual as any other customer. "Why did they do that to him?"

"They are Turks—Savvas was a Greek."

Ben was annoyed by the stereotypical idiocy. "They don't torture every Greek."

"He was living with a Turkish woman. They are very righteous about some things."

"I don't believe that was all of it."

Falkos's eyes narrowed a little. He's assessing me, Ben thought, questioning whether I'm worth an answer to my question. "The Turks wanted to use him," the schoolteacher said. "In his restaurant, he was in a position to hear things. But he refused to give them information. His business depended on maintaining the friendship of all kinds of people, he said—Greeks, English, Turks, Americans, everybody. He had to be neutral." Falkos paused for an instant, as if weighing whether his assessment of the medic warranted his going further. "Point is, that Menas was not neutral. He was working with us. And the man found out."

"What man?"

The teacher smiled. It was the most engaging smile, all charm, with ice at the heart of it.

"Cabrir," he said.

It was a name the Greeks used for scaring naughty children—and traitors. His full name was Ihsan Guhl Cabrir; he was a Cypriot Turk who had worked with the British. Although Ben had never met anybody who had actually seen him, Cabrir was always described in the same cardboard villain way—a handsome Turk with a Mephistophelean mustache and a preposterously romantic scar on his left cheek, from jawbone to eyebrow. In the early days, he was a venal informer, paid by the English to betray his Greek neighbors. When the British were no longer an enemy, he became a Turkish Robin Hood who stole from the Greeks and gave to his own people. During the disorders of '64, the terror surrounding his name had intensified. He had become the essence of evil. He was not, except by accident, a killer; he was a torturer. An artist in the administration of pain, the Cyprus *Mail* had called him, an exquisite of cruelty. Real though he was, he became a hobgoblin in the Greek mind. Where there was ingenious atrocity, it was Cabrir's.

Falkos seemed mesmerized by the view of the dead man. He smiled grimly; almost, it seemed, in admiration of the torturer. "What an idea . . . to use a press . . . blood into wine . . ."

Ben couldn't tell where the horror left off and the reverence began. Chilling. "Have you ever met him?"

"Cabrir?"

Ben nodded. The interval was heavy. Just as he was expecting he would get no reply, Falkos said, "Yes, I have met him."

If there had indeed been any approval of what the teacher was regarding, it was gone now. Only loathing remained, as deep as an ache. "And I will meet him again. When I do, I will personally, with my own fingers, tear out one of his eyes, then wait a week and tear out the other."

His voice sounded nearly as ugly as the sight of the dead man. Ben pointed to it. "You won't be able to equal that."

"Perhaps not. But I will try."

"Good for you."

Falkos heard the sarcasm and his face constricted. Angry, he retaliated, "How is it you're still here?"

"Where should I be?"

"At the Monastery—all by your neutral self—tending an old priest."

Ben flushed; the taunt hit home. "You made it clear that I wouldn't get there."

"What difference does that make? A public-spirited man like you—respected all over the island—you're not a coward, are you?"

It was a rhetorical contempt; he expected no answer. Nor would Ben have validated the question by giving him one.

The teacher muttered something in Greek to Pig Hands, and they started away. At the doorway, unexpectedly, he paused. His

anger had disappeared. He was again the cool-headed, faintly iron-
ical man.

"You don't happen to know where I can find Kalya, do you?"
he asked.

The question was unaccountable and Ben was taken by surprise. Instinctively, he felt that Falkos's purpose was to shock some
revelation out of him, some exposure of himself, or perhaps of
Kalya.

"I don't even know her," Ben said.

Falkos looked from Ben to Yannis. The old man was good at
concealment. His face showed nothing. The teacher smiled and
went away.

No, the contempt was not rhetorical, Ben reconsidered, it was
a challenge. And it stayed in his craw. But it was a booby-trapped
challenge, only a fool would get tricked by it. If he went up to the
Monastery alone, somewhere on the road—he knew it as certainly
as if it had been spelled out—a mine or mortar would go off; or
one of their Grivas belts—a chain with explosive attached—would
tighten across his headlights, there would be a shatter of glass,
burning petrol, ambulance, American. He needn't blame himself
for deciding not to take the dare. Some gauntlets, a realistic professor once told him, should be left in the dust. But the confrontation
needled him.

The whole afternoon was discouraging. The radio news from
Geneva said the peace conferences were bogging down. Turkey
was refusing to withdraw her troops, which Greece was demanding
as a condition for continued discussion; and suddenly they were
wrangling over the whole Cyprus constitution, as if they were preparing it for the shredder.

Meanwhile, as the invading army was pushing further and further southward, the Greeks were retaliating by driving Turks out
of their homes, off their farms, into prisons, into camps. In the mu-
nicipal soccer stadium of Limassol there were 1,750 Turkish in-
ternees. Midafternoon, when Ben heard about them—knowing
there would be medical problems there—he and Yannis drove to
the stadium to offer assistance. The Turkish prisoners were broiling in the August sun, without water or shelter. At night, they said,
they had frozen in the cold sea air. The illnesses had begun. The
Greek guards were hostile and abusive; a maddened internee had

been shot; there was little food; the latrines were a corruption. When Ben complained about the sanitary conditions, two guards raised their rifles at him, ruled him off, and forbade him to return.

Then, pesky things. Late in the afternoon they had a flat tire, the valve on the oxygen tank went totally to pieces, and toward sundown the Larnaca hospital dispatched them to the wrong address.

The final distress: "I want to go to my village," Yannis said.

It meant that the old man was at the lowest of his lows. He had been moody all day, not only hungover but disheartened by the murder of Menas and a cease-fire without peace. He had to be desperate indeed to want to go back to his old village, where he had nobody anymore. His old friends were gone, his family had died or disappeared; the place was full of grievous memories.

"You don't really want to go," Ben said.

"Yes, I do—for one night."

"The last time you went, you were miserable for days."

Doggedly: "I will go."

It was over fifty miles away, mostly on bad roads. "Let's go, then, it's getting late."

"I will go by bus."

"No, I'll take you."

"Take me back to Limassol, to the bus."

"You want to be that alone, do you?"

". . . Yes."

So he drove the old man to the bus stop, forced a few extra pounds on him, and watched the dusty vehicle pull away.

Poignantly, he felt the old man's loneliness, and it made him realize how lonely he himself was. It's only a mood, he said, and I'll nip it in bud; I won't go to a taverna for dinner tonight, I'll battle it out on my own. He knew only too well what had depressed and shaken him.

Falkos: "You're not a coward, are you?"

Am I?

It would not have been so plaguing if he hadn't asked it of himself a thousand times. And if he wasn't, what was he, a man avoiding what an army captain had once called virile combat. A pacifist was a euphemism for what?

His father's question, the nagging repetend: "Define yourself."

"How the hell can I define myself, Father?"

"Damn it, you have to! You didn't wait to get drafted—you

volunteered. That's damn decent of you. The only worm in that apple is—you're really a conscientious objector. But you couldn't *wait* to get into the uniform—so what the hell did that mean? Are you a C.O. or are you a blood and guts soldier?"

"Do I have to be either?"

"You have to be whoever the hell you *are!* You quit school because you don't want to be a doctor. And you sign up for the army—specifically as a medic! Define yourself!" His voice became quietly confidential. "Well, I'll tell you, Ben, if you can't do it, I can do it for you. You're a doctor."

"No, I'm not, Father."

"You are. You've gone nearly all the way through med school, you've always been high in your class, you've got a real talent for the profession, and you're ready to go to work in a hospital. By God, you're a doctor!"

"Don't plan on it, Father. When I come back from Vietnam— if I do come back . . ." There weren't any conclusions, not even to the sentence.

"What the hell will you be?"

"I don't know."

"What are you now?"

Father to son: the cruel question. Who was he? Not a doctor with a sense of mission, as his father was; but not apathetic—there was hardly anything or anybody he had no feeling for. Once his shouting and marching days were over, he had not voted with regularity, but if he couldn't vote he would feel that he had lost an ethical muscle without which he couldn't stand erect. Not prudish, but if he went to bed with a woman he didn't at least *think* he loved, the night was long. Who was he? A mid-course man, living in the unhappy medium.

In war, he felt no guilt about carrying the red cross as a protective shield, and he wondered if the whole company of ordinary men, to which he belonged, did not prefer a shield to a sword. It was less romantic, perhaps, but he would not admit that it was less heroic; and he was certain it made more sense. But, as between sword and shield, what was the morality? Compromise? Wasn't it moral double-talk to say a man must carry both? And . . . to be a medic—in a *war*—wasn't that a moral dodge?

"I'm trying to find a viable compromise, Father."

"A viable lie, did you say?"

"You really think I'm lying?"

"I don't believe in the golden mean, Ben. The people I've known who talk it—they're generally being mean to get the gold. They use words like that to be acceptable."

"So do all of us—so do you."

"That's not true—not me! I don't give a shit about being on the acceptable side. I've been a Democrat when it was smart to be a Republican, and vice versa—and being either one of them gives me a pain in the ass. And your mother—she's never in her life been on the acceptable side, but she knows who she is! That's a great deal better than *my* mother. My mother could sing like an angel and write like a demon and talk at a dinner party as if she had it straight from the Lord, but she didn't know for damn what she wanted to do with herself—and dear God, she died of an *unidentifiable sickness!* Can you imagine that—there's a terrifying curse in it. The wife of a doctor and the mother of one, and she doesn't know what ails her—and there's nothing in the skill of the two people she loves best, there's nothing in all their tomes of art and science, there's nothing in their *love* that'll help her know what's made her sick all her life! . . . Now, Benny, I beg you— don't get sick like that. *Identify yourself!*"

"Do I have to find a label?"

Without umbrage, he replied, "Don't be so high and mighty about labels, Ben. If we don't put labels on things, the whole Rx turns to chaos, and we wind up dispensing piss. . . . Anyway, you've already written the label, it's right in your hand—now, have the gumption to stick it on the bottle."

"I'm not a doctor, Father."

"Then find out who the hell you are."

. . . And the same question, asking it of himself today, still could not be answered with any dauntless affirmation, but only in the negative:

I am not a man who drives an armored tank to a monastery.

Nor am I a man who commits suicide by driving up alone.

An old and ailing priest notwithstanding, I can do neither one.

So I do nothing.

Who am I, then?

. . . Toward dusk, he bought some *halloumi* cheese and some cracked green olives and a bottle of white wine. He drove toward Zyyi, but well before he got there he turned southward to the shore, and went out among the rocks. It was a place he knew, little frequented, where the sea churned more than usual, as if there were an underwater Poseidon and Triton, father and son going at each other in a futile contest, roiling the deep.

It was nighttime now, but bright as daylight nearly, with a full and naked moon, and the sky as greenish blue as peacocks. He finished the wine and tossed the remaining bits of *halloumi* outward to the gulls. He wondered how they could see the morsels on the water, how so many of them had fluttered in so soon, and where they had flown from.

At first he thought the sound was the greedy bickering of birds on the water, but then he heard it behind him, landward. It was his radio, going full blast, some distance from the shoreline. An unusual sound so late, in this seaside area. Unlike the capital, these places went to bed at night; so did emergencies.

Cape Roulis, the message said; no more than that. Not whether it was man, woman, or child, and not the nature of the exigency. It was one of those vague ones, an *afixis,* discover-on-arrival. He hated that kind; it meant somebody had a bellyache from overeating, or an arthritic pain he couldn't help with much more than aspirin; or, worse, something serious he might handle better if he were warned ahead of time.

He drove the truck recklessly. Without Yannis to monitor his speed, he stepped it up past the trembling point—he needed something to shake him up tonight.

Cape Roulis was a narrow spit that reached far into the sea. A strange place for an emergency, he thought, unless it was some kid who had swum off the point and been pulled in, waterlogged. He drove as far as he could go, to the end of the road. The rest of the distance was all rock and pebbles and sand, then sky, sea, horizon.

He didn't see a soul. If there were an emergency, he would have had some sign of it by now—lights, for example, a flashlight or kerosene lantern or one of the road torches. But nothing. And it wasn't that it was too dark for visibility—the entire shoal was bright, every rock clear, as white as if the land were snow-swept. There was nobody.

Then he saw her. She had been sitting on the seaward side of one of the rocks, perhaps; now she got up and, standing on a slight rise, was looking in his direction. He barely recognized her at first —she was dressed as he had never seen her before, in a soft thing of some sort, a skirt somewhat longer than the custom and a blouse with more material than necessary, so that there was a blown look about all the cloth that enveloped her, and she seemed wind-caught. The most striking thing was the scarf she wore. Stark white and covering her hair and her high cheekbones, it was tied tightly at her neck so that all that was visible of her face was a long, narrow oval of burnished gold in a moon-brightened frame. He had never imagined that she would dress like this, so delicately, so yieldingly. There was an unlikelihood . . .

All of it was unlikely. What false emergency had summoned him here, and who had arranged it? And why in this setting? Before he had seen her, the vista had been as elemental as nature can be—only the barest rudiments of sky, rock, and sea—but now, with her startling presence, it had ceased to be natural, it was bizarre. And, thinking of Menas's death, threatening.

Was there someone else there, he wondered, and where? He looked in every direction and saw nobody. He imagined someone as invisible as she had been, behind the rocks.

The time, the place, her presence—they were too oblique to be trusted. He had an impulse to retreat, but didn't. He kept his distance from her, didn't move. Warily, his glance scanned the tiny headland, the closer rocks, the further ones, the finger of sand that drifted off the cape, into the bay. He thought—to the seaward side of her, on the beach—he saw a shadow.

"Is someone here with you?" he said.

"No one." She spread her arms in a gesture that said: I am alone, I am fully revealed, and as unguarded as you are.

"I'm sorry about your—about Menas."

"We're in a war." Then she added simply, without making a slogan of it, "Cruel things are commonplace."

"Did you expect . . . ?"

"Yes, we were always in dread of it."

He knew that her calm was costly to her, but it still seemed extraordinary to him. "You got away from him just in time, didn't you?"

He hadn't meant how it sounded, the implication that she played things less for feeling than for caution; but even though he saw her wince, she answered him with disarming simplicity. "Yes. I left when our child died, which was . . . just in time."

If he had been unconsciously probing for her susceptibility, he had found the aching nerve. But she wasn't parading her pain; if she was making an ostentation of anything, it was her pride. He could sense her working at it as if it could be accomplished by the simple control of muscles, by lifting the head, by carrying the bosom a trifle higher, and by looking slightly upward, past the shoulder of the outside world. Even her involuntary muscles were under her command. She was no longer a madwoman in a ditch; she was a strength.

"Was it you who called the hospital?" he asked.

"No."

"Who, then?"

"Falkos."

"You mean he sent you to me?"

"Yes."

"To intercede for him?"

"Yes." She was having difficulty. "To ask you to change your mind about going up with the ambulance."

"I told him I would be willing to go—by myself."

"I know what you told him."

"What makes him think you can change my mind?"

She faltered. Clearly, she had no confidence she could change anything. Putting off her answer to his question: "He asked me how well I knew you and I said you were . . ."

She couldn't make it. He helped her. "Attracted to you."

"Yes." Then, gathering courage, "He thought you might be willing to go up the mountainside . . . with me."

It was another deal of some sort she was suggesting. He felt a surge of resentment. Was she offering herself to him if he would go? And what was in it for her?

"How would that work?" he asked.

The wind fluttered the scarf a little, and as the white material stirred slightly away from her cheek, she raised her hand to keep it securely close to her skin, as if she wanted herself to be seen only minimally.

"He will need some help in the ambulance—but nobody must be Greek. He asked if I would be willing to go—and I said yes." She paused. He had the sense that she had carefully rehearsed in her mind what she would say to him, and the words were gone. "We—you and I—if we were seen anywhere, together, the word would get out that the American was living with the Turkish . . . woman. The Greeks would assume it, and so would the Turks. It would be useful for people to believe that."

"Especially when we go up the mountainside."

"Yes."

"With Falkos hidden in the vehicle."

"That's right."

"With guns."

". . . Yes."

"If Falkos makes it, a lot of Turks will get killed. They're your own people. Doesn't that bother you?"

"No. I hate the Turks."

He thought of the raids they had made on the restaurant, and their responsibility for hastening the child's death, and the spoliation of the grave. And the torture of Menas. "You've become a Greek partisan, then?"

She smiled bitterly. "No. I hate the Greeks as well." It was as if she were a detached spectator observing a corrosive satire, comical but not pleasurable. "I also hate the English and the Americans. Since those are, for the most part, the only people with whom I have come in contact, I do not hate any other nationalities."

Apparently he wasn't meant to enjoy the irony. He didn't. "I'm sorry, but I won't go up the mountain with you. I don't hate any of those people."

Her smile was still grim. "You're a little Jesus in that ambulance of yours."

"Bullshit! I'm not a little Jesus, but I certainly won't be part of this catchall vengeance of yours. Is that what you're doing it for?"

"Vengeance? No."

"What, then?"

She paused, seeming reluctant to confess the word: "Employment."

With a cutting edge: "You've tried everything else?"

She pretended not to hear the sarcasm. Speaking with absolute directness, she didn't make the slightest bid for sympathy. "I left Savvas last night and went down to Limassol. I stayed in a cheap pension—I only had six pounds. There's an employment agency—I went there and said, 'I can do many things—read English and write it—I'm not a fast typist, but I can get faster—I can cook, I can wait on tables.' They said I was a Turk, and why didn't I go to Iros Square? So I went. One of the Turkish restaurants had been burned, and another had been vandalized. There was window glass everywhere, and all the Turks were gone. I had only one pound left. I went to Nicosia and it was the same thing. In the afternoon I decided to cross the Green Line and go to the Turkish area. But I had no papers. Even if I had—they knew me; one of them said I had been living with a Greek. As he said it, he did to me what the Turks do. He licked his palm and held his hand up so I could see it was wet—it has a foul meaning. The other one said, 'Go back.'"

She had been talking with her head averted. Now she faced him. "Go back where?" she asked.

"So you called Falkos."

"Yes."

"How much money is he giving you?"

She flared in anger. "I didn't say money, I said employment. I must have something to *do!*" Her tone was fugitive, and reckless.

"What will your work consist of?"

"I don't know—cook—translate from the Turkish—question prisoners—anything!"

Including, perhaps, sleeping with Falkos. It was a hasty thought, and hastily he discarded it. For no reason he could substantiate, purely on insight—or, more accurately, because he wanted to see it this way—he didn't think sex was part of their arrangement. However—more repellently—Falkos was acting as her procurer, with Ben as john. And this would be part of her "employment." A steady job—the last resort of a homeless, rootless, outcast woman, a pariah. He must guard against feeling sorry for her; it was a trap he had fallen into once; he must not do it again. But the word came anyway. "I'm sorry you have to do this," he said lamely.

"What? Sell myself?"

". . . Yes."

Bitterly: "All women sell themselves for a price."

It was not only a platitude but, to him, a false one. He offered his own: "Some women don't settle for anything but love."

"Love is also a price."

If her cynicism is a shell, he thought, it's impermeable. At least to me.

"I'm sorry," she went on, "I'm doing this badly. But I thought it would be easier. I thought you . . . wanted me."

He responded as detachedly as he could. "You made an offer like this once before and—"

"For Savvas, not for myself!"

"I wasn't blaming you. I was—" He stopped because he guiltily knew he *was* blaming her, as if the fault were singularly her own and easy to designate. But the reproach, just or unjust, *was* easy enough to designate: they were both—she as well as he—calling her a whore.

"*You* would not be paying for me," she said, "somebody else would."

Dryly: "Tell him thanks."

"As a matter of fact, it would not be a gift. You *would* be paying something."

Yes, by way of foregone scruples. He wondered how she understood him so well, and had such contempt for him. She thought him a prig, clearly, self-righteous when it was easy to be that way. For her, obviously, nothing had been easy. And now she was cornered and desperate, a war casualty. The most defenseless kind of war casualty, hated by both sides, a target for everybody. No wonder she had to join something: simple safety. For a proud woman to have to settle for such a meager necessity—he felt deeply sorry for her. But then he warned himself: beware pity. Pity was his flaw. Not a tragic flaw, only a pathetic one; not the size of a heroic fall, only a stumble. Anyway, beware.

"I didn't expect you to say yes immediately," she said. "If you want to talk further, I'll be at the Alasia Hotel in Nicosia."

He thought acridly that the Alasia was not a deluxe hotel, but it was respectable, it cost money—and she hadn't any. Falkos would be paying for it.

She started to go. As she got a few feet away, his voice stopped her. "By the way," he said, with a show of amusement he didn't genuinely feel, "how did you come to choose this place for our meeting?"

The question unsettled her. "It was Falkos's idea. He chose the most romantic place he could think of—so that I would seem as attractive as possible."

Tentatively, she put her hand on her cheek. Since she had been talking about attractiveness, he thought it was the typically feminine gesture of a woman smoothing back her hair, but her hair was altogether hidden beneath the scarf. Abruptly, an outlandish thought occurred to him:

"What's the matter with your face?"

"Nothing." She was startled, caught.

"Let me see."

Without deliberation—impulsively—he reached and pushed

back the scarf. Her cheekbone was badly bruised. It looked swollen, raw.

She made a sound: frustration, pain.

"How did that happen?"

"Never mind," she said, and started to flee.

He stopped her. "Let me look at it!"

"No!"

He held her. "What happened?"

"At the Green Line, as I turned back, somebody—a Greek—saw me leaving the Turkish sentry post. He knew I had been trying to cross the line and he called out, 'Intern her! She's a Turk, intern her!' Then somebody else and somebody else! I was terrified—I ran. Somebody started to throw stones."

"Kalya—"

"Don't pity me!"

"Wait—!"

"Don't pity me!"

A shriek of rage, of savagery. As if his pity angered her more than an insult, it was a physical assault, more painful than the stones.

She ran. He rushed after her, but only a few steps, then halted. If he caught up with her, he knew he would be invading the last bit of self-respecting privacy she had. He saw her hurtling away from the beach, ascending the incline, onto the main road. She's in the middle of nowhere, he said, where's she rushing to, with her clothes flying in the wind? Then he saw the car. It had been parked at some distance, perhaps, and now its headlamps sprang alight and it was advancing toward her. It stopped, she got into it and was gone.

Later in darkness, on another beach, he lay down and tried to sleep. The night was warm, the sky was as close and soft as an eiderdown, and the balmy zephyr came from a distant time, a distant place . . . and he could love that woman. Only it wasn't a woman, it was a child—Mee Lanh—and why did he dream her as a woman?

Stay back, Mee Lanh.

A tiny flame, no greater than a match light, exploded in his mind.

It's not fire, he said, it's only a brief glimmer, it will go.

He reached down and touched his thigh, roughly kneading it.

There was total feeling in it, not the least bit numb. He flexed his leg; it moved, it twisted, it followed every command. No fire, he repeated, not crippled.

He stood up quickly. Too quickly; he was a little dizzy.

Keep away, Mee Lanh. Stay where you are.

His head wouldn't clear; still dizzy. You're in deeper trouble than you thought, he said.

Stay back.

She wasn't Kalya, the Turk, she was the Vietnamese girl, and one had nothing to do with the other. Or did they? Were they, after all, two faces of the same apparition, or of himself? Was the child a promise of the woman, or a warning of her?

He saw the face staring down at him out of the lightlessness, the VC face, a man this time, painted for night patrol, hideous and spitting blood at him, and he awakened.

Even awake, he heard the jungle noise, he saw the gangrene in the soldier's belly, smelling like cat piss, he heard the *rracckk rracckk* and didn't know whether it was the jungle mynahs or automatic weapons. Then there was the napalm face, black and smoking, and finally The Grave.

It was not a single grave. His assistant, Ludwig Stroudt, in writing up the report, would call it a Mortuary Multiple. They looked down into it.

"How many in there, would you say?" Ben asked.

"Counting by arms or gizzards?" Luddy said.

There could have been twenty down there, reckoning the way the dreary joke went, count the arms and legs and divide by four, except that for some reason more legs had been blown off than heads, so the head count wouldn't tally. How long before they cover this one up? he wondered. There was an ooze lifting to the surface and it would cover a lot of it. Luddy considered it might be seepage from the subsoil, but it was very red for that.

They were giving a transfusion. "We're running out of blood."

The assistant pointed to the Multiple. "Siphon some out of there."

No need for blood right now—he was wide awake on a Cyprus beach. No need for any of that anymore—another war, and this is cease-fire peace, try to lose it if you can, as it was lost.

But he couldn't. Mee Lanh appeared. Go away, girl, he said, let me alone. But she wouldn't.

The transfusion wouldn't have done the boy any good anyhow. Maybe the chaplain would.

"I don't know nothin'," the bandaged head said to the priest.

"Never mind, son."

"I don't know nothin' but my asshole."

"Our Father which art in heaven . . ."

Rracckk rracckk.

The sound wasn't in the jungle, it was sea birds, flying against a southern sky, winging toward Limassol. Mee Lanh, you don't belong in Cyprus, you're in the wrong place, go away. What the devil have you got to do with Kalya? What can you tell me about her, a strange world, a strange language, a Viet child speaking to me of a Turkish woman, someone you've never seen or heard of? Why do you meddle? What the hell do you mean, you're two faces of the same apparition? What the hell do *you* know? Stay out of it—let me be rid of you—stay back!

"What you want I do?" Mee Lanh asked.

"Try to walk."

Was it her inability to walk, or his own? "Try to walk," he said again.

"I do walk, Ben."

"No, don't limp. Walk naturally. Try."

It had been four straight days of lay-them-out-and-treat-them-on-the-ground—and dope everybody up as best you can, and keep on moving. Except that moving was impossible too. The road had been bombed, and the wagons, carts, trucks, donkeys, water buffaloes, tanks were detouring into what used to be rice paddies. It was all reeking swamp now, with people, animals, equipment mired in it. That made no difference; more moved in.

"Where the fuck are they going?" Luddy said. "Can't they see we're up to our ass in it?" He cursed the bog, the Nams, the VCs, everything. Cursing had come late to him; he didn't do it well. He was Pennsylvania Dutch, barely nineteen, a renegade from the Amish—the black beard and the blue Bible, he said—and he was bright, troubled and profane. He had a right not to go to war, his father had told him, an Amishman could be conscientious. But Luddy had replied that he believed in America, not in a bearded God; and his father had said he would be shunned. Ben predicted he would go back to the Amish one day, and back to church, but Luddy said frig that, he had gotten too young screwed

and too old fucked. You'll die young, dumb, and sorry, Ben said
. . . They liked each other.

Luddy stuck his head out of the ambulance window. "Let's
go, asshole!"

They were just out of the swamp and beginning to pick up a
little speed, when they saw the child's body on the road. It was
moving a little.

Rracckk.

"Stop," Ben said.

"What the fuck for?"

"There's a kid."

Rracckk. Luddy pointed to the gun spatters, like huge rain-
drops on the road. "Are you whacked up?" Luddy said, and kept
on going.

They drove a minute or so. There was another jam and
nobody moved. Ben got out of the ambulance and started running
back along the line, took a shortcut across a mucky rice field, back
on the road again, looking for the kid. When he got to her, she was
dead.

He looked at her on the ground, a Vietnamese girl, perhaps
nine or ten, no more than that, her leg bleeding, not very much.
She had no right to be dead with as little wound as that; he had
seen guys come to life with nothing left below the waist.

Then he noticed that the leg gash was oozing in a slight beat,
rhythmically, not lifeless blood at all. He touched her for the second time; she was cold. He touched his fingertips to an eyelid,
lifted it. Son of a bitch, he said, this thing's alive.

Gently, he lifted her off the ground and started to carry her
back to the ambulance. But when he got to the rice bog, he got
sucked into it, caught as if in quicksand. The stalled line of vehicles began to move. I'm going to get left, he thought in panic, this
kid and I are going to be ditched in a strafing-targeted quagmire.
But the motor line came to a stop again, and he saw Luddy scud-
ding back toward him, sweating and cursing.

In the back of the ambulance, he tended to her. For once, the
slow movement of the line was an advantage; he could put a tight
binding on her leg and clean the road dirt out of the wound.

In the night, just as they were entering the relative safety of
Dak Quan, she came to consciousness. She had a fever and he gave
her antibiotics and kept pouring water into her, by IV at first and

then by mouth, forcing her to drink it. She wet herself and began to cry.

"I am for shame," she said.

She could get along in English very well. She had been an American "mascock," she said, for three years. She either couldn't pronounce the word mascot or some wit of a soldier had told her that was the right way to say it. She wasn't sure whether Mee was her first name and Lanh her last, or the other way around, so she asked to be called by both. Her family? She put her hands over her eyes when she talked about them. She knew her father and two brothers were dead, but wasn't sure about her mother. It had been three years since their village had been bombed—a faraway land, she said—and in those three years, one after another American soldier had taken care of her. Ben said he would take care of her as well. She would go along with them in the ambulance and be their mascot. He taught her how to say the word correctly, but she liked the old way better.

Two or three days after Ben found her, he asked, "How old are you, Mee Lanh?"

She didn't respond immediately. Then she said, "Nine years?" It was distinctly a question, not a statement, as if she wished she could be sure.

Mee Lanh recovered rather quickly, because she insisted on it. In a week, she was hobbling around, favoring her bandaged leg, trying to help them in their work, getting in their way. She showed no horror of the blood and entrails; she had already seen her share. Soon, she could shove an intestine back into an open gut, and hold it while a tentative stitch was taken. And then an hour later, if they had a breath of quiet, she was a happy child, laughing to the point of stomach-ache at something Luddy would say. She thought Luddy a clown and Ben a sage, considered them both funny, and seemed to love them equally. For Ben the war was less terrible after Mee Lanh came.

The day he took the bandages off her leg, she walked proudly away from him, but she still limped.

"Walk straight," he said.

"I do walk straight."

"You're limping."

"I no lumping, I no lumping."

"Don't tell me. Here's what you're doing." He caricatured her walk and she died laughing. He gave her a hug.

"I lucky," she said. Her face went grave. "I no roppeed."

He didn't know what the word meant; it didn't sound like pidgin English and he thought it must be Nam. When he said he didn't understand, she seemed reluctant to explain it. But Luddy kept asking her questions, and she kept trying to get away with half answers. At last, in an agony of embarrassment, she pointed to her vagina and shook her head a number of times, vehemently, no, no. Never raped. Nine years old and proud not to have been raped, she didn't seem bitter or even angry that others had been. Nor was she partisan about it. "Cong man—Nam man—you man—all man do same," she said; rape knew no nationality. Perhaps she doesn't quite understand what it means, he thought, perhaps she's too young.

On a summer's day when the air was so muggy that Luddy said it was like inhaling beer suds, Mee Lanh behaved in a strange way. All morning she had been uncharacteristically mopey and irritable; slow-moving, too, as if stripping a Band-Aid were a major undertaking. By a coincidence, they had just run out of benzies, and Ben wondered if she had been pinching uppers, pill popping. It would account for her customary liveliness, her unflagging good cheer—and for her depression today, without the lift of the amphetamine. It bothered him and he watched her covertly.

Lunchtime, to get away from the mosquitoes, they had driven to a dried-up canal and parked the ambulance in the open sunlight. It was murderously hot and, even in the baking glare, the air was steamy. They were eating lunch. The food was freeze-dried sawdust, Luddy said, the water in their canteens was buffalo sweat. In the middle of lunch, with elaborate casualness, Mee Lanh got up and meandered away. Not many minutes later, Ben saw her slip into the back of the ambulance. If she was really on the stuff, and looking for it, he thought he'd better find out. He didn't know exactly what he would do about it . . . nine years old.

He followed her. Moving silently to the back of the ambulance, not betraying his presence, he looked in. Sure enough, she was searching for something. Poor brat, he thought; and what bastard started her on the junk?

Then he saw her do a strange thing. She brought out a roll of gauze bandage. She unwound a sizable quantity of it, folded it end on end, neatly and carefully, and when she had a number of layers of it and had patted them down, she picked up the scissors and made the cut.

"What are you doing?" he said.

She jumped as if shot. Her face turned purple. She shoved the gauze behind her back. "Go away—go away!" she said.

He suddenly realized. You fool, he said to himself, you dumb idiot, she's menstruating. It accounts for the mopes, the lassitude—and now, the secrecy.

He wanted to leave her to her privacy, yet it occurred to him that this might be her first period, and he wanted her to know she need not be embarrassed by it, or ashamed—or even frightened.

"It's all right, honey," he started, not sure where he was going or what he would say when he got there. What he was finally inspired to say was threadbare maxim, the bumbling half truths of which parents beget themselves on the grand approach of the menarche. "It's okay—it's natural—women get it—it's a good thing—you understand—it's a *good* thing."

"I know what it is." She said it quietly, with slightly offhand dignity, not making an event of it.

"You do?"

"I have it. Two years I have it."

"You said you were nine."

She flushed as if mortified to the soul. "I lie," she said.

"How old are you, Mee Lanh?"

"Thirteen."

He found himself looking at her flat breasts. Her confusion grew worse. "I see what you look. I have not much. And what I have is tie tight."

"Why?"

He thought for a moment that she couldn't stand it, she would run away. Then she held her ground. "A woman tell me, do not say your age. If they think you are not child—you are woman—you will get roppeed."

He nodded. He was just as disturbed as she was. Quickly he left the ambulance and walked away.

The next day there was a change in Mee Lanh. What she always wore, because she had nothing else to wear, was a worn and faded cotton blouse buttoned up to the neck, a pair of cotton slacks that were made for a schoolboy, not a girl, and a pair of scuffed and misshapen leather sandals. She was meticulously clean —she bathed at every uninfested watering place and washed her clothes on any pretext—but those were, he thought, the only clothes she had, not a stitch of anything else. It never occurred to him that she wore underwear. But she must have, at least before what he called "the change." He was sure that now—today—she had discarded whatever she had worn as a brassiere. He could see, for the first time, the tentative statement of her breasts.

"The kid's getting boobies," Luddy said.

"Yes," he answered quietly. "She lied—she says she's thirteen."

Luddy whistled.

Inexplicably, Ben was offended by the sound.

As he noticed Luddy thinking differently of the girl, he knew that inevitably he too would come to think differently of her. He refused, however, to admit there was any ferment in his new way of seeing Mee Lanh; it was the way it used to be, he told himself, except for his compassion for a child who had been forced to come so furtively to womanhood. And it saddened him that she might not be quite so innocent as he had thought.

He knew it saddened her as well. She didn't laugh as readily as she used to; and hardly ever when Ben tried to be funny—only Luddy was the comic now. Bothered that she took him so seriously, he felt she was asking forgiveness for some offense she never could have perpetrated.

One afternoon, after five days of rainstorm and flash flood, he saw her bathing in the canal. He watched her at a distance. The long loose-fitting blouse she constantly wore had always suggested that she was as straight as a boy, but she wasn't, she was as rounded as a woman. Her breasts were not large but they were fully formed. He continued watching and couldn't turn away.

When the Vietcong started their October offensive, Ben got orders from the field hospital to move inland across a high-crested ridge. It was a senseless maneuver, there was no movement that meant anything, and just as they got to the saddle of the hill, the cab roof caved in. It didn't even seem like gunfire—at worst, it could have been a bit of mortar shrapnel—because there was hardly any damage to the ambulance.

Only to Luddy. He sat there, still holding the wheel; the ambulance was still moving. His body was just as sturdily upright as ever, his hands as capable, except his skull had a cleft in it like the split in a gigantic and overripe tomato, and the red juice ran down his temple and onto his cheek. It was only after they moved him that his muscles lost their tone, and he went to uselessness. As Ben wiped his face, he prayed that Luddy would die immediately. But he didn't. Unbelievably, he lay there, staring, talking from time to time in a dwindling voice, asking for nothing, not even speaking of pain. But he knew he was going to die, and he said, quite simply, "I don't want to do that."

"Then don't," Ben said.

The boy tried to run his hands down his body but couldn't manage. Not knowing where the damage was, he was taking an inventory. "Do I have everything?"

"Yes," Ben said. Everything but your brain, poor bastard.

"How long will I keep it?"

"I don't know."

"Not long, huh?"

"I don't know, Luddy." Then, quietly, "Shall I do something? Shall I find a chaplain?"

"God sucks."

It was the last thing he said, but it was at least another hour before he died. Ben didn't know what to do with him, how to bury him. It was all rock and stone up here, no earth he could dig into, and nothing to dig with. So he carried the body to a place where the rocks were smallest. He pushed a number of small ones around with his hands and he rolled the big ones, and tried to cover his body in some way, but couldn't do much of a job of it. Mee Lanh helped him. All the time she was scrabbling on the ground, pushing stones around, she kept nodding to Ben and nodding, as if to say they were engaged in a worthy enterprise.

Then it was finished. Ben sat on one of the large rocks. He didn't know the tears were coursing down his face, but she apparently did and couldn't stand it. "No," she cried, and took him in her arms and rocked him, kissed his cheeks and his eyes, kissing his tears away, and his hands, which were bruised and bleeding from the stones. "No," she said.

The ambulance didn't even need any repairs. There was a small hole in the roof, that was all. During the next few weeks, when he was driving, the gust of air that came through blew on his scalp in exactly the place where the shrapnel must have hit Luddy, but it didn't bother him; it was as if there were something left of the boy, an afflatus that was friendly.

Except for driving Mee Lanh did all the work that Luddy used to do. Some things she did better, some things worse. She even griped like Luddy, using some of his obscene words. He wondered if she said them to appear as tough as a soldier, or to comfort him by filling a vacuum that Luddy's death had left.

He loved her a great deal, not as a woman, but still, her burgeoning body notwithstanding, as a child. He had no notion what sort of love she had for him, until one night when they had descended to the valley and were awaiting orders from the field hospital. It was the first chilly night of the year, and they were in an abandoned hut just off the road. They had found a stray chicken and had roasted it over a tiny bonfire. And now it was time for sleep.

She said, "I have story to tell you."

"Yes?"

"One time I am nine year old—I am *true* nine year old. But American soldier think I am six, seven—I don' know. He give me all-time good candy, good ration. He have little house in village, Keiku. I clean for him—dish, floor, shoe, shirt, scrub back, everything. One night I am sleep, I hear terrible noise, someone is cry. I look all place, I not find. Then I know—is come from where he sleep, and person is hurt him. So I not know what to do. I get big knife from kitchen and I open door. He is nake, all nake—and she is nake too. And she is one who make big terrible noise. And I think he is hurt her, he is lay on her and make choke—maybe kill —so I say no, no. And he get up and she get up. And they both laugh at me. So I run away and I am shame—and I do not know why I am shame. Tomorrow come, and I say in my mind: I think I know what they do, but I am not sure. But he tell me more later, he tell me is not to be afraid, is make fuck-fuck, is very nice. He say, 'Is *true* very nice, Mee Lanh.' And then he touch me and he say, 'You want to try?' And I want to try, but I remember how she scream and I am afraid. So I say no. And he do not touch me anymore, and he do not make fun of me. He is nice man. And by-and-by, he get kill. And never in my all life do I make fuck-fuck— and never do I want . . . Excep' with you."

He told her that he loved her, but that she was too young and he did not want to touch her.

She said, "Do not be afraid."

"No, Mee Lanh."

"I will make fuck-fuck to you, then," she said.

He smiled.

"Is wrong way?" she asked.

"No," he said, and laughed a little. It was a gentle laugh, in affection, but she thought he was making fun of her. Humiliated, she started to run away, so he reached for her shoulder to console her.

"No—let me, let me," she said.

But she didn't run. She started to cry. This time he took her in his arms, he held her. She was filled with confusion and mortification, and a little fright. He realized it had taken all these many weeks to gather this much courage, and now it was all forsaking her.

"Mee Lanh," he said as comfortingly as he could.

"Ben . . . please."

It was deep night, with only a ray of moonlight on the earthen floor, and he could hardly see her. He felt her move close to him, giving her whole body to his, pressing her breasts against him as if they ached, trying to become one with him. He let his hand touch her shoulder, her arm, the curve of her thigh, and she trembled as she became aware of it. Then she was touching him everywhere, his cheeks, his lips, his eyelids, and she was undoing the buttons of his shirt. He felt her mouth on his breast. Abruptly, she stopped everything and was gone, and he wondered if she had panicked and fled. But in a moment she was back, altogether naked, moving her naked breasts against his, rubbing herself against him. Then, as he felt her fumbling clumsily at his trousers, he removed them and became as naked as she was.

As he started to touch her, "No—let me," she said.

So, for a while, he let her, and he became quickly aroused.

"How you call this?" she said.

"It's a penis."

"Do you make it grow so big or do I do it?"

"You do it."

"Oh, do I—do I?" The ecstasy of the thought seemed even greater than the ecstasy of the feeling.

"If I stop touching, will it go away?" she said.

"Not immediately."

"Oh, I will not stop," she said reassuringly. "If you touch me, will great thing happen?"

When he touched her, she was already moist. As his finger went inside her, she cried out. "Oh no, I cannot stand, I cannot."

"Did I hurt you?"

"Oh no!" And then the thought occurred to her: "If you put

yourself inside me, will hurt? Is this why woman of soldier scream?"

How to let her know the distinction between the first-time pain and the pleasure-pain that comes later? No woman he had ever heard of had found the first time painless. He tried to explain, but she thought the pleasure-pain explanation was comical; which was it, one or the other, yes or no?

Smiling, he wished he could answer it as simply as it was asked. "Yes and no."

She thought it was funny. "All time yes and no?"

"All time."

She laughed happily. "I don' like say fuck-fuck, I will say yes and no."

Abruptly she became overwhelmed with how much she loved the touch of him and, without thinking, certainly without knowing what it was she was doing, or that there might be a name for it, she was kissing his penis and sucking it. Unable to stand it anymore, he turned her over, and as she lay back ready for him, waiting, he entered her and thrust as gently as he could, then more roughly, then without any restraint at all, and she wanted all of it.

"Yes and no!" she cried in pain. Then, in a little while, there wasn't any no.

In the next few weeks Mee Lanh wanted to make love all the time and so, in fact, did he. There was a febrile excitement in both of them, a glow as if their temperatures were always a few degrees above normal. They were constantly touching, stroking, reaching for each other. Accidentally, as they did their work, their bodies would brush against one another, as though the world had become a more congested place, and they had to graze while passing. Whatever injuries the war had done to her, she came to lovemaking without angers, without prejudice or hypocrisy, with a yearning to know and search and explore everything. There was no form of it she did not pleasure in, nothing he ever did was unenjoyable to her; she would do anything he wanted, and there was never an occasion when she said no to what his hands were doing, his mouth, his tongue, or any part of him. He could do no wrong, as long as he did something.

She carried on a separate and tender and very private love affair with his penis. It was as secret an intimacy between them as if the organ had nothing to do with Ben. She adored it for its sake alone, ascribing to the member its own differentiation, its own personality. Not enough that she kissed and stroked and sucked it, she talked to it as well, and pretended it was a two-way conversation— a colloquy conducted in such utter secrecy that she did not speak to it in Ben's language, but her own. With this friend and relative —and lover—she had the most voluptuous and yet the most companionable liaison. In Vietnamese, she confided everything to it, secure that Ben would not understand, gave voice to her sexual appetites and temptations, her naughtiest delights, her dreams, the mischievous gossip about the ludicrous ways that people make love, her small-girl embarrassments about her own imaginary lusts. Sometimes she would tell Ben what they were saying; more often, not. But even if he expired with curiosity to know their secrets, he didn't press his questions, for this was a privacy she deeply cherished. It was as if she had comfortably married a boy from home—she, who would never be able to marry the American she loved—and they spoke the same language and lived in the same neighborhood which they would never have to leave. Thus, with this companion, she was not a total stranger to her past, and her life would somehow have continuity. . . . And the thread of it was so delicate that Ben would not allow his curiosity to snap it. Sometimes, altering its role, she talked to it as if it were her Vietnamese child, slumbering in a cradle of warm grass, whom she would dress and dandify with one kind of kiss or another, and put to sleep. Frequently, however, when she was awakening it, it would cease to be either a child or Vietnamese: what big boy you are, she would say in English, what big boy, and she would praise it until it was inside her. Lovemaking, to Mee Lanh, was not only a devotion, not only an erotic passion, it was a child's game, an ecstatic make-believe, a fantasy of happiness too beautiful to be solely real.

Ben's sexual craving for her, in some anomalous way, obscured the fact that he genuinely loved her. But he felt a disquiet about his love. It was not a unitary thing, with a single and undivided integrity; it had a disturbing dualism. In the darkness, in the fever of wanting, she was—the Nams had an expression—his passion pillow. But in the daylight she was his beloved child. She was never a whole woman. In a deeply disconcerting way, as if foredooming eternal childliness, he couldn't conceive of her ever becoming a woman. Always the helpless innocent, the urchin he had found dying by the roadside. And no matter how she worshiped him, he could not make himself think of her as the mature love of his life, and he felt guilty for it, as if he had tried too little to love her, had given too stingily of himself. Yet, the part of him that did love her—as a child—was the purest part of him, the part he cherished most about himself.

One day, thinking of this, he had a revelation. It was so clear, so unassailable, that it astonished him. He discovered that his love of Mee Lanh had saved his life. More than his life, his soul. Luddy, in his death, had bequeathed him a name for his despair: God sucks, and so does life itself. There was all the crying and the dying to testify to that. There was all the solid, liquid, gaseous cruelty of war to testify to it. There was the hopelessness. It was unbearable.

And then, with Mee Lanh, it was no longer unbearable; he could endure it. Not that she was lovable—which indeed she was —but that, in the midst of this grotesque ugliness, he could feel some beauty in himself—he could love. That he had been blessed with a gift for it! And he realized that never in his life, as long as he could love someone, could he fall into an abyss of despair. Love would be a salvation he could always count on.

It was a time of quiet for him; in all the boom and babel of war, a time of silence in the spirit, of peace.

All at once, the war became louder, and shattered it.

The October offensive started moving westward, and they were in it. Not too dangerously at first; then, overnight, everything. A few Cong choppers for a day or so, then the planes, skimming the ridge top, the orange bombs, the brown shit-blasts, as Luddy used to call them, then the chemicals. Soon the recon patrollers appeared, night after night, in their tiger and monkey suits, and there was talk that the regulars would inevitably be next.

Where the *people* came from, the ordinary fleeing people, Ben couldn't imagine; this was countryside, there were no towns or cities to be emptied. But suddenly the ridge road was jammed with refugees. In the early days of flight, they carried things—packs and bundles and bits of bedding and animals on tethers—but later they came only with their fear.

In the midst of the chaos, Mee Lanh heard a rumor. She had accidentally encountered a cousin who had come from Dak Binh, their village. He was not going back, he said, because his parents were dead, but he had heard that many people had been allowed to return; it was reported that Mee Lanh's mother had been one of them.

Relating the rumor to Ben, she trembled; her face was drawn. "You will take me back?" she asked.

"Take you back—in the ambulance?"

"Yes."

"Mee Lanh—honey—how can I do that? I can't just take off. I have to do my work, I have to get people to the field hospital—I have orders."

"Is not far. Is other side of Bien Tum."

"My God, that's nearly two hundred miles from here—on a road that probably doesn't exist anymore."

"You can take me."

It was the dogged, quiet oversimplification of childhood. But it was her mother she was talking about, and he realized that whatever oversimplification he heard, her utterance was pure pain. Still, how could he take her, with a war carnage in the making, and every hand vital? Yet, how else could she get through? And would she go without him, would he ever see her again? The thought of it had a density that made breathing difficult.

"Mee Lanh—I can't."

The whole thing was taken out of their hands. The offensive came. In a single afternoon, the valley was ablaze and the ridge top seemed to have been shorn away. Nighttime, the Cong came in, not patrollers now, the real thing, the road was blasted behind them, there was no longer any route back to the field hospital, not a track or trail.

Within a few daylight hours, the refugees were scurrying westward. Now the ambulance was cut off not only from the field hospital but from the military. There was no access to the wounded, no soldiers to attend to. When the civilian casualties had been succored, Ben realized that his greatest utility, indeed his only one, was westward where the refugees were going—in the direction of Mee Lanh's village.

The ambulance became the rear guard of the exodus. Daytimes he would stop and tend the wounded; at night he would try to pick up speed. But he never attempted to outstrip the faltering column of sick and injured exiles. He and Mee Lanh worked ceaselessly from dawn to darkness; they had, it seemed, an inexhaustible store of energy.

But not of supplies. Everything was running out—antiseptics, palliatives, bandages. Now, even their energies began to diminish.

Ben's hands started to tremble, he started dropping things. And on the fourth day of the hegira, Mee Lanh began to limp again.

"What's the matter with your leg?"

"Nothing."

"You're limping."

"I no lumping."

She knew how to say the word properly now, but was hoping he would smile. He didn't. "Are you in pain?"

"Who say?"

"I ask."

"No pain, no pain."

"Let me look at it."

She rolled up her pant leg and he stared. It was swollen from the ankle to the knee. It had a bad color, purple going to gray.

"When did that start?" he asked.

"I don' know. I think yesterday."

"Why didn't you tell me?"

"I don' know."

"Does it hurt here?" He poked a few inches above the knee where there was no discoloration. She winced. More gently, he pressed the flesh a bit lower on the leg and she twisted her head away.

He couldn't understand it. It had been such an obvious kind of wound and it had healed. If there had been something continuingly wrong, it would have shown up long ago; it was months since he had treated her. There had been nothing like a postoperative infection—there had been no operation; besides, it would have been over and cared for by now. Yet, an infection . . .

Her temperature was 102. Her cheeks were flushed, she was breathing unevenly. He gave her two compatible antibiotics, one by injection, one by mouth; he gave her aspirin.

But that night her temperature was up another point, and by morning she was delirious. She talked in a kind of pidgin English he had never heard her speak before, then she would lapse into Nam and be totally incomprehensible. She was burning up.

He kept examining her calf, her knee, her thigh. The infection was spreading, the swelling was enveloping the whole inflamed leg. She was deathly sick, he could do nothing more for her, and he wouldn't believe his suspicion of what it was.

It was osteomyelitis, the bone infected by staph or strep, or some obscenity of this war-diseased country. It was sickness to the bone, to the marrow, the kind that attacks the young.

He gave her more antibiotics, and more. Even if he weren't running out of them, it would make no difference, they were doing her no good.

She was dying. If there were a hospital that was reachable, if there were a surgeon . . .

Dying.

Do it, he told himself, you can do it. Do it.

He thought: I'm not a doctor, I'm certainly not a surgeon, I have no expertise in this, I might pull her through an amputation, and then those other catastrophes, shock, hemorrhage, embolism, anything might happen.

She's dying. Do it.

She kept murmuring and murmuring, as if asking someone to answer her, but he didn't understand a single one of the foreign words, and all he could do was make comforting sounds and touch her now and then.

He had the equipment for it, knives, a surgical saw, gut for sutures, clamps, Demerol, a bottle of ether somewhere.

The bottle might be empty. Ether was volatile. No matter how tightly it was stoppered, somehow the liquid always disappeared.

The bottle was nearly full. There were no excuses.

Do it.

Her voice seemed stronger. Perhaps the fever would subside. He would wait a while.

The day had passed, the light was nearly gone—he wouldn't be able to see her clearly. But tomorrow might be too late.

Her murmuring had stopped.

Do it.

He wired two flashlights together, his and Luddy's, and suspended them from the ceiling of the ambulance. He thought at first that he would operate on her where she was lying on the stretcher. But he realized it might not be steady enough, for there would be motion and force. So he moved the supplies case and the instruments cabinet together; there was, luckily, very little difference in their heights. He put a plastic poncho down and a white rubberized reception cloth on top of it. He lifted her off the litter and onto the improvised table.

Then he gave her a sedative and, while it was taking hold, he prepared the instruments. She seemed to be breathing more deeply now, more regularly. If only he himself could get a deep and regular breath.

He didn't need to shave her leg, there wasn't a hair on it, but he did wash it carefully, with soap and water first, then with alcohol.

He made a neat wad of gauze and poured some ether on it, then placed it gently on her nose and mouth. Lightly, he held it there, thinking: How will I know how little or how much? Observation of her eyeballs or eye activity would be unreliable under this inadequate light; besides, he wouldn't know exactly what to look for; so he would have to rely on watching her respiration, and on the principle that too little ether was better than too much.

She was deeply under now.

Below the knee, he lanced the skin. Instantly he knew that it was useless down this low; the gangrene was sickening. The putrefaction was rank, and this part of the leg was not salvageable anymore, it had mortified. As she stirred a little, he poured more ether on the gauze and started on the thigh.

If it was going to be a mid-thigh amputation, he would have to cut a slight bit lower so that he could undermine the flesh and leave enough to make a flap over the bone. He cut through the skin and into flesh and, with the first spurt of blood, he had the clamp ready, and then another and another. There was some mortification here too, but not as much, and he could cut it away. He was surprised at how well he had contained the bleeding.

He was working faster now, and almost as if he knew what he was doing. She made a little sound, like moaning, and he gave her more anesthetic, pouring quite a lot this time.

Then he had the saw in his hand. For the first time since the operation had begun, he started to shake. He could not believe that in a moment he would have to saw a human bone. Don't call this a saw, he told himself, and don't call this bone; one is a surgical instrument and the other a femur—neither, in this instance, has humanity in it. Technology.

His heart stopped—the lights went out.

No, not the lights, only one of them. The other flashlight, albeit the weaker one, was still illuminating the operating table. Even the remaining one had a flicker in it, and he prayed it would last some minutes longer. He was almost through, he was already sewing things up again, and the patient was still alive and breathing. He debated whether to suture everything or leave part of the wound open so it would drain. There might still be some infection, although he felt reasonably sure that he had gotten all of it. Still, it might be better if he didn't sew it totally closed.

The operation was over.

He took the gauze off Mee Lanh's face. Her cheeks were brilliant scarlet; it was ether flush. Soon she would perspire, she might be nauseous, he thought, even before she became conscious again. Meanwhile, he was certain she was not in pain. Later, when she came awake, she might be dizzy and complain of headache, or of thirst. He would be here, he would tend to her, he would make her as comfortable as he could. And somehow, as soon as they could get somewhere, he would make arrangements for a prosthetic leg; it was not too soon to think of it right now, even now. She would be well again. . . . He had done it.

He watched her sleeping. Her slumber didn't seem so unnatural anymore, it had a deep sound, steady and tranquil. He would stay here, not move away, in case she needed him, keep the vigil every minute of the night.

He said: I love you very much. With the feeling came the overpowering gratification: he had saved her life.

However, sitting in the airless enclosure of the ambulance, his spirit began to languish a little. He smiled ruefully at the notion that the postoperative depression was being suffered not by the patient but by the doctor. In a wave of self-doubt, he was not so certain that he had indeed rescued her. She was still heavily under anesthesia and anything might yet occur, and she might die. And if it were to happen, he would have to face the fact that it had been, largely, his fault. He had allowed the infection to progress too far, had taken too much time to decide that he should perform the operation, and that he *could*.

His mood turning blacker, he faced a more probing question. Wasn't it possible that, not knowing enough, he had performed the operation badly, and he could have performed it more skillfully if he had been totally trained to do it, and had become a doctor? He was afraid of the answer to the question, for it might reveal a deeper deficiency than a mere lack of skills. Perhaps the same worm worried at the heart of his indecisive delay in operating on Mee Lanh as in his irresolute failure to finish medical school: he could not take the responsibility for anyone else's life. There was a dismaying void in him that made it unthinkable for him to be a doctor. And he came upon the tragic omission: he lacked the conviction of godliness that would make him equal more to saving a life than to taking one.

He was afraid. If he hadn't been afraid, he would not have delayed the operation until the infection might have become irremediable. He could not make a life and death decision, he could not hurl defiance at mortality, he could not make the irrevocable commitment to being either a doctor or a soldier, a healer or a killer. He was the medial man, the soldier-medic.

But if Mee Lanh were to die, would he have to carry the guilt of it? Was nothing to be said for someone who had demonstrated a competence in shrilling wartime emergency, in Herculean difficulty, in agonizing sights and smells and fears, and had given all of himself to the saving of lives? He had seen the double-edged knife that can cut a soldier in two directions: the self-recrimination for killing and for being alive when others are killed. Was he also to suffer a double-edged guilt? How could he live with it? If Mee Lanh were to die, what name other than self-loathing could he put on it? Would he be reduced to calling it rage, loneliness, grief, the obscenity of a war that sucks and a God that does the same, and the muscle-binding, brain-crippling helplessness that knows there is no retaliation?

But she would not die, he said.

His depression, he realized, had had something to do with the stifling air inside the ambulance. Not daring to open a window for fear of chilling Mee Lanh, he had been unable to dissipate the ether fumes. They were making him dispirited and drowsy, and if he fell asleep, his resolve to watch over her through the night would be vitiated. He wished the oxygen tank were not empty; he needed a bracer, a quick jolt.

He looked closely at Mee Lanh. She was quite all right, sleeping profoundly. If he were to go outdoors for a sharp gust of air, race along the ridge for a few minutes, run his lungs clean, he could be back before she came to consciousness. He felt her forehead and her pulse, covered her a bit more securely, then slipped out.

The night was cool. Just below the ambulance, on the shoulder of the hill, there was a tiny village—only a few wattle houses and some tiny hooches, nearly all thatch and bamboo, in deep thickets of grass, glimmering like a moonlit fairy tale. He breathed deeply, still a little fuzzy from the ether. He must rout the giddiness quickly, he said, and hurry back to his patient. He started to run, easily at first, not pushing too strenuously for fear of a reactive dizziness. The air felt wonderful and lifted him. In a fleeting fantasy, he was back home again, sailing in the bay off Marblehead, with a sweet zephyr filling the sails of the skiff, and he was flying free in the company of the west wind.

Running, running, and all at once, as if cued by a streak of lightning, he ran out of the world, and into oblivion. He was shouting Mee Lanh's name, and fire, as if the two outcries meant the same, they were interchangeable. Fire, again and again, shrieking for the girl, certain she was dead. How he knew she was dead he could not tell, or if indeed she really was. All he knew was that the war was gone from his mind, the ambulance as well, the little village of bamboo, the thatched houses, everything gone, the whole ridgeline and valley a vast and interminable emptiness. Only, at times, the flames existed, a fullness of them, blazing in his mind, quickening all his consciousness to pain and outcry, and to the torment of fear and fault.

Fear, fault, and fire . . . he didn't know where they came from, or what they meant, or what the fire-fault had been. He kept screaming the terrifying word—how long did he scream it, days, weeks, months?—until he knew he was lying on a white bed in a field hospital, hobbled of body and mind.

Would he ever discover what the fire was, or if indeed there had been any, or if it was a reprisal that his angry mind had devised to set his inhuman world aflame? Would he ever remember a specific event that had occurred, or had something simply snapped in his brain, setting him adrift to wander away from Mee Lanh, forsaking her to her postoperative helplessness, an abandoned cripple? He could imagine any horror, so many horrors having been real to him, but he could not *remember* any. Not knowing was, perhaps, the worst horror of all.

Why, after three years, had so much of the past, yet not enough of it, returned to him tonight? Why, on this safe seaside, was he sending this long-delayed message to himself? And what was the message? Why, particularly, had it come in the form of a triad, with Kalya as the third part of the trinity. Now, subtly and peripherally why was another name intruding? . . . Falkos. What did the guerrilla-schoolmaster have to do with it? What did his going up to the Monastery or not going up—with Kalya or without her—what did it all have to do with his recollection?

The sea was calm. He heard gulls crying. He walked along the strand, letting the water edge up to his shoes, dampening them. The sound of the seabirds was far away.

What did the memory say?

Define yourself, his father had told him, and he had come to Cyprus to do just that, had come to this far-flung island, Mid-East, nearly mid-life, mid-stream, mid-nothing. And what name had he come up with?

If he had to define himself in terms of soldiering or doctoring, or by any of the tenets of his parents, he was something less than magna cum laude. But there were other criteria, more lenient and more human, softer perhaps, not the hardware of accomplishment. If he had to define himself in terms of Mee Lanh, he could say— and be proud—that his love of her had helped to make her happy, had mitigated her wartime terrors, her loneliness, had in a way saved her as it had saved himself.

Precipitously, a clear, awaiting thought, a latency begging to be summoned, came to him. In this flash of insight, he saw the relationship between the Vietnamese child and the Turkish woman, and why the little girl had returned so vividly tonight. The lesson he had learned from loving Mee Lanh was luminous. Why had he forgotten it? It was the revelation he had had while she was still alive:

In the season of the worst horrors of Vietnam, when life had been unbearable, his love had made him able to endure it. It had been his salvation. At no time in his existence, in fact, had he known so securely who he was, and where his benefaction as a man might be. It was the one thing about himself that he knew was constant and inalienable: his gift of love, and his need of it.

But . . . to the question of who he was, could he simply answer: I am a man who needs to be in a state of love, and only then can I be useful to the world? Was it as simple as that? He knew that in a loveless era, when rage was more modal than affection, there was a vestigially romantic notion that love was the answer to everything. Even if the idea was pap, and he couldn't believe in it, mightn't it be true of *him?* If so, what a tiny compass within which to define himself—solely and exclusively, a man in love. Would he be willing to settle for such a narrow confine? Were there no other attributes by which he could describe himself—his decencies, his generosities, his competence in the work he did, the ideal of peace he believed in—did none of them count when he identified himself? Yet, none of those qualities in himself had ever moved his mind and muscle with such strength and certainty, none had moved his heart with such overwhelming happiness as his love of Mee Lanh had done.

And, he suspected, as his love of Kalya might do. So—could it be that neither the death of Mee Lanh, if indeed she was dead, nor the terror of fire was the message of the memory, but that love was the message, his dependency upon it?

Not that he had any certainty he would find it with Kalya, but that he was magnetically drawn to her. In fact, he was angry at himself for letting his mind become so entangled. He resented the compulsion he had toward the woman as he had never resented his love of the Vietnamese girl. Why was he so waywardly tempted by her? What insanity to say it was because she was beautiful, she was sensuous. He had known sensuously beautiful women before, and more to his taste—leaner, younger, not so exotic as to be alien—without noticeably losing his common sense. He ached for her distress, knowing that anybody's suffering made him vulnerable, but he had known sad women, tragic women who had not made him obsessional. And even if he were to add to her attractions that she was perceptively intelligent . . .

Wait. How much more need she be than beautiful, intelligent, and afflicted for him to be in love with her? The core: it wasn't what he knew about her that excited him, it was what he didn't know.

A woman of discrepancies. A collection of shards that could not be put together to make a single artifact. She was a feral, mad creature in a ditch, yet a sensible person who studied her limited alternatives and made a deal. She was a woman too proud to be pitied, too proud to show the grief of her heart, yet she would sell her body for quotidian employment. She was a vulgarian who could spit into a cone of currency, yet with those same lips she could fashion words with fastidious precision. She was primitive, she was civilized.

She might turn out to be as ugly as she was beautiful. She might be as capable of inflicting pain as she had suffered it. She might already have done it; might have committed an unnameable horror in her life.

So be it, then—he was bewitched by the mystery of her, by the illusion of what she might turn out to be. And what was wrong with that? How much reality could there be in love, anyway, how much did it depend on keeping afloat the glittering bubble of the dream? Love didn't live in the realm of matter, but in myth. In the realm of Aphrodite.

Wasn't this why he came to her island? A realist, hadn't he consciously come to an isle of illusion, a Cloud-Cuckoo-Land where there would be eternal peace? Hadn't he come to find a goddess of love, since he could not live without the myth that she existed? Hadn't he come for some fantasy he could live with, his real view of life-as-hellfire being intolerable? Myths, fantasies, illusions—was he perhaps not the realist he had always hoped to be? Must he face the fact that he needed illusion, to stay alive?

He had hardly slept at all. It was almost daylight. He could not wait for the morning to come, so that he could call her at the Alasia Hotel. And as he contemplated the call, he shoved into the back of his mind the disquieting thought that, no matter whether his decision to go with her was good or bad, the reason he had made it might be wrong. Love might not be the answer to anything.

5

At nine o'clock in the morning, Ben drove to the Limassol bus stop to pick up Yannis. As he waited for the bus to arrive, he tried to think of a way he could tell the old man that he had called Kalya and they were going to be meeting with Falkos at eleven. It would be difficult. To a pacifist like Yannis, converting the ambulance into a moving arsenal—even for only a few hours and in the cause of his own people—might be an enormity he could not handle. Perhaps he would quit. It was a possibility Ben did not want to face. He was even fonder of the old man than he had realized.

The bus arrived and a new Yannis alighted. Yesterday he had departed for his native village in a mood of suicidal depression. This morning, he was roseate with good cheer, his eyes glinted with delighted mischief, and he seemed fifteen years younger. Whatever happened last night, Ben thought, has made him happy, and I mustn't spoil it with a sober occasion. So, for the moment, he told him nothing of Falkos.

As they drove toward Nicosia, Ben asked, "Was it a woman?"

"What?"

"You heard me—was it a woman?"

"What woman, what?"

"That made you happy."

He grinned. "Who's happy?"

"You."

His smile turned sheepish. He wiped his chin with his gnarled hand, looked embarrassedly out his window, then started grinning again. "Not a woman," he said. "A raisin."

"You spent the night with a raisin?"

"Yes." Bellows of laughter.

"What the hell does that mean?"

"You don't know what is a raisin? A raisin is a dry grape."

"I know what a raisin is. I'm trying to figure what game you can play with it."

"Is not a it. Is a she."

"I was sure you wouldn't be out with a he-raisin."

"They call her I Stavitha—which means she looks like a raisin."

"Does she like to be called that?"

Abruptly the old man's face became serious. "No, she does not like to be call a raisin. It makes her feel bad."

"Then don't call her that."

Outraged: "Me? Never! I never call her that!" Then, quietly, almost to himself: "Until last night."

Under the glee of the old man, this was clearly something bothersome. "This woman—her name is Gannoula—she is maybe fifty years old, and she is never married. You know why? Because she is maybe the ugliest woman in the world. Her face is—how you say—it has so many wroonkles in it that they call her I Stavitha. But not me—never—I never call her a raisin—never. I never say she is ugly, I never turn my face from her. When I see her, I say, 'How are you, Gannoula—how are you today? The sky is beautiful, the oranges are big, we have good plums this year.' But yesterday—you remember?—I am very unhappy. So I get a little bit drunk, and then a little bit more drunk. And I am walking in my village and I am near the church, and she is there, and she sees me. 'Oh, Yannis,' she says to me, 'you have come home to your village—I am glad to see you.' And I say to her that the plums are good and she answers yes, they are. And then she says to me, 'Yannis, I have made some special wine—I will bring you a bottle.' And do you know what I say to her? I say, 'What kind of wine? Raisin wine?' And when I say this drunken joke, I see her eyes close a little, and she goes away. And I say to myself, you rotten drunken bastard to say such a thing to this poor woman. And I cannot stand how I feel, I want to die. So I drink more, and I feel worse. And it is nighttime, and I say to myself, you goatshit, you go to her house, and tell her you are a sorry man for saying this. So I go. And I am so drunk that I cannot find her little house. Even if I know every stone in that village, I cannot find where she lives. So I am in her neighborhood, and I am calling out loud,

'Gannoula! Gannoula! Come and spit on my face! Come and tell me I am goatshit for saying a bad thing to you!' In some time, a door is opening and she comes out. She is wearing an ugly night-gown and she says, 'Shut up, you goatshit, you will wake all the chickens and all the sheep. Shut up, you drunken goatshit!' . . . So . . . she takes me into her house. And in my shame and drunkness, I start to cry. I say to her, 'I am sorry I say this word to you—raisin—I am sorry I say this, Gannoula.' And she says, 'Do not be sorry, Yannis. I have to tell you something. In this world, I am not the ugliest, and you are not the oldest.' And when she says this to me, there is nothing more to cry about. And I say to myself, 'If I am not the oldest and she is not the ugliest—then this is the most beautiful thing that somebody has ever spoken—or even in writing, on a piece of paper.' . . . This is truly beautiful, yes?"

"Yes, it is."

"So we sleep together."

"Congratulations."

"No, is not congratulations. Not yet. When I am in the bed with her, I do not want to tell her a lie. So I say, 'Gannoula, I have to tell you something. I am here, but my *vila* is in Athens.' So she says to me, 'Is all right—my beautiful face is in Athens also.' Well, we have much laughing, and I go to sleep with my belly against her behind. And I have to tell you, Ben, a belly against a behind is like warm bread in your mother's kitchen."

Ben agreed totally. The old man looked at him quickly, to see if he was being laughed at, and, noting the sobriety of the American's face, he nodded a little in appreciation of the other man's appreciation.

They drove in silence for a while. Ben didn't interrupt the sweetness of the old man's reverie. But as they made the final turn that took them on to the Nicosia road, the Greek noticed that they were going toward the city without having been dispatched there.

"Nicosia? Why?"

"We're going to a meeting."

"Who? What kind of meeting?"

"Falkos and Kalya."

Yannis held back, seeming not to want to engage the question. Then: "What happen?"

Ben told of last night's meeting with Kalya.

"Why does she do it?" Yannis asked.

"She works for Falkos—he gave her a job."

"Why do *you* do it?"

"There's an old sick priest up there."

"Why we don't go there without them?"

"We'd never make it."

Inferentially, the Greek understood the risks. "Then don't go."

"The old priest will die."

"We will all die."

"You don't have to go if you don't want to, Yannis."

The old man didn't say yes, he would go, or no, he would not. Instead, unexpectedly, he asked, "You like it in Vietnam?"

Irritated, he snapped, "No, of course not."

"Then why do you go to another one?"

"If there are wars, there are wounded—and I'm a medic. I've never carried a gun—and I won't carry one this time."

"The others will—and there is a cease-fire."

"Who's observing it?"

"I am. You and me."

"That's great—but we've always observed it. How about them? Did you hear the morning news? The Turks are still advancing southward."

"Which way are you advancing?"

"I'm not advancing."

"Yes, you are—up the mountain—with Falkos."

Ben lost his temper. "What the hell do you think he'll do without me—just sit on his ass and do nothing? You think the Greeks won't attack the Monastery? They'll bomb the gates open! Even if he says they won't, we know they will—they have to! They'll destroy the place!"

He stopped short. He was finding the logical, perfect extenuation for joining Falkos. And it shook him how quickly he had come to justify it. As he was on the verge of rescinding the argument . . .

"You are perhaps right." The old man was still worrying it. "I will go with you."

"No. I don't want you with me."

Yannis was bewildered and hurt. "We work together."

"It'll only be a day or so. I'll leave you in Nicosia and pick you up when we're finished."

He could see how torn Yannis was. The old man was pitting

his loyalty to an idea against his loyalty to someone he loved. "I am your friend—I will not let you do this by yourself."

In a little while they entered Nicosia.

The place where they all met was a wine cellar called Skotos, the darkness. It was well named, for hardly anything was visible— a few tables, a few vats, Kalya's face still wrapped in a scarf, Yannis's very drawn, and Falkos across from Ben. With the waiter still hovering, the teacher postponed discussing the major transaction. Instead, he said to Yannis:

"That boy you sent me—Mark Achille—do you recommend him?"

"Recommend? I only see him two times."

"He claims you recommended him."

"He says he wants to kill Turks, and I say you are the right man to see."

"Then why *don't* you recommend him?"

Ben said, "He has epilepsy."

Falkos smiled without amusement. "That was quite a joke, Yannis—sending me a boy with epilepsy. Why did you do that?"

"Alexander the Great also has *epilepsia.*"

This time the teacher's smile was genuine. He turned to Ben. "Is it of an incapacitating kind?"

"He had four attacks within a few hours." Then he added, "I don't know what you had in mind for him."

"Nothing specific. He seems a bright boy—with a genuine American passport. That could be useful." But he raised his shoulders and gave up the idea. "Too bad—I rather liked him."

The waiter returned with the coffee, served them, and departed. Yannis had ordered nothing. The others had all ordered *metrio.* Kalya drank hers quickly, then dumped the grounds onto her saucer and in them was studying her fortune. She rarely looked up; when she did, Ben wondered at her eyes; they had always seemed coal black to him, but now he saw many depths of dense purple, like grottoes within grottoes.

"If you do precisely as you're told, there should be absolutely no danger," Falkos said. "You are three people above suspicion. You and Yannis have been Good Samaritans to Greeks and Turks alike. As to Kalya—being a Turk, and if we dress her as a nurse— she will certainly not be challenged."

He finished his coffee and put the cup to one side. "On the other hand, I don't want you to think it will be as gentle as a running brook. From our standpoint—but not from yours, Coram—it will be a risky enterprise."

"What is the enterprise, exactly?" Ben asked.

"I'll tell you what you need to know in order for you to do your share of the work. Since you want to do very little, you will have to know very little." His voice was ingratiating. "Believe me, Coram, I would like to tell you everything—I'd like you to be one of us."

"I'm not one of you," Ben said quietly. He made the definition as distinctly as possible. "I'm a medic, I'm not a combatant. I'm going up to tend to Father Demetrios. While I'm there, I'll take care of anyone who is hurt—Greek or Turk."

Kalya looked up from the coffee grounds. "We took that for granted. Why did you feel you had to make a point of it?"

The question ruffled him a little. She had caught him protesting too much. "Falkos is recruiting," he said defensively. "I don't want him to think I can be enlisted."

Falkos smiled ruefully. "We keep wooing America—and we think we have her in bed with us—and the next thing we know, the Turks are firing M-16s."

"I won't give them any M-16s—or fire them."

"Let's go on from there, shall we?" the teacher said. His tone became flatter. "I would like the three of you to start off—without me—late this afternoon, say at six. Is your ambulance in good working order?"

"Yes."

"I'd like to have it checked, if you don't mind. I'll tell you where to go. And of course, there's a little carpentry to be done."

"What will be done?"

"Those three drawers that are under the built-in bed—they have a good many implements in them—do you use all of them?"

"Most of them."

"You'll have to store them elsewhere. The faces of the drawers will be sawn off, and battened together in the rear. Then they'll be hinged back on. Later, when I join you, I'll ride in the space that the drawers formerly occupied."

Ben, wryly: "With your own implements."

"As you say."

Falkos reached into the pocket of his wilted summer jacket,

pulled out a small note pad and a tiny stub of a pencil. He scribbled something and handed the piece of paper to Ben. "This is the address of the auto mechanic. He'll do everything—even the carpentry work."

"Before going there," Ben said, "I'll pick up the dialysis equipment at the hospital."

Falkos looked blank; his mind had wandered. An old priest with a kidney disease had been mentioned only once in the course of the conversation. To the teacher, the patriarch's involvement was merely incidental. "Yes," he said cursorily, "get whatever you need."

"When do we go up to the Monastery?"

"Tomorrow morning."

"Why not this afternoon?"

"Well, there's work to be done on your vehicle. And by the time we get up there it might be nightfall."

"Wouldn't the dark suit your purpose better?"

"Not at all. It must all seem as innocent as morning."

Ben felt a shiver. With conscious rationality, he had engaged in a madness. He wanted the affair to be over as quickly as possible, yet he knew that as soon as it terminated, his excuse for being with Kalya would vanish, as she herself might vanish. If being with her was the heart and purpose of this lunacy, why did he want to quicken it to an end?

He looked at Kalya. Her face was very still, an exquisite mask; he wondered what havoc was under it. Then he looked at Falkos. The man was too cerebral and too sensible; there was something chilling about him. He spoke too benevolently about violence. He was too friendly. Ben felt as if he were being licked affectionately by the tongue of an untrustworthy animal. Sitting beside him, Yannis was motionless, he barely breathed; the old man was frightened.

"All right, then, tomorrow."

As he said it, Ben realized that he could be alone with Kalya sooner than he had expected. They could have the whole afternoon together. He would hurry to the hospital, borrow the equipment he needed, take the vehicle to the mechanic, and then . . .

Falkos broke into his thoughts. "I will meet you all in the morning. There's an old copper mine—it's halfway up the mountain road that leads to the Monastery. You will get there this evening, near sundown. Kalya will show you the way."

The meeting was apparently over, but the schoolmaster made no sign that it was time to leave; on the contrary, he seemed more rooted than ever. "There's just one other thing." He said it as an afterthought, which clearly it wasn't. "Tomorrow, when we leave the mine to go up to the Monastery, there will be a time when I'll come out of my hiding place. It will be—in a sense—the start of the action. You, Coram, will be driving. I will station myself at the large right window of the ambulance, and Kalya will be at the left one." He paused an instant. "I'm going to ask you, Yannis, to station yourself at the rear window."

Yannis barely moved. He simply slid his hands off the table and put them quietly in his lap. "For what cause?"

"Kalya and I will both be armed . . . and so will you."

Softly: "I do not carry arms."

"I know you don't. But you will, won't you?"

"No."

Ben tensed. "Let him alone."

"I'm not talking to you, Coram."

"I said let him alone."

Yannis interrupted. "Is all right, Ben—I can do for myself."

Ben knew that Yannis was not equal to the schoolteacher, but there was a tenet of self-esteem involved, a question of the impotence of age, and the old man had to do it on his own. The medic withdrew a little.

"If I have to carry a gun, I do not go with you," Yannis said.

"You have to come with us," Falkos said evenly. He spoke with the patient reasonableness of a skilled teacher who believes that the student to whom a proposition is sympathetically explained will inevitably be willing to agree with all its implications. "Yannis . . . this operation is extremely delicate. It is a trick that can succeed only if everything looks—*ordinary*. Nothing out of the usual, understand—everything routine—a typical ambulance call —hardly even an emergency. And it is done by two men who are known as friends of the Turks. Not one man, Yannis, two. You and Coram—everybody always sees you together—you work together—you go to the gambling casino together—you even have your picture taken—by a Turkish newspaper—*together*. Now, this is our strength. Already, we are weakening things a little by taking a chance on Kalya, but she is Turkish and will be dressed as a nurse, and we will get away with it. But we cannot weaken ourselves any further, Yannis. We need you. If you are not there—"

"I said I would go, but not with a gun."

"You won't have to kill anybody, Yannis—I promise you that. You will be given a gun, but it is only to be used as a deterrent. You will open the rear window of the ambulance and spray the road with bullets. The *road*, Yannis, not people—only the road. You will hurt nobody—you will simply prevent an action behind us, that is all. I give you my word."

"I will not hold a gun."

Still with the caution of kindness, his voice became firmer. "I have to remind you, Yannis, that your sons were killed by Turks."

"They were killed by a *war!*"

Kalya said softly, "Leave him in peace, Falkos."

The anger he had spared the old man he turned on her. "You're a Turk—you're here for money—stay out of it!"

The old Greek had his palms together and both hands tightly held between his knees. His head was bent down, he was staring at his lap. It was impossible to see his eyes. Falkos pursued him. "Yannis, it isn't as if you have an alternative, you know."

Ben couldn't restrain himself any further. "Yes, he has! He wants to be out of it—and he's out!"

Falkos, steadily: "It's not your decision, Coram."

"Yannis, get out of here," Ben said.

"You're being brave with someone else's skin," Falkos said.

It was the first ugly note. Yannis had begun to move but the threat stopped him. Tracking a wounded animal, Falkos pursued him. "Yannis, don't listen to him. He's an American—and he can be a big hero at your risk. If things get too difficult for him here, he can leave. And he will. But you can't. You'll have to live the rest of your life on a small island. If you don't come with us, it will be remembered of you. Wherever you go, it will be said that you're not only a coward, but perhaps also a traitor. It will be said—you know the Paphos expression—you empty your bowels on your sons' tombstones. You will be alone in every taverna, in every church you go to."

"I'm alone anyway!" the old man cried.

"You do not know what alone is . . . until you have to run from angry people."

The old man couldn't take anymore. He nodded in assent.

"Thank you, *patriotis*." Falkos said it warmly, without mockery.

When Yannis raised his head, his face was ravaged. He was

boxed into the booth, against the wall, and needed to flee. "Let me out," he said.

Ben got up quickly so that his friend could escape. "Shall I come with you?"

The old man said no, muttered thickly about needing air, shuffled hurriedly up the steps and out of the basement.

"You bastard," Ben said, "you did that very well."

Falkos turned to him. The schoolteacher was not gloating over his conquest of the elderly. On the contrary, he seemed genuinely perturbed, as if all the wounding arguments he had used had been tortured out of him, and he was ashamed for having inflicted them. He appeared grateful for Ben's contempt; it made it less necessary for him to suffer his own. When he recovered, his mood quickly changed to a rankling anger. "I'll do just as well with you, mister."

"I won't give you the chance."

"You've already given it."

Ben had thought they would spend the afternoon together, he and Kalya, while the ambulance was being altered. He had no notion how things would happen between them, or where they would go, but there was one thing he knew for certain, without ambiguity, with painful clarity. He wanted her. No matter how mismatched they might be, no matter how out of joint the occasion, he saw himself making love to her. He remembered her as she had come wetly out of the lake, her silhouette, naked, he recalled the outline of her body, knew her closeness, felt the softness of her breasts as if he had had her at one time and she had slipped from his embrace. He knew everything about her flesh, he told himself, except the exquisite knowing, without which he felt he could never again take a full breath. So he was prepared to go to her hotel, or take her to another one, or rent a car and race to the nearest seaside and make love to her on a blazing beach. The afternoon heat of August did not matter, nor any observance of form or custom; he felt only the ceremony of desire, and the satisfaction of it was all he wanted.

But it was not to happen.

She was arrested.

Not five minutes after they left Falkos, as they were walking away from the wine cellar, two men approached them, two youngish Greeks, one in plainclothes, the other in police uniform. They asked her if she was Kalya Menas, and she replied warily that she had been known by that name, and they announced that she was being taken in custody as a material witness in the death of her "husband," Savvas Menas.

Ben hastily defended her. "She was nowhere near the place where he was killed."

Before he could go on, she asked him not to be helpful, they weren't charging her with anything. "Don't be concerned for me." Turning to the officers, she said she would gladly go with them. As they led her away, she looked back at Ben. "I'll meet you on the Kanning Bridge at six o'clock." Then she added, "Don't be late."

There was not the slightest doubt in her voice, not a quiver of apprehension. It was the calm of someone who was going to discharge a minor obligation, an irksome chore the nature of which she knew precisely; she could predict exactly how many minutes she needed to dispose of the nuisance, and she would be back promptly at sundown, don't be late.

He watched her walking between the two men, the crown of her head as high as if she were royalty and they were minions. Even though he admired her self-respecting courage, he wanted to shout caution to her. Remember the threats to intern you, he wanted to yell, remember the throwing of stones; don't be so damn proud, you're not royalty, you're Turkish trash to them, and they know how to beat you and leave invisible welts.

He worried about her, and didn't know what to do. He didn't share her confidence that she would be free in a few hours. A few days, if at all. How could he get to Falkos, he wondered, and did the teacher already know, through the ferreting underground, that she had been arrested? If he didn't know, he should be told—the guerrilla was bound to have considerable influence, sub rosa; a word from him might oil squeaky hinges, she might indeed be free by nightfall. But suppose he hadn't been told, how could Ben find him? Leaving them in the murky wine cellar, the man hadn't actually departed, he had simply evanesced into a black wall. And whom could Ben ask in Nicosia? The capital was certainly not a safe place to inquire about a fugitive partisan.

Nicosia was not safe for anything. The war, cease-fire or not, was still a raw-wound fact. There were still night raids and seizures; and informers were everywhere. The embittered citizenry talked about "a fool's friend," meaning a friend who didn't exist,

172

everybody was a potential enemy. It wasn't only the enmity of Greek versus Turk—that, after all, was an open danger, and one knew to be armed. But there was the hidden peril, the blood-congealing dread that is inherent in a civil war: the perfidy of friends. Yesterday's beloved neighbor was today's assassin—by glance, by whisper, by Judas kiss. It was as if the enemy were exhausting a lethal fume into the air, the poison gas of paranoia.

Everything that happened was suspicious; the slightest change in the habitual order of the day was cause for alarm. This was particularly true in the old section of the city, Nicosia within the walls, where the twistings and turnings of the tiny streets and the cobblestoned alleyways lent themselves to tortuosities of the mind. If the jeweler on Ledra Street closed his shop an hour earlier than usual, what secret meeting was he going to? Why did the wine seller near Venizelos Square—in wartime—suddenly stock a larger quantity of Morphou wine than he had ever sold before? Where did he get it, what was in it, what deal had he made? What did it signify that the dentist, Ialos Haralambos, who had once said that the *hamam* was a louse-infested Turkish bath, was now going there faithfully on every men's day of the week? Why had the Phillipos children been taken out of the *gymnasion* two weeks before the school year was over, and sent to their grandmother's house in Episkopi?

In a city that was in siege to suspicion, Falkos would not make himself too overtly visible. He was still a youngish middle-aged man, but an old campaigner. As a guerrilla who went back to Grivas days, he had washed his hands of many bloods—English and Turkish and, yes, Greek, when countrymen had betrayed a man or a hiding place. The families of many of them would gladly cut him open. No wonder he vanished into shadows. He would be hard to find.

Even Yannis was hard to find. Ben had expected the old man to be nursing his shame in the Rivoli Cafe, near the wine cellar. But he wasn't there. Nor was he at his other haunt, the Delos Hotel. When Ben asked questions, all reports about the old Greek, like rumors of the progress of the peace talks, were contradictory.

His concern about Yannis deepened. The old man had probably gotten drunk, and would have no idea how to find Ben, would have forgotten that the ambulance was in the mechanic's garage, and not know where to go. Yet, maybe if his assistant didn't show up, it would be the way out for him, a liberation from a task that sickened him. But it would be only a short reprieve. Falkos would not allow him to get away, or go unpunished; some way or other, he would have to pay for it.

He was wrong about Yannis being drunk. When Ben arrived at the mechanic's garage, the old man was already there, waiting for him. He was in fact soberer than Ben had ever seen him. When they drove away, the Greek was resigned, like a man who rides in a tumbril.

The mechanic had done an excellent job. The motor was tuned to perfection; the slight miss in it that Ben had grown accustomed to was altogether gone. The tires were slightly underinflated so that the vehicle rode not so hard as before, with better traction for mountain roads. Under the cot, the drawer faces looked exactly as they had looked before; no hinges were visible.

They had only to pick up Kalya and be on their way. Ben drove through the narrow streets, came to the Kanning Bridge, and parked just south of it. He was still a bit ahead of time, but at six o'clock there was no sign of her. Six-fifteen, six-thirty. It was exactly as Ben had dreaded: the police were going to detain her. Perhaps, some way, delicately or brutishly, they would work her over.

It was ten minutes of seven now, and he didn't know what to do. Since there was no way of reporting her absence to Falkos, he had no alternative—he would go to police headquarters and talk, ask questions, offer alibis for the woman. He had just put the ambulance in gear, had just turned it toward the Lykavitos Police Station, when he saw her.

She came running as if she had been let loose in a wilderness, a wild creature, a large lithe animal, crashing through underbrush.

"Wait!" she yelled, as if the vehicle might pass right by her in the street. "Wait!"

He pulled to a halt. She opened the door and as Yannis pushed into the middle she climbed in beside him. She was out of breath, quivering with excitement. And she was laughing.

"What happened?" Ben asked.

She couldn't answer, she was laughing too hard.

"How did you do it—how did you get away?"

"I told them everything they asked me."

"What do you mean, you told them? What did you tell them?"

"They said—you should have seen their stupid faces—they said, 'Who do you think killed your husband?' and I said, 'The Turks.' Then they looked at each other skeptically, and one of them said, 'Will you tell us their names?' And I replied, 'Certainly. Why not?' And they said, 'You have no reluctance to expose your own people?' And I couldn't help myself, I started to laugh, and I said, 'I haven't any people—I don't like them any more than I like you.' Well, one of them thought I was 'well water'—very refreshing. 'Go on, then,' they said, 'who do you think did it?' And I answered, 'Ihsan Cabrir!' This made a great impression on them, but I was not sure whether they believed me or not, and they asked me a hundred questions about him, none of which I could really answer, until they asked me if I had ever seen him, and I said that I had."

Ben looked at her quickly. *"Have* you ever seen him?"

"Yes—once."

"When—recently?"

"Oh no—months ago."

"Where was he?"

"In our restaurant."

"Did you talk to him?"

"No. I was in the kitchen. I didn't see him until he was leaving. Savvas pointed him out to me."

"Did Savvas know him?"

"No."

"Then how do you know it was Cabrir?"

"It's a face that can be identified. The most romantic—the eyes, very black—the luxuriant mustache—and of course, the scar."

"Did you see him after that?"

"No, never."

"Then what makes you think he killed Menas?"

She thought about it. "Because Falkos believes it."

It was as if Falkos knew everything, and what he believed was incontrovertible, an article of faith.

Fleetingly, as he drove, he glanced at her. Something strange had happened. She wore an expression that was new to him. This had been another day of persecution for her, but she was not behaving as he felt certain she had behaved when they threw stones. She was exhilarated. Her movements were swift, her eyes danced. Something euphoric was going on.

"You had a good time, didn't you?"

She turned brightly, with a flashing smile. "Yes, I did!"

"Why?"

"Because there were five of them and only one of me—and they asked me a thousand stupid questions, and I was quicker than all of them! And they were all men!"

The last word was a shock. Then the startling thought occurred to him: always, it had been men who had persecuted her. Women, in her experience, didn't go on raids at night, they didn't smash doors and windows, didn't vandalize restaurants and abuse sick children. Men had been her tormenters, and she the victimized. Always on the losing side. And today, for the first time, she had been a winner, she had had a moment of triumph. It elated her, she exulted in it. It was a new kind of excitement for her; it had power in it, and even perhaps a renegade sexuality. . . .

It might be that this enterprise was, for her, more than mere employment.

They were going in a southeasterly direction when, after a brief time, she told him to slow down at the next crossroad and go westward.

He had the sense, when they turned, that an event had taken place: their venture had begun.

For about twenty miles, as they drove toward the setting sun, the conversation was sparse. Yannis, in deep dejection, contributed nothing to it; Paphians, it was said, could become morose without reason, and the old man had reason enough. He must have felt, moreover, that he was in the way, that Ben wanted to be alone with Kalya; so, when they stopped for petrol, he said he had a headache, would lie down on the cot, and spend the rest of the trip in what he called the *klinikos*.

The Greek's absence from the front seat, instead of making conversation easier, made it more labored. Being alone together intensified their awareness that they would soon be alone in a more intimate way. And it was as if they had made a tacit pact not to discuss it but would simply let the episode happen, a point of civilized behavior, as it were, to let it take care of itself, like a phenomenon of nature. Beyond that silent understanding, he didn't know what she was thinking, and felt that she did not want him to know. Each time he tried to reach her in some private way, she evaded him by asking him something about himself, nothing that solicited very much from him, or from her. Statistical questions:

"When did you arrive in Cyprus?"

"In 1970."

"How long have you been a paramedic?"

"Ever since the war. Vietnam."

"I knew which one you meant."

She said it as if he had been trying to insult her learning or intelligence. Since she had used the word "men" so resentfully, he was sure the subject was an inflammation to her. He wondered how deeply her bitterness as a Turkish woman went. Was she at pains to remind herself she was modern, educated, not a harem creature, veiled, showing her eyes through a slit, walking ten paces behind the male?

"Why don't you tell me who you are?" he asked.

It was point blank and it stirred things a little. She looked at him more directly than before, but didn't answer. He sensed that he had broken through. But guardedly he decided to follow her lead and ask only impersonal questions, the innocuous ones that she might answer to a census taker, and not feel threatened.

"Where did you go to school?"

"Cyprus—then Istanbul."

"College?"

"Yes."

"What did you take?"

She smiled, seeing through him: he was asking commonplaces, and she could answer bromides; it was a game.

"This afternoon—when they finished their interrogation—they made me sign a paper. Will you do the same?"

He smiled too. "No. You're safe—I'll take your word for everything."

"You're also on a hunt, aren't you?"

Joking, he melodramatized, making a title: "The Quest for Kalya."

She laughed. "What was your question?"

"Not incriminating. What did you take in college?"

She was embarrassed. It loosened her a little. "It was called Cultural History."

"What's that?"

"Who we are in terms of art, drama, poetry."

"Who are we?"

"Oh, we're very nice!" A touch of vinegar. Then she expanded on it as if she were back in school, writing a collegiate satire on the subject. "We're poets, all of us—the aesthetic phrase for the ugly moment—pain recollected in beauty. Or we're dramatists—love requited—death to the wicked—war, ennobling."

"Is that the way you said it when you were a student?"

She enjoyed being caught; she brightened. "Yes, I wrote it in my third year."

"What happened then?"

"I quit."

"Why?"

"It was a fake. Art history is beautiful and real history is cruel —and the one is always justifying the other."

Well, he thought, it served him right. He had retreated to undergraduate questions, and deserved undergraduate answers. He wished he could break out of the game of vapidities, for he was certain she had more colorful answers to give, and was withholding them. Not that she was trying to conceal her disenchantment with life—her cynicism was plain—but that she was hiding some other aspect of herself, something objective. Particularly, he questioned whether she had revealed the exact reason for giving up her education. He had the suspicion that the truth of her decision had not been as abstract as she had stated it, but something quite specific —a stony fact, a crisis in one of the realities of her life.

"How did you get into Cultural History?"

"My father. He was an old-fashioned man. He thought the arts were very becoming to a woman, like a fine necklace. When I said I wanted to be in touch with something spinier, like science or business, he said there was no necessity for me to do anything difficult—he was proud to be able to support me, and when I got married, he felt sure my husband would feel the same."

"What work did your father do?"

"He owned a cannery in a fishing village."

"Where?"

"You mean the town?"

"Yes."

It was a simple question, but it seemed to confuse her. She took too long to answer, forcing it, perhaps.

"Nexos," she said.

The name was familiar. He had been to a village of that name, but he could not remember it. As he was trying to recall it, she was talking more rapidly than before.

"He had ten employees," she said. "And my mother was an *ev kadini*—that's a term of high approval in Turkish, it means a model housewife."

Uncommunicable before, she was chattering now. It puzzled him.

He had an eerie sense: lies.

His feeling was totally irrational. There was not a word she was uttering that seemed incredible, yet he didn't believe her. The quirk had to be in him, not in her. Everything she had said should have been totally convincing; she had spoken it straightforwardly, seemingly without prejudice, without paranoia, with far less animus against life than her experiences justified; in fact, with remarkable detachment. Perhaps that was it: there was hardly any feeling at all. It was as if she had been reciting something she had learned, and was repeating it mechanically.

Tantalized, he probed further. "Why did you live with Menas?"

Only a breath's pause. "Because I thought I was in love with him."

"What made you think that?"

"When someone is kind—and you haven't had much kindness . . ."

"And then you got pregnant."

"Yes."

It was easy to fill in the remaining spaces. She didn't want to abort the child, she didn't want to marry the father. . . . But there was another question.

"Have you ever been in love?"

"Yes—my husband."

It was the simplest, most direct answer she had given him. He had touched a deep ache. As if probing for infection, he went deeper. "Is he still alive?"

"No."

"When did he die?"

"A long time . . ." She looked away. "I don't think I can manage this." The wound, no matter how long ago it had been inflicted, was still open.

They rode in silence, watching the terrain change from flatland to rolling hills. As they started to ascend onto higher ground, she said, "Did you decide not to become a doctor, or simply happen not to?"

"I think I decided."

"Good. I don't like doctors."

She said it without any biting aversion, almost facetiously, and he teased her. "We've had the nationalities. Let's start on the professions."

"I beg your pardon?"

"You said you hated the Americans, the English, the Greeks and the Turks. Now—about the doctors . . ."

She didn't mind being teased. With mock grandeur: "Doctors have a special place in my disaffection."

"Why?"

A glint of mischief. "Parable?"

"Parable."

She told a story of a Turkish farmer whose wife could not bear him a child. He tried everything, she said, seaweed and seafood and bargains with the moon, and still she couldn't conceive. Once, in a drunken rage, he beat her with a sheep's bladder because he thought she was barren out of spite. At last, he faced the crushing possibility that it might be his own deficiency, so he went to see a doctor. He was given tests and tests, he spent money and sperm, and finally the physician told him the bitter truth: he was sterile. Then an appalling thing happened. Shortly after learning that he could not possibly impregnate anybody, his wife became pregnant. He couldn't stand her faithlessness, and the fact that she was bearing another man's child—so he strangled her. He had loved the woman deeply, and he despaired over what he had done, and almost submitted to the law. But at the last moment, he ran away. Fleeing to another part of Turkey, he settled there, took to farming again, and began to manage his life fairly well. Except that he was deeply lonely. He determined, however, that he would never again give himself totally to an inconstant woman, he would never remarry. One day he met a prostitute. He had no love for her, but he needed a woman to do for him, and she was willing, so he offered her a home. Unfortunately, he began to grow fond of her, and as his affection increased, he became terrified that once again he would be the victim of a woman's infidelity. So he moved to the coldest, loneliest heights of the Taurus Mountains. He farmed land that was nearly as barren as he was, but it was exactly what he wanted—an isolated place where there were no people— no men—no danger that his female companion would be unfaithful to him. One late afternoon, when he came home from the fields, he saw an elderly woman coming out of his house. She had come a long distance, from the nearest town. She was a midwife who had just examined the prostitute. She is pregnant, the midwife said. And he thought: I will kill the whore as I killed my wife. Then it occurred to him: there could not have been any other man —he himself was the father of the child—as he must have been the father once before. So he went into the barn and threw himself upon a pitchfork.

She finished the parable and smiled as if she had been teasing.

"You think he should have pitchforked the doctor?" Ben said.

"Yes, I think so."

Her smile, which was fixed now, implied that the story she had told was not particularly elegiac, but simply one of fate's practical jokes. Kismet, the dirty trick, with a doctor administering it. Yet, he knew she was not a supercilious woman, to tell murder and suicide as if they were trivialities. He sensed that the parable didn't begin to illustrate the real reason for her anger against doctors. "I don't think your dislike of doctors has a damn thing to do with that story."

"Don't you really?"

"No," he said quietly. "What was wrong with your child?"

She took a deep and difficult breath. "It has nothing to do with my child."

"I think it does. And with a doctor, probably."

She didn't immediately comply with his demand upon her. Finally: "Yes it does . . . for the second time."

"You've had two children?"

"Three. I had two with my husband, and one with Savvas. My first child was five months old when she became ill—she had a ruptured appendix. A doctor diagnosed it as colic and she was dead in two days. The third child—whose grave you saw—was ill with a fever, and no physician would come because I was the Turk who was living with a Greek. So I bundled up the child and took him to a doctor thirty miles from Seismos. He too was a Greek who didn't approve of my living with a *patriotis*. And I'm certain he didn't want the child to live."

"I can't believe that."

"He said, 'Take the baby home, keep him in bed, do not move him, and I will come and see him tomorrow.' He didn't come. We called him five times and he didn't come. And no other doctor would come—nobody."

"When I was there—while the baby was sick—why didn't you ask me to help you?"

"I . . ." Her voice faltered.

He persisted. "You knew I was a medic."

Unevenly: "The baby was not—he was not so sick then—and we were still hoping the doctor would come."

"But later, when he didn't come, when you couldn't get anybody—why didn't you call me?"

She began to tremble. "I don't know," she said.

"You mean because I had made a pass at you—you were so goddamn proud that you—"

"No!"

"—wouldn't let me help your child?"

"No—stop it!"

She was trying not to cry, shoring up her defenses so no breach would develop. And at last, dry-eyed, she succeeded.

But he knew that she was suffering, and was sorry he had goaded her. Wanting to apologize, he didn't do it immediately, and wasn't sure he should. However, about twenty minutes later, when she was calm, he said, "I'm sorry, Kalya."

She turned slowly and looked at him with low-burning resentment. "What is it exactly that you're sorry about?"

Her manner had no compromise in it; unforgiving. It disturbed him. "I baited you into telling me things you didn't want to."

She smiled grimly. "You didn't do the job very completely, either," she said. "I've had three children. I told you about the first one, and about the last. But you didn't ask about the second one."

"What happened to the second one?"

"He was butchered by the Greeks."

Spoken coldly. She reported the cruelty with her own cruelty, as if in retaliation for his.

As the sun was setting and the dusk became cooler, the name of her native town—Nexos—recurred to him. He had once, on a walking trip, passed quickly through it, and he vaguely recalled the place. But it was not, as she had told it, a fishing village; it was an inland hamlet on a dry and dreary plain. He was going to mention the discrepancy to her, but he had a reluctance; he was afraid he might catch her in a lie, and he didn't want to think of her as a liar. Then he told himself it was relatively minor; besides, he himself might have made a mistake about the town; a wrong name, perhaps. So he put it out of his mind.

He knew these quiet foothills, knew them very well. He had spent many days and nights in them—in the months before he had bought the Land-Rover—had made his own trails, had climbed the mountain to the Monastery, had seen this forest green in spring, and white with snow. Once, he had spent one whole afternoon watching two wild sheep grazing, the beautiful red-amber moufflon, and they hadn't run from him.

But, as they drove up into it, there was something alarming about it this evening. What had once been a peaceful woodland, a cedar forest, might now become a jungle. Woods, a sergeant had once told him, is what you got at home, with a girl in it; jungle is the same trees, with killers.

They proceeded upward slowly, into the darkness of it, on a dirt road that was rocky, washed out, and too precariously canted. In wet weather, going a shade too fast, you could slip off a nonexistent shoulder into an abyss.

"Falkos wants you to know that the road is not to be trusted," she said.

It occurred to him that it was not to be trusted in other ways as well. "Is it mined?"

"He didn't say that. But there's no doubt there are Turks here."

The dimness was almost impenetrable now. He pulled the knob on the dashboard and the headlights sprang to brightness.

"No, don't!"

"Don't what?"

"The lights—turn them off!"

"It's pitch black—I can't see a thing."

"Stop. Turn off the motor."

Uncertainly, he brought the ambulance to a halt, turned off the lights and motor. She opened the door and got out. He heard her in the rear of the vehicle, in a brief colloquy with Yannis. Then she was back. She had a few keys in one hand and a flashlight in the other. The glow it shed was blue, a blackout bulb. She held it up and pointed the beam through the windshield. Like a pale blue ghost, the glittering ray shivered on the road.

"That won't be seen from the air," he said. "But it'll be visible a mile away on the ground."

"Falkos says a few yards, not a mile."

They started to move again, following the weak beam into the darkness. He pointed to the torch. "Did you get that from the cupboard under the cot?"

"Yes."

"What else is in there?"

She looked at him sideways. "Do you really want to know?"

There was a taunt in her voice. It was Falkos talking to him, using her as his medium, provoking him. "No," he said.

He didn't know what her expression meant; it could be curiosity, or it could be disbelief.

They made a slow turn to a higher elevation, then seemed to level off.

"Stop here," she said.

He did as he was told, although he couldn't understand the reason. They were nowhere. Except for the slight rise, the road hadn't noticeably changed its topography, there was no landmark, no special tree or singular rock she could have seen to tell her this was the appointed place to halt the vehicle.

"What are we stopping for?"

"We're supposed to turn to the right."

He looked where she pointed the torch. It was woods and scruffy brush, the kind of low-growing alders and water rushes that indicated marsh.

"It's a bog," he said.

"Drive right through it, between the two poplars."

"It's a bog," he repeated. "We'll be up to the windows in swamp."

She directed the flashlight to the ground. "You see those vines —they're growing over gravel—there's a hard path there. Go down it."

"He said a copper mine."

"Yes. Go down, please."

"There can't be a mine down there," he said.

"Please."

He started slowly, heard the crunch of vine stems, felt the ground give way soggily underwheel, then not give way at all, and it was just as she had told him, gravel. He picked up a little speed and she slowed him down. Don't be too nervy, she said, you're still crossing swamp, go carefully. The road made a sharp turn, rightward; it was going uphill gradually, then more steeply. And the swamp was gone.

He couldn't believe what he saw. They were on a small plateau—trees all around them, swamp growth on three sides, and on the fourth side, blue black in the torchlight's glow, a drift of cedars thrown downward, as it were, from the mountaintop. The narrow shoulder of the hillside was a tableland of grass and wild flowers and, shining over everything, a sky so full of stars that there didn't seem room enough for half a dozen more. It was so illimitably distant and yet so close that he wanted to get out in it, put his arms up, and take armfuls of the firmament.

He wasn't aware he had slowed down, or that he had come to a halt. "Why are we stopping?" she said.

He pointed upward, "My God, look at it."

He realized he had said it as if she couldn't have been aware of the beauty. "Yes," with unconvincing matter-of-factness, "I noticed it."

He gave his attention to the mundane things. "There's no mine up here."

"There it is."

The dark patch against the cedars could not have been there an instant ago. There was an oblong of it, a blackness, like a cave. He put the car in gear again and started across the plateau. The distance was deluding, and the shoulder of the mountain was not as flat as it had appeared to be; they were still moving upward.

As they came within a hundred feet of the black opening, she said, "Pull as close to the hillside wall as possible, and stop."

The instant he applied the brakes, she opened the door and got out. He heard her walking on gravelly ground, and he too alighted. They had ascended quite a height, and this level place was a high saddle on the mountainside. The wind was strong. He heard Kalya at the rear of the ambulance, heard the door open and close, then she emerged carrying an oil lantern, unlighted. Immediately behind her came Yannis, squinting into the night, and scrunched up as if his joints had petrified. "I was asleep," he said. "What is this place?"

"You will soon see," she said.

Carrying the still unlighted lantern, she led the way across the moonlit plateau. The ascent was more gradual than before, the walking was not difficult. Here it was now, the shadowy opening, the passage into opacity. Without looking back at either of them, she entered, and instantly was swallowed by the cave. Ben followed her, and heard Yannis's footsteps on the gravel, close.

A match burst aflame. It flickered a moment, threatened to go out, came brightly aglow. Kalya raised the chimney of the lantern, applied the match, and the cavern sprang to light.

Ben was dazzled by the bright amazement. The walls were every color imaginable, every color copper could become, brown as bronze, red as fire, the olive of chrysolite and—the glaze on everything—a cuprous green like the decay of churches. In some places, where water seeped through the walls, from mountain streams perhaps, there were luminous drippings, like hanging emeralds. It was as if everything, in this underground obscurity, were light-permeated, beautiful and blinding.

Moving slowly, they came to the empty mining pockets in the mountainside, the little cubicles that had been lodes of copper ore, now deep gouges in the glowing, shimmering walls. One cave after another, and caves within caves, chewed out of the unwilling opulence of the mountain—dying cavities gone to decay, like caries.

He had seen copper mines on the island, one underground and one open-cast, but none like this. There was a weird prophecy in this one, a mine whose story foretold itself, describing the colors that the ores would become, even before they were smelted.

"This place is a myth," he said.

"It *is* actually a myth," she responded. "It's called Aphrodite's Cave."

Out of the darkness behind them, Yannis said, "There is not an Aphrodite's Cave."

She winked to Ben. "They say this is it, Yannis."

"It is only wine talk," the old man scoffed. "Aphrodite is a sea goddess, she never lives in a cave—never. Also, I know every goat track—" He stopped himself, realizing the oddity. He was assuming the reality of the goddess as if he personally knew she existed; only her habitat in a cave was controversial. They laughed, and even Yannis smiled at the eccentricity.

"We grew up arguing like that—was there ever such a cave?" Kalya said. "Legends—lies—back and forth, believing nothing, believing everything. And then one of Grivas's men said he found the cave."

"Grivas?" Ben asked. "Was it a hideaway?"

"It still is."

"How hidden can it be after all these years?"

"You would have ridden right past the place where we turned off. So would I, if Falkos hadn't told me when to start counting and what to look for."

"The English never found it?"

"Nor the Turks."

"Do they know of its existence?"

"Only the way they know of Aphrodite's sea-foam and her fountain. Fables."

"How can you be so sure?"

"Falkos told me."

Again. Incontestable truth, divinely revealed.

"He trusted you," Ben said.

She winced. "I do not betray." She intoned it like a bit of rhetoric, with classical augustness. He had not insinuated anything, but she had heard the insulting stereotype: treacherous Turk.

"What I meant was—it's a dangerous piece of information to give away."

"It's dangerous to have."

And now he had it. And didn't want it. The possession meant that more and more, through his imbecilic innocence and their guile, he might become one of them. It could happen with the craftiest subtlety, a word spoken, a word hinted or meant to be overheard, no more audible than Chinese droplets, and the new knowledge he possessed would be like an incriminating weapon, and he would be their accomplice. He must beware and not ask a question, however innocuous. . . . And yet, he knew he would ask questions.

They had descended perhaps two hundred feet, and still had not come to the bottom of the mine. From somewhere in the corridor they heard the sound of flowing water and, walking further, they came upon the source—a little springhead gurgling from an outcrop of rock; near it, a number of bent tin cups, a broken saucepan, and a green bronze ewer. Over the spring, on the face of the rock, someone had started to chisel the word "enosis," but had stopped before the final sigma.

Now the channel they were walking through widened and became a level space, a circle of underground floor the diameter of which was perhaps thirty yards across. Opening onto the level area was a warren of cells—rooms, actually, some only large enough for a cot and a chair, some with shelves built into the mountain-side, with mattresses upon them; also, a number of spacious chambers, one of which was large enough for three beds, a long table made of wide planks that rested on sawhorses, a stack of painted, sheet metal drawers.

Ben noticed the unlighted oil lanterns in niches in the walls, and, on a protuberance of rock, a double-burnered spirit stove. He imagined the fumes, the oil smoke. "How did they ventilate the place?" he asked.

Kalya didn't know. She was as caught in the mystery of the caverns as he and Yannis were; the sense of concealment beyond concealment. When they lighted the lantern on the wall of the large room, and then a lantern in the small chamber that adjoined it, they felt they could not truly illuminate any darkness here, there would be deeper darknesses, and deeper still. Something, someone, some legendary being out of a past beyond recall, would always move away, out of the sphere of light—there were unfathomable depths of shadow where it could hide.

In this underground night something happened that made them all silent, and he didn't know what it was. Not a myth-minded man, he didn't carry talismans or wishbones, but he felt a disembodied presence. And so, apparently, did they.

Then they heard it, the slightest stir, like treetops whispering far away. And they felt the breath of it; you could hardly call it a wind or breeze. It was the faintest sigh of air, a sifting through passageways and past them and disappearing into the outer stillness. Yet, faint as it was, and despite the glass chimney over the wall lantern, the flame flickered.

He had had his answer to how the place was ventilated, but another question sprang to mind. What had caused the draft? Having entered from the direction by which they had come, how did it exit? Well, it was not, after all, mystical hocus-pocus; the caves simply had to open somewhere else, another entrance. It would be another *exit* too, he realized, with some cautionary notion he knew he would have no use for—they would be out of here tomorrow, and he would then put his mind to forgetting this place.

Exploring the caves, they were all doing it together and then —how it occurred he could not tell—they were doing it separately, in different corridors. From time to time, he heard a footstep, that was all. After a while, from a distance, Yannis called. "Plenty of places to sleep." Their voices were hollow, with an echo, as if all the overtones were sucked into a distant vacuum.

The old Greek's voice once more: "I go to sleep again."

He had apparently found a cell for himself, and was laying claim to it. This would be another flight into slumber, as if he could narcotize the next twenty-four hours out of his life.

And Kalya . . . which cell had she discovered for herself? He would go in search of her. Again, the questing word had come to his mind, sending him on a prowl in a shadowy cave, to find a goddess or a gorgon, some creature he could love or fear, who would satisfy his hunger—for what? For tenderness or violence, or both; for a craving of the heart and loin, and nothing that his mind could comprehend.

He wandered through a twisting corridor, almost too narrow for passage, and suddenly was in a good-sized room. And she was there.

She was sitting on the edge of a largish bedstead. It was only a mattress, actually, flat on the ground, and to sit on it was an inapt thing—her knees were almost up to her breast, and she looked awkward there. He had caught her at being young. It was a fleeting glimpse, a trick of the eye, and there she was, the adolescent girl, discovered unaware, and vulnerable.

But only for an instant. Quickly she got to her feet and was her own poised pride again.

"I've been waiting for you," she said.

They stood across the cell from one another, hardly more than a dozen feet apart, yet the doubt between them was a long one, a world away. The span could be shortened, he speculated, if the right word of revelation were spoken by one of them, a hint of emotion in surprise, a syllable of need, of passion. But there wasn't any. It was simply payment time, and cold. And yet there *was* emotion—his, only his: he wanted her. So don't think too much, he said, this is what we bargained for, two grown-up people in a deal, this is how contracts are consummated.

He crossed the room and touched her. It was the lightest touch he knew, a hand raised to her wounded cheek, tender and tentative, a hand that said: Let's be still a moment. She understood him and seemed in need of it. Slowly she took his hand in both her own, held it gently as if to let it breathe, a wild thing she didn't want to crush, then lingeringly raised it to her lips. His heart began to quicken. Slow down, he said, she's not loving the hand, she's merely thanking it, grateful for the obverse reason than you would want her to be; she's relieved that it's being tender and not passionate; she doesn't want you to be aroused by her, she would like for you to touch her soothingly a moment, and go away.

Even knowing this without a trace of doubt, he reached for her. With the hand she had just released he touched her again, just as provisionally as before; he laid it gently on her breast. Through her clothes, as if she were wearing nothing, he felt the softness and the warmth. She seemed almost not to notice. As he moved his hand, he wanted to feel some change in her, a rising of her bosom to meet his touch, a quicker breathing, a firming of a nipple, but it didn't happen. Slowly he edged closer to her, his body next to hers, his mouth on hers, his tongue searching, and she opened to let him in, and she was kissing him as he was kissing her, and he should have felt: she wants me. But he wasn't sure.

Slowly, she disentangled herself from him. She paused a moment, then started to undo the buttons of her blouse. Soon it was discarded and she was in her bra; she kicked her shoes off, slid open the zipper of her skirt, stood there in her underwear, not moving.

Starting to undress, he thought: I've seen her naked before, and felt the wanting, and yet it was nothing like this, an ache of needing I've never known before, and I won't be able to stand it, I'll come like some pubescent kid, down my pant leg.

They were both naked now. And just as he was starting to embrace her, he felt her tighten and retreat. He wanted to clutch her tautly to his body for fear she would not come back, but he warned himself: Give her breath, a latency.

"We both know I'm not a naïve girl," she said. "I know what these pleasures are made of—for a woman—and for a man as well."

He didn't know where she was going. Puzzled, he heard more wryness in his voice than he had meant to show. "Do you? Tell me."

His tone unsettled her a little. "Well . . . there's his own satisfaction, of course, but I think most men—especially sensitive ones like you . . ."

She couldn't make it; he helped her. ". . . derive their greatest pleasure from knowing they've satisfied a woman."

"Yes." With an effort, "And I think you should know—beforehand—that you won't have that pleasure."

Off balance. "Is that an apology or a challenge?"

"Neither. I simply don't want you to expect more than either of us can give."

He felt humiliated by her, and by his nakedness. "You're welching."

"If that means I'll cheat you—I won't."

"You've already cheated me. You contrived the perfect thing to cool me off, to soften me up."

"I didn't do it for that reason."

"What other reason did you have for calling me impotent?"

"I didn't say impotent—it wasn't in my mind."

"No, but you put it in mine! I couldn't satisfy you—that's what you said. I'm incompetent—I might as well run home with my tail between my legs."

"I only told you the truth. What did you expect me to feel? You made an arrangement with a whore—you implied the word yourself. Do whores have ecstasies?"

"Not often, perhaps. But they certainly don't cut down their customers. You're not even a good whore!"

Suddenly the thought occurred to him: maybe she *is* a good one. Maybe this is a preliminary to lovemaking, a hostile aphrodisiac. Maybe this is a message that I've started too tenderly, that she wants me to be rougher with her, needs anger as incitement.

With a sharp movement, he reached and grabbed her. Pulling her tightly to his naked body, he pressed himself against her so she could feel his hardness. He kissed her without gentleness with his lips, his tongue, his teeth. As he did, he closed his hand upon her breast, cupped it tightly, pressed it.

"Don't," she said, and tore herself away from him.

It's not a forbiddance but a challenge, he said, it's foreplay, go after her. One step closer and he snatched at her again, his arms around her nakedness. As he felt her trying to tear herself away, he made a wrenching movement, angry, violent.

Her hand struck out. He felt it, a slash across his cheek.

"You bitch," he said. "You want me to hit you back, don't you?"

"No!"

"You want to taste a little blood, don't you? You want me to rape you!"

"No!"

"You're a liar—it's what you want! So that you don't have to make the choice—it was *done* to you! Another persecution! Maybe you enjoy them! Well, I don't! You can go fuck yourself!"

Enraged, humiliated, he started to put his clothes on. She made no movement to dress; and that too, in some contorted way, added provocation.

He hurried away and left her there. Back through the narrow corridor, lost and wanting to be lost, he made turns he had not made before, and suddenly was outdoors on the level place, not many paces from the ambulance.

Again the sense of rout, she had put him to flight somehow, had made a fool of him. She had touched him in a place he had not known was sore, and he had run away. He took deep breaths to calm himself. The night was balmier than it was before, too warm for a mountainside, a light wind had risen, a sea wind, and yet he knew they were miles from the sea. The sea's in everything, he thought, even on this hillside, the sensual moisture, the Venus moisture, the woman rising from the childbearing sea.

Goddamn her.

Without knowing why he was sure she was behind him, he turned. She too was dressed now. She came slowly toward him.

"I'm sorry," she said. "You were right about what I did—and I *am* sorry. . . . Will you come back?"

"No."

"Come back," she said quietly, without pleading.

"Go away."

"Don't be a romantic—come back."

"I'm not a romantic."

"Of course you are—you're an American."

What a vacuous thing to say, he thought. Then, still resenting her, he decided to lead her on, let her speak her generalized inanities, and secretly or openly deride her. "Are Greeks any different? Or Turks?"

"You're giving me rope, aren't you?"

Not inane. How shrewd she was. "Yes."

"I'll take it." She accepted the summons as if he had brought her to trial and there was a mootness she had to answer. She smiled a bit sadly and started her case. "A Turk thinks a woman is his infirmity. If he wants her, it's because he's weak, if he loves her . . . Will you come back?" She started to touch him, but desisted.

"If he loves her," he prompted.

"If he loves her, it's because he has an illness, if he sleeps with her, she's stealing his potency, sapping his . . ."

"Strength."

"Yes, his strength."

"A Greek?"

"A Greek thinks he *is* a woman's strength. Without his love, she will not be beautiful, without his wisdom she'll be an idiot, without his seed, she'll fade and wither." This time she did touch him. "Come back."

He moved away a little. "And the American?"

"Completely different. Woman is his total mystery. She's the religion he has given up, she's the romance he wouldn't for a moment suffer in a business conference, she's the fantasy he learned in his mother's lap. He's frightened to death of her—he's frightened that she'll outwit him, that she'll castrate him, and that she'll desert him. And because he's terrified, he'll give her anything she wants —even her freedom to leave him. The one thing he will never do for his woman is: understand her."

Angry, "I've been trying to understand you," he said, "and I've been the one who asked questions, not you! But you've only answered the superficial ones—and I don't know a damn thing about you!"

"But that's what you find most attractive, isn't it?—what you don't know about me."

"I might find you more attractive if I knew who you are."

"I doubt it."

"Why don't you risk it?"

"I did risk it!" she said in a temper. "I tried to tell you the truth—that there was no ecstasy in it for me—and you became a bully, and then you ran away. You were afraid you couldn't make me love you. And probably more afraid that *you* couldn't love *me!*"

"That's not true!"

"Yes, it is! That's what's most terrifying to an American. He has to be in love all the time. And he has to be in love with every-thing—with his business, his president, his wife, his mistress! And it's when he's *making* love that he's the most frustrated. The Turk and the Greek will settle for an emission, but the American will settle for nothing less than the realization of a dream—that the mysterious creature he lies in bed with will have a mysterious ecstasy, and he'll have given it to her. It's romantic—and it's absurd!"

It was as if she were talking not about Americans in general, but about him specifically: he needed love at the center of his life, as the motive for all his actions. Love conquers all, indeed; the pursuit of it was certainly conquering all of him.

When she spoke again, her voice was gentle, conciliating. "What I said to you in there—I think it was foolish of you to take it seriously. If I don't have an ecstasy, it's not important. I've had them in my life, and not been happy. More often, I've been happy without them." She pointed to the cave and said softly, "Come inside."

His resentment was gone now, but so was the moment. "No."

"Come. Let's be naked together. Come."

"Thank you, Kalya. You've discharged your obligation—you needn't feel indebted—thank you."

He didn't say it meanly, but with kindness. He wanted her to know that their tawdry bargain was over, that he was ashamed he had ever entered into it, that the shabby and prurient side of their relationship had come to an end. And if they were to have anything together, he and Kalya, it would have to be different; for they were both worth more than they had exacted in the deal, that each of them—in need—had settled for the going market price, beneath their own justifiable appraisal of themselves. Cheaply.

But he felt empty, and he ached, and couldn't say it.

Oddly, as he glanced sideways at her, he sensed that without his uttering anything, she understood. Then she smiled—with some new, higher measure of him, perhaps—but there was still sadness in it, as though she regretted having encountered him in such times. And she went away.

When she was gone, the wind rose a little and he had a night chill. He felt witless and still not totally cleansed of a contamination. The worst part of it was, he himself had perpetrated it—in the name of love. He had made an airy illusion of a grubby circumstance—all for guess-what and the world well lost—and he had consecrated it. So long as the sacred word, love, was invoked, however it was corrupted, there was a bending of the knee and a hallowing of the voice. He thought ruefully how sanctimonious the love sentiment can be.

He had a moment of wanting to blame it all on this damn island, this sickly Aphrodite-land, this love-infected Cyprus where every vapor from the sea, every drift of fallen leaves, every rustle in the grass, every downdraft from the mountaintop whispered love, love, love. There was an amatory disease here, Venus-generated, a primordial venereal illness that overheated the heart and gonads, and maddened the brain.

But he spotted it as a grandiloquent alibi, and contemptible. He was damn well aware that the fault, dear Brutus, was not in the Cypriotic stars, nor in the mythical love goddess. The fault was singly, and without extenuation, in himself.

He knew what his conscience had directed him to do: go up to the Monastery and tend to the dying priest—not with the others, but alone. It was an obligation to the faith he had in himself as a peace-loving, compassionate man, which was the only faith he could pragmatically live by. It was the only obligation he had to fulfill.

And it was not too late. He could still do it. If he did, good things would happen. He would rid his guts of his quavering guilt, he would flee from an erotic enslavement he did not understand, and he would free Yannis. He could imagine the lightening of the old man's spirit when he realized he didn't have to carry a gun, that they didn't have to become war accomplices.

Go up the mountain, then, on his own?

He knew he wouldn't do it. He was still ensnared by that woman. And he was—why didn't he face it?—afraid. As Falkos's ally, however unwilling, he was temporarily safe. As a deserter—knowing as much as he did about the teacher's enterprise—he was a danger to the Greek, and would be in danger *from* him. If he were to start out, he would probably get no further than the main road. A guerrilla patrol, a sudden burst of fire. They would take his ambulance and, most certainly, his life. Afraid.

Ben thought of the old, palsied patriarch, painting an icon with quaking hands, and taunting him with the question: "Afraid?"

"Yes," Ben had admitted.

"Why not? What are you, an oaf? You want to be unafraid of everything?"

"No, not everything, but—"

"Yes, you do," Demetrios contradicted. "You want to be unafraid of everything."

"Is that bad?" Then, the reverie: "Wouldn't it be wonderful to live in a world where you never had to be tested for courage?"

"Nor tested for virtue either?" There was the faintest note of raillery in the old man's voice. "How about intelligence? Kindness? No tests? How about breath or pulse?" His banter stopped, and he asked gently, "Is it your fear of life that you don't want tested, or your fear of death?"

"That too."

"Not that *too*—that above everything. That's why you're afraid of being a doctor—because you don't know that your fear is your strength."

The old man's thoughts scampered too haphazardly, a windstorm in the brain. He could see that Ben was trying to assemble what he was saying, yet the priest had no clearer way to express what he meant. So he asked his guest to leave him alone for a few hours—he wanted to start on a new painting, privately. Late that afternoon, he came in through the cloister archway and summoned Ben to the winery. He placed the young man in a position directly in front of the painting he had been working on, and apologized for showing it to him in this as yet uncompleted state. But even unfinished, it should say something to Ben.

"What do you see?" he asked.

Ben couldn't see very much. A face was just beginning to emerge from the primitive, abstract globs of paint. He was at a loss.

"Who is it?" Ben asked. "Another saint?"

"Oh, quite the contrary."

"A sinner, then?"

Demetrios thought about it weightily, couldn't arrive at an answer, grew pettish, and told Ben to go eat his dinner.

The following night, through his bedroom window, Ben looked across the snow-covered courtyard. He could see the window of the old priest's cell. A light was burning. It flickered, for he had no electricity in his room, only candles. Toward dawn, when Ben awakened, the light was still fluttering.

In the morning the picture was finished and the old man showed it to him. They were in the refectory where the sun poured goldenly through the windows, but Ben might just as well be viewing it while blindfolded—no image came out to him. He felt terrible. The patriarch, exhausted from having worked all night, his palsied hands shaking, stood almost within breath's distance of him, waiting for the young man to utter some sound. But he couldn't.

Then Ben saw it.

He saw himself.

And he couldn't believe that anyone could ever look at Ben Coram and see a vision so gentle and so touching. And so strong.

"Am I . . . ?"

"Yes, you are."

"Why did you call it a sinner?"

"I didn't—you did." Demetrios pointed to the face in the portrait. "That one has a beatitude in him."

"Which beatitude?"

"Blessed are the meek for they shall inherit the earth."

Ben smiled ruefully. "The beatitude has it wrong. The meek never inherit the earth. A glimpse of heaven, perhaps."

"That too. But the pronouncement says the earth." The old man was watching him in puzzlement. Unexpectedly, his face brightened as if illuminated. "Ah, I see. You think of meekness as a kind of cowardice. But it's not. It's another form of courage."

It was a Christian sophism, easy to believe when the faith was strong and the facts were weak. And Ben's facts *were* weak—some fear of fire, hidden beyond recall. But even so, not knowing where a specific terror came from, he knew he could not accept the patriarch's rationalizations. Courage, he thought, was by definition bold, not meek; not altogether rational, as fear itself was not altogether rational. Courage might, in fact, be the most precious bequest of the beast. The delay that culture counsels before the blow is struck, the other cheek of Christian forgiveness, the beatitude of meekness, might all be debilitations.

Meekness, another form of courage? Nonsense. Tonight, a few miles and a number of years away from Father Demetrios, standing on a windy plateau within sight of his ambulance, he needed a tougher beatitude. If he had it, he would be up at the old man's bedside—by himself.

Instead, he loitered in the darkness. Slowly, without objective, he walked past the ambulance, along the roadway, down the hillside, feeling the crunch of vines and creepers underfoot, and the gravel hard beneath them. He heard the summer swamp sounds to the right and left of him, the rut of frogs in their guttural lewdness, and a night bird mourning somewhere.

One step in the wrong direction and the ground gave way

under him; he was ankle deep in muck. He had continued straight ahead when the pathway had turned, and he could already feel the pulling of the swamp, sucking him into itself. He yanked one foot free, dug it into gravel, then twisted sharply and was clear of it. Brushing the mud off his trouser legs, he pulled his shoes off and, as best he could, shook the muck away.

The sound he was making was not the only human sound he heard. He couldn't tell where it came from, or how many there were, but there were voices.

He remained very still. The night became still as well. Utter silence now, except for the nature noises. Perhaps the voices had been imaginary.

But there were Turks in these woods, he had been told, and Greeks as well, and the voices might not be altogether in his mind.

Back on the roadway, he heard the squeak of wetness underfoot, and the gravelly complaint. But there was that other noise again—not voices, perhaps he had been wrong about that—footsteps, not his own.

If someone was following him, there was no escaping—right and left were swamp. He could only go straight ahead, or back. Either way, the other one—whoever he might be—would have no trouble finding him.

Get back to the parking area, he told himself, as quickly as possible. There's space, and there's the ambulance. Get inside, lock the doors, get the motor running, take off. He hurried now, raced uphill, hoping he wouldn't lurch—wrong direction—into swamp, get caught in it.

He heard the footsteps behind him, just as fast as his own.

He stopped. There was a turning here—somewhere—he mustn't mistake it, or he'd get lost or mired. Where? He stopped.

The sound stopped too.

Whoever it was, a pursuer, was not trying to get closer. Why not?

Could he, after all, have been mistaken? Had there indeed been no sound behind him? Or if there had been, had it been innocent? An animal, perhaps, a hedgehog, one of the wild sheep of the hillside? Yes, a moufflon, that's what it might have been. Was it possible there had been no danger behind him? If so, then perhaps he was even more fear-ridden than he had thought.

He listened. He listened as tautly as if hearing were the only sense he possessed. He heard nothing.

Then he felt the thing in his back, the rigidity of it.

"Hold still," the voice said.

It seemed forever, and nothing happened. The man was taking his good time. Then quietly the voice said, "Turn slowly."

He turned.

Falkos.

The moonlight picked up the shine of his smile. All smile, pernicious glee. "I hope I alarmed you," he said. "It would be the best way to illustrate the principle that these woods are not for strolling."

"Thanks. I could have learned it just by being told."

"Kalya didn't tell you there are Turks here?"

Sheepishly, "Yes, she did."

"Then you didn't learn, did you?" The pedant's tone.

Ben indicated the gun. "Put that down."

Falkos lowered it. He stood quite close. Ben was not certain but he thought he smelled liquor on the teacher's breath.

As they walked toward the caves, "I wasn't expecting you until the morning," Ben said.

"I always lie about my comings and goings," he said breezily. "Besides, it's safer to travel by night."

That would be true of him in any event, Ben thought. He was a nighttime man, burrowing into a secret nether world, mole of mind.

He was sure of it: liquor. Falkos had had a good amount of it.

"What the devil are you doing out here?" the Greek asked. "Why are you . . . awake?"

The hesitation before the last word—Ben knew what it signified, why aren't you in bed with Kalya? He muttered something about being a light sleeper, restless.

"Restless—why? Isn't lovemaking the great soporific?"

"Do you expect me to discuss that with you?"

"Only in the abstract." His manner was ingratiating. "We needn't mention names."

Something crawly. Ben had the creeping suspicion that the man wanted avidly to discuss what had happened between him and Kalya, wanted to hear it in detail. The teacher's eyebrows were lifted in a kind of supercilious detachment from the subject, yet Ben could feel his lickerish curiosity, like a wetness, the oozing of a snail.

Ben turned away and hurried upward toward the caves. He

heard Falkos hastening to catch up. "Have you found out anything about her?"

The question sounded odd. Ben slowed down. "Like what?"

"Like anything. Who she is—where she comes from."

"Don't you know?"

"Oh yes, I've heard it a number of times—and it's always consistent."

"Well?"

"I think she tells it by rote."

Ben felt queasy. At first, it had been exactly his own perception—until she had mentioned the name of her home town, what was it now—Lexos—Naros? The fact that he couldn't remember the name might mean that he himself was wrong. And yet, for whatever reason, both he and Falkos were dissatisfied with how she told her past. He wondered whether to discuss it further with the schoolmaster, but some uncertain ethic stopped him.

Falkos had already gone beyond the subject. "How's Yannis?"

"Not very well."

Reflexively. "You mean ill?"

"In a way, yes. He's silent."

"Is that ill?"

"With Yannis, yes." Then, hoping that the man's concern might be genuine, he asked, "Why don't you let him off the hook?"

"What does that expression mean?"

"Let him go."

"Off the hook." He was assaying the word. "What a cruel image—like the hanging of a butchered animal."

"Yes."

"I can't let him off the hook." Then, quickly. "I'm sorry about Yannis—really I am. But you and he, you're like a—what is the term?—a set. I've thought of breaking you up—honestly, Benjamin, I have—but I can't find a believable substitute for the old man. There was that boy, Mark Achille—he's American and he *looks* American—he might have been a possibility. But, an epileptic." He considered. "Are you sure the boy can't be used?"

How wily he is, Ben thought, to throw the onus on me. And what reply could the medic give that wouldn't sound mealy-mouthed? There's an unfair prejudice against epileptics? They can behave more normally than people think, and too often they're not allowed to do what they *can* do. All true, but weasel stuff—no answer to Falkos's question. The *fact* was the only answer: the boy had had a number of bad seizures within a very short time, and some doctors might hospitalize him. . . . Put a gun in his hand?

"The army would never take him," Ben said.

"There you are, then . . . Too bad."

They were in the parking area, within sight of the ambulance. There was more moonlight here, now that they were off the tree-canopied road, and more wind. Falkos pulled his coat tighter; he was cold.

"I'm going to get some sleep," the teacher said. "I suggest you do the same."

"What time will we be going?"

"What time?"

"Yes—what time in the morning?"

"We won't be going in the morning."

"When, then?"

"Not for a few days."

With a clutch of anxiety, "Why is that?"

"Ask Chartas."

"I'm asking you."

Falkos pondered it an instant, then seemed to see no risk in discussing it. But he was guarded. "There's been a change of plan. There will be other attacks which must be timed simultaneously. We have to wait."

Ben felt tricked. Angrily, "How long?"

Also angry, "I told you—a few days."

"There's a dying priest up there."

"Relax, Coram," he said. "Have a good time—go back to Kalya."

"You son of a bitch!"

Surprisingly, instead of making the teacher angrier, Ben's outburst amused him. His face relaxed. "Are you really angry at me, Benjamin, or at yourself? Why did you come up here—for a dying priest? Come now, was it really Demetrios, or was it Kalya? You know the answer—why don't you settle for it? It's not so heinous, my friend. We all do it—we mix our metaphors all the time."

"I don't know what the hell you're talking about!"

"Yes, you do. You say Demetrios and you mean Kalya. I say Cyprus and I mean Cabrir. We live by mixed metaphors—mixed, mixed!" He laughed with unnatural hilarity; he was drunker than Ben had realized. "You want to hear a little secret? In the daytime, I tell myself I'm a patriot—I love Cyprus, I love my people—and that's why I'm in the war. But at night, with a drink of truth in me, I don't give a fart about Cyprus—I'm in it for *Cabrir!*"

His laugh was too loud for safety. Too loud, also, to be believable. There was too much passion in the way he had said the Turk's name, a depth of virulence under it. Ben was convinced that the hatred was older than the death and torture of Menas; its origin was in Falkos's own life, a primal malice.

His vexation with the teacher was suddenly secondary to his fascination. "Why do you want to kill him?"

"I don't want to kill him," he replied. "I want to torture him."

"Him especially?"

"Him especially—and him alone. If I can torture him, I will try not to hurt anyone again for the rest of my life. No one! I will live in kindness with everybody, even Turks. I will speak generously, I will let my hands get soft. If only Cabrir . . ."

"Why him?"

Briefly—the flash of an eye—he thought Falkos was going to tell him. But: "We've strayed from the point. The point is, we wander into the wrong dream—and suddenly we're on a mountainside instead of Famagusta."

"Famagusta—is that where he is?"

"So Chartas says. Two of his lorry men saw him in a road taverna right outside the city." Then he added, with bitterness, "And I am here, with the nightingales."

He made a vague gesture to the cedar tops. It was only after he made the motion with his hand that he became aware that he had actually been hearing the sound of the birds. Apparently it had been subconscious to his thought, and now that he was mindful of the rich throaty notes of the birdsong, he paused to listen.

"Nightingales," he said again, as if he had never heard the music before. "A special kind—a honeythroat. If my wife were alive . . ." He stopped as if arresting a sentiment. Then, without nuance, "She was an ornithologist," he said.

The birds lost their charm for him and he started away. When he had walked a few steps from Ben, he stopped, thought an instant, then looked back. "Don't think of leaving here by yourself, Benjamin. The main road is patrolled, so are the side ones. Don't do anything Homeric."

Unhurriedly, the teacher strode toward the cavern, and Ben watched him until he had disappeared into the density of the mountain. He felt as if Falkos had just done something sinister to him, had operated on his brain and left a small foreign object inside. He would have to open himself up again.

The mixing of metaphors . . . Kalya or Demetrios. Was it as simple as that? Choose one or the other?

Don't do anything Homeric.

Why *should* I do anything Homeric?

Why, indeed? Why should he risk his life for the old man? Was Demetrios a worthier symbol than his love for a woman? A sick old man in his middle eighties, his art behind him, his lifework done, an obsolescence of a man, a priest by no means perfect, not Christlike or forgiving, with rages against people he had never known, with crotchets, and now full of rot and perhaps full of pain —why not just let him expire, say a prayer or two, and forget him?

As a matter of fact, it was difficult to *remember* him. He was able to conjure flashes of individual features—the deep eyes, the white beard, the sublime mass of the man consuming all the space in a doorway, but the descriptive components refused to coalesce. The old man would not return to him as a person, but only as an idea. "Only" an idea—as if that weren't enough. If the image isn't as significant as the fact, of what use is thought? The dying priest himself had little to do with Ben's morality; the man was a metaphor. He stood for the old, the sick, the weak, the untended to whom Ben had dedicated his life. The patriarch might have no universal newsworthiness, he might be nobody else's world symbol, but in an essential way, he was a symbol of Ben's world. A world that might be dying. It was certainly being fed intravenously, with wires and tubes and catheters all desperately trying to nurture and purge it. There might be some who would say—as it might be said, with some justification, of Demetrios—that it should be allowed to die . . . but Ben was not the one to pull the plug.

If Demetrios was a dream that exceeded his grasp, he would have to know by how much he had fallen short of the mountaintop. But even suspecting that he would fall short, he would have to *try*—or he would be damned in his own eyes, and despise himself. Not that he would climb the mountain to affirm that the man and Monastery existed, but that the world existed, and would not perish in war or rage or entropy, there would be no doomsday. For, no matter what suffering he had seen on earth, he still held a hope for life's continuance. Everywhere. He was not a partisan; he had no nation but his love. And he would not be a traitor to it.

So he had to go there, to Demetrios. He had to go up the

mountain—alone. Not in a few days, as Falkos had said, but to-night. Now.

He looked in every direction. There was nobody visible, and probably nobody observing him. He wondered what time it was. No matter. The ambulance, as if spotlighted, was bright in the moonlight.

He wouldn't dare start the motor; the noise would bring some-body running, Falkos certainly. If he could silently release the brake—and not even shut the door after him, for it would make a report—he could let the vehicle drift slowly backward, down the hill.

He started to hurry across the parking lot, but haste made too much noise, the gravel crunched loudly underfoot. He slowed down. Everything, he told himself, would have to be done slowly, carefully.

As he got to the ambulance, the question occurred to him: what would he do with the weapons they had concealed in the cab-inet under the cot? The quickest thing would be to forget they were there, and get away. But what if he were caught with them—by anybody, Greeks or Turks—how would he explain them? A medical mission—why the armament? Whatever explanation—hard pebbles, the Greeks would say, and the Turks would use its correlative, something that translated into stone testicles, which his would be. He had to get rid of the guns.

But where, and at what stage? If he did it up here, someone might hear him. He would have to do it down below, on the little crossroad. But that would mean he would have to break his momentum, park and unload the weapons closer to where the pa-trols might be. No, if he did it up here—quietly, before the whole maneuver began—he wouldn't have to stop, he could keep on going.

He went to the rear of the ambulance, silently released the catch, and opened the doors. It was pitch dark inside, he didn't dare turn on the light. On his knees, he felt for a cabinet latch. There used to be three that worked, now only one of them did. He lifted the panel, reached inside. He could feel them in the rear, the loathsome objects, the whole vicious arsenal of them. Treat them gently, he told himself, as gently as you would treat children on the Dak Binh road. It was surprising how much armament they had

stashed into the narrow space. Unloading all of it, he laid it carefully on the ground, on a bed of creepers that cushioned the sound.
He looked at it, spread out. Guns, ammunition—not merely
enough for the three people who were supposed to use them—con-
siderably more. Some of the rifles were new but others were well
worn, a hodgepodge—five Lee-Enfields, a couple of carbines he
couldn't identify, a Sten submachine gun, grenades of three or four
kinds, perhaps fifty altogether, a few pistols, and something that
was disassembled and looked like a diminutive cannon, possibly a
mortar. Part of a real military operation, yes; both sides breaking
the cease-fire as if peace talks weren't going on, the bastards.

He closed the rear doors. It was easy to do those quietly, but
the front doors—he must remember not to shut them. And no
lights, of course. Not altogether a hardship here, in a wide open
space with all this moonlight, but it would be more difficult on the
pathway downward, where the trees hung over. Besides, without
the headlights on, the brake light would not function. So he would
be guiding the vehicle downhill, in reverse, with only the moonlight that sifted through the treetops. One tiny faltering twist of the
wheel and he would be mired, engorged by bog.

He stood at the front door, not yet opening it. He looked at
the declining grade. Quite good, quite enough to break inertia.
Without making the slightest noise, he turned the handle, pulled
the panel, and climbed in behind the wheel. He took a deep breath,
reached forward, and released the brake.

There was no movement.

Move, he said. But the heavy truck was inert, rock-solid in its
refusal to budge. He pulled the brake tight again, then released it
more joltingly than before. Still no motion. Hoping to wobble the
wheels a little, he rocked himself in the seat, backward, forward,
sideways. There wasn't a tremor. Move, you dumb clod, he said,
move!

He slipped out of the cab. Hurrying to the front of the vehicle,
he spread his arms, put both hands on the front bumper and
pushed. Nothing. He kicked at the earth behind him, a few feet
from the ambulance, dug a hole in the ground, then shoved his
heel and sole into it. He braced himself against the earthen foothold and shoved.

The vehicle stirred. Feeling the motion away from him, he
pushed harder, with all his weight. The ambulance began to roll. It
drifted downhill, backward. Hectic, he hurried alongside, pitched

himself upward into the cab, grabbed the wheel, twisted it just in time, and the Rover was on its way. Down the decline it went, faster and faster—and silently. He was making it!

If only he could keep the wheels on the pathway, and out of the bog, if only his momentum would last the whole distance down to the narrow crossroad where he could start the motor and turn the vehicle around.

He felt the sick softness. Rear right wheel, he said, in swamp. He turned his hands scarcely an inch and felt the gratifying firmness again. With luck, he would do as well at the curve—that part might be trickier. It should be another hundred feet or so, and now—here it was. Turn quickly. Back now, and straighten out. No, be careful of the softness—straighten out, *straighten out*. Good, it's firm again. Downward—faster than before—the road steepening—faster still—plummeting. And . . .

There it was. The little crossroad.

He stopped the ambulance. First objective—he had made it.

Rushing now, he turned the ignition key, heard the engine answer with a roar, pulled the door shut, put the car in reverse into the pinched road, stopped, went into low gear, quickly, second, third, and he was on his way, forward.

He could risk the headlights now, the low beams anyway—he was beyond earshot and gunshot of the caves, they would not be able to hear or catch him, he was safe.

Even safe from Turks, he realized, if he were stopped by them. His vehicle was innocent, and so was he: a medic going up to minister to an invalid—headlights candidly ablaze, a clean passport, an American neutral, a man of medical mercy.

But the Greeks . . . They were patrolling, Falkos said. Still, what would the patrols know of this venture, how much information would be entrusted to them about a secret mission to attack a monastery? And why wouldn't Falkos have lied to Ben, to scare him out of action?

Relax, he told himself, it's nighttime, nobody sees you and the road is deserted. Already he had crossed the swamp, he probably had less than a few hundred feet and he would be down on the highway. He reduced his speed as he approached it. Also deserted. Not a vehicle or a human being in sight. He turned left and entered the main road.

He must have driven a mile or so—upward, always ascending —when the road started to narrow. It had stopped being asphalt a little while ago and was now hard dirt, its dust flying blue in the moonlight. Presently, he drove into a stretch of darkness, no sky visible, black cedars pressing in, both sides of him. There was too much dust, it settled on the windshield, he wished he could see better, wished the road were less rocky and the incline less steep. He wished, especially, that he could come out into the open where he might begin to see the Monastery.

Crack!

It sounded like rifle fire, but it wasn't. Impact. His head snapped back. His neck hurt. The ambulance had stopped.

He heard the rattle of chain, the clank of metal against metal. When he felt the hindrance tighten, he knew what it was—a Greek *havia*, a snaffle bit, the linkage of metal bars that pulled taut and yanked a vehicle to a halt. Sometimes, often delayed, there would be a detonation. He held himself, waiting for the blast.

No explosion. The constraint loosened a little; the vehicle settled.

"Stasu!"

As if the command to stop were necessary; he couldn't be any more static than he was.

He heard a muttering of men's voices, Greek, in disagreement. *"Na min vyi exo,"* one said, don't let him out; another one dissented, wanted the American searched. Then he heard Falkos's name mentioned a number of times, with varying interpretations of what the schoolmaster had ordered.

A scowling face, bearded, appeared at the window. A blue-lensed flashlight glared in the medic's eyes.

"Come out," the beard said.

Ben opened the door and stepped down on the ground.

"Not be foolish," the man warned, and one of the other men muttered behind him.

"Ochi," the searcher said irritably, quickly running his hand over Ben's clothes, feeling for weaponry.

"Pockets," he said.

Ben didn't understand, assumed he had already been inspected for dangerous articles.

"Pockets, pockets," he repeated, with more annoyance.

Turn them out, he meant. Ben showed him what they contained: a few shillings, four pounds, a ballpoint pen, a handkerchief, a stopwatch, a thermometer in an aluminum case.

His examiner looked at each article carefully, even at the currency, as if there might be something tricky about it, then handed everything back.

Ben saw that there were four of them, two young, two middle-aged. One of the young ones held a gun on him while the three others went into a hurried conference, muttered and unintelligible. The bearded man left the group, walked to the back of the ambulance, opened the doors, jumped inside, poked around for a while, then came out and studied the locks on the rear doors.

He approached Ben. "You have lock inside, you have lock outside."

"Yes."

"Why you have lock inside?"

"In case one of us is in there with a patient—he doesn't have to wait for the driver to open the door."

"You do not lock from outside?"

"Sometimes. Not always."

The beard considered it a moment; he was not altogether clear about the explanation. His companions thought something was tricky. Two of them hurried to the back of the ambulance, inspected the doors, returned, and had another consultation with the beard, who was apparently the leader. Then Ben realized what they were thinking. The inside lock didn't matter. They could lock the American from outside, which meant only one man would be required to take him back to Falkos; the others could remain at their posts.

"Mikis," the leader said. He gestured for the youngest man to go to the ambulance.

Mikis got up into the cab and sat behind the steering wheel.

"Back door—what key?" the leader asked.

"The ignition key."

Mikis heard him, pulled out the ignition key, handed it to the bearded one, who gestured Ben to precede him to the rear of the ambulance.

"In," he said.

Someone shoved him toward the step and he went inside. At once, the doors were shut behind him and he heard the key turn in the lock. Another brief murmuring of the men, then the repeated chig-chig-chigging of the motor—he'll run the battery down, Ben thought—and the engine turned over. The driver overraced the motor, kept it interminably at the roaring level, then flicked the headlights on and off a few times. The vehicle turned tentatively back and forth, reverse and forward, then started slowly down the hill.

He stood looking out the rear window of the ambulance and, when everything indicated he had failed, he obdurately refused to believe it. They would not take him back, he resolved, they would not return him like a faulty object. Someway, the old man in the Monastery would see him up there—tonight—beside his bed. And he realized, with a twinge of chagrin, that one of the ancillary penalties he refused to suffer would be his mortification when Falkos would inevitably mock him in the presence of Kalya. What a petty thought, he said, that aspersion in her eyes would bother him, when the old man's fate was all that should have concerned him. Vanity, humanity. He had to get out.

His breath was steaming up the window. He wiped it and saw that the vehicle had passed from the dirt road onto the macadam; they had come out from under the trees. He looked up and he could see the summit of the mountain. And there—in brilliant moonlight—he saw it—the Monastery. The three-domed roof of the basilica was backlighted by a sky full of stars. How beautiful it looked, and how close. He had gotten much nearer to it than he had imagined—a mile or two at most. From the point at which they had caught him, he could easily have walked the remaining distance. He could still do it.

Walk. If he could get out, he could make it on foot. Of course, he couldn't take the dialysis equipment with him, it was too bulky, but he had his medical bag and an emergency kit. He could pack the bag with diuretics—he had two kinds, thiazide and mercurial—and with an acidifying agent. Also, his blood pressure apparatus, a catheter, a hypodermic needle, and some analgesics in case the old man was in pain. The more quickly he packed, the less distance he would have to walk. It would take less time if there were better light; he regretted having blocked up the side windows when he rebuilt the Rover. But no matter, there was a little illumination through the tiny rear windows, and most of the things he could identify even in the dark. He could manage. Except . . . how to get out?

The side doors, right and left, had never been used since the remodeling of the vehicle. On the cot side, the door would be inaccessible; the metal frame of the bed had been welded to the wall. But on the other side, he could move the drug cabinet, it was merely bolted with butterfly nuts that could be turned by hand.

The first two bolts were easy; they rotated with little resistance. The second two were rusted tight. If he could bang on them with something—but it would make a noise. He'd loosen them with alcohol, perhaps, or baby oil. But time, time. He reached for the spirits bottle, opened it, doused one wing nut, then the second. He tried the top one; it wouldn't give. The bottom bolt—locked tight.

Losing time. Getting further and further away from the Monastery.

While the rust was softening on the bolts, he filled the leather bag. In a rush, in a panic, he opened the drawers of the cupboard, made his selections in the blackness by the feel of things. He could be choosing all the wrong stuff, he thought, so he had better add substitutes and extras. The bag couldn't hold any more; it bulged, he could hardly snap it closed.

Now, the bolts. The top one stubbornly refused. He tried the bottom. It turned a little, got stuck, then gave up willingly. Back to the top one. It turned instantly—no recalcitrance at all—it went all the way.

Cautiously, inch by inch, he pulled the cupboard away from the side door. He looked at the panel, felt the square stem that the door handle had fitted on. If he had the handle, he could turn it easily; even with his fingers he might twist it up. He tried; it wouldn't give. With a pair of pliers—but there wasn't any. Perhaps a scissors. He opened the leather bag again, rooted around in it, found the surgical shears, and with them he grabbed at the metal stem. The grip was not firm enough. Then he heard the tiny snap of the scissors blade being nicked, and suddenly the grip was tight. He turned and the handle moved.

The door was free—all he had to do was open it. He kicked it hard. It sprang open. He grabbed the bag and jumped.

He felt the ground under him, felt his knee give way, dropped the bag, recovered it, heard the door flapping noisily against the side of the vehicle, heard the tires screech to a halt.

He was in the woods. Running, falling, rising, rushing, no direction certain, only flight. He would get back on the road at a later time—the distance from the ambulance was all that mattered now.

The thought struck him: when the driver saw that it was the right door that had opened, he would correctly assume his prisoner had taken to the woods on the right side of the road. Ben would have to switch over to the left side, instantly, before he could be seen. Reversing himself, he thrashed back through the underbrush, came to the shoulder of the road, saw that the truck was just maneuvering to return, hurried across the roadway, and into the woods on the other side.

A better side to be on anyway; the road curved leftward and uphill, which was exactly the direction he was going. If he could cut across a segment of the half circle the road would have to make, he would come out of the woods on the other side of the crescent, and out of sight. It was faster here, too; there was an animal track—wild sheep, perhaps—and he might follow it. No good —it turned and went deeper into woods. He started the other way.

Below, he heard the ambulance. It was moving slowly uphill, but closer and closer. And then it stopped. That was worrisome. So he lay down in deep brush.

He could barely see the road from here. The sound of the ambulance advancing; then the vehicle in view. It was inching forward, crawling to a halt. He hoped the young man, Mikis, was not very bright. The guerrilla got out, hesitated, then disappeared. Not good, Ben thought, if that means he's coming into the woods on this side.

Trying to be absolutely motionless, trying not to breathe too loud, he waited to see if the man would come this way. But there was no sign of him. Then suddenly, there he was, the other side of the road, already going into the farther woodland, deeper and deeper, and downhill.

I can exhale now, Ben said, and I can move again. Slowly, softly, on hands and knees, he crawled across the segment he had diagrammed in his mind. He was beyond the open place and shielded by undergrowth behind him; he could get off his knees and walk. Rising carefully, he remained quite motionless. For the first time he realized that his knee ached. He lifted his pant leg and felt the bruise. It was only a little damp, just bloody enough for a scrape, nothing more. Anyway, he had no time for it to be any worse than that, he had to keep moving.

And there it was—the roadway—just where it was supposed to be. Warily looking to the right and left, he stepped out onto the dirt-and-gravel path. Hugging the shoulder of the road, hanging close to the shelter of the cedars, he trudged his way upward. If only he could get another glimpse of the Monastery, he thought, it would give him a sense of being closer, the goal attainable. It might be miles further than he had imagined—he had no notion how far downhill the Greek had driven him. But then, by going across the segment, he had shortened the distance.

Another curve, and it was his again, the Monastery, not as close as he had seen it before, but close enough. It seemed even more aglow than before, the Greek crucifix glistening, a shine of blue silver on the mountaintop. Twenty minutes and I'll be there, he thought.

He heard the vehicle before he saw it. He was certain, at first, that it was the ambulance coming up the road. But the sound was from the other direction. He scurried back into the shelter of the woods.

Then he saw the jeep. It wasn't coming fast—quite slowly, in fact. An old-fashioned American vehicle, it was familiar everywhere; he had seen hundreds like it. But there were no Americans in it. The two men could be Greeks, they could be Turks.

Alert and not budging, Ben watched it. In a few moments, it was gone.

I'll walk upward through the woods, he decided; going by way of the road had been a foolhardy risk, he wouldn't try it again. It was bound to be slower going, but there was no safe alternative, and he should have realized it before. Anyway, there was no rush now that he knew he could make it. He could take it more easily, with an occasional breath. Upward, steadily upward.

This time the noise was not a vehicle. Nor was it on the road. Somewhere in the woods, ahead of him. Not voices, movements. Again he thought: An animal, perhaps; but animals made sounds with softer edges. . . . Human.

Then, unaccountably, the noise seemed like an echo, and the real source of it was at a distance, behind him. The distance shortened and he was about to turn to it. Too late. He felt the arm at first, not certain it was an arm; then the blow, not certain it was a blow. He ran, he heard the scurrying after him, the hoarse commands. He didn't see the drop ahead of him, like a deadfall, but all at once he had tripped into it. Then pain, like noise that wouldn't stop; loud noise, volume up too high, too many decibels to manage, too loud, too loud.

Then silence.

6

He heard voices, or perhaps it was the singing in the sail; he was back in the cave, or perhaps he was running his skiff in a quiet sea, off Marblehead; there were two men carrying him, swaying his body a little, or perhaps it was the lilt and roll of Dru's sloop, undulating in the softest billowing of waves.

"There's going to be a squall," she said.

He had just been thinking how peaceful the day was, how far from storm. There was a feathery air that filled the sail with a bellyful of snugness, the little craft glided on the sea as smoothly as a swan, and he felt a warm cradle comfort in the late sun of a summer's afternoon. There never was a less threatening end of day.

"Squall?" he answered. "You mean that itsy cloud?"

She pointed the other direction, south. They were due southeast of Marblehead Neck, no land visible. "Down there," she indicated, "toward the Cape."

Larger than the northern cloud, this was a cumulus of puffs and mounds, towering a little but not formidably, and he didn't see how she could think it ominous. The threat, he knew, was not in the sky but between themselves; they might make rough weather.

He tried to tease her out of it. "Shall we get both engines roaring and run like hell?"

Generally she didn't mind being twitted on her double-engine caution, but today she didn't smile. "When it hits, it'll be a bastard."

He'd have to face it, then. "Say it, Dru."

"I can't believe you've done it."

"I have, though."

"And waited to tell me until now."

"I only did it yesterday."

"Without a word . . . ?"

"I knew what you'd say."

"Why, for God's sake? Have you suddenly become a hawk?"

"No—holy—! Of course not."

"Well, it's certainly not the act of a cooing dove, is it? Somebody who's been marching for peace and love and bless-the-universe. What the hell are you *doing* it for? Giving up your medical degree—giving up everything—what *for?*"

It was such a reasonable question, a penetrant beam of light, a laser shooting through his dark irrationality. "I don't know," he said, in distress.

"Don't know—is that a reason? Just go out and risk your life because you don't know what you want of it? Isn't it time enough to do that when you've got a passion?"

"I don't know," he said numbly again. "I've been defaulting—playing it safe . . ."

"Why shouldn't you? You're not a hero—you were never meant to be. You're too smart to be a patsy—it's not in character. You've joined the rallies, you've shouted and thrown your pebbles, and gone home to lobster thermidor. You know which side your life is buttered on, and that's what I love about you."

"Is that what I am?"

She saw that she had overshot the point, and changed her sights. She pretended none of it was all that solemn. "It's quaint, isn't it?—a medic, did you say? What's that mean—succoring our boys?"

"The Congs too, if necessary."

"Good lad."

"Don't be a crud."

"You'll be wasted, goddamn it!"

"Dru—"

"Get out of it, Ben—please, get out of it."

"I've enlisted, I told you. All I have to do is pass my physical."

"Fail it."

"What?"

"Fail it. Flunk out."

Quietly: "I can't do that, Drusilla."

"Yes, you can. A shot in the arm will do it. I'll give it to you myself."

He turned away, and watched the gray thing moving closer; perhaps she was right, a squall.

She reached to his shoulder and tried to twist him toward her. "What the hell are you proving, for God's sake—that you're not a coward?"

"I don't think so."

"Yes, that's what you do think, but you're proving quite the opposite. You haven't got the courage to be a coward!"

"Quit that."

"You haven't got the guts!"

Something went haywire. Her head twisted as if he had hit her, so he must have done it. She called him a bastard, and something else happened more quickly than it had a right to, a pressing darkness, it was the squall, he thought, the scream of it, the blackness without warning, the stabbing pangs of lightning.

He saw her rush to shorten sail, then—hectic—hurry to the larger engine, to start it up. He heard the roar of it, then she let it scream its own way, and, slipping in the wet, rising quickly, scurried back to lower the mainsail. She's playing it safe, he said, sound cautionary sailor that she is, racing the storm on engine power, to port on gasoline, under bare poles, a motorboat. She was tugging at the wet stop knot, cursing it, and he roughly pulled her away. He heard her mutter something about the halyard, something that made no sense, but the wind was louder than voices.

He shouted, "We'll sail it out!" He rushed back to the engine, reached for the starter to turn it off.

"What the hell are you doing?" she yelled.

"No engine!" Then again, "Sail it out!" He called out some idiot thing about its being the name of the sport.

"Are you crazy?"

She tried to shove him away from the engine. She's strong, he thought, an arm like a mainmast, and as the rain came pouring down and the boat started to heel, he pulled one gas line, then another, fouled both engines, felt the spray of oil in his face, my God, he said, there'll be a fire, but the storm drenched him and the engines, it beat down like flying nails.

"Are you crazy?" she kept screaming. "Are you crazy?"

The tempest struck, full rage. All the elements altered. Air became water, and sea became mountain. Great crags of waves crashed against the craft, gray palisades rose and loomed and came cracking down, in avalanches. The sloop surged and reared and carried them aloft, then dropped them into chasms, only to lift them to the mountain peaks again. The deck was awash, not only rolling and pitching but ramping, upright against the fury of the deep. Clearly, as if separate from the tumult of the storm, they heard the screech of cracking wood, like the shriek of an animal, and the jib was gone, the mainsail ripping. The ocean was all roar and anger, and cliffs of water kept smashing and battering at the sloop, and suddenly they fell from a great precipice of wave, down into a trough of calm, the valley held them quietly, and the squall had passed.

Spent and speechless, they gazed at the departing northbound traffic of the black tempest, and saw it darken out to sea. Limping, the craft moved landward, not to Marblehead, but toward the Neck, which was a glimmer of light in the now twilit distance.

Sailing was a sport, he had said, or some such inanity, and she had answered that life was not.

Mountain climbing, too, was a sport . . . but who had made *that* observation? Who, and what mountain had there been, and was there something at the top of it? A monastery? . . . Had he reached it?

His head hurt. Through the ache, he couldn't tell the difference between seas and caves and mountains, which insanity he belonged to, if any at this moment, wherever he might be.

Nor could he identify the voice he was hearing; might it be his doctor father? More likely, it was the voice of the professor who taught the course called Medical Ethics.

"Where are you now?" the lecturer inveighed against him. "Have you no grace, no gratitude? Before there were doctors, there were priests, and they healed the wan and wounded. Before there were madhouses, there were confessionals that gave remedy to the tortured of soul. Before there were hospitals, there were monasteries—and a monk opened the door to the maimed and the withered and the sore of heart. And now—where is the physician who has been called to heal the ailing monk? Where does he lie, malingering?"

Ben said: Perhaps the healer, then and now, was waylaid by a metaphor. Or perhaps he ached somewhere; perhaps he wanted water.

"My head hurts."

"It will get better," someone said. It was an old voice, a man's, and familiar.

He tried to make some sense of what "get better" meant. The expression was perhaps something he was not required to hear. The thing he *was* required to do was move.

"Do not get up." He knew the sound now—it was not Demetrios, but Yannis.

There was someone else present, someone silent, standing in the corner of the room. Her arms were folded across her breast, as if she were cold. He tried to figure whether it was the time of year to be chilly. She was a beautiful woman, and he suspected who she was; in a little while, he would even know her name . . . Kalya.

He slowly raised his arm. His hand felt something, not his forehead, but something wet. He removed it: a compress. There were pink stains on it.

"Am I bleeding?" he asked.

"No," she said, and no more than that.

He wondered why she spoke so little. Were they keeping something from him? Why didn't they let him up? Not that they were physically hindering him, but they weren't helping, either.

The deadly thought: I'm crippled again. And, just like the first time, nothing wrong with my leg, no ache, not a stitch of pain, and yet I can't walk.

Then—blessedly!—he felt the sharp stab in his knee, as if a bone had been damaged or a knife had been pulled.

"Has my leg been amputated?" he asked.

Yannis looked alarmed. "No, your leg is hurt, but is not bad. Why you say that?"

Never mind, he thought relievedly, it has nothing to do with Mee Lanh, only with last night. Remember something, he commanded himself, remember a bearded man. The night returned. The ambulance, the flight through woods, the Monastery on the summit, the four men, one of them bearded.

"Have I been back for long?"

"Last night," Yannis said.

"Asleep?"

"Well . . ." He was holding something back.

"Unconscious?" It was a trade word, he knew what it meant.

"You are talking a lot last night," the old man said. Ben wasn't really interested in what he had said—his head and leg ached too much—but the old man apparently thought he was comforting him. "You ask for people—we do not know who they are, these people. And you are trying to fix something—we do not know what it is."

"And you wanted licorice," she said.

"I don't like licorice."

She didn't smile. "Then I'm glad we didn't give you any."

He remembered more now: She had been naked, and he had almost been to bed with her. Something sad had happened, something unfinished, he couldn't remember what. Only that she had smiled gratefully for something he had said or done. What was it? Her face didn't tell him.

He decided: I'm going to sit up, whether they like it or not. They were not obstructive. Strange, his head didn't hurt as much as when he was lying down.

"What time of day is it?"

"Morning," Yannis said. "Ten o'clock."

It puzzled him why he couldn't tell it was morning. Then he realized: no windows. The cave—day and night were the same.

But this was a different room from the others he had seen last night. This was larger, capacious enough for a huge round table, with chairs and small benches and seating places made of tree stumps. In one of the alcoves there was a tier of two cots roughly framed out of cedarwood, and another alcove was a pantry lined with shelves where food was stored—tinned goods and canisters, clay crocks, odds and ends of pottery. There was something uncanny about the room—it was both soothing and awesome at the same time—and he realized again how ineffectual the artificial light was against a darkness as dense as solid substance. There were three oil lamps in wall niches, but it was the blazing fire that was the riddle of the room. It was a wood fire that burned in a recess of the mountain wall. The flames snapped like red and yellow flags, and yet the flare of them seemed incredibly unable to throw the light any further than the hearthstone; nor did the heat warm a chamber that should have been roasting if this was August. Yes, he remembered that it was. Even considering that the cave was hundreds of feet underground, it ought to be warmer than this, and why wasn't it smoke-corrupted? Something was wrong, he couldn't tell what, for it was blissfully cool, with a primitive purity that suggested that the air was new, unused, it had just freshly emanated. That, perhaps, was the most beguiling wonder of the place; where did the smoke from the lanterns and fire disappear to, where did the innocent air come from?

It was not a fearsome fire, but a comforting one. Hypnotized by it, Ben wished reality wouldn't come back so starkly, and so fast. With each new clarity, a new uncertainty—and the unambiguous fact that last night he had failed. He didn't yet know how he felt about it, what he wanted to do, or what he could do—and was not lucid enough to know which question had priority.

"Falkos . . ." he started to say.

"Is here," he heard the voice reply.

The teacher stood in the archway. He took no cognizance of Kalya or Yannis—as if they were not present. "Are you well enough to talk?" he asked.

Ben wasn't sure but didn't want to admit the weakness. He nodded.

"I'm sorry you were so badly hurt. That much was not necessary." His vexation was emphatic. "Those chickenheads—they would take a cannon to a gnat." The gaffe was inadvertent and he said quickly, "That's tactless—I'm sorry for that—and for everything."

"Balls."

"You think I don't regret . . . ?"

"No." He didn't know why he said it. There was a sudden flood of memory. "I saw a man you burned to cinders."

"Do you suppose I wanted to do that?"

It was the pious demurrer of a war-disciplined man. Ben was not up to dealing with it. "Tell me something. That *havia* chain—it can't be in position all the time. How did they know to get it up in time to stop me?"

It looked as though Falkos enjoyed the question but wasn't going to answer it. So Yannis did. "He has an instrument," he said.

Falkos seemed at pains to hide how annoyed he was. He smiled with fixed amusement, and then said evenly, "Would you both mind—I would like to have a minute or two with Benjamin."

Kalya was out of the room almost before the sentence was finished, and Yannis immediately followed her.

"Yes, an instrument," Falkos said. He reached into his pocket and pulled out a black case the size of a deck of cards. It was the smallest walkie-talkie Ben had ever seen. The sight of it made him feel juvenile. They had been skirmishing in these guerrilla woods for nearly a generation, these Greeks; how could they not be equipped with gadgetry? "This one is very good—both voices can speak at once—it's American." He put it back in his pocket.

His manner became congratulatory. "You surprised me, my friend. When I said no Homerics, I didn't think there was a chance you'd be insane. What are you trying to do—kill yourself?"

"I'm going up again." He was surprised by his own words. Thought had nothing to do with them; they came from his will alone. Once they were spoken, he had a sense that they were right; his mind couldn't improve on them.

"You *are* insane, aren't you?" the schoolmaster said.

"I'm going up as soon as possible."

Tauntingly: "Today—tonight?"

"If I can."

"Let's see if you can. Get up."

"What?"

"Stand up."

Ben, to himself: He wants to prove I can't do it, the crud, he wants to show how weak I am. But maybe it's worse than he thinks, maybe it's in my head.

Ben started to move his legs off the cot. The right one was hot with pain; not fire, ordinary pain. Relieved, he took a breath.

"Can't do it, can you?"

Again, Ben started to move. The pain was worse. Falkos watched him without blinking. He wasn't crowing over the medic's discomfort, but his very presence was an affronting challenge. Compulsively, Ben had to be able to put himself in motion.

He pretended he had no ache, no distress at all. The first stage was simply to stand; he had to make himself do that. There was nothing wrong with his left leg, he told himself, it would be perfectly capable of bearing all his weight; the right leg would have to take care of itself.

Move the left leg off the mattress, he said. Slowly, do it slowly. Well done. Now the other. Slide it over, bring it in line before you raise yourself on the right one. Patient, you're doing fine. Now get your weight off your ass, put your hands on the mattress so they can push up when you start to go. Ready, now—all the weight on the left foot—go.

He did it.

He remained upright for an instant. Then the right knee screamed at him, he couldn't stand the knives, and, just as he saw Falkos moving toward him, a moment's darkness.

Light returned and the schoolmaster was supporting him, holding him gently.

He sat down. Presently, his breath came back, and with it sharper clarity than he had had before. The pain should have dulled my mind, he thought; yet I feel I'm bright enough to deal with him.

"That leg may be broken." The teacher's solicitude seemed genuine.

"It's not broken," he replied, with inordinate calm. "It's in my knee—one of the ligaments, that's all. Give me a minute and I'll name it for you."

"Name it for yourself. . . . You're not really serious about going up there again?"

"Yes, I am."

"Why, for God's sake?"

"I have no alternative."

"Yes, you have. You can stay with us."

"I'm not a soldier."

"You go up there alone and you'll get killed as if you *were* one."

"I'm not a soldier," he repeated stubbornly. "I'm not a sadist."

Falkos blinked and rubbed his eyes; they seemed tired. Ben hadn't had Cabrir in mind, but he guessed that the teacher was referring the remark to the torture of the Turk and perhaps regretting the drunken confidence.

"Sadist?" The Greek said the word as if it were a corrosive on his tongue. "You think there's no sadism in medicine?"

"Oh, Christ."

"Do you know the Greek word for remedy?"

"Pharmakon."

"Yes. It also means poison."

"So?"

"You have to kill to cure. Soldiers and doctors, both. You think there's a doctor in the world who isn't sadistic?"

"If you mean knife-happy surgeons—"

"Them, yes—but even the so-called honest doctor. Do you know what his honesty often signifies? Cruelty. Have you ever seen an honest doctor tell a man he has cancer, tell a boy he's going to cut off his arm, tell a woman she's going to have a breast removed? Can you accurately estimate how much is causing him pain and how much is giving him pleasure? . . . And do you think it's all pleasure for me to burn a man to cinders?"

"And you do that for the common good."

"You think I dare to believe otherwise?"

"All right, you've made a choice. However ugly I think it is, it's yours. Why can't you let me have mine?"

"I've already given you a military reason. But if that doesn't satisfy you, I'll give you a personal one." The man was serious. But to give himself an escape route, he pretended a supercilious manner. "I would like to have you come along with me."

"Why?"

Grinning: "I like you."

Ben put his hand over his mouth, hiding it.

"You don't believe I like you?"

"No."

"My God!" Falkos laughed. "I thought it was plain. I've been sending candy and roses!"

Under the japery, a note of pleading. It was as if he didn't dare to make a sober offer of friendship—to Ben or to anyone—for fear that it might be rejected. Yet, he had a hunger, and had to declare it. Albeit jokingly, he had a need to offer the cheek of amity, hoping someone would kiss it, at least not strike it.

Facetiously as the overture was made, Ben knew that it was sincere and that Falkos was exposing a woundable part of himself. Perhaps by exploring it the medic might find a means to get away, shake himself free of this enterprise.

"What do you like about me, Falkos?"

He seemed prepared for the question; the answer was ready. "You're a brave man."

It was a shock. Falkos meant it. His flippancies were past; he was in deep earnest, and offering the tribute with dignity. It stirred something in Ben. He heard Demetrios calling him meek, and saying it meant strength, while to Ben it had meant weakness. And now . . . brave.

"Thank you." As Falkos smiled, without affectation and with surprising modesty, Ben asked, "What kind of teacher did you used to be?"

The question took the Greek unawares; he was pleased by it. "A very good one. Very kind. In all my years in the classroom, I never raised a hand to anyone. I was very . . . loving. And as I look at you, I have a certain . . . nostalgia."

There it is, Ben thought. He yearns to get back to an earlier self, to someone I remind him of, someone he may think brave and idealistic and, as he says it, loving. He sees himself in me—with an ache, perhaps—with a rage that he has become this torture-yearning man. But the corollary struck Ben as well: If Falkos likes me for that reason, he probably hates me for the same reason. Envy, like acid. He wishes he had remained as I *am,* and regrets having changed. He needs to know that he *had* to change, that everyone must, that inevitably men must turn to bitterness or vengeance or atrocity. And that I will turn as he did. He wants to see me do it. He would like to *make* me do it. There was depravity in it.

Ben smiled as charmingly as he could. "I'll be very wary of your affection, Falkos."

The teacher seemed injured. "Why do you say a thing like that? I'm not trying to hurt you. On the contrary, I'm trying to save your life. I ask you not to go up there alone, Benjamin—I beg you!"

"I have to do it."

Falkos's nod said that he had expected no other answer, but it saddened him. He turned quickly, walked through the archway, and was lost in the darkness of the corridor.

The exchange with the teacher had taken something out of Ben. His head ached again. Putting his hand to his forehead, he saw there was blood on it. Not much, only a little. The basin which contained the compresses was on a low stool not far from the bed. As he extended his arm to it, he realized that the distance was further than it seemed, and he barely touched the rim of the basin.

"I'll do that."

It was Kalya. With a decisive stride, she crossed the threshold and approached his bed. She picked up one of the compresses, wrung it out, placed it on his forehead, raised his hand so that he had to hold it in position. Murmuring about the need for fresh water, she lifted the basin and left the room with it. In a short while, she returned and put the basin back where it belonged.

Ben still held the compress to his forehead. She took it from him and lay it on the stool. When she started to unbutton his shirt, he was puzzled until he looked down and saw a gob of caked mud on it. There had been no time to clean it, she said, and she would do it now. Dropping the shirt on a bench near the hearth, she picked up a few scraps of clean toweling and returned to his bed. He sat on the edge of it, naked to the waist, watching her. Her grace was in her assurance, he thought in the economy of motion; she was like a lithe panther that knows its track. He heard the soft splash of water being squeezed through cloth. Then she came to wash him. The water, fresh from the mountain flow, was icy cold. For an instant, the shock on his face, on his bare chest, was unbearable. Then, almost simultaneously, he felt a surge of vigor, like a fresh supply of blood. Her hands were quick and nimble-fingered, like a conjurer's. She made no effort to be tender with them, simply directed them to do her work. She rubbed him vigorously; she seemed to be infusing his body with her strength. But each time, as soon as the warmth of his skin tempered the coldness of the cloth, she would return it to the basin for more water—glacial—and bring a fresh frigidity to his skin. And it became unbelievably erotic. He had heard of ice being used for the shock of sexual excitement, and had even been told of a woman of Amazonian stature who used an ice phallus in a velvet sheath, but she was weird, and this experience was ordinary, a commonsense washing of his face and torso, the water being, by happenstance, rigorously cold. Yet, for all the wet frostiness that stabbed him with ice needles, he had gooseflesh that was not the simple tingle of freezing temperature. There was a special titillation in it, his shivers were alternately freezing and fiery, chills and fever, and he sensed that what she was doing to him might soon be more than he could stand. He had never in his life discerned any real sensitivity in his breasts, but now as she stroked him he felt as though his nipples were a woman's, and it was so disturbing that he could hardly tolerate it. He tried to hide from her that he was becoming aroused; he tried to measure his breaths, and to swallow with an even continence, and he prayed that he would not get an erection, for she would inescapably become aware of it.

Then a tiny incident happened. Her cloth had too much water in it and dripped down his back. Involuntarily his hand went behind him, to wipe the excess moisture away, near the base of his spine, at the waistband of his trousers. Seeing his movement, she quickly muttered an apology and added something precautionary about getting his clothes soaked. Without preamble, in the most matter-of-fact way, she loosened his belt and pushed his zipper tab down a little. Quickly, as competently as a masseuse, her hand with the cloth in it reached down into his trousers, under his shorts, to wipe away the superfluous wetness. She stroked him at the rear at first, his ribs, the base of his spine, down to his coccyx, but not a millimeter further. It's nothing, he told himself, no major event is developing, don't make too much of it. But he couldn't help himself; in his trousers a major event *was* developing, and he crossed his legs to hide it. Her hand moved forward now, to do a thorough job of it, to dry the front of him; again, his waist at first, then his navel, and downward. The cloth was no longer chilly but felt like the temperature of his skin, enkindled, hot, and he was randy as a hare, full and hard, held tightly, imprisoned between his thighs so that she might not know the horn he had for her. Oh, Christ, I want you, he thought, I want you.

Abruptly, the washing and drying exercise was over, and she was murmuring something about his shirt being mud-stained, and she would clean it. He wondered why—really—she had loosened his trousers, why she had continued her ministrations to a place so private. For an instant, he thought she had been deliberately tantalizing him, cock teasing, but she had not in fact gone an inch too far in her hand's exploration of him, and her manner had been as coolly detached and professional as the service of a practical nurse. And whether or not she had been aware of his erection, she had not in any way, by word or eye-blink, alluded to it. No, he was merely responding to the tantalization of himself *by* himself, an autoerotism that the woman aroused in him. And he must stop, he told himself, he must stop thinking of her as an aphrodisiac. Not only had she warned him that there was no gratification in it for her, but it was aimless for him as well—it confused his purpose. It had done so once, dulling his determination, and would do so again. He must keep his mind clear of her: there was a mountain to climb.

She said something about hanging the shirt near the fire where it would dry in a few minutes. He thanked her for everything she had done and told her how much better he was feeling. Then it occurred to him that she probably had had very little sleep last night, while looking after him. Her reply was vaguely about sleep being inconsequential, but she said she would go and have some rest.

As she was about to leave, something held her in the room. Then: "Did you mean it—you'll go up again?"

"Yes."

"You're a fool—and I hope they kill you."

He was jolted. He turned quickly to look at her. Her face was full of contradictions. She hadn't meant the words, only the anger. And even the anger seemed to refute itself—as if not knowing where the fury should be directed. Most incongruous of all, some other emotion than rage was under everything, something as ramp-

ant as he himself had felt, something yearning and erotic. And perhaps she was angry at that as well.

Toward noon, the bombing started.

Ben was lying on the bed. There was nobody else in the main room. When he heard the first sound, and it seemed underground, he thought it was an earthquake. Then, more logically, a cave-in. It wasn't a loud report, it couldn't have been too close, but there was a tremor in the cave, the mountain shuddered. Then he heard the second noise and the third and knew they were detonations. But he couldn't tell how near.

There was a lot of running in the corridor and a confusion of men's voices. What they were saying he didn't know, except that nobody in the mine could determine the distance of the explosions.

And the bombardment didn't stop.

In a little while Falkos rushed in. He carried his tiny walkie-talkie, which chattered unintelligibly. Proud of the instrument before, he now swore at it because the voices weren't coming through. He yanked at a cupboard door and pulled out a large and obsolete intercom, which he began to swear at as well. Paying no attention to Ben, he kept trying to reach Chartas, but kept getting others he didn't want to speak to, none of whom could tell him anything. After a half hour of impatience, he heard his superior on the little walkie-talkie; the voice was steadier than his own, but not altogether calm.

The Turks were bombing Martoulas, Chartas said, a village some fifteen miles from the cave, the other side of the mountain. If Falkos was feeling it at this distance it might be because the town was on the same fault as the cave, not because the bombing was dangerously close.

Falkos said that fifteen miles was close enough and, in his consideration—with the Turks closing in—they should not delay the assault on the Monastery, but put it in action instantly, at least no later than tomorrow morning.

Chartas disagreed. The Turkish planes on the Monastery's vineyard-airfield were not being used, he said, and might never be used unless the peace talks fell apart. But they might be, Falkos countered; it wasn't as if the cease-fire were being observed. The two Greeks were abruptly both talking at once, quarreling. As

Falkos uttered an abusive word, the other one went dead still. It took the teacher a moment to notice the silence, and he too became quiet. Chartas began to speak again in a measured and moderate voice that was almost inaudible. He was midsentence when Falkos made an angry movement at the intercom and flicked him off.

The teacher sat there seething and thwarted. Then, compunctious, he put an elbow on the table and his forehead in his hand. He was worried. He switched the walkie-talkie on again, asked for Chartas, and apologized.

He kept his anxiety to himself, referred none of it to Ben by so much as a glance.

The bombing continued. Particles of lava and limestone fell from the ceiling. There was a metal rattling somewhere on the hearth; Falkos went to it, removed the kettle from the trammel hook and placed it on the hob.

An hour after it had begun, the bombing stopped. It was lunchtime. Some of the guerrillas generally ate outdoors, some came to the cave; there was no ordered plan. They entered in pairs or singly, they gobbled their food hurriedly out of cans that they took from the shelves.

Kalya came in and made a thick lentil soup, also out of cans, adding spices that were none too fresh. In the course of the mealtime, perhaps a dozen men appeared. Some ate standing, some sat down. As Kalya hurried from one man to another—feeding them, taking their soiled dishes away—Ben saw a curious thing. She treated them not as men, but as boys, even though a number of them were older than she was. She was their war mother, she might be telling them, and they could rely upon her for food and fortitude. As she played the role, he could see that the need was more hers than theirs, and that she might be happy if the world were all children. He thought of three children lost, and an emptiness that she might believe would never again be filled. And perhaps it wouldn't. Watching her, he felt forlorn, with the sad, the helpless sense that there was no palliative he could give her, there was no analgesic for a void.

One of the men had a straw-covered bottle of wine. They passed the bottle around; some drank from tin or plastic cups, some drank directly from the bottle. By the time it got back to its owner, the bottle was empty. The men made a joke of it, but the owner was angry.

His name was Kostas and Ben recognized him as one of the men who had beaten him last night. He was an unkempt man, squat and stubborn as a tree stump. His gray shirt lacked a full complement of buttons and his trousers were thick with grime, but his Lee-Enfield rifle, although ancient, shone. He hated being laughed at.

The guerrilla who laughed hardest was Louka. Slung over his shoulder by a leather strap was a crudely made kithara, partly a guitar and partly a santuri, with more strings than either. He had a bearded, beaten-up face that had once been handsome. He was the bearded man of last night.

He saw Ben staring at him and, with a tin cup of lentil soup in his hand, advanced toward him.

"I hope you do not know me," he said.

"Yes, I do."

"I am sorry, then. But I want you to understand—I did not hurt you. It was the others—Mikis and that stupid Kostas."

"You were the leader—you gave the orders."

"No, I did not. We could take you without to muss up your hair. I would not give order like that. I am more smart—I am professional soldier."

"Good for you."

"You bet, good for me. They hurt because they *want* to hurt. This is their fight, this is their anger. But I am not angry at anybody. I do this for money. I will go anywhere—Angola—Cambodia—I am money soldier."

A mercenary, and stiff with pride about it. Now the man relaxed a little. "You see? This is my *business*. I say this to American—who understand business. Right?"

"Right!"

The beard didn't hear the sarcasm. "Thank you for this understanding. And I give promise to you, nobody will hurt you again. I will be your protector."

"For a fee."

This time the mercenary did get it and he laughed. "You are fine sport," he said. "I like fine sport. My name is Polycarpos Louka. All people call me Louka."

The bombing started again. The cave quaked. Food got spilled. One of the walls of the fire recess seemed to be moving a little. Two of the men rushed to beat the fire out; Kalya suffocated it with pots and pans.

The men were tense. They did not meet one another's eyes.

Louka said to Ben, "You are scared of the bombing?"

"Yes, aren't you?"

"Oh yes," he said with hurried candor. "I am scare like shit."

The mercenary had taken a fancy to Ben, he stayed close to him. "You know what I will do with soldier money? I will go to America. I have talent with my kithara." He made a strumming sound on his instrument, then rapped it with his knuckles. "I can sing in night club, in film—in big film. Also, I make up song—I am compositor of song. You would like to hear a song?"

Kostas heard the question and bellowed, "No!"

This time the laugh was on Louka, and it pleased Kostas. But it pleased the musician as well—he glowed in any light.

Another bomb, and another.

The men, as if by consensus, pretended not to hear it. Kostas got louder, overshouting the detonations. The men laughed at jokes they would not normally consider funny. Louka played fortissimo and sang at the top of his voice. Kostas, trying to get added applause for an only-once-used joke, yelled, "You want to sing song, Louka—go sing yourself in Hollywood."

Laughter.

"They will make a grape out of one of your *orhis*," Kostas continued.

Bombs, and bellows of laughter.

"But one *orhis* is enough in Hollywood. I saw this in a cinema. You know how they make the *fou-fou?* The woman is on top. This is the law of Hollywood—the woman has to be on top. If a man will break this law, he will lose his last *orhis!*"

They screamed with laughter, kept on screaming it, hardly hearing the bombs at all.

It was only when the bombardment ceased and the silence came that they saw no further humor in anything.

"Why do they bomb Martoulas?" one of them asked. "What in sister's ass is there?"

Somebody said there was nothing there, only old people. Somebody said only old people and goats. Somebody said it was a junction of dirt roads, none of which went anywhere.

Then Louka mockingly said that perhaps the Turks thought they had a major military objective.

This was the best laugh of the day. In a way, it got back at the

Turks for their vandalous stupidity, and the room vibrated with hilarity.

Then somebody suggested that maybe the Turks thought Martoulas was a cell of resistance, maybe they thought there was a hideout of guerrillas in the village.

Or nearby, somebody else said.

They looked at him.

Slowly, by degrees, the men stopped laughing.

Ben had had a few bad hours. The ache in his head had gone, but his leg had become more painful. He had lied to Falkos about being able to identify what was wrong with it. The knee was too swollen and, without an X-ray, he couldn't tell. It could be a torn ligament, a fracture, an injury to cartilage—the only certainty was pain.

Besides, it was stiflingly close in here. The walls of the cave, which had been assuagingly cool this morning, were suddenly copper-hot. All the imprisoned metal seemed to be smelting itself to escape. What troubled him most was that he wasn't certain it was the walls; he might be getting feverish. So he had taken quite a bit of aspirin, and as his eyes got heavy, the thought occurred to him: Don't doze off. There's a mountaintop—you have to run for it. On what, he said, run on what? And fell asleep.

Some soft stir in the room awakened him. He felt cool again and didn't mind that Kalya had rebuilt the fire. The kettle was back again, boiling.

Yannis was at the table drinking tea. Kalya asked Ben if he wanted any, and before he could answer they heard the hurry of footsteps in the hallway and two men came in. The older one he recognized—his name had been spoken last night—Mikis, the guerrilla who had driven the ambulance. He seemed more mature today, as rugged as Macedonia, his mustache heavy and his eyes enormous. He introduced the younger one as Petros—twentyish, with a face like Hellenic statuary, so perfect in its stillness that it was a pity that the mouth must move or the eyes blink. He seemed pathetically shy and did not acknowledge the introduction. It was a breach of manners that Mikis could not stand. Say *herete,* he said to Petros, say *herete.* It was as if he had asked the boy to make a vast public pronouncement, impromptu; he couldn't utter a word.

"He stammers," Mikis explained.

Petros spoke: "I—do—not—stammer—in—English."

Mikis smiled with comic sufferance. "You can imagine this? In English he can talk, but in his own language he has a short tongue."

"My—name—is—Petros—Drakos."

Kalya nodded and Yannis murmured *herete*. Ben gave him his hand and the boy smiled, breaking the beautiful marble mask.

They heard Falkos calling to Louka, something about doubling the watch, then the teacher entered.

"You brought him?" he said to Mikis.

"Yes. He is in the upper gallery," he replied.

"He drove?"

"All the way."

"Did he drive well?"

"As well as I do."

"Send him down," the teacher said.

Shortly after the two young men had left, the other one came in. Ben remembered him instantly, but not his name. In his mind he was simply Mark, a boy not yet a man, epileptic.

It seemed important to the new arrival to let it be known that *his* memory had not lapsed at all. "We've met before," he said. "At the port."

"Yes. How are you?"

"Very well." With a little asperity. "Hello, Yannis," he said, as to an old acquaintance.

Kalya hung back, at the perimeter. Falkos made a gesture to her. "Mark Achille—this is Kalya Menas."

She acknowledged the introduction with the slightest movement of her lips.

"You're the Turkish woman," the boy said. There was no insulting inflection in it, no discourtesy. It was stated in the most unmodulated voice, without stress. That was its provocation.

"Yes," she responded politely. "I am the Turkish woman."

There were grits of abrasion; Falkos hastened to brush them away. "We're a mixed assortment here," he began, with mock solemnity. "And it's not to be expected that we'll see eye to eye on everything. Still, there's no need for dogs to tear one another apart when there are wolves about. Since Mark is now one of us, Mikis has told him a few things—and I will tell him more. We won't keep any secrets—and I won't keep any from you, Benjamin. You tried to get away once, and you say you'll try again. This time I have to believe you—and this time you will probably be killed. In which case, we have no ambulance driver who would not seem suspect to the Turks. So, with your permission—or without it—Mark will spend the next few days driving your ambulance, as your substitute. Yannis will go with him. They will go only to Nicosia—that's all they'll have time for—and make themselves as conspicuous as possible, in tavernas, in cafes. In that way, it will become known that another American is now driving the ambulance. He and Yannis—"

"I will not go with him," Yannis said.

"—will spread it about that you have gone home for a while—an illness in the family—and you will come back before long." He smiled quizzically. "If you should come back sooner—in time to drive your ambulance—with us, the way we originally planned it —we would heartily welcome you back."

It was a resourceful maneuver. Whatever its faults, it told Ben he was no longer indispensable, there was somebody warming up behind him. Ben looked at Yannis, at Kalya, at the boy. The old Greek stood slightly apart from the group, his eyes lowered. Kalya was gazing at Mark, appraising him. The boy seemed calmer than all of them. He was quite erect, quite still, attending only to Falkos, the leader.

Ben said, "Are you going to trust everybody's life to someone who shouldn't be allowed to drive?"

"He's already satisfied me on that point." Falkos turned to Mark. "Answer him."

"I've driven a vehicle safely for three years."

"Without an accident?"

A flicker of hesitation. "I had one accident. It had nothing to do with a seizure. I was avoiding a drunk, and I hit another car."

"You never had a seizure in three years of driving?"

"I didn't say that. If I saw one coming, I pulled over and . . . worked it off."

"Did you always see one coming?"

". . . Yes."

"When I took care of you at the port, you didn't see one coming."

"That was different. When I'm driving I can always see one coming."

"That's convenient, isn't it?"

"Yes, it is." The boy was not as calm as before. His stillness was becoming rigid. "It's a breath of air—it's like somebody sighing inside me—it's—" He stopped, confused and nettled. "If you're a doctor, I don't have to tell you about *aura epileptica,* do I?"

It was true enough, what the boy was saying about the phenomenon, except that the symptom was unreliable. "He'll be under terrible stress—you can't trust your lives to him."

"We'll trust them to you, Benjamin."

Falkos turned and went away. When he was gone, his last statement stayed behind, like a dangerous object ticking.

Nobody looked at anybody. There was an irresolution among them, everything suspended and alarming, as if they were strangers in a doctor's waiting room. How sick am I and how sick are all the others, who's in pain, and who'll be dead before the year is out?

The boy seems the most resolved of all of us, Ben thought, but we know what he's got—unknown, incurable—remissions, that's all. Poor bastard.

There was a flight of planes. Even in the cave they could hear it. They all looked up as if they could see through the mountain.

Mark was excited. "Mikis says they're Turkish. He says they're landing on the Monastery airfield."

"It's not an airfield," Ben said, "it's a vineyard." The distinction mattered.

"How many planes have they got up there?" the boy asked.

Ben didn't know. However many they had yesterday, they have more now, he thought; they were adding them a few at a time, not too conspicuously.

The boy, as revved up as the planes, was a trouble in Ben's mind. Mixed with his pity—annoyance. "Why did you get into this?"

Mark, for some reason, looked quickly at Kalya, but said nothing.

Yannis answered for him. "He hates Turks."

Kalya appeared unruffled. "There is a Turkish expression: Know us more, like us less."

Yannis tried to grin. "We say the same in Greek."

She gave him a grateful glance. "About yourselves or about us?"

They all tried to smile. Nobody managed it.

Overtly, she turned all her attention to the boy. "You're an American—why do you hate us so much?"

"It's an unpleasant story."

"I didn't expect to chuckle over it."

This time they did manage a smile, she and Mark, but it was a friendly compact to despise each other.

Ben's leg, in an access of pain, started to give way under him and he realized he was standing, and had been for quite a few minutes. He was glad that he had been able to do it, but as he sat down, his face must have betrayed the hurt.

Mark pointed to the leg. "They didn't do that to you, did they?"

"No, that came later. I think I fell."

"Mikis says they beat you up."

"Yes."

"He made a point of letting me know that. As if I'd ever do anything they'd beat me up for."

"You never can tell."

"Does it hurt much?" It seemed important to know.

"It'll pass."

"That's the lucky thing about what I've got—no pain—nothing like that."

"Only mysterious breaths."

The boy heard the sarcasm and spoke with urgency. "I told you the truth about the *aura*. I do get those breaths. And other auras too. Honest to God I do."

He's pleading with me to believe him, Ben thought. He's attaching himself to me. He knows I'm not a doctor, but he's going to treat me as if I were. Not to flatter me, but because he needs to think I *am* one; probably needs a doctor around him all the time.

He didn't know how he felt about the boy. There was something terrible about him, and something kindly and touching. Nineteen years old? Yes, perhaps, but twelve one minute and forty the next. Aberrational. A genius, the kid had said he was, and it might be true, one way or another. Master's degree—book-brilliant and world-stupid. Painfully innocent.

"Why don't you believe me?" Mark persisted.

"I do believe you," Ben said. "Except that the symptoms don't always happen."

Mercurially, the boy switched from pleading to anger. "What the hell do you know? The doctors tell me what I'm feeling—and they don't know a damn!" As if persecuted, "What are you trying to do—discredit me with Falkos? You think I don't know what to do about it?"

Kalya said, "What *do* you do about it?"

Her voice was not friendly, only civil. And it was clinical. The boy had expected no such interest from her. He was off-balance. "What?"

"Do you take things for it?"

"Medications, you mean?" He snarled the words. "They don't do any good. I've had them all—and they're worse than the fits. They make me sick in the stomach and dead in the brain. I hate them all! I hate the goddamn sickness—and I hate talking about it!"

He shook with anger, uncontrolled. *Furor epilepticus.* He could have a seizure any instant, Ben thought, and there would be no preventing it. Yet, how different it was, seeing it now, from what it had seemed when he had read about it. This epileptic rage was no sicker than other rages he had seen, and God knows the stricken boy had more reason to rage than most. Then, what was it, what was different about it? What was its unearthly thing? An electrical storm in the brain, someone had called it; and someone else, correcting, had said it was in the soul.

"I hate it!" the boy repeated.

But there were no spastic motions, no writhing, no fit.

Nor did Kalya seem to view it as if any of those signs would appear. Quietly, she asked, "Do you hate it worse than you hate the Turks?"

At first Ben thought how cruel she was to get back at the kid with such a mean requital. But then he saw that she was asking the question with no hostility at all, had even inquired with a certain kindness, as if she had forgiven his assault and would be charitable to a sick boy no matter what his answer might be.

Her compassion, instead of soothing Mark, rattled him. "I hate it," was all he could say.

"It hasn't always been hated."

Abruptly, some new awareness stirred in him. "No? When wasn't it?"

The directness of the question seemed to unsettle her for a moment. A demand had been made on her to quote facts and sources; she was trying to dredge something out of her past, out of a book somewhere. Ben caught a fleeting glint of a Cultural History girl.

But she couldn't summon what she needed; it was gone. "Something about the gods—I can't remember," she said. "The sickness of the gods—isn't that what they called it?"

"Of the gods, huh? Then it's an honor to have it?"

The boy was leading her on, making a fool of her. "Well . . ."

"You've got it wrong," he said flatly. He was having no such difficulty as she was having. Facts and sources came easily to him; his mind recorded footnotes. And he was, particularly on this subject, the ultimate authority. "It was called *morbus divus*—and it doesn't mean anything noble like the sickness of the gods. It's not a disease they *have*, it's a disease they *inflict*. It's a curse!"

"It depends on—"

"It depends on nothing, it's a curse!" Contemptuously, he turned from her and looked at Ben. "You tell her, Doc—tell her what a curse it is!"

"I don't think it's either an honor or a curse," Ben said quietly.

"Then what is it?"

"It's only a disease. Like measles, only we haven't found a vaccine for it."

He stopped. They were both defining it in romantic terms, and he, by defining it in realistic ones, was belittling it, robbing it of its compensation, its enchantment—a dramatic fantasy. He wanted to go on and say that by calling it an honor or a curse they were saying it was beyond substantiality—and therefore, invincible. The way tuberculosis had for so long been invincible—the poet's ailment—the white affliction—such a beautiful malady! There were all those flush-faced, burning-eyed love scenes in the Alpine sanitariums—in exquisite technicolor, with only the blood hues missing. Or, on the other hand, there was the *ugly* picture, bewitchingly ugly—the black evil—the devil's curse— unconquerable. So it had had its own way, galloping consumption, too beautiful to banish, or too satanic to be banishable. And meanwhile people were sweating the nights and burning the days, and hacking real gore, not in technicolor, and dying. Then some prosaic drones went to work in a laboratory—and they didn't get bewitched by a pretty picture or get terrified by an invincible devil—they attacked a bacterium.

"Someday they'll find it," he said. "The way they found streptomycin for T.B. . . . And that'll be the end of epilepsy."

It seemed such a workaday thing to say, so colorless compared to their vivid deities and curses.

"You think it'll happen, do you?" the boy said skeptically.

"Yes, I do."

"I'll stick around."

His snideness gave over to fatigue. His resistance was suspended; he seemed drained. Yannis, apparently thinking the boy might pass out, went quickly to him, and offered to show him to one of the smaller cells where he could lie down.

When they were gone, Ben saw that Kalya's mind was still on the boy. Her eyes were fixed on the archway through which he had gone as if he were still there, as if they were silently communing with each other.

Ben had a twinge. The boy was attractive. Even sexually so. There was that perverse refusal of the two sides of him to become one, the child and the man, the brilliant and the naïve. He was an exciting sport of nature, with a lightning streak of madness that could strike two places at once, at himself and at her. He wondered if it had struck.

"What are you thinking, Kalya?"

"He's so much younger than he thinks—and he's in such pain."

He heard the responsive pain. Her voice sorrowed with it. Perhaps it was totally different from what Ben had thought. Perhaps she had not seen a handsome young man, a genius, a sex object, a flash of lurid light; nor even an objectionable boy who was trying to offend, a Greek insulting a Turk, an enemy. Perhaps she had seen only a child who was afflicted. Maybe nothing about him had any reality to her except his adversity, his need, his angry desperation— and it was all she spoke to. It was for that reason that she had referred to epilepsy as the sickness of the gods, to lift the boy's spirit, to put a poultice on his pain. The thought was poignant to Ben, and he hurt for her more than for the boy. He yearned to console her for *her* afflictions, which he was sure had been more agonizing than the boy's. He wanted to move closer to her, to hold her soothingly, to give her comfort as she, likely, wanted to comfort Mark.

"Did you believe what you said to him?" Ben asked. "About the gods?"

"Does it matter?"

"No, not really—you were being kind. But did you believe it?"

". . . I think so."

"Really?"

"Yes."

"Then you believe in God?"

She was disturbed by the question. Perhaps it had not been an imposture with the boy, but something she trusted in, a matter of creed. Fate. Turkish, this could be a tenet out of her Islamic heritage. She was accepting her lot, her portion of the world's outrage, bowing without whimper to whatever blows and buffets had been meant for her, Allah be praised, kismet. But there was something wrong with the picture: she was a fighter. She drew excitement from besting bullies, like the police who had arrested her; she allowed no water to damage her child's grave; she would take arms against an unjust deity.

He pressed the question: "Do you believe in God?"

"No—nothing so sublime as that . . . Only in the gods."

"The Fates, you mean?"

"Yes, fates." She said it contemptuously, as if she was reducing the capital to lower case. "The little ones, the mean ones, the spiteful."

"Small—and therefore manageable?"

"Oh, less manageable because they're small."

"What do they do?"

"Petty mischiefs that all add up. Dirty little accidents that wreck your life. Hopes that are really evils . . . blights."

"And we call it bad luck—is that what you think?"

"Yes . . . coincidences."

It occurred to him that words like "coincidence" and "accident" had little meaning in life, and little usefulness in thought . . . and that they were retreats when we can't see the whole design, or when the design was too painful to contemplate. He wondered what other retreats she might have.

Dinner, like lunch, had come drearily out of cans except for the wild thyme, a shrub of which Kalya had found outdoors. The main room of the cave still smelled of it. Thyme and brandy.

Falkos had had little to eat and was drinking as if he had a goal. Ben's single glass of brandy was still half full. Kalya, clearing the afterdinner mess, hadn't had any, and now she paused a moment, tipped a little liquor into a plastic glass, took a single sip and resumed her work.

It was quiet. The radio intercom had not squawked for hours. The men on bivouac, and the few who had cells in the cave, were probably asleep, except for those on watch. Yannis and Mark had said good-night a while ago. The mood was somnolent.

"Have you two made love as yet?" Falkos asked.

The silence was a caesura in a slow-tempoed verse. Then the line went on again, Ben drinking, Kalya putting away the last of the utensils.

"What are you waiting for?" the teacher continued.

When he got no answer, he poured himself another drink. Now he did not address both of them but only Ben, who sat across the table from him.

"Do you think because you haven't consummated anything with her, you needn't consummate anything with me? You're wrong, Benjamin. We've made a pact with each other, and I'm going to hold you to it. When the time comes, it won't be Mark, it'll be you who'll drive the ambulance. And I hope you'll do it willingly. In fact, I had hoped that you would already be happier about it. But if you're not, I don't think you're altogether at fault. The job hasn't had any attractive perquisites, has it? Bad food, no money, an injured leg . . . and no love."

He turned his attention away from Ben. "And you, Kalya— I'm quite disappointed in you. I hired you as Aphrodite, and you're playing Medusa."

"I'm not playing anything."

A low command, smiling. "Then play, Kalya."

"Why don't you stop being a pimp?" Ben said.

Even if that's what he was, Ben thought, he could hardly blame the teacher for invading a privacy that had no sanctity; after all, Falkos probably assumed they had settled for a tawdry, meretricious relationship. But what *was* nettling was that this clearheaded, canny man should imagine he could openly negotiate an erotic match between the two of them—and why did he need to do it?

The schoolmaster was unruffled by being called a pimp. He merely chuckled, took a sip of brandy, and waved airily to someone in the archway.

It was Mark. He stood on the threshold adjusting his eyes to the brighter light.

"Can't sleep?" Falkos asked.

"I kept hearing planes."

"There haven't been any." Then, cordially, "Come in—have a drink."

A curious instant. The boy looked quickly at Ben: the doctor. Then he said, "I don't drink very often."

But he did join them at the table. The expansive host, Falkos asked amiably, "We were talking about Aphrodite. What do *you* think? Wasn't it her function to foster love?"

The boy looked from Falkos to the others, suspecting an off-color joke. Guardedly, he said he didn't know.

"Don't know? Didn't you say you were doing research on Aphrodite?" On a note of supercilious amusement: "And Benjamin tells me you're looking for her grave."

Injured, "That's not as silly as it sounds."

Falkos leaped to his defense. "Who says it's silly? This is *it!*"

It *was* a joke, the boy's expression said, and he was the butt of it. "This is what?"

"Her grave."

"I thought it was called Aphrodite's Cave."

"Her grave and her cave are the same thing," the teacher responded. "At least, that's what the myth says."

"What myth?" Mark asked.

"The one that starts with Aphrodite's trial." He turned to Kalya. "It does start with her trial, doesn't it?"

She tried to remember it. "Was Aphrodite on trial?"

"Of course—on Olympus."

"A legal trial, you mean?" Mark asked.

"As legal as possible. Olympus was corrupt."

"What was the charge against her?"

"Lust." He smiled; so did Kalya.

"What happened to her?"

Falkos looked to make sure they wanted him to tell it. Then he did.

They had their share of hypocrites on Olympus, he began. Zeus himself—and he was judging her—was not above a bit of lechery. When he had a hunger to seduce, he would resort to anything, to the most unscrupulous disguises—he was a white bull, a cuckoo, a swan, a shower of gold. And the goddess who brought the charge against Aphrodite was not much purer, she was that bitch of so-called chastity, Artemis. She brought witnesses—those she herself had slept with—Apollo, Hades, Hermes, all of them. And she accused Aphrodite of seducing every deity who had a *phallos,* and a number who hadn't. Every one of them had believed he was singular in Aphrodite's affection—because each time she had believed, in all her parts, that he *was* singular. But now, seeing there were so many of them, they testified in rage against her. Some said she was the liar among the gods, some said unfaithful, some, licentious. Hephaestos said she had stolen all his flames, and Hades said she had diseased him. They all lied a little—she was too beautiful.

Dionysos defended her, but he was drunk. She never had a chance.

When all the testimony had been given, Zeus asked if she had anything to add, and she had no answer except to take all her clothes off, and stand before them, naked. She always felt that nudity was a persuasion. And she said: "You all know me. I have not changed. I am as I was when I was born. What they say of me is true. I have loved them all. But each time that I loved, I loved for the first time. And there is not one of them to whom I lied with my eyes or my mouth or my heart or my breasts or my openness. And I am still a virgin."

The gods began to laugh and she covered herself in shame. When Zeus had silenced their mockery, he raised his arm against her and said, "You are the whore of Olympus. And I sentence you to Earth."

So she fell down, down through all the hypocrisies of heaven, and it seemed to her that she had died. When she came to life again, she was ascending through the waters of the sea. She lived, then, on all these islands—Cyprus, of course, which became her home—and Crete, Rhodes, all of them.

When she was sentenced to Earth, Aphrodite thought that she had been exiled only from Olympus, but she came to realize that her punishment was worse—she had been banished from innocence. She did not know whether she would be able to endure the ambiguities that mortals suffered. She had always thought, in heaven, that love was only a blessing; on Earth it was also a malediction. She thought that music was a sound of joy; on Earth it was also a lamentation. She thought red was the color of passion; on Earth, of blood.

She had never known loneliness before, and now she knew it. I do not seem the same to myself, she thought; perhaps the light is different. Or perhaps I am changing and am not so beautiful as I used to be. . . . She was not a goddess and would never die; yet, she began to know the feeling of age, of growing older. And worst of all, she was a stranger here, alien from Earth and heaven. She did not know the mortal language. The goddess of love could speak no endearment that anyone would understand, and no sound she heard had a caress in it.

So she began to sicken. And when she could bear it no longer, she decided to learn the earthly ways. She started to walk as mortals walk, as if to hide themselves. She started to say one thing and mean another. She practiced temporizing. She came to understand that while love was a simplicity, passion was largely paradox, and mortals wanted both at once.

Also, she learned to tantalize. When addressing herself to a man, she might speak of the smoothness of a flower petal in such a way that he would understand the smoothness of her skin. When she finished speaking, she let her mouth remain slightly open so her tongue might be seen, suggesting that it might have other messages than words. When she touched a man's hand she made possibilities spring into his mind that she was touching him elsewhere, and more lovingly.

She knew about men and moistures. If she purposely did not wipe away the drop of wine that remained wetly on her lips, she was certain that a man would stare at it and want to lick it away. The liquid of her eye when she got a mote in it, and the closeness of a man when he removed it; the damp vapors of her mouth, the droplets in her armpits, all the warm wetnesses of weeping and eating and kissing, she knew that they all promised the great moistures of love, the deep waters of Aphrodite's sea.

She knew she had an evocative power. She knew how to sit in such a way as to suggest that she was lying down and waiting; she knew how to lie down in such a way as to suggest that a man was within her.

In her presence, a mortal male imagined love was always approaching climax. He could be halfway across the world from her and, if she meant it that way, he would believe that he was kissing her, fondling her, sucking at her breast, her mouth on him, his love inside her, loving, loving, penetrating profoundly into the wet deeps from which she came.

Men to whom she did give herself were in bondage to her forever. Menelaus did not go to Troy for Helen but for Aphrodite. It was not Circe that Odysseus loved; after one night with Aphrodite he spent twenty years in search of her, wandering a loveless world. She was the eleventh labor of Heracles—the task was to satisfy the goddess—and he failed.

No mortal man ever satisfied her. In heaven every time she had ever loved she had been fulfilled. On Earth she was always empty. She had thought that by learning to make love in mortal ways, she would put an end to her loneliness. But she discovered that love and loneliness have little to do with one another, and loneliness was the human condition which mortals had learned to endure. But she could not endure it. She longed for Olympus, she longed for home. She cried to Zeus, "Let me come home again! Or else let me not be immortal any longer. Let me be an earthling, and die. I have lived too long. Let me go back into the sea, and disappear. Let me perish."

But he would not hear her, and she lived.

Then one day she saw a stag. He was in a wide green meadow with the sunlight on his antlers, and no other deer around him. He was of a great size, the most powerful buck she had ever seen. Black, everything about him black, his horns and his hooves, and his gleaming coat, and he was a black fury as he ran. He was the most beautiful wild male she had ever seen. As she watched him, everything he did had a respondence in her. When he was still, she felt a stillness like the sleep of childhood. When he tilted his head to question the wind, she felt that there were answers she might tell him. When he leaped, her whole spirit leaped with him.

Suddenly, he raised his antlers, must have caught the breath of her, bounded one direction, then another, and started to flee from the meadow. No, don't go, she cried, stay and I won't disturb you, I'll stop breathing, no, please, come back! . . . But he was gone.

She said: I will find him, and I will mate with him. It is a mortal creature, she told herself, and I am a goddess, and I will find a way to capture this beautiful stag.

She enlisted all the ruses that she had ever learned from the goddess of the hunt, her enemy, Artemis. She made confusions in the winds so he would not know from which direction danger came. She changed the scents of verdure so that the aroma of growing things that stags loved would lead him to her. Brooks, freshets, rivers—she altered their courses so he would come to drink where her currents led him.

But he eluded her and would not come. Many days she had no glimpse of him at all. If, rarely, she got close, he took to flight. And once, only once, she got near enough to touch him. When her fingers barely grazed his horn, however, he reared and kicked at the air, he made a sound of frenzy, and fled.

That day she knew that she must have him, or suffer a greater agony than exile. It would be the final banishment—from her senses. This wild thing she needed with all her immortal soul, for it was as though the simple beast was her lost innocence.

It was then the mating season. In the middle of a stand of birches there was a glade, and in it she saw her stag and a young doe, joined. She watched them until the act was over. Now, Aphrodite became so jealous that she said: I will kill her. So she tracked the doe, and tracked her. But she was too elusive. At last, one night, the goddess came upon her. She heard her thrashing in the underbrush, and she saw the thicket shaking. Entering the brake, she saw the deer ensnared by vines and creepers. The creature crashed about in the runners and tendrils and could not free herself. When Aphrodite lay a hand upon her, the doe's terror became more desperate. Then, moment by moment, when she sensed that help had come, the animal started to be soothed. As she was disentangling the creature, the goddess could smell the doe's fright. The aroma was a strange one, as fragrant as greenwood, yet pungently bestial. And she realized that the odor was more than fright, it was the scent of the female's estrus. Excited, an inspiration struck the goddess.

Before letting the deer go free, she undressed, stripped herself naked. Then she rubbed her body with the moisture of the animal, rubbed her thighs and her breasts and all her private places, and as she lay down naked in a clearing by a stream, she changed the zephyrs so they would carry the scent of her through the woodland, while she waited. She waited and waited, and the stag did not come, and at last she fell asleep.

In the darkness she felt the touch upon her bosom, she felt the rough tongue over her breast, her belly, her thighs, and as she spread herself and his mouth was upon her, her mouth was upon him. She tasted his musk with her tongue and with her lips and sucked him, then made him come in upon her. And she had never had such passion, never the enormous fury, never the wild fulfillment, never the joy. And she had the stag again and again.

When he was gone, she had a child by him, an earthling. All

that could unequivocally be said of the infant was that it was male. It was neither god nor man nor beast; it was monstrous. Two-legged, it had black horns and a face of fury. Its cry, like the mandrake root, was frightening. The first time she suckled it, it could not be satisfied. It clung to her breast and would not release her. She struck at it and struck at it and cried and struck, until it was dead.

Then she mourned for it so terribly that she grew ugly, and could not bear to look at herself by daylight. She realized that for most of her life on Earth she had mourned, and the truth came to her: she had been mortal for a long time, without knowing it. And the one gift the gods did not possess was the mortal blessing, mortality. So, in a craze, she searched for perpetual darkness, and at last wandered into a cave, where she perished.

It is said that this is the cave of Aphrodite.

When he was through telling the story, Falkos poured himself some brandy and refilled Ben's glass. Mark was still not having any, and Kalya did not want any more.

"Well, what did you think of the myth?" the teacher asked.

"I don't believe there is such a myth," Mark said. "You made it up, didn't you?"

"Of course. All myths are made up."

"The ones of older vintage sound truer."

"Why?" Falkos asked. "Because what's ancient is believable?"

"We're comfortable with the old lies," Kalya said.

"But we've run out of them," Falkos said. "We have to manufacture more."

"Why?" Ben said.

"For new times, new purposes, new people. If only for the tourists."

Kalya thought the boy was being deprecated. "He's not a tourist."

Mark turned to her. "I don't mind being called a tourist."

"When he says tourist, he means fool," she explained.

"I know I'm not a fool—I don't need you to defend me," Mark said.

He underscored the "you"; it meant "Turk." And Ben thought: Wouldn't it be nice if that were the remark of a simple snot instead of a sick kid who can't accept the smallest favor from a Turkish woman?

And there she was again: turning the other cheek to a rigid little fanatic who had vowed vengeance against her own people. And she was holding him to account for nothing—he was a trick of the gods—another malevolent accident in her life.

The boy, aware that his churlishness had ingratiated him to nobody, wanted to make amends, but didn't know how. He muttered something about going back to his imaginary airplanes, and left the room.

As if he hadn't been able to wait to have them alone, Falkos looked at Ben and Kalya. "Well, what did you think of my myth?" When neither of them answered, he stared pointedly at the Turkish woman. "Well . . . well?"

Her look was quizzical. "I was thinking that in your Olympus, the god is a god, and the goddess is mortal."

He was having a good time. "Do you think that's chauvinist of me?"

"Well, it *is* a man's myth, isn't it?"

"Yes, but my Aphrodite *wanted* to be mortal."

"Why?" she asked. "Because there was death in it?"

"Because there was choice. A goddess can't die even if she wants to."

"But why was that the limit of the woman's choice?"

Flushed with brandy, he didn't answer her question but laughed excessively. Turning to the American, "What did you think of my fable, Benjamin?"

"I don't like Spanish fly."

"What's that—an aphrodisiac?"

His correct guess at the meaning of the term betrayed his purpose. "Yes, I confess it," Falkos said. "That's what I had in mind. I wanted the two of you . . ."

As he lifted the brandy bottle again, his hand was not steady. Ben sensed that the man didn't know how drunk he was.

"Don't be too hard on me for that, Benjamin," he said. "I want you to be with us—but whether you *are* with us or not, I want you to be with her. Believe me, I mean that. I think you are in need of each other. I would like to see you together—in my mind—I would like to see that."

It was so frankly voyeuristic that it amazed Ben. He could not believe it of Falkos. Aside from how perversely it described him, it seemed irrelevant to all his other qualities as an integral person. Voyeur. He felt a wave of sympathy. The man was a creep, but that was not the essence of him. There were too many other things —inconsistent—how could he be despicable and admirable and pitiable all at once? Beware, Ben said, don't say pity; feeling sorry is your weakness, your pathetic fallacy. The man was insidious, a rodent burrowing into the libido, leaving his night soil behind him. No matter how selflessly he played the selfless matchmaker, he was offering them a bed for a piece of the action. He might pretend that he was waiving his seigneurial right, but he was retaining the most formidable right of all: control over both of them. Power. A potent aphrodisiac in the pharmacology of sex. And by bestowing the erotic gift, he was actually snatching it away—stripping the American of his sexual initiative. Enervating him. Paralyzing him so that he couldn't mount a woman or a mountain.

His knee ached like hell. It had no right to ache that much. It was Falkos, he said, crippling him.

Kalya said nothing.

The teacher was watching him.

Then there was a scuffling in the corridor. Somebody ran, with someone after him. Then a shout: be careful. Another outcry. A gunshot.

They rushed into the corridor and saw a scramble at the far end of it. There were three men, unidentifiable at first, the light was murky. As one of them got thrown out of the melee, into the orbit of the candle lamp, they caught sight of Petros. The second was tall and bearded, Louka.

The third wore a dark uniform and a green beret. He was a Turk.

As Falkos rushed toward them, there was another shot, a skirmish. For an instant it looked as if they had the man. Louka's arms were locked around him. Suddenly, another confusion of bodies, and the Turk was gone.

Somebody shouted *here,* and there was another shout, from a further passageway. A voice called from up high, from a gallery above, then there were yells from intersecting corridors.

Soon the main corridor was a tumult—Louka and Petros, where they had been before, Mikis at the other end, Kostas rushing in and out, from one tunnel to another, and someone calling to a man with a lamp, Evagoras, Evagoras!

The man had escaped.

Louka had the Turk's gun in his hand.

"He is still here, Falkos—he has to be here," the mercenary said.

Mikis agreed. There was a guard at the upper exit; nobody could have passed him, and there were two men posted at the opening to the copper road. There was no way for the Turk to get out.

Falkos fumed, "If he can't get out, how did he get in?"

Nobody answered. Someone had napped, someone had walked away, someone was looking the wrong direction.

"But he is still inside," Louka insisted.

The teacher nodded. He sent two men to reinforce the exits; two others to the intersecting tunnels. Louka and Mikis were dispatched to the upper galleries. Kostas and Evagoras were ordered to the downgrading adits, deeper into the earth.

As the men were about to depart, Falkos took the Turk's gun from Louka and gave the command: "No guns."

"The man has a knife," Louka said.

"So have you," the teacher said. "I want no further noise."

"It won't be heard outside," Kostas said.

"No more chances. Besides, I want him alive. I have to find out how he got in."

Kostas muttered under his breath and went with Evagoras. The others departed as well. Falkos flicked his intercom and called: "Lambros—Photis—come inside by way of the copper road. Georghiou and the twins—the other way. Be careful—we have a Turk in here."

He needed more men to probe the corridors. There were literally hundreds of tunnels, passages, adits, galleries where the enemy could hide. He set up his command post in the main section, called "the open place," into which most of the upper galleries descended. When Ben hobbled slowly into the area, Kalya was already there; so were Mark and Yannis; all were ordered to the perimeter darkness. It was curious, Ben thought, that Falkos allowed them there, but not so strange when Ben saw him in action. He was in complete command, and good at it, and he wanted them to know he was, it gave him pleasure to have an audience. The voyeur liked looking, and being looked at.

Soon, the outdoor guerrillas started coming in. Some of them had small torches; Lambros had a large one. But there were not enough flashlights to go around.

"If you do not have a light—talk!" Falkos ordered.

"He'll hear us," one of the men said.

"Talk!" he repeated. Darkness was as dangerous as the Turk; a Greek could knife a Greek.

The torches cut through the black. There were spasms of light. Passages appeared where there had been a mountain wall. Tunnels exploded into brightness. The beams struck one another and fled.

Falkos, in the middle of the open place, had to shout his orders—there were distances to travel and walls of rock to pierce. "Georghiou—to the second gallery, and work down. Vasos—there's already one torch there—go to the tunnel. Talk, Georghiou —talk!"

Most of the men tried to sound conversational, although their voices were strained; some shouted; Louka sang.

"I'm here," one said irritably. "Go the other way."

"Turn the light downward."

"Who's that, Vasos?"

"Yes, Vasos."

"Talk, Vasos."

Occasionally in a dart of light a knife would flash. Once, there was a dumping sound, followed by a soft cascade of rock and all of them went still, nobody moved, until they knew it was minor, not a cave-in of any kind.

Falkos called, "You've been there, Photis—twice—go up this time! Petros, don't walk backward on the gallery—look, look!" Then: "Parpas!"

"He's down below."

"Parpas!" he called again. Still he got no answer. In some passages, the voice got lost. Somebody would be talking and then it was as if a switch were flipped: silence. "Parpas—somebody find Parpas!"

"My father's *orhis,* what do you want?" Parpas shouted.

"Answer me, you bastard!"

"I did—three times!"

He sent the young man further upward. The lower tunnels, of which there were fewer, had been well searched by now, and he was deploying all the men higher, gallery by gallery. Louka and Mikis were on the topmost gallery—far aloft—almost out of sight.

One of the torches died and someone cursed. Somebody stumbled and also cursed.

"Louka—there he is!" Falkos cried.

The Turk was as high as he could get—on the sixth elevation. Where he could have been hiding was unknown—the balcony had been explored.

"Take care! Behind you!"

Louka turned but didn't see him. The Turk ran one way, then another, and vanished.

"Mikis!" the teacher yelled. "To your left—toward Louka— the low tunnel!"

Mikis ran toward the dark patch on the wall.

The Turk appeared on another part of the gallery, halfway between Mikis and Louka. Now, seeing he was caught, he jumped to a lower gallery. Louka jumped too, and Mikis after him. The Turk was faster than either of them. He was running, flying. His uniform looked black. He was a bat. Maddened with fright, he darted five feet one way, ten another, trying to find an exit, a crack in the mountain, any slight cleft he could fly into.

The men were converging on him. Kostas suddenly appeared in what had seemed an alcove. He bore down on the Turk. The bat fluttered. Now it was openly terrified and made sounds.

"Photis—come down, come down!" Falkos yelled.

The black thing wielded a knife.

"Petros—stay back!"

Louka got to him first.

The knife flashed.

Mikis was there, behind him. He grabbed the hand. Now, three of them, together, the bodies indistinct—which was which? —only the knife had clarity. They grappled, skirmished, then the knife fell, and someone kicked it. It dropped below, to the rock floor of the open space. But the men were still clutched and struggling, moving toward the gallery's edge. Mikis, the closest, the likeliest to fall, stepped back, felt rock give way and, moving sideward, released the Turk.

"Louka—pull back!" he yelled.

The mercenary loosened his grip and let go.

The bat raised both arms like wings, teetered for an instant, then fell backward.

His body struck the ledge of rock not twenty feet from where Falkos stood. The head got the worst of the impact.

The men converged. They didn't get too close, as if they were allowing the corpse some air. Some of them, held momentarily by what they saw, stood and stared; others looked away.

Photis said, "Kostas, help me—we'll take him out and bury him."

"Not out," Falkos said. "In. Find a place inside the cave."

He turned from the dead Turk and addressed the men. "The others—all of you—into the main room."

He was calling a meeting, not only of those present, but of his whole command. Ben wondered why he wanted everybody, but Falkos obviously knew what he was doing. His voice was level and certain, without the slightest hint of hesitancy. There was no sign that he was drunk.

Ben turned to look at Kalya. Her eyes, horrified, were on the dead man. But now he saw them—as if at her conscious injunction —leave the body and look upward at the gallery from which the Turk had fallen. Her head stirred in short, quick starts, her eyes darted—she seemed to be living the chase again, the scurrying of men on the heights above, the shouts, the play of light, the hue and cry, the fight, the fall. And the horror in her eyes had given way to excitement.

The men in the main room waited. There were fourteen of them, and eighteen more had been summoned. In all, Falkos's command numbered forty-five men; thirteen would remain out-doors, on guard. While waiting for the eighteen to arrive, even though it was nearly midnight, they did what they always did in the main room: they ate.

They ate anything that was easy, anything they could open quickly that they didn't have to cook or mix or wait for, especially sweet syrupy things. Jarred peaches, the ideal. Sometimes they used spoons, sometimes not; either way, their faces ran with juice.

They made a point, apparently, of forgetting the dead Turk. They knew they were in this room because it was an emergency, but they didn't know what kind, nor what would be expected of them. Therefore, they were nervous; therefore, they made jokes. The best joke was the insult, although they didn't try to pink the skin. It was a game of butts—somebody had to be the object of ridicule. Their humor eschewed subtlety as if it were desertion from the cause. It dealt in depth with questions of quantitative comparison—whose belch was loudest, whose penis longest, whose fart the most redolent. Fundamentals.

The butt right now was Georghiou. He was the kindest of all of them, also the most stupid. Middle-aged, he had been, in civil life, a salt gatherer. With his donkey he used to go to the flats near Larnaca, gather salt from the ground, pack it into two sacks which he would sling over his animal's back, and plod through the streets of the city calling *alati, alati*. Tonight, somebody, behind his back, had put a tablespoon of salt into his peaches and some were saying *alati*, and dying of the wit.

When nearly all the men had arrived, Falkos started to bring them to order. Ben saw him differently now. The men openly respected him, some liked him, and possibly a few were afraid of him. But their approval of him was, in one way, exceptional. They didn't behave as if he were a guerrilla leader or military commander, but as if he were the man he had been, a schoolmaster. To them, he was still in the classroom, treating his men like boys, no matter what their ages. Whether they were more expert at guns than he was, or stronger, or more gifted at warfare—they were his students. With their respect inbred from childhood, they clearly had no resentment of his discipline. And Ben wondered whether the great benevolence in being treated as students instead of soldiers was that it made them feel they were civilians performing military tasks that were provisional, and would shortly be over; soon they would be happy at home with their peacetime labors. Even those who had been guerrillas for many years, doing battle with the British—had they come to believe that in the schoolmaster's company all this was temporary, that peace was the true permanence?

"*Stasu,*" Falkos said.

It was a traffic signal, not a call to order, but the men responded as if he had asked for silence.

"Who saw him first?" the teacher asked.

Somebody said it was Louka who had seen the Turk first, but Louka said it was Petros. The boy came out from behind the others. He didn't speak but he nodded it was true that he had seen him first.

"Where did you see him?"

With everybody present, the stammerer was having a difficult time.

Patiently, Falkos rephrased the question. "Where did you actually find him—where I saw you with Louka?"

Petros started to answer him in Greek. He stammered and instantly switched to English. "No, I had to run after him and—"

Kostas laughed. Angry, Falkos looked at the man, and the laughter ceased. The schoolteacher turned to observe the boy. His voice was firm but there was no hint of unkindness in it. Despite the emergency, he exerted no pressure. "In Greek. Talk slowly. I will wait for you."

He put all his concentration on Petros, and it was as if he would not allow the boy's eyes or attention to wander to anyone else. "Go ahead," he said assuringly.

The boy spoke slowly and without a halt. He said—in Greek —that he had been asleep, had heard a strange sound, like someone falling. He had gotten up and heard the sound of rocks, and had thought it was a cave-in somewhere.

"A cave-in?" Falkos was startled. "Where?"

The boy started to tell him that it wasn't a cave-in, only some rocks that the Turk had disturbed at the end of—

As he was about to finish the sentence, Falkos stopped him. "Never mind," he said, "it's not important."

Clearly, it *was* important. His alarmed expression had said it was.

Petros began to speak again and, for the first time, Falkos was curt with him. "I said it's not important, Petros."

With a gesture, he silenced the boy. It seemed strange to Ben, as it must have to the others. But Falkos hurried on.

The Turk's appearance might not be anything to cause concern, he said. The man might be a deserter, or simply lost from his company. But he might be something else. "Until now it was safe to suppose that the Turks have had no knowledge of the cave. But there have been bombings in Martoulas—and perhaps they suspect guerrillas in this general area. So it would be wise to question whether this is not one Turk alone, but a member of a search party. And if he is, to find the rest of them."

"When?" Louka asked.

"Tonight."

"Tonight?" Kostas asked. "In darkness?"

"Tomorrow may be too late." Then he raised and lowered his shoulders, to relax them. "It will not be as difficult as you think."

"How do we find the Turks in the darkness?" Georghiou asked.

"We don't find them. We let them find us."

The men looked at him and at one another, puzzled.

"How?" asked Mikis.

"How do you attract animals at night?"

Louka said, "With light."

"Yes . . . One of us will stand on the high point, above the swamp, where the ridge begins. He will smoke a cigarette. It is a good place that can't be seen as far as the main road, but can be seen over the cave area. He will be covered—at suitable distances —by the rest of you. If there are any other Turks—and if they move in on the smoker—you are to wait until they are as close to the decoy as possible. Knives—again—would be better. We don't want to alert the whole mountainside. Is it understood?"

They nodded. Everybody knew the next question, but nobody was ready to ask it: Who will be the target, who will take the biggest risk?

"Who will smoke?" Kostas said.

"I will," Falkos replied. Then he added, "I will need one of you to be my back-man. Will someone volunteer?"

"Yes—I do."

It was Petros. He had said the words instantaneously, in Greek, without stammering.

There were no further questions. Falkos sent them out in twos and threes, directing precisely where they should start, what progressions toward the decoy they should make, and how to set their watches.

When all of them were gone except him and his back-man, "Come, Petros," he said.

They started off, and an insanity happened.

Kalya said: "I'm going with the men."

Her face was inflamed as if she had been standing inches from the fire. There was desperation in her, but ecstasy as well. She seemed possessed.

Falkos, unsettled, looked at her, saw her disarrangement, didn't know how to deal with it, and again—without a word— started to depart.

"Wait! I'm coming with you!"

He had to confront her. He treated her demand like a rational request that must be answered with military precision. All his words were italicized. "*You, Yannis, Mark, and Benjamin are another unit—and the most important one. I cannot risk any of you.*"

"I'm coming anyway!"

"I have no time for this," he said. He turned to Ben. "She'll be hurt out there. See that she stays here."

He hastened away into the corridor. Kalya took a few steps after him and Ben blocked the archway.

"Get out of my way!" she said.

"Are you crazy?"

"Let me go by!"

"What are you doing this for? Are you out of your mind?"

She started to push past him; with a movement of his arm he thrust her back. As he did, he was off balance and his bad leg began to give way under him. Seeing him lurch, she tried to get past him on the other side. With a curse, he shoved her hard. Her head hit an outcropping of rock on the jagged archway. She held her arm up as if he had struck her and there might be another blow. Unsteadied by the impact, not knowing which way to go, she stumbled back into the room.

Her head clearing, she cried, "Let me go with them! Please— let me go!"

"For Christ sake, why?"

"Let me go with them!"

"Why do you want to do it? Why do you want to risk your life?"

"*I have to know what it is!*"

"Know what? My God—what?"

"War! I have to know what it is—I have to know what it feels like!"

"It feels like death!"

"Then what do men get out of it? I have to know! I have to feel it! What is it to them? Is it a game? The one after they've been beaten in all the others? Is it a gamble?—loser take all? Is it a test? What does it prove? Manhood? Cunning? *What is it?* Is it rage? Is it a scream against God? What gives them the stupidity for it, what gives them the *courage?* What is it? I have to feel it, I have to touch it! *I have to know!*"

Then—insanely—she directed it all at him alone: *"What do you get out of it?"*

"You're talking to the wrong man!"

"No—you—*you!* What do you get out of it?"

"I hate it!"

"You're a liar! You love it as much as the rest of them do!"

"That's not true!"

"When you went up the mountain—what was that? Was it an act of peace? What did you expect—that they would let you do it? It was an insult, it was a challenge! It was as if you had fired a gun!"

"No!"

"Why do you deny it? Are you ashamed? Why are you ashamed? Why doesn't it excite you? Why aren't you proud that you did it? Why aren't you proud that you were a man? *I* was proud of you! Before you did that, I thought you were a coward—and I didn't want you to touch me! But when you came back—I was so excited—! I had all I could do to keep my hands off you!"

Suddenly, as if the madness were a fever that had broken, she began to tremble, and her trembling frightened her. In a panic, seeming terrified she was going to quake apart, she extended her shaking arms into an empty space and cried oh God, oh God.

He went to her. He pulled her to him. Holding her as tightly as he could, he pinioned her to his body, didn't let her move, contained all her shuddering within his embrace.

She made a fitful movement and he thought: The hell with the ache in my leg, if she tries to run again, I'll go after her. But she wasn't fleeing. Abruptly, she bent over and he felt her mouth on his bare arm, biting it, kissing it, biting it again.

When he couldn't stand the pain of it, he pulled her up so that he might see her face. He kissed her and as she tried to wrest herself away, he clutched her violently and kissed her once more. In a moment, he could feel her tongue, and her lips holding his, and again the bite of her teeth.

She twisted away and tore at her blouse. She opened it so that her breasts were exposed, and she lifted them to him. He took her in his mouth, he held her, kissed her as she had kissed his arm, heard her cries of pain and wanting, her wild impatience. They were naked, then, naked as their desire, and lying somewhere, they didn't know where, all his bodily ache gone except for the torment of needing her, and then he was inside her, and her agonies cried against her pleasures, and his raptures filled the cave.

Later, they lay unclothed in the other room, the cell where he had seen her naked. As they stared into the darkness, he started to talk about her outcry against the war, but she would not discuss it. What she had screamed was the size of her feeling, she said, and she did not want it reduced to a composed aftermath. It was a subject for madness, not for tranquillity. So he let it go for the moment, and they tried to talk of innocuous things. But they couldn't. The best they could manage was news chatter about the cease-fire and the peace talks and whether they thought the truce would hold and whether the Turks had really taken the villages at the foot of the Monastery mountain. Even when they mentioned Falkos and the men, who had not yet returned from their search-and-destroy, they didn't refer to Kalya's frenzy to go with them.

But it was an undertow beneath the calm surface of their talk, and with distressing clarity he saw that this was why she had come on this venture. Without knowing it herself, perhaps, she had engaged herself to it not for employment alone—although it had been the conscious part of it—but for the heartsick need to know what this was, this illness of her time, this plague of war. And that she wanted to go on the search-and-destroy tonight as she would want to go to the Monastery in an armored vehicle at another time. She would *have* to go, in fact, for she would have to know what the chaos was that had wrecked her life, and that might do so again; she would have to test her strength against it to know whether she could endure; have to test her sanity against the madness.

It saddened him that she needed to be part of the war as desperately as he needed not to be. But they didn't talk of it; they had had enough of chaos, and they lay softly in a provisory contentment. She told him, without being asked, about her first two children and her husband, and how she had adored him. Ben could see that she didn't know what pangs she was giving him, for she didn't know how he loved her, nor did he really know himself, unless aching was an indication.

As she related bits and pieces from her childhood and her married life, he found himself confused. There were some details that didn't seem to agree with others, there seemed to be an inconsistency of times and places, and, shadow after shadow, he had the sense that he had had once before: She's lying.

He recalled Falkos's observation and realized the teacher was only partly right. She did tell her past by rote, up to a certain point; but there was some complexity, some catastrophe perhaps, that she would not recall, or would not tell. Somewhere in that entanglement—the lies.

He remembered the name of the town.

"Did you say you lived in Nexos?"

She looked at him quickly. "Yes."

"You said it was a fishing village. . . . I went through it once, it was a flat plain, I think—inland."

A silence. He could feel her struggling with it. At last:

"I lied."

He was not surprised, but he was puzzled by his disturbance. "Why?"

"I . . . can't tell you."

"You mean you don't know—or you can't?"

"I can't."

A gray thought came to him, groundless he knew, a bottomless conclusion he had jumped to, as if into an abyss: she had lied earlier tonight as well, while making love. She had matched his rapturous outcries with her own, as if the event had been as epochal in her life as it had been in his, she had arrived at a joyous terminus, totally gratified. But it wasn't the truth, she had had no such climax. He felt certain his suspicions was right, and he deeply wanted to be wrong.

"Tonight . . . ?"

She knew what his question was going to be, and tried to forestall it. "Let's not talk," she said.

So that was the answer, he supposed, yet he had to hear it spoken, had to know whether she would tell the truth, or lie. "Did you, or not?"

"I . . . didn't."

"You pretended."

"I didn't pretend—I wouldn't!"

"You screamed as if . . ."

"It was only—wanting."

She was right, he shouldn't have asked. It bothered him more than he thought it would; he had asked for the truth and gotten it, between the eyes. For all her wanting . . .

They lay there, in the ponderous darkness, altogether silent, barely moving, and he wondered why he was so upset by what she had told him. How many countless times had he been with a woman and not achieved a perfect congruity of orgasm; how many times, for some women, had there been none at all? What school-boy ideal of perfection was he expecting with this one, what erotic conjury was he demanding of himself and of her? What was the base of this irrational melancholy, this eccentric sense of defeat which he had never experienced so frustratingly?

The silence lengthened like a thread unwinding from a spool. How separate they were, he thought somberly. The distances between them that had never seemed divisive—of nationality and custom and ordinary sensibilities—were now wide disparities, almost irreconcilable. And that too was senseless, totally inapposite to what had or had not occurred between them. Cursing the maladies of lovemaking that infect the other faculties he wished that he could quarantine his mind from his gonads . . . and wished that he and Kalya were not so far apart.

In the darkness he felt her hand moving, wandering under the light cotton covering. He thought at first that she was going to be touching him the most intimately, but she came to rest on his hand, covering it, comforting it. He turned his palm to hers and their hands held firmly, each one offering what neither of them was yet prepared for, a friendly encounter. He remembered the warmth and sensual need in their first handclasp, and how her eyes had lowered to gaze at his dimensions, and suddenly it came over him, engulfed him, his need to make love to her again. He disengaged his hand from hers and turned on his side to face her. Too soon, he realized, before she was ready, he would be big with hunger for her, so he pulled rein on the stallion in himself, held the animal in tight constraint. Make her want you more, he said, make her need you, tempt her, bait her, plague her into such a desire that she's already home before you've come in sight of it.

He moved closer to her and, putting his hand on her shoulder, let it drift gently down her arm. He felt her turn a little, then move slowly until she was facing him. Her breath was warm and deliciously, palpably heavy, and he recalled a fable about the liquefaction of the breath of a satyr. She murmured something that he thought were words, but he realized they were only nighttime undertones, ambiguities of time and place, dreamy modulations on love and warm pleasure and simple comfort. As she started to mumble the sound again, he stilled it with his mouth. Not a kiss really, only a touching, the lightest tangency of lips to lips, and slowly, almost imperceptibly he came closer, then slightly, very slightly separated her lips with the tip of his tongue. Almost instantly, he felt her tongue darting back to him, recklessly darting like a tilting swift, caged in his mouth and fluttering to be free. His own mouth tried to capture it and couldn't, tried to hold it between lips and teeth, but what came of it was the agitation of two creatures trying to mate, glancing and falling away from one another, tasting and losing one another, wanting what they couldn't have or know. When he reached down to touch her breasts, her nipples were already risen and firm, as hard as acorns, and there was a heat in them that he had never known was possible. She's as ready as I am, he thought; but it was only a hope, he warned himself, he mustn't stake an outcome on it. Tease her, he said, harry her a little. He slid away from her mouth as her lips tried to restrain him, he kissed her neck and the nape of it, he kissed her arms and under them, he ran his tongue down the whole curve and crescent of her body, and came to rest on her belly, which he kissed and pulled at gently with his mouth, then went nibbling on the small ridge around her navel, and turned upward toward her breast, his mouth getting hungrier and the ache in his testes becoming almost unendurable. He was under her bosom now, kissing her breast, lifting it with his tongue, then upward over the tenderly luscious parabola of flesh, the breast of having and wanting, and his mouth came at last to the edge of the areola. He circled it with the finest tip his tongue could make as if delineating its outer limit, his tongue never completing the circuit of its delight, going round and round and never coming to an end of it. But he could feel the skin tightening and that too was a ravishment to him, but there was still the center to taste and touch, and his mouth moved to it. With lips almost too chaste to open, he held the nipple gently. Then, like starvation, he opened his mouth and took it in, sucking it with his tongue, drawing it tightly with his mouth, nibbling, pretending to eat, to consume it, to make it part of himself, to carry it back, far back into his throat. He could not tell his sounds from hers, the suckling sounds and animal hungers and moanings of incompletion were all one.

"Touch me there," she said. "Please touch me there."

He let his hand slide downward over her belly, her abdomen, the violin curve of her side, her thigh. Then with both hands he

went on a voyage of discovery, his palms rising to every knoll and
hillock of her body, his fingers searching every grotto, every
orifice, every recess, his tongue lapping and tasting at her ears, her
eyelids, her hidden places. He chewed and nibbled at her, he
caressed and ate where he could eat, hurt and healed her. But the
one place he did not touch was where he knew she most wanted
him.

"Touch me," she said again. "Oh, please."

At last, when he could feel her quiver in every part of her
being, he let his hand slide down, and his mouth slide down her
belly until his lips came to the hair-grown delta of this Venus that
he wanted to devour. Slowly he caressed her groin, on the right
side and the left, and still did not really touch her. Now, on the
delta, his fingertips smoothed the silken down, as fine as the
tomentum on the stem of a leaf or the pistil in a flower, and
combed the softness as if to separate each hair, to love each one
with the singling out of it. Suddenly, by pretended accident, a
fingertip happened upon dampness, and drew it up on the dune of
hair, then another finger found the dampness, then another, and at
last one of them found the source of it, and entered into the deep
moisture, entered and came out again as if to tell the others, entered the paludinal luxury . . . and he couldn't bear how big he
was.

"Come in," she said. "Come in to me."

But he didn't. Two fingers, seeking, found what they were
after, and held the tiny thing, the minuscule nub of pleasure. They
rubbed it between themselves, gently at first, then crushed its
wetness with one fingertip, then with another and a third, and then
a knuckle, hard, went at it, so that she screamed with ecstasy akin
to pain.

"Come in! Don't tease me anymore—come in!"

With a heave, he went astride her body and, moving upward,
thrust his penis between her breasts, drawing them together, covering it with their heat, only the tip of him showing at her throat. In
a spasm, she bent her head forward, to catch him in her mouth,
but she could not reach him, and she moaned again for him to stop
tantalizing her and to come in upon her.

Now he quickly pulled himself away from her breast, turned
himself around, and brought his mouth downward, to kiss the hair
he had combed and the tiny bud of pleasure his fingers had discovered. He had her in his mouth now, and he could hear her making

convulsive sounds, could feel her hips moving back and forth, her body shaking, trembling.

"Oh, please!" she screamed. "Take me—please take me!"

He pulled himself up from her and drove his prick inside her, drove with all his force and might and love and anger and desperation and desire, fucking her and fucking, needing her to come as he came: how prodigiously he came.

Under him she gasped for breath, threw her arm up as if to ward off injury, ran her hand through her hair, kept on panting with an insufficiency of air. He tried to lighten himself upon her, but as she felt his weight diminish she drew her arms around him to hold him close, she wanted him to stay. How warm she was, he thought, and how moist all over, and he didn't know whether the perspiration was hers or his, or whether even in this they were indivisible, a monad. Her breath returning, she licked her parched lips; seeing how dry they were, he bent to moisten them with his own. He could see her smiling through the kiss, knowing his intent, and grateful. How strange, he thought, marveling at the triviality, that all of her was wet and her mouth was as sere as if it had been burnt. Where tricklets of perspiration coursed down her forehead, he raised his hand to her eyes and with delicate fingertips lowered her eyelids, wiped them of moisture, then smoothed her brow, drying it with his hand. She opened her eyes again and watched him as if she could not completely comprehend his kindness, or could not believe it; scrutinized this aspect of him more acutely, this sweetness that only a moment ago had been a wild aggression.

"You are so good," she said with hushed amazement.

He was profoundly, almost unqualifiedly, happy, and wondered why he had thought "almost." He must not question his happiness, he warned himself, must not catechize his mood or he might find an exception. Some dull apprehension told him that there was indeed an exception, somewhere; better not look for it.

"Don't frown," she said.

"Was I frowning? I wasn't aware . . ." He was indeed aware, but wanted no point made of it, wished she weren't so perceptive.

"Why were you?"

He hesitated. "It's nothing."

"No, it's nothing." She agreed too quickly. "Try to remember that."

He knew, then, that there had been a reason for his "almost"; he hadn't imagined it at all. She was telling him—openly, without guile—what he had subliminally suspected: close as she had come, she had not come at all. He felt a wave of disappointment—overly acute, he knew he was exaggerating it beyond significance—an irrational sense of his inefficacy.

"It doesn't matter—it's not important," she said urgently. On impulse, she put her hands to his face and drew him closer. "Ben." Her voice was anxious, full of entreaty. "Ben—please—it's me, not you. You're a wonderful lover—you are! You do everything I want you to do. You make me feel beautiful everywhere, and you make me scream. You make me feel that my life is ending and just beginning, and it's pleasure and wonder—and you do it! You, Ben. Why do you look like that, why does it seem so earthshaking to you?"

Why, indeed, when it never had before, never had seemed of galactic consequence before, why did he need her to have a titanic orgasm with him, why was it so imperative to carry her to some unbelievable apotheosis of lovemaking?

Abruptly, with arctic certainty, he knew the answer. It unnerved him. He recalled her warning to him, the first night they had seen each other naked: men, especially sensitive ones, she had said, derive their greatest pleasure from knowing they've satisfied a woman—and Ben would not have that pleasure. She said it starkly, like a Delphic prophecy, without a time limit, world without end, an augury so unchallengeable that it became an irremediable fact.

"You warned me," he said.

"Yes."

"How could you be so certain?"

She faltered. "Because I know."

"You know what?"

"Please, Ben."

He would not release her. "You know what?" he insisted.

"That . . . I can't."

"Why can't you?"

Unhappily she tried to smile, muttering something about how heavy his body had become, and would he move a little so she could breathe more easily. He stirred away from her, lay beside her, on his back, not looking at her, not looking at anything. He had a yearning to comfort her, to offer tenderness or palliative, but he didn't know what was hurting her, or where, or how deeply, and wasn't sure she wanted to be humored at this moment. So he heard himself speaking with a clinical timbre, and didn't particularly like the sound he was making.

"Have you ever had an orgasm?"

"Yes."

"When?"

"Do you have to write it on a chart?"

"Yes . . . when?"

"When I was married."

"Never since then?"

"No, never." Then, quickly, sensing he might think there was an ethic or a formalism involved, "But I'm sure marriage hasn't anything to do with it."

"Then what does?"

"Ben—please—it doesn't matter anymore."

"What the hell do you mean, it doesn't matter?"

"I don't hope for it anymore."

"Why not? Are you dead?"

She lashed at him. "Why don't you let me alone? Why are you badgering me?"

"Something happened to you—what was it?"

"Let me alone!"

"Tell me!"

"Oh, God . . ."

He could feel her trembling beside him, unable to control herself. Contritely he reached to console her. She flinched and again begged him to let her alone. At last, she was quite still, but he felt that there was a harrowing shudder inside her, a trembling in the shadow of some bygone horror, some atrocity that she could not bring herself to put into words, for she could not bear to hear them spoken. A bloody violence had been done to her, no doubt, a warborn barbarity, a rape, a debauchment, a sexual plunder. There had been a sick carnality somewhere in her past that was too terrible for him to imagine—and if it was too terrible for him, what must it be for her? What crime had been committed to her vitals, to the center of her womanhood, what recollected evil did she have for a night companion? And would she ever free herself of it?

He wanted to help her do it. He had an urgent need to see her through this darkness in her life, this malignity from which she could not liberate herself. He saw, with a revelation, that helping her to have an orgasm could be more than merely one of the amatory ministries that people offer to one another, but might be her rescue from atrocity, from the memory of a malevolence that had blighted her spirit and might possibly have destroyed her life. He wanted, desperately he wanted, for her to have a great gratification at his hand, his mouth, his heart, his genitals, any part of him that would bring her joy again. It was not only a function of his male pride, not the strut and clank of machismo, but his need to compensate for some grisly malice that had been done to her, with an act of goodness and tenderness and love. If only he knew what her horror was, her evil; if only he had a potent prescription that would cure it!

Softly: "I'm sorry I 'badgered' you," he said.

She reached over and lay her hand lightly on his breast; it was a hand of forgiveness. But he sensed that the subject was not yet over, that she wanted to say more about it but didn't know how to approach it. So he remained silent, letting the stillness become emptier until she had to fill the vacuum.

"I hope you won't ask me any more questions," she murmured.

"I can't promise that I won't."

He could feel her dread gathering again. "Then . . . I will have to lie."

"As you did about Nexos?"

"Yes."

"Will you lie about us?"

"Oh no," she said quickly. "While we were making love, I was tempted to say I love you—but I didn't. I wouldn't lie about that."

"I wish you had."

She looked at him wanly. "No, you don't."

He suspected she was right.

"I would never lie about that," she said. "Only about the past." An unsteadiness in her, as though she were on a shaky ledge. "I can't tell the truth about it—I have to imagine things were different—or I can't stand it."

An obscure notion, dark, shadowy, like a phantom, occurred to him: the evil in her life might have come from more than one direction, she might even have perpetrated part of it herself. A violation might have been committed upon her . . . or *by* her. The remembered cruelty of others might be excruciating to her, but guilt might be worse. . . . Whatever the specter in her past, he told himself, he must face the possibility that she would never tell him. She might always remain in the darkness to him—an anomaly who might have done no wrong, and yet was guilty—or had committed unimaginable offenses and was still one of the war's innocents. He knew it was a meaningless paradox, one he might have contrived when he first met her, when mystery was what had drawn him to her. But now he did not need the mystery in order to love her. In fact, what he did know about her made him love her more—her strength, her kindness, her quickness of mind, her potential lovingness . . . even if she did not love him.

He believed her on that point: whatever her lies, she would never lie about loving him. Perhaps that would be all the truth he would ever need of her. How many married people had even that much?

"Will you go up the mountain again?" she whispered.

". . . Yes."

"Alone?"

"Yes."

"I don't want you to."

She was talking about danger, and how inconsistent she was. She herself would have gone with the men just a few hours ago; and when the time came she would go unflinchingly with the ambulance; in fact, all her excitements were being tuned to it. Yet, for *him* to go . . .

"Why you and not me?" he asked.

"Because you will be killed."

"And you . . . ?"

"It's a useless question. It will happen—to one or both of us —and we will have nothing to do with it."

"Or with anything, you mean."

"Or with anything."

That fatal fatalism of hers—he hated it. Even if he could make her love him, they could never make a life together; they were too different. She mothered the weak and he doctored the weak, and in that way they were similar, but in all other things they were worlds apart. She lived by a kismet that was her personal kind of existentialism. Why be respectful of the past since it has bequeathed us nothing but cruelty, why think of the future since it is a visionary's conjecture? Existence always before essence, and, instead of freedom, only the anguished slavery to fortuitous incident and one's tyrannical self.

She had no world dream, none at all. There wasn't a human tear she would not want to dry, yet there wasn't a flag she wouldn't spit at. She could tremble with compassion for a wounded man or a sick child—even a dead one—her own or anyone else's—and let the race be damned. Her kindness was not sentimentality; she was a tough woman, and had the mettle to remain tough—but there was no cant in her; she had no causes.

Nor was she a cause to herself. She considered that she was merely the dupe of a fatalistic practical joke, the victim of a vandalous determinism. But not important in any way—she was a minor accident, someone who had happened on the wrong planet at the wrong time. Her whole life was An Unfortunate Coincidence.

But he could never think of life as meaningless. He was by religion a scientist; he believed. He had to believe that there was a pith somewhere, an essence, that every cause did indeed have its effect, and every effect its cause. And if he accepted the notion that the First Cause was a kind of birth, divine or otherwise . . . he could not yet accept that the Final Effect was death.

Perhaps the quality about her that most achingly touched his heart was her loss of faith in life itself—her disbelief in the efficacy of hope, her sense that we were all minor mishaps, and if the race were to die, good riddance.

Since, between them, they could not have some consonance of image about these things, how could she ever love him? And yet . . . he was falling in love with her quite deeply without it.

"Please," she said softly, "don't go up the mountain by yourself."

He was profoundly stirred. Not only by the entreaty in her voice, but by something else: she was trying to change the course of predetermined events, she was fighting against her fates.

"Please," she said again. "Something terrible will happen."

"Can't it happen if I go up with the rest of you?"

"No—I'm sure it won't. I think Falkos's plan will work. I think they will be so surprised—it will be quick—it will even be quiet."

"Like church on Sunday."

"Don't joke. It will be safer with us, Ben—it will! Nobody will be trying to kill you—and you alone. But if you go up by yourself, this time they will hunt you down—only you. You will be their only prey. And this time they won't dare to give you a chance—they'll shoot you like an enemy!"

He knew she was right; he had had the same thoughts. But: "I have to go, Kalya."

"No—please! Why?" It was an outcry. "For what? For an old man whose life you can't save? And what difference will it make if you come two days later? Or even after he is dead?"

"It hasn't anything to do with Demetrios."

"With what, then?"

"With what he is to *me!* He helps my life make sense! He lets me see myself more clearly than I've ever been able to. He tells me I don't drive a tank, I drive an ambulance. He tells me I'm not a killer, I'm a healer. He tells me I'm not a coward, I'm a man. He tells me there's something worth living and dying for, and it's not hatred, it's love. He tells me who I am!"

As he repeated the thought with which he had once so totally convinced himself, he realized that he was no longer persuaded by it. The argument was only an achievement of his mind and, as such, it was reasonable enough. But reason hadn't everything to do with it. The greater part of his motive was plain obsession, mindless, driven, perhaps a bit deranged, maybe even suicidal—and he could not have molded the manic reason into any truly convincing form. Something compelled him upward and alone, something perhaps that had to do with fears and fires, some need for trial, for a criterion of courage to judge himself by, something unknown that he ached to know and—like Kalya's specter—might never get to see in any daylight of his mind. So be it—let the obsession have its way with him.

To Kalya, however, the reasonable reason had been persuasive, and it defeated her. She had defied the fates, and failed. For the longest time, she made no rejoinder. She did not move closer, nor further away. She didn't touch him. When he gently put his hand on hers, she didn't respond to it nor did she remove her hand. Then she turned her head away. It occurred to him that—softly— she was crying.

"I must not . . . ." she began, and stopped.

"What?"

". . . let myself love you."

"Yes . . . let yourself."

"No . . . you will be killed."

He told himself—and her—that she was wrong. And silently he vowed: I will put my heart to it, I will put my mind to it, I will put everything I am to it—and I will not be killed.

7

He could not tell what time it was when he heard the men returning from the search. It must be nearly dawn, he thought. Kalya's sleep was profound; she obviously did not hear them. Nor did she stir when he quietly got out of bed and dressed.

As he limped out of the room, the pain in his leg was worse. Don't think of it, he said. The corridor was empty and dim. The candle in the wall sconce was low, the wax guttering, the light flickering. He hadn't heard many voices, only Falkos and Mikis clearly, the others were just murmurs. Now, at the end of the passage, where it intersected with the corridor that went to the open place, he saw someone crossing.

It was Petros. The boy turned, saw him, and Ben beckoned. The young Greek came quickly.

"What happened?" Ben asked.

Petros gave him a warm smile of relief. The plateau was clear, he said; no sign of Turks or anybody—at least they didn't respond to the decoy. Not a sound or trail of them. So everyone, he grinned, had come back.

They nodded to each other as if they were both to be congratulated. It was a useless search, Petros said, then added quickly— loyal to Falkos—that it was a shrewd idea and an excellent operation, and now everyone could rest more easily and go to sleep.

When the boy had departed, Ben thought of his last words: everyone could sleep.

This would be the perfect time to get away.

Making a quick turn, he felt a pain so excruciating that his sight went black. He threw both arms up, put his hands against the wall, and let his torso carry part of his weight. The candle flame seemed to have too many aureoles; they overlapped one another. I'm going to faint, he said. He moved one hand, struck his fist against his forehead, substituting pain for pain, and the aureoles vanished. I can't stand here all night, aching, he said. I need to take something—a pill—a downer or upper, either one.

If he could get Yannis to go out to the ambulance . . . But which was his room? He seemed to remember the old man going to the right when he had entered the hallway from the main room. He started in that direction.

Trudging, he favored the bad leg. It was doing hardly any of the work, and he shouldn't—by any logic—have heard what he did.

Click.

He stopped walking. Even motionless, the leg was no better. He moved again.

Click.

With each movement, he heard the muted, almost inaudible clicking in his knee. Now that the swelling had gone, the cushioning of congestion gone as well, bone was rubbing bone. Oh God, he thought, can it be merely a dislocation? Not a fracture, not even a torn ligament, perhaps—could it be that the femur and tibia were askew from one another and . . . with some help . . . ?

"Yannis!"

Better not shout, he said, better not alert everyone. If the knee *could* be mended quickly, and if someone saw him able to walk without pain, the surveillance over him would become more vigilant—and he wouldn't get away. The thing to do was to tell only Yannis, not even Kalya. For whatever reason—his sake, hers or Falkos's—she did not want him to go. Tell only the old man.

But where was he, which cell? He had already limped down half the corridor when he heard the trumpet in low tremolo. The old man's snore. He followed the sound down a tiny passageway that entered the corridor diagonally. In the cubicle, he could barely see the sleeping man; the light from the passage was dim.

A whisper: "Yannis."

Damn the old man's noise. "Yannis." He shook him a little.

"Yes—what?" The Greek's voice was a bellow.

"Not so loud. Now, listen."

He told him what he thought was wrong with his leg.

"Then what do we do?"

"I will lie on your bed with my leg extended over the end of it.

I will hold onto the wooden frame, and you are to grab the leg and yank it."

"What?"

"Pull it."

"Pull?" He couldn't believe it.

"Yes—hard—with all your might."

"I will hurt you."

"Yes, for a minute. But do it."

"Holy Mother!" He made a gesture of rejection and walked away from the bed.

"Come back. Now go on—do as I say—I'm holding—now grab it."

"No."

"Goddamn it!"

Slowly, the old man came back to the bed, paused a moment, crossed himself, grabbed the foot, held it an instant, then pulled.

Pain. In every nerve. Not only in the leg, everywhere. How many meddling bastard neurons had to get into the sonofabitching act, he said. Pain . . .

And nothing had happened. He would have known if it had worked. Something would have told him—a click perhaps—a sense of rightness in the knee—more motion in it—something. Oh, murder.

"You didn't pull hard enough."

"Yes I did."

"Do it again. Harder this time. Everything."

A stifled sound from Yannis, like a moan. Then he grabbed the foot again, but did not tug at it. The old man was steeling himself, his breath coming hard. Ben felt one hand tighten on his foot, the other on his ankle. Then—

No.

"Christ—let go!"

The pain had been wasted. It hadn't happened.

"Let me do it." A whisper at the doorway.

How long Kalya had been standing there he didn't know, or how she had known to look for him. His absence from bed, perhaps, or his call to Yannis. She must have been there quite a while, for her clothes were pulled together and her face was calm; it would have taken her time to make such a controlled picture.

"Are you sure this is what should be done?" she asked quietly.

Ben thought: I wonder if I can stand once more, I don't think I can. "Yes, I'm sure."

The only sign that she was frightened was that her hands were icy. How wonderfully cool they felt, how soothing to his pain, how—

"Oh, God!"

Blackness, then aureoles again, then a hand caressing him, his cheek, his wrists, his hands, and her voice saying his name, over and over, his name. Then her face, and Yannis's behind her.

The pain was still there, but it was different, somehow. He wished he knew what the difference was, as if it mattered; pain was pain. No, it *did* matter. If he could raise his leg and flex the knee, perhaps the ache would go away. He tried it slowly. It was easier in the bent position than it had been when straight.

"I think . . . it may have gone back in," he said.

He started to sit up.

"Be careful," she said. She had been utterly calm in the crisis; now that it could be over, she might go to pieces.

He touched her reassuringly, then indicated for her to move to one side so he could get out of bed.

He stood up—left leg first, then, gingerly, his right. His weight was all on one side for an instant, then he shifted and equalized it. The pain was considerable, but only a soreness; he knew that kind —first day's pitching practice, only this was not in the arm. A bearable pain, an almost measurable pain.

He walked. He *could* walk. Another day or so, and there would be no sign of the agony, none.

He turned to them. "The operation was successful." He grinned. "Thank you."

Yannis giggled with nonsensical happiness. Kalya smiled reservedly, watching Ben in a sidelong way. She turned to look elsewhere, with an odd shyness, like a young girl being told her bosom is burgeoning, then murmured something about going to bed. That too was on a note of shyness, but there was a quiet pleasure, a conjugal security in the sound.

An hour later, lying beside her, it occurred to him that his leg was well enough for him to try to escape again.

But could he leave her? Even for an hour, could he leave her? And if he did attempt to escape, how could he go? No chance with the ambulance again—Falkos would assuredly have it watched from now on. The exit as well. But there was a second exit—could he find it?

He didn't *want* to find it.

He didn't want to go. He wanted nothing now, nothing but Kalya, nothing but her body beside him, all the sweet mercies and cruel pleasures and warm moistures of lovemaking, the music of murmur and outcry, the satisfactions and frustrations of the flesh, all the lost lovings that might be recaptured, and held, and never lost again. He wanted to caress her and hear her speak and be happy with her—oh Jesus, to be happy with her!

He didn't care—not here, not now—about an old priest dying on a mountaintop, he didn't care about *any* of the dying, any of the wounded, any of the sick and sad and afflicted; he had had enough of them. Enough, and more than his share. He didn't care whether he was a real doctor or a pseudo-doctor, whether he was a healer or a soldier, whether there was a principle at stake, a cause to beat his brains in for, or even an elemental decency to defend. He didn't care if he was betraying a vision of himself that he needed if he was to survive. The hell with all of that. What he did need was love and making love; it was the hunger of his heart and balls; it was his *right*. If it was survival he was thinking about, love was the heart of it, not the valor of muscle or the persuasion of mind, but love.

Try to escape again? And get himself beat up, or killed? No, he would not try to break out of the cave. On the contrary, he would go deeper and deeper into it, deeper into its warmth and pleasure . . .

. . . and safety.

Waking . . . and Kalya, gone.

How long had he slept? Was he still asleep? It was half-past eight.

Kalya gone? He couldn't stand it. Had she slipped away for a minute, had she vanished forever? He wanted to shout her name, to beg her to return.

He got out of bed quickly. The leg was only memorially sore; he could easily walk on it. He hurried down the corridor to the main room.

She was there, alone, at the fireplace, holding a long-handled copper cup just barely in the flames, and the smell of coffee was a redolent welcome. He couldn't find the words for the size and particularity of his happiness, so he made do with the commonplace that the coffee smelled wonderful. She poured it slowly, as if it were a lingering flow of time, a prolonged continuation of the night.

"I have a message for you," she said.

"Yes? From whom?"

"Falkos. He says you're not to try anything . . ." She searched for the word.

"Homeric."

"Yes. The ambulance and the path to the main road are guarded by Kostas and Photis. He said that of course they were armed."

"Thank you for the message." His voice was level. "Why didn't he tell it to me himself?"

"He's gone for the day."

"Gone? Where?"

"He didn't say." She left the table and started to open a tin of biscuits. "Yannis went with him."

"Yannis—with Falkos?"

"Yes. And Mark as well."

"Why? What for?"

"I don't know. I didn't ask, because I didn't imagine he would tell me."

He couldn't discern whether she was worried or merely puzzled. "Did Yannis want to go with him?"

"No."

"Then . . . ?"

"You think he had a choice?"

It was unaccountable and it bothered him. But he wouldn't let it trouble him too deeply, he told himself, for it had its cheering aspect: they would be alone together for all the hours that the others were gone; they would have to deal with no one but themselves.

"What would you like to do today?" she said, as if the choices were manifold.

He didn't mean to smile so goatishly, but her smile was only a shade subtler than his own. "I mean—besides that," she asked.

"Explore the cave?"

She was delighted. It was to be an adventure, a sport. "What's it called? Spe—spe—?"

"—lunking."

So they went in search of some purposeless pleasure, some diverting magic in the nether world. And they found it. Taking the central corridor, they started inward and downward, going deeper into the mountain. For a few hundred feet, the passage was illuminated by oil lamps and candle sconces. The lights flickered on schists of mica that shimmered in the semi-darkness. There was no feeling of dankness in the passage they moved through, no mustiness at all, even though in many places water seeped through the walls. Where it dissolved marls and ores, the colors were luminous, like falling rainbows. It was the water, he thought aloud, that made the rocks so beautiful.

"Yes," she agreed, "by eroding them. As it destroys them it makes them vivid."

He was about to say that vivid meant alive, but she had a distant, distressed look on her face, and he reflected that the notion would not be of any comfort. Looking at her, he thought of Aphrodite, wandering, alone. He took her hand.

The lights became fewer and the passageway darker; the channel also became narrower. The underground coolness which had seemed so pleasing was now a damp chill, mean and biting to the bone. Yet, despite the cold, the air was incongruously sultry, there was a swelter of old leftover suffocation, and creatures dead of its noxiousness. It was an ancient death, long since invisible, yet still inhalable, the smell of dread that had never been put to rest. Then, at one turning, they noticed—hanging from the ceiling of the cave—a stalactite deposit they had seen before. They were going around in circles; they were lost.

Stories occurred to him—people wandering in caves, some never found, some never sought, wasting with hunger, turning skeletal. He pondered whether goddesses got lost, and if it frightened them, and whether Kalya was frightened.

Then he felt an oddity, something in his hair, the slightest stir. An insect, he thought at first, but almost at once he realized it was a breeze that was touching him, breathing on his hair—the answer to his curiosity about the ventilation of the cave—a slight wind blowing through one opening and toward another. Kalya too had felt it; she raised her hand to it. The draft was coming from the passage on the left. Hurrying toward it, they entered.

The corridor was not wide and not straight. Almost immediately, it started twisting backward and forward upon itself, as if it might return to where it had begun. Then, unlike the other passages they had traveled, it started to ascend.

It's going where it should go, to ground level, he said, and became excited. Then it made the sharpest turn of all, and they saw a light. It was far away, a glimmer at first, and not straight ahead but reflected. Hastening, not questioning where the reflection would lead them, he rushed toward the opening—and daylight.

In a spurt, they were outdoors. Not merely outdoors, but on a shoulder of the mountain that was so green and full of summer, with a view so far that they imagined they could get a glimpse of the sea. Not that one could catch the slightest glimmering of horizon or of waves—it would be impossible, there was no magic of compasses or bearings that could bring the sea within view—yet there was a beauty here that promised a vista of water.

It was only a narrow shelf on the hillside, not more than fifty yards wide, and nothing had a right to grow here. Except that the mountain's curve had made a sheltered place, and wild grasses flourished. There were poppies too, and a few volunteer anemones and a hibiscus larger than the eye could hold. And one olive tree, arthritic with age, catching the wind in its silver-grizzled branches. It was a place too unbelievably figmental, a hypothesis of beauty utterly contrary to fact. Let us suppose a place like this, it said, let us set our better minds to imagining it, to finding a loveliness that has no use, and needs no questioning.

They had discovered a momentary neverland, where they could make believe that no wars had ever happened or portended, that no one had ever died of anything, that love was the eternal life, and that the fantasy of love was the fact of it. They lay down under a carob tree on a bed of jade green *lihon* moss as fine as thistledown, and felt the warm balm of the breeze, hardly a breath of it, like a satin coverlet. In a little while, Kalya was so motionless that he thought she was asleep, and he too began to feel the lulling of the lenitive morning, and a sweet somnolence.

Out of his languor—it seemed almost a part of his drowsiness —he felt her move. She was sitting up, her arms clasped around her knees to draw her legs close to her breast. It was a ruefully girlish posture and, through half-open eyelids, he watched her. She was staring toward the edge of the precipice, long distances in her eyes. She seemed impenetrable; he would have given something to know her thoughts. Slowly, almost it seemed by stealth, as if thinking him asleep, she arose and started to make her way toward the brink of the cliff. She did not stop walking until she came to the utter limit, where the plateau fell off into nothingness, the chasm. She stood very still; the breeze was still as well, hardly a breath to stir her hair. Then, unhurriedly, with slow deliberateness, she unbuttoned her blouse, took it off and listlessly let it drop; she kicked her shoes off, and continued, by the most even degrees of circumspection, to undress. Now she stood there, wearing only her underthings, which she began to discard. Oddly, she kept her brassiere on until the end, lingering in it; her hips, her thighs, the rest of her all naked. At last, slowly, hook by hook, she unfastened her brassiere, drew her arms out of it, and freed her breasts from their confinement. They were, to him, a perfect equipoise: if they depended very slightly because they were large, they also were gently uplifted because they were full and firm, the nipples turning almost imperceptibly upward, with a pride. It occurred to him that no object in the world had ever been so sublimely designed to excite the sense of touch.

Barely moving, quiescently, almost like an inert object, she nakedly stood at the edge of the precipice, her head tilted, as if thinking or listening, or testing the direction of the almost nonexistent wind. Then, seemingly on an impulse, she turned and leaned a little, to gaze down the escarpment, to descry the bottom of the abyss. She sucked in her breath, her hand flew to her throat, and for an instant Ben had the terrible thought: she's going to hurl herself into space, down into emptiness. But slowly she turned from the brink, and gazed at him. Again she became motionless, did not stir, but stared and stared, and he suspected that she did not consider him asleep, had in fact known that he had been awake all the time, watching her, studying her nakedness, wanting her. And his need, moment by moment, grew more pressing, alternately dull and sharp, like the two edges of a knife. As if he had never made love to her, he recalled the reverie of the half-naked woman in the kitchen of the restaurant, and his desire for her now was part dream, part fleshy reality, with his cock as large as his trousers could hold. But, pretending to be asleep, he did not fully open his eyes, and did not move at all.

Nor, naked, did she; barely stirred; merely continued to hold him in her fixed, hypnotic gaze. Then, at last:

"Fuck me," she said.

And still he didn't move. But by the time he had risen to start undressing, she was back on the mossy carpet, under the carob tree, wildly tearing at his shirt, ripping at buttons and buttonholes, wrenching at his trousers; and with a suspiration that was a sigh and a moan, she was down on her knees, to take him in her mouth. As he felt the wetness of her tongue, her lips and teeth were a snare, trapping him, and for an instant she did not release him but held him so firmly, so tightly that he could feel the throb of pulse, and the ache of it. Then she let go a little, sucking him and sucking, pulling at him with her mouth, making sudden vacuums which her tongue would fill as if to rescue him from the anguish of nothingness, then all the rest was a drawing and pulling with her lips, her tongue like a warm salve draining taint and poison, a blissful panacea against pain. For a breath or two it was a poignant pleasure, stinging, quickening his senses, then her teeth seemed suddenly to sharpen, he felt an acute pang and another, a cutting, stabbing pain, as she began to chew at him. No, he said, and no again, but she clung and would not remove herself, hurting, afflicting. He grabbed her head, her hair, and tried to tear her away, and when she still clung, his hand struck hard at her face, and he twisted her away.

"Christ, Kalya!"

She flung herself back again, her mouth agape, to snatch, to masticate, to devour all of him. He grabbed her and as he held her off, she cried out, "Fuck me! Why don't you fuck me?"

He pushed her down onto the green carpet, and, because he was not quick enough, she began to cry obscenities at him, gutter words in Greek and Turkish and English, a single language being insufficient to make him understand her rage, her sick famine, her lust; fuck me, she cried over and over, fuck me, fuck me. He plunged inside her, and felt her nails scrabbling, scratching down his back, long ripping strokes of fingernails, scoring her anger into his flesh. But the pain was nothing to him now, for there was another exquisite agony; he rammed into her, against barricades, choking the passageway as if it were a throat that he was stifling. Fuck her and kill her with his penis, he said, to avenge the pain of his back, and to quit himself of love and ache and hunger.

"Oh, make me come!" she cried desperately. "Oh, please—oh, make me come!"

There was anguish in it so terrible, so racking that only her rage could cope with it. He heard her scream and curse and abominate, and then her mouth was on his breast, her teeth in his flesh and, biting and sucking, as if his sperm might not be enough, she tried to draw his blood. His last surge, then, his last full shout of it, his voice echoing across the plateau and up from the abyss, his shriek of coming, and he gave all of it in one agonized surrender, and would gladly have given blood as well if she could have come with him. But she kept clamoring and clamoring, and was not satisfied.

Separately, they lay back again on the green softness, and he could feel the turmoil in her, some deep, conflicting harassment that pulled her back and forth from one remembered torment or another, and he wondered what bygone suffering had quickened the present one. She was ashamed, he knew that much, and covered her eyes as if the sun which was not shining in them was more light than she could stand.

She did not look at him. "I'm sorry I hurt you."

He also was sorry she had hurt him, not for the pain but for whatever had caused her to perpetrate it.

"Do you think I'm perverted or something?" she asked quietly.

"No."

"You don't think I am . . . *nymphomanis?*"

"No, I don't." It hadn't occurred to him that she might be. "Do you think you are?"

"No, I'm not." She said it undefensively, as a quiet fact that she did not feel constrained to prove. She turned to him a little, and looked at his breast, where she had bitten him. She saw the flecks of blood. "I'm not a vampire, either." Trying a smile, she could not achieve a convincing one. "And I'm not cruel."

"I don't think you are." He spoke matter-of-factly, knowing that excessive solicitude would sound disingenuous, and her ear was finely tuned to detect even the slightest falsity. But still she looked at him doubtfully, not trusting that what he said was what he meant. "I don't, Kalya," he said assuringly.

"But there *is* something wrong with me," she murmured, in misery. The pain went so oceanically deep in her, there were so many currents, that he wondered if he could ever sound the depths. "And there has been . . . for many years," she added.

If you go slowly, he cautioned himself, she may tell you all of it. "Since when?"

"Since . . . then."

The word was conclusive. He realized there would be no more, not today; she had gone into her depths again, her drowning and unfathomable depths, and would stay there, alone. At least for now, alone. And perhaps, for always.

He took her in his arms and held her securely. He could feel her need to be held, to be enclosed and protected, even imprisoned, so that the world would not invade her. He felt her fingers on his back again, this time gently, as light as remedy, to soothe the pain her nails had caused him, to beg forgiveness for the wounds. At last he could sense that she was comforted by her own comforting, and more at peace again; carefully, with tentative uncertainty, he released her. Oddly, she was soon asleep, her hushed breath as sound in slumber as if there had been no cry or crisis. And he too, in a little while, began to doze.

It could have been a half hour later, hardly as much as an hour, that she was in his arms again, and as he began to touch and fondle her, she responded with a more tranquil need of him, sensual and deep but not turbulent as it had been before. They made love clemently, needing a forgiveness, and he tried not to mind that she was doing everything for his gratification, and letting him do nothing for hers. Leaving the reality of pain behind them, they returned to the dreamlike beauty of the plateau, making love in a hallucinatory way, as if even their bodies were an illusion. Then Kalya went one step too far and said that love itself was an illusion.

Affectionately he scoffed at her. "Yes, a grotesque one."

"No, I mean it," she said. "The illusion that it can last."

"Bizarre. And comical. It's the big ha-ha."

"Be serious. Have you ever known two people for whom it has lasted?"

"Yes—my father and mother."

"Really? How did they manage it?"

"By not seeing each other."

"The big ha-ha," she mimicked. "They were probably pretending in your presence—so that *you* would have the illusion."

"No—I think it was real."

"How could you tell?"

"In my father's case, it was simple. He had no sense of humor. I never heard him make a joke except with her or about her. When my mother went on a lecture trip he would make up whopping stories about them getting a divorce—she deserted me, he'd say. Then when he'd see the shock on people's faces, he'd howl with laughter. And when she died, he again made a joke about it. He grinned and said, 'Deserted me again' . . . and I don't think he ever knew how to put himself together after that."

"How do you know *she* loved *him?*"

"Because she was so jealous. She was always afraid that in her absence, he'd run off with another woman. Once she sent him a letter from Cleveland. She enclosed her travel insurance—the kind you buy in an airport. And her note said, 'In case I die, here's money. Use it to buy yourself a nubile woman, screw yourself to death, and join me as quickly as possible.' When she came home, he gave her the insurance policy and said, 'Indian giver.'"

"What's an Indian giver?"

"Someone who gives you a present and takes it back."

"Like this day." Her voice had gone quiet and grave.

"Nobody will take it back," he promised.

"Even while it's happening, I feel it's being taken back."

Her malevolent fates again. It disturbed him more than he revealed. "Kalya . . . you've got to make yourself believe that you and I are going to have a life together. This war you've lived through—so many years—you've got to trust that it'll be over soon. And we'll both come through it safely—and you can let yourself love me."

"Another illusion?"

"If that's the only way you can love me . . ."

He had changed his mind. It wouldn't hurt him if she pretended the words, as long as she said them. Sooner or later, he believed, she would hear the sound of them, and believe what she was saying. But even without her saying the words, he was happy. And for the moment, he was sure that she was, as well. How could that be? Could it be that it takes far less to make two people happy than he had ever dreamed? Could it be that happiness is a measure of the store of love that two people make together, irrespective of how much each contributes? If it was true, then his contribution was making up for both of them, and he could go on contributing more and more. If it was wanted . . .

He was happy. Look at yourself, he said, you're happy. Remember this moment, put a label on it, a mnemonic so that you'll never forget it: happy.

Then, more illusions—glinting like crystals in his mind—he saw her in another place—the two of them together—sitting on a terrace, looking out to sea. San Francisco? Viareggio, perhaps— what was the pale saffron drink in her hand?

"Where are you?" she asked.

"Viareggio—no, Dubrovnik. You're with me."

She liked being with him. Illusion was not such a bad game after all. "What language are we speaking?" Her voice was eager.

"Something Slavic—Croatian, I think."

"What am I wearing?"

He smiled. "Long—it's long—it trails the ground. We bought it in another country—in a *souk* somewhere."

"Oh, good—it's a *djellaba*."

"Yes—with nothing underneath."

"Then touch me. Let me taste your drink—and touch me."

He did as he was told.

"And now what are we doing?" she asked.

"Now or sometime?"

"I know what we're doing now. Tell me sometime."

"Drinking, touching, dancing."

"I used to dance."

"Again. We're on a ship somewhere. The *Ile de Something* or the *Something Maru*. And we're the only couple dancing—and we're a whole cotillion."

"Enough of that—I have to work."

"You *do* work—you *are* working."

"Where?"

"Let me look closer."

"In an office—with papers?"

"Oh no—with people. Children!"

"Oh yes! Thank you—yes! Children!"

"And now it's after work—and I pick you up in a dumb little car—and today you're annoyed, and tomorrow you're happy, and yesterday one of the kids gave you something."

"A present?"

"Wrapped up—with ribbon."

"And I have it still."

"You'll keep it always, won't you?"

"Yes, oh yes!"

He imagined them together far away, off Marblehead. They

were in a sailboat, his skiff, far out in the bay, becalmed, not a breath of wind billowing the whiteness of the sail, and they didn't care if no breeze ever blew them landward. Wherever they were was agreeable, it was all one, soft and contented on a sunlit sea. She lay naked on the deck and he swam naked in the summer warmth. She talked and he said what, what, I can't hear you, and she said don't swim so far that I have to shout, you idiot, and he said, what, and she said cornmeal mush, and he said yes, indubitably. Then he heard her yell that she was getting hungry, and should she do something about the sail and he said yes, why not, yes. He heard the *chwish* of the canvas, and was suddenly aboard and lying on top of her, making love no differently from anywhere else, and everything would be the same, wanting one another wherever they went, and they would make it work somewhere, the two of them together, oh yes, love, they would, in Marblehead, Valparaiso, Oshkosh, Tashkent, Xanadu, Boston, Saigon, Dak Binh— Dak Binh—!

A quickening pain, in every part of him and nowhere, an outcry of the mind.

"Fire!"

A soundless scream. I'm gone, he thought, something has ripped, I'm torn away, and back somewhere.

"Fire!"

Where's Kalya, he asked, where did she go, Kalya come back, tell me what it means. No—Mee Lanh—*you* tell me! Tell me what it means!

Mee Lanh!

It was hot in the ambulance, and airless. If he opened a window, it might chill the girl, but he had to get the ether fumes out of his lungs or he would fall asleep. He looked closely at his patient. She was quite all right, and still deeply anesthetized. He took her pulse and felt her forehead, covered her somewhat more securely, then went indoors.

The night was a little chilly. On the shoulder of the hill, just below the ambulance, the tiny village glimmered like a starry fairy tale, wattle houses, tiny huts of thatch and bamboo in deep thickets of elephant grass. Still a little dizzy from the ether, he breathed deeply. He must clear his head, he thought, and hasten back to his patient. Starting to run, he didn't exert himself too much at first; he didn't want to get too giddy. The air was bracing, it lifted him. In a quick-running reverie, he was back home, sailing, a sweet zephyr in the sail of the skiff, flying free in the company of the west wind.

The noise behind him was not action of any kind, certainly not VC gunfire. Hardly anything, the snapping of a straw. More accurately, it sounded like an inhalation, a sudden suck of breath, then the release of it. He stopped and turned around, and saw nothing. Then the light, a faint burst of it, high and far away, an orange glimmer in the sky. One flare and, at a distance, a second one. They hung there, in the company of stars, suspended, not falling, at last drifting down the blackness of the night, their tiny parachutes swinging back and forth. They didn't seem dangerous in any way, only like a pair of brightly lighted toys, flying plastic mice, mechanically squeaking a little as they descended.

As if not related to the flares at all, he heard another sound. Before he could identify it, he heard the louder one, its base note trumpeting, then the phosphorus grenade blasted, the white smoke at first, dense and brilliant, and the village was in flames, snapping softly, no louder than the cracking of eggshells. All at once the wrath exploded, mortar shells and *rracck rracck,* the hill shuddering, the thatch and bamboo burning, the elephant grass a running course of flames, a man racing with a flaming pole upon his back, children screaming, a goat running free, a buffalo bawling, a woman with burning hair crying down the moon, a child with its dress aflame, slapping at her belly's fire.

The ambulance was not in the path of the flames, but the wind was capricious, variable. He raced toward the vehicle.

"Mee Lanh!"

Where the new gusts of flame came from he could not tell. He thought they were torches at first, ordinary flashlights stabbing the darkness, but then he heard their roar and anger, and knew them: flamethrowers. He saw the three men, two along the ridgeline, one below, all carrying the pipes and hoses, the VC faces lighted and lighting, the ear-cracking noise, the raging whoosh of flame. Running, streaking toward the ambulance, his mind exploding, he kept crying why, why burn, why here, there's nothing here, why, and suddenly there was a detonation and the ambulance was ablaze.

Something—like his own violent death—stopped him.

"Fire!"

He couldn't move.

"Fire!"

He ran. Not toward her, but the other direction. Not to the

ambulance, but away. Ran, ran, crying fire, ran from Mee Lanh, fire, from his need, his love, his courage.

"Ben," Kalya said. "Ben, where are you?"

"I'm here," he lied.

"You look deathly. Are you all right?"

"Yes—fine." He saw her concern. "Really, Kalya—I'm all right."

"Is your leg bothering you again?"

He was grateful for the cue, it made evasion easier. "Only a little." He looked in the direction from which they had come. "Shall we start back?"

"Yes."

Returning through the passages and tunnels, he tried to carry his share of the conversational burden, whether the purple was porphyry and the yellow was pyrite, and whether quartz was good for anything. He felt that he was doing well; Kalya didn't comment again upon his looking "deathly."

He considered whether to tell her about Mee Lanh. How would he do it?

I was a coward, he would say. Four years of withdrawal were in that single moment, four years of blood and agony, of scurrying like a rodent from the mortar blasts and phosphorus bombs and the sickening black embraces of napalm, four years of terror in one moment of flight, the abandonment of a woman-child I loved. The solitary instance incapsulated all the years of waning valor, of immanent *desertion* . . . and labeled me a coward.

Strange, it wasn't the fear of her condemnation that kept him from confiding in her. He had a dread that she would console him, offer extenuations for what he had done, or had failed to do. Suppose you *had* run back, she might reason, what good could you have done? Was there a chance in a million that you might have saved her? There was an explosion, the ambulance was in flames, the Cong were all around you. It would not have been an act of courage, but of suicide.

But even if there was only a chance in a million, he would say, if there's *any* chance, a man runs back—the full distance. When his legs don't run in the right direction, they stop running altogether, he is hobbled, he's a coward.

Nothing more than that? she would argue. Did your four years in Vietnam count for nothing? Did the horrors you lived through, the lives you saved, the bath of blood you endured, did they count for nothing?

It would be a reasonable question, of course, if one could rationalize a bedevilment. And it wasn't as though he hadn't tried. But what good had reason done him in the hospital, how had it prevented his defection from medical school, how effectively had it dealt with his gut-corroding guilts, his helpless immobilizations, the lacunae in his memory? Well, there was no gap in remembrance any longer—he had it all now, with searing clarity—everything blazingly allegorized in one instant of terror, one act of desertion.

And what rational remedy did he have for healing the ache of culpability, of self-shame, the afflictive pain of failure? None.

But why need the remedy be rational? Go up the mountainside, alone—did he need a reasonable justification for an insanity? Why need he search for it? Insanity—why not? How had sanity ever helped to exorcise a demon, to fortify him, to steady him, make him less a coward than he saw himself? What had sanity done to still the fire cry in him; what haven, for Christ sake, had sanity offered from blood waste and obscene brutality? What sane, rational, well-cerebrated argument could give him courage to stand and face it, when all sound reason counseled him to run? What sober, steady-minded exegesis on morality could move him up to a mountaintop—that an old priest stood for all the sick and lame and old that he had dedicated his life to serve? That a monastery attested to a belief he held with all his soul that a decent and peaceable world must somehow be made to endure? How potent were the reasonable arguments? How effective, the rational man?

How much more power and passion there were in madness! Well, if he needed a deranged obsession to fortify himself, to exorcise the coward—he had it. Truth was, he had had the obsession all along without identifying it, without recalling the trauma from which it had sprung. Now, with the actual remembrance of the flames, he was exposed nakedly to himself. Painfully, repellently, he saw his image and felt estranged from it; the cowardly act had been perpetrated by a Ben Coram he did not want to know. His whole being ached, he was isolated from something too vital to live without; he was lonely, personless, in exile. Someway, by any act

—of madness, if necessary—he had to fight his way back to the lost country of his courage.

When they got back to the main room for a belated lunch, some of the men who had not gone to Limassol with Falkos were just leaving the table. There were stuffed grape leaves for the mid-day meal, and olives mixed with cheese and pimiento, nearly everything out of tins, and everything the same temperature, tepid. Ben and Kalya ate pensively. He felt that he was still successfully hiding his somber mood; at least, she was asking no questions about it.

As they were finishing their coffee, Louka came in. The merce-nary wasn't hungry, he said, and wanted only a little wine and cheese, to both of which he paid scant attention, but plucked at his kithara with a sensual address to the curves of the instrument as if they were a woman's. Not all his attention was on his music, how-ever; from time to time he would look up and cast a quick glance at Kalya or at Ben; there was something on his mind. At last he arose, let the kithara hang loose by its strap, and approached the table.

"I have to warn something." He was discomfited; he paused. "I see you today—where the cave is opening to the path."

Ben's first presentiment: it was a mercenary shakedown. The man had seen them making love, and thought there might be a shilling in it. But Ben discarded the idea—he saw no leer, no innu-endo in the soldier's manner.

"Warn us of what?" he asked.

"Do not try to use the path."

"I didn't even see the path," Ben replied. It was true; nor had they looked for one.

"There is a path," Louka said dourly. "And it is guards there. I am above and Georghiou is below. . . . I tell you this because I do not want your trouble."

He was a hired man doing a hired man's work, the minimal; he wanted no extra chores or hazards. Ben assured him that he would make no difficulties for the mercenary, and Louka smiled histrionically. He was a studied charmer. "I hope you will not have this against me—that I cannot let you go."

When Ben said he wouldn't, Louka showed happy teeth, did a quick strum on his instrument, and told the American he was a man of true friendship. He finished his wine with a flourish of the plastic cup, and offered a little gift—a song without words. When he wasn't serenading himself in privacy, he needed public applause, and he played well enough to get it. It was a quick song, tricked with virtuosity. Finished and appreciated, he thrummed a few busy chords, then cleared his voice to speak.

"I have a favor to ask you," he said. "Three months from now, maybe only two, I will have enough money, I will leave Cyprus—goodby, sweet island—and I will go to America." An instant of interlude, then he intoned the incantatory word: "Hollywood."

Ben offered felicitations.

Louka, encouraged, proceeded. "I will take with me a few pounds sterling, my kithara, and my beautiful voice. I know how I sing—very good. I know how I make up the music—very good. But I also know how I make up the words—is perhaps *not* very good. So I ask favor. You listen and tell me how to make better."

Ben saw Kalya smile and turn away. His impulse was like hers, but the man was staring at him, in pitiful earnest. He was the bashful and unabashed amateur, money- and fame-struck, who wanted to be a star, and was auditioning—for Ben, primarily, because all Americans are specialists on the subject of Hollywood. Ben marveled at the credulity, the artless simpleminded infatuation of a middle-aged, war-toughened man who could believe in such a lotus land. The artist, innocent and corrupted.

Much though Ben tried to hide his wry amusement, Louka saw it and was offended. "You think because I am mercenary, I have not talent, yes? Is not truth. A soldier has much time on his hand. I *use* time. I work, I study, I learn English, I copy songs—I am not *erasitehnis!*"

Not a dilettante. "I'm sure you're not—you play beautifully." He gestured to the kithara. "Please."

Nervous, Louka tuned up a little, stalling. "Is better in Greek." The artist's disclaimer.

"Do it both ways," Ben said.

He strummed softly, along the neck of the instrument. His plectrum was rubber-banded to his little finger, but he caressed the strings with his naked fingers as well. Gently, they inched toward the sounding box. The instrument was a womanly companion, he fondled it.

He sang the song in Greek, a lament, full of Aegean languors

and longings. It sounded like a threnody, a plaint for love unwilling or love gone. Then in English:

> *Please not to trust how I love,*
> *Please not to trust what I say,*
> *False is my music, my tone,*
> *People I love I betray.*
> *Better you go all alone.*
>
> *But if you say I not love*
> *And if you say I betray,*
> *Then is my heart die alone,*
> *Then is the sun turn to gray,*
> *Then is the sea turn to stone.*

The lines were ungrammatical and yet, for all Ben knew, the
prosody might be perfect; the idea was banal Tin Pan Alley, but
with an Elizabethan naïveté and sweetness. He sang and played so
tenderly, his heart was so ingenuously being offered gratis to the
listener, that the song was touching.

"Is good . . . or bad?"

"Good, Louka, very good," Ben said.

"You say true, yes?"

"Oh yes."

The artist could show off now; he took an elaborate, theatri-
cally displayed inhalation of relief. "You can give idea to make
better?"

Yes, he could make it better, Ben thought, and wreck it. "I
don't know anything about songwriting, Louka—I certainly
couldn't do as well as that."

This was the encomium; he glowed. Turning to Kalya, "You
the same?"

"Me the same, Louka," she said.

"I make a million dollar, you say?"

Ben and Kalya laughed. "Oh, at least," he replied.

The performer made his exit as if to thunderous applause.

But when he was gone the melancholy of the kithara still lin-
gered in the room, and the words still echoed . . . a song of betrayal. He wondered if she sensed betrayal in his dark preoccupation. The early time of the day, when they had been together on
the plateau, had been flawed but so beautiful that it had tacitly
suggested he would not try to escape from the cave, would not risk

his life again. He had made no such promise, but his happiness had promised it, and now he knew he had no alternative, he must go. Not that he was doing something valorous—there was no such luxury of glory in it. He was not, to use Falkos's term, Homeric; not a hero—no Achilles, no Hector—nor did he have any higher admiration for the warrior-hero than for the coward. Simply: courage was the medical specific; it would save his sanity, perhaps his life. Valor was the better part of discretion.

But if it had been difficult to escape the first time, it would be more difficult the second. Both exits, as Falkos and Louka had forewarned, were carefully guarded. He was locked in, imprisoned. He thought how ludicrous brave occasions can become; he thought how preposterous he was to imagine there was a way out.

Except . . .

How had the Turk gotten in?

And why did Falkos not allow Petros to finish the sentence about the cave-in?

Could there, perhaps, be a third exit?

But why would that one not be guarded?

Unless, for some reason, it couldn't be. Which might explain why Falkos didn't want it discussed in Ben's presence. Or in anyone's presence, for that matter—apparently the other men were as puzzled as Petros was about how the Turk had entered.

Only Falkos wasn't puzzled, because he knew. It could be that he was the only one who knew.

How could Ben find out where the exit was? From Falkos himself? Not very probably. And yet . . .

I have to talk to Falkos, he decided. By some device, by some inspiration—without taking Kalya into my confidence—I have to get it out of him. But how?

"Did Falkos say what time he would be back?"

"No, he didn't." She looked at him. Perhaps, in the studied casualness, she saw the tension. "Why? Is it so important?"

He must disarm whatever suspicion might be stirring in her. "I wanted to ask him when we're going up," he answered.

He hoped the only word she heard in his empty reply was "we." And his hope was granted. She turned quickly to see if he really meant it, and when he smiled quietly, he knew that she believed him. The day with her had been precious to him, his smile had said, and Louka's warning had convinced him that escape was impossible, he had given up the idea of ascending the mountain alone. He was choosing the safer alternative—with the others. It was easy to make the lie credible; it was what she wanted to hear. Her eyes shone with gratitude; she had no doubt he was telling the truth.

As he saw her belief, an idea came to him: he would tell the same lie to Falkos—and lull him into a sense of security. Then he would work on the teacher's most vulnerable weakness: the man was a drinker.

There was a third exit.

The first to return was Mark. It was nearly eight o'clock in the evening when he stood in the doorway of the main room. More accurately, he took a stance there, his legs apart, his head high, proud. He carried an English rifle, an old Enfield, held it possessively with both hands, so that it crossed his body at the level of his thighs. He was exhilarated. Everything about him seemed energized, his eyes darted quickly, like an animal vigilant over dead prey. His responses were anticipatory, he was ready for large incident, and wanting it.

Kalya's question deflated him a little. "Have you eaten?"

He was irritated by the perennial mother embarrassment; took it to mean she was belittling him. "Yes, we went to a restaurant."

"Where'd you get the rifle?" Ben asked.

This was much more to the virile point Mark was trying to make. "Falkos." His swagger suggested it came from Zeus. "He's teaching us how to shoot."

"Who's us?"

Mark pointed to the doorway. Yannis was there. The old man carried no rifle. He looked exhausted of all his energies, robbed of everything.

"You too, Yannis?" Ben asked.

The Greek didn't answer, went toward the fire, ignoring everyone; nobody was in the room.

"Where did you shoot?" Ben said.

"Not anywhere near—it's a danger zone." The boy sounded like a model soldier dutifully repeating the orders of the day. "Limassol—a warehouse near the old port." He was chesty with pride. "I'm quite a shot."

The old man muttered to himself. "For one day he puts his finger on a trigger and he will never put it anywhere else again."

Mark laughed and took it as a compliment. He tapped Yannis on the shoulder; it was not patronizing but affectionate. "You're not so bad yourself." With proprietary warmth, he turned to the others. "You know what the old boy's score was? Forty-three."

Ben said to his assistant, "If you won't be required to shoot *at* anything, why is Falkos giving you rifle practice?"

The old man winced. "I don't know."

Mark defended Falkos for ordering and Yannis for obeying. "What do you mean, you don't know? Put a gun in a man's hand, and if he doesn't know how to use it, he can kill himself." Then, comforting the old Greek, "You don't have to be ashamed of doing well with it."

"Go piss your pants," Yannis said.

Mark didn't hear it as a derogation of the nursery but of the locker room, and laughed with rattling masculinity.

The night had turned chilly and the boy's hands were cold. He went to the fire, lay the rifle down on the hearth, and held his hands to the blaze. Without a word, Kalya lifted the Enfield off the hot stonework and carried it to the jog, where she stood the rifle up in the cool corner. As she returned to the hearth, the boy was watching her speculatively. Their eyes met. "Thanks," he said. But there was no gratitude in it, so she gave it no reply.

Ben heard Falkos's voice in the hallway, and his muscles tensed. With the others around, how could he work on the man?

The teacher came in, with Mikis and Petros at his heels. He carried a demijohn of raki and he was already on his way to being drunk. His mood was foul. All his usual affability—or his pretense of it—was gone. He slammed the raki bottle roughly onto the table and when a plastic glass rolled off and hit the floor he kicked it. Seeing them all stare at him, he was embarrassed.

"Why is everybody standing around?" he growled. "Mikis! Why the hell are you standing around?"

"I do not stand around, *kirie*. I wait for orders."

"Get out—that's your order—get out!" As Mikis and Petros hurried away, he barked even more angrily, "Standing around— everybody standing around—while the Turks take Morphou!" He turned directly to Ben. "Did you hear that? Did you hear the news? Morphou—they've got Morphou! And meanwhile, in Geneva we're allowing the Turks to stick dumdum bullets up our ass! Do you know what they said today—the Turks—do you know what they asked for? The division of Cyprus. Dumdums up our ass! And what do we do about that? We stay here! While they collect their planes on the mountaintop—we stay here!"

"When will we go up?" Ben said.

"I don't know!" he raged. "I don't know!"

So self-centered was his indignation that Falkos didn't hear the "we." It didn't register that Ben had capitulated and was at last willing to join him and the others.

"They don't tell me when we'll go up!" he railed. "I tried to get Chartas on the phone today, and I got his stupid Platigoras. Since when do I talk to lieutenants, I said. Tell him we have to move, I said. When will we move, I said! Dumdums up our ass!" He turned to Ben and painstakingly mouthed the words: "To answer your question, I—do—not—know."

Falkos reached for the raki bottle, started to open it, realized he had already had too much, and disquietedly abstained.

If I could have him alone for only a little while, Ben thought, I could get him drunker. Then—with a trick and a bit of luck . . . Meanwhile the thing to do is lull him, make him feel he's won me over.

"You have no guess when we might be going?"

It got through. The man saw some vista outside himself. Turning from his indignation, he looked at Ben.

"Did you say 'we'?"

"Yes."

He tried to focus more accurately. "Do you mean it?"

"I . . . think I do."

"No more exploits on your own?"

Special caution now, he told himself. If you say yes too willingly, he won't believe you. . . . Minimally, he averted his head.

The man was not as easy a mark as Kalya had been; belief came more circumspectly. But the teacher was succumbing. "What changed your mind?"

Don't say her name, Ben warned; just give her a quick glance.

Falkos saw it. He looked at Kalya. Back to Ben. Then at Kalya again. "Is it true?" he asked her.

If she had said yes openly, that she believed it to be true, it might not have been as convincing as her silence. He saw her own trust in the fact, and the modest credit she took in having brought it about. He saw in her stillness that they had slept together, had been together, one way or another, all of last night and all of today. What he had hoped would happen—what it was in his *plan* to happen—had happened. It was a tribute to her, yes, but even more it was a tribute to himself, to his guile, to his aphrodisiacal storytelling, to the teacher as leader and schemer and matchmaker.

He was on the verge of letting himself be moved. "It's really true, then, is it?"

"Shall we have a drink?" Ben said.

It was ceremonial and therefore credible. Falkos's eyes brightened, he let his happiness show. "Welcome, Benjamin," he said, and he extended his hand. It was a firm, warm handclasp. "Yes, let's have a drink." Then he kept repeating welcome, welcome, everybody have a drink.

He wanted the others to share his happiness; he was making a celebration of it. He poured the glasses full, but only four of them, excluding Mark. "Raki—it's very good raki." He was a little giddy with enjoyment.

"May I have some?" the boy said.

Falkos turned deferentially to Ben. "Is it really bad for him?"

Ben didn't want to be the boy's spoilsport, but the raki was poisonously strong. "Yes, it's bad for him."

"I only want a little," Mark said.

The boy was already pouring it, and nobody was stopping him —except Kalya. She moved to the table. "Don't drink it," she said quietly.

"It's none of your business," Mark snapped. He might have drunk it a little at a time, but there was a challenge now. He tossed the drink back, taking it all at once.

"You jackass," she said.

"Kiss my jackass!"

Falkos had meant a gaiety, and it was being spoiled. "Enough of that, you two—enough." He seemed desperate, after a day of frustration, to get the merriment rolling. He turned to Yannis. "I was proud of you today—you handled that gun very well."

It was the wrong compliment. Yannis turned his back, went to the table, and started to refill his glass. Falkos was too unclear in his head to realize he was taking a mistaken direction with the old man, and went further. He started to tease him in a way that he thought was good-natured.

"It's wonderful what a gun will do for you," he said. "You know the old saying: a big gun in the woods, a big gun in the grass. Do you have a woman, Yannis?"

"Your sister."

Falkos pretended not to hear it as an insult and laughed immoderately. "Do better, Yannis. I have no sister."

"Your mother, then."

There was no ignoring the provocation any further. Falkos offered sugared venom. "It's all right, old man. You can insult me when we're drinking, and come crawling when we're not."

"Go get an abscess," Yannis muttered, and went to bed.

One gone, Ben said, and two to go—and then I'll have the man alone.

To recover from his social defeat, Falkos turned to Mark. "If I compliment you as a rifleman, will you insult me too?"

Mark smiled. "I'll say thanks."

He meant it. Clearly, he admired the leader; the man made him feel able-bodied and potent. Besides, the drink had relaxed him and given him a new certainty. With studied nonchalance, he started to pour himself another one.

"Please—no," Kalya said.

He kept pouring.

"Ben—" she murmured.

The medic said quietly, "I wouldn't, Mark."

"You wouldn't and I would—and tell her to mind her own business."

"But it will hurt you!" she said.

He turned to her. He didn't understand that he was a child to her, with an illness, and there had been others in her life. "Keep your goddamn mouth out of it!"

Both Ben and Falkos moved between them. The boy was inflamed now, by rage and raki, and he shouted past them, "Tell her hands off! Tell her to keep her bloody hands to herself!"

"My hands are not bloody!"

"They're Turkish!"

There were other voices, but hers was above them. "What've you got against Turks? What the hell do you know about Turks?"

"I know they've got a taste for blood, that's what I know! I know they're cruel! They lock a man in a cell with his own dogs. They starve the animals and cut slits in the man's neck—so the dogs will smell the blood—and devour him! And do you know when the Turks circumcise their males? Not at infancy the way the Jews do—but when the boy is twelve years old—so he can feel it, so it can hurt him and humiliate him!"

"They're atrocity stories! You read them in a book! They've got nothing to do with you!"

"You want to hear one that has?"

"You've been brutalized!"

"My mother!"

The rage was full of pain. Then, silence. When he spoke again, there was a dreadful calm in him.

"Do you have breasts?" he said.

She was as austerely quiet as he was. She didn't answer, except in an indeterminate stillness, as if confessing by her silence to the fault that she had breasts.

"My mother was Greek, my father was Turkish," he said. "He cut off her breasts."

Something impalpable happened, like the slightest change in atmospheric pressure. Actually, the only change happened to Kalya. She looked ill.

She seemed barely able to utter the words. "If your father did that, he was demented."

"He was Turkish."

She was gathering her wits. With bitterness, expressing an evil: "I hope you find your father—and I hope you discover that he never did such a thing. I hope you find him a decent man. . . . I mean that as a curse."

Falkos said, "I hope he doesn't find him at all."

Kalya's voice was grimly positive. "He'll find him. The Fates have long arms, and it's a small island. They wouldn't miss a trick like that."

"Like what?" Mark said.

"Some spite or other. Your father was decent—and your mother was a murderess or a whore."

The boy was as grim as she was. "It won't happen that way."

"What if it does? What if there's nothing to hate your father for? What will you do with your rage?"

"Kill myself."

"You should. . . . The Fates would approve of that."

Without warning, she gave up, unequal to any more. She rubbed the back of one hand with the palm of the other as if she didn't know what to do with either of them. Summarily, she left the room.

In the quieter last moments of their quarrel, the boy's attitude to her seemed totally to have altered. He had been listening to her talk about the Fates as if he either believed in them or had an awe of her belief in them. Something of her grim dread and her talk of curses had surrounded him, capturing a part of his spirit, perhaps alarming him a little. Or bewitching him.

He put his glass to his lips, took one sip, then another, and finished the rest of the drink. Carefully setting the glass on the table, he went to the jog where his rifle was leaning. He lifted it, held it loosely, with a level assurance. As he started out the door, Falkos called after him.

"Your room is the other way."

"I want a little air," he answered, and left the archway.

Falkos looked quickly at Ben. Although the boy had shown no signs of seizure, they had both had the same thought.

"Is he on the verge of another one?" the teacher asked.

"Who knows?"

"What did you think of their little altercation?"

"Don't belittle it."

"Why not? You think it's momentous, do you?" he sneered. "Does she really have breasts?"

Not answering, Ben stared him down. Was it another one of his watcher questions?

Falkos said, "Don't look so disgusted, Benjamin. Don't you think she acted strangely when he told about his mother?"

"Strangely? No. I thought she was going to be ill."

"Wasn't that strange?"

"It's hardly anything for a woman to yawn about."

"For her, it might be. She's seen more horrendous things than that."

For a while, watching Kalya's encounter with the boy, Ben had forgotten his own concern. But now that they had all gone, and he was alone with the teacher, he could begin his questioning —except that the Greek had been somewhat sobered by the quarrel.

"I need some raki," Ben said. Rather than let Falkos pour it, he got up quickly and filled two glasses nearly to the top.

Falkos looked at the quantity of liquor he had been given. "Are you trying to make me maudlin?"

With meticulous care, "No—only myself."

"Why? Are you so unhappy about your decision to come along?"

"It wasn't easy."

With warm sympathy, "No, I'm sure it wasn't. But I'm very pleased to have you, Benjamin—truly I am." He showed his pleasure unreservedly. He seemed to be trying to recapture his celebrative mood, attempting to mend the torn streamers of his party. "You know, my friend, you made me sick with jealousy that someone could hold on to an illusion of peace the way you did. I've tried—dear God, I've tried. And lost it. Why?"

"I'm certainly not an authority."

"Pretend to be. It's your national perquisite. Why did I lose my illusion of a peaceful world?"

"Because you don't want a peaceful world."

"That's sheep turd, Benjamin. It's like saying I lost my youth because I no longer want it. I lost my youth because my muscles went to mush and my heart went to stone. It's middle age, it's the end of the noble dream, and making do with . . ."

"Cabrir."

"Yes, Cabrir."

His hand shook. Good. The man was not so sober after all.

Start now.

"You needn't 'make do' with as little as you think. You're an excellent teacher—you're admired by your men—you're a superb commander."

Falkos looked at him sharply, to catch signs of sarcasm. He didn't see any. "You wouldn't know that, would you?"

"Yes, I would. When the Turk got in—I saw you handle that situation."

"An orderly could have done it."

"Not really. You did it exceptionally well. Not only the way you deployed the men through the tunnels, but—this is more important, I think—"

"What?"

"The personal thing."

"What personal thing?"

"You didn't get angry at anybody. The way you treated Petros, for example."

"He's teacher's pet. I'm very fond of him."

"Yes, I noticed that. But even with the others—you didn't get angry at *any* of them."

"Why should I? They're good men."

"But quite clearly, somebody fucked up. Yet, you didn't wound a single ego—you didn't blame anybody. Why didn't you?"

"Because nobody fucked up."

Ben tensed a little, and tried to look even looser than before. "Come on, somebody did fuck up. Somebody was asleep at one of the entrances—or where he shouldn't have been."

"Nobody fucked up."

"Then how did the Turk get past the guards?"

"He didn't get past the guards."

"How did he get in?"

"Through another entrance."

"Another entrance? . . . Really?"

"Yes."

"Where?"

Falkos didn't reply for an instant. Then, with the quietest contempt, "You bloody slime!"

Don't move.

"You lying, bloody, fucking slime!" Falkos said. "You've joined us, have you? You've given up your illusions, have you? You bastard, you're trying to do me for a bit of information, aren't you? Trying to play me for a goddamn fool! Trying to find a way out of this goddamn cave! You slime, you slime!"

Then everything went bizarre. The man's drunkenness and mortification and perversion caught him, everything at once. He ranted and wept and panicked, all at the same time.

"And after what I've done for you! That woman you're humping—she was my gift to you!"

"Leave her out of it!"

"Out of it?—*she is IT!* She's my gift to you, you bastard! My gift—and you've given me nothing! You—have—given—me—not —one thing! Give me something, you slime! Give me something back!"

"What do you want?"

"Tell me about her!"

"Tell you what?"

"Tell me—tell me everything! What does she look like? When you've got her to yourself—what does she look like? When she's naked! You owe me that, you bastard! What does her body look like—her breasts—what does she feel like? Are they full? Are her nipples large—what does she feel like?"

"Stop it!"

"You owe it to me, you son of a bitch! Tell me about her! How does she look? How does she spread herself to you—"

"Stop!"

"—does she moisten quickly—does she rise to you—"

"Quit it, Falkos!"

Falkos shook; the paroxysm was over. "Oh, my God," he said. He held his head in his hands. "Oh, God!"

Ben felt none of the revulsions he would have expected. No loathing, no anger. Not the faintest quiver of disgust. Only pity.

"Oh, my God!" The teacher's body shook convulsively. He was crying.

Ben thought the man would never stop punishing himself. And then something stopped him.

A shot.

It was a rifle shot—muffled—but no question about it, as identifiable as if it were in the next room. The sound had come from outdoors.

Ben rushed to the passageway. He heard Falkos immediately behind him.

Another shot.

In the background, Kalya's voice, then her footsteps hurrying after them, and her voice, in panic.

Another shot.

8

Mark hurried through the passageway, not wanting to be confined. Outdoors, he felt the cool clarity of the star-filled night. The wind was brisk and he inhaled the fresh air deeply, needing more than his share of it. How close the moon was, with a toylike beauty, an illuminated frisbee, sailing. It seemed buoyant and he had the same sense of weightlessness, everything about him levitating, a lightness in his head, in his walk, in the feel of the rifle.

He had had a prodigious day, and he was proud of himself. Never in his life had he held a gun in his hands and today he had taken to it as if it were a pocket calculator. And he had driven that miserable jeep both directions, with a secure mastery of the tight mountain curves, keeping his speed up all the way. Then, tonight, he had stood his ground with that Turkish bitch.

But best of all, no seizures. Not the faintest sign of one, not even now after two shots of raki, no flashes of light, no anger stripes, no icy drafts of wind. And none of the No Place grays. A stupendous day.

His need for air had simply been his sense of incarceration—he hated caves—anybody might feel that way. If he walked energetically and sucked in big drafts of air, he would be over it in five minutes.

Swiftly, he descended the gravel path until he got past the swamp. At the intersection, he paused for breath. How sweet the cedar trees smelled, to the left of him. There was a green, a vital exhalation coming from them, and a faint soughing of the larger ones, like voices calling. Cautiously treading the ground to make sure it was solid under him, he entered the woods. Firm as the earth was, he could feel the pliant undergrowth—ferns, mosses, creepers—welcoming his feet with a yielding softness. The deeper he got into the woodland, the sweeter it smelled. What a harmony he felt with it.

He heard a sound. It startled him. It might be one of the darkness birds, an owl or a nightingale. He suspected it was the latter because, although he knew very little about nature, he had heard in Limassol today that this year the mountain nightingales were so noisy that people couldn't sleep.

He thought once more about how good the day had been. The only thing he regretted was Nexos. It was the town where his Turkish father had last been heard of—at least according to Uncle Lexi. Mark had gone there on the day after his meeting with Falkos, that hopeless meeting when he thought the teacher would never get in touch with him.

His uncle had remembered only vaguely where Nexos was— way the hell and gone, the western end of the island. It took Mark five hours to get there. The town was spiritless, on miserable dusty flatland, with no hint of mountain, grove, or sea. The people lived in squat gray boxes, not the cheery whitewash of typical Greek islands. Gloomy place, the inhabitants gloomier. How could they possibly help him, they said, if he didn't even know the man's name? Besides, there were no Turks here, nor had there been for many years. Except that there had been a few Turkish families that lived *outside* the town, on the old road that nobody used these days, the one that went to Prodhromos. He hitchhiked part of the way and walked the rest. The whole area was dust-swept and abandoned. There were four houses, one empty and three in rubble. How long ago the Turks had forsaken the place he couldn't tell; years, perhaps.

But on the door of the remaining house, there was a name crudely painted—Aytul, B. Going back to Nicosia on the bus, he made a note that some way he would track down Aytul, B. and get what information he could about a Turk without a name. It would probably be an ineffectual step, but he had no others to take, and he regretted that Falkos hadn't called him a few days later, so he wouldn't have had to stop so early in his search. Still, this wasn't really the end of it. . . . Some way, he would find his father.

The second drink was beginning to go to his head, to his spirit, lifting him still higher than he had been before, in a transport. This was the life—happy—a man—a fighter for a cause—

why need he regret not having found his father? He had had two of them—the surrogate had brutalized him, and the real one had brutalized his mother. Loathing both of them, he had a brightening thought: I've got two new ones.

It struck him as funny, it was so pat—two bad ones and now two good ones. As between Falkos and Ben, which one did he like better? Well, Falkos, probably. He was the one who had the faith to put a gun in Mark's hand—and had taught him how to shoot. A wonderful teacher, he had treated Mark without patronization and with respect, had made him feel like a healthy, full-grown male.

But Ben had treated him like a child, a sick one—avoid driving, drinking, guns. The medic was more of a worrywart than some of the doctors he had had back home. Perhaps because he cared more. That was the thing about him—no matter how old he got, he would probably never become apathetic, he would always go on caring. But that kind of man could be dangerous. Trying to please a man who cared . . . If you disagreed with what he cared about —firing a gun, for example—you could get yourself in trouble with him. You could be injured by his disfavor. Or worse, you'd find yourself polishing up for his approval, doing things you hated doing, cadging handouts of affection, free grants, beggarly fellowships of love. Balls to that. Beware. Don't like him too much.

And yet . . . Why couldn't he have been his father? Or Falkos? Why couldn't he have had a father he could love instead of one he must hate? Why had his real father given meaning only to the angry tempest in his brain, to the hands that palsied with rage, to the mouth that foamed, to the curse that drove him senseless into a No Place of wrath?

There he was, calling his malady a curse again—against the medic's plea that it be called a disease which one day would be cured.

But Mark's mind ran to curses, as Kalya's did.

Curses of a different kind, however. Hers came from the mean little Turkish kismet—the Fates have long arms and it's a small island, she had said—and you wait passively until the Fates have at you. But his curse made him obsessional to *act*—to find and kill his father. "I hope you find him a decent man." Kalya's curse. Fuck you, you Muslim, he said now, and wished he had said it to her face. He hated her, not only because she was a Turk but because she was beautiful. She blurred the clear, distinct lines of the racial stereotype he needed if his purpose was to remain sharp. She was in no way coarse-looking. Although her face was strong, every one of her features was as precise as if it had been etched by a needle. She was pushing forty, he would guess, yet she didn't have the dumpy look that fit his stock image of the prime-of-life Turkish woman. She was lithe and slim . . . and yet, voluptuous. He had not meant to call her voluptuous, had stumbled on the word. He didn't want to think of her that way.

The nightingale again. Damn it for frightening him.

It was her movements that were voluptuous, it was her looks and glances. He had caught an accidental contact of her eyes with Ben's, and there was such wanting in the woman—he wondered if they were having it together. They must be having it, for the same look was all over him, and Mark could see that they were trying to avoid any physical closeness, the slightest tangency, which suggested to him that they were onto one another. How long they had been screwing he couldn't guess, nor whether they were doing it now. He could be giving it to her in the middle of the night, right here in the cave, and never have the self-shame that Mark would have at banging a Turkish woman; there'd be no guilty coitus interruptus, not for either of them. But there would be for me, Mark said.

It was her mouth that excited him the most.

He had an erection. He couldn't remember when was the last time he had had one, but here it was again. It wasn't the woman who had brought it on, he told himself, it was the raki. It had exhilarated him, elevated him, literally. He could feel it thrusting in his trousers, at practically the same angle as his gun, and just as stiff. Bang, he said, bang. It was the raki.

Liar. He wanted to make love to her.

No, he daren't say love, not in the same breath with the word Turk. It was more rudimental than that, closer to the gonads, he wanted to fuck her, that was all, just to ream her, violate her. Yes, that was the essence of it. Not contrary to his feelings about Turks, but an ancillary expression of it: rape. He wanted to tear her clothes off, force her to the ground, hear her outcries, press his knees between her thighs, assault her, break her open, enter, thrust and thrust and desecrate.

But wouldn't it be better to seduce her into it? Wouldn't it be better for the classic wily Greek to trick the stupid Turk, button by cunning button, pretending love while loathing her? Wouldn't there be an extra pleasure in the deception?

No, he couldn't pull it off. He couldn't pretend love that he didn't feel. If he were to attempt it, he would probably start to believe his own impostures, he would make them a verity, and would truly be spellbound by her. By himself, actually—by love as a self-deception. He couldn't go through with it, anymore than he had been able to go through with his lie about being here in search of Aphrodite's grave. Love was a delusory myth, fabricated as Falkos had concocted the story of Aphrodite's cave. He mustn't get taken in by it, ever. It could be hallucinatory, it could delude him into believing, as Ben believed, that all diseases could be cured in time, and the world would be better for it, and that Turks could be kind and brave and—oh yes!—beautiful. It could cause him to destroy the whole cosmos of wrath he had built to live in. It would be like committing himself, his whole existence, to a new syllogism, an illogical one, like believing in a false mathematical axiom which divided his life by zero. He would have none of it.

He felt less light-headed now, and his erection was gone. He had turned around and was almost out of the woods, in view of the path, when he heard a sound. Not the bird this time, not aloft but in the brush. It was somewhere behind him.

Alarmed, he walked faster to get to what might be the safety of the path. The sound was not behind him now, but to his right, as if there might be two of them.

Perhaps he was imagining that there were two. He stopped walking, he listened. There was no sound at all.

He decided not to run. Walk as softly as you can, he said, as carefully. Perhaps he was frightening himself unnecessarily. Not only was the woodland silent now, but even if the noise should happen again, what could it signify? Possibly only small animals in the underbrush.

Did he hear it again, and was it closer than before?

No noise now. The rustling in the trees had ceased, the wind had died down. There was not the falling of a leaf. Summer night stillness, no bird sounds, no cricket noises. Wryly he added: I certainly don't have to go far to find anxieties, I can pull those rabbits out of a bottomless hat. What a foolishness he had scared himself with. If there had been anyone nearby—one of Falkos's people, for example—he would have shown himself. Where the hell are you going? the man would have said. If it had been a Turk, there would have been a shot, or the flash of a knife, and he wouldn't have had time to be frightened. The fact that he had *heard* the noise lent safety to it. If you hear the thunder, the saying went, the danger of lightning is already past. The thought relieved him. He was no longer afraid. Anyway, he had the rifle; there was courage in it.

The sound again. Not imagination, real. Clearer, closer.

Reversing his direction, he ran.

The noise, repeated. It didn't stop. A sound of running, like his own. He thought it was all around him, had the senseless terror that one man, only one, was running in circles, making a tighter and tighter perimeter around the quarry, cutting off Mark's retreat. The circles kept diminishing, the man was coming closer. If only I could see him, he thought. A mistake: don't ask for sight of him, don't think of sights and rifles.

The sound, closer.

He dropped to his knees. He didn't move. His hand tightened on the gun. But Falkos had been clear: no noise, no betraying that we're here.

Silence now. Perhaps the man had gone, perhaps it had worked, his dropping to the ground to be covered by brush; perhaps he was safe.

He saw the motion. It was ahead of him.

A gray stirring in the undergrowth. No illusion; altogether clear. And the motion was slowly coming toward him.

He couldn't see the man, only the flutter in the dense thicket. Mark wondered if his own stillness was as clear as the movement the other one was making.

The brush still moved, closer now. The stir was as close as breathing.

The gray figure rose.

It disappeared for an instant, then he heard him, within reach of overpowering dread, a live presence, indeterminate, dark and terrible. He raised his gun. He heard the gunshot—his own gunshot—not knowing when he had decided to pull the trigger, not even certain he had done it. He pulled the trigger again.

The gray shadow leaped.

He heard a beating at the undergrowth, a whipping sound like a scythe cutting at long grasses, then another noise, a gasping.

Hectic, in cold sweat, wanting to flee, yet exultant too, he ran toward the noise and saw the creature in the small clearing that its thrashing body had made.

It was a sheep, a moufflon, a gray wild thing of the mountain, struggling with its death. He had hit it all right, and the moonlight made the shoulder blood look black. The beast pawed at the ground with its forelegs, scratched at the earth as if the action would keep it on its legs. It twisted to one side, one shoulder trying to slant away from the other shoulder's blood. It raised its head, dropped it, raised it again. With one curving horn it tried to do what its forelegs had not done, grabble something from the earth. Then utter stillness, and a tremor. The graceful thing became an ugly awkwardness. It fell, a heap.

Still, it was not dead. One spasm, then another, convulsion to convulsion, all pain.

Kill it, he said, it's suffering.

The beast's spasms would not stop. At last, shaking, he raised the rifle, again heard the blast as if someone else had caused it, felt the recoil, wanted all the ache.

He couldn't tell how long he stood there.

Behind him somewhere, another sound, and another. He heard the thrashing through the woods. Then voices:

"Mark!"

His hands would not stop shaking. He mustn't tremble, he told himself, they mustn't see him trembling. And he must drop the gun. But it wasn't there anymore, not in his hand. Gone. Where? Where was it?

"My God, it was only—!"

Falkos's voice. The man was looking at the dead thing on the ground.

"What is it?"

"Where? What is it?"

"A moufflon!"

Suddenly the Greek twisted around and reached for the boy. "You stupid—!"

"Somebody—" Mark said. "Somebody—" He pointed vaguely one way, then another.

"I told you not to!" Falkos, enraged. "You'll have the bastards coming—they'll come looking for us!"

"Somebody—!"

"Give me the rifle," the Greek said. "Give it to me!"

"I—no—" he said. What he meant was he didn't have it, had dropped it.

"You stupid—give it to me!"

"No—"

Aimlessly—possibly to show he had no rifle—he raised both arms. The other arm struck out, the Greek's. He felt the blow, he heard the bluster in his head, the hurricane.

"No, don't!" The woman's voice.

"Let him alone!" Ben said.

He saw the two bodies, clashing, the two men, the fists raised, the slashing of the air, the cries.

"Oh no," he heard the woman say. "Oh no."

Then he lost them all, and was No Place.

9

He was right behind Falkos, who blocked his view, so he didn't immediately see the boy, but only the dead animal on the ground. When he did see Mark, it was too late. You stupid, was all he heard from the Greek, and the boy was saying somebody, somebody. He was back there in the darkness, out of the moonlight, still muttering somebody when Ben saw him raise his arms, and didn't know the reason.

Falkos hit him once.

"No, don't!" Kalya said, as Ben rushed between them.

He pulled at the Greek, then he felt the man's fist in his face. And suddenly there was blood, whose blood Ben didn't know, and they were fighting.

"Oh no," he heard Kalya say. "Oh no." He didn't know what she was saying it about, or to whom.

Again he struck at Falkos, and again. He felt the other smashing back, smashing as if the Greek needed all his force to break through rock, and Ben must take it until he burst or broke.

"Oh no," he heard her again. "Oh, help me, help me!"

That quickly the fight was over, and the men saw why it was that she needed help.

The boy was thrashing in the brush. The scream, the unearthly tumult of the larynx that makes its own outcry, then he stumbled outward, toward the clearing. He fell in the patch of white moonlight, as white and maddened as if moonstruck, his head turned toward one shoulder, then clonic seizures, one after another, the spasms of ligament and muscle, the violent crack of limbs as if they were whips to slash the air, the stertorous breathing, the choke and spasm, choke and spasm, the wetness of mouth, the froth, the terrible malevolent scum of the terrible mal.

"Oh, help," she said. But she was nowhere near the boy. She stood at a distance, dismayed and hypnotized, her eyes wide, wanting to do something for him, and too repelled to move. Oh, help, she kept saying, oh help him.

There was little Ben could do. He loosened Mark's belt, pulled his shirt apart; there was no tight collar to release. Holding his mouth open with one hand, he reached for a twig, wiped it on his trousers, pressed it between the teeth like a horse's bit so that the gnashing would not cut the tongue. As he saw the boy's arms flailing at his own face, he gently spread them once, then again, holding them loosely, letting them go.

And he waited.

In a few moments, it had passed. Kneeling by him, Ben still waited. Then he heard the sound—the long, drawn sigh, like the most agonized lament, a cry from another world, an even darker one perhaps.

Hearing it, Kalya too cried out, a moan, nameless, full of pity. She dropped to her knees on the other side of Mark, lifted his head a little, cradled it in her arms, and rocked him a little. As she did, she said the hushing word, the soothing, lulling word. *"Siopi,"* she said, as if to a child, *"siopi, siopi."*

Later, when the boy could walk, they brought him back to one of the larger cells, better ventilated than the one he had slept in. Mark stood over the narrow cot, trying to focus on it, not certain it was meant for him. As Kalya patted the pillow she had brought from another cell, he tentatively let himself lie down. In a little while, he was asleep.

When he awakens, Ben wondered, what will he remember? Were there goblins in seizures as there were in bad dreams? Epileptics didn't say there were, but that might be simply because they couldn't recall. Might it also be true that so-called normal people have the mals and never know it? The petit mals of forgetfulness; seizure as an escape from pain. It was a mystery ailment, still an enigma, an arcanum into which many great people had fled. From what? From greatness itself, from genius, as this boy might be fleeing? But epilepsy—and forgetfulness—were not reserved only for the great. Lethe was for everybody.

Kalya was lying on a low bench, not far from the bed. She was wide awake. Ben sat on a ledge of rock, as silent as she was.

"I think he'll be all right," Ben said. "Go to bed."

"And you?"

"I'll sit up with him a little while."

"So will I."

She wanted to prolong the illusion that they were needed—parents caring for a sick child. "He's sleeping as if nothing had happened."

"Perhaps nothing *has* happened."

"But something has." She was perturbed. "A tempest like that—it seemed like a madness—like The Furies."

"It's not a madness, Kalya," he said quietly.

People were frightened by it because they thought it was. Yet, he had never seen the slightest sign of derangement. He had been in high school with an epileptic who was the best basketball player on the team, swift, agile and, above all, fair-minded; when he was a medical student, he had known an epileptic girl who had a steady-eyed view of the world, and knew a joke or two.

Kalya shivered. "When I saw what was happening—the gagging—the violence—I was so horrified—I wanted to run. . . . I'm so ashamed."

"Don't be. People *have* run—and still do. There've been others who have thrown stones, who've beaten the thing to death."

"Beaten . . . ?"

"There've been cases where looking at a seizure has caused a seizure in someone who's never had one before."

"From . . . horror?" She heard herself say the word and quickly looked at the boy. With a sound of startlement, she put her hand on her breast. "What if he heard me?"

"You think he hasn't heard that word before? His own friends . . ."

"Oh, poor child."

In the darkness, they heard Mark's voice. "Kalya . . ."

It was the first time he had called her something other than Turk or Turkish woman. He had probably been conscious for quite a while. There was not the faintest aftermath of convulsion in his manner. On the contrary, he seemed totally self-possessed and keenly aware; he was anxious to talk. "I heard your . . . sympathy," he said. "I want to thank you for it—but I want you to know I don't need it."

It was genuine, a gesture of decency, no more. By no means

an apology for having treated her offensively, it was not an effort to end hostilities. But Kalya looked deeply touched, as if it were.

"Thank you," she said simply. She seemed to sense that he was still on his guard. "And I'm sorry."

"For what?"

"For cursing you."

"It was only half a curse—the rest was a blessing."

"A blessing?"

"Yes. You said, 'I hope you find your father.'"

"If you do find him . . ." She paused, unwilling to continue.

"Yes?"

"Do you really think you'll punish him?"

"That's the purpose."

"I don't think it is."

He looked surprised and interested. "What's the purpose, do you think?"

She started to answer him, then faltered. After a lengthy hesitation, she tried again. "A number of years ago, I went looking for my father—I hadn't seen him since I was twenty years old. He had been very cruel to me—and I was going back to avenge myself. Within the first hour of our meeting, he pointed out that I had forfeited the possibility of a fine career, I had lost my husband, my children had been killed—and all my misfortunes were my own fault. And when I left him, I realized that I had always known that he would say exactly what he did say. And that those were the things I had gone back to hear."

"Not to punish, but to be punished?"

"Yes."

"You think that's why we go in search of our parents?"

"In search of our past, yes."

"Even when it was happy?"

"Oh, especially when it was happy—that's the worst punishment!"

They both smiled, and Ben—the spectator—sensed a curious rapport in their conversation, shy, tentative. The rancors were losing some bitterness, they were not talking like enemies, but like strangers in a pleasant contest of the minds, enkindling one another's curiosity. They were exploring, not necessarily for one another, but for a common language.

"Even Aphrodite . . ." Kalya began.

"Was looking for one thing and thought she was looking for another?"

"Yes. Was it love or darkness?"

"Which was which?"

"Well, I think—even in Falkos's story—she was looking for the man who had punished her—Zeus." She paused, and then said quietly, "And Zeus was her father."

"Now, *you're* making up the myth."

"Yes . . . so are you."

". . . Me?"

It troubled him. But it intrigued him, too.

She was charming the boy. Ben wondered how much of it was conscious guile. Again, the question struck him: was she the liar she had confessed herself to be? Or was she a fantasist who could bear to live only in the world of myth? Had she, in some amorphous way, slipped through reality, to live a lie so enormous that it could not be distinguished from the truth?

Could she have known the boy's father?

Two Turks—might they have been fugitives together? Was his father perhaps related to her—a brother, a cousin? Had she seen the cruelty of a woman whose breasts had been hacked off? Had she had anything to do with it? Could this be among the atrocities she had to keep in the darkness of the cave?

As Kalya and Mark continued talking, they hardly noticed when Petros came in. The Greek said quietly to Ben, "Kirios Falkos wants to see you."

Not disturbing them, the medic slipped away.

He dreaded the meeting with Falkos. Whether Ben had to deal with the consequences of having tried to trick the teacher, or the man's humiliation over his sick breakdown, or the fistfight over Mark, in some way the leader would want his pound of flesh. He was not likely to go without demanding some requital, a bitter quid pro quo—and Ben saw no way out of it.

As he approached the main room, he heard the squawk of the intercom and Falkos's voice, reporting Mark's three shots at the moufflon. The teacher was repeating the word "wait" a number of times, questioning it as if he loathed the term and all it signified. When Ben entered, the man was no longer occupied with the radio but with the raki bottle. He poured a second glass, which he set across the table for the American.

Clearly, he did not want to talk about the moufflon. "Nobody should ever drink this libation all evening," he said. "It tells you how beautiful the world is, how happy you are, how everybody respects and loves you—and suddenly it counsels suicide."

Putting the clown's face on his agitation, he smiled engagingly. He was muddling through a bad place, grinning too much, not doing very well. Twice in Ben's career as a medic he had tended people who had tried to kill themselves; one of them had succeeded. The latter showed the same derring-do against heartache, against the futile sense of being trapped within a lonely and loathsome self, with no escape to anything but destruction. And Falkos was not taking it out on the American, but on himself. Or so Ben thought. Until:

"I don't blame you for trying to deceive me, Benjamin. If you think I'm your enemy, what else are you to do? But I would like to point out that you have been deceiving not me, but yourself."

"In what way?"

"Have a drink."

"No, thanks. In what way?"

"You have a wrong picture of who you are. You're a gentle, peaceful man, are you? Nonsense. You're more meanly militant than I am."

"You have a way of measuring these things, I suppose?"

"Yes—look."

He had been sitting in an unnatural sideways position. Now he turned to reveal the other side of his face. His jaw and cheekbone were badly bruised.

Ben hadn't realized the fight had been that violent. "I'm sorry for that. But it wasn't deliberate—it just happened—self-defense."

"Self-defense? Did I attack you first?"

". . . No."

"Benjamin . . . I think you enjoyed that fight."

"That's not true. And if I did it was a temporary . . . lapse."

"I don't think it's so temporary. I believe there's a pattern to it —I believe you're *looking* for altercation. You've tried to escape— that's asking for a fight, isn't it? Wouldn't you say that's part of your predictable behavior?"

Was he indeed deceiving himself? Kalya had said practically the same thing—that he had tried to escape in order to challenge. If this was true, it might be that he had no such peaceable bent as he believed he had. There was no scale by which to measure cowardice and courage and belligerency; and if the bully was often counterpart to the craven, what was Ben Coram's counterpart? He had the unwelcome thought: Perhaps he was being self-righteously above the combat while sickly seeking it; perhaps he had as deep a hunger for encounter as Kalya did, as Mark did—and others detected this in him. Why didn't he detect it in himself? He was certain of only one thing:

"I'm not a militant."

"Are you sure?" Falkos said. "Let me ask another question. . . . Why did you come to Cyprus?"

Warily, "Why shouldn't I?"

"You knew it was an embattled country."

"When I first saw it, it wasn't embattled."

"There were disturbances here in '64. There will always be disturbances. It's Greek versus Turk—it's gone on for centuries—it has never stopped and it never will. It's in the blood—and you know it. Why did you come?"

"Because it was peaceful, it was beautiful."

"Tahiti is more peaceful and more beautiful. Why not there?"

Ben relaxed a little. "No Greeks."

"You love the Greeks, do you?"

"Yes."

"Why?"

"What do you mean, why? Anybody who's been educated in the west has Greek roots."

"Particularly in the ancients, right?"

"Yes."

"Great people, the ancients," Falkos said bitingly. "They loved poetry—democracy—wisdom—the arts." Then, iron-hard: "And they had a passion for war."

"Not true."

"Don't tell me, Benjamin. It was their only passion. They didn't give a damn about women, they had no real devotion to family or to daily life, all they cared about was battle. Even their Olympic games were rehearsals for prowess on the battlefield."

"Their dramas were against war."

"Dramatists are liars, Benjamin—like you. You want the truth, look to the philosophers. Socrates, Plato, Aristotle—they never said a word—not a caviling word against war. Do you know why? Because they knew that war was man's great occasion. They knew that the gods were not kindly or forgiving or just—the gods were terrorists. And only in war could we prove we were not afraid of them. Heroism is a defiance of an unjust god."

"Cut off your head to spite their divinity."

"Spite is the only weapon we have."

"I don't want it!"

"Then get out of the world." Abruptly, the thought struck him. "Holy Mother, that's really why you want to go to the god-damn Monastery, isn't it? You want to stay there! You may not know it, but you want to spend the rest of your life there! Why don't you do it, Benjamin? Why don't you get out of the world?"

The teacher was having his vengeance, all right. Ben felt hectored, his mind was disoriented, he had no answer for the man.

Luckily, there was a distraction. Someone talked loudly in the corridor, a flurry of voices, and Mikis entered. He said that Chartas was there. Ben was surprised; he had assumed it was Chartas that the teacher had just consulted on the intercom, but apparently it was a lieutenant. Falkos too seemed surprised.

"Chartas?" The schoolmaster was off-balance, disturbed. Quickly, he left the room.

Get out of the world, the teacher had commanded, as if banishing him. How differently Demetrios had said precisely the same thing, but as a welcome—to St. Timotheos.

"You love it here, don't you?" the old priest had asked.

"Yes."

"Then why don't you stay?"

The invitation had come the day before Ben had departed from the Monastery. They had spent the whole morning—Demetrios, Modestos, and the American—hanging the patriarch's best paintings on the walls of the baptistery. One wall surface of the octagonal building was taken up by the entrance door and the towering Byzantine windows above it; the seven other walls were being hung with two pictures per surface, fourteen altogether—the Stations of the Cross. All the pictures were good, a number were excellent. There were two that were particularly awesome—Jesus' first fall, and the meeting with his mother. But the painting that caught Ben's breath was the stripping of Christ's garments; it was an agony of shock and shame.

In the early afternoon, there was still one painting to hang, and Ben did not see it among the packings. The missing picture was the Twelfth Station—Jesus on the Cross.

"Did we forget to bring it from the studio?" Ben asked.

"No."

That was all Demetrios said. Modestos moved away, as if he wanted no part of the subject.

"Where is it?" Ben asked.

"I don't know," the old man said. There was a baffling avoidance in his manner. Something was perturbing him.

"Has it been sold? . . . Taken?"

"No." He walked to the temporary trestle table and assembled bits of wrapping muslin and strands of wire, busied himself with nervous nothings. Finally, he said, almost inaudibly, "I haven't painted it."

"Why not?"

"Jesus on the Cross . . ." The old man started and stopped. "All the others—they can pass as *paintings*. But on the Cross—!"

The old man could not continue. Then the words, like wrenchings, "An *icon* is wanted!"

And he couldn't paint it. The patriarch turned away to hide his agitation. His palsied hands shook more than usual.

It was the old insufficiency again, the man who wanted to be an icon-maker—a healer—and had to fall short by being an artist. To paint Christ on the Cross—and heal the viewer as he hurts him —! It was the dream of his life, and he could never accomplish it, he could no longer lift a brush to try. He had never attempted the canvas, but was filling his days with what he knew in his heart were the lesser daubings of his life. He was pretending to be appeased with his inadequacy. . . . So there would be an emptiness on the wall, as there was in the old man.

The rest of the day was a grievous one for the patriarch. Twice Ben tried to stir him out of his despondency, to cheer him, but the priest would not be consoled. At last, right before vespers, as the lavender shadows lengthened on the snow, and as the old man was lighting the first candles of the evening, Ben did not try to console him for the third time, but attacked him instead.

"If I were to behave as you have behaved all afternoon, what would you say to me?"

Demetrios blinked uncertainly. "What would I say?"

"You would scold the devil out of me. You would say I was stubborn and vainglorious and full of pride."

"Is that what you're saying to me?"

"Yes, I am."

"Why?"

"Because you want to paint a miracle."

"Why shouldn't I want it?"

"Because you're not a saint."

"Good heaven, I don't pretend I am."

"Yes, you do. You judge yourself as if you were a failed saint —you can't paint a miracle of healing. And you're ungrateful for the great gift God has given you."

"That's not true—and may God forgive you for saying it!"

"God forgive *you*, Father."

"You are insolent—and you are stupid! You're a sliver under my fingernail, a thorn in my flesh, and a fool who doesn't know balsam from beeswax . . . and I shall miss you dreadfully when you are gone."

He said nothing further. Later, after evening prayers, he asked quietly, on a note of pleading, "Why don't you stay?"

"It's not what I want, Father."

"Don't lie to yourself, Ben. You don't want the purgatory that's going on out there, do you?"

Purgatory was a test of his courage to stay alive; did he want it? "No."

"Then . . . ?"

"But I don't want this either."

"You will—when you give yourself to it."

"No. I'd spend every minute in doubt."

"Who says that's bad?"

"Doubt? In a monastery?"

"Yes—we *need* it here. There used to be five hundred of us— and now there are only fourteen. Fourteen believers. Fourteen monk-priests who live by rite-and-canon, and never falter in their faith. They get *soft* in it. Their heads get soft, and their souls get soft—and the faith itself gets soft."

"How can the faith . . . ?"

"Faith has to be tempered in doubt."

"As if it were a sword?"

"Don't disparage swords. You think Christ had no metal in him? You think he was a pudding? Didn't he battle the money changers? . . . The Church has always needed soldiers."

"Here too?"

"There's no escaping conflict, Ben . . . And don't delude yourself that you're not a soldier."

They had all said it. Demetrios, Kalya, Falkos. You're a soldier. And there was no world—secular or religious—without an army. You got drafted everywhere. Get out of this world? And into which other one?

Falkos, you bastard, you're sucking me into your suicidal mood. There's only one world I have to get out of—this goddamn cave.

He heard the voices—the Chartas meeting going on in another room. They seemed far away and he wondered where they were. Perhaps they were in the open place—where the Turk had fallen.

A wild thought: Falkos was showing Chartas where the man had been apprehended and killed. Perhaps—thin hope—he would also tell his superior how the Turk had gotten in.

He rushed out of the main room. The instant he got into the passage, he stopped. They would see him coming if he went by way of the central corridor. Reversing himself, he ran to a nearby turning, veered to the right, took a narrower hallway. Then he entered a tunnel that went steeply upward; he would listen from a higher gallery.

Above, in a shallow alcove, he hung back in the darkness. They wouldn't see him here, he thought, they wouldn't think to look this high, unless in pointing out how the man had fallen . . .

They were talking of other things. There were four of them—Falkos, a short man with a high forehead and a thin falsetto voice, a youngish man who paced in and out of the group as if sampling tidbits of the conversation, and Chartas, towering over the others.

He could not make out what they were saying. The teacher was not looking up to where the Turk had been, but pointing to where he had fallen on the rocks. Ben could hear the tones and modulations of their voices, but could not hear the words. The discourse became a mumbling monotone, and, his heart sinking, he realized that the talk about the Turk was over. They were having an argument.

Falkos: "Are you saying I am drunk?"

"I merely say you would not make such a rash suggestion if you had not had so much to drink." Chartas spoke with dignity and almost without reprobation. For a lean man his speech was oddly orotund, full of golden notes rarely heard in the Greek tongue. "You misunderstand me, Manolis Falkos," he said. "I am not reprimanding you. I am merely trying to tell you that I am concerned. Not only about the success of our tactic—although you know how vital it is—but about you personally. We have been friends for many years. You know how I regard you. But suddenly —in the last year or so . . . I cannot understand how you have become so . . . erratic."

"I am not erratic. There were three gunshots. They will have been heard for miles around. The Turks will not know that only a moufflon has been killed. But they *will* know that one of their men is missing—and the shots came from here. By tomorrow, they may have found the cave."

"Do you suggest that we attack tonight?"

"At least by dawn tomorrow."

"It's impossible, Manolis."

"Not all the attacks—only ours, Pavlos. You say the Monastery is more important than the other two hills—then, let me take the Monastery."

"Let us go," Chartas said to the other two men.

"No—please, Pavlos!" Falkos said. "I am told that not a single plane landed on the vineyard today—and no planes have departed. Which means they have all they need. And tanks too, I'm sure. This morning they took Morphou—in Geneva the talks are breaking down. Do we need any more, Pavlos—do we need any more? There will be a second invasion!"

"There will be no second invasion, Manolis." He spoke gently, as if to a child.

"Get your head out of the sand!"

"Stop being a hysteric."

Chartas was right, Ben thought; the teacher did sound like a hysteric. Poor sick man, he believed in nothing, he had no faith in anyone, he had nothing to live for but Cabrir.

Chartas in the lead, the men departed from the open place. Falkos, a few paces behind the others, trailed them in a disconsolate way, totally defeated.

The open space was deserted. The tunnels were dark. The galleries were still.

Ben heard the kithara. It sounded distant, another existence, coming not so much from another place as from another time. Old longings, old sorrows, old betrayals.

Why had he thought betrayals? He listened and recognized

the reason. Louka was playing his own song. Some of the words clung to the memory . . . something about better to go all alone, people I love I betray.

Betray. And the man was a mercenary.

The notion in his mind could not possibly make any sense. Louka would know nothing, he would agree to nothing, he could not be trusted.

But already Ben was en route to the sound of the kithara. He homed on it as if it were a beam, he got lost from it and found it. He wandered for hundreds of feet, in a bright tunnel and a dim one, listening intently, losing the sound and hearing it again, praying that the music which gave him his direction wouldn't stop. And finally—

"You are out of breath, *kirie*," Louka said.

"I've been trying to find you."

"Where you look? I am here." Glowing with hospitality, the bearded man offered an expansive welcome to his cell. He was glad to see Ben—the American was his kindred spirit; they spoke the same Hollywood language. With a cry of felicitation, he pointed to Ben's leg. "Is now all right, yes?"

"Yes, I can walk on it."

"Good, good."

"I can even run."

He tried to load the word with meaning, but the Greek did not notice, or pretended not to.

"Where do you run to?" His tone was innocuous.

"Wherever you tell me."

"Me?"

"Yes . . . I need you to help me get away."

Carefully, the mercenary put the kithara on the bed beside him. It was unclear whether he was interested or not. "You have the wrong man," he finally said. His cordiality had regressed a little.

"No, I don't think so."

"I am a Greek."

"You're not a Cypriot, you're a mainlander. It's not your war."

"I do not betray."

"Your song says you do."

He raised his shoulders, extended his arms widely, and laughed.

"My song! I am a poet. A poet will say anything for a good—how you say—*aisthima*."

"Sentiment."

"Yes—sentiment." The definition: "That—is a poet."

"How about a mercenary?"

"A mercenary works only for money."

"That's what I'm talking about."

Silence. Then: "I am writing a new song. You would like to hear it?"

"No."

"How much?"

"How much do you save in a month?"

"In American dollars—maybe two hundred."

"I'll get you a month closer to Hollywood."

"If I do this, I would want to get away more quick than that."

"Five hundred."

Louka was tempted, but he walked away. "We are talking foolish. It is impossible. There is no way out that is not guarded."

"The way the Turk came in."

"Now that is also guarded. Falkos put the twins there."

The man didn't say it flatly enough. There was some reservation. "That's not the truth, is it?"

"That part is the truth."

"What part isn't?"

"There are many exits, *kirie*. But most of them are where there have been cave-ins. Either they are closed by the mountain, or they are closed by man."

"You mean blocked? Doors?"

"We call them—I do not know how to say in English—*phragmos*."

"A barrier?"

"Something like this, yes. Some are old, very old."

"Can they be moved?"

"I do not know, *kirie*. There is one near the copper road, and there is another that . . ." He stopped. "I do not know."

"Can you try—tonight?"

"Tonight—in dark? Impossible." Annoyed to have to admit his inadequacy, he said, irritably, "It is not easy, *kirie*. And it is something which it must be done from outside. If I will do it from inside, a mountain can fall on me."

"Will you do it tomorrow?"

"I will try, yes."

"In the morning?"

"I am on guard—I cannot. I have to wait until late in afternoon—I have three free hours. I will make with those hours an extra hour for my meal—this will give me four. If I can do it, I will do it. But I will not be able to be back here until it is dark."

"How will I know it's done?"

"I will play kithara. Yes?"

"Yes."

"Same song. When you hear me play, you come."

"Here?"

"Yes."

"When?"

"Maybe—I do not know—before nine o'clock."

"Nine o'clock." Ben nodded.

The mercenary smoothed his hair, his beard, his mustache, as if to put everything in order. "Now . . . where is money?"

"It's in the ambulance. After you've opened the driver's door —above the seat—center—hanging from a hook—there's a safety helmet—a big hat—metal. It has a removable lining in it. Take the lining out, and take two hundred pounds—that's over five hundred dollars. But no more."

"There is more there?"

"Yes—about three hundred more."

"You are going to leave it there?"

"Yes."

"Why? You think you will see your ambulance again?"

Ben had a twinge. "No. But Yannis knows where the money is. I want him to have it. . . . You won't take any more than two hundred, will you?"

"No—I promise." Then, with a grimace. "I was stupid. Why I did not ask for more?"

On leaving Louka, he had no doubt of it: the mercenary was an excellent choice. The man had no scruples about helping him get away. A scruple, Ben recalled from the back pages of his pharmacopeia, was an apothecary's unit of weight, equal to twenty grains. That was the way Louka measured scruples, by grains— two hundred was not enough, five hundred tipped the scale. The rest, for Louka, was all prudence: how to do it shrewdly, from the outside instead of the inside, how to do it without getting caught, without losing one's payments, or one's life. In an act of betrayal, the mercenary was the perfect ally.

As he came to the end of the narrow passage, Ben paused to listen. There was no sound coming from any direction. Turning the corner into the main corridor, he saw a bewildering sight. Falkos, perhaps five hundred feet away, was performing a strange act of ablution. He was standing by one of the trickling waterfalls. His shirt was open, and he was scooping up handfuls of the freezing water and dashing it at his face in a kind of frenzy. Frustrated by the meagerness of the flow, and by how slowly his hands were filling, he fought the waiting time with frantic tosses of his head, like a wild horse trying to snap its tether. Then, maddened by this detention of his spirit, he dropped to his knees, reached into the icy puddle on the ground and doused himself with water—his head, his neck, his chest. He made spastic motions with his body, animal sounds of pleasure and shock, and it didn't seem that he would stop. Ben thought he had become deranged.

Caught by the sight, the medic moved closer. The teacher looked up and saw him. He didn't seem in the least bit embarrassed. Jumping to his feet, he clutched at Ben. "Help me—something has happened—help me!"

But it wasn't the hopeless plea of the suicidal man he had seen a little while ago, it was euphoria; the depressive had become manic. He grabbed Ben's arm and, dripping all over the medic, pulled him into the main room. "Everything's changed, Benjamin —the world has a new face!"

Ben realized what the washing signified: an event had occurred—an emergency that also might be an opportunity—and Falkos was desperate to sober up and be equal to it. Now, in an effort to get dry, he was shaking water off himself, looking for a towel, not finding any, quaking with excitement.

"What happened?"

"Benjamin, I need you!" The words would not come fast enough. "I ask you—I beg you—don't give me any more trouble! When the time comes, drive your ambulance—be one of us!"

"What's changed?"

"Come to the Monastery!"

"Tell me."

"Cabrir is up there!"

"You said Famagusta."

"No—he's there—he's *there!*" He was berserk. "Just before

Chartas left—as if it were the most trivial thing in the world—he told me Cabrir is there!"

"How does he know?"

"Two people saw the man—two of them—one of the park workmen and a veterinarian. They saw him in a car going up the mountain. Chartas says it's not certain he went all the way up, but where else would he be going?" He was in a rapture. "I know it—I feel it in every nerve—he's up there!"

"I hope you never reach him."

Like another face of insanity, his mood changed to anger. "That's what I thought you'd say—and I don't want to hear that! You've got to be on my side, Benjamin! I can't stand it! I've got to get Cabrir—I've got to, or I'll die! I shake inside at the thought of it—and I musn't shake—I've got to be a rock—I've got to believe that—! You've got to help me!"

"Me?"

"*Approve of me!*"

The man *was* insane. It was pointless, talking to him, listening to him. Ben turned to leave.

"No!" Falkos rushed after him, grabbed him. "Don't go! Please, Benjamin, don't go! What do I have to do—how can I beg you—what can I give to get you on my side? What can I do to get your approval?"

"Approval? Christ!"

Again Ben started for the archway. This time—maudlin—bathetic—angry, weeping—Falkos threw his arms around Ben, and begged, "Listen to me—don't go—you don't know about Cabrir—don't go—just listen to me—*will you please listen?*"

The man's anguish was too unbearable; Ben couldn't leave him. Slowly disengaging himself from Falkos, he sat down.

The man shook. Then, painfully, muscle by muscle, it seemed, he pulled himself back to sanity. He started to help himself to more raki, but decided against it. Finally, when calm returned to him, it was as inordinate as the frenzy had been. Then:

"When I was in my early twenties," he said, "I was teaching school in the village where you met me, Lythia. I was unmarried. My parents had been dead for many years, and I was long past grieving for them. I had their little house which I loved, I had a secondhand Vespa motorcycle, I had a certain respect in the town, and I was very contented. In the summer I used to ride up into the mountain resorts—Platres, Troodos, Kakopetria. I gambled a little —not much—and I made love to any woman who attracted a second glance.

"In those days—it was nearly twenty years ago—General Grivas had just organized his revolutionary guerrillas, the EOKA. At first, there was no violence, only little flashes of surprise. A British flag would be burned, leaflets would appear out of nowhere, a sign would get painted on a barn in the middle of the night—Free Cyprus, Limey Go Home, Enosis. Nobody knew Grivas was behind it—he was a mystery man—he used a *nom de guerre*—Dighenis, he called himself. It was the name of a fabulous hero from Byzantine times. Very romantic. The Greek Cypriots were hungry for a legend, and they adored him.

"Then came the raids. A munitions dump was blown up, a military warehouse was attacked and emptied of all its armament, a soldiers' barracks disappeared in broad daylight. Sabotage, strikes, explosions . . . and, of course, casualties. And the certainty was growing—Cyprus would be free.

"But what did I care about freedom? I was already free. I was making a decent salary, I had wheels and I could go anywhere, I enjoyed every child in my class, I slept with any woman I wanted. What did I want with a legendary hero? I was my own hero.

"Until I met a woman named Nina Zavris. She was a creature I could never have imagined. Very strange, very ethereal, almost unearthly. She was an ornithologist and it was the most befitting work for her. She was like a bird, a linnet—never at rest, dancing in flight, making quick swoops at life, then sweeping away from it. I couldn't understand being attracted to her—she was not like any woman I had ever been drawn to—she was too insubstantial, too disturbing, too capricious. But the very first time we met, I knew I was in love with her. Yet, I felt quite sure that, while she tolerated me, she was not enravished, by any means—in fact, she was probably bored to death. It was hopeless for me, it was an agony to be in love with her.

"For weeks at a time she would totally disappear and I wouldn't know where she had gone, what had happened to her or whether I would ever see her again. And there was one preposterous thing about it. She had this ridiculous bicycle, and attached to its frame was a little saddlebag in which she carried her binoculars and a sketchbook—and she would get on the damn bike and rush off to watch the birds somewhere—and I wouldn't see her for a month. Where have you been? I would ask, and she would give me a lot of gibberish about black terns and warblers and whitethroats—and somehow I would never believe her. Do you know why? Because even when I thought she had begun to like me, she would never let me make love to her—never let me touch her—and I suspected she had another man somewhere, and that's where her trips were taking her. A married man, perhaps. Or she herself was married. Anyway, there was something unexplained.

"Then one day I noticed a strange thing. She had been away three times in a six-week period, and each time she returned, she had a new bicycle. I said to her, Nina, how does that happen? And she replied that the first bicycle belonged to her sister, and she had returned it; the second one was defective, and she had returned that one too. But then I saw something else that was suspicious. Every time she reappeared after an absence, she had a new pair of binoculars. I was on the point of asking her about that, but something told me to restrain myself, and wait.

"Meanwhile, we seemed to be getting closer to one another. One evening, I told her that I had a friend who would lend me his Renault for a few days, and would she like to ride with me out to Cape Andreas, which is wild country with an exciting sea. Her eyes went absolutely dead, and I saw a curtain closing over them. And she said, 'No, I can't go. Tomorrow morning I have to go away again.'

"So I decided to follow her.

"She lived in a guesthouse in the center of Limassol. The following day, I drove there in the borrowed Renault. I arrived in the dark, before dawn, and stationed myself where I could see the doorway, but a safe distance away. It was barely daylight when a small enclosed lorry appeared, and stopped in front of her door. In a few moments, she came out of the house and down the steps with her bicycle. A young man got out of the lorry, opened the rear door of the vehicle, and put the bicycle in. She didn't go up front with the driver, she got into the rear of the lorry, and he closed the doors on her. When the vehicle drove off, I followed it.

"We rode for a short time, until we were on the other side of Khalassa. I had to be very careful. There was no problem on the main road, but when the lorry turned onto a narrow one, I had to increase the distance between us so as not to seem suspicious. Then the road began to twist and wind up into the mountains. As it started to descend, I saw the lorry for a little while, and suddenly it was gone. I didn't know those back roads, and they did. Besides, it was the height of the grape harvest season—the macadam was slippery with crushed fruit and wet vine leaves—I had to slow down. And I didn't catch up with them. The lorry had totally disappeared. I went up and down every side road—for miles and miles—and didn't see their vehicle. Finally, I had to give up, and started to make my way up the mountain again.

"As I got to a broad shoulder of the hillside—at a place where one branch of the road goes down to the citrus villages, there was an electrical power station. Not a big one, not important except that it served a British patrolling camp in the mountains. And leaning against the rubblestone wall of the power station was Nina's bicycle.

"How stupid I was—I came to a totally wrong inference. All I could think of was my own rejection. There's a man inside that building, I said to myself, the man she came here to see, the one she really loves. She's in there with him now, they're whispering together, he's holding her in his arms. And as I thought of it, I was haunted, I had to see him, I had to see the two of them together, I had to face up to my own jealousy, to compare myself with him, to know the extent of my own inadequacy.

"So I turned the car around, drove up the hill a little way, to a position where I could see the door and not be seen. I parked and waited.

"Not long. Only about ten minutes. Then the explosion.

"It was loathsome. Two people ran out—not people—you couldn't tell whether they were men or women—just objects, bleeding. Generators—transformers—the whole power station, ripped apart—wild wires thrashing like snakes—snapping, spitting fire . . . And there wasn't any remnant of the bicycle, not a token of it.

"I didn't see Nina for two weeks. In that time the newspapers reported two other bombings, the runway of a British naval airstrip, and a convoy of three army lorries, one of the vehicles smashed to bits.

"Do you know how something appalling can turn into a macabre joke? It was the view of Nina Zavris riding a new bicycle. When I saw her I kept patting the handlebar of it, laughing at a horror.

"'You're a terrorist,' I said.

"'I'm a Greek Cypriot—and so are you.'

"The implication was that I was a slacker and a coward, that I should be doing something, throwing a bomb, laying a mine, risking my life.

"But I had no provocation to do that. My life was easy, I hated nobody, not even the British. Nina, however, had good reason to hate them. Her parents had been farmers—respectable middle-class people. Her father was a Greek patriot, even before the Grivas days, but he was not militant in any way. One afternoon a Greek guerrilla appeared. He was a fugitive and badly wounded. They let him come in and took care of him. In a few days, a detachment of British soldiers came to the Zavris farm. They found the guerrilla and when he tried to escape, they shot him. The sergeant in charge then accused Zavris of hiding other terrorists, and where were they? He denied hiding anyone else, and they started to club him. When Nina's mother interfered, they beat her as well. Her father died that night; her mother died two days later. Neither of them had been armed.

"'Everybody has a story like that,' I said to Nina. 'Some are true and some aren't.'

"I hadn't meant to imply that *she* was lying. But it was a doltish thing to say. When she heard it, it was all over between us.

"At first I tried to think: The hell with her, she's rabid. But I came to realize that she wasn't, that it was possible for a bright and reasonable woman to be willing to give her life for a patriotic cause. And I thought of that—and of her—incessantly. She—and the war—started to take over my whole mind. If I picked up a newspaper, it suddenly seemed full of British bigotries, British treacheries. If I was teaching a history lesson, I would find myself an ardent Cypriot, even to the point of altering the facts and twisting the chronicles. And one evening, in my own house, with a group of friends, I was having a rational discussion about Dighenis, and I found myself hysterically defending all his terrorism—as if my guests were disagreeing with me.

"I had talked myself into being a patriot. And I wanted to be a guerrilla.

"I went to see Nina. It was Good Friday—the sun was warm and kind—the air was like a feather. She wore a lilac-colored dress which made her blue eyes look lavender, and, gazing at her, I thought I wouldn't be able to utter a word.

"But at last: 'I want to join you,' I said, 'but I'm frightened.'

"She took me in her arms and held me, and that night, for the first time, we made love. . . . Lavender is now a bad color for me.

"That summer I lived in an abandoned granary near Limassol with twenty-six men and eight women. We were a sabotage unit, and Nina was an auxiliary arm of it. One of our men was an electrician's apprentice—seventeen years old—he made grenades out of pipe joints and petrol and adhesive tape; he put fireballs in wine bottles. He could make a bomb as big as a fruit basket, or small enough to fit into Nina's binoculars. We ran raids on army lorries and police stations and transit dumps and military warehouses.

"In the middle of summer I was put in charge of my own detachment—six men. I wanted to meet Dighenis—I didn't even know his name was Grivas—but I was always put off. I got my orders through visiting lieutenants. They would arrive, give instructions, and disappear.

"One day one of them told me I was to go on a raid with Nina. She was to be in charge—did I have any objection? No, I had none—she was far more experienced than I was. And, to myself I had to admit, far more courageous.

"Besides, this particular plan was entirely Nina's. She had negotiated the use of a meat provision lorry that supplied the mess kitchen of Camp Prassas. I drove the lorry and she dressed as a butcher boy. The mess hall of the camp adjoined a row of Nissen huts. We rode up to the gates of the encampment, the contents of the vehicle were thoroughly inspected by the guard, and we were directed to the mess hall. We delivered the eight pig carcasses, and over forty kilos of assorted meats. Sewn into one of the carcasses was a ten-pound bomb.

"On our way out, one of the chefs gave us two huge sugar macaroons. As we started to eat them, a mile away from the camp, we heard the detonation. I couldn't finish my macaroon, but Nina finished both of them.

"You mustn't think from what I've said that Nina had a heart of stone. She didn't. She was a tender woman, she was deeply compassionate. I've never known anyone who was willing to give so much of herself, so much love. And the love she gave me . . . It sounds terrible to say that in the midst of all that ruin and bloodshed I was happy—but I was. And so was she.

"We were married the day before Christmas of that year. We decided, war or no war, we would have a child immediately. The two of us had—between us—so much joy of life, that two bodies were not enough to contain it. We even knew what name we would give it. There was a birdcall that Nina especially loved. It was the sound of a certain linnet that lives only in Cyprus—and the sound is *zito, zito*. It's a wonderfully cheery sound, full of spring hope. And—agreeably—*zito* in Greek means hurrah. We used to say the word to each other, sing it to each other, *zito, zito*. . . . But the child did not come.

"Still, it was a wonderful time for us.

"Unfortunately, it was not wonderful for the Greek cause. Things were going badly. Archbishop Makarios had been exiled. There had been a cease-fire, ostensibly to negotiate a compromise peace between the Greeks and the British, but Field Marshall Harding had betrayed it. Suddenly, in the midst of the peace negotiations, thousands of British soldiers landed. The island was saturated with them, and our Turkish neighbors were now openly on the side of the British. Many of our best men were captured or killed. And that winter, as our fortunes began to decline, the faint hearts proliferated, there were defectors, traitors, informers.

"And somebody informed on me.

"That was how I came to meet General Grivas. We met in a cement bunker under the floor of a grocery store in Limassol. I was not impressed with his personality—he was vain and rigid and humorless. But what fortitude he had! He was in his sixties then, he was thin as spite, his teeth hurt and he had a bone-chilling influenza. He had just come over the snow-covered mountains, literally crawling on hands and knees—miles of it—so as not to be seen by the patrols. One of his hands had frozen and he was just beginning to be able to move the fingers. In three days, I was to learn later, he went back over the same route in the same way.

" 'You will have to have a new identity,' he said. 'New name, new papers . . . And I will have to transfer you.'

" 'With Nina?' I asked.

" 'No—alone.'

" 'If she stays, she will be in the same danger as I am. Everybody knows we are married.'

" 'I am transferring her as well,' he said. 'But somewhere else.'

" 'Why not together?'

" 'Because—as you say—everybody knows you are married. You are dangerous to each other—like arrows—follow one and find the other. . . . But don't worry—it may be only for a little while.'

" 'Where are you sending her?' I asked him.

" 'If you're caught and they question you—do you really want to have that information in your head?'

" 'No . . . Where are you sending me?'

" 'To Afxentiou.'

"We had all heard so much about Afxentiou that we felt we already knew him. In my opinion, he was the greatest hero of our revolution. He was a very young man, but the fact that he was still alive seemed impossible, for some of the risks he took were maniacal. It was a scarifying thought to be transferred to him, and I couldn't understand why I was so thrilled by it. Hearing this, I said jokingly to Grivas that it would be very difficult to keep such exciting news from my wife. The General did not see the humor.

" 'It won't be difficult. She has already been transferred.'

"I didn't even get to say goodby to her. I resented Grivas for that; it seemed a terrible lack of trust. But the man was right—no precaution was extreme enough—for by this time we were being betrayed everywhere. Mostly by our fellow Cypriots, the Turks. At the beginning, they had pretended to be neutral, but they had an underground organization called Volkan, many of whose members were secret agents of the British. Soon they were not even underground any longer, but were openly part of the Auxiliary Police. The final stage—the most terrible one—was the campaign of the Q Patrols. They were small mobile units of strong-arm men— British and Turkish—who were directed to gather informers and information, and to question prisoners. 'Question' was a euphemism, of course. They were the night raiders—they would awaken families out of sleep. They were called, in Greek, the darkness visitors. Even loyal Greeks, when captured, couldn't be expected to withstand the 'questioning.' To possess any secret knowledge was not a privilege but an affliction, and I was glad that neither Nina nor I was burdened by it.

"The place I was sent to was in the Pitsillia area—magnificent mountains. Afxentiou and his small band of men had been hounded from village to village and had finally made a hideout in a hillside cavern. They were being fed by monks and priests in the nearby churches and monasteries, and by the neighboring villages. It was uncanny how many Greeks knew his exact whereabouts, yet the British didn't. Nobody would betray him. In the first two weeks I was with him, we made eight raids, we were seen—and recognized—by countless men in vehicles, women in the fields, children even, and nobody ever exposed us. I never heard Afxentiou's name mentioned, not by anyone; it was as if he had never existed, a hero out of legend. They idolized him.

"And so did I. There is a Cypriot poem that says only in wartime can men admit love for one another. I think I could have admitted it to Afxentiou, even in peace. He would dare unimaginable dangers. Yet, he was like an anxiety-ridden mother who shook with fright if any of us took an unnecessary risk. There was not one of us for whom he wouldn't have given his life; he imperiled his life for Cyprus every day. And he was so attuned to beauty—he could stand excruciating physical pain without tears, but not a lovely poem; he was sentimental over sunsets; a moth could make him weep.

"When news came to me, through one of our reconnoiterers, that Nina would be passing through the village of Alona, less than three miles away, I knew that Grivas would never have allowed me to go in search of her. But Afxentiou did. It was only a short distance to walk, but it was difficult terrain—I didn't dare use the roads. Yet, I cannot tell you how joyously I flew across that mountainside.

"She was staying in one of the back rooms of a taverna, and as I approached the place—even before I went inside—I saw her walking toward me. She was dressed in old clothes, dun colored, but she seemed more beautiful than ever. Without having any intimation that I was nearby, she came hurrying toward the entrance. I called her name. She turned, she put her face in her hands, she began to cry. I kissed her, I lifted her, I kissed her, I laughed at her tears, I kissed her.

"We went indoors. In the semi-darkness of the taverna, three men approached us from different directions. One of them was in plainclothes, the other two were in British Army uniform. In the darker background, another man arose from a table. I couldn't see very much of his face, except that it seemed handsome, with a picturesque scar.

"The plainclothes man searched us, asked for our identity papers. He knew instantly that the documents were false—he knew us both by name. And Nina had a gun in her coat pocket.

"Outdoors, we were ordered into an army lorry and driven a long distance, it seemed, but still in the mountains. The snow was falling heavily. When the vehicle stopped on a level area, all that was visible through the snow and darkness was a huge Quonset hut and, in the distance, a number of makeshift cabins.

"Nina and I were put in separate cells in the Quonset hut. The room I was in was absolutely bare—not a cot, not a chair—only an agate basin into which I was to deposit my excrement.

"I stayed in the hut for three days, sleeping as best I could on the frigid earthen floor. The meals were minimal, porridge mostly. Through those three days, nobody came near me except for the man who delivered the food and removed the slops, and he would answer no questions about Nina.

"The worst part of the cell was that it was freezing cold. I huddled into a corner, making myself smaller and smaller to concentrate my body heat. I hoarded the warmth of my breath. If I felt I was congealing into ice, I would get up and run around the tiny room, rushing after the vapors of my pantings and wheezings. Another few days of it, I thought, and I would be insensate, beyond thaw.

"It was almost a relief when the interrogation began, for they started to question me in a warm place. It was a room with two paraffin heaters in it, and a desk between them. On the other side of the desk sat an English subaltern.

"Even before I asked about Nina, he quite considerately informed me that she was as safe as I was, and added abashedly that he knew the accommodations were not, as he put it, country garden. He was a pleasant young man who suggested old English inns, wainscotting, crackling fires, shepherd's pie. He was understated, sad and remote, a pipe smoker. Sometimes I could hardly hear what he was saying, he barely opened his mouth even when his pipe was not in it.

"All he wanted to know, he said, was where he might find Gregoris Afxentiou.

"I told him I didn't know.

"He replied that quite obviously I did know since I had just come from him and, when my visit with my wife was terminated, I would return to him.

"If he believed that to be the case, I said, why didn't he just wait until my visit was terminated, and have me followed?

"He blushed. He then admitted two things. He didn't know for certain that I *was* going back; and second, that they had tried to follow guerrillas twice in these forested mountains and once had lost track, and the second time lost soldiers, three of them, shot. Then he added, with disarming modesty, 'We're not as good at this as you are, old boy.'

"To which I answered, on a confiding note, that Afxentiou was not in these hills—the last time I had seen him was in Limassol.

"'You're trained to talk that way when questioned, aren't you?' he said. 'Add one useless truth to every falsehood.'

"He summoned a corporal, nodded to him, and in a few minutes Nina was brought into the room. I was astounded at how steady she looked. If she was living in the same sort of accommodations as I was, she showed no sign of it. Her clothes were rumpled, of course, but not herself. Her head was not lowered, her face was composed, her wholeness was as undisturbed as her eyes.

"Now the subaltern questioned both of us together. He made a statement first, reading a list of raids we had perpetrated, separately and together. Some of the items were true, some false; the list was formidable. He suggested that any random two of those offenses were sufficient grounds for having us shot.

"'If you really mean "grounds,"' Nina said, 'then you cannot shoot prisoners. Those are military offenses.'

"He smiled at her ingenuousness. 'Has a war been declared?' he asked.

"I was amazed. It went on that way, abstract talk—there was no real ominousness in the man, none at all. I had the feeling that nothing about the officer would allow him, in all British decency, to perpetrate any real violence upon us.

"Nor did he, ever. He brought us into his office many times during the next week, sometimes each of us alone, sometimes together. Occasionally, he tried to set us off against each other, but never with lies as deceitful as my own. He was playing a cricket the rules of which I could not understand, but brutality was certainly against them. He never raised his voice, and certainly not his hand.

"He left it to Cabrir. That was the young Turk's name, the man with the scar.

"About ten days after we were arrested, I was moved to a larger room in the Quonset hut. It had a cot, a small table and two chairs, and it had a paraffin heater. It was, after my gelid cell, a hearthstone of warmth. Alone in it, I sat in the chair closest to the stove until I couldn't stand the heat anymore, then I switched to the other chair. I lay on the cot, I got up, I rested my arms on the rough wooden boards of the table, I luxuriated in the feel of furniture as if it were human.

"Then Cabrir came in.

"I was standing and so was he, at the door. He indicated both chairs and asked me where I would like to sit. He was as civilized as the subaltern, offering a choice as if he were in a gentlemen's club just off St. James's Square. His voice was as softly modulated as a muted string instrument; his English was better than mine. He was leaner, taller than the average Turk, and he was handsome, with a luxurious but carefully tended mustache—black eyes—and a quickness of movement that always caught you off guard. Nina once called him a birdrat—it's a terrible rodent which destroys nests and eats young birds before they can fly, only wounding them so it can devour its prey slowly while it is still alive. Later, it became a name for Cabrir—Birdrat—and he hated it.

"When I sat down, he watched me silently but did not sit. He was diagonally across the room from me, as far as he could get, as if not wishing to crowd me.

"'The subaltern tells me he has given you ten days,' Cabrir said. 'He now gives me only four more—so that it will be an even fortnight. In that time, I must find out where Afxentiou is. Will you kindly tell me that?'

"'I don't know.'

"'I'm glad—for a start—that you refuse to tell me. Most interrogators pretend they do not like to torture people. They don't even use that word. I am more honest. I do. I will ask you a second time. Where is Afxentiou?'

"'I don't know.'

"'Now. To make complete the ritual of three. The last time: where is Afxentiou?'

"'I don't know.'

"He walked unhurriedly across the room and struck me across the head. Instead of falling from the chair, I got up. I faced him. I did nothing.

"'Strike me back,' he said.

"I didn't.

"'Strike me back—I'm not angry enough—strike me back.'

"I hit him as hard as I could. I hit him again and again, and he just stood there. Then, with the coldest rage I have ever seen, he beat me so that I could barely see. I fought back, but it was useless

—he was more experienced, he was stronger, he had fists like mallets, and when they did not punish me enough, he shoved me against the wall, and crashed at me with his elbows, then he pushed me against the doorframe and pounded my head against the wooden jamb, until I no longer knew he was doing it.

"When he left, I lay bleeding on the floor, I don't know how long. It had been daylight when he had come in. The light through the tiny window had gone and come again, and still I lay on the floor, unable to move.

"That afternoon he returned. 'Where is Afxentiou?'

"I muttered that I didn't know. Again he beat me. Just as he was leaving, he turned at the door.

"'Would you like to know what is happening to your wife?'

"He stood there without expression. He didn't say anything else, didn't tell me a word about Nina, simply departed, leaving me to think of her, a new torture.

"It revivified me. I started to scream her name. I didn't know where she was in the building, or even if she might be in another one. I screamed and screamed in the hope that she would hear me and yell back. Not that I thought our shrieks would serve any purpose, except that I might know she was alive. In any event, I *had* to scream.

"I didn't hear any sound of her. No responding call at all—not from my wife or my jailers—hardly even the echo of my own voice. Thinking of Nina, I began to cry. What could I do without her? If they were going to use her as an instrument of torture, I would totally disintegrate. I might be able to endure the beatings, I might endure any other unnameable horrors, but if they harmed Nina, and threatened to harm her more, I would do anything they told me, I would betray Afxentiou, I would tell them everything.

"The following day Cabrir came back with two other men, Turks. One of them had a mound of iron chains in his outstretched arms, and all I could think was: If you're going to beat me with chains, that many are not necessary, a short length will do. But that was not their purpose.

"I was slumped in a chair, every cell in my body aching, scarcely able to move. Cabrir took the other chair, sat astride, his forearms on the back of it, paying no attention to me, watching the men. There was a metal bar that extended diagonally across the room about eight feet off the floor. The men were attaching three pulleys to the bar, and through them they threaded the chains. In the middle one, they attached a leather strap which they caught back upon itself, and it became a noose.

"They were ready for me now, they said.

"The two men moved me off the chair, pulled me to the corner of the room, and held me while Cabrir strapped me into the contrivance. The noose hung around my neck, not tightly at first. The two side chains were a harness through which they pulled my arms, so that the chains drew firmly around my shoulders. Suddenly the men drew the metal lines through the outside pulleys and I heard the rattle of iron, and felt the chains tighten under my armpits.

"I was too terrified to utter a word. I started twice to say *ochi*, *ochi*, but even 'no' would not say itself.

"'This is called the *Yular*,' Cabrir said. 'It means the Halter. *Yular* is a Turkish word, but actually we owe this clever contraption to the French.'

"He then went on as if he were demonstrating a parlor game. The chains would lift me slightly off the floor. The weight of my body would be borne by the left and right chains, which would be slightly more taut than the halter chain, in the middle. My arms and shoulders would be carrying my weight. The pain would be in those places. If, however, I should let go and not carry my weight by the side chains, the center chain would carry it, and the halter would tighten around my neck.

"As he was saying this, they were tying my hands behind my back. Whatever they were using—thongs, I think—cut into my flesh. When he saw me shrink away from it, he said it was the subtlest intimation of what was to come.

"'Where is Afxentiou?'

"I didn't answer.

"I felt the soft flap of the chains on my shoulders, loosening a moment, then the bite of iron in my armpits. As my body lifted off the floor, I moaned. He looked at me quickly and I stopped making the noise. He said for me to go on, I wasn't gagged, I could make whatever sounds I wanted.

"I didn't feel the full force of the pain until the men left the room. The chains chewed into my flesh, my bones turned to knives, and the sheer ache of carrying my own body seemed unendurable, as if I had become mountainous. If I could touch the floor for an instant, if one single toe could bear some of the burden, I could suffer the rest. I tried to stretch myself, my torso, my thighs, my calves—only another inch, a fraction—but I couldn't reach. And it occurred to me that the very closeness of the floor—that too was part of the torture—the earthly foothold just barely beyond reach.

"I don't know how long I hung that way—perhaps a few hours—when I knew I couldn't stand it any longer. The pain in my shoulders was intolerable. And from my armpits I could feel the warm wetness of coursing blood. Desperately I knew I had to let up a little, allow my arms to hang looser, relieve them of some of the tearing strain.

"Gently, I said, let go gently, one erg of energy at a time, gently. Even before I gave myself the easement, the thought of it comforted me, and I indulged it. As I got myself ready to let go, the sweat poured down my forehead and into my eyes. Now, I told myself, now is the time for a breath of relief.

"The deliverance was an ecstasy. Maybe he lied to me, I thought, maybe it will be a lesser pain than I can endure. Then I felt it. First, at my throat, choking me. Then the sudden tension, and the terror. Quickly I lifted myself, crying out against the biting of the chains. As I supported my body once more, I thought: What if I should faint? If I stop carrying myself, I will either be strangled, or my neck will be broken. Must I then be conscious every instant of the agony, can't I even be allowed the respite of unconsciousness? No, I was not permitted any collapse—except of the mind and will.

"I heard Nina's voice. A scream, it cut the air. It was a more tormented outcry than I had ever uttered, or heard.

"I don't know how many times I shrieked her name. Then there was deathly silence, and it was the worst time of all. Like a hedonistic corruption, my physical pain became a pleasure that I yielded to, rather than thinking of what might have happened to my wife. I counted the pangs as a function of breath: how many inhalations per how many spasms; then, more refinedly, how many excruciating agonies per how many bearable aches.

"There is a small mercy about pain that, when it gets too afflictive, it gives no indication how much one is suffering. It was a mercy they took away from me, by bringing Nina in so I could see her.

"She had been beaten. But the terrible part was not what *I* saw, but what *she* saw. She looked at me, enchained and bleeding, and she cried out oh Jesus, oh Jesus.

"I told her not to look at me, to turn away, to close her eyes, I begged them to take her away. Oh Jesus, she cried.

"At that moment I wanted to terminate her agony more than mine. 'Shall I tell them what they want to know?' I said.

"But she would not answer. No matter how much Cabrir urged her, she would say neither yes nor no to me. But he kept at her and at her. Finally, she couldn't stand it any longer—she called him Birdrat, and she struck him. He did nothing to her, merely nodded to the two men, and all four of them went away.

"Something blessed happened: the night. I realized I had seen the day through and the throes were no worse. By morning I had developed a grim expertise: by striking a balance of weight on all three chains so that my neck and arms carried their burden equally, I could lessen the pain everywhere. Not that it was less than racking, but it was almost tolerable. Sometimes, when my reflexes failed me, I would upset the aching equilibrium and scream; sometimes, when I felt I might faint or fall asleep, I purposely upset it, and screamed mostly to vivify awareness.

"In the middle of the morning, Cabrir came again. It was his fourth day, his last. Nina was with him, between the same two guards. She looked deathly. Not as if she had been beaten again, but the deathliness of one who has become mortally ill, and has willed it. She stood as straight as she always did, her head as lofty, but there was sickness in her.

"Cabrir studied me from head to toe—clinically—as though I were already a cadaver and he was going to perform a postmortem on me. He looked behind me to gaze at my bound hands, he leaned to feel a muscle in my calf, reached up to see what the chain was doing to my neck.

"Then he said, 'Afxentiou?'

"I didn't answer.

"He said he had no more time—only today. 'Afxentiou?'

"Again I did not answer.

"He then asked me if I understood Turkish, and I replied that I knew only a few words. That disappointed him, he said, because it would have given him pleasure to tell me in Turkish what they were going to do to me. Then he used the words *hadim etmek,* and repeated them two or three times. There's an obscene Cypriot joke that has the word *hadim* in it. It means eunuch.

"Nina spoke. Her voice was no louder than a reed in the wind. She asked what he was going to do.

"I begged him to send her away.

" 'No—tell her,' he said.

"She kept repeating her question, what were they going to do?

"When Cabrir saw I wouldn't tell her, 'Geld him,' he said.

"She made wild movements with her hands, as if she were fighting an attack of rodents.

"They were already undressing the lower part of my body. Not haphazardly; they were making a ritual of it, so that the portent would be as tormenting as the experience itself—and I would have time and trial to reconsider.

"My boots were off, my stockings.

"No, she kept crying, no.

"I was naked from the waist down. Then she saw Cabrir with the knife in his hand.

" 'No!'

"She broke away from the men and ran to me. Cabrir stepped aside to allow her to do so. She took me in her arms, clung to me. 'Tell them!' she cried. 'Tell them what they want to know!'

"Gently, quite deferentially, Cabrir led her away from me. When she was again in the hands of her captors, he turned to give me a questioning look. She had done his work for him—the man could see that I was going to do what Nina said. He spoke softly:

" 'Your wife has saved your manhood.'

"Manhood . . . the word was suddenly ambiguous. I hardly knew what it meant, what part of me it was, whether it was in my brain or my spirit or my testes, whether it was in my love of a woman, or of myself, or even—I am not a religious man—in a love of God I never knew I had.

"Something occurred that I will never understand. At times—later—I was tempted to call it my single act of heroism. But over the years, I have come to perceive that it was something less than that—it was my instant of great perversity. Cabrir had blundered. If he had made me witness *Nina's* torture—or if he had never brought my wife into my presence—or if he had never said 'manhood'—the likelihood is that I would have told him what he wanted to know. But with Nina in the room—a woman who would sacrifice her courage—sacrifice what she held most dear about herself for my sake—I had to know where my true 'manhood' was.

" 'Where is Afxentiou?'

"I spat at him.

"I felt the first knife cut, the pain, the flow of warmth. I felt the second too.

"I do not know what happened then, I was unconscious. Afxentiou told me later that Nina had tried to interfere, a guard had grabbed her, and Cabrir had said something about the torture continuing, this time upon herself. The knife that had been used on me was on the table. She tore herself free for an instant, grabbed the thing and plunged it into herself. But not well. She was alive when Afxentiou's bomb went off. I was supposed to have returned ten days previously, and when I didn't, he guessed that I'd been taken. They went to the taverna, heard about our arrest, and started searching for us. When they found us, Afxentiou dispatched one of the men—Pavlos Chartas—to set off a distraction bomb.

"Later, I was told that Nina lived for a few hours after Afxentiou arrived—but for days I was not aware of everything that had happened, I was not aware of what had been done to me. When they finally told me what I had become, I hardly heard them. For a long time, all I knew was that Nina was dead. The other knowledge came afterward."

Falkos sat in utmost quiet. He drank the last drop of nonexistent raki out of his empty glass. He stared at nothing.

"How did Cabrir get away?" Ben said.

"Nobody knew. He always seems to disappear. It plagues me to think that he gets some favorite smile of fortune. I can't believe that his gods can be more powerful than ours. And they won't be. I've almost had him a dozen times. This will be the last. And then . . . the war will be over."

"I don't believe it."

"Oh yes—over! *Cabrir is the war!* And I've planned how to put an end to it! I will make it die in torture! And I will see it happen—in *him!* When I catch him I won't kill him, understand, I'll nurture him—because he's precious to me. I'll keep him alive as long as I can, so that the death of war will be a ritual I'll always remember. It will be sad to see war die, because it is our greatest venture—but it will be joyous as well. So I'll prolong his agony. At first I'll feed him, and later I'll watch him being gnawed by hunger. I'll give him nectar, and then I'll make him drink acids that corrode him. And toward the end, I'll invent special gouges, special racks—things that will burn and contort him. I'll never let him get bored with banal agonies, I'll devise a new one as soon as the old one palls. There will always be some new torture he can choose for himself, like a child's dream of toyland, so that he will never spend one day of commonplace suffering, and his whole life will be an ecstasy of pain. I'll never give him relief from it, and if he should die before I do, I'll mourn him."

Ben turned from the horror of it. He thought of Falkos as a young man, leading a good life—a cherished and cherishing teacher, in his first true rapture with a woman, loved and loving, capable of limitless felicities. How beautiful the world must have seemed to him then! And here he was, a ruin of a man, wrecked not because of the damage that had been done to his body—others had triumphed over worse impairments—but because his spirit was devastated beyond repair. The tragic, joyless man—begging for the forgetfulness in raki, and in the vicarious pleasure of peeking through keyholes at other people's loves. Tell me about Kalya, he had said, tell me! As if he himself had never known such an ex-perience—tell me about love!

Falkos's manner was quieter now, but his voice was fervid.

"Cabrir is up there." He said it, then softly repeated it, a lit-any. He leaned across the table, and with a desperate need for Ben's partisanship: "This is not a wanton cruelty on my part, Ben-jamin—you see that, don't you? I don't go about brutalizing peo-ple—I don't. I'm asking only for the most essential retribution—I need an end to this—a final justice. You do understand that, Ben-jamin—don't you? Don't you, Benjamin?"

He was pleading for confirmation—a license, a sanction, an absolution—as if Ben were his judge, his father, his priest. The medic could cry for him, but . . .

"How can I agree with that?" he said. "I can't believe—I can't ever believe that revenge is the better part of justice."

A silence.

"Will you come with us?"

Ben hoped the question would turn out to be academic. With some luck, Louka would get him out of the cave.

"Will you?" Falkos persisted.

"Would you let me out of here if I said no?"

"No . . . I would have you killed."

"Then there it is again—I have no choice. I'm not suicidal—yes, I'll come."

"Willingly?"

Ben smiled grimly. "Love me, the rapist said."

"Yes—love me! Be my friend—love me! Or be my doctor—treat me—give me something—I'm in pain!"

"I'm sorry, Falkos. I have nothing for your ailment . . . And you may die of it."

He hated hearing himself say it, and wanted to take it back, but couldn't. He hurried away from the table and went through the archway. In the corridor, confronting himself more honestly, he realized that, mixed with his shame for having pronounced the man's mortality and for the complacent superiority that an ethical position confers, there was the tiniest quiver of satisfaction in being able to have his own revenge. Only moments before, he had decried revenge as the crueler part of justice, and here he was, finding satisfaction in it.

Hating the role of retributive judge, he recalled Falkos's charge that doctors were sadists. The so-called honesty of the physician, he had said, signified cruelty, especially when announcing the death sentence. The teacher's remark now had a cutting significance to him. He himself—uttering death—had been cruel. But if he had been vengeful, he defended himself, it was because of the sickness in the man, and against the sickness, not the man. It was the *disease* that was the doctor's enemy, it was the fear of conquest by the disease that provoked the word of cruelty, the cry for reprisal. Could it be that this was not altogether an evil impulse, and that he might be weak in thinking it was? Could it be that, hidden deeper in this thought, there was an explication of his fear of being a doctor? . . . He felt he might be onto something, but he was reluctant to pursue it. Lurking, there was an indeterminate dismay somewhere.

In the hallway, he wasn't paying attention to where he was going. If he had put his mind to it, he probably would be going to his own cell. But he found himself, instead, in the narrower passageway, outside Mark's room. On the verge of turning away, he remembered that Kalya and the boy had been talking raptly when he had left them, and now there was not a whisper coming from the dark. Strained and curious, he took the few steps to the threshold and looked in.

Kalya was asleep. She lay on the earth floor, huddled as if cold. Across the room, on the mattress, the boy too was asleep. He looked more comfortable than she did, serenely undisturbed, no hint of care or riot, not a sign that he had ever had a troubled visitation.

They had turned the lamp down quite low. It fluttered as if it wanted to expire. He speculated whether to turn it out entirely and let them sleep, but then Kalya made a murmuring sound, an unhappy one.

He wanted to wake her with the word "beloved." He had always thought it a maudlin term, he had never addressed it to anyone. But now . . . beloved, he wanted to say. It was a self-exposing word; one daren't say it unless certain that the beloved would say it in return.

He heard the murmur again, a soft lament.

"Kalya."

She didn't hear him. Then, when he touched her gently and whispered her name again, she awakened with a cry, "No," she said. Then no, a number of times.

"It's all right," he comforted. "You were having a bad dream —it's all right, Kalya."

". . . No," she said. This time the no was not part of the dream, but of the waking. Even half-conscious, she was saying that whatever it was it wasn't all right, no. But when she saw his face so solicitously close to hers, as if to retract the syllable, she touched him gently on the cheek, and put her mouth to his. Beloved or not, he thought, I'm a respite from her dream.

As she tried to move, she winced a little, with a crick from having lain on the cold, rocky earth. Laughing, she made a joke of the petty tragedy. "If you can't sleep on the ground," she said with mock sententiousness, "then youth has fled."

"And hope has flown." They smiled to each other. "Tell me what will comfort you."

"Take me to bed," she said.

She looked across the room at the sleeping boy. "Will he be all right?"

"He would have been all right—without either of us." He realized it wasn't altogether true, that he might be reacting a bit jealously to their closeness.

"You're wrong," she said quietly.

She stretched a little, tried to adjust the lamp so it wouldn't flicker itself out, then looked at Mark again. She crossed through the dimness and stood over his bed. A long time she gazed at him. Then slowly, without reservation, unmindful of Ben's presence, she

leaned over and kissed the boy on the forehead—tenderly, as if he
were a child whose prayers she had just heard. It was a fragile kiss,
innocent, there was nothing amorous about it, yet Ben felt as if he
were watching an erotic secret between them, and he would rather
not have seen it.

When they were undressing, he wanted to refer to it but
couldn't. Then, when he realized it was his own guilty secret, not
hers, and that Kalya had nothing to confess with regard to the boy,
he asked, "Why did you kiss him?"

"Because . . . I was leaving him alone in the dark."

He was about to point out that there was a light in the room,
but he knew she meant nothing so literal. She simply regretted
leaving him—wanted to be there, in case he awakened, to tell him
anything that would console him; she would, in as many ways as
the word had meanings, lighten things for a night-stricken boy.
Ben wished she would do the same for him—if only the darknesses
with regard to her past. Would he ever know the truth of her? He
felt as though they were parallel lines moving along at a distance
from one another, waiting to meet in some doubtful infinity.
Infinity had always seemed a future, not a past.

This would be their last night together. How could he tell her
how much he loved her without her hearing a goodby in it?

When they were in bed, "I love you, Kalya."

"Don't love me too much."

But as if giving the lie to the words, she clung to him with the
desperation that dreads a parting. Not that they gave utterance to
any farewell, or even hinted at it, but there was an evanescence in
their lovemaking. They loved and didn't know why they loved,
feeling like witless people who knew just enough about one another for their passion to be genuine, yet feeling that they had not
been initiated in a vital rite of the human mystery. He was certain
he was more benighted than she was, and it grieved him. Where do
I go to find you, he felt himself begging, what past agony do you
hide in, where can I go to give you pity, if you want it, and the
kind of loving tenderness you gave the boy, how can I bring you
the love gratification you haven't had in years, where do I go to retrieve whatever joyous part of you that life has pillaged?

He tried to find her by kissing her, by touching her, by probing every secret part of her person, searching for the rest of her.
And as if she were trying to say with her corporality what she
could not say in words, she exposed her body more openly than

ever before, divulging herself to him in all her orifices, wanting him to enter everywhere, inviting him to discover her in her most clandestine places. And as he came, the discovery was almost complete and he thought any moment she too would be coming, and he would hear in her orgasmic outcry what it was she had needed for this long time, and that he had helped her find it. But something thwarted her, there was no climax, and there was no revelation.

They fell asleep simultaneously, it seemed, but soon he was awake, aware that in some loving way she had insinuated herself into his arms. He wanted to lie there, open-eyed and alert, to savor the pleasure of it, his hand on her breast, feeling her warmth and the soft rise and fall of her breathing. He thought he was managing very well to prolong this bittersweet vigil, and was totally unaware that he had again fallen asleep.

Something startled him awake. He heard the signal—the kithara. Louka, calling him; time to leave.

Jolting, he got out of bed. Not thinking—still half asleep—hectic—he started to dress.

"What's the matter?" Kalya said.

"I've got to go and—"

He stopped. He had almost given himself away. Abruptly it occurred to him what an idiotic blunder he had made. Louka wasn't playing the right song—and it wasn't even the right night. It was *tomorrow* evening that the signal would be given.

Kalya too had heard the strumming music. "Did the playing awaken you?"

He could risk her knowing that much. "Yes."

"Why were you getting dressed?"

"I don't know—a dream—crazy."

Her silence told him she knew it was a lie, that she might even suspect it was a signal of his going. Yet, this time she was accepting what she knew. She did not try to dissuade him from his obsession, as she would not be dissuaded from her own, to carry a gun. She had reconciled herself to his departure and the likelihood she would never see him again, as she had long ago reconciled herself to all departures, finalities, deaths. She knew there was no promise that could be trusted, and she knew the world would end. The termination of all existence might indeed be what she wished for; she expected no more futures, nor did she think mankind deserved them.

And if she seemed stoical about such things, it was the bravery to deceive. She ached. And loving her, he wanted to impart his hope of life, his high romantic hope that love does indeed break freshets through the rocks, that neither of them would ever die, that this was not goodby, he would not listen to goodby, that they would be together when the assault was over, and that if they loved . . .

There was the rub, of course. Love was the potent energy, the magic power that might make it possible. And if she did not have it . . . Suddenly he realized that whether or not she was in love with him was not a matter of the heart alone, but also of the will; being in love was a question of courage. In a world of hatred, to let one's self be in love was an act of valor, and perhaps she was no longer equal to it, perhaps this was the desideratum without which she would never reach the orgasmic zenith to which she achingly aspired. . . . If he had pitied her before, this was his most poignant compassion.

The darkness in the room seemed to become a substance; it thickened. Almost inaudibly, she said, "Ben . . . I have something to tell you."

"Yes?"

"The other times—when we made love—I always took special care . . . but this time I didn't. I don't want you to think it was an oversight. If a child is born, it won't be an accident."

He was astonished. He didn't know how to interpret what she had said. "Why, Kalya?"

"Because—obviously—I want to have your child."

"Perhaps you love me more than you say."

"I don't want you to think that. I had Savvas's child—and I didn't love him."

Then why was she telling him? Because it was a new way of keeping him from going up alone? He couldn't believe it was the time-tattered use of pregnancy to get a man to do something he doesn't want to do, marry the woman or take the job, or both, or agree not to climb a mountain. If she was lying to keep him safe, why didn't she tell him a more powerful lie—and say she *did* love him? It would be even more effective with Ben—why didn't she do it?

Perhaps, because she was not lying at all. She did want his child, even if she didn't love him, even if he meant no more to her than Savvas. So he mustn't get sentimental about what such a pregnancy might signify to her.

But it did signify *something*. He was wrong about her fear of letting herself love someone: she had the courage to have another child. How could she do it? Would it take a lesser order of devotion, a safer hazard than committing herself to a man? It occurred to him there was another reason: she had a greater faith in the future than in the present. Tomorrow could not possibly be as cruel as yesterday; her child's world would be kinder than her own. She wanted a child—his child!

And it made him happy. Whatever reservations were attached to his relationship with Kalya, he hoped that the child would know that it had not been conceived without love. And that on the night when its mother had said a child might be born, and life should continue, its father had been filled with joy.

If only it had happened sooner. Or on another island, or in another world.

10

How bizarre it felt, the following evening, to be so glibly talking at a dinner table, knowing that before the night was over he would be running free, or dead . . . or, of course, still imprisoned in the cave. Covertly, he looked at his watch. It was 8:03. Louka had said nine o'clock. Within less than an hour, he would hear the sound of the kithara . . . or not hear it.

It had been a harrying day, the air charged as if on the point of spontaneous explosion. Mostly, it was the planes. Falkos had been wrong. The flights had not ceased. On the contrary, the day had been a bluster of them. From early dawn until now, the onset of darkness, they had been coming and going, without discernible pattern, swooping down from high altitudes, then whipping wildly out of sight, amok in the sky. Or they had simply hovered as slowly as helicopters, two or three at a time, never more than four. A constant drill was going on, in preparation.

In the afternoon, Georghiou, the salt man, had come in with the dressed moufflon on his shoulder. There had been an argument, almost to the point of blows, between him and Mikis, as to whether the meat of the wild sheep could be eaten without having been hung and aged. Even after Kalya had settled it by saying she knew a special way of cooking it, the argument broke out anew with insults and recriminations.

The most recent disturbance was the report—from Georghiou —that Louka had gone off on his free time a half hour earlier than scheduled, and nobody knew where to find him. Nor had he returned by dinnertime. Somebody said he might be drunk; somebody said there could be a woman, somewhere. Their speculations were disquieting.

At the table, Georghiou said, "I admit it—it is not aged enough." However he took another helping of the roast meat.

Mikis accepted this as an apology, but said grudgingly, "It is not aged at all. We are eating live flesh."

But they were gorging themselves on it. So were Yannis and Falkos. Even Mark did not seem to mind that he himself had killed the animal; he ate quietly and steadily, as if he were keeping a schedule. Ben had a few bites and inconspicuously slowed down, then halted. He was too on edge to eat. When he glanced at his watch, he tried to do it unnoticeably, his hand in his lap. It was only 8:10.

He looked at Kalya. Like him, she was not eating at all, but she had a better pretext than he did. She was waiting on the men. How gracefully she does everything, he thought. She might be serving dinner anywhere but in this cellar of a cave. She could be in Seismos, or on a fashionable hotel terrace somewhere in Famagusta, or on a height overlooking the sea near Kyrenia, or under a grape-leaved arbor on a beach near Limassol. More and more, in reverie, he kept imagining her in a future peacetime, on a city street, in an art museum, reflected in a shopwindow, on a seaside, barefooted, making footprints in the damp, tide-forsaken sand. He heard her voice, and gulls, and murmurings of water. . . . No, Kalya, he vowed in his mind, I will never say goodby to you.

The men were complimenting her on the food. Falkos led the way. He raised his wineglass to her. "You make a cave seem like a salon."

Yannis was the most appreciative. "Even my mother would say it is good. How did you marinate it so fast? What do you call it?"

"*Tavas*," she said.

"*Tavas* is made with lamb, not with wild sheep," Mikis said. He was the only dinner dissident.

"*Stifadho, yahni*," she replied. "Call it what you like."

"I will call it sheep with garlic and onions," Georghiou said. He had an enormous mouthful; the brown juices dripped on his chin.

Mikis said, "You know, it is illegal for us to eat this."

Falkos corrected him. "It's not illegal to eat it, it's illegal to kill it."

"How do you eat it if you do not kill it?" asked Georghiou.

Mark didn't put the forkful in his mouth. "Why is it illegal to kill it?"

"It's an endangered species."

"So are we," Yannis said.

Some laughed, others ate.

Mark stopped eating. Mikis pointed to Mark and then to Ben. "You see? The Americans do not eat very much."

"So is what?" said Yannis.

"So—in all my life I do not kill a moufflon. And come the Americans and a sheep is dead. But I eat—and they do not."

"So? You enjoy the taste of the animal, and the American does not. There is a lesson in this?"

Mikis was getting tempery again. "Yes, there is. We do not kill for no reason—and because of this, we have no guilt. So we can eat."

"This is very deep, what you say," Yannis rejoined. "Deep like a pile of sheepshit."

"Softly, softly," Falkos said to both of them.

"What, softly?" Yannis said. "It is talk like this that makes people angry at one another. It is talk like this—"

In the middle of what looked like a peroration, the old man farted. It was loud and he was embarrassed to have done it at the table. He apologized. To those who hadn't heard the fart, he explained what he had done so that his apology would not seem pointless. Ben laughed, delighting in the old man, and Yannis, seeing himself appreciated, joined Ben's merriment. The laughter was theirs alone at first, not so much at any jollity that had occurred, but with a kind of happiness that they understood one another, and had one another. Oddly, it was Mark to whom this gladness was first communicated. The old man had in some way endeared himself to the boy and now, on impulse, Mark hugged him and called him *Pappos*. The Greek had probably never been called grandfather, and, liking it, he farted again, and the men praised his virtuosity—no longer an accident but an art.

"Fill your glasses," the teacher said. "I want to propose a toast."

There were two wine bottles on the table. As Georghiou reached for one of them, Falkos lifted the other, filled his own glass, then—after a cursory reference to Ben—began to fill Mark's.

"That's enough," the boy said. He stopped the teacher before there was more than a half inch in his glass. He had had nothing to drink all evening, and Ben thought a little wine wouldn't hurt him, not like the two shots of dynamite raki that had exploded in his brain last night. Besides, the boy had been tense all day, wretched, and it looked now as if the laughter and his fondness for Yannis had released him a little; the wine also might be good for him.

"A toast!" Falkos said. "An hour ago I received word from Kirios Chartas that the time will be—tomorrow!"

The table clatter stopped. Only silence, then the glances. There was a confused traffic in the rapid darting of eyes, quick looks that flew past one another, all wanting to alight somewhere. Ben's glimpse of Kalya was brief; she blinked and turned away. Yannis's eyes went back and forth from Falkos to Ben, and so did Mark's. Even the eyes of the guerrillas were not still.

"So this is a toast to the morning—and to all of us," Falkos continued. "Tomorrow—as the sun rises—we go up to the Monastery. It will be—for me—the end of darkness. So I toast the new day."

Not giving utterance to it, he was offering a salute to Cabrir, a fanfare not to a detested enemy but to a cherished friend. The others raised their glasses with him. But they had not caught his febrile mood; his news had subdued them. Whatever lofty toasts he intoned about sunrises and new days, there would be gunfire tomorrow, and grenades and Christ knew what else; and fewer of them to raise glasses tomorrow night. When he sat down, they all made little mouthings, hardly audible, but nobody arose to offer another toast, and nobody uttered one aloud. Yet, Ben had the sense that each of them was offering a libation to something or somebody, and a few of the prayers were standard to men afraid.

His own toast, also in the quiet, was not a prayer: Father Demetrios. I hope you're still alive. I hope—if you're in pain—that I can ease it a little for you. I hope you're well enough to speak with me again. I hope I can thank you. Not for being a great man or a great artist or a great priest. Not even for being there. But for a vision I have of you—real or imaginary, sane or deluded . . . a vapor on a mountaintop that I must climb to reach . . . a dream I have of myself that I must make true . . . a vital madness.

It was 8:35.

A pall had come over the table. Now, to add to it, they heard the planes again, louder than ever. Only briefly this time—a whirr, a whooshing sound, and they were gone.

Falkos's reflex to the noise was swiftest. Of anyone, he seemed the most unnerved by it. So it was he who made the most elaborate effort to restore the cheerfulness that his toast had dispelled. With excessive exuberance, he raised his arm and his voice: "Kalya! I have to have some more of this *tavas!* It's the most luscious delicacy I've ever eaten in my life. It has some special flavor, some special condiment. What's the spice in it?"

"Anxiety," Mark said.

The word was so caustic that there was an instant of nothing. Then Falkos howled with fabricated laughter. "What a brilliant notion! How clever of you, Mark! Have some more wine!"

His fake gaiety didn't hide how the boy had nettled him. Before Mark could object, the teacher had filled his glass to the brim.

I hope he doesn't feel challenged by the man, Ben thought, I hope he doesn't feel that he must drink it.

Mark looked at Falkos, at Ben, at Kalya. Then he slowly reached for the glass, and as steadily as possible placed it alongside Falkos's plate.

"I've had enough—you have it." As he saw the start of a demurrer, "Go ahead—you can drink it out of my glass—what I have isn't catching."

"Are you sure?"

"Yes. I'd be more likely to catch something from you."

The teacher who had been openly admired by the boy was now being attacked by him, and he didn't know why. "Me? Catch something from me?"

"Yes."

"What?"

"Fear."

"You're not seeing fear in me tonight. Quite the contrary, my boy. Excitement."

"You've lost your nerve about *me.*"

Here it was, then. "How do you know that?" Falkos asked.

"I've seen it—all day. A kind of contempt. Just because I shot that moufflon, you've given me up, haven't you?"

Falkos saw the hurt in the boy. He was suddenly the good teacher again. His voice had a gentle strength, a reassurance in it. "No, I haven't, Mark. It's simply that Ben is going with us after all.

But there will be room for you—somewhere—I give you my word."

"Thank you, Falkos." He was subdued. "I'm sorry I was a shit."

The leader arose, and the dinner party was over. Georghiou was the first to depart, and a short while later Mikis followed him. Falkos muttered something about preparations, and Ben wondered what they might be. There would be intercom instructions from Chartas, of course, and to his own men. And what about the planes—what did they signify? Ben tried not to think about any of it; he had his own tactic—not tomorrow, tonight. If he heard the signal . . .

It was 8:40. Unless it happened in the next twenty minutes, it would mean that Louka had failed. . . . 8:41.

Falkos loitered at the archway. "We leave right before daybreak, Ben—you understand?"

"I understand."

The teacher pointed to Mark. "Can you get yourself up, or shall I wake you?"

"I can get myself up."

Falkos departed. Almost the instant he left the room, Mark said, "I like that man."

"Why?" Yannis said. "Because he will let you join him? He has to. You know too much. You either go *with* him, or he will leave you here—dead."

"Don't say that, goddamn it! He's better than all of us!"

Yannis was startled by the outburst. His affection for the boy was genuine; they had made a warm correspondence with each other. He hadn't meant to damage it in any way. "I am sorry," the old man said. There was no pretense in the apology; the Greek was upset. "We have a saying: When you go into battle, it is the best to believe that the corporal is a general." He put both hands on his belly. "I eat too much, I drink too much and I talk too much. I will go for a small walk."

Kalya didn't watch the old man go; her eyes were on Mark. "Do you really think Falkos is better than all of us?"

"That's not the point." Defensively. "Why shouldn't I like him?"

"What do you like about him?"

"I don't know—I've got a thing about teachers." Then, unthinking: "Have you ever been one?" He blushed.

"Thank you," she said. "Was your first love a teacher?"

The boy, last night, had begun to be drawn by her magnetism, but all through the day he had seemed to regret it—as a weakness—and had retreated to mere civility. Now he retreated still further, almost to his original insolence. "No, my first love was a crybaby named Lissa. One night, when I was having a seizure, she peed in her pants and ran home."

"Didn't a teacher ever run out on you?"

"Never. On the contrary."

"What's the contrary of running out?"

"Somebody who's there until you see it through. I had a math teacher—her name was Mrs. Merrill—she was wonderful. She taught me algebra as if she were letting me in on a personal secret. She let me invent the binomial theorem."

"She let you 'invent' it?"

"Yes—I was nine years old. I had a problem I couldn't solve and I had no idea there *was* such a thing as a binomial theorem. So I made it up."

"And she didn't tell you it had been there before you were born?"

"No, I thought it was mine, and she didn't have the heart to take it away from me. She let me keep it for a while."

Kalya nodded. By allowing him to prove his point, she had won her own. Another obstacle between them was down. "Yes, that does prove to the contrary."

"Does it?" Ben looked at Mark. "Didn't it hurt to have it taken away?"

"A little, yes."

"Wouldn't it have made you just as happy if she had told you—right off—that you had earned your membership in the society of great mathematicians?"

"*No!*"

Mark and Kalya said it so loudly and so perfectly in unison that they both laughed. Then they laughed louder because Ben joined them, and then they laughed simply because they were laughing, not quarreling anymore; they were actually listening to one another, not probing for weaknesses, for vulnerabilities that could be attacked. It was Kalya who had done it, adroitly. She had made them seem to be a family more real than Mark's foster family; and—to hear him tell of his last beating by his foster father—more charitable to his sensibilities.

"And after he gave you the beating," Kalya was asking, "what happened?"

"I stopped calling him father and started to call him Frankos."

"What did you call your foster mother after that?" she continued.

"Nothing. I just said You—her name became You."

"That was mean." But she smiled. "If he was a monster, it wasn't her fault."

"Yes, it was. She never backed me up, she never risked a damn thing for me. And for a long time she played me a dirty little trick. She was dumb—and she used her stupidity like a cat-o'-nine-tails—that was her way of beating me. If I said anything she didn't understand, she would make me simplify it and simplify it until I was making mush, and then she'd laugh and smear it all over me. It was her triumph—she made me as stupid as she was."

"And as cruel."

Vexed, he struck back at her. "And as cruel."

"They were Greeks, did you say?"

"You think you're smart, don't you?" His temper flared. "Tricking me into saying ugly things about the Greeks!"

"I didn't trick you—you wanted to say them."

It was, as the boy saw it, a mousetrap to snare a man; it had belittled and caught him. Clearly it was not premeditated on Kalya's part, but had come out of some involuntary necessity.

The collapse of a peace talk, Ben thought ruefully. Ethnic idiocies—afraid to lose their animosities. It was too bad; she had generated a warmhearted mood—singly, at first, without anybody's help—a friendly, brightening climate where everyone had been accessible, and now it had gone somber and cold. What a sadness it was; it had promised so much, this kindly perception they had had of one another—why had it endured so fleetingly? Two mind-gifted people—why did it seem so inevitable that one or both of them would botch it? Why had they finally agreed on the single wrong conclusion, hostility? Especially since neither of them wanted it; both would have settled for any other conclusion, love, understanding, even cold justice. Why had they settled for rancor?

He asked it. Neither of them answered.

At last, Mark spoke quietly. "Maybe we need the enemy."

"Bullshit."

"No, I mean it—what if he's the only one we can rely on?"

"Perhaps he's right," Kalya said, subdued. "Who's more likely to tell us the truth? If life is bad news—who's going to report it? I'll rely on the enemy."

"The enemy's your trusted friend," Ben said derisively. "Then why try to kill him?"

She turned quickly. "I'm not trying to—"

"Yes, you are! Why will you carry a gun tomorrow?"

She was as still as if in a spell. He recalled the havoc in her on the night when the men had gone on the search-and-destroy, and her hysteria at being left behind. Now there was no hysteria. Her voice had a deathly quiet.

"I know the suffering that war causes, but I don't know what it *is*. I've always thought it was an insanity. But surely, after all these centuries . . . can we go on, deranged? Yet, maybe it's *not* an insanity. Maybe it's not the enemy I've always thought it was. The dementia might be in me. There might be something missing in my mind—something I haven't seen, or haven't understood— something, perhaps, that I've distorted. Either the world is mad, or I am. I have to know."

She spoke it rationally, as if all she needed were the two sound premises of a logical syllogism, and she would be rewarded with a valid and inevitable conclusion. And there was no hint in her manner that the expectation, in itself, was an irrationality, on the edge of madness.

8:47.

Withdrawing from a battlefield, Kalya was taking refuge in a demilitarized zone of small talk. "But your foster parents did give you something you like—a fine Greek name. What was it— Markos?"

"Yes. Achillides."

"Did you ever find out what your real father's name was?"

"No, that's what makes it seem impossible to find him."

"Where did you look?"

"I only had one place. It's a small town in the western end of the island. Nobody's ever heard of it."

The quiet was longer than it needed to be, Ben thought. "That's where I come from—the western end," she said. With more deliberation than the movement required, Kalya put her hands to her hair and smoothed it back.

"What's the name of the town?" she asked.

"Nexos."

She only closed her eyes, and opened them.

She's going to tell him, Ben thought, that she knows Nexos, knows it very well, her village; that she knew Mark's father, a neighbor at the turning of the road, a friend, a cousin's cousin; that she was there, in Nexos, when the horror happened, there were screams that night, that morning, there were charges, rumors. Or, more to the point—reminding herself that the Fates wouldn't miss a trick like this—she's going to tell him that she knows where his father is, the village he now lives in, or knows who can tell him how to find the man.

But she said nothing. She made a gesture Ben had never seen her do before; eerie. Putting the tips of her fingers to her cheek, she slowly, gently ran them downward from her temple to her chin. And he thought: If she had done it faster and with more force, her nails would have torn gashes in her flesh. Her face was ashen.

"Is something wrong?" Mark asked.

"She hasn't had a thing to eat," Ben said. "I watched her all through dinner."

She looked at him gratefully. "Or drink," she said.

Ben poured the wine quickly and she had a gulp of it.

Stillness again. Across the silence, a roar of planes, a swath of noise, then gone.

At 8:49 the kithara music began to play.

Time to go.

He listened to it for a few bars of the melody and thought how beautiful it sounded, and how melancholy, a lament. He remembered one of the lines of Louka's betrayal song: better to go all alone. Yes, far better.

Kalya too had heard the music, but he could not tell whether she knew its specific portent. In fact, he could not tell at all what was going on in her mind, and he wondered if even she might not know. She looked like a woman who had suddenly become fragmented, unable to reassemble herself.

The music continued. Go, Ben said. No need to say goodby, for he'd be seeing her, and soon. Tomorrow, now that the assault was scheduled; only the next morning, in fact, merely a matter of hours between his going and theirs. Why did his departure so few hours ahead of them mean so much to him, what would be lost by delaying? The rational question, like a pain between the eyes . . . Go—don't wait, don't find good reasons for cowardice—go with the madness. The pain—pinpoints in the retinas—began to seem more real. Go!

He started toward the door, and with the first step of action, the pain began to lessen . . . Yes . . . departure time.

Tomorrow, Kalya, my love. Don't notice that I've gone.

Out of the room, in the corridor, he leaned against the wall, took a deep breath, looked up, looked down, looked every way for some certainty he was going to make it tonight, and couldn't find any. It was a vacuous thought; if there were certainty, there would be no danger.

He hurried to his cell, found his medical bag, and started through the passage toward the sound of Louka's kithara. He caught himself running, and slowed down, debating for an instant whether to go back to Yannis's room and let him know that he was going. No telling what might happen, who might hear, or how—inadvertently, of course—the old fellow might give him away. Better not.

He heard the squawk of the intercom perhaps four hundred feet ahead of him. It would be coming from Falkos's room, which he would have to pass. Perhaps the teacher was deeply enough preoccupied with plans for tomorrow that he might not look up to see him passing. If Falkos got off the intercom, however, and there was a danger that he might see Ben, the medic would have to drop his black bag in the corridor, stand at the archway and say—casually—that he was going up to the parking area for a breath of air. Nerves, he would say; the man would understand that. But what if, in a spirit of comradeship, he offered to go up with him? Go up, then, the pair of them, breathe the air, walk about, return —and then try again, if possible.

Very close to Falkos's room now. The squawk was louder here, of course, and he could make out the messages the teacher was hearing. Once he thought he heard Kostas's voice, and then, almost immediately following, the sound of one of the twins.

Ten feet away. Slow down. Amble. Evening promenade.

The walkie-talkie did not stop its chatter. He rushed past the doorway—and no voice called out to him. He could speed up a little now. Not much, only a slight quickening of pace.

Just as he made the turning, he saw the figure ahead of him. Twisting, he retreated into an alcove, not a deep one, too shallow for the darkness to protect him. He hadn't had time to identify the man, had only seen a shadow moving toward him. Of course, it might be Louka coming to fetch him, but the kithara was still playing, at a distance. He wished he could know who it was, before they were abreast of each other, but he didn't dare lean out to look, not so much as an inch.

He heard the footsteps getting closer. It occurred to him, with a sinking sense, that while the other man had not been in the light, he himself had been.

Closer. The footfalls only a few yards away.

"Ben."

"Yannis! Oh, thank God!"

The old man looked at him oddly. "I watch you walk. Then you see me and hide. Why?"

"I didn't know it was you."

"If it is somebody else—so?"

"Never mind." He wondered if he shouldn't change his mind, and tell the old man, after all. No, there would be complications.

"Where've you been?" Ben asked.

"I walk. Up top. Is a beautiful night."

"That's where I'm going."

"Come," the old man said, starting to join him.

Ben stopped moving. "You've just come from there."

Yannis also halted. He looked down at the black bag, then up at Ben. "You lie to me."

"The Monastery."

"By yourself?"

"Yes."

He started away, but Yannis stood in his path. "No, wait," he said. "I go with you."

"No—you can't."

"Ben—please—I have to go with you!"

"Not so loud, for God's sake."

The old man lowered his voice. With desperate shrewdness, he gave up the tone of pleading and turned to prudence. "Now, you hear me, Ben—do not make again the same mistake. It is too dangerous for one person to do this all alone. They catch you once, they will catch you again. If I am with you, this will not happen. I will be an extra pair of eyes and ears."

Ben was about to say it would be even more dangerous with an old man hobbling him; in time, he caught himself. "Either way it's dangerous. Yannis—I can't risk your life."

"I *want* to risk!" he cried. "If I stay here, I will have to risk with them—I want to risk with you."

Ben found himself mouthing what Kalya had said. "If you go up with them, you're one of many, Yannis—nobody's gunning for you alone. But if you come with me—"

Doggedly, "I come."

It was the stubbornness of a child who can't bear to be left behind—take me with you—who cannot believe the reasonable exclusions, can't even hear them. But not a child, Ben knew; this was a strong old man, who had not flinched at the sight of gore and broken bones and disaster, who had gone into accidents and burning places without fear, and had never taken safe positions outside them. Ben looked at the deep furrows of life in his face, and thought what a great old face it was, and how beautiful.

"I can't take you, Yannis."

Since sensible arguments had done him no good, the old man routed them. "I will come anyway," he said. "I will follow—I will run after you!"

He knew how unhinged he sounded, and he stopped. He tried logic. "Ben—tomorrow—with Falkos—you know I cannot carry a gun. If I could not carry a gun in company with my sons two weeks before they are dead, can I carry it with anybody? I cannot do it, Ben. If I am alive so long, and I believe what I believe, can I deny this in the last days of my life? Can I deny, Ben? Can I say my whole life was not the truth, Ben? Can I deny, Ben? Ben—can I?"

With an aching need to embrace him, he took Yannis in his arms. He held him, released him, then they started upward along the passage, together.

As they were approaching the tunnel that led to Louka's cell, he told the Greek about his deal with the mercenary. "Is good," Yannis said.

He could feel the old man's excitement, like the need to applaud. He'll laugh when we get out of here, Ben thought, the dear old bastard will scream with laughter. At the last intersection, the medic paused to decide which way to turn. When he veered leftward, the old man said it again, "Is good, Ben—is good."

It hadn't anything to do with the proper passageway or the wisdom of decision, it was simply that the old man was saying that *everything* was now right and proper and felicitous. The Greek's approval lifted Ben's spirit, he felt buoyant. On a burst of giddy merriment, he echoed his friend's words, is good, is good!

Louka was waiting at the entrance to his cell. He was impatient. "Where in hell are you?" he said.

"Which way do we go?"

Louka looked at Yannis, then at Ben. "You do not take the old man, no?"

"Yes, I do."

"No—you will not make it."

Before Ben could respond, Yannis took over. "Why, you fool? I cannot walk? I am too old?"

"You are too Greek. There are Turks in those woods."

"So he is an American—and I am deaf and dumb. How can they know what I am?"

Exasperatedly, "How can they know, how can they know!" Then, more practically, to Ben, "Do not take him. It is an old tunnel. They closed it because the walls are weak."

"If they are weak for me, they will be weak for him," Yannis said. "If something happens, two people are better than one." Then, turning away from the mercenary, "Please, Ben."

"He's going with me," the American said.

Louka made a dry spitting sound: on your head be it. Then he led them on to a low gallery and into a passage Ben had never seen, through tunnels of dampness and darkness, until they came to the mouth of a small channel, no larger than the opening of a fireplace.

He pointed down to it. "Through that is where you go," he said. "I do not go with you from here." This was the extent of the risk he would take; the rest was up to them. "You will have to crawl—maybe it is five hundred feet. Then it will get big and you will be able to stand up. But do not walk together—only one behind the other—be narrow—do not touch the walls, they are soft like sand. The walk is maybe five minutes, no more—and you will see some light. Not much light—only enough to squeeze through. . . . And you are out of the cave."

"Where will we be?"

"Is a *monopati tou chalkou*—copper trail—in old days they carry copper dirt down mountain. Is very difficult, with rocks—this will take you down to main road. But you cannot walk on main road because there is Kostas and also one of the lorries. You have to find goat track. When you get to main road, you do not turn left like you are going up the mountain to the Monastery, but you turn right, like you are going down. Away—you understand?"

"Yes. Then?"

"Then you will be on highway for perhaps a thousand feet. This is dangerous because you are on main road—open. You look for sign. It say, 'Public Park. Not Hunting. Please Not to Smoke in Woodland.' You go around sign, and on other side of sign—there is goat track. Is more wide than goat track—and it will go almost to Monastery—maybe only two hundred meters away."

"Is that it?"

"No—one more thing. When you are walking on goat track, it will be wood—trees, yes? At certain point, there can be Turks. You will walk first, then Yannis—with your hands in air—show them you are not armed."

"At what point?"

It was a poser. "At what point? How do I know? If you are professional soldier, you would not ask this question. There is a point—if you take one more step or whisper one more word—you are dead. I do not know when this is. One says the right moment is when you are hungry, another says when you have to piss, another says when St. Chrysostom talks to you. So what is going to tell you —your belly, your prick, or God? Me—I hear a note of music."

Although he saw they were anxious to go, Louka stopped them once more. "I already have money. Two hundred pounds. I did not take more. Tomorrow you will see I said the truth."

He pointed to the tunnel. They bent down to enter it; as they did, he tapped each one on the back and said *epitihia*, and they muttered their thanks.

The crawl space was narrow and damp; its floor was jagged, lacerating their hands and knees. But it was over sooner than they had expected, and it opened into a passage that offered enough head and shoulder room to suggest that they might, indeed, walk side by side. But Louka's warning was justified. Every ten paces or so, they would hear a low fluttering sound, like a scare of birds. It was the detritus of the walls, slipping away, falling alongside them, sometimes right in their path, as if the mountain had been inexpertly made of wattles and mud which were now crumbling to ruin. They had to walk carefully and slowly; not like walking at all, but the resolution of tensions, the release of one strain and the start of another.

Adding to their difficulty, the tunnel started to ascend—

gradually at first, then becoming inexorably steep, without a single level place to give relief from the climb. When the ascent became even more precipitous, Ben called back to ask if he was going too fast. For response, he felt a shove from the old man, who was closer than he had thought. But in a little while, Ben heard the Greek begin to wheeze.

"Shall we stop for a moment?" he asked.

"Save your goddammit breath. Go."

They went. The tunnel made one final upward thrust, then there it was—the sliver of sky! It couldn't have been more than a foot wide, a vertical oblong of deep blue like an enormous jewel, a baguette of sapphire.

With a lurch of happiness, forgetting caution, Ben plunged ahead, rushing to the beautiful light. Reaching the crevice, he turned sideways, stepped upward a bit, and he was through— standing on a narrow plateau—free in the moonlight.

He heard the sound behind him.

Again, it was a scare of birds. Abruptly, however, the sound changed. It was a groan, a low murmur of resentment, then he saw the crumble, a slow subsidence, as if the mountain were slipping down onto the plateau.

"Yannis!"

He heard nothing of the man, nor did he see him—only the last stir of the rock slide, then the soft slurring aftermath.

The fissure Louka had opened for them had closed again, and there was no sign of the old man. All Ben saw in the moonlight was a wall of rock, not a solid wall but a scraggy debris, with fissures and breaches in it, some narrow, some deeply receding into darkness.

"Yannis!"

He thought he heard an answering sound, but it could have been the echo of his own voice.

"Yannis—Yannis!"

There was a response—muffled but audible.

"Where are you?"

"Ben!"

"Christ, where are you?"

"I see you—I see you!"

Then Ben caught a glimpse of a whiteness, something moving. It was the old man's hand. For a terrifying moment, he thought there was not much more than head and hand that had not been buried, but as he hurried to the fracture in the rock, he could see the old man's face, appearing at the opening and disappearing—he was moving freely.

"What's back there?" Ben said.

"The tunnel—where we came from."

"Is it clear?"

"Behind—yes."

"Then go back."

"Where?"

"To the others."

"No!"

Almost instantly, he heard the movement of debris. The Greek was scrabbling at the hole with his hands. Ben reached to the hole and did the same from his side, scraping and scratching at the aperture. When the opening was somewhat larger, he heard the old man stop. Unexpectedly, his head came through and then one shoulder.

"It's too small, Yannis."

"I was born through a smaller one than this," and he was laughing.

"Get back, you goathead!"

"No—I can make it—pull me!"

"Back!"

"Pull—pull."

Ben was already yanking at the Greek, one hand on his head, the other on his shoulder. The old man wriggled more of him through—his head and both shoulders, now one arm. "It's too small, goddammit!" Ben said.

"I am also small—pull!"

One more yank and the Greek was through. He fell in a heap on the ground, bruised and breathless and howling with laughter. They rolled on the narrow ledge of rock, both of them screaming in hilarity, losing their breath in it, catching it to shout again, laughing with relief and release.

They were free. They were in moonlight, out of darkness. They were in an open world of illimitable vista, not in the dismal durance of a cave. Weaponless, and no longer under coercion to carry weapons, they were once again armed—with themselves. They had recovered their strength. Stealing a moment from their purpose, they sat there quietly together, breathing this breath of freedom, grateful for it, and for each other.

The ledge they were on seemed like a shelf suspended in the sky. There was an unearthly breeze—too pure and rarefied to be mundane—that seemed to come from another universe; yet, somewhere close by, testifying to the worldliness of their station, some night-blooming flower breathed on the wind with a pungent perfume. As they took ease in the beauty of the place, Ben thought of Kalya, and tried not to. Think of the impending peril instead, he told himself, it's far less painful, think of the path you'll take down the mountainside, then the main road you have to cross, then the ascent again; think danger.

Not danger, Ben, his mother used to say: think venture. Think the exciting side, and then she would add the whack for alertness: a risk can't hurt you except if you lose. Lose what?

Only your life. And the old man's as well.

The road downward, although narrow and rocky, was not treacherous. True, there was an abyss to the left of them, and there were times when a misstep might send them crashing, but the brilliant moonlight was a torch that illuminated every stepping place, and the ancient trail seemed to have been forgotten and unpatrolled.

A figure arose from the underbrush. They had come a good distance down, to a widened area forested with cedars, when they saw him. It was Georghiou. He would not have been visible if he had been still. But he came out of the greenwood into the open area to a tiny point of land that extended from the trail and overhung the abyss. Standing there, silhouetted against the sky, he turned one direction, then another, listening. He had heard a sound of them, but couldn't tell its direction. He unslung his rifle.

They hung back into the darkness of alder and laurel, and didn't move.

How long would he stand there, Ben wondered, and how long could they remain here, undetected?

Georghiou looked and listened a while longer, turned back toward the woods from which he had come, then stopped and reconsidered. Holding the rifle in both hands, he started to ascend the pathway, toward them.

Yannis, tightly close, turned to retreat upward. Ben grabbed him and told him silently: stand still. The old man froze.

They didn't see the guerrilla for a minute or two. Nor did the brush move between them and the spot where he had been. Perhaps he too was frozen, waiting.

They saw a silver sway of undergrowth. Closer, now. Then there he was again, coming toward them.

Carefully, stirring by slowest degrees, Ben reached to the ground to find a pebble, a stone. He found one, edged away from Yannis only a few feet to give himself a clearing space, then pitched the stone as hard, as high as he could, into the greenwood behind the guerrilla. They heard the sound aloft, in a treetop somewhere. The man whirled to it, and just as he did, Ben reached for a second stone and hurled it in the same direction. Another swish in a treetop—and Georghiou turned his body to it. But he made no other move. Ben had the bitter thought: You fool, I see you clearly and you don't see us, and what a target you would make. And yet, if you do catch sight of us, unarmed, we're pigeons.

Still hesitant, the guerrilla was motionless. Then, slowly, he started away from them, in the direction of the treetop sounds. Perhaps it was only a bird, he might be telling himself, perhaps there was no danger, nothing to worry about. That's right, Ben thought, no danger, not from us.

Ben made a gesture to the old man and they moved downward, hugging the mountainside. Soon, the road was no longer the copper trail, but a valley between two hillsides, and any path that descended had to be the right one.

Deeper, they plunged deeper into forest, neither of them speaking, neither questioning, always downward. The descent became steeper, almost as sheer as cliffside, but Ben took it as a good sign: they were going in the right direction, toward the highway, and faster than he had hoped.

Once, stopping, they thought they saw a ribbon of moonlight down ahead. It's the road, he said, don't you think so? But as they walked onward a hundred paces or so, it had disappeared, he couldn't tell where.

Then, alarmingly, the descent stopped. They were walking on level ground now, and the flatness could tell them nothing about the right direction, whether to go toward moonlight or away from it, right or left.

Without warning, they were in it: swamp.

He cursed his thoughtlessness. He knew damn well there was a swamp on the other mountain plateau; why hadn't it occurred to him that if both roads were ultimately going to the same place, there might be a swamp on this plateau as well, since both of them were one?

He could feel the bog, softening underfoot. Yannis, trying to find another pathway, was up to his ankles in it.

"Wait," Ben whispered.

The old man either didn't hear or wouldn't. He pulled one foot free, stepped sideways, slipped off balance, and sank deeper.

"Wait, I said!"

He circled around the Greek, kept one foot on hard earth, and reached. "Don't worry about your left foot, pull your right—but not yet. Wait till I pull," he said. Then: "Now!"

He tugged. Yannis fell headlong toward him. Clutching tightly at the old man, he pulled him onto solid soil.

They stopped now, distrusting every yard of earth, uncertain how to move or where. If only he could detect a downgrade someplace, but how to find a downgrade through a bog? He wondered how abysmally deep it might be, whether it was a real quagmire or only a shallow marsh. How far would he sink into it, he speculated, before finding out?

Yannis apparently saw what decision he was on the verge of making. *"Ochi,"* he said.

But what alternative was there—immobility? He walked along the edge of the bog, testing, poking with his foot, trying to make some logic from a terra firma that belied its name. At last he found a likely spot. He extended his leg, felt the sucking underfoot, but not too badly—his tread came to a solid stop. Encouraged, he tried the other foot. Down, suckingly down, a swirl of muck—and just in time he twisted his body onto the heavy earth, and fell on it, free again.

"Shit," he said. Yannis agreed that it was.

They stood there, as balked and senseless as if they were drugged. They said nothing. In their silence, they heard a rippling sound. Not loud—very faint, in fact—but clear, like water burbling out of a bottle. A lovely sound; nature, chuckling.

"It's a brook," Ben said, "or a spring, or something."

If they could find it, if it was not too deep, if it had a pebbly bottom and not a marshy one, they might wade their way in the bed of it, downstream, down the hill. But what if they had to go to the middle of the swamp to find it?

They started to move separately, exploring the perimeter of the morass again, getting further and further away from each

other. When Ben had gone as far as he could go—without success
—he turned. Yannis had disappeared.

Disturbed, Ben hurried back to where he had left the old man.
No sign of him. He followed the direction that Yannis had to have
gone and, still not seeing him, looked upward. There was nothing
except the ugly marsh grass, the sump reeds, and the scrubby
alders.

He heard a thrashing. It was behind him in the upland from
which they had come. Yannis was spilling, falling down the hillside
in a cascade of glee. "I find it! I find the water!"

They scrambled upward together. How logical it was: if there
was a stream coming down the mountain, it would have come from
a higher place than this, and the old man had gone directly upward.

It was neither a brook nor a stream and it hadn't, as Yannis
put it in Greek, any certainty. It was really only one tiny head-
spring of water after another which might, in wetter seasons of the
year, be a respectable rivulet of sorts, but which was now the tiniest
rill—flowing, of course, downhill.

It was all they needed if it didn't turn to swamp. They walked
into the middle of the minuscule waterway. The ground was rocky
underfoot, but firm. Icy cold as the water was, it did not feel unpleasant, only invigorating, with a chill that enheartened.

There was no doubt any longer where downhill was; the current told them. They walked, they stumbled a little, occasionally
one or the other lost his footing and fell. Before they were aware of
it, they were in the middle of the swamp, crossing it safely by way
of its watery roadway, seeing the stream deepen ahead of them like
a ribbon of silver.

Silver—this was what Ben had seen from the higher ground,
thinking it a roadway, which for them it was. But there was a dry
roadway they would later have to travel. He hoped it would be as
peaceful as this one. Soothing, how warm the water had become.
From bone-cracking cold, through refreshing chill, to warm as
baby's bath. He regretted the end of it.

The end came when abruptly the stream, of considerable
depth now, went underground, and they realized they had successfully crossed the swamp. But why did the watercourse go so suddenly underground, Ben questioned, as if it had been made to do
so, unnaturally?

Perhaps it had indeed been made to do so. He started to step out of the dry stream bed and onto the bank. But the channel was deep and the incline was grassy, with little brush or tree to offer a handhold. As he made his way upward, he saw that Yannis was having difficulty. He reached down to the old man, who grabbed Ben's wrist and pulled himself out of the trough.

They were on top of a high bank now, and saw it—the main road. Ben's speculation that the stream had gone underground unnaturally was right—it had been made to flow into a culvert built under the macadam bridge.

They looked at the highway and at each other. Yannis tried to hide how pleased he was. He smiles with old world shyness, Ben thought, like a child embarrassed to be praised. The Greek kicked his right leg to shake off water and muck, then kicked his left. He mumbled grumpily about *engrotis* and *kopros,* wetness and dung, but he was fooling nobody—right now he felt friendly to both. So did Ben. He tickled the old man, and Yannis made giddy, happy noises and punched at him, saying that Ben was a perverted American who took pleasure from wet-footed old men.

There were sounds behind them.

They thought, at first, that they might come from the sighing trees, but there was not wind enough. Then they thought the gurgle of the stream, but there was not flow enough. It was men.

The pursuit had started. More than started, there were probably detachments on all sides of them, for certainly a message had gone out on the intercom.

"We have to cross the road, yes?" The old man's voice had tightened.

"Yes—at the roadway sign. Do you recognize where we are?"

"We have to go to right—not up."

"Ready?"

"Yes."

In a dart, they crossed the highway. Just as they reached the other side, they heard the truck. Its lights were not visible, but the rumble of it came from the direction in which they were going, around the bend of the roadway. Presently it appeared—its headlights not turned on—lumbering heavily in their direction. They moved swiftly into brushwood, further from the road, and dropped flat on the ground. Slowly the vehicle kept advancing. It was an open truck with three men in the rear, two looking toward the hedgerows to the left, and one to the right. They all had rifles.

Lying prone, Ben and Yannis didn't risk a breath.

The truck was close enough so they could hear the muttering of the men. Then the thing passed. When it got to the little bridge over the culvert, it came to a stop. Two of the guerrillas got out; one stayed on the flatbed of the conveyance as it went into a lower gear and started climbing the hill.

The two men whom the vehicle had left behind took positions one on each side of the bridge, one looking upstream, the other down. They were assuming, Ben realized, that the two fugitives had not yet come down to the main road. How stupid they were to take for granted we haven't yet made it, he thought. He wondered if he and Yannis dared take advantage of their blunder and move. The truck would no longer be a threat, he reasoned, but the two men might hear them if they made too much of a stir.

Crawling, barely raising his body clear of the earth, Ben started to inch his way along the ground, in the woods, parallel to the roadway. He could faintly hear the old man crawling after him. Not hearing him too well gave Ben confidence that the patrols could not be hearing them at all, so he crawled faster. If they could make it safely to where the road turned, they might risk standing up.

He felt a tug at his shoe. He turned to look at his companion. For the first time, the old man was asking for a respite. Ben paused. After a brief interval, scarcely a few breaths later, he felt Yannis slapping his leg. They started to crawl again.

The tiny pause for rest had been good for both of them. The second lap—to the bend—seemed shorter than the first. They were there.

Slowly Ben pulled himself to a kneeling position, looked all directions, saw nothing dangerous, stood up. So did Yannis.

They took a longer pause this time, then stepped out toward the roadway. "Can you run?" Ben asked.

"Fast, yes—but not far."

"Let's see."

It wasn't a steady sprint, more like a scamper from shadow to shadow, a hesitancy, then another short one.

They saw the sign, a big one. In Greek, Turkish, and English, it said that hunting was illegal, so was littering the roadway or landscape, and that this was beautiful countryside and should be kept that way. The final line was an exhortation: be proud.

They slithered behind the sign, dropped unexpectedly a few feet, stumbled upward a few more feet, and were on the goat track.

It was even wider than Louka had described; not a goat track at all, but an old wagon road.

They were going upward, rapidly upward—toward the Monastery. It suddenly all seemed easier than Ben had imagined—how exaggerated his misgivings had been! He knew it was too early to feel this relieving sense of fulfillment, he knew there were dangers yet to come. There were Greeks and Turks to be wary of—everything on this mountainside was hazardous. Yet, having come this far, having eluded them this distance, he sensed that if the dangers had not diminished, his apprehensions had. It signified that, although he must beware of recklessness, his courage had increased in proportion to the perils. Minute by minute, he was getting stronger, becoming equal to the bastards, and he could win without raising a hand, without spilling a drop of blood.

The Turk arose from nowhere.

He was young—he couldn't have been out of his teens—he was probably as frightened as they were, and he was clumsy. If he had fired the pistol immediately, once, twice, he'd have killed them both. But he was indecisive between murder and flight. He took one step forward, one step back, pulled the trigger on the backward step, a single shot, and missed—and by that time Ben was upon him, thoughtless, reckless, bringing the boy to earth, twisting at him, twisting, while Yannis tried to wrest the gun away.

Suddenly they were all standing, flailing at one another like clumsy amateurs, the pistol out of sight, fallen somewhere into darkness.

"Get it!" the old man muttered, pointing vaguely to the other side of Ben where he thought the gun had gone. "Get it!"

But the medic saw the flash of the knife over Yannis's head, and didn't grab for the fallen weapon but for the assailant. He reached one hand upward to the lifted arm, clutched and held the wrist, tried to wrench it, turn it, then threw the other arm around the young Turk's neck.

"Drop it," he said. If the boy didn't understand the words, he'd get the tone. "Drop—drop it—drop it!"

He felt the soldier writhing in his grasp, felt the head straining forward, one foot kicking backward, mouth making noises, no words, choking sounds. And Yannis, searching the ground for the gun he had just seen but now could not find.

"Drop it!"

The Turk shouldn't have tried to twist in that direction, Ben thought, and not so hard. Nonsensically, he heard himself saying too much torque, the twist not warranted.

He heard the sound of the young man's neck. It was an innocent sound. In high school Ben used to produce the same small crepitating noise by the cracking of his knuckles. This time, in the boy's neck. Not knuckles, he thought. It's broken.

The knife slipped away, the arm dropped lightly, floatingly, like a kite string. No more twist in the body, no torsion, no struggle of any kind. Ben held the boy's weight by the arm around the throat. Like an embrace, he said, a love clasp.

Oh Christ, I've killed him, he realized, I've killed a kid in a darkness, oh Christ, oh Christ.

He let him go.

The boy sank by stages, as if he knew to slip to his knees to break the fall, and then face forward on the woodland floor.

Oh Christ.

"Listen," Yannis said.

He had only half heard it himself, the sound of the truck motor, the movement of men in the forest.

Something about the others hearing the shot, Yannis was saying, and not getting through Ben's mind. Oh Christ.

"Ben—come on!"

Yannis started ahead of him. Ben took one last look at the dead boy. Come on, the other was saying, come *on*.

Then two things occurred at once:

He heard the voice back there, not many paces away, a familiar voice—Mikis perhaps—saying in Greek, "I've got him." What Mikis had hold of Ben couldn't imagine. Did he think he had one of the fugitives?

And the other occurrence:

He saw Yannis reach to his left shoulder, in some pain. Then Ben saw the blood. The dead Turk had a small posthumous revenge. His bad shot had wounded one of them.

The blood was not a trickle, it was surging forth, gushing in an ominous rhythm. Ben hurried to the old man and, as the Greek tried to pull away and urge them forward, the medic grabbed, restrained him.

Not light enough to see, he thought, but he wondered if the bullet had gone through the other side. Reaching behind the old man's shoulder, he felt for wetness and found none. The bullet was still inside him, in the shoulder, stopped by flesh and bone.

"Come on!" Yannis said.

Too late.

He saw Kostas first, then Petros. Too many guns raised, Ben thought, you don't need that many guns to capture us. I'd have come anyway, to tend this old man, I'd not have gone without taking that murder out of his shoulder, too many guns.

Then Mikis arrived with Evagoras. Between them they had their prisoner, a middle-aged Turkish man. His face was covered with wet earth, muck; a leaf was sticking to it. And Ben had the preposterous thought: He's mud and leaves, the rest of him is terror.

Kostas was in charge. He pointed to the dead boy on the ground and looked at Ben.

"You shoot him?"

Unable to bear the question, he evaded it. "I haven't any gun."

"We hear a shot."

"His."

"Where is gun?"

"Somewhere . . . I don't know."

Kostas told Petros to find it. Turning back to Ben, "How you kill him?"

"I . . . how? I—his neck—I broke it."

"Good."

Evagoras was searching the dead soldier, turning his pockets inside out, finding papers, identification, anything.

Ben looked for Yannis and didn't see him. "Yannis?"

He heard the old man answer. He was under a tree, leaning against the trunk of it, standing, refusing to fall.

"What is with him?" Kostas said. It was too dark under the branches, he couldn't see the blood.

"He's wounded—hurry—help me—I've got to get him back!"

Without haste, the bullock of a man walked to Yannis, looked him over. "Is only shoulder wound."

Ben scrounged on the ground for his medical bag and couldn't find it. By the time Petros brought it to him, the medic had torn part of Yannis's shirt away, where the blood had wet it. He wadded the cloth and stuffed it into the old man's wound. The Greek cried out in pain, *"Oh, Christo mou!"*

Petros offered to help Ben carry Yannis. As they were lifting him, Evagoras found the young Turk's pistol and, adding it to the dead man's other effects, shoved it into his pocket. While Mikis held a gun on the prisoner, Kostas grabbed the legs of the carcass and pulled the body off the goat track and into the brush. With his feet, he kicked dead leaves and branches over the corpse, made a busyness of the activity, then sloped the hillock gradually to the ground so that it looked no different from a natural windrow, forest made.

Ben and Petros carried Yannis to the truck and lay him on the flatbed of it. With a slight movement of his gun, Mikis ordered the prisoner into the truck, then the rest of them got in.

Yannis was perspiring, the sweat in his eyes made him blink and blink. With his hand, Ben wiped the perspiration off the old man's face, and smoothed his grizzled hair out of his eyes. The Turk was sitting close to him, making soft, unidentifiable sounds.

When they got back to the cave, they lifted the old man out of the truck, opened the back door of the ambulance, and laid him on the cot. He was still bleeding quite a good deal, but not as much as before. His breathing was a little unsteady but his pulse was surprisingly strong; and, blessedly, he was unconscious. How long he would remain that way while Ben probed for the bullet, he couldn't guess, but he had some chloroform and some ether; he didn't know which he would use.

The paraffin lamp that Petros brought him was not very good. But he had worked with worse light than this, once with two flashlights, one of which had gone out. Anyway, it wouldn't be too difficult. The thing was to do it fast, cauterize, and sew him up as quickly as possible.

As he started, he heard a noise outside the ambulance. Kalya stood at the open door.

"I'll help you," she said.

The space inside the ambulance was small, but she seemed to use up little of it. She had an intuitive sense of what he needed; she was in charge of objects, she made them do their task. With her helping him, the surgery went swiftly, and he even enjoyed doing it, knowing the old man would get well. He felt her watching him, and her admiration, and it made him work even better than he knew he could. I could be happy now, he thought, near her again, doing work I am meant to do . . . . if only I hadn't killed that boy. I could even forget that once again my attempt to escape has failed, I might make do with fire fears, with a compromise of sorts, with the felicity of healing beside a woman I love, if only I hadn't killed that boy.

As the bullet came free, the old man cried out. He was conscious, and the job was not yet finished. Kalya looked at Ben, not knowing what to do. Without a word, he reached for the roll of absorbent cotton and the bottle of ether. He poured some on the whiteness, placed it over the man's nose and mouth, and Kalya held it. She didn't know how long she had to administer the anesthetic; she looked at Ben, not the patient, needing to see the signal. He paid her no attention, and still she watched him steadily, only occasionally glancing down at her charge. The old man was breathing deeply now, no pain, no consciousness.

Each time the needle sank into the flesh, she turned away. He caught a glimpse of her flinching, and thought how strange that she winced when the worst was over, with the bleeding totally checked, and hadn't made a sign of shrinking from the bloody mess she had seen before.

Barely looking at her, he nodded, and she knew the signal meant she need not administer any more of the anesthetic. The job was done, and neatly.

The old man was resting easily, unconscious still, with apparently no distress. What suffering would come later might not be all that bad; no bone had been injured. And if the pain was tolerable, he would probably not complain; he was a strong old man, and gutsy.

They were cleaning up after the operation. How did she know where things went, he wondered, how was she so sure of what she did, and so uncertain of what she knew? Correcting himself, he realized that the uncertainty about her was his more than her own.

They held one another. He kissed her gently. "I'm glad they didn't hurt you," she said.

"I killed a Turk."

"I know. I'm glad it wasn't you."

"He was a young boy."

"I'm glad you're safe."

He tried to say more so he might feel less, but he couldn't. He wished he could cry.

To be alone with what he felt, he turned from her to go outdoors. As he stepped down off the ambulance, just as his feet reached the ground, somebody in the darkness grabbed his arm. It was Kostas, his rifle at his side. "You are not permit to go someplace," he muttered thickly.

"Let him go," a voice said in the darkness.

They turned. Petros was coming from the cave. He too was armed, a revolver in his hand. "Falkos wants him."

Kostas loosened his grip on Ben's arm and released the prisoner to the younger man.

As they started toward the entrance of the cave, Petros said, "If you will not cause me trouble, I will walk beside you instead of behind you." A boy with compassions, he wanted to be comradely, not a jailer. Assuming from the silence that Ben wanted the same, he walked abreast of him.

Mark was standing at the mouth of the cave, waiting in the archway. The boy was nervous, his eyes had a glitter. "You killed a Turk," he said. It was congratulation; there was elation in it.

Too perturbed, Ben walked faster, away from him. That quickly, striding alongside, the young man changed his tone. "How's Yannis? Is he badly hurt?"

"He'll be all right."

"May I go see him?"

"He's asleep."

"I won't wake him. But I thought—if he needs anything—while you're inside—"

"Kalya's with him."

"I know."

Of course he knew, Ben mused, he wants to be with her, not with Yannis. But it was unfair—he was certain the boy's affection for the old man was honest; there was something even generous in it.

"Go on," he said.

As Mark brushed past him, Ben got a whiff of something, wine perhaps. He heard him running across the gravel, and no sounds of anyone stopping him.

Falkos sat behind the bare table in the main room, staring at the doorway, waiting for him. They were running out of paraffin, he said, that's why there were only candles on the table, in ruby glass, vigil lights. The underside of his chin was illuminated starkly, also his nostrils and the ridge of bone above his eyes, fire and brimstone.

But the man was kindly and, considering that tomorrow was

the day, inordinately relaxed. He had the warmth of a patient father who was again forgiving a truant child for running away from home. Nothing mattered more than the runaway's return. There was not a warp of falsity about his welcome; he was sincerely fond of the renegade.

"I'm glad you're back, Benjamin. Are you all right?"

"Yes."

"I have a question or two—I hope you don't mind." As Ben made no rejoinder, he continued. "On the copper trail—how did you manage to get past Georghiou?"

He told about the throwing of the stones. It was so nitwittedly simple that Falkos, embarrassed for the salt seller, covered his eyes.

"Who told you about the tunnel?"

"Nobody," he lied. "When you were away—rifle practice—I explored the passageways."

"Hm. I thought it might have been something like that. Very resourceful, Benjamin—you're to be commended."

The words were mocking. "Don't rub it in—I know I've failed."

"You've failed in trying to escape, yes. But you've come back a hero."

"I'm not a hero—and not trying to be."

"Are you sure? Single-handedly—unarmed—you've killed an armed enemy."

"He was not my enemy."

"In modern warfare we always claim we have no personal animus against the people we annihilate. We're simply defending ourselves. And indeed we are. He was trying to kill your friend, so you had to kill him."

How shrewd he is, Ben thought. Without putting it into words, he's saying that I've proved his point—my pacifism is fake, I'm as warlike as he is—as "meanly militant," he had said. He's nailing me as a killer . . . and that's what I am. No, Christ, it's not true . . . But I did kill him.

"I was not *trying* to kill him!"

"I never believe it when a man—in a hand-to-hand struggle—kills someone and says it was an accident. I think you meant to kill him—and you did it very well."

"I only wanted him to drop the knife."

"But you're not stupid. You knew that wouldn't be the end of it. If you had let him go—only for an instant—he'd have murdered both of you. You had to make a choice—him—you—Yannis. So you didn't let him go—you broke his neck—"

"I didn't mean to kill him!"

"—and saved the old man's life. My God, Benjamin, against an armed man, you saved your friend's life. Don't you really think that's heroic?"

"I'm not a hero—I don't want to be a hero—I didn't mean to kill him!"

Falkos ignored the pain he heard. "It's not an insult, being called a hero."

"To me it is!"

"Well, to me you've performed an act of bravery, and I'm grateful. You've killed one of our enemies—and you've helped to bring back a very useful prisoner."

The word "useful" was ice. "What are you going to do to him?"

"Question him."

"What do you expect to get out of him?"

"The usual things—where he's posted, who else is there, how many, what weapons they have. It would be especially good if he could tell us about men and armament in the Monastery."

"Where's Afxentiou?"

Falkos didn't blink. "No, nothing like that—this is routine. We won't torture the man—we probably won't have to. He's middle-aged, he's got a wife and three kids. If he's got a favorite daughter, we'll talk about her, and his mouth will miraculously open."

He thereupon reached into a side pocket of his coat and pulled out a number of objects. A spectacles case, a crumpled package of cigarettes, a ballpoint pen, two pages of an as yet unfinished letter, and a blank envelope that had never been used. From another pocket, he brought forth a finger ring crudely carved out of a black burl of wood, and a small plastic container of peppermints. The last object was a springblade knife, closed and innocent-looking now, but deadly when open—*kiyasiya kavga*—war to the knives, as the Turks put it. It was the weapon the boy would have killed Yannis with. Falkos snapped it, the blade sprang gleamingly to life, and he set it on the table. He made no further reference to it, but it was between them as they talked.

"This trivia belonged to the soldier you killed. If he had been questioned, he'd probably have given us a great deal more trouble than the older one. He was seventeen or eighteen, the men tell me, and at that age these Turks carry the burden of destiny. Their mothers write them letters saying, 'Come home a victor or come home dead.'"

He reached for the unfinished letter and held it up for Ben to see. "He was probably writing to his mother to tell her to start twining laurel leaves. . . . I don't read Turkish, do you?"

"No."

"We'll ask Kalya to translate it for us." As Ben perturbedly looked away. "Do you think it's distasteful of me to have her do it?" he asked.

"I have to go back to Yannis. What did you call me for?"

"Just what I've said. Especially to congratulate you." Then, pretending it to be an afterthought, "And to remind you—dawn tomorrow."

Ben left the main room. In the passage, Petros was waiting for him. Starting through the corridor, en route to the ambulance, Ben wondered where they were keeping the prisoner. He was on the verge of putting the question to Petros when he decided he did not want to know. Whatever information the questioners got from the Turk, however they pinpointed his identity, Ben wanted to keep both of them—the living and the dead—anonymous. He certainly didn't want to *look at* the captive; he had no wish to see his own offense in the face of another man.

Outdoors, he thought he heard the sound of planes again. But they were too far away, or not real. He thought, then, that he heard the sound of the sea. The same could be said for it.

Then, Kalya's cry.

Real.

She came rushing out of the ambulance—too fast for Kostas to stop her. Running, hectic, the guard after her, her hair flying, her face white in the moonlight.

"Ben!"

He raced toward her. "What? What is it?"

"Yannis—he can't breathe—he can't breathe!"

He ran past her, quick as panic.

Mark was in the aisle between the cot and the instruments counter. He was on his knees, kneeling beside Yannis's bed, looking into the old man's face. The patient didn't seem deathly at all, one of his arms was effortlessly relaxed, lying on the pillow beside his head, his hand on his forehead.

The boy was in the way. "Get up!" Ben said.

"He's not breathing!"

"Get up—get out of the way!"

Mark arose and slipped past him.

Ben reached to feel the pulse, touched the old man's face, pulled his shirt open, kneaded his chest, thought of wild and useless remedies, incisions to massage the heart, nitroglycerine and digitalis, he thought of prayer, he thought of pretending it away. The old man was dead.

"Oh, Jesus," he said.

Irrelevantly, he took the gray face in his hands, held his palms on the cold cheeks as if to warm them; slowly, absurdly, he patted them as if he would gentle them to their dying.

"Yannis—"

Seeing his misery, she wanted to lessen it with motion or procedure. "Ben, get up."

Lost, he looked at her. "He was getting well—why did he die?"

As if she had an answer to the incongruity. Everything at random, she might have said. All she had was silence.

Mark broke it. "They killed him—those Turkish bastards killed him!"

He stood in the doorway of the ambulance. Abruptly, he too seemed unable to breathe. To worsen it, he put his hands over his face, covered his nose and mouth with them, to keep the breath from coming, to stifle himself. Then, the glazing of the eyes.

"No!" Kalya said.

"Help me!" The boy was choking.

She rushed to him, encircled him with an embrace, did what one is supposed not to do: gave him no freedom to thresh the air. She held him tightly, almost too tight for breath, held him in restraint. Murmuring his name, she did not loosen her confinement of the boy, but kept murmuring to him, forcing him to become aware that he was in her arms, that he was *somewhere*. Mark, she kept repeating, Mark, infusing him with her strength, as if she were pouring blood into his veins. He seemed desperately to clutch at her, to grasp at what she was saying as something that might save his life, pull him to a shadowed safety, pull him away from some other place he didn't want to go to.

He shivered once, then again. The glaze was gone; he was seeing her. Seeing her, and needing her and using her, to guide him back.

She led the boy out of the ambulance. Putting her arm through his, she helped him down the step and walked with him, slowly, closely, into the night.

Momentarily—without her—Ben felt bereft. But soon he was glad that they were gone. Slowly, he turned to the body again.

For a long while—he couldn't guess how long—he sat with the old man's death. Foolish notions he had no belief in came to mind. I'll keep him company until he gets used to it, he thought; I'll lighten his loneliness. He knew well enough it was his own loneliness he needed to lighten, as heavy as the dead weight of mortality. Then another foolish notion: take my loneliness with you, he said to his friend; where you're going, it won't matter— take it. And still another: tell me what it is.

I must bury him, he said. I must carry him outdoors somewhere, and bury him. Not tomorrow, tonight. God knows what will happen tomorrow. Now.

He started to take the dead man's hand off the clouded face so he could rearrange the limbs before they became rigid. The arm was already stiffening, and he was glad he had thought of it. But how quickly it was happening. How uncharacteristic of the man, he reflected; there was never a muscle of rigidity in his friend, not a thought that wasn't yielding, that wasn't lovingly pliant and giving. Don't stiffen too soon, he said. He bent down and, before closing the eyes, questioned quite reasonably: Why did you have to die, why did I have to lose you?

As if the old man had responded, he heard the answer: You're being punished, Ben, for having killed the boy. Punished by whom, by what? By himself, by the local Fates, by God? If it was God, the punishment might be endurable, the Deity being, by Christian reputation, compassionate. But if by himself . . .

Bury me, Ben, and finish the night.

Then, precipitously, everything was in doubt, his whole world trembling in a quake of ambiguity. He thought of Demetrios and Yannis, the old men in his life, the one a symbol and the other real, and he denied that any quest up any mountainside, that any terror exorcised, that any abstract vision of himself was worth such aching loss. Not visionary loss but real, as tangible as a cold corpse, as categorical as grief. Lost, earth lost, and perhaps no heaven to gain.

He wondered what the guards would do when he carried the body out. No matter. Let them do what they do.

Bending, he lifted the carcass off the cot. He had thought dead weight before, but had been wrong. He was a little man and surprisingly light, even in death.

He carried him out into the night. The guard, following his every footstep, offered to help him bear the burden, but he wanted to do it alone, just as he wanted to bury him alone. He had no shovel to dig the grave with, so he put the body in a shallow pit, covered it with stones, then threw dead leaves over it until they were a mound.

Still, he didn't go away. Nor did Kostas urge him to. The guard stayed quite a distance from the grave, where he could watch but not be an intruder. Ben walked around the leafy place a number of times, not knowing what purpose it served or what comfort it gave either to himself or the other one.

He had no idea how much later he heard someone approaching and thought it was the guard to tell him that he could not remain any longer, he would have to go somewhere else, back to the ambulance, or to the cave.

But it was Kalya. She couldn't see him at first, but knew he was somewhere nearby, the guard had told her so. She saw the grave before she saw Ben. She seemed to stop looking for Ben, simply gazed at the freshly built mound, studied it as though it might be something she misunderstood.

At last, seeing Ben, she said, "Come back."

"Not yet."

"Come back. Don't grieve anymore—come back."

"I killed him."

"Don't say that. He didn't die of anything you did to him. He only died because he was an old man."

"The boy was young."

"No, Ben—please."

"I killed them both! Oh, Christ—I did!"

He began to cry.

"No! Oh, don't cry, please!"

He stood in the darkness, weeping, shaking with sobs, convulsive.

"Oh, please," she said. "I can't stand you to cry!"

Then, for the first time, she told him that she loved him, and he heard her and thought that her love should soothe all heartache, should cancel every loss and redress every wrong, should bring him consolation for the death of the old man, but it could not comfort him.

11

Mark lay in the darkness of his cell and pretended to be asleep. He was sure she was in the room, although he could not see her. She was probably sitting on the hard, uncomfortable bench within arm's reach, watching him, tending him, caring for him.

If I extend my hand I can touch her, he thought—and I want to. But it was a treacherous affinity.

She had performed a miracle. There had been times in his life when, by taking a deep breath or lying down or changing his position in a chair, he had prevented a minor seizure from taking hold. Or, if it did happen, he would be no more aware of it than a brief lapse in the ticking of a clock. But with a major one—even if he could detect its onset—his only recourse was to halt what he was doing, put the pen down, pull the car to the right and park it, stop speaking mid-syllable, and let himself be abducted. Tonight there had been the sinking feeling, the chill, the rush of wind, and just as he was being snatched to No Place, she had grabbed and taken possession of him. She had not let him go, she had shaken him, had murmured something in his ear or into the ear of the demon, some incantation—his name, his name—and the abductor had been routed. She had saved him from being seized.

Then she had walked with him, her arm in his, slowly in the night, like the steps of a religious ceremony, moving toward a sanctuary. And as he had lain down on the cot, she had unbuttoned his shirt and loosened his belt so that he could breathe more deeply, and had not left the room. He was sure she had not left the room; he was certain he could hear her breathing.

Oh, Kalya, I love you. The thought stormed in his brain.

He had been right, years ago. He had wandered into the truth about the illness in his fantasies of the therapist Amélie Françoisette. His yearning for her had lessened his mals, had made them less frequent and less bleak, had flushed the grays with color. Could it be then, as he had suspected, that his ailment was an inanition of love, a hunger for sexual satisfaction? Certainly what had happened with Kalya tonight suggested it was so. The force of her, the magnetic galvanism of the woman had drawn the electrical storm out of his brain, grounding it. How potent her energy had been, more powerful than any drug he had ever taken.

Thinking back, he realized what a prophetic lie he had told— about coming to this country to find Aphrodite's grave. He had found the love goddess, all right, but not dead and entombed— alive—as erotic as the myth Falkos had told. Perhaps the woman was as false as the myth, perhaps she had no reality, not even any beauty outside Mark's image of her, but it was enough. He could live on illusory things, he could make substance out of vagaries. He had no need for the facts of existence; none of them had been generous. He could make do with the one fact he lived by: the cruelty of his father. He could generate his energy from his hatred of the Turks.

What about the other energy, the love of Kalya?

He told himself: Put it out of your head that she is Turkish. Touch her. Reach out into the darkness. Put your hand on her. Don't let yourself think that love will enfeeble your anger, that Delilah will shear the hair of it. Besides, there was no such thing as love uncorrupted by hatred. Rage was a booster rocket that lifted love into an outer atmosphere, an ecstasy in space. He suspected there was no great erection in tenderness alone. His love could be a caress and a ravage, which might be the perfect passion. He recalled a woman in the university library who sat behind one of the desks and knew where every book was. She was so delicate that he often wondered if her fine, blue-veined skin was a capable integument; and her voice was tissue paper. But she was married to a bull with arms like sledgehammers and hands that appeared to have no fingers, they were ingots. Mark was certain that he raped her every night, and she was happy.

I've got to reach out and touch Kalya. I want her tonight and I know she wants me. I could tell, this evening, after dinner, the way she spoke to me, the way she looked at me. She listens to every word I say, she refers to me after she has spoken to see if I've heard, if I agree, if I like her. She wants to know if I love her, wants to touch me as much as I want to touch her. When she undid the buttons of my shirt, her hand caressed me; when she loosened my belt, she wanted to slip her fingers inside, she wants me. Why don't I reach for her? Am I going to let myself be cursed by the word Turkish? Or is it just an excuse for not daring to touch her? Am I afraid she'll reject me, that she'll reduce me in age, in size, in potency?

Reach for her! Touch her!

He touched himself. If *she* would only touch *him*, he thought, if she knew how large he was, how much he needed her, how his hunger was more than the fear of seizure, more than the dread of No Place, how not having her *was* No Place. . . .

Slowly, tentatively, he extended his hand into the darkness. His fingers caressed the air, then he lowered his hand until it rested on the unremitting wood. Like blindness, he felt along the surface of the bench. There was no one there.

Perhaps she was elsewhere in the room.

"Kalya . . . ?"

There was no answer. He said her name again, louder this time, and waited.

She wasn't there. It was nothing to be upset about, he told himself, it was his own fault. He had wasted too much time in indecision, vacillating, saying nothing, doing nothing, so she had thought him asleep and had slipped away. One word from him at the proper moment, and she would have stayed—but he had lost the moment.

She hadn't, however, rejected him. If anything, he had seemed to reject her. She had made every large overture, hoping he would make a small one, and she was still waiting for him to do so.

It was the most heartening thought of all, the image of her, waiting. In her room, perhaps, lying on the bed, just as awake as he was. Waiting.

He was not lying down now, but sitting on the edge of the cot. Sitting and appraising himself, realizing how strong he was. He arose and felt himself equal to what he wanted to do.

Without haste, he walked out of the tiny cell, into the passageway. It led, through dimness, to an intersecting corridor where a sconce held a flickering candlelight. He walked into the glow, then out of it, to the room where he knew she slept.

He was on the threshold now, unable to see anything, listening. There was no sound.

"Kalya . . . ?"

She did not answer. Could he be wrong, was she not awake? Slowly, he advanced into the room, step by cautious step. The edge of the mattress touched his shin.

"Kalya," he said again.

Carefully, his hand traversed the bed. There was nobody in it. He felt a wave of disappointment, at the brink of nausea.

She's in Ben's room, he said.

Then it came back to him. As if a torch had flared, his brain became clear, and he remembered something that his arrested seizure had darkened—the death of the old man. Pity and rage came to him almost together. The Turks had done it.

The kind old Greek was dead in the ambulance. And that's where Ben was. And Kalya. Only they probably were no longer in the ambulance, but somewhere outdoors, in a grassy place—with the old man still not cold in his death—having it with each other. Jealous, he welcomed the return of anger.

He realized that he had been saved from making a terrible blunder. He might have tried to make love to her tonight, and been rejected. Or, worse, he might have succeeded with her, and failed in everything else.

She might have emasculated his rage. And he remembered that she had concurred with him:

The enemy is all we can rely on.

12

There were a half-dozen vigil lights on the table of the main room. The schoolmaster carefully arranged all of them in a semicircle at one small segment of the table, where Kalya was sitting.

"I would like you to translate the Turkish soldier's letter for me," Falkos said. He put the letter on the surface in front of her, within the arc of light.

Considerately, he turned to Ben. "There's no need for you to listen to it, Benjamin, if you don't want to."

He certainly did not want to. He had no morbid desire to hear a personal letter—written home—by a boy he had killed. He had an impulse to thank the schoolmaster for his thoughtfulness, but he didn't follow it. The man's generosity was patently not altruistic. He was still trying to pervert Ben's pacifism. Exposing the American to one of the emotional aftermaths of his having killed a young soldier would not be to the purpose.

Falkos saw Ben's hesitation. "Why stay? Simply to blame yourself?"

Who else was to blame him? The law? It was a wartime act, even though there was no declared war; it was the act of a soldier, even though he was not a soldier. People were getting away with it all the time; military expedient, not murder. Who was to hold him to account? . . . Only a dead boy.

"I'll stay," he said.

Kalya, he was aware peripherally, had watched him every instant. Her eyes were wide and staring, anxious. Hurting, she was trying to lighten his onus. Don't, he wanted to say; you only make it heavier.

She looked away from him and down at the letter. She adjusted the lights around it. Her hands were not steady.

"Read it," Falkos said.

"The light . . . And the handwriting is not very clear," she said.

"Then read it slowly." He was encouraging a pupil.

"Dearest Yama," she began.

"I've never heard that name," Falkos said. "Is it a man's or a woman's?"

She glanced quickly at the first paragraph. "I think she was his . . ."

"Sweetheart?" Falkos said the old fashioned word with studied delicacy.

"Yes," Kalya answered. Then she read the letter:

"How terrible I feel that I won't be home for your birthday. I was promised a fortnight's leave, but at the last minute they decided they couldn't let so many of us go, and they're making me stay."

She stopped. "I cannot read the writing," she said.

"Why?" He moved around the table, looked over her shoulder. "It's not as unclear as that. I can almost read it myself."

She made the word out. "It's a name," she said. "It's Mehmet." Then she continued reading, still with difficulty.

"Mehmet was lucky, however, and will be allowed to go, so he will bring you my love, he will hold you closely for me, and give you the present I am just finishing for you.

"It is not much. I found a beautiful burl of wood in the dead leaves of the forest, and I have been carving you a ring. Your brother says it is an olive burl, but I think it is carob. Of course, you know how Mehmet is—the minute he finds out it is not olive, he will deny he ever said it was. I want it to be carob, because it will be unusual, it will be special, it will be something nobody has ever seen before—the way you are, and the way I love you.

"Anyway, olive or carob, it will be finished by the time Mehmet has to leave, at which time I will send this letter with the birthday gift."

She paused. Again she seemed to stumble over the words, and again Falkos seemed puzzled. But she recovered and went on:

"How good you are to go and see my mother and my aunt. Oddly, I think Aunt Nemeka must appreciate it more, because she has nobody, and her beautiful piano is silent unless I come and play it. Tell her not to send any more presents to me here; they get lost and I have not received any of them. I have written her the same, but she insists on sending, sending. Convince her that I mean it, and give her a special hug.

"I had looked forward to getting back to Istanbul before this. I hate the Birdrat for having taken me off the going-home list. Behind his back I called him Birdrat which is a name he hates, and somebody told him about it, so he punished me by putting me on night patrol. Three weeks now I have been on night patrol, and in the daytime I cannot sleep, especially because I miss you. I miss you very much. I miss you by day as well, whether I am on night patrol or not. When I finish the ring . . ."

There, apparently, the writing left off, and so did Kalya.

Since Ben had stayed to hear the letter as a punishment, he had just had it, like a scourge. He was deeply shaken.

Falkos too was perturbed; his face was waxen. His whole body seemed drained, as if drawn of blood; he was holding himself erect by spirit alone. He spoke with utmost control:

"Are you sure you read 'Birdrat'?"

She looked down and studied the handwriting more closely. "Yes—*Kuş-siçan*. It occurs twice in the letter."

He repeated the name to himself, a whisper. He was seeing the man again, now and years ago; perhaps hearing his wife's outcries, feeling the knife. He touched his mouth with his fingertips in a way that seemed autistic. Then, as if pulling himself out of a hallucination, he put his hands down to his sides, and summarily left the room.

Contemplating his departure, Kalya looked at Ben. "I wonder who Birdrat is."

"Cabrir."

"He sees Cabrir in everything," she said. "He thought Savvas was tortured by him."

"Do you know why he sees him in everything?"

She knew only rumors, and he related what Falkos had told him. She listened with a strange immutability, as if she only half heard him. They did not trust themselves to discuss what preoccupied both of them: Falkos had gone personally to question the prisoner, in whatever way he must.

But there was one aspect Ben did not understand. Suppose the schoolmaster were to find out that Cabrir was, after all, not in the Monastery itself, but somewhere in the woodland where the prisoner had been captured—what could the teacher do about it? It was now well after midnight. In a few hours, the intercom would splutter, the signal would be given, and they would all be en route to the mountaintop. And if Falkos did learn that Cabrir was not indeed up there, but in the woods, would he go to rash extremities to find him, would he endanger the attack on the Monastery? Ben speculated that if Cabrir was truly the totality of the war to Falkos, there would be no boundary he would not cross, no command he would not disobey, and sanity would have nothing to do with anything.

In another war, on the edge of the jungle near Phin Tsen, Ben had heard a sound he had never heard before—the cry of a macaw. It was macabre, it gave him the creeps. Tonight, this very minute, he heard the sound again, like a vicious parrot's voice, the screech of a bird mocking the madness of men. But the noise was made by a man.

Ben rushed out of the main room, with Kalya behind him. In the passageway, Petros was on guard.

"Where's that coming from?" Ben asked.

"Go back," Petros said.

"Where is it?"

The cry again. He started in the direction of it.

"Please—do not!" Petros said. He raised his revolver and pointed it at Ben's feet. Grimly, the medic guessed what his instructions had been: maim, but do not kill. Probably no different from the instructions about the imprisoned Turk.

The outcry was not repeated. Petros, frustrated by Ben's forbidden presence in the corridor, made a sharp movement with the gun. An instant longer they listened in the passageway for a repetition of the cry. When it didn't occur again, they returned to the main room.

And waited. They hardly spoke. There was an unusual stillness in the cave. Except for Petros, nobody passed the archway, there didn't seem to be anyone anywhere. Yet there was an etheric oscillation in the air, an inaudible vibrato, just a decibel too soft or a quaver too swift to be heard; its motion was like a quickening of the blood.

When nearly an hour had passed, Ben conjectured that the questioning was over, the prisoner had succumbed and told the schoolmaster where to find Cabrir. What did that signify, that

Falkos—in the middle of the night—had derangedly gone in search of him?

Just before one o'clock, the teacher appeared. Walking with taut control of every muscle, he could not conceal his agitation. Nobody need be told that he had had no success with the prisoner; he looked frenetic. "You'd better get some rest, or tomorrow will be impossible," he said.

It was a curt order. Kalya departed immediately. But with a motion of the hand, Falkos detained Ben. As the medic waited to hear why he was being held back, Falkos didn't speak, apparently not yet trusting his command of himself. His tormented face had turned to burning scarlet, like the blaze of crisis before the break of fever. Everything that would test him, all the trials he had prepared his angers for, were all coming at once. His time was dwindling—he had only a few hours to get the information from the Turk. The counting had begun on him, in ever decreasing numbers—a few human breaths before flash point. He was a radioactive dust, waiting for the spark.

"As you can imagine, I'm under more stress than usual," he started. "I don't want to drink any more—no sense in getting befuddled, is there? Do you have anything I can take?"

He meant a barbiturate or a tranquilizer. But he had been swilling even more than his reference had suggested, and in fact still hadn't stopped. "Considering that you've had a bit to drink, I don't think you ought to take anything else," Ben said quietly.

"Yes . . . I thought you'd say that."

He looked haunted. His whole being seemed shaky, spasmodic, without a stabilizer. "Try to get some sleep," he said. "And please—it'll be useless to do anything quixotic tonight, Benjamin —there will be a guard outside your room."

As Ben got to the archway, he heard the cry again. It was not at all like the earlier screams of pain. It was a mournful, forlorn sound, like a memory of torments long past, an old grief.

Ben spun to face him. "Tell them to stop it!"

A petty evasion. "I'm not doing it. It's Evagoras and Photis."

"On your orders. You said you weren't going to hurt him."

"Yes, when the questions were routine. But this is Cabrir."

The scream again.

"Stop them!"

"It's nothing to what they've done to us!"

"You bastard, stop them!"

"Stop Hiroshima!"

The man was berserk. "What?"

"You're an American—what would you rather have—Hiroshima?" he said fiercely. "Dresden? Cambodia?"

The question was unbalancing. "What have they got to do with it?"

"What would you rather do—kill the enemy at a distance, or torture him close at hand? You'd rather do it at a distance, wouldn't you? Drop a bomb on a *map,* so you don't see the child who gets it. So you don't see the father, the mother—only a console of levers, with buttons, with little lights that flicker. So you don't feel self-convicted—because you didn't do it—the instrument did it, the government did it. Is that what you'd rather have? That's *civilized* warfare—is that what you want? Well, I'll take the *primitive* kind! It's close, it's personal—I see my victim, I look him in the eye! I see my enemy suffer, I hear him cry for mercy, I watch his blood flow, I'm there when his parts are taken away from him! When it's over, I agonize over having caused it! I've seen what I've done and I'll remember it! I'll never erase his face from my mind! If I'm free of him by daylight, he'll haunt me at night! The guilt is with me all my life—I'm never absolved of it!"

"You think you should be absolved?"

"No! But guilt is *something,* isn't it? You don't even suffer that! How guilty do you personally feel about Hiroshima? *You* didn't do it—it was those others who dropped the bomb!"

"Christ, do you think I would try to justify Hiroshima?"

"You're an American—your citizenship 'justifies' it!"

There was a disturbance in the corridor. Petros and others were shouting, and Ben could hear Kalya calling. He rushed to the archway.

At the far end, he saw Mikis trying to keep Kalya from entering the passage. When she saw Ben, she shouted his name.

Behind him, he heard Falkos: "She's probably found the prisoner." He beckoned to the guard to let her approach.

She came running. "They're killing him!"

"How do you know?" Falkos said. "Have you seen him?"

"No—Mark has. They wouldn't let me in, but I was right outside the cell. Stop them—they'll kill him!"

"On the contrary, they'll try to keep him alive. We'll let him go entirely when he tells us where to find Cabrir."

"Will you let me tend to him?" Ben said.

Falkos turned to him. The thought gave him pause. He appraised it. "No, he's not that far gone. But perhaps—in a little while—if he starts slipping away from us."

It was trade cant, the professional jargon of torturers: death would be a slipping away of information, nothing more.

Falkos was still mulling Ben's question. "I'll make a deal with you," he said. "As a medic, you want to save his life. Perhaps you've got a nostrum worth a thousand bandages."

"I won't be one of your inquisitors," Ben said.

"I will."

Ben could not believe Kalya had offered it. "No," he said.

"I don't care about your talk—yours or his," she said grimly. "There's a man being tormented, and he's a poor fool. He thinks there are rules to the game, and he's following them. He doesn't know there aren't any rules, and there isn't any game. I'll talk to him in Turkish, I'll tell him that everybody lies to him, on both sides. I'll tell him to save his life, to answer anything they ask—I'll beg him."

Falkos nodded, trying not to show how gratified he was. He looked from one to another of them. Then, when he saw that Kalya was determined, he dispatched Petros for Ben's medical bag. Stepping between them, he led the way down the passageway.

They went up an incline, then through a tunnel, and when they came out of it, they were on a narrow gallery high above the more familiar corridor. Everything seemed different from the passages below, even the air seemed different, closer, more humid, with a faintly mephitic atmosphere of decay, as if this level of the mountain had died more recently than the places below. The last gallery upward was guarded by another sentry Ben had never seen before. He handed Falkos his lighted lamp and stepped aside, and they continued upward.

The Turk was in a cramped cavity of a room, an upright cylinder of darkness—or near-darkness, the candle in the niche throwing a mean little light. As the three of them entered with their lantern, they saw the prisoner. He was bound by ropes that were attached to a rusty iron grapnel, an old mining hook, which hung from a heavy metal bar that had been driven into the rocks. Although his feet were on the floor, they were tightly fettered, and his knees were bent; he would have fallen if the ropes had not held him upright. Either by accident or design, his hands were fastened in a tangled way so that his arms seemed twisted out of shape, and gave the illusion of one being longer than the other, and thinner.

Last night Ben had not noticed that the prisoner's hair was graying, and he was slightly bald. He wouldn't be a mainland Turk, Ben surmised, because nearly all those soldiers were youngsters, conscripted, like the dead one; this man would likely be a native Cypriot. He was fighting for what he knew and needed, his family, the right to be heard, a *dönüm* of land. Forty years old, perhaps, maybe fifty, it was hard to tell through the blood. There was much of it, some dried, some wet on the forehead and the neck, and oozing through the gray-green shirt. His mouth, too, was wet with it. Probably most of his pain came from his right hand, Ben would have judged; it was mauled and the thumb hung too loosely.

Photis sat on the ground, his back against the wall, resting. Evagoras stood near the prisoner. As Ben started toward the bound man, Evagoras moved between them. Ben shoved him aside and the Greek looked quickly to Falkos, who waved him out of the way.

The medic reached for the Turk's damaged hand. When he started to lift it a little, the man whimpered. Ben couldn't tell what was wrong with the wrist, but something was broken in it.

When Petros arrived with the medical bag, Falkos took it before Ben could lay hands on it. "Not yet," the teacher said. "I want you to be clear about procedure. The man has told us a dozen things—all immaterial and all lies. I only want to know where Cabrir is. He says he doesn't know. The Captain disappeared a week ago, he says, and left the patrolling company in the hands of a subordinate."

"What if that's true?"

"It's not true. He repeats it from memory—it's instructed information."

He gave his attention to Kalya. "Talk to him in Turkish," he said. "Convince him you mean him no harm. I want the truth— where's Cabrir? That's all I need to know. If he tells you, he'll be free—I give my word. When we go, I'll leave him here with food and without a guard. As soon as Benjamin can be spared, he can come down and take care of the man—and he's on his way—he can go back to his family. . . . But if he doesn't tell you, the next hour will be terrible for him—tell him that. Make him understand one thing. It's not a military question I'm asking. If he wants to save himself some pain, he has to do the same for me."

He said it nakedly, without shame. Then, unpredictably, a sensitive consideration occurred to him. "If it'll be easier for him, I'll clear the room of Greeks." He motioned to Photis and Evagoras, telling them to stand guard outside the cell. As they left, he started to follow them. Bethinking himself, he said to Ben, "If it should occur to you that the better part of mercy is to put him out of his misery—don't. I want the man alive."

He departed.

Ben hurried to the wounded man. He lifted some of the matted hair away from the bloody forehead. As he did, the man moaned and muttered.

"What does he say?" Ben asked.

"He only wants you to let him alone," she replied.

Ben opened his bag, reached for a vial of sedative and his hypodermic needle. As he was preparing it, "What are you going to do?" she asked.

"Put him to sleep—so he'll be no good to them."

"Don't. They'll kill him trying to wake him up."

She was probably right. He had no idea how far their barbarities might go. "I'll just give him a little," he said. "If I don't, he won't be able to stand it when I treat him."

"Wait—let me ask him—"

"No."

"I may save him more pain than that will." She pointed to the hypodermic.

Before he could demur any further, she turned to the Turk. She spoke quickly to him, in their own language, the sentences spilling out of her, pleading. The only term Ben understood was the name Captain Cabrir.

The man turned his head away from her and lifted it, as if to withdraw his consciousness from this place.

"Lûtfen," she said. It was an entreaty. "Lûtfen." She said it over and over again.

At last the Turk looked painfully down at Ben. His tongue and his accent were thick. "Tell her go to hell." Then he added quietly:

"She not fool me—she is not Turkish."

Kalya stopped beseeching him. The Turk had disabled her.

She seemed suddenly defenseless, incapable of asking him anything else. She turned away.

Not Turkish.

Quickly Ben finished filling the hypodermic. He reached for the Turk's arm, thinking it was an uninjured place. But the man let out the terrifying cry, the parrot shriek, once, twice, continuously.

Ben administered the drug and waited. It wouldn't be enough to knock him out, but it would mitigate the pain. In a little while the prisoner stopped screaming. His breath came in gasps; he was not unconscious. Ben cauterized and bandaged his hand. Without an X-ray, it was only makeshift work. He cleaned the head wounds, swabbed them, didn't feel that he was healing anything or even soothing, only purging a little, possibly fighting an infection.

How long Mark had been there he didn't know. He stood at the entrance to the room, watching as silently as if he were a student in an operating room amphitheater. He was phenomenally calm. He's getting his revenge, Ben thought, watching the anguish of a Turk.

Kalya apparently interpreted the boy's expression similarly. "Go away," she said.

"No." There was no contention in his voice. "I have to see."

"See what?" Ben said. "See them tear him apart?"

"See . . . everything." He was steadier than Ben would have imagined possible. "When Photis was beating him a while ago, I was in the passageway. I heard what he was doing to him. The man was trying not to scream, not to make any noise. Then Evagoras came with a bar that had nails in it. That's when he started to scream. And I thought: He's a Turk—I should be glad. But it made me sick."

He was not talking about epileptic sickness, but a revulsion that was stronger than seizure.

"Kill him," he said quietly.

Ben realized he had mistaken what he had read in the boy's face. Not revenge, but pity. He was suggesting that Ben perform an act of mercy. And he wondered how many killers had thought their hands were merciful, and whether death might sometimes be the only mercy left.

"Kill him," he pleaded again.

"Go away," Ben whispered.

"He'll only suffer—kill him."

"Kalya, please—take him away."

She didn't move.

Unhurriedly, Mark turned and they could barely hear his footsteps in the passageway.

The Turk's breathing was as calm as peaceful slumber. Anesthetized as he was, he was still conscious, and Ben recalled a quibbling question raised when he was a medical student, whether there was any difference between insensibility and absence of feeling, and the professor's supercilious query: Whose feeling, yours or the patient's?

Kalya was staring at the wounded man almost as if she were afraid for him to speak.

"Do you want to question him any further?" he asked.

"No."

It was a mordant thing to ask, and he had spoken it compulsively, needing to know what she might reveal. She had failed—not only with the prisoner, but in a way he could not comprehend. He put his hand on her arm and led her out of the room. She might have been sleepwalking.

As they passed the men, he saw Evagoras reentering the room, followed by Photis. A little way along the tunnel, Falkos came out of a shadowed place. He looked at Kalya, then at Ben, and knew they had not succeeded. He hurried past them. At the place where the gallery passage joined the corridor, Petros was waiting for them. Following them down the corridor, he maintained a discreet distance, but he was vigilant.

They heard no sound from the prisoner. Even when they had arrived at the entrance to Kalya's cell, no sound. Ben wondered if the anesthetic had weakened the Turk's will, and he had spoken. If so—ironically—it was Ben's mercy that had contributed to the surrender of the man.

When they were alone in the room, away from Petros's view of them, he stared into the dimness—the room, the bed where they had made love.

She was watching him, and quite tense. In a frightened voice, "I don't want to be with you tonight," she said.

"I know."

And he also knew why. She could not make love without, at last, facing the lie. He tried to help her. "What did he mean by saying you're not a Turk?"

It was like a midnight instant, neither today nor tomorrow; this was the instant of Kalya, neither truth nor falsehood. He thought she was going to tell him; then she couldn't. "I don't know," she said evasively. "I think he was . . . repudiating a Turk who was a traitor."

Her answer sounded reasonable enough. Yet, having said it, she panicked. Her glance seemed fugitive, no place to hide. Another lie. He touched her tenderly on the cheek, and turned to leave the room.

She clung to him and laid her head on his breast. "I love you very much, Ben. I've never loved anyone as I love you."

She didn't want him to leave with a lie in his mind, her embrace was telling him. He believed that it *was* the truth, that she loved him. And while it counted for nearly all that was good in his life right now, nearly all he wanted, it wasn't everything.

"I love you too, Kalya," he said.

In the passage, on the way to his own cell, he kept saying the other words to himself:

Kalya is not a Turk.

The prisoner was not abstractly repudiating a Turkish woman who had betrayed her people—he was concretely denying that she had ever been one. It was, to the man, a matter of determinate fact: not only did she not act like one, she didn't speak like one.

Nor did she read like one, Ben remembered. The young Turk's letter was not illegible, it was precisely written, and a Turkish woman educated in a Turkish university . . .

And the larger lie: Nexos.

She had lived in the town. Inland or by the sea, whatever small prevarications she chose, it was a village that she knew. Which meant she knew Mark's parents, knew the horror that had happened there. When the boy had mentioned Nexos, it had been a terror of some sort, she had been barely able to cope with it. Yet, she had not said a word about ever having seen the place. Even in Ben's presence—when he knew she had lived there—her silence had been a lie.

But the most lamentable falsehood of all . . . He did not want to gaze too intently at it. Perhaps it was not really a falsehood, only a gross misapprehension, a question that had gone unasked, and was unanswerable:

Her affinity to the boy. But the closeness meant nothing. God knows there had been enough animosity between them. Yet, under the enmity, and even as a part of it, there was a sexual attraction. However, it was more than the libido of hostility on Kalya's part, there had been a heart of pity in it, of womanly compassion for a boy afflicted, of motherly tenderness for a child. If she mothered Mark, so had she mothered Ben when he was hurt, and Yannis. Mothering was her essence.

No more. He mustn't get seduced by Kalya's persuasion that life is ruled by the Fates, and we are their whimsies. He could not believe that we are the toys of coincidence. Those two, strangers, a woman and a boy living half a world apart, suddenly cast together by an offhand irony—no, Ben said, our lives are not controlled by such malicious accidents. Not that he was a rigid scientist who believed in the infallibility of numbers and measurements. Nor was he a doctor who felt that every symptom had a logical explication; but while not making a religion of the canon of cause and effect, he did put trust in it; and he could not believe we were helpless in a world of caprice. Oh murder, he thought, haven't we been able to light our way out of the cave of chance?

Chance? Abruptly, he realized that he *was* falling into Kalya's fatalistic trap, blaming everything on the Fates, the stars, the gods of ironic accident. But how much coincidence could there be in the boy's discovering his true parentage? Wasn't that what he had come here for, wasn't that his *purpose?* He had even had a specific place in mind, Nexos, a tiny village on a small island where the adage went that to turn a corner was to run into your cousin or your enemy, never a stranger. He was not a world rover, wandering without intention or destination, he was an impassioned boy on a single-minded search, in quest of his past—and sooner or later he would be bound to find it. Sooner or later—Nexos always being smaller than we imagine—he would have found his parents and re-created them . . . as we all re-create them, to our necessity. He would have found a past that would justify his future. Not an accident, not a coincidence, Ben said: *Mark* made the meeting, not the Fates.

And Ben had the feeling that if the son found the father, and killed him, he would not blame the gods, but would take it all upon himself, all the pain and penalty, for Mark was a modern, not an ancient. What an unrecoverable loss, what a sad loss, on the day we learned that we no longer had the Fates to blame!

But, he asked, what if she really is his mother? Would there be—finally—no Fates to blame?

About a half hour later, lying on his bed, fully clothed, unable to sleep, he heard footsteps in the corridor. He hoped it would be Kalya, but it wasn't. It was Mark.

He did not fully enter the room but hung back, barely inside it, hesitating, absently rubbing his neck as if he had just gotten out of a tight collar. He didn't move, just stood there, diffident and misplaced.

"I saw the flicker of your light," he said. Then his voice went lamely to nothing. After a moment. "You can't sleep either?"

"No."

"Strange—I'm not scared. I'm not even thinking about going up the mountain . . ."

He wanted to be asked the question. "What are you thinking about?"

"The prisoner . . . the Turk."

". . . Yes."

"I haven't heard another sound, have you?"

"No."

"What does it mean?"

"I don't know."

"You think he talked? . . . Or is he dead?"

"I don't know," he repeated.

"Why are they torturing him?"

"Falkos wants him to tell where Cabrir is."

"I know that. And I've heard who Cabrir is. . . . But why are they torturing him?"

The boy was not making sense. He had asked a question and had had a direct answer. Apparently he knew enough about Cabrir for the answer to be comprehensible to him. But he was refusing to understand it. Seeming to deny his intelligence, he was allowing himself to be witless. Yet, there was an extra animation about him; his eyes were unnaturally bright.

Uncertain how to reply, Ben merely observed him. Mark continued. "He's only an ordinary soldier, isn't he?" His mind was running too fast, falling all over itself. "He doesn't seem bright— he's not an officer or anything—he's only a soldier. What I mean

—not *important*. Why are they hurting him? Is he important enough to hurt?"

"He's too important to hurt."

"I mean—he doesn't seem as bright as I am, or as you are. Nothing will be gained by hurting him—nothing. Why are they hurting him?"

It was not a reasoned question, Ben realized, and the boy was not expecting a reasoned answer.

Mark rushed onward. "Suppose it's—what the Turk was telling them—suppose it's true. I believe it *is* true—that he doesn't know where Cabrir is—then why are they torturing him?"

"They don't believe it's true."

". . . I think they do believe it."

There was a horror in his mind, a hideousness the boy could not face: cruelty for its own sake. Brutality, not as an ancillary pleasure, but as the innate hedonism of war. But the boy might be suffering another confusion. Wasn't this what he had come to Cyprus for, to commit a savagery against the Turks?

Ben saw his agitation. "Mark, *you're* not doing it to him."

"I'm . . . not sure." Then, mercilessly studying himself, "When you came back—and they said you killed a Turk—I envied you. Then when Yannis died, I thought: I can't wait until tomorrow, I can't wait to get the rifle in my hand. And then . . . when I heard the man screaming . . ."

"But you still want to carry the rifle."

". . . I don't know."

The boy seemed feverish. He kept licking his lips, they were parched. And it looked as if he wanted to be here, but wanted to run. Then, the cry:

"What shall I do?"

"You don't have to go tomorrow, Mark."

"Yes, I do."

"No—you can get out of it."

"You're going."

"Not by choice. And I won't be carrying a gun. I'm going because Falkos said he'd kill me if I don't—and I believe him. But he'll do nothing to you. He'll write you off as being ill—which you are, Mark—you have a right to get out of this."

"What do I do, have a seizure? Every time I'm frightened or in a rage—is that what I run to? Is that going to be my answer to everything?"

"It's not your answer to anything! It simply gives you a legitimate excuse for getting out of it."

"I won't use my illness as an excuse for being a coward!"

Ben's throat tightened. The sore word again—discordant and deviate—he mustn't respond to it by confusing himself with the boy. He didn't speak. At last, when he felt sure he was seeing Mark separately:

"You're not a coward. That's not why you would be getting out of it—because you're scared. You're getting out because you're *revolted*. That Turk up there—looking at him tonight—you can't be part of that. And it's not cowardice."

"What if it is? What if some things we call decency are really only a . . . preference for safety."

Quietly: "If you're willing to risk your life for them—that's not a preference for safety, is it?"

Equally quiet: "You're talking about yourself—and you don't have to prove anything, Ben . . . but I do."

Suddenly the boy was desperately important to him, and he wanted compellingly for him not to go. "You don't have to prove it here, Mark—and you don't have to prove it tomorrow. You'll find other ways to prove it—believe me, Mark, you will. And you won't have the aching doubts about them that you have about this one. You'll be sure. They'll be your own imperatives, Mark. They'll clarify everything for you—and they'll give you strength. I promise you—that'll happen. Just wait, Mark. Don't go up tomorrow."

The boy was touched, but trying to distance himself—not from Ben, but from what he was saying. Still, man and matter were inseparable, and the medic obviously cared so genuinely, so deeply.

"Let me think about it," Mark said.

Ben realized that he would not be pushed into a promise tonight, nor did he want to prevail upon him. Let the boy persuade himself, he said, if he's to be persuaded at all.

Mark seemed to be emerging a little; he was even able to attempt a smile. "Thank you, Ben. I feel much better." He discovered something that pleased him. "You're a good doctor."

This moment, Ben said to himself, I think I could be. I think I care too much about healing for me not to be, as if that were all of it. With a surge of optimism, he thought: The boy won't go tomorrow; I feel it in my bones, he won't—and I'll have helped him decide that way.

Abruptly, a glowing thing happened between them: they simply stood there and smiled at each other; no more than that, but it was just as good as a handshake, or even an embrace.

"Where's Kalya?" Mark said.

"In her room."

"No, she's not."

"I left her there a little while ago. She probably couldn't sleep either. Did you look in the main room?"

"She's not there. I thought she might be with you."

Disquiet. Something namelessly alarming about her not being in either place. "She may have needed a breath of air. Did you go up to the parking area?"

"Yes. Kostas didn't see her. Nobody did."

Ben hurried past the boy, into the hallway. Petros was sitting on the earth floor, his back against the wall. Half asleep, the young man stirred quickly and jumped to his feet. "Wait," he said.

"I'm not going anywhere," Ben said. "You can come with me."

Not waiting for permission, he hastened down the passageway with Mark and Petros following him. He made the same stops as Mark had made, Kalya's room first, then the main room, and she was in neither place. Just as he was about to climb the passage to the outdoors, an image flashed: she was with Falkos and the prisoner.

It was too erratic, it didn't make sense. Yet, some kink in his thread of reasoning made him sure he was right.

He was almost right. As they left the incline and started up the rocky stairway that entered the gallery, they saw her. She was sitting on the topmost step, huddled into the corner against the wall. Quite a distance and a number of levels away from the room in which she had pleaded with the prisoner, she was many hundreds of feet closer to him than she would be if she were still in her room. In trouble herself, she had gravitated, as she always did, to the more troubled.

She was in a daze. She looked as if someone had dealt her a terrible blow that had stunned her. And she seemed to have dwindled, to fit the small darkness she sat in.

"Kalya . . . ?"

"I haven't heard a sound of him, have you?" she asked.

The same questions, the same answers, had he spoken or was he dead?

"Come on," he said softly, "let's go down."

She was totally submissive, seemed relieved that someone had come to fetch her. As they started down the steps, she shivered as if cold, and he put his arm around her. She looked at him gratefully and smiled. It wasn't only because Petros was there that they said nothing; he knew she had a constraining need to be silent. Yet he also knew that under a fragile membrane she held back a flood of words that had to be spoken.

When they got back to her room, the quiet seemed even more ponderous. The only disturbance of it was a sound from the hallway, perhaps fifty feet away, Petros yawning. None of the three of them was yawning, however. We're all too vigilant, he thought, watching for what?

She sat on the edge of her bed; Mark, on a three-legged stool, leaning forward, his arms on his knees, looking at the ground. When the boy raised his head and both their faces were caught in the candlelight, Ben thought: They resemble each other. He changed his mind—it was purely imaginary. A professor had once told him that he short-circuited neurons, built faulty synapses. When the dissociation of phenomena was too frustratingly confusing, the man had said, you fabricate relationships between elements that can be nothing but strangers to each other.

These two were strangers.

Yet, he had to know.

How could he go about it? He was not an inquisitor, like those others. And any question he might ask could be a rack, a wheel of torture to her. He couldn't do it. He knew that in the middle of the inquiry he would break down and go no further. If there was a doubt, he would make her a present of it, not a gift but a forfeit.

Suppose she did tell him the truth about herself, was he equal to it, no matter what it might be? What if she were hiding something so horrendous about herself that he could not continue to love her? He could not imagine such a thing. In any event, what he did not know about her was what separated them, what had always separated them. Incongruously, the mystery about her was what had attracted her to him, and now it was keeping them apart. It had stood between them tonight, preventing them from making love. It was the limbo that kept them isolated from one another, each of them alone.

"What did that man mean—not a Turk?" he started.

"I told you," she replied, almost inaudibly.

"I don't think he meant he was repudiating you as a traitor," he said.

"What do you think he meant?"

"That you talk like a Greek."

"I've lived with Greeks for many years—nearly all my life."

"In Nexos?"

They heard the boy take a startled breath. "Nexos?"

She looked to the doorway as if to flee. Ben said, "Wait, Kalya."

"You've been to Nexos?" Mark asked.

She did not answer.

"Yes, she has."

"You've lived there?"

"No!" She was chaotic now, as if flight were in every direction. "I used to visit and I—" She was unable to continue. "Go away," she said roughly. "I have to talk to Ben—go away."

"You knew my parents, didn't you?"

"Go away!" Pleading, to Ben. "Please send him away!"

"I won't go away," Mark said. "Tell me what you know about my parents."

She darted away from him, then toward the doorway. Mark ran ahead of her and stopped her. "You did know my father and mother, didn't you? You probably had something to do with her death, didn't you? Didn't you? You were probably one of the Turks who—"

"I'm not a Turk!" she cried. "I never killed anyone, I never hurt anyone!"

"You're lying!"

He was out of control, wild. He raised his arm as if to strike her and Ben moved quickly between them.

"Tell him, Kalya," he pleaded. "You have to tell him."

"I can't!"

She trembled. The sobs shook her. One last time, she started to flee, but Ben took her, held her steadyingly, trying to keep her from shaking apart.

"Kalya, tell him."

After a while, she stopped quaking. Gently, she disengaged herself from his strength. She was doing quite well, he thought, in charge of herself again. Although she was not quite fortified enough to look at them when she spoke, her voice was surprisingly composed.

"I'm a Greek, and my husband was a Turk," she said. "I met him when we were children, when our being together seemed a—a quaint thing—I mean to our parents, a quaint thing—not like child and child, but like a child and an endearing pet. How sweet they are together, our parents used to say."

She stopped. She put both hands to her mouth. When she saw the tremor in them, she quickly put them down again. "I can't do it," she said.

All three were silent. Moments later, she went on.

"My father owned a cannery in Akti. It was one of the few good fishing villages on the western coast of the island. We were well off, my family. It was a beautiful town—I loved it—I practically lived in the water. They used to call me *galani*. It's a fisherman's name for a beautiful blue gull that seems to swim but actually sweeps the surface of the water with its wings.

"Akti was almost totally a Greek town, but there were a few Turkish families. They were all quiet people, there was never any problem. My father used to say, 'The Turks are peaceable people, they are satisfied with fishbones.'

"But there was one who was not satisfied with fishbones. His name was Tero Sormak. He was only a few years older than I—the quickest, brightest person I had ever met. He taught me everything I ever learned about the sea—how to read the sky and the seaweed, how to live with the tides, how to interpret every scrap of flotsam that came drifting up at daybreak.

"I can't remember when I was not in love with him. It seems that with my first strokes into the sea, as I tried to swim out toward him, I was swimming to someone without whom I could not live.

"When I was nine years old, our family moved to Limassol into a fancy house with three floors and as many books as I ever wanted to read. I think my parents moved away from Akti not only to send me to school in the city, but because they were desperate to separate me from Tero. But my father kept the cannery, and summertimes we went back to the sea, my mother and I, and my father would come only on Sunday. That would be the day I didn't see Tero.

"When I was fifteen years old, they knew how serious it was, and from that time on, we didn't go back to Akti at all. I didn't see Tero again until I was seventeen. I was being sent away from Cyprus—to the university in Athens—and the thought of going so far from Tero was so unbearable that I wrote to him, and we stealthily met each other on the beach. And we made love for the first time. When my father heard about it, he beat me and locked me in my room. He didn't let me out until two hours before my plane left for Athens.

"Tero's schooling had been over when he was sixteen. He didn't mind the lack of it—he wanted to be a shipwright. So he had apprenticed himself to Alekos Leonides, who was the only shipwright in Akti. He was a good old man, very proud of all his Greek ancestors who had lived by the sea. He was truly fond of Tero, and it never mattered to him that the boy was not Greek. In fact, I never heard Leonides say an unkind word against any Turk.

"The old man had a son who was also an apprentice. They called him Yotis, and he had something wrong with him. We never understood what it was. Nothing physically wrong, but a kind of verbal perversity—he twisted everything you said, and made it sound vulgar or dishonest or foolish. He was the first person I ever heard say anything mean about a Turk—and he said it about Tero. He called him a Turkish *karoxa*. It is the name of an ugly and filthy fish that is caught by trawlers. It will devour anything, even its own waste matter. The sport fishermen will not use them for bait, they contemptuously throw them back into the sea.

"Yotis was actually an excellent shipwright—even more skilled than Tero—but he was very envious. Partly, I'm sure, because I was in love with Tero—but mostly because everyone loved him. When the fishermen came into the shipyard—even the Greek fishermen—they took their damaged boats to Yotis only if Tero was too busy.

"You would have thought, in those days, that no Greek would ever lift a finger against this twenty-year-old Turkish boy—they loved him too much. However, they didn't know how seriously he and I loved each other—and giving him work was one thing, but intermarriage was another. Especially since the trouble with the English was starting to frighten everybody, and it was now being said that the Turks were betraying their Greek neighbors to the British.

"Things were getting worse and worse between Yotis and Tero, and old Leonides was having difficulty maintaining the peace between them. Then quite suddenly Leonides died. And the very day Yotis came into ownership of the yard, he discharged Tero.

"So Tero let it be known that he was a shipwright on his own —and he would mend boats outside the shipyard by paying rent at the public wharf. It was a hazardous thing to do—a Turk going into competition with a Greek in a tiny fishing village. But for a while he did very well—and we optimistically decided to let it be known we were in love with one another—especially since most of the village already knew it. When we were open about it—except for an insult or two and a little scuffle in the taverna—the villagers didn't harm us. That summer—I had just finished my second year in college—Tero sold his small boat and started to build a larger one with a sizable cabin in it, and I helped him build it. When it was finished, we began to live in it.

"I can't tell you how I hated going back to college, but I went. Very shortly afterward, I realized I was pregnant. I wrote to Tero and he said come home quickly and we'll be married. But when I told my father about it, he sent me a very brief letter—on his company's business stationery—and he let it be known I was no longer his daughter. Much as that hurt me, I was happy to go back to Tero. So I met him in Nicosia. Since he was Muslim and I was Greek Orthodox, we had decided we would have a civil ceremony only—and we were married by a British justice.

"We had no intention of keeping it secret, not even for a few months. We didn't anticipate any real trouble. How the people of Akti found out about the ceremony before we even returned, I don't know. There was a rumor that my father told them, and I believe it was true. Anyway, when we got back to the village, Tero's new boat was gone—we couldn't find it. The following morning we discovered it in one of the coves. It had been torn apart, chopped to splinters, and neatly piled into a mound of firewood, ready for the match.

"And the most ominous part of it: everybody in the town professed to be shocked by it. Neighbors came, offering food and bedding. The priest arrived and commiserated. The man who owned the taverna said we could eat there as long as we liked and stay in a back room free, until Tero could build himself another boat. And nobody in the village had the vaguest idea who had sailed the boat out of the tiny harbor, and who had smashed it to bits.

"Tero did build another boat. It was the same size as the first, but more beautiful. It was a present for me, he said. He called it the *Galani* and carved a figurehead out of cedarwood, the most uncanny likeness of me, with the wings of a blue gull. That boat was the happiest home I have ever lived in. And in it my daughter was born.

"She was an exquisite child, as perfectly formed as a child need be. She was free of the slightest taint of sickness. And when she was five months old, she was dead. The doctor said he didn't know what she had died of. He said croup, he said a heart failure, he said there were accidents of birth. I said it was murder. Tero sided with the doctor. I was getting paranoiac, he insisted—I was seeing persecution even from our friends. But someone, one night in the taverna, was reported to have whispered that the doctor had known all the time that the child had an infected appendix; he had let it rupture, and let her die.

"I wanted to move from Akti, but my husband was doing well again, people were coming to him with their damaged vessels; some were asking him to build from the very hull. He had even built his own little boatyard.

"I became pregnant again and had the second child. It was a boy. He was as beautiful as his sister—and you have never seen such a vigilant mother. I would not let anyone come near him except his father, I studied books so that I could doctor him myself if he became ill. I watched over him day and night. I was even suspicious of food that came in tins, and I was still nursing him when he was nearly a year old.

"One night a gray-green lorry drove into the village. Four English soldiers got out and arrested two Greek men. One of the Greeks was a cousin of Yotis. His name was Ernos. He was a fisherman who had a large caique—and the English charged that he was smuggling arms to the guerrillas. When the lorry left the village, Yotis told somebody that Tero had worked on the caique, had mended it, and was the only one likely to have known what Ernos carried in it—therefore, the only one who could have betrayed him to the British.

"We didn't know any of this was happening—we lived on our boat, which was moored in the cove. But in the middle of the night, we saw an automobile approach. It stopped where the gravel ended, and we saw a man rushing toward us. It was the priest, Father Vasilios. Get out, he said, leave the village, everybody thinks you informed on Ernos. Hurry, he said, don't even wait until the morning.

"He offered to drive us to Mesoyi, which was a town quite a distance away, where there was a constabulary of British. At first Tero wouldn't go. If we went for the protection of the British, it would be an admission that he had betrayed Ernos—and he hadn't, it wasn't true—Ernos had always been a better friend to Tero than he had been to his own cousin. But we convinced my husband that the truth hadn't anything to do with vengeance. We bundled up our child, we took what we could carry, and drove with the priest to Mesoyi.

"It was impossible there. The three of us were confined to a tiny room in a small *panthohion* where the other boarders were mostly invalid, and the hallways smelled of disinfectant. Besides, we had little money—Tero could not be a shipwright in an inland village. And we longed for the *Galani* and the sea. Through Father Vasilios we learned that Yotis had not damaged our boat—he was counting on it to draw Tero back to the village, and then they would lay their hands on him.

"One morning, Tero was gone. He had left me a note saying that the innkeeper was going to drive him to a bus which would take him close to Akti. He would arrive there in the darkness. Somehow or other he was going to board his boat and sail it around the little headland. When he got to a safer port, he would get in touch with me and we would start our life over, somewhere else.

"I didn't hear from him for three weeks. A dozen times I telephoned the priest, but all he knew was that the boat was gone, and nobody spoke of it anymore. There were no rumors, no speculations. It was as if the incident were totally closed.

"Then—on a morning in April—I got an excited telephone call from Father Vasilios. He was in a state of bliss. He had had an anonymous message—a handwritten note—saying that my husband had finally succeeded. Tero had managed to board his boat and take it out to sea, but he had had difficulties with it. However, everything was now in order, and he would meet me at a cove near Pomos at sunset today. The priest said he would come and pick me up in the late afternoon, and drive me to the cove.

"For a moment, I had a terror—it might be a trap. They might want to kill me, or my second child, or both of us. But if there was any chance I could be with Tero again, I had no alternative, I had to take it. And the priest was not a bad man or a foolish man, and he trusted the note, so I felt that I too could trust it.

"That afternoon Father Vasilios arrived at the *panthohion* and drove us across the hills and downward to the sea. I can't tell you what I felt when I breathed the damp salt air again, and as we made our last descent toward the seacoast, I imagined I was on those cresting waves. And there it was—the *Galani*—just as it always was—moored where the rocks touched the strand. Oh, how lovely it was!

"Drive faster, I said to the old man, drive faster, can't you drive faster? And then, just as we were a stone's throw away, he stopped the car, and I heard him say oh no, oh no, and he began to sob.

"I had momentarily glanced down to my son as if to share my joy with him, and when I looked up I saw what the priest had seen.

"The figurehead on the boat was not the form of a woman, it wasn't my likeness. It had been replaced. Impaled on the rod of the figurehead was the head of my husband.

"I ran toward it—not believing it was real—not believing that I saw it—I had to touch it, I had to feel if it was true flesh. But I couldn't seem to reach the boat. It was there—it was not moving —and I was running toward it—but I couldn't get any closer. I felt that I would die if I couldn't find out for certain. But the distance got longer and, no matter how fast I ran, the boat got further and further away. And I never reached it.

"It was dark before I became aware of anything. I could hear the waves, but I could barely see the water. The sky was so close that I thought the stars were part of my clothes. And I was totally alone. There was no sign of the boat. Father Vasilios was gone too, and so was the car.

"I couldn't find my child. That was the only reality—my child was missing. Already, I was telling myself that all the rest had never happened—I had not come here with any priest, I had not seen any boat, I had not seen the bloody head of my husband. There was only one truth, one trouble I must manage: my son was gone, and I would have to find him.

"Searching the beach, I never let it occur to me that my child might be dead. In the darkness, I made my way to the nearest village. Everyone was asleep. I knocked at the door of a bakery and from the rear, a woman came outdoors to see who it was. I don't know whether she believed what I told her, but she knew nothing of the whereabouts of any missing child. All she could do was give me coffee and offer to dry my clothes, which had become wet with the sea damp.

"For two days I wandered through the village and to the nearby farms, knocking on doors, asking everybody. I tried to telephone Father Vasilios in Akti but his housekeeper said he had not been seen for two days. But I wasn't sure she was telling me the truth. So I went back to the bakery, and borrowed money for the bus fare that would take me to the hill above Akti. When I arrived I walked down into the town and went directly to the church.

"It was locked. There was nobody anywhere—not in the church itself, not in the house close by where Father Vasilios lived. I waited and waited, and toward dusk the housekeeper came. She was a senile woman called Ismene, and it was difficult to make sense of what she said, but she repeated that she hadn't seen the priest in a few days, and didn't know where he was. She was certain of only one thing: it was dangerous for me to be in this village.

"But she was kind to me. She took me into her own little house, and hid me while I waited for the return of Father Vasilios. Nearly a week went by and he didn't come. I couldn't just do nothing but hide in that little back room, so at last I determined to go to the harbor. I entered Yotis's dockyard and found him working. I tried to be as cunning as I could, never even mentioned the murder of my husband—as if I didn't know it had ever happened—I simply asked him where I could find my child.

"He pretended to be puzzled by my inquiry. He didn't know anything about anything. He had not stirred from his home and dockyard in over a fortnight. As I continued to ask questions, he got angry that I should involve him in what he called my Turkish perversions. I would do well to take my troubles to the Muslims.

"I walked along the inlet to the village square. I asked everybody I knew, and hardly anyone would talk to me. When I greeted old friends or neighbors, they turned away. Someone spat at me. Two boys followed me and called me the wife of an informer; they called me Turkish whore.

"As I approached Ismene's house, she came rushing out to me. The village telephone exchange had had a message that Father Vasilios had died in Nicosia. Nobody knew anything else about him, she said, except that he had asked to be buried in Akti, where he had spent forty years of his priesthood.

"His body arrived the following morning. On the day of the

funeral, Yotis confronted me and, in the presence of the towns-people, said I had been responsible for the old man's death. How I had been responsible he didn't say, but it was implicit in his charge against me that he knew more about the whole occurrence than he had pretended, and that others knew as well.

"I began to get frantic. I followed every clue, I pestered any-one who was willing to glance at me. If someone gave me the slightest hint of my son's whereabouts—no matter how mocking it was—I followed it.

"Bit by bit, I became aware that they were treating me as the village madwoman. And I didn't care. In my secret mind, I felt they were right. Because I was beginning to have delusions. Al-though I had accepted the reality that my husband had died, I began to imagine it had happened in a way I could endure. I saw him lying under a beautiful tree, and dying of a painless ailment. I saw him die while we were making love. Sometimes I made compromises—he had died horribly, but not as horribly as I had witnessed. For example, one night there was a torchlight parade in the village—with flaming besom brooms as torches. I imagined they were burning our wharf and all the boats—and my husband had jumped from one of them, and had swum into the distance, be-yond endurance, and had died in the sea.

"Then I began to have nightmares about my son. I saw him murdered in the same way as my husband had been murdered. And the townspeople contributed to my nightmares. It was a fur-tive kind of torture. I would get messages that my child was alive. One day a note was placed under Ismene's door. 'Go to the lacemaker's house. She has your baby.' But there was no lace-maker in the village, nor in any village within thirty miles. An-other day, a fisherman stopped me on the street. He whispered that there was a rumor my son was alive, but crippled, and that was all he knew. One morning I was asleep when I heard a knocking on the window. I opened the sash and nobody was there. But I saw a paper bag on the sill. In it was the cotton sweater my son had worn on the last day I saw him. I had a terrifying visit from a wizened old woman who sold charcoal. She had been instructed to tell me how my son had been killed. They had butchered him and thrown his scraps to the *karoxa* fish.

"That night I heard the screams. They were my own but I didn't know it. I awoke in the middle of a vast darkness and I saw an animal—I cannot describe what it looked like—it started to tear at my skin. I could feel the gashes it was making, ripping flesh away. When I turned the light on, there was no animal, and my hands were bloody.

"Another time, when I was coming out of the church, a man pushed me down the steps, saying I was filthy, I had fouled my clothes. Which indeed I had.

"What happened in the street one morning—I cannot tell how much of it was real, and how much I imagined. I saw the little boy, that much was real. He looked the image of my son—the same age —the same hair that turned off his forehead in a crooked way. And I swear—at least I swore it at the time—that I believed he was my son—even if he wasn't, I *believed* he was. He was playing at the place where the cobbles ended and the wharf began. There was a pile of sand there, and a pile of heavy rock—they were building up the breakwater. The boy was pouring sand into a little enclosure of pebbles, filling it, very industriously filling it. His hands were my son's hands—or so they seemed to me—the same fingernails, everything. I didn't rush to him. I recall how proud I was of my self-control—I watched him and watched him and didn't stir a foot or make a sound. Then, when I was certain it was he, I walked slowly to where he played and I talked softly to him. He smiled, he spoke, he wasn't afraid. Suddenly I had to hold him in my arms. I bent down, I picked him up, and something in my manner—perhaps my intensity, perhaps I began to weep—it frightened him, and he cried out for his mother. I said I was his mother, and I begged him, 'Don't cry,' I said, 'don't, I won't hurt you, don't. The people will come—stop crying—don't!' And I put my hand over his mouth, and ran with him in my arms. There was a shout from the wharf, and another from the tackle shop—'She's stealing a child, she's stealing a child!' And from every direction, people came running. I raced down the alleyway between the fishing shacks and the boatyard, and the shrieks terrified me, the people running, the screams, so many screams. Then they grabbed me and I clung to the child, I wouldn't let him go, I could hardly feel the hands that were laid on me, the fingernails in my eyes, the blows, the tearing of my clothes. And as they snatched at the baby —a terrible thing—he fell. I don't think he was badly hurt, but his forehead was bleeding, and a woman was yelling at me, cursing me, and I was in pain, and I couldn't stand it.

"Then—I don't know—it may have happened—or only in my mind—I was lying on a table, and men were at me, not one but many—my legs were spread apart—someone was fingering my vagina, hurting me, making me shriek—and one of them did something to me with a sharpness, I don't know what it was, and when I cried out he said it was nothing he had done, it was the pain of syphilis, I had been infected by a Turkish filth, I was diseased, I was festering. While something told me it was untrue, a terrible lie —I believed it because I was persuaded by sickness, I was persuaded by evil. They spoke of pus and decay, they said I was dying of it, they said that one of my labia had rotted away, that I stank, and one of them rubbed his hand on my vagina and raised his finger to my nostrils so I could smell my own putrefaction, and it was real to me—the reek of myself was unendurable.

"When they left me, I thought my breasts were bleeding. And from that time on, I had the nightmare many times, that my breasts were bleeding—not one nightmare, but many. I would scream awake, with blood all over me. And suddenly I realized that I had the nightmare in the daytime as well—I would be wide awake and there would be blood, and I couldn't stop the flow. Then one day I ran shrieking through the streets that someone had butchered me—my breasts were gone, my breasts were gone—oh, butchers!

"Two days later, I was arrested for making a disturbance. They said that on Epiphany Day I had desecrated the sanctity of the occasion by shouting obscenities.

"One day I fell and fell and fell . . . and I couldn't stop falling.

"The first thing I can recall holding onto was a spoon. It was a small spoon, too tiny for adults to eat from—perhaps it was a toy. But I began to see that it was usable—I was feeding a child with it. At first the porridge that went into her mouth was more real to me than her face. I had never seen her before, she was a stranger. And soon she disappeared.

"Then there was the falling again.

"But the child returned. And other children, older than she, and I began to tell them apart. The two larger ones did not need feeding, only faces to be washed. The little one and the infant did need feeding, out of a small cup or a spoon.

"The falling didn't happen so often anymore.

"It was a large family, and they were Turkish. The parents barely existed for me at first. And even the children were not altogether distinguishable from one another, except for what they ate, and how much washing they required. Then one day something happened in me, like a gleam: if a child was cross and you fed it, it would smile. I cannot tell you how exciting it was to have the thought—and to know that it was mine, it had occurred to *me*.

"Shortly after that time, I had my first yearning: I wanted to bathe the infant. I wanted to do it without help, by myself. And one morning I was permitted to do it. I was watched, of course, but not once did the mother interfere. She only nodded to me from time to time. As I was bathing the baby, I realized she was a girl. No matter how many times I had diapered her, it had never occurred to me what sex she was. Now, suddenly, she was *somebody*.

"And her mother became somebody. And the others as well. The two oldest were boys, the two youngest were girls. The father was a man.

"They were all kind to me. They liked me and never made fun of me. One day—I don't remember why—they said that they were Turks, so I said that I was too; I didn't know that I wasn't. And when I said it, they didn't deny it. They didn't deny me anything. If I said I could do something, in a little while they would allow me to do it.

"One summer morning, I was sitting in the grass with the baby, and I realized she was not an infant any longer, she was walking. And it puzzled me. That's when they told me I had been with them for two years, but I didn't know whether that was a short time, or long. I wondered if I would ever know.

"However long that was, I had never been outdoors by myself. Then, at last, they encouraged me to go for a short walk. But I returned quickly, ill at ease. Not that there was anything to be ill at ease about. There were only four houses huddled together, quite a distance from the town, which was Nexos. And all the people who lived in the three neighboring houses were also Turkish—nobody to hurt me. The family said that Nexos was their village, so it was mine as well. The name Akti started to come back to me, and every time it did it frightened me. It still frightens me to say the name.

"I spoke only Turkish in those days. I could hardly recall a word of Greek. I had no idea whether I was speaking it well or badly—they always understood what I said, and nobody made fun of me. Except once. One day the older boy got angry at me and said I was a Greek, and I began to cry. The mother scolded him and told me that he was wrong. I was kind and good, she said, and I was Turkish. Nobody ever called me Greek again.

"It was a small house, not large enough for so many people, and the husband, who was a stonemason, kept saying he would build an addition one of these days—he would convert his wife's chicken house. She would laugh and ask him what she would do with the chickens and geese. And nothing would come of his promise, because nothing needed to come of it—they were happy people.

"I was happy too. I did the work that I could manage. I cleaned, I began to cook again—but mostly I tended the children. Until I thought that they were mine.

"Nobody ever told me I *shouldn't* think of them as mine. But when I saw myself imagining it, I began to be frightened. And when I saw that I could be frightened, I saw that I might be getting well. And I didn't want it to happen.

"But it was happening rather quickly. And with each return of something from the past, it hurt more and more. And at last, one evening, I found that I was strong enough to bear it.

"I stayed with them for a few months more, then took a job as a housekeeper with another family in a neighboring town. Also Turkish. Then, I was a waitress in a small Turkish restaurant in Larnaca. Then I became a cook.

"My Greek was coming back to me, but I still refused to speak the language. If one of my own countrymen came into the restaurant, it would never occur to him that I was Greek. But I'm quite sure the Turks knew that I wasn't one of them. If the question ever came up, I would say I spoke a dialect—Anatolian—or I had learned my Turkish in America. When I said that, they would laugh understandingly. Whether they believed me or not, they never made a point of it. They were never—not ever—unkind to me. . . . until years later, when I was living with Savvas, a Greek. Then they thought Savvas was betraying them, and it was true—he was. When they found out, they were as cruel as the Greeks had been.

"There is no difference, really. There never was, where rage was involved. The cruelties may be of blood and bone, or of the mind—but they both run to cruelty . . . Greeks and Turks . . . both.

"The worst cruelty, of course, was in not telling me my son was still alive.

"I don't know how cruelty begins. It has no beginning and no ending."

Then she was silent. She did not dare to look at the boy.
Nor he at her.
Suddenly he couldn't stand it, and ran from the room.
"Mark!" she called. And she ran after him.
Ben had an impulse to follow, but he stopped himself.
He hoped for the moment that she would not catch up with him, that he could lose himself in the cave for a while, so he would not have to confront her immediately. He hoped that she too could momentarily lose herself. He wondered if they could ever really find each other.

13

Run, the boy said, run.

Don't let her catch up with you. Don't let her make it any clearer than she did, hold on to the confusion, keep as much of it as you can, wear it like a suit of armor. Run.

Don't let her be your mother. She's something you can't answer for, she's not part of the falling sickness, not a symptom you can tell a doctor. Even the pain is different—you never wrote a pain like this in any of the questionnaires, never. She's not in your medical history. Or in any history—she's a stranger. You do not belong to each other. Run.

"Mark!"

Don't call after me, he said. Stay away.

What passage can I run through? What corridor, what cave can I hide in? Where won't she find me? How did she find me here?

No, it was I who found her. I came looking for her. No, not true—I came looking for my father, looking for someone to loathe, to kill, and not to love . . .

I love you, Kalya . . . Mother.

No, not anybody. I don't love anybody.

I tried to touch her. Last night I tried to make love to her. I reached for her in the dark, I would have kissed her, I would have run my hands along her body, I would have seen her naked, I would have touched her breasts.

My mother's breasts were mutilated.

No, it was a lie.

"Mark!"

Go away.

What cave can I hide in? But I'm already in a cave, not dark enough, no hiding place in it.

"Mark!"

She says he was a good man, my father. She lied, of course. She's told lots of lies, she said as much herself, she confessed to any number of them. The very first time we met—all that made-up stuff about the sickness of the gods, as if I were a fool to believe that, as if I couldn't tell she was trying to ingratiate herself to me, to give me false comfort, cure me like a miracle doctor who can heal an illness by a laying on of hands and hearts. My father was a decent man: a lie.

She's a liar, and Christ knows what else. A thief.

She's trying to rob me of my rage.

How can I live without it? Can I give up the gun? Can I hang back tomorrow? What will I do, while doing nothing?

How can I live without my rage? How can I account for the curse that's on my brain? I have a right to this rage, goddamn you! It's little enough compensation for the sickness. And if you steal it, what can I have in its place? What passion can equal—?

You cannot rob me of it.

"Mark!"

Where can I hide, where can I run to? What if there's no place to hide, what if there's No Place?

What if she catches up to you? She'll say there are Turks and Turks. Some of them are kind, she'll say, some Turks have love in them. But there are others, I'll say—all the others—who kill and maim and torture, and butcher the breasts of women. Not your father, she'll say. Some people are this, and some are that—

—and some are liars, I'll say. Some are mythmakers who tell phony fables about Aphrodite going in search of her father Zeus— and dying in a cave. Some are lunatics, which she is; by her own admission, insane.

Perhaps that accounts for her story. Demented. She has disordered everything as she herself is disordered. She doesn't recall that my father was a torturer who abandoned her, bereft and breastless—

No, not breastless. But perhaps she *is*.

—breastless and insane, to run in pursuit of blue gulls, in pursuit of—

Me.

"Mark!"

Stay away. Stay away, I hate you, I love you, I want you for my mother, I want you to make me well again, I want you for my woman and my nurse, I want you for my bed, I want you because I ache, I'm sick, I'm full of shame, I'm lonely. . . .

"Mark!"

Stay away.

She stood in the doorway, then, and he hung back in the furthest corner, hoping the dark would cover him. But as if she had lifted a covering off his bed, she saw him.

"Please," he whispered, "go away."

"Come out of here."

"You lied, didn't you?"

"No, I didn't," she said.

"Then you're still insane, aren't you?"

"No."

"You're not my mother, there's nothing about you that could be my mother—no resemblance—nothing that speaks to me of you—"

"Yes, there is."

"No!"

He felt the surge. The cold wind, the grays. His eyelids moved too fast. Oh Christ, he said, not now.

A petty one, thank God, and gone.

"You've robbed me!" he cried.

"Of what, of what?"

"My rage!"

"I haven't robbed you of it—you're raging now."

"Why did you have to tell me? Why did I have to know who you are? Why couldn't you remain a stranger?"

Why couldn't she remain a stranger who could hold him, caress him and be caressed, a stranger whom he could love and make love to, whom he could see naked, whose breasts . . . ?

He felt lightning in the cave, a brightness unendurable. He started to reach for her.

"No," she said. "Don't!"

Oh Christ, I can't, he said. But he imagined her breastless, and had to know. His hands clawed at her, clawed at her clothing, ripped.

"No!"

He saw her partly naked. Saw her breasts, full and real.

"Oh no," she said.

She pulled him to herself. She held him close against her naked bosom, and he could feel the softness, the terrible softness, and his mouth began to lose itself. As he slipped down, as she tried to hold him, his mouth made sucking movements, tried to suck at her, and he could feel the flesh, the warmth in his mouth, and his own wetness, and he was in No Place.

14

Waking from an unquiet sleep, Ben thought he was smelling the tar of pines. It is called friar's balsam, the old patriarch had said years ago, it has a soothing effect, it goes deep into the lungs. The medic had known that it did no such thing, but it had been pleasant and comforting, reminding him of home remedies in his childhood. Then it will be doubly curative, Demetrios had said, and it turned out to be so. . . . Why was he smelling balsam now, these years later, in a cave?

His watch said it was 3:40, which meant he had slept less than an hour. He would have guessed more. It seemed ages ago that Kalya had gone running after the boy. How strange that all her murky, shapeless lies had clarified into a crystalline truth, too sharp to bear. He thought of the refugees of war, of the war-lost parents and children he had seen, of the endless, heartbreaking quests of loved ones for loved ones, and the joys of the reunited. But he wondered: after the first exultant glances of recognition, after the perusals to read the facts in one another's faces, could the void in the chronicle ever be filled? Sometimes, he thought, lost was better lost.

And he had been one of the agents of the finding. He had urged her to tell the truth as if it always brought a benefaction, but he suspected it was only a copybook maxim, and neither of them would ultimately view it as a precious present. Beware of Americans bearing gifts.

Dimly, the sound of a single plane going over, or he thought he heard one. Where would it be coming from, where would it be going, dead of night?

Not night—almost morning. This was the day, then, this was

it. Perhaps there was another hour or two left before daybreak. Very little time, possibly very little anything, maybe not so much as a whole day left for some of them.

He deeply wished Kalya would return for these two hours. But when she did, he didn't hear her footsteps. A faint whisper of clothing in the darkness was the first sound he heard of her, and he realized she was there and getting undressed. Soon she was lying beside him, naked, clinging to him desperately. Her body trembled, he thought she had a chill. Then she begged him, "Take me, please —oh, take me."

He heard the airplane again, and heard her make a strange sound to accompany it, a high, treble descant on a single exquisitely painful note, and he felt that tonight of all nights she needed an epic remedy, and he had none for her. He could not promise her a great fulfillment. Poignantly he wished he could help her to it, and realized that all he could do was ache for her if she could never have it.

Take me, she repeated softly. There was a silence as they loved, then a sigh somewhere, of wind, of water, an emanation from the dead rock, through passages of darkness, through tunnels of hazard—far, far back into oblivion. The cave came alive in all its colors, real and mythical, the magic of the metal ore and the magic of the mind, the memory of ancient days, of fables realized, of gods and superstitions come to truth, of the cuprous green of dead enchantments born to glow again, of bronzes as red as fire, of olive chrysolite, of rust and rime and hanging emeralds; with all its cry of colors, the cave gave up its warnings and its horrors, surrendered all remembrance of atrocity. Then it happened for Kalya, it fully happened, like walls of copper glowing, and the dark cave came alive!

"Oh God," she said, "oh God."

As her body surged in one last ecstatic spasm of consummation, her outcries filled the grotto. She rejoiced and mourned, she wept for the wonder as if it were the first time it had occurred to anyone; she wept for all the years of loss and being lost, for the terrible alienation of her present from her past, which were now a continuum again; she wept for the years when she had been ugly and sick and filthy, and a loathsomeness to herself—and wept exaltedly because she was now beautiful and whole and clean again. She wept for felicity and agony, and for the release from the prison into which the world had cast her, and the prison of her own memory within which she had immured herself, terrified to be free. She wept and wept and couldn't stop. Oh Ben, she cried, oh Ben, oh Ben.

It had occurred so uncomplicatedly, he thought, as if by a random encounter in an unfamiliar place. He had performed no sleight-of-hand of lovemaking, no extraordinary feat of manhood, scarcely more than a caress, a kiss of glancing love, a murmuring of need, then entering. Again, like a late arrival, he had scarcely reached his destination when she was already there, had come on wings. Oh, thank you, beloved, she said, oh, thank you, as if he had materialized everything from nothing, had fabricated the total ceremony by himself; and when he demurred, she said he had given her the other times, the times of waiting, and the loving had led to this; that her ecstasy had not been of this night alone, but was the whole summation.

Then, however, as they lay tranquilly together, he felt her move in a way that puzzled him. And made him apprehensive. She's going to endanger it, he told himself, if she wants so quickly to make love again. He had a dread that her first climax with him might have been the single benefaction of the night, a happy fortuity that could not be repeated after such a brief interval, and that it might be tempting her Fates to try again. But he suspected that she too dreaded it had been only an accidental bliss, perhaps even a little imaginary, too sublime to be true, and she had to test not only to see if it was real, but to see whether love was not a coincidence perpetrated by the Fates, it was of their very own doing, his and hers. Don't distrust it, he wanted to say, please have faith in it; but already her hunger had surrounded him, cutting off escape with embraces and touches and kisses and a hot urgency that not only was full of passion but was quickened with alarm. Even when he felt she was not yet ready, she said come now, hurry, now, please now, and when he did enter her, she was indeed ready for him, and came instantly, and laughed as she did, and kept on laughing. Then—miracle to tell—hardly minutes later—still once more, the third time, and she said with wonder that three was the mystic number, and he said she was silly, and she agreed and laughed even more joyously.

Yet, in a little while, he heard her crying again. But it was a soft crying this time, full of benignity and thanksgiving, and he could not imagine what else, except that it was the first time that someone's tears had seemed like a beatitude.

Next, almost without a sign that she was doing so, she fell asleep. But very soon she was awake again, saying that if they kept their eyes shut they might protract the darkness and delay the daylight. To preserve the stillness, they pretended they did not hear the distant sound, a whirring noise. But it could not be ignored.

"Whose plane is that, do you suppose?" she asked. "Theirs or ours?"

Obliquely, on the edge of smiling: "What do you mean, 'ours'?"

"Greek."

For an instant he had the ill-considered notion that she had become a partisan. But he knew it could be nothing like that, not with Kalya; all of them be damned. It was simply that she was closing a parenthesis, finishing a statement she had started long ago, and now at last had the courage to complete. A finality, identifying herself. He wondered what her next sentence might be. But he decided not to ask her about herself, only about the boy.

"Did he have another attack?"

"Yes."

"Was it bad?"

"Yes."

"Is he sleeping?"

"Yes . . . I can't believe how soundly he can sleep afterward."

Then she told him everything that had happened and, although he could hear how afflicted she was, there was no lamentation in her voice, and not the faintest sigh of self-pity. She viewed the spectacle of her life not as a tragedy because of what had occurred, but as a tragedy because of what had not been resolved. Its conclusion now was like the ending of a barbaric ritual which had been ceremoniously cruel, but had finally offered a rubric of relief. She had been holding her breath for half of her life, and could now release herself. Freer, perhaps, than she had been for years.

His mind jumped a hurdle. He questioned how truly free she was. "How much has changed, Kalya?"

"I love you."

If that much hadn't changed, it was what he needed most to hear; but he had meant another thing. "Do you still feel you have to go?"

"Up there?"

"Yes."

She delayed her reply, seemed to need certainty that could be expressed without agitation. "I have to go," she said.

He felt a sinking disappointment, as if he had been cheated. He realized how overly romantic it was to hope that one night's felicity in bed—or even many nights—would be the panacea for all her ills; she was not, after all, only a creature of gonads. And yet . . .

"Do you suppose . . . Can you really kill someone?"

He could feel her rigor, as if her supple flesh had turned to stone. "I have to see it through. If I go on being terrified . . ." Then how would she know she was cured? the implication was. She had to see her madness to its resolution, whatever it might be, look the horror in the face, and find a name for it that she could bear to utter. See where the lunacy would take her—to reality or endless nightmare, to one lie or another, to the scream of breastlessness, to a myth she could live her life by.

But he pursued the question. "You haven't answered me. Can you kill someone?"

Again she responded evasively. "It *is* a war, isn't it?"

"It's an insanity."

"If men do it, it's valor. If women—it's insanity."

"It's always insanity."

And all of them, he realized—Kalya, Mark, Falkos, and himself—all were obsessive. Not Kalya alone—but Mark and Falkos, with their monomanias of vengeance, and Benjamin Coram with his single-minded compulsion to conquer fire and attain Demetrios, as if Demetrios were not a human being but a blissful state of existence, a salvation by faith and love and courage. All of them, mad, all trying to make visions appear or disappear, trying to conjure myths out of manias. He, with a generic similarity to the others, was a mythmaker who had fabricated a legend of himself to make life—beautiful?—well, at least endurable. If theirs were myths of rage or vengeance or madness, and his was a myth of love, was there more than an aesthetic difference? Perhaps only through the smug self-service of his own morality could he say that his quest for a metaphoric vision of himself was one bit more sane than theirs, more just or real or full of grace, that love for humanity was a lunacy more viable than hatred. And how much hatred was buried beneath his love? . . . He had killed someone.

And perhaps at the root of all their lunacies was the single madness, war, the poisonous rootstock out of which so many other insanities grew—the homicidal manias, the paranoias, the hallucinations of racial superiority and national destiny, the sadomasochistic passion for pain, and the tragic delusion that death is heroic, death is beautiful.

Perhaps it was a madness that they would never cure, simply because it was incurable. Perhaps the pitiful illusion was that we were born to live in peace and love—in sunlight—when the reality was darkness. The reality was war. Perhaps it was the aboriginal padded cell, the snake pit of rage and terror and brutality and despair and loneliness; perhaps it was the dark cave from which we might never emerge.

He felt a cold dread that one of them would be killed today. He had forced the possibility to the back of his mind, denying death as if it were his special privilege to do so, rejecting it as if he had inside information that it was an erroneous error. Because here there was a difference: he had come upon the great love of his life, the love that is a refutation of death, that makes mortality seem a calumny. It was a love he would give his life for— ironically at a time when love had made his life more precious to him than ever.

Now, with the pain that is the concomitant of common sense, he knew that it would all soon be over, and they might have to part —one or the other of them killed—and that this eternal love might have been only an interlude between wars, an item in the cease-fire.

How little time they had left, he thought again: an hour perhaps. Sixty minutes for nothing but farewells. How can I say goodby in such brief time? How can I let her know how much I love her, how everlastingly I would love her if we both could live? How can I tell her, with minutes ticking by, that she has filled me so profoundly, yet left me hungry in places I never knew were empty—and that filling the emptiness was the life with her I had hoped for? Goodby, Kalya, my love. And goodby to this place, this cave, this brooding darkness. . . . Goodby to Yannis . . .

There was a stirring in the corridor, the movement and whispering of men. He heard a burst of static from the intercom, a chatter of unintelligible voices, then the volume lowered.

A figure stood in the doorway, beckoning him to come. It was Petros.

"Is it time already?" Ben said.

"Not yet," he answered. It was another summons from Falkos, perhaps the last.

Ben started to follow him and so did Kalya. The young Greek seemed a bit discomfited. "He say make sure he will come alone."

She nodded, let her hand linger on Ben's arm for a moment, then returned to the room.

As they arrived outside the main room, Petros stopped. This was as far as he would accompany Ben. He seemed tentative, clearly wanting to say something not easy to express. "I am sorry I gave difficulty."

Ben nodded understandingly, and realized there was termination in the young man's manner. "Are you leaving?"

"Yes." He raised his hand to indicate he had been ordered to the mountaintop.

Ben made a wry joke. "If you don't guard me, I'll escape."

Petros shrugged. "Where?" It was an unanswerable question. "Anyway, is too late."

That too was unanswerable. "Be careful," he said to the boy.

"You be also careful," Petros said. Starting to say good luck in Greek, he stammered. "Be with God," he said.

"You too, Petros."

Turning away, Ben entered the main room.

Falkos had the two-way radio on the table and was listening to Chartas's voice. He was nodding energetically, unable to contain how eagerly he agreed with everything the man was saying. Whatever difference they had had between them was now over; this was at last the day of action that Falkos had been urging, it had come. Watching him, Ben realized he had never seen the teacher so buoyant and so confident.

When he disconnected, Falkos turned to Ben and gave vent to his excitement. "I was wrong!" He was jubilant. "Thank God, I was wrong! They haven't budged one inch up there—and there has been no second invasion anywhere. And we'll be going up in perfect time! Did you hear that plane?"

"Yes."

"It's ours! It gave Chartas a report of the Monastery airfield. There are twenty aircraft up there—all lined up in the old vineyard. And they're *sitting* there—just waiting to be taken. And we're ready, Benjamin, we're ready. We've got four tanks on the other side of the mountain, and five armored vehicles—and they haven't the slightest notion that we're anywhere!"

"How do you know that?"

"They'd be bombing the hell out of us if they knew!"

Energetically, he slapped his arms together as if embracing himself, took a profound breath, and tried to control his enthusiasm. He looked at his watch. "It's almost time, Benjamin."

"What's going to happen to the Turkish prisoner?"

Falkos's mood sobered. He was regretful. "He got away . . . he's dead." Then, to convince Ben that his regret was genuine: "I didn't mean for him to die—and didn't think he would. I questioned him myself last night—without even touching him. Only that damnable question, and he wouldn't answer it. I thought I'd try him once more in the morning. But about twenty minutes after I left him, Photis came down and said he was dead."

"What a nuisance." Bitterly. "Three children, did you say?"

Falkos made no pretense that he didn't feel the sting, but did not reply. He studied Ben as if to take a final conclusive measurement of the man. "I want to give you something, Benjamin." He reached into his pocket and brought out a gun. Holding it flat on his palm, he gazed at it: an old keepsake.

"This is a Browning automatic," he said. "I've had it for sixteen years. While I don't rhapsodize over guns, I'm extremely fond of this one. It's fully loaded now, and all you have to do to make it operable is press this safety catch. It's yours. I give it to you as a present."

He carefully placed it on the table in front of Ben.

"You know, of course, that I won't accept it."

"I urge you to change your mind."

"I won't." As he turned toward the door, "Call me when we have to leave."

"Wait, Benjamin—please wait," he said. "I don't want you to be killed."

"If that's your real reason—thank you. But I don't think it is."

"What, then?"

"I don't think you can bear to see me . . ." He couldn't bring himself to finish a statement that he knew Falkos would ridicule.

"Uncorrupted?" the teacher prompted.

"I wasn't going to say that. I'm not uncorrupted—I've lied a good deal—to you—to others—to myself."

"Then what? I can't bear to see you what?"

"Still in love."

"With Homo sapiens?" There was a hoot in his voice.

Ben knew he would have to face the derision. "Yes."

For a flashing instant, as if someone had snatched the mask of contempt off his face, Falkos was revealed, envious—like the last person, left behind, forsaken. Recovering quickly, he said, "If you're in love with life, don't kill yourself."

"I'm not trying to."

". . . Have you ever owned a gun?"

"No."

"Have you ever fired one?"

"Basic training—targets."

"You've shot at nothing alive? A rabbit, a rat?"

"Nothing."

"You were in Vietnam. You never shot at anyone?"

"Never."

"Were you ever under direct fire?"

"Not really, no."

"Do you suppose—if you *had* been under direct fire—with someone pointing a rifle at you—you'd wish you had one of your own?"

"No. I wouldn't shoot it. I wouldn't kill anybody."

"You're sure?"

"If I'm not sure of that, I'm not sure of anything."

"Have you ever tested yourself?"

"Tested? In what way?"

"If you're standing in front of a man who points a gun at you, and you have no gun, and therefore cannot shoot him—you're not testing any principle. But if you're armed as well as he is, and you know that if you don't pull the trigger, he'll shoot you and you'll die—and *then* you don't pull the trigger—by *choice* you don't pull the trigger—*that* tests your principle. . . . You haven't had occasion to test yourself, have you?"

"No."

Falkos moved to the table, lifted the gun, and challengingly handed it to Ben. "Are you afraid to test yourself?"

"It's a stupid test."

"No, it isn't. Take it. Test yourself."

"It's stupid. It's like saying, drink a cup of hemlock, see what's stronger, you or the poison. I know what's stronger—the hemlock. Unless I don't drink it—and then it's weak as water. It's the same with that gun. I'm stronger than that thing—until I shoot it."

"Which was stronger, Benjamin—your hands or the neck of that young Turk?"

"That was an accident!"

"That's what you say, but it upsets you to think about it, doesn't it? Even if momentarily you saved your friend's life, it still upsets you. Why? Because you're not sure it *was* an accident. You're not sure—if it happened again—you wouldn't do exactly the same thing. And you'll never be sure. All your life you'll remember that you killed a man. And every time you say 'accident,' you'll know it's a lie. And it'll torment you. It'll torment you until you test yourself. Until you stand in front of an assailant, and as he fires his gun, you don't fire yours. Until you do that, in your own mind you'll always be a murderer." He extended the gun once more. "Take it!"

"No."

Kalya stood in the archway. "Take it," she said quietly.

"Go away," Ben said.

She moved closer to him. Pointing to Falkos, "Every word he says is wrong," she said intensely. "He's using lies and stupidities and tricks. But there's only one thing, Ben—if you don't take the gun, you may get killed. Take it."

"No."

"Take it—please—I beg you."

"No."

"Then *you're* the insane one!" Her anger flared. "Who are the crazy ones?" she cried. "Those that want to kill or those that want to die? While you both battle the world ethic, I lose the men I love, I lose my children! Why do you want to help nature destroy us all? You think it can't manage by itself? You think there aren't enough diseases and floods and earthquakes? You think there aren't enough evil accidents? Do you have to help? Why can't you let us live? Who are the insane ones? Which is crazier—the illusion that we love one another or the illusion that we hate one another? And if both of them are insane, why can't we settle for the myth that love exists?"

"It does exist! That's why I won't kill anyone!"

"Then don't kill yourself—and don't kill me! Take the gun!"

He thought: Perhaps the goodbys were premature; perhaps she is the only sane one: she insists on living . . . and insists that I do.

He took the gun.

The sun was up and the day was already warm, although it was barely dawn. Only moments ago, drifts of mist had been hanging low, but now they were going quickly, nearly gone, not lifting as they usually did, but seeming to leach into the verdure, soaking the already moist woodlands from which they had come. The trees were as green as they needed to be, he speculated, if they had to take cover among them; but there would be no taking cover, they would move out overtly on the open road, displaying themselves.

Falkos stood beside the ambulance, demonstrating the rifle to Kalya. He would hide the weaponry in a moment, he said, in the drawer space where he himself would be hiding, but he wanted to make sure she knew how to use it; all guns are a little different, aren't they? he said.

Especially the one I have in my pocket, Ben mused; it is very different from anything else in the world.

Mark had not appeared. Kalya hadn't as yet told Falkos about her true relation to the boy—she would not do so without her son's concurrence and she was behaving with extraordinary detachment. Ben knew how anxious she was, yet she asked about Mark only once, with studied casualness; and the leader answered vaguely. I can answer more specifically, Ben reflected with a lift of spirit: the boy's not coming. If they went in search of him, they would find him ill, or pretending illness. At least that much had been accomplished; one of them would remain behind. It was a gratuity he thankfully accepted as an offsetting compensation for other unfulfillments.

The boy came out of the cave. He had a distant expression, as if he had just come from a deeper cavern than the mountain could hold. Ben wondered how much of the young man was not yet present, how much he had forgotten of last night, whether what he did remember he imagined as a dream. Mark remained at the mouth of the cave—perhaps a hundred yards away—not moving, adjusting his eyes to the light. When the day was in focus, he scanned the presences with a look of foreboding, as one who is facing a firing squad. His survey stopped with Falkos.

Like a failing student, he'll go to the teacher now, Ben speculated, making his apology, asking to be excused. And Falkos—did
he really need the boy to fill Yannis's place?—would he let him
go? Ben had decided not to face that problem until the last minute.
Which was now. He would have to add his weight to the boy's argument, and Kalya would do the same.

Mark's waiting time was over; he started to walk. When he
had crossed half the distance, Kalya moved a little way toward
him, and stopped. She did not take her eyes off her son, and Ben
was bemused by how unabashedly she stared at the boy, no longer
reserving her motherhood, her anxiety naked. Her lies were altogether in the past; overnight she had become guileless.

When the boy got closer, she started toward him again. It was
a mistake. He didn't want to speak to her. He gave her one fleeting
glance, then studied distances again. As he passed, she asked him
something, whispered it so nobody could hear. His reply was inaudible, not even addressed directly to her but to the anonymous air.
So he had remembered enough, Ben concluded, and was choosing
not to. But how much had he remembered of his conversation with
Ben? And what would he say to the teacher?

He came closer—and did not go to Falkos. He went to Ben.

"I have to talk to you," he murmured.

The boy withdrew from the others; Ben followed him. When
he was certain he was out of earshot, Mark said, "I'm going with
the rest of you."

Ben felt a heaviness, a sinking regret.

"No, Mark—go back."

"I can't."

"But everything's changed," Ben said. He started to point out
that the configurations in the boy's world had altered, that a libel-
ous history had been rectified, that afflictive dispositions of the
mind could be discarded, that vengeance against the memory of a
decent father was not only unjust but meaningless, that the man
had never brutalized his mother, that before he could commit himself to violence he had to give himself time to realize that today's
world was different from yesterday's, and he would have to be
different as well. "Everything has changed!" he repeated.

"I haven't."

"You will, Mark—believe me."

But only the facts had changed, and facts did not matter to
the boy. The image of atrocity he had lived with was far more real

to him than any objective phenomena could ever be. Like mathematical numbers, like zero that was nothing but was also the end of nothing, such phenomena had fascination for him only when they became abstractions, and seemed insignificant until they were larger than his mind could hold. The atrocity had been a postulate in his life, and he believed in it, it was a tenet of faith. More than form and substance, it explained his ailment to him when doctors were unable to do so; it even justified a weakness. More than drugs, it was the counterirritant, it was his rage against rage, his fury that fought the *furor epilepticus*. It made it possible for him not to despise his infirmity but to dignify it as a worthy enemy, to ennoble it as a fatal curse. It had given him a passionate energy—

"Rage," he said.

Rage against whom? Ben replied—and knew it was useless—against the Turks who were kind to the boy's mother and made her part of their family, against his father who loved them both? Somehow, he thought, there must be a way to draw a thread of reason through the Gordian knot; could only a bullet do it? "Rage? Is that all you want?"

"It's all I've got."

"Even when the object of it is gone?"

"What difference does it make?"

"It has to make a difference. You can't live with a fury that has no reason, it'll make you—!"

"Make me what? Ill?" The boy smiled bitterly. It was exactly what Ben had kept himself from saying, realizing what a bare truism it was. "Things equal to the same thing are equal to each other," Mark said. He was not letting Ben get away with any such easy axioms; he *was* ill, it was a given in his life, too self-evident a proposition to question further. Then he added, gently, "Thank you for being kind to me, but don't concern yourself anymore. This won't be a hardship for me—I'm used to it—it's part of the mal—it has a momentum—I can't stop it . . . and I'm not sure I want to."

His voice was not angry, nor was it cold with cruelty, only a statement of a symptom, as if he had finally formulated a description of his malady that reconciled inconsistencies and satisfied his mind.

He walked away, leaving Ben separate from the group. Come back, Ben wanted to call, as if there were any sense to it. Then he told himself: Stop crying about the boy; write him off. Write him off as another war casualty, a war that happened nineteen years ago, nineteen hundred years ago, nineteen thousand. Write him off with Mee Lanh and Luddy Stroudt and the Turkish soldier you killed, and Yannis. Write him off as you will write others off today, perhaps yourself. But he knew that writing off was a bad anodyne; the pain was there.

Mark approached Falkos, who pointed to the ambulance and gave him whispered instructions. The young man listened, nodded a few times, went to the vehicle, opened the window, tried the handle to see how quickly he could turn it in either direction, then went back to the teacher, who tapped him once, lightly, on the shoulder. And handed him his rifle. Inspect it thoroughly and give it back, he said.

The boy looked at Falkos, at the gun, and then at Kalya. This time, however, it was not a sidelong glance. He faced her squarely, confronting her gun-anxious face. His eyes were impassive. He didn't utter a word, but what he was saying was clear and deliberate: I cannot manage my life by trusting to anyone's love; I have to make do with hatred.

Falkos directed Ben to inspect his ambulance. It's no different from an ordinary day, the medic tried to tell himself; this is the early morning survey before the daily emergencies. The dressings were neatly stacked, the instruments were properly in their plastic trays, the trays all interlocked so movement wouldn't jiggle things; the oxygen valve was tightly closed, not leaking any longer, the litter and braces in their brackets so they wouldn't fall. Even the money he had meant for Yannis was still in his crash helmet; Louka had been honest in how much he had taken. Everything in proper order; the ambulance was ready for the calls. Just like any other day.

Not just like. More like Til Menh or Vet Lokh, walking in red puddles. And not even like those.

He had never carried a gun.

So this was a day not only different, but one that could never take its place in the continuity of his other days. It would not fit into any chronology—a day apart, and he might never understand it as a day of his own, but might pretend it belonged to a stranger. If he lived to pretend it.

He was mortally afraid. For the first time in his life, he was not ashamed of it. There was not one of them, he was quite sure, who did not feel the same dread of death or mutilation. No matter how the bravos among them might call it the excitement of battle, still—underneath even such a transport—there was fear.

And why not? Why need a man be a coward or a hero? Did the process of natural selection recognize no middle state, did it destroy all but the warring valiant? Was there no place for the ordinary valors of the ordinary man, the living with the quotidian aches and pains and nuisances, the making-do with pleasures instead of joys, with data instead of discoveries, the compromises with impurity, the erosion of the dream? Wasn't living in itself an act of heroism? Wasn't the fear of death—no matter when it happened, even in old age—a sufficient trial of courage?

Wasn't it enough to die just once? Not only cowards died many times before their deaths—lovers, as well. He had died with the death of Mee Lanh and of Yannis, and with the death of the Turkish soldier he had killed. And with them all, he had known that in one way or another he had made it happen. Even with Luddy, struck down not by Ben but by enemy shrapnel, he had felt: there, but for the grace of God. There was guilt in it, that he had been spared. And with all of them, a little death of his own.

Wasn't it enough to die just once?

Was that, then, the evil dismay that prevented him from being a doctor? That he couldn't finally and irrevocably dedicate himself to the guilt of killing, and the daily dying? Was that, too, the heart of his pacifism—that he could not endure the death of another, because it was his own? Could it be that he was looking at two faces of the same fear? And was it a fear he had to overcome?

The terrible question: Was Falkos right? Was he *obliged* to test himself? Was the gun in his pocket a means of doing it?

But need he be a warrior in order to be a doctor? No. *Firing* the gun would not liberate him from any fear of death. But *not* firing it . . .

If, to be a doctor, it took more courage than he had had at one time, he would see how much there was of it now. Enough? he wondered. Enough to face death, and *not* kill anyone? Could there be any healing in all this?

He saw Falkos, with the rifles in his hands, get into the ambulance. The leader pulled the cupboard door open, stowed the guns between the submachine gun and the long carton that held the grenades. Then he came out again.

He spoke to Ben. "You've been to the Monastery, you said?"

"Yes."

"Do you remember it?"

"Very well. But it was winter—there was snow on the ground." And not, then, an armed camp, he thought.

Falkos gave instructions. He spoke concisely, every word measured and distinct, his diction rigidly precise. "The purpose of the operation is to take the Monastery and the twenty aircraft that have been deployed to it. The objective is actually an old fortress, but it is also a religious institution, so we do not want to destroy it. If our entrance is a total surprise, it will be possible for other combat vehicles to follow us and seize the airfield and the cloister with a minimum of damage to everyone."

The preamble was over. He paused, then began on the specifics. "There are two sentry posts. The first one is minor. It is at the start of the alleyway between the basilica of the Monastery on the left and the old winery on the right. There is only one man at this post. He is armed but he is not important. He will stop you, ask who you are, what you want. You will identify yourselves—two Americans and a Turkish woman. You are a doctor and you have come to tend the old patriarch. The guard will probably want to look inside. Treat it routinely—do not glance at the cupboard where I'll be hiding—don't look at it at all. Directly after you pass the first sentry, I will come out. I will give Mark and Kalya their guns and I will spread the grenades on the surface of the cot. Ben will drive very slowly through the alleyway to give me a little time —it is only a distance of three hundred feet.

"I will station myself at the right window, Mark will be at the left, and Kalya will be in the rear. In those three hundred feet, we will pass the winery on the right and the basilica on the left. Most of the winery windows are clerestory—too high to give us any trouble. But two of them are not. If there are armed men in the windows I will pay no attention to them, I will not open fire."

He turned specifically to Mark. "During those three hundred feet—on your side—you will be passing the basilica. There are four buttresses that extend from its walls. If there are armed men behind these buttresses, you are to pay no attention to them—you are not to open fire. Do you understand?"

"Yes, I do."

Falkos looked at each one, then resumed, his manner becoming more trenchant. "We now approach the second entry. This is the danger point. On what used to be the loading platform of the winery, there is a gun emplacement. It may be large—possibly a battery of guns. I shall have to dispose of it. Sometimes the sentry stands on the loading platform alongside the soldiers who man the guns. Sometimes, however, he is in the sentry box which is on the left." Again he turned to Mark. "If he is in his box—or near it— you are to wait until you hear me open fire, then you are to fire as well—at the sentry. And you are not to stop firing until you are certain he is dead. Yes?"

"Yes."

His last instruction went to Kalya. "When I start firing, you do too. I do not anticipate any trouble through the rear window, but if there is any, it is up to you."

Kalya nodded.

It was Ben who got the concluding instruction. "The instant you hear the shots—without waiting to see whether we have been successful—you are to drive forward into the cloister yard. You are to turn left immediately, toward the entrance of the basilica, and clear the alleyway for the tanks and armored vehicles that will follow us through the alleyway. Your work will then be over. Enter the basilica, go through it into the old baptistery. The infirmary is directly behind it, through a covered ambulatory. Father Demetrios is there."

The infirmary. He would be seeing the old man in the room where he had originally met him.

Swiftly, sharply, Falkos inquired if there was any question. There was none.

"How loud does your radio play?" he asked Ben.

"Quite loud."

"Do you get the Nicosia music station clearly?"

"Up here—I would think so."

"Try it."

Ben went into the cab, flipped the radio switch, turned the dial. It was a love ballad, music set to the verses of Lipertis, sung by a woman whose voice was like a shepherd's flute.

"Not loud enough," Falkos said.

Just as he was about to switch to Limassol, the same song came on being played hard rock, the melody barely recognizable. Loud, blasting.

"Good," Falkos said. "Can you turn it higher?"

So that we seem innocent, Ben thought, heralding not hiding our approach—the bedlam-loving Americans, blaring lustily at the tranquillity of the morning.

"Are you ready?" Falkos asked, as if readiness were a decision *they* could make. Mark and Kalya said they were.

The schoolmaster mounted the single step at the rear of the ambulance. As he did, the radio went crazy, the music tore with a ripping noise. Then, no sound at all, like the cut-off of electrical current. A dead moment or two, not even a crackle of static, followed by a shout—a man's voice:

"—in full force on the northern coast. Kyrenia again—and which one?—are you sure?—Dhavlos—!"

The voice stopped. Music an instant, jagged and irrelevant, a shriek in the background, another voice, a woman's this time:

"—wave after wave of them—Phantom jets bombing Famagusta! The Turkish army—a second invasion—no, Famagusta has not fallen—"

Another voice interrupted: Famagusta, he said, had fallen.

Falkos stood on the rear step of the ambulance, unable to move.

Then he was berserk. He ran across the parking area, ran derangedly into the center of it.

"*Ochi!*" he yelled. *Ochi, ochi,* as if it were the only word he had ever learned.

He looked up at the sky, scanning it for planes. He kept running across the parking area, this way, another way, trying to find a more open place where his view could sweep the heavens for a sign of aircraft. The sky was empty.

"*Ochi,*" he shouted. "I don't believe it! It's a lie—I don't believe it! The planes haven't taken off! If it were true, they would have gone by now! I don't believe it—*ochi*—I don't believe it!"

Frantically, he raced back to the ambulance. As he was getting in, he shouted to Ben, "Hurry—oh Christos—hurry!"

He got into the vehicle and swiftly opened the cupboard. He slid in, pulled the door behind him, and Ben heard it click shut.

The others got into the ambulance and Ben shut the door. He went to the front and got into the cab. He started the motor. Just as it began to roll down the hill, he saw Yannis beside him. The old man was as poignantly real as if he had been there, chewing on St. John's bread and smelling of too much wine. Go away, Ben said, and stay. Then he thought: Yannis might actually still be here, in the flesh, if I had carried a gun. Well, I'm carrying one now.

A second invasion. He couldn't believe it anymore than

Falkos had. The schoolmaster had been right; the cease-fire had failed, the peace had failed, and some would say the second assault was a foregone conclusion—war, inevitable. Ache: was it always inevitable?

The radio had gone dead again. Now, with a screech, it came alive with music, clamorous. As it racketed, he opened the window to the hot sun. He could smell the pines and cedars; there were balsam and wild savory and spicebush in the air. (*War, inevitable.*) Although he could still get lost in these woods, he felt he knew them as intimately as if he had lived in them, knew the whole island, knew how green and soft it was, (*inevitable*) knew a hillside that burned with poppies, a field that was all marigolds and daisies and cyclamens and anemones, that flowered in and out of season, and told no time but beauty. It was an island he loved, give or take a heartbreak or two, give or take a rage, a malice. In a world he loved, and he would be loath to leave them. . . . *Inevitable?*

The ambulance arrived at the bend in the pathway. It was his last chance to see the entrance of the cave. He looked back. It was only a small blur of grayness, receding, becoming a thing of the past. If he came through alive, he would probably forget the grotto with the passage of years, but it would always be somewhere in the dark of the mind, a cache of shadows where blood and pain and torture lurk, where love grows like an anomaly, a flower in a dungeon. He wondered if he would ever think longingly of the place, if there might not be a nostalgia not only for good but for evil. As he made the turn from the cave . . .

. . . his thoughts turned to the mountain. He could barely see it. At the top of the long ascent, the basilica caught the sunlight and glowed with it, its terra-cotta resolving to scarlet, its sienna to blazing hues of fire—and further away, the slender bell tower with the belfry was perforated by a sky of blue innocence. It was more beautiful than he had ever seen it, and more terrible; it was a fortress. Ringed around with low breastworks of stone and, beyond them, tall ramparts of native rock, it seemed impregnable and forbidding.

Almost before the woodland was behind them, they were there.

He saw the first sentry, five hundred feet ahead.

The man's hand rose, and slowly Ben stopped the ambulance.

The guard uttered a command in Turkish, and asked a question. Then, in rough English, "Who are you?"

"Ben Coram." Perfunctorily he offered his passport. While the man looked at it, Ben said, "I'm an American. Paramedic—from the hospital. I'm here to take care of Father Demetrios."

"From what hospital?"

"Nicosia General."

The man looked at the windows and saw Mark. "Inside—who is there?"

"My assistant—also American."

The man looked somewhat confused. He was not yet wide awake. His clothes had been slept in; perhaps he was at the end of the nighttime watch. Had he not heard that elsewhere his countrymen were invading again? And hadn't the twenty aircraft heard? Why were they still on the ground?

"Open the back," the guard said.

Ben got out. "It can be opened from either side," he offered. It sounded disarmingly manifest, with nothing concealed.

The sentry glanced at Kalya, then stared more fixedly at Mark. He used the English rote he had learned. "Who are you?"

It was Kalya's change of expression that made the thought strike Ben: The boy's last name was originally not Achille or Achillides, it was Sormak. And although Kalya had actually mentioned it, he was certain the boy would not remember, nor ever want to hear the name again.

Mark wasn't answering anything—he merely handed the man his passport. It was glanced at and returned almost at once.

Then the sentry, not crediting the possibility that the woman could speak, asked Ben, "Who she is?"

"Her name is Kalya Sormak."

"Turkish?"

"Yes—she's a nurse from the hospital."

"Then why she is not there?"

"The Greeks discharged her from her job."

Cogent. The sentry shut the door and waved them on.

Ben got behind the wheel and looked through the rear window of his cab. Mark was sitting on the edge of the cot, his hands folded in his lap. Just as he was thinking that the boy was not afraid, the latter smiled and betrayed that he was. Kalya caught her son's eye, and she too smiled, letting him know she was as terrified as he was, and might need to borrow courage.

He was driving slowly now, as he had been instructed to do.

But he mustn't crawl, he told himself, or it would look suspicious. He heard a shuffling noise behind him, heard the opening of the cupboard and the closing of it, saw the man's form, Falkos, standing in the path of the rearview mirror. Get down, he wanted to say, you'll be seen back there. It was unnecessary, however; the three hundred feet were nearly two-thirds gone.

There was nobody at the winery windows on the right, nobody behind the buttresses on the left. Ahead of them, the sentry was not with the men on the platform, but standing on Mark's side, in front of the sentry box. Eighty more feet and they would be at the post.

Seventy. His heart was going faster than the motor.

Sixty. Slow down even more now, the guard's hand is up.

Fifty. Stop, he says.

He saw the gun emplacement. A machine gun, mounted. One man stationed behind it, two men with rifles . . . then:

Without warning:

Before the first shot had been fired, they heard the sound of planes. A single plane at first, then another and another—five of them in quick succession—lifting from the vineyard-airfield, taking to the sky.

"Oh no!" It was Falkos.

Another sequence of planes, five more.

Now five again.

"Stop them!" he yelled, as if anyone could. Stop them, stop them.

Five more planes. Twenty aircraft.

"Too late!" Falkos cried. "We've lost them—we're too late!"

Forty more feet to the sentry.

"Too late!" But his submachine gun was at the ready.

Thirty feet.

"Stop!" The sentry too was ready.

Twenty.

"Stop!"

He heard the sharp crack of Falkos's gun behind him, on his right, then Mark on his left. Again, again, again. The men on the platform—one of them looked skyward, for no reason—the planes—while the other one raised his rifle. The machine gun swiveled, but fired nothing. The Turk behind it fell; the gun continued turning a little, nobody moving it.

The sentry simply dropped to his knees, then forward on his face. The first shot might have killed him, but there was another, and another. Then Mark's rifle stopped.

The last man on the gun emplacement was sprawled on the steps.

Not a single shot had been fired through the rear windows of the ambulance—and for that brief blank in time Ben told himself that Kalya would not pull the trigger on her rifle. But then, in his mirror, he saw her reflection as she raised the gun. She held it indecisively for a spell, and then she fired. She fired twice, then again and again and again.

But an astonishing event was happening back there. For an instant he turned and looked, to confirm what he hoped he had seen. Yes, it was true! She was firing, but not at the ground, not at any level that human beings inhabited, but upward at the sky. And she was jubilant. Round after round at the sky, as high as Mount Olympus, at the gods that had betrayed her, at the Fates that had persecuted her all her life. She was defying their curses, exorcising herself, breaking out of the darkness in which they had imprisoned her, taking arms to destroy them so that she could live. Triumphantly, she was shooting them down, denying that they had any power over her from this shot onward, from this battle forward. She was having her final madness and—for the first time in her life —making a rapture of it.

Oh, Kalya, my love, you've won the war!

But the war was not over.

"Faster—move!" Falkos called. "Turn left—move!"

He heard the bullets hit the hood like hail. He didn't know where they were coming from until he brought the vehicle to a stop outside the basilica entrance. Then he saw the man on the second floor of the refectory building, across the cloister yard. Opening the door on the far side, away from the machine gunner, he reached across the seat for the aluminum suitcase which contained the dialysis kit, and for his medical bag. As he got out of the ambulance, the first armored vehicle came roaring in. It was a flatbed with four machine guns and he couldn't tell how many men. They started throwing grenades almost instantly. He didn't know what their targets were. A second truck, then two tanks blustered in and started diagonally across the cloister yard, en route to the airfield.

To what, you automatons, to obsolete orders that have missed the point, to an empty airfield?

The rear door of the ambulance opened. Falkos was shooting out the window on the right, and Mark was beside him.

"Kalya—Mark—come on!" Ben shouted.

She hung back, waiting to see what the boy would do. He kept on firing.

"Get out—both of you!" Falkos ordered. Then, when the boy did not move, he roughly shoved him. The teacher, firing, remained inside.

As the three of them hurried to the basilica entrance, the shooting was all to the left of them, eastward, under bright sunlight. Opening the door, he turned back to see two more tanks roaring toward the airfield. Behind him somewhere—he could not tell what direction, but no longer from the ambulance—he heard Falkos shouting at the armored vehicles.

"Where are you going, you fools? The planes are gone!" His voice, a futility, kept screaming through the din the ordnance was making. "You fools!" Then some hoarseness to the effect that they were attacking an empty birdcage. "You fools!"

Indoors, the basilica was in shadowed darkness. They hurried through the moted shafts of stained glass light, and across the open passage, then into the baptistery.

The early morning sun poured through the great Byzantine windows and flooded the octagonal chamber with a glowing incandescence. The baptismal font of white stone glistened as if there were mica in the marble.

And Ben saw them again, on the seven walls, the patriarch-painter's thirteen Stations of the Cross, more beautiful in the golden summer light than in the gray shades of winter when he had last seen them; and more real as well, because this was more nearly the glare of Golgotha where the torture was perpetrated, in high illumination. Hardly moving from the entrance, he gazed at the paintings straight ahead of him—the first fall, the meeting with His mother, the stripping of His garments—as deeply moved, as startlingly shocked as if the narrative were new to him.

Constrained, he moved toward the middle of the room where the font was, and when he reached it, he turned slowly, his eyes drifting from one painting to another, regretting that there would be one space on a wall that would be, forever, empty. But as his body turned toward the entrance through which he had come, he caught his breath.

There it was! The missing picture, the Twelfth Station of the

Cross—Jesus crucified. Staring at it, he could feel the quick motion of his heart, as if in flight, and the panic that his consciousness might not be able to keep pace. Not only because the picture was *there*, not only because it was the most beautiful of all, but because it was a revelation totally discrete from all the others. It was a private and secret utterance of pain, as if the Son spoke His suffering to the Father alone, not meaning others to know the unbearable agony of it. As he gaped at it, Ben felt that he was invading the most personal intimacy, spying on the last mortifying secret of Christ. Overwhelmed by viewing something he was not meant to see, so excruciating and so sacred, he started to turn away, when he saw the greater thing.

He was a Christ of most amazing joy. He thought at first that it was impossible, that joy was discrepant with such pain; but no, it was the paradox at the heart of a marvel. The torment seemed the lesser matter in the crucifixion; the ecstasy was nearly all of it. Always, in every Calvary picture he had ever seen, the head of Jesus, in death, was lowered, sunken in the last repose. But in this one, even while there was no doubt that He had given up the ghost, His head was uplifted, still taking succor from the skies, and radiant. Even the hands, for all the reality of blood, seemed not so tortured, the right one closed with the spike not visible, the left in shadow. Nor was it the nails that supported Him upon the cross; He was held aloft by the ethereality of His spirit, lifted from earth by heaven.

Ben wanted to cry out. The pang he had felt on first seeing the picture was gone; in its place, a surge of such exceeding happiness that he could barely contain himself. It was a masterpiece, and served as a masterpiece must serve—to hurt and to heal. And if healing was in it, then this was the icon of Demetrios, as all sublime works of art are, in some sense, icons. And the patriarch had finally painted it. . . He couldn't wait to talk to the old man.

He heard a sound close by, as soft as a deep sigh, and turned to see Kalya crossing herself. He wondered if ever during her years as an apparent Muslim she had found herself doing that. Mark was not looking at the paintings at all, only at his mother. He was hypnotized by her, the onetime Turkish woman crossing herself; his face was enrapt with wonder and confusion.

Outside, the gunfire hadn't really stopped or lessened, and yet seemed muffled, from another place, at a far remove from the beatitude in here. It was as if the genius of the patriarch's art had painted a glowing agony on the walls which dimmed the other one, in the cloister.

Ben heard a whispered, terrified voice behind him. "Dear God," it said in Greek, "what is going on?"

The medic turned. It was an old priest, sallowed, squinting through thick spectacles, quaking with fright.

"Greeks," Ben said, as if an onslaught by people of his own race would comfort the cleric, but it didn't. Starting to speak to him in Greek, the American couldn't say the words clearly enough, and saw that the man was hard of hearing. Loudly, in English: "I've come to tend Father Demetrios."

"With guns?" the old man answered. He was indignant.

Unexpectedly, Kalya was talking to him in Greek, swiftly, a spate of it. The priest interrupted her with some asperity, and she went back to explain something again, and soon his voice became more genial.

She turned to Ben. "He says Father Demetrios has been in and out of coma for over a week. He is not conscious now, but you can go into the infirmary and see him."

The priest directed Kalya and Mark out of the baptistery and, through a passageway, into the portico, further away from the gunfire. Then he lighted a lamp and guided Ben through a more shadowy passage, down a few stairs onto the covered ambulatory that led into the infirmary.

Brother Modestos sat in a corner of the room, listening to the gunfire, frightened. He got up when the others entered, greeted Ben in monosyllables, then pointed to the portieres around the old man's bed; there was a draft, he said. He drew the curtain. The patriarch lay in the stark white shelter that had been made for him, his face as white as the hangings around him. Everything about him was blanched, not as if he were ill but as if all the colors of his life, the chromatic splendor he had painted, had been etiolated, bleaching him to extinction. His coma was profound and nearly perfect, and he seemed at total peace.

Ben reached for the old man's hand, lifted it, felt his pulse. It was practically gone. "I wish I could have seen him sooner," he said. It sounded like the classic medical regret, signifying that help might have been available to the sick man, but all he had in mind this moment was the glorious painting, and the realization of the old man's dream.

"Has he been in much pain?" he asked. "I mean before the coma?"

"Oh no," Brother Modestos said. Ben had forgotten what a giggler the man was; he was doing it now, tittering eccentrically. "We played a trick on him. We brought a Turkish doctor in—Dr. Dikmen—a very good man. He came in every day. But Father didn't know he was Turkish. They got on splendidly."

They got on splendidly. How ironic that he had not been needed here, a Turk had tended the beloved, bigoted old man. And they had handled it so expeditiously—simply by denying that the enemy existed. But why did it take mortality to make it happen?

Gazing at the dying man, there was something else he could not understand, that troubled him deeply. Demetrios was altogether different from Ben's remembrance of him. In memory, he had had a grander, statelier head and a beard more majestic, on the scale of Michelangelo's Moses, with a look of thunder in him. But the head of the dying man was of an ordinary size, and his beard was not so full and gleaming as he had remembered it; in fact, it looked scraggy and lusterless. Perhaps in these three years, the illness had changed him—it certainly could—or age had done the work. But perhaps—and this was the sorest nerve of the speculation—Ben's mind had changed him. The real Demetrios had not needed a magnificent beard, only Ben's symbol had required it. In this brief span of time, he had glorified the man in his mind, had made him nobler and more awesome. Year by year, he had increased and exalted him until he was the size of Ben's need, the stature of his vision. Like Mark, he had mythologized an image. Luckier than Mark, his was an image he could love, but still . . . an ordinary man.

And yet, this ordinary man had created works of staggering beauty, this average sized human being, of no greater breadth than the narrow cot he lay upon, had transfigured the agony of Christ. If only he could talk to him about it!

He felt the bitter taste of disappointment. He had struggled up a mountain of turmoil and peril for this last moment with the dying man, and was not to have it. Sometimes the ironies were worse than the tragedies, when one was expected to laugh at a great jest, the point of which was unrevealed. To have been cheated of one, final, farewell conversation . . .

He again took the old man's pulse, raised an eyelid, lay a hand on his heart. The medical bag and dialysis equipment were unnecessary, beyond any usefulness. Death being so imminent, he didn't want to be here. He started to turn away when he heard the old man's voice.

"Who is it?"

Ben took a step back, toward the bed. The priest's eyelids fluttered a bit but did not open; the mouth quivered unevenly.

"Who?" the dying man asked again.

"It's Ben, Father—Ben Coram—do you remember me?"

There was a long silence. Ben had the poignant sense that it was not a silence in which the old man was trying to remember, but simply that he had wandered from any interest in his own question.

"Ben Coram—I was here a number of years ago—do you remember me?"

There was no response. The old man had slipped away again. Ben repeated his name, and then once more, tried it in a slightly higher pitch, a lower one; he bent close to the patriarch's ear and whispered it. There was nothing. Was this going to be all of it? he wondered. Abruptly, he had a need, a burning necessity to have the old man recognize him.

"Father!" he said. "Father Demetrios!"

No sign at all. He reached down to the small table beside the cot, picked up a spoon. Lifting the priest's wasted hand, he placed the handle of the spoon in the palm and closed the fingers upon it, and he held the hand so it would not open.

"Do you know what this is?" he asked. "It's a brush, Father— it's a paintbrush. Do you feel it?"

There was a slight fluttering of the eyelids, but that was all. When Ben released it, the hand would not hold the spoon, there was no energy in it, not even enough for spasm: the palsy was gone.

"Please try to remember me," he said again. "Ben Coram."

The eyelids fluttered again, and this time remained open. He had the uncanny sense that the old man was seeing him, and refusing to recognize his presence.

"Please, Father!"

No answer. But he was sure of it now: Demetrios was aware of him. Angry without knowing why he was angry, he blurted,

"You have no right—!" Then, like an escape, the words burst out of him, echoing the past. "You're stubborn and vainglorious and proud!"

The old man's lips moved but no sound was heard.

"What? Tell me again. What did you say?"

"Who . . . is it?"

"It's me, Father—Ben."

"Who is it?"

"Ben—Ben Coram."

". . . I do not know . . ."

"Yes, you do! You know me! Look at me, you know me!"

". . . morning prayer is not that color . . ."

"What color is it, Father?"

"You are painting it wrong."

"You're the painter, Father. I'm—"

"—Ben."

"Yes, Ben! Yes!"

". . . I cannot paint it."

"Yes, you can."

"No. My hands . . ."

"It hasn't anything to do with your hands."

"I . . . cannot."

"Because you want to make an icon?"

". . . Yes."

"Just paint it, Father. Just lift the brush—do as much as you can—only paint it."

In an almost inaudible whisper, yet with extraordinary intensity: *"I did paint it."*

He was present, almost totally present now. Ben reached for the old man's hand. He held it tightly in both his own. Yes, he was there again, returned, blinking a little, trying to see his visitor, trying to understand who he was, to *believe* who he was.

"Is it . . . really Ben?" he said.

"Yes."

It was deeply difficult for him; he took a long time reassembling memories. It was as if he had to come to some meeting place in his mind. When he arrived: "Did you see it?"

"Yes, Father."

He was about to tell the priest how the picture had stirred him. But Demetrios seemed strangely frightened. "Don't talk about it," he said.

"Very well."

"When you left . . . my hands . . ."

"Yes?"

". . . I could not use them. . . . I thought—what you said—I could not stop thinking . . . Ben . . . And one day, my hands . . . I painted His hand . . . Did you notice His right hand?"

"Yes, it's clenched," he answered. "You can't see the spike."

The old man tried to smile. "Perhaps . . . there is no spike . . . When I didn't have to paint it . . . I could paint the rest."

"It's a masterpiece, Father."

"I do not care about that."

"It's an . . . icon."

Hitherto, there had been no sign of emotion in the old man's face, nor of any physical pain. But now, hearing the word, he seemed tormented. "Oh, please . . ."

"It is."

"I no longer hope for it."

"But it is! It's full of hurt and full of healing!"

"Do you . . . believe that?"

"Yes, I do."

Ben felt the faintest pressure of the old man's hand, that was all. Then there was a long stillness; even the guns seemed to go still for a moment. The old face had a benignity of gratitude in it, and grace.

Ben sensed, then, that Demetrios did not want to speak anymore, wanted to be alone.

"Can I do something for you, Father?" He meant in mundane ways, the specifics of relief from discomfort, a sedative perhaps.

The old man's voice was the faintest murmur. "No. You have already . . . healed me."

Then we have healed each other, Ben thought, and this was what I came for. This was the vision the mountain had promised him, or it was part of the vision; this was the doctor dream, the therapeutic of the soul.

But still there was a void somewhere, and he would have to fill it. He took the old man's once palsied hand to his lips, and kissed it, and went away. If the patriarch had filled an emptiness in him, why did he still feel so incomplete, so hollow . . . ?

He walked through the rear doorway of the infirmary and onto the glassed-in portico. Kalya was nearby, at one of the embrasures, looking out on the courtyard. Mark was further away, also staring across the cloister.

Outdoors, there was a larger detonation than usual. Momentarily, Ben had forgotten it was going on, as if the infirmary was not at all related to the explosions. After a while, he thought, the firing will stop, and there will be wounded to tend. . . . He was back in Vietnam again, the dead, the mutilated.

The firing seemed closer now. He heard a sound, a quick sound, sharply repeated, like handclaps. He recognized it, the rapid applause of an automatic rifle. There were other guns, heard more clearly here, and occasionally a grenade; not many pauses. Sometimes the panes in the windows rattled. A few feet downward, toward the end of the colonnade where it joined the library building, a threesome of monks were huddled, looking through the windows, murmuring, praying, one of them mutely crossing and crossing himself as if to cease meant instant annihilation.

At their perimeter, part of them and yet apart, Mark stood near the window, mesmerized by the shooting. The young man moved his head quickly, his eyes darting to the sources of the gunfire. He looked up at the gallery on the second floor of the refectory building, where most of the Turkish fire was coming from, then, like a spasm, to the cloister yard where the armored truck was moving, pouring fire upward and toward the colonnade far to the east. Some of the Turkish fire was coming from the winery, from the high clerestory windows. The boy held his rifle in his hand, loosely at his side; he seemed to have forgotten he still carried it.

Ben felt Kalya move past him. She didn't look at him, nor at her son. She moved quickly between them, and stood at the arched window, the center one, and he wondered why she was gazing at the ground. Then he saw. She was staring at the dead.

There were many. A number of them lay on the loading platform of the winery, some near the sentry box. On the gravel that diagonally bisected the cloister yard, two men lay sprawled in almost identical positions, half turned on their sides. One was a Turkish soldier, the other was a monk. There were any number on the grass. Three of them, grenaded, were only parts of men. Not far from them lay two Greeks. They looked familiar, at least their clothes did, but he couldn't recognize them. Strange, Ben thought, how uncertain I am who they are, yet how certain that they are dead. The dead, even when they are whole, lie in parts; their bodies lose integrity.

Among the fallen, some still stirred. When the shooting stopped, he would hurry to them.

Again he didn't see Mark leave. Suddenly the boy was outdoors, scurrying into the courtyard, hugging close to the stone wall of the library, moving quickly, sprinting, pausing, spurting toward the entrance of the refectory building.

He knew what the boy was after, and couldn't believe it. He was going for the machine gun on the second floor balcony.

Ben heard Kalya cry Mark's name.

He saw her running, not knowing where the door was, starting one direction, turning the other way, frantic to pursue her son.

"Mark!" she cried. "Mark!"

"Kalya—stay here!" Ben called.

She found the door and was racing through it, racing after the boy.

"Kalya—come back!"

He rushed after her. She kept on calling and calling her son's name.

As Mark was cutting across the angle from the library to the refectory entrance, he stopped, drew a bead on the second floor gunner, and fired.

The man hadn't seen him before, but now, hearing the shot, he whirled to see where it came from.

"Mark!" she called.

The idiots, Ben thought, two idiots calling attention to themselves.

The machine gun chattered. The boy was almost at the entrance now, but Kalya was still in the open. As Mark, with one final spurt, hurled himself at the door, the machine gun spat at the grass around Kalya. The boy was indoors now, momentarily safe, but she was not. Then the catastrophic thing—she stumbled and fell—the rain of shot around her. Miraculously, she arose and ran —twenty paces, perhaps, and through the doorway. Not such a miracle after all, he realized, for the gunfire had been diverted from her, upon himself. A clod of grass tore up from the ground ahead of him, spattering in Ben's face. He changed direction, went zigzagging across the diagonal, ten feet more, five. Hugging close to the refectory building, he too made it indoors.

The hallway was a huge one, dark; all he could see was the pallor of Kalya's face. The boy was nowhere in sight.

"Where did he go?" she said.

There was a confusion of doors and two alcoves off the hallway, but no sign of any stairs. He knew where to find them, but didn't want her to follow him. As he rushed past her, as she started after him, a shrewdness occurred to him:

"Stay here—watch for him here!"

Seeing her hesitate, he ran through the farthest doorway. It led to a corridor which was pitch black. He could see nothing, and he heard no sound of Mark. Good, the boy had gone the wrong way and was lost. If he himself could get to the top of the stairs, he could block them, in case Mark should find his way here.

Hurrying through the darkness, he went the full distance of the corridor, his hand outstretched ahead of him. He felt the newel-post, the bannister, and started up the steps. As the stair turned, he saw a knife-edge of light—the door that led to the balcony. He would not open the door and go out on it; the gunner was there.

Then he had the terrible recollection: there was a back stairway. What if the boy had found it? If he had, he would be coming out on the balcony on the other side of the machine gun, and what could Ben possibly do about it? Distract the gunner and direct the fire against himself?

Use his own gun to save the boy? No.

But something—he was Kalya's son—something—!

He opened the door slowly, hair by hair. Getting it ajar a few inches, he looked at the way it was set. Luckily it was deeply framed, the stone of the wall was thick. Quickly, in the sunlight, he slid toward the hinged side of the door. Pulling himself thinly back against the wooden panel, he peered around the corner of the stone.

The balcony was perhaps two hundred feet long. More than halfway down the ambulatory, the gunner, behind a metal baffle, had his weapon concentrated on the alleyway through which the armored vehicles had come. There was action there, and men. Ben couldn't see the extent of it. From time to time, the gun would rattle, then go still.

The gunner was all that Ben could see, and for whatever good he was going to do, he would have to know if Mark was near. It meant he would have to expose himself to some extent, hoping that the man's concentration was on the alleyway.

As he leaned out a little—too late he realized that the man had seen them enter the building. He pulled back quickly, but the machine gun was turning toward him now. As it almost got into firing position, he heard the shot—not machine gun fire, but a ping. A rifle ping. Then another one, and another.

The machine gunner thrust one hand into the air as if to clutch at something out of reach. Then the same hand dropped and slapped against the barrel of his gun. He slumped and held to the mount, pulling at it with both hands, then released himself.

Ben took a step out of the doorway and saw Mark at the other end of the balcony. In case he might need to fire once more, the boy still held his rifle in position. Seeing Ben, he lowered it.

Just as they thought it safe up here, the Turkish officer appeared. He came between them from the passage at right angles to the balcony. He was tall and thin and his visored cap had a glint of captain's black-and-gold on it—not a mainland Turk but a native one. He saw the dead man and saw Ben before he knew the boy was behind him. The officer raised his pistol, sighted it on Ben. There were two reports, his and Mark's, but the boy's was first, and the Turk's meant nothing. Then Mark shot again and the Captain didn't seem to fall, but merely to subside. He stayed on his knees a moment, fired another shot, and fell peculiarly—sideways—as if to the very end he might have risen if he had not missed his footing.

Slowly they converged on the dead men. All they saw of the gunner was his back; he had fallen forward. But the Captain was lying on his left side. Only the first of the shots had hit him, in the back. It had probably shattered his spine, and gone as close to the heart as necessary.

The officer must have been handsome in his life. It was a face more romantic than was credible, with jet brows and a luxuriant mustache, well tended, black gone to gray. And from the temple to the jawbone . . . a long scar.

There was a lull in the gunfire for some moments, the slightest caesura, as if the spokesmen for the battle were pausing for breath. Somebody shouted that the balcony was safe, the machine gun taken. Then Ben saw three figures, down below, hurrying toward the refectory entrance—Falkos, Mikis, and the superior officer, Pavlos Chartas.

Soon they came through the same doorway Ben had used, Chartas in the lead. He advanced toward the dead Turks, looked at the bodies, and at the machine gun. Turning to Ben, he asked, "You?" The medic shook his head. Chartas saw Mark's rifle and nodded approvingly.

But Falkos said nothing. He glanced only briefly at the dead gunner, then slowly, from the perimeter of the group, made his way toward the fallen officer. The corpse, in a profile position, did not give him the conclusive evidence he needed, so he unhurriedly —and with remarkable gentleness—turned the dead man on his back. Very delicately he ran his thumb down the length of the scar, as though feeling the depth of it. From his kneeling position on the floor, he looked up. He was not addressing himself to anybody, nor did he want any reply to a question that had already been answered:

"Who did this?" he said softly. "Who did this?"

He spoke as though a heinous crime had been committed.

"I did," Mark said.

"Why?"

Mark was bewildered. He looked at Chartas, who—knowing —turned away, then at Mikis, who was as perplexed as the boy.

Falkos did not rise from his kneeling position. His eyes were glazed, he was as pale as the death in front of him. He started to tremble; midsummer, he was cold. They heard him try to catch a breath, another, but they were fugitive. Then, the hoarse cry, "Oh, Cabrir!"

He kept repeating the man's name, all heartbreak. It didn't seem to matter to Falkos that his capture of the Monastery had been a successful failure, that they had lost the aircraft, that the whole tactic had been a futility and waste; it didn't matter that he had predicted the second invasion and the catastrophe had happened. Only this single passion was of consequence to him, and it was all consequence, the total of his life. He couldn't stop repeating the name, the lamentation for a cherished enemy, the death of a love that was irreplaceable. Oh, Cabrir, he cried over and over, oh, Cabrir. Suddenly, he was an ancient Greek, suffering a wild, anachronistic grief. He reached to the breast pocket of his jacket and, with a wrench, tore it away. Then, when there was a slash in the fabric under it, he started to tear it, yanking, ripping it downward, cry by cry, "Cabrir, Cabrir!"

"Manolis—no," Chartas said, and tried to restrain his hands.

"Cabrir!" He rent his clothes, so that his friend had to turn away from him, murmuring to Mikis not to stare but to move apart, to take charge of the captured gun. Then the tall man ordered Ben and Mark off the balcony, where they were too dangerously exposed, to the relative safety of the baptistery. Turning once more to the now numbed schoolteacher, he led Falkos away, and they descended the stairs, not far from the fire.

When Ben and Mark got down to the main hallway, Kalya was gone. As they started opening doors, they heard a man's voice in the dining hall. Entering, they saw Kalya with one of the monks who was guiding her back to where she had started. Lost and wild-eyed with worry, she shook with relief on seeing them.

It would be easier to cross the diagonal this time, Ben thought, for Mikis had them covered from the balcony. As they were passing through the corridor of the refectory, the gunfire seemed to have lessened, but at the slightly opened doorway into the cloister courtyard they halted, for the firing had resumed. Mortars were being hurled somewhere, probably on the airfield side, Ben speculated, where the tanks and trucks had gone. From the winery, four or five Turks appeared, two with submachine guns. In a little while, there were more, from another place, it wasn't certain where. Then there were fewer of them; finally, no more were visible.

As they stepped out of the refectory building, the tanks started returning from the airfield. There were only two of them at first. They moved ponderously, more sluggishly than before; having performed no function, and still having none to perform, they had no destination. They crossed the cloister single file, one of them going toward the winery, the other turning to depart through the alleyway by which it had entered.

Nobody knew where the mortar was positioned, or even if in fact it was a mortar shell that exploded. It burst on the near side of the second tank, which was its target; the wellhead, closer, went up in a fine shower, flying all directions, as if it had been made of sand, not stone. The tank halted only for an instant, but, unable to spot its assailant and having no other objective, it resumed its forward motion at a quicker speed. Another mortar and another, both missing their mark, as if the shells were being fired blind. Then a closer one, within yards of the tank, and as the earth shuddered, Ben felt the familiar mortar rush, his heart pumping more than his arteries could carry, the charge of adrenalin, the high jag of fear.

Somebody yelled louder than the bombardment, and something detonated. Christ, Ben said, it's the infirmary. As he was praying to be wrong, he saw the havoc, a delayed response, an afterthought, the building seeming to tremble, wait, and then explode. There was no further delay, the rest was rubble, clouds of dust, the stink of cordite, nostril-filling smoke, and a dirty gray haze on everything. He started to run to the destruction but Mark and Kalya held him. Foolishness, he knew, great foolishness to go there, nothing left, the man was dead, somewhere in the rubble or in the ashen haze. Demetrios, he cried, Demetrios, and even while an allaying voice tried to tell him that the old priest had been moribund and would have died of natural causes at any moment, a mortar was an unnatural cause, oh Demetrios.

There was no time to grieve, for the mortar struck again. He could have sworn he heard the whistle in the tube, the far, far distant whine, then the *kerrumm,* and it was the baptistery. The small octagonal building seemed to take it like a wound. At first there was a wisp of fine, thin smoke, as white as phosphorus; he thought it strange how pale it was. Then the great breath came, as if the baptismal place were expanding with too much air, inflated with an overweening pride, then punished with a fulmination that echoed in the cloister yard and across the mountain peaks, and finally hardly anything to hear or see except desolation and debris, a white smoke and a darker one, nearly black, and from somewhere a long and wailing incantation. Oh no, Ben said, the baptistery, the hall with fourteen glimmerings of the human passion. He could not hold it in his mind's horror. He remembered every one of the paintings, every icon, the day they hung them on the walls, the dazzling color, the ache of aching, the frailty of the stumbling Jesus, the strength of the spat upon, the pity of Man and Mother as if pity were the totality of their lives, and the final agony of crucifixion where the pain could not be mitigated by saying it was passion, and exquisite. All blown to bits, to nothing, gone. The old man's toil, his dream, his heart's devotion, all the heavenly aspiration to heal, all the rapture of the artist and the icon maker, gone to a white smoke and to a black one, like napalm. All lost to ugliness, to hatred, to obscenity. Oh no, he kept murmuring, and wept, unable to stop the torrent of tears, kept crying no, the waste, the wildness.

Then he felt a rage, a hatred he had never known his heart could tolerate. He wanted vengeance against a distant artillery, a remote cruelty that could cause such an intimate torment. He thought of the thousands of bodies he had dumped, with mismatched appendages, into shallow graves; he thought of morseled brains and eviscerated guts, of the scream of women violated and of the dead eyes of young men still alive, and of this last inexpiable ravage of soul's breath and beauty. And he hated. He felt a loathing, ugly and malignant, a heartful of venom. He could kill now; no compunction, he could kill. Nor did it matter who his victim might be, Turk, Greek, American, anybody in the inhuman race; he could maim and lash and mutilate. And kill.

Then, something in his rage, which had been so imperatively clear, became incomprehensible, like bad grammar, a sentence he couldn't parse. He saw Mark run across his line of vision in the courtyard, and he thought: Watch out, you crazy bastard, you'll get hurt. But the boy was full of destinies today; had killed a gunner, and now—Ben's erratic speculation—was off to find the mortar emplacement, to wipe it out. While it was a wayward surmise, he knew the boy had heard the same whistling in the tube, and had run into the colonnade which led in the direction of the sound.

He ran after him. Not such a rash place to be, if they could stay there, protected by the overhang and the shadows, along the narrow porch of pillars, out of the range of gunfire. The boy was almost out of the colonnade, and Ben was halfway down the passageway, and then . . .

It was baffling. There was nobody ahead of him in the long ambulatory except Mark and an elderly monk; and surely the cleric could not have fired the gun. But clearly there was a shot. Mark was perhaps a hundred feet ahead of Ben, where the columns ended in wide, arched casements. The boy had both hands against the largest window, scrabbling at the pane with his fingertips, trying to hold to the crystalline glass, so that he might not fall.

Ben heard Kalya behind him, a few paces, and to his right. He turned to her. She had stopped, unable to bear it; she was transfixed.

But where did the shot come from?

Starting toward Mark, Ben saw the Turk. He was at the far end of the corridor, lying nearly prone, armed with a rifle. Pointing the gun, the man fired again. And struck nobody. Yet all the targets were clear and easily within range.

The medic halted. Mark held on to the sash, not falling. But in order for Ben to get to him he had to make himself a closer and closer target.

"Ben—your gun!" Kalya cried.

Yes, his gun, and his rage. He pulled the pistol out of his pocket. But he didn't release the safety, and didn't know why.

Mark fell.

Unthinking, Ben lurched toward the boy. He saw the Turk raise the gun a little, saw it shake, and the man trying to steady it.

"Ben—shoot!"

He released the safety. But don't shoot it yet, he told himself, until you're close enough; then make the anger pay. The killing must not be done dementedly, in the heat of tantrum, but as an act of cool hatred, totally detached.

He saw Mark twist, like a mistake in the nervous system, and saw the Turk steadying one arm with the other, and suddenly realized why the soldier had fired at him and missed. The man was wounded, no doubt badly damaged. For an instant Ben felt his resolve waver a little, but he steadied himself: wounded, yes, and that much easier to kill. But why was he delaying?

The Turk fired again.

"Ben—shoot," she cried once more.

He put his finger on the trigger. How easy it will be to press it, he thought. One last step toward Mark, and he was on his knees, staring at the wound. No need to look at it, he realized. There was nothing he could do for him; the boy was dead.

He arose from the body. Another dead one, Kalya's son, another flag of rage. He felt the trigger getting warm. He raised the pistol. Then a wrench happened in him, a terrible contortion of what he saw and what he remembered, what he was and what he hated, the grief-rage-love-vengeance-forgiveness agonies that were suffered almost alike by lunatics and men of reason. The Turk was Luddy Stroudt and Yannis and Mee Lanh and Mark and the boy that he himself had killed, and all the other innocents who had died in consternation, and he knew that he could never kill another man, and his rage was over.

Again, the Turk fired.

Ah, then, there was another question. Could he answer it?

"Shoot!"

Could he answer it?

He would have to say what he had always said to the wounded. "You're hurt. I'm going to lift and carry you."

He didn't walk away from the wounded man, but toward him.

The rifle cracked again. I'm getting closer, he thought, and so is he. No matter how blind he's shooting, the closer I get, the clearer he sees me.

He walked.

He heard Kalya call his name, and then he heard the outcry: *"Fire!"*

His hand trembled and was still. Oh please, he said, don't let me run away again. For an instant he could not move, his legs were numb. He thought: I'm hobbled now, as I was then. Keep going, he said, keep going forward. He moved a bit, a step or two.

The Turk's rifle, a shot. He felt the swift air of it.

Keep going, he said.

Fire: the cry again.

But this time it did not stop or terrorize him. Forward, he was moving forward. Not running away, but forward.

The Turk steadied himself. Maybe he has only one shot left, Ben thought, maybe he'll make it do.

Suddenly he was there. With the gunman. He knelt beside the soldier, and gently took the rifle out of his hands. It was easy, there was no struggle. Pushing the Turk's gun out of reach, he dropped his gun.

He lifted the wounded man so he could carry him through the arcade, indoors somewhere, away from the gunfire. But he had hardly moved a few steps when he felt the spasm in the man, and the sudden stiffening. Slowly he put down his burden. As it lay on the floor again, he studied it a moment to make sure. There was no doubt. He looked at the young man lying there, his dead body already crooked. He was no older than Mark, he would say, and no older than the Turkish boy Ben had killed. Well . . . this one he hadn't.

Rising, he turned to find Kalya. For an instant he did not see her, then his glance went to Mark. She was sitting on the floor beside her dead son—not weeping, not touching him, not doing anything. She did not know him well enough to weep for him, this onetime genius boy, this stranger, her son, except there was a crying of the blood, and a crying for a wasted one who had died young and lonely, in a foreign place. And a crying that she had wandered for so long, through too much glare and too much darkness, to find him. And having found him, they had never been close enough to call each other the mother and son names they so sorely needed to say and hear. So that the lost was never surely found. And a crying of release that she was now cleansed of an indecency of the mind, of a myth that was made of madness; and this at last was the end of it.

As Ben approached them, she did not look up at him, her eyes did not change their focus on emptiness. He had an aching need to help her, to lift her, to take her with him, but he thought it would be better to leave her for a while. He walked past them and started toward the refectory. As he got beyond the casements, he heard her voice:

"Ben."

He turned. He looked across the distance and their eyes met. She was not staring at emptiness, but at him.

"Wait," she said.

He thought it one of the most regenerative words he had ever heard. She had left her rifle somewhere, it said, and now she was leaving her dead as well; and if he would just be patient, she would catch up with the living. Wait.

He waited.

The gunfire sounded remote. Somebody had located the mortar emplacement, and eliminated it. The courtyard was still; there were no figures moving in it. He heard men's voices, also a long way off, shouting. Then he realized that there *was* gunfire, almost beyond hearing. This hill had been taken, but the shooting came from another hill—perhaps miles and miles from here. In Vietnam, he thought, it might have a number, not a name. Numbers, somehow, didn't hurt as much—but he hoped in Cyprus they would keep their names; hurting wasn't all of it.

Kalya, walking, was almost within reach. He wondered, now that she had seen and spoken the truth about herself, whether she would someday be able to look back at her life with other remembrances than pain. He wondered too—about himself— whether he could ever tell his own story without reference to a war.

He heard the airplanes—far, quite far. They had come from here, he supposed, and had been bombing, but he no longer heard any detonations. Soon, the sound of the planes themselves died away, and the sky was still.

Here too it was quiet. There was a stillness in him as well, and he could imagine a stillness everywhere, except for the wounded.

In a little while, as soon as he could get to the ambulance, he would go out into the cloister and do what he could do. Meanwhile he filled the empty silence with remembered sounds: the soft snuffling of the sea tide against the rocks, the voice of Yannis, and the hushed breathing of a woman in her sleep.